THE CHILDREN OF WRATH

THE CHILDREN OF WRATH

The Renshai Chronicles:
Volume Three

Mickey Zucker Reichert

DAW BOOKS, INC.

DONALD A. WOLLHEIM, FOUNDER

375 Hudson Street, New York, NY 10014

ELIZABETH R. WOLLHEIM
SHEILA E. GILBERT
PUBLISHERS

First printing, June 1998

1 2 3 4 5 6 7 8 9

DAW TRADEMARK REGISTERED
U.S. PAT OFF. AND FOREIGN COUNTRIES
—MARCA REGISTRADA.
HECHO EN U.S.A.

PRINTED IN THE U.S.A.

To Koby Moore,
whose very presence
allowed me time to finish.

ACKNOWLEDGMENTS

The following people assisted in making this a better book:
Mark Moore, Sheila Gilbert, Jonathan Matson, Jody Lee, Caroline Oakley, and the PenDragons.

Also thanks to my support staff:
Sandra Zucker and Ben, Jon, Jackie, and Ari Moore.

Contents

Prologue

DRY leaves of myriad hues rattled on their branches, and evening's grayness settled over the kingdom of Béarn. Autumn winds whipped Tae Kahn's hair around his Eastern-swarthy features, hindering vision. Aided by self-made bracers fitted with steel claws, he clung to castle walls carved directly from the mountain. He knew King Griff stood on a balcony on an adjacent side of the keep, the king's voice and the cheers of the crowd beneath him wafting to Tae as a distant cacophony of muffled sound. The smoothed granite afforded the Easterner little purchase. The claws ticked and skimmed from the rare irregularities, and the slipping of his booted feet seemed more regular than the solid footholds he gradually managed. Impatience and curiosity had driven him to such unorthodoxy, accompanied by a silly need to appear collected and in control ingrained in him from his years alone among Stalmizian street thugs.

The sun disappeared behind the west tower. Tae paused in a precarious position, one hand winched around a fourth-story sill, relying on friction to keep his feet in place. With cautious movements, he flicked black hair from eyes nearly as dark and wiped sweat from his forehead with the back of his sleeve. *Father would disapprove.* Tae rolled his eyes at the thought. Not long ago, he would not have cared if Weile Kahn dropped dead in a crowded market. So much had changed over the past several months, including the embroidered silks and expensive travel leathers that had taken the place of his ragged linens and vest.

The irony drove a smile to Tae's lips. *Here I am assailing Béarn Castle yet worrying about my father's reaction to four months without a haircut and dirt on my clothes.* Shaking his head, he continued his climb to the fifth story, singling out the queen's private chamber as much by the delicate weave and colors of the curtains as by its location. The excitement of a recognized goal made many men careless, but experience kept Tae from falling prey to a mistake that might cost him his life. He inched toward the opening more slowly than before, metal claws rasping across stone to settle into minuscule depressions. At length, he reached the queen's window, studying the interior through the gauzy film of curtains.

The room seemed to stretch forever, ending in a dark rectangle that surely represented a door. Bureaus, wardrobes, and shelves lined every wall; clothing, knickknacks, and bric-a-brac cast strange shadows that Tae could not wholly interpret. A massive bed stood in the room's center, tall and canopied. A person reposed on the mattress, large yet with obvious female proportions, unequivocally a Béarnide. She clutched something in her arms. Tae grinned, memory filling in the details of Matrinka: thick, ebony hair that flowed past her shoulders; soft, doelike eyes; gentle features pleasant, though few would consider her beautiful. Her kindness had brought him and his friends through harshness and bickering, and her knowledge of herbs and healing had rescued several of them from death. He had not seen her in a year, since before she became the queen of Béarn.

Balanced on the sill, Tae removed the gauntlets, drawing the claws into the leather so they would not click together as he moved. He tied them to the right side of his belt to avoid the long knife at his left. Silently, he shifted the curtains, the gossamer fabric slithering along his cheek. Matrinka carried a bit more weight on her already Béarnian-large frame; yet she appeared otherwise unchanged from the last time he had seen her. She wore a loose-fitting robe best suited to sleeping. The bundle in her arms wiggled. She studied it, oblivious to his sudden presence. Tae eased into the room.

Another was not caught so unaware. A calico cat leaped from the coverlet and galloped to Tae, claiming him with raucous purring and fierce rubs against his ankles that all but knocked him back through the window.

Mior. Tae hefted the cat, hugging her to his chest. In a moment, he knew, Matrinka would learn of his presence, too. Cat and queen shared a unique bond that few would believe, a form of mental communication.

A moment later, Matrinka whirled toward Tae. Brown eyes sparkled beneath a fringe of bangs, and a smile split her broad mouth. "Tae," she said, the quietness of her greeting making it no less exuberant.

Tae's gaze fell to the baby in Matrinka's arms. Born that very day, it still carried flecks of blood and vernix in its dark hair. A generous nose for one so young poked from tiny, doll-like features. Matrinka laid the baby on a blanket. Startled by the movement, it jerked, then settled back into placid sleep. A moment later, Tae realized Matrinka struggled to rise. He moved swiftly to the bed, saving her the effort.

As Tae drew to her side, Matrinka lunged for him. Mior scrambled to his shoulder, claws piercing silk and gliding around leather to tear flesh.

Tae winced as the queen caught him into a wild embrace and Mior rescued herself from a crushing . . . at his expense. "Tae. Oh, Tae."

Tae wrapped his arms around a friend whom he loved like a sister, savoring her warmth and presence. He sought the proper words to maintain his dignity without belittling their reunion.

Matrinka beat him to speech, whispering into his ear. "Tae, you're the East's diplomat to Béarn, as well as a prince. You don't have to sneak through windows any more."

Tae chuckled, loosing Matrinka. "Old habits die hard." The words emerged without thought, adequate but untrue, at least in the current circumstances. "So this is the heir to Béarn."

Matrinka hefted the baby again, love evident in her eyes and expression. She had never looked so attractive to Tae. "Beautiful, isn't she?"

Tae rubbed at the fresh line of scratches Mior had gouged into his right shoulder and chest. "How could she not be with you as her mother?"

Matrinka's cheeks flushed.

Tae peeled the cat from his shoulders and placed her on the bed. "I believe this is yours, too."

Matrinka rolled her gaze to Mior, then frowned, obviously in response to something the calico had communicated. "Your father sent a message announcing your imminent arrival." She cradled the infant in the crook of one arm and took his hand. "You really should have used the door. The guards could have rightfully shot you. Not only would your death sadden me, the king, and several others, but it could spark war."

Tae dismissed Matrinka's concern. He had long ago learned to consider death inevitable, to rely on caution and accept the consequences should it fail. That philosophy had kept him alive for nineteen years. *Barely*, he reminded himself. Before his father had turned from the East's first crime lord to its king, Tae had dodged enemies daily. At the age of ten, he had suffered sixteen stab wounds, drifting toward oblivion hearing his mother's dying screams. Yet he had survived that and so much more. If fate decreed he would die plummeting from Béarn's walls, he had little say in the matter. He resorted to the truth. "I could have gotten into the castle but not to you. I wanted to see the baby."

"You would have seen her."

"Not today."

Matrinka laughed. "Tae-logic. Risking death and war to glimpse a tired, disheveled friend and a baby before its naming."

Tae dodged a discussion that no longer mattered, attentive to every movement and sound around him. He watched Mior pace an indignant circle on the coverlet, then settle against Matrinka's leg. "You and Griffy." He shook his head at the strangeness of the coupling. "Who would have guessed?"

Matrinka stroked fine hairs from the baby's forehead. "We call him King Griff now." It was a warning as well as information.

"King Griff," Tae repeated thoughtfully, unable to banish the image of the childlike bear of a farm boy whom he, Matrinka, and three friends had rescued from the elves' prison. He glanced back at the baby, noticing the elegant patterns on canopy and blankets as he shifted his gaze. "I hope the heir gets a fancier, more royal-sounding name than her—" He broke off suddenly, recognizing the large, straight nose. "This isn't Griff's baby," he blurted, his usual composure lost. *Damn me to the pits, did I say that aloud?* He stiffened, avoiding Matrinka's eyes.

"Of course, she's Griff's baby." Defensiveness coarsened Matrinka's tone. She hesitated, as if to reveal a secret, then finished simply with, "He's my husband." She did not add that, spoken by a Béarnide, the accusation Tae made would be considered treason.

Tae said nothing, simply turned a measuring stare on his onetime companion. Long before they had bonded as a team to rescue the heir to Béarn's throne, Matrinka had loved Darris, Béarn's bard. Struck by a curse that passed always to the bard's oldest child, Darris suffered an inhuman curiosity that drove him to learn everything, though he could teach others what he discovered only in song. Most found him an entertaining oddity, tedious when the bardic malediction forced him to arias in the middle of conversation. Somehow, the two had seen beyond Matrinka's softhearted shyness and Darris' prolonged silences to discover a depth of love few shared in a lifetime. Unfortunately, Matrinka's royal blood forbade them from marrying. Presumably to strengthen the waning bloodline of Béarnian nobility, Matrinka had wed her cousin instead.

Matrinka sucked in a deep breath and loosed it slowly through her nose. She would never lie, especially to a friend. She caressed the baby's hand with a finger. "Is it that obvious?"

"Noticing details keeps a boy alive on the streets." Tae squeezed Matrinka's fingers. "And hope had a lot to do with it. You and Darris belong together."

"The king thinks so, too."

Tae's eyes widened. "Griff knows?"

"Of course, he knows. It was his idea. What kind of adulterous whore do you think I am?" Even as the words left her lips, Matrinka cringed as if she worried she might have offended Tae.

Freeing his hand from Matrinka's grip, Tae searched among elaborately carved furniture for a chair. Finding one in front of a desk, he pulled it to the bedside. High-backed, plush, and patterned, it smelled pleasantly of polish. He crouched rather than sat. "I have to hear this."

"There's not much to tell." Matrinka shrugged. "The populace demanded our wedding, and their king denies them little. But Griff and I are friends, not lovers. He also worried that the closeness of our bloodlines might result in cretins."

Tae wondered if the bloodline alone might do so. Béarn had a long history of naive, simpleminded kings. He wisely kept the thought to himself.

"Being the bard, Darris serves as the king's bodyguard and most trusted adviser, not to mention my beloved." Matrinka shrugged, a slight smile tugging at her features as she gazed lovingly at the baby. Nothing further needed saying.

"I came here because I heard King Griff announcing the birth of his daughter from the balcony. Darris was with him, of course. Neither one mentioned the deception."

"It's not really a deception," Matrinka insisted. "Béarnian law defines parentage by marriage at the time of birth, not by blood." She hugged the baby closer, as if to remind herself of its reality. "It's not exactly a secret. A few people know, and she will, too, of course." Matrinka glanced at Tae. "I'd rather you didn't speak of it. It's really Marisole's decision who to tell."

"Marisole," Tae repeated, believing nothing could reassure more than changing the subject. The arrangement pleased him, and he would never have believed Griff capable of such cleverness. "Is that her name?"

Matrinka nodded. "It will be."

"Worthy of a princess." They both knew Tae meant as opposed to "Griff." Born to the exiled, youngest son of King Kohleran, Griff had never been expected to sit upon the throne.

The comment begged no answer, so Tae continued, still working to dispel the awkwardness that followed his discovery with conversation. He lowered his center of balance. "My children will have to be called 'something' Kahn."

"Kahn? Like Tae Kahn?"

"Not Tae Kahn, no. That would get confusing." He grinned to show he was joking.

"Why 'something' Kahn?" Matrinka settled into a gentle rocking motion. She shifted on the bed, supporting her back against the headboard. Childbirth had tired her.

"It's a family thing, though not a long-standing one. My father started it. My grandfather gave him two names: Weile and Kahn." Tae's wiry shoulders rose and fell. "I don't know why. Maybe he couldn't agree with my grandmother. Anyway, it's considered disrespectful to shorten a person's name in the East, so my mother deliberately gave me a one syllable name. Who could shorten that? My father thought it too brief, so he added the Kahn and claimed it as tradition. It's worked out well. Since it's a whole separate name, people can drop it without offending."

Matrinka yawned, then added sleepily, "I don't know how well 'Kahn' will fit with a Renshai name. Assuming the Renshai accept him, of course."

Her words made no sense to Tae. "Accept who?"

"Accept . . ." Matrinka trailed off, stiffening. "You don't know, do you?"

"What don't I know?" A clump of hair slid across Tae's forehead. No matter how often he promised himself he'd attend to the soft locks, they always wound up in a snarl and in his eyes. His thoughts raced. Twice he had slept with their Renshai companion, Kevral, whom he loved; yet their friend, Ra-khir, had captured her heart as well. She had promised to choose between them once Griff took his throne, but circumstances had delayed that decision. Now, if he read Matrinka rightly, Kevral had borne him a child. His heart rate quickened to wild thumping, and he leaned forward in the chair. "Matrinka, you have to tell me."

"I'm sorry I said anything." Matrinka reached for Mior, and the cat wriggled under her free hand. "I made a mistake."

"Matrinka," Tae fairly pleaded. "You can't leave me hanging after an announcement like that."

"I'm sorry." Matrinka's tone revealed the sincerity of the words. "I really am. I made a mistake."

"Matrinka—"

"I'm sorry. It's not for me to say more. You'll have to talk to Kevral."

Restlessness assailed Tae, and he sprang from the chair. "Is he—is he—?"

"Tae, I can't tell you anything. I'm sorry."

"Can you at least tell me where to find Kevral?" Tae paced toward the window.

"Fourth floor. Same wing. And, Tae . . ."

Tae slid out before Matrinka could finish the sentence, the words chasing after him.

". . . use the door."

Tae refused to waste even the few moments it would take to negotiate the hallways, let alone explain his sudden presence to the guards. He scrambled down the granite without bothering with his gauntlets, preferring the risk of death to delay. It seemed he had a son, Kevral's son, and surely the hand of his lady as well. His father had made many mistakes raising him that he would never repeat. Tae's son would have the perfect upbringing. Whatever he wished to become, his father would not be the cause of any failure, would support any endeavor the child chose.

The first few windows granted Tae glimpses of empty libraries that left him mad with impatience. As he gazed into the third, he discovered shelves covered with toys and two bassinets. Anticipation shivered through his chest, and his throat suddenly felt engorged. Planting both hands firmly on the sill, he eased through without a sound. The faint snores of a congested infant touched his ears. He crept around the tiny cribs. The noise emanated from the first, a chubby baby with sparse red-blond hair and tiny pink lips pursed in sleep. Tae turned his attention to the other: smaller, lighter, its skin nearly as swarthy as his own. Raven hair draped over its forehead, and dark eyes rolled toward his face. Though Easterners and Béarnides looked similar, the thinness of the hair and the slightness of build suggested the former. Tae stared, unable to move, certain he looked upon his own child.

I'm a father? The thought failed to register. Tae tried again. *I'm a father!* Nothing. He hefted the infant, its weight meager in his arms. "I'm your papa," he whispered, worried he might awaken the other occupant of the nursery.

The baby thrust a hand into Tae's face, clumsily grabbing the hair flopping over his eyes.

"Hey!" At that moment, a rush of understanding hit Tae low in the stomach. Love seemed to pour forth like water through a broken dam. Nearly overcome, he tightened his hold on the baby and reveled in the tears filling his eyes. "My son," he said, hoping he spoke truth. Nothing had ever seemed more significant, and he hoped he had not hopelessly and eternally bonded with a stranger's child.

Tae had to know immediately. Pausing only long enough to bind the baby to his chest with one of its blankets, he again slid out the window. Even as he did so, he cursed his impulsiveness. *That's right, stupid. Demonstrate your love by getting both of you killed.* Hand over hand, he worked his way to the next window, acutely conscious of the additional warm weight against his chest. A peek through the opening revealed a bedroom, and he recognized Kevral's boyish figure seated on a bench beside Ra-khir's massive form. Not bothering with more details, Tae shoved aside the curtain and sprang inside.

Desperate instinct seized Tae. He glanced up, catching the blur of a descending sword. He dove into the room, rolling, curling his body protectively around the baby. The blade skimmed his shoulder, painless, the warm trickle of blood his only warning of injury. The additional weight threw off his usually graceful timing. The baby wailed.

Tae rose to a low crouch, one arm raised to block, the other supporting the infant. "Kevral, stop!" he managed, skittering from the path of a second attack. "It's Tae." He had barely dodged the Renshai's awful speed in the past. Now, it seemed hopeless.

"Kevral, no!" Ra-khir's strong voice boomed, too late.

Tae cringed, anticipating a third strike he could never avoid. He looked up into Kevral's calm blue eyes and Northern-pale face. The year had added touches of femininity to her sinewy figure. Approaching seventeen, she had finally developed breasts, and a hint of hip flared her warrior tunic. The blonde locks remained functionally short and feathered away from her face, so as not to interfere with battle. Though she refused to wear her own hair long, she had expressed appreciation for Tae's own wild locks, the main reason he had allowed them to grow during his months of travel from the Eastlands to Pudar.

No longer menaced, Tae turned his attention to their companion. Dressed in the formal attire of the Knights of Erythane, Ra-khir wore a tunic displaying Béarn's tan bear on a blue background. On the back, Tae knew, he would find Erythane's symbol, a black sword thrust through an orange circle. As always, Ra-khir appeared immaculate, from the shoulder-length strawberry-blond hair to his unwrinkled garb, to his regal bearing. His features defined the male ideal, though he seemed not to notice. As he had so many times in the past, Tae marveled at the idea that he could compete for Kevral's affection with this paragon.

"What in Hel are you doing?" Kevral slammed her sword into its sheath. "You could have killed him!"

The baby's howls ended, and it snuggled against Tae, its breaths post-cry snorts and sobs.

Tae hugged the infant, trying to dispel the tension with humor. "As usual, a rousing welcome." His quiet entrances had nearly earned him death at her hands before, though every other instance had occurred in battle. He had not anticipated violence in her own chambers.

Kevral's features bunched tighter, and her mouth thinned to an angry line.

"You're right," Tae said in honest apology. "I shouldn't have carried him through the window. I won't do it again." He could not help adding, "But you're the one who almost cut us both in half."

"I'm sorry." Rage disappeared from Kevral's demeanor and she hesitated, as if uncertain whether to hug Tae or retreat to give him air.

Tae made the decision for her, standing and embracing her with a caution that did not menace the baby.

Kevral glanced at Ra-khir before clamping her hands around Tae's shoulders. She jerked back immediately, blood smeared across her right palm. "Oh, Tae."

The baby went silent, quietly watching.

The sight of the blood brought an abrupt rush of pain that excitement had previously held at bay. "Just a scratch." Tae managed to keep his voice steady and hoped his eyes did not betray him.

"We're going to need a bucket to collect the blood from that so-called scratch." Ra-khir jerked a handkerchief from his pocket, clamping it to the wound with a firm suddenness that doubled the pain. He led Tae to a chair.

Kevral slipped the baby from Tae's makeshift pouch, cradling the child in her arms. "You're all right, little one." She wiped tears from the tiny eyes.

"Tell him his father is an idiot," Ra-khir said from behind Tae.

"Ahh," Tae quipped. "So he *is* my son."

"Yes," Ra-khir admitted. "But we're hoping he'll inherit his mother's survival instinct." He continued pointedly, "And his mother's *Renshai*." He sounded amazingly good-spirited for a man who had, apparently, lost the competition for his beloved. Surely, Kevral would see the need to marry her baby's father. "We're glad you're back, of course, Tae. But you should know better than to surprise a Renshai, especially when there're more lives than just yours at stake."

It was a point well-taken. Renshai became warriors the day their baby fists could close around a sword, and their lessons began as soon as they could walk. Dedicated wholly to dying in the glory of battle, their training included instant, violent reaction to threat. "So this wasn't punishment enough?" Tae waved in the general direction of the injury, swiveling his head to see Ra-khir behind him. "I have to suffer through a lecture as well?"

"A lecture?" Ra-khir snorted. "Come to a ceremony led by knights sometime. A man hasn't been born who can sit through one of them without fidgeting. Except the knights themselves, of course. It's part of the training."

"I think I could forgo that punishment and still consider my life complete."

Baby tucked into the crook of her left arm, Kevral made a broad gesture with the right. "How's it look?"

Removing the handkerchief, Ra-khir examined the wound. "Not all that bad. The bleeding's stopped. We'll have a healer take a look at it in a bit. Right now, you have much to talk about, and I'd like to excuse myself if neither of you minds." The humor disappeared too quickly, leaving tension in its wake.

Tae nodded stiffly, and Kevral waved in dismissal. Ra-khir headed from the room. The door clicked closed behind him.

Still clutching the baby, Kevral turned away. "How did you find out?"

Tae refused to implicate Matrinka. "It doesn't matter. You should have told me."

"When?" Kevral turned back to face Tae. She walked to the chair. "This is the first chance I had."

"What's his name?"

"He doesn't have one yet." Kevral studied the baby, watching his eyes droop shut and his breathing settle to the slow rhythm of sleep. "The Renshai have to interview you to decide whether or not to accept him into the tribe. If they do, he'll undergo the training and be granted the name of a warrior who died in glory. One who will watch down on him from Valhalla."

"Oh," Tae said, other matters more pertinent at the moment. "Well. This may seem a bit late, but circumstances being what they are . . ." He slipped from the chair to his knees. "Will you marry me?"

Kevral winced.

Tae would have preferred almost any other response. "I thought you might want to marry the father of your baby."

"I did marry the father of my baby." Kevral placed the infant on the bed.

Tae's heart froze in his chest. His mouth refused to function, but his thoughts raced back to words Matrinka had spoken: *Béarnian law defines parentage by marriage at the time of birth, not blood.* "Oh, no." Tears filled Tae's eyes, and now he looked away. "Oh, no." He could still feel the impression of the baby against his skin. *I've lost Kevral* and *my child.* He wondered if his presence could have saved that bond, cursed the day he had decided to return to the East and make peace with his own father. For the second time in less than an hour, he discovered only irony. The price for finding a father turned out to be losing a son.

Kevral's free hand circled around his. It felt hot compared with the chill that numbed him. "Didn't you notice two babies, Tae? They're twins. Boys. The other one is Ra-khir's."

"Twins?" Confusion partially displaced grief. "With different fathers? That's impossible."

"Everyone says that. Including me, at first. It's rare but not impossible."

Realization became more important than arguing. "You married Ra-khir?" Tae found himself incapable of looking at Kevral. He had never doubted she would do so, but the reality struck harder than he expected, especially after he had become so certain that he had won her hand.

"I'm sorry, Tae. It was a difficult choice. Almost impossible. Had things happened differently, I might have married you. I love you."

At the moment, the words consoled little. "But not enough to parent my own child."

Kevral's hands tightened around Tae's. "Of course, enough for that."

Tae jerked his fingers free and finally looked directly at Kevral, eyes glaring and jaw fiercely clenched. "Don't toy with me. I know the law."

Kevral met his gaze with innocent bewilderment. "What law?"

"Béarnian law. The one that defines a baby's father by marriage prior to its birth."

Kevral's lips twitched. "First, I'm Renshai. I'm not constrained by Béarn's *social* order. If I were, the babies would have no fathers at all. We only married a few weeks ago. The twins are three months old."

Tae blinked, uncertain where Kevral was headed, and thus unable to concentrate on a single emotion. Grief and anger trickled away but did not disappear. The wrong words could spark either to a bonfire.

Kevral placed an arm around Tae's shoulders and led him back to the chair. She pulled up another beside him. Only now, he noticed the furnishings, plain compared to Matrinka's yet clearly Béarnian. Bears predominated in the carvings, the dressers, chairs, and bed sturdily constructed. "Ra-khir's mother and father parted ways when he was little. She quickly remarried and attempted to convince Ra-khir his stepfather was really his father. When he discovered the truth, his mother told terrible lies about his father." She shook her head, though whether at the foolishness of Ra-khir's mother or the idea that anyone could believe ill of Knight-Captain Kedrin, he did not know. "Eventually, she forced Ra-khir to choose to associate with either her or Kedrin, not both."

Tae nodded. He knew much of the story from conversations he and the young Knight of Erythane had shared alone. The hatred Ra-khir still harbored for mother and stepfather seemed the only chink in an otherwise flawless sense of honor.

Kevral studied Tae as if her next words should seem obvious. When he only waited for more, she finally continued. "He's not about to steal your son."

My son. Tae found himself smiling. He rose and took the baby, who awakened at the jostling. For second place, he had done as well as he could ever have hoped, his life permanently entwined with the woman he adored, their son a living testament of their love. He studied the darkening eyes that still held a hint of their birth blue. Thin, black hair trickled over the forehead, so like his own. The facial shape, narrow in the forehead, softly rounded cheekbones, and gentle chin resembled neither himself nor Kevral but, Tae realized suddenly, his own father.

Tae did not know how long he sat in silent discovery, but he abruptly became aware of a prolonged hush and that he rocked the baby without realizing he did so. The small lids drifted closed again, and Tae could not suppress a proud, admiring smile. However, the words he had to speak quickly banished the grin. Prolonging the question would not change the situation. "What happens now?"

Kevral's gaze drifted to the baby, and a softness crossed her usually too-somber features. "We need to present you and Ra-khir to the Renshai's current leaders. They have to decide if they think your bloodlines add enough to the tribe to admit one or both of the boys."

Tae grunted, anticipating. "So, when they find Ra-khir worthy and not me, what happens then?"

"There're three other possibilities, Tae."

"Uh-huh." Tae dismissed them. "The answer?"

Kevral shook her head, as if irritated beyond argument by Tae's foregone conclusion. "First, most fathers wouldn't consider acceptance of their sons into the Renshai tribe a 'worthy' thing."

Tae knew Kevral spoke truth. Though the Renshai protected the heirs to Béarn's throne, most feared their violence and rigid dedication. Legend proclaimed them golden-haired devils, from their wanderings nearly half a millenium past. Then, exiled from the savage North for brutality, they traveled the world, waging war on innocents for food, gold, and the joy of slaughter. Ancient tales survived the Renshai's ancestors, centuries after they'd settled peacefully on the Fields of Wrath, their swords now in the service of King Griff. Yet becoming Renshai still meant a life dedicated to dying, likely young, in the glory of battle.

"Second," Kevral continued, "I'm making no guesses. Neither should you. Renshai children take the tribe of their mother."

Tae cradled the sleeping baby, turning Kevral a narrow-eyed look. "I thought the tribe was Renshai."

"Right." Kevral sat, one leg on the floor, the other gathered to the seat. She could rise and fight in an instant should the need arise. "But there're three branches within the tribe. That goes back to a point in distant history when only six of us remained. The tribe of Rache carried no original Renshai blood, the tribe of Tannin carried half, and the tribe of Modrey was full-blooded."

Tae shrugged, wondering about the significance of the lesson.

"Of course, the tribes have interbred, so the differences have become less pronounced with time. Through the years, several Renshai have married outside the tribe. If they choose well, their children are often accepted, because new blood can bring new skill. Unfortunately, the leaders rarely accept outsiders into the tribe of Modrey because it has the purest blood."

"And," Tae guessed, "you're of Modrey."

"Right." Kevral shook back the yellow-white locks that fairly defined the Renshai's Northern origins. "So I don't know if they'll take either of the boys."

"Colbey Calistinsson believes redheaded Erythanians descend from Renshai."

At the mention of her hero, a light flickered through Kevral's pale eyes. She had emulated the ancient Renshai turned immortal, quoting him and patterning her life after his until discovering he still lived among the gods. "That may give Ra-khir an advantage," she admitted. "But it's not a contest. The Renshai may take one, both, or neither. Confirming one does not eliminate the other."

"And if they accept him?" Tae massaged the baby's palm with his thumb.

"He undergoes the training, the Renshai maneuvers, philosophy, and language. He is Renshai. When not with his *torke* . . ." Kevral used a word in her own language which interchangeably meant swordmaster and teacher. ". . . he can play and learn from us."

"Us," Tae repeated. "If I remain here."

Kevral made a noncommittal gesture, though her expression revealed that she hoped he would stay. "That's your choice, of course."

"Not wholly. I'm a diplomat now. And, apparently, a prince." Tae maintained doubts about the latter. Weile Kahn had intended to maintain the title "leader" when he stole the Eastern throne from corrupt and feuding princes. From citizenry to foreign kingdoms, others insisted on calling him king. He had requested that Tae succeed him, as master of the Eastland's criminals as well as his new duties of state. Tae had not yet agreed, though time and circumstances steered him, more and more, in that direction. "I have responsibilities in the East."

"Tae." Kevral reached over and stroked the baby's head. He snuggled deeper into Tae's arms. "You're his father. And I'm his mother. He has a right to both of us, and we have equal responsibilities to him. But if you don't think you can fulfill that commitment, Ra-khir would treat him no differently than his own son."

"I know that." Tae hugged the child protectively, and he stirred in his father's arms. "You agree our roles are equal."

"Yes." No hesitation from Kevral.

"I'm likely to spend years in Béarn. Eventually, though, I have to go back East," Tae stared at Kevral. "When I do, why can't I bring my son?"

Kevral closed her eyes, then opened them slowly. They seemed moister, though he saw no actual tears. "You may. Perhaps his brother, Ra-khir, and I would accompany you. If you'd have us."

Tae could scarcely believe he had won a battle against a Renshai. "I'd be thrilled."

"Assuming he's not accepted into the Renshai, of course." Kevral's words sounded suspiciously like a retraction.

"What do you mean?" Tae asked.

"Renshai train daily. Until he accomplishes the sequence of skills that define Renshai coming of age, usually around eighteen, he's bound to his *torke.*"

"You mean he couldn't travel."

"He could, but only with a Renshai of sufficient skill to teach him at whatever level he's attained."

"Like you?"

"Maybe."

Tae put the whole together. "So, if he's accepted as Renshai, he has to remain on or near the Fields of Wrath. He might come visit me, but he couldn't stay."

"Right."

Tae examined his son again, the tiny features the epitome of perfection, the miniature limbs embodying potential. Weile had made so many mistakes. Tae's son would not suffer a similar fate. "And if the Renshai don't accept him, he lives with me."

Kevral swallowed. Hard. When she finished, she nodded stiffly. "And the two of you visit me as you can. Or we'll travel to you."

"That's it?"

"That's it," Kevral repeated. "What more do you want?"

"Nothing," Tae said quickly. "I'm just surprised there're no conditions. I don't have to prove myself wiser than forty sages or hurl myself into a bonfire or battle you to the death."

Kevral managed a smile. "Not this time. Just be the best father you can. And I'll try to be the best mother."

Tae had watched Kevral fling herself eagerly upon hordes of enemies. She had climbed the gates of Valhalla to battle its undying warriors, without thought to her own mortality. Once, Weile had defended the errors he had made with his son, some nearly fatal, by stating that Kevral would understand when she had children of her own. Now, she did; and the idea that she might make similar mistakes became an anxiety that, this once, violence could not dispel. Sensing her need, Tae rose, enwrapping Kevral and the baby together into his embrace.

They clung for several moments, Kevral's body pressed against him inciting a passion Tae fought to contain. He would savor the times they had had together, but he would never betray his friends. *More irony.* Tae let his thoughts follow this tangent to force them from the wonder of Kevral in his arms, a pleasure soon only Ra-khir would know. He had joined Kevral, Matrinka, Darris, and Ra-khir initially only to use them to help battle the enemies that hunted him for no better reason than his parentage. Once, Tae had exploited his friends without guilt. Now, the very idea shocked dread through him. *I've come a long way. I only hope I can teach those values to my son.* "I'll do my best," he promised them both.

CHAPTER 1

The Fathers' Worth

Every time a sword is drawn, it's a real fight.
—*Colbey Calistinsson*

PERCHED upon an elegantly carved desk chair, King Griff ignored the austere furnishings, unable to pry his attention from Tem'aree'ay. The elf lounged on her bed, the canopy shadowing her golden curls and stealing the touch of elfin red. An ever-present smile lit her dainty oval face, her delicate figure a stark contrast to the whale-boned Béarnides. Even the bulge that housed their imminent child did not mar the fragile-appearing figure; the excitement of its presence trembled through Griff every time he glimpsed or thought of his lover, which was often.

Tem'aree'ay's eyes glittered in the lamplight, and Griff regretted that rain kept them indoors. In sunlight, their pure elfin coloring, unmarred by the starlike cores of human eyes, closely resembled sapphires. "Your daughter is beautiful, Sire."

Griff grinned with pride. He could not imagine any child more so. It did not matter to him that the black hair, dark eyes, and bulk came from the baby's mother and not himself. The previous evening, Béarn's populace had welcomed the new princess with a feast and the nobility with a ceremony flawlessly executed by the Knights of Erythane. Dragged into an eternity of pomp and speeches, Griff had found even his own elation giving way to boredom. Just once, he wished the knights would forgo a few spare details of their ritual; but his bodyguard/adviser, Bard Darris, had assured him that to request such would not only disparage the procedure but gravely insult the participants.

Now, Griff believed, Darris needed some time alone with the queen and the infant he had sired. And that left Griff free for his own favorite pastime: Tem'aree'ay. Emotion swept him suddenly, and he found himself unable even to blink as his dark eyes drank in every part of the elf. Once, he had believed his love ludicrous, like that of a sheep for a cat.

Innocent exploration had proved him wrong. A virgin until his night with Tem'aree'ay, he still did not know for certain whether elves and humans shared anatomy; but their companionship had turned naturally into lovemaking and, eventually, created the child in her womb.

So much more than becoming an illegitimate prince or princess lay upon the infant growing inside Tem'aree'ay. Only thirty-seven of the two hundred and forty elves lived in Béarn, in harmony with mankind. The others, the *svartalf,* sought to destroy humanity and had nearly succeeded using magic that rendered human women sterile. Only those pregnant at the time of the casting, or not yet of reproductive age, remained fertile and then only until their cycles started or resumed. The elves faced their own crisis that only a few humans knew: though freely sexual, they conceived only after the death of an elder due to age. Stripped of memories, the ancient soul then entered the newborn.

Griff saw the baby as the product of a love he once believed he could never consummate. But those who knew of the coupling, most of them elves, saw the continuity of life itself in the tiny, developing being. Here might lie a solution to both problems, yet no one wished to act until the results became clear. The human/elf might die outside the protective world of Tem'aree'ay's womb. A twisted, hideous monster might emerge or a soulless creature despised by the gods. Elfin magic would tell them more about the baby than Griff's eyes ever could, but the deeper truth did not matter to him. Whatever the result, he could not help adoring the child. *Perfect, no less.* Griff's smile widened, innocent faith carrying him past the concerns of elves and advisers. *The gods care for us too much to let else be the case.*

"Why so quiet, Sire?" Tem'aree'ay's question seemed odd. Elfin lives spanned centuries or millennia, and they never seemed to notice lapses that could make even a Knight of Erythane squirm.

Griff rose, knelt in front of Tem'aree'ay, and took her hands. His beefy fists engulfed her long, slender fingers and tiny palms. "Tem'aree'-ay, would you agree to marry me?"

The elf blinked once, expression blank. "Marry?" she managed.

Griff nodded vigorously, coarse black bangs slipping into his eyes.

"Elves don't . . ." Tem'aree'ay started, then stopped. "I mean we've never . . ."

Griff understood. "So you'll be the first. Like you're the first to carry a human's baby."

The homogeneous eyes studied Griff's gentle, rotund features. "What would I have to do, Sire?"

"Just stay with me forever . . ." Realizing the discrepancy between her life span and his own, Griff amended, "Well, that is, as long as *I* live. And allow me to love you."

Tem'aree'ay wet her heart-shaped lips with her triangular tongue. "Sire, I'm not going anywhere. And don't you already love me?"

"Well, yes," Griff admitted. "But this would make it official. And our children heirs to the throne, too." Ancient law and custom did not allow illegitimate offspring to rule.

Tem'aree'ay nodded, eyes narrowing slightly in confusion. Experience had taught Griff to read beyond the subtlety of elfin expression. "But, Sire, aren't you already married?"

Griff released Tem'aree'ay's hands, lowering his head until the hair fell into a full curtain over his eyes. He wanted to hide the tears resulting from Tem'aree'ay's hesitation. "The high king can marry as many times as he wants. In fact, it's encouraged. It varies the line and makes for more heirs if something happens." He thought of the previous ruler, his grandfather. King Kohleran had not taken the throne until age forty, by then pledged to only one wife whom he adored too much to share with others. Though she had borne him eight children, who, in their turn, produced twelve grandchildren, and four great grandchildren, this had nearly proved too few. Aside from Griff, those not assassinated by elves had failed the staff-test created by the father of the gods, Odin, to assure the appropriateness of Béarn's heirs to rule.

Thoughts of the staff-test raised other concerns. The leader of the *svartalf*, Dh'arlo'mé, had stolen the Staves of Law and Chaos before Griff could undergo his own testing. Nobility and commoners alike believed Griff the proper heir and had crowned him without challenge. He alone seemed to harbor doubts about his worthiness to rule, a worry Darris had assured him boded well for his fitness as king. Kevral, Ra-khir, and Tae had later discovered that Dh'arlo'mé bonded with the Staff of Law and its near-infinite power. The immortal Renshai, Colbey Calistinsson, had taken up the Staff of Chaos for the purpose of restoring balance. And Colbey's son, Ravn, had assured Griff that he, as all the Béarnian kings before him, represented the focal point of the worlds' equilibrium. Without him, the universe would crumble into ruin.

King Griff ran a hand through his beard, coarse hairs rasping against his fingers. "I married Matrinka for the populace. Now I want to marry for love."

Tem'aree'ay's voice penetrated the barrier of hair he had placed between them. "You love Matrinka." Woman and elf served Béarn as healers. Not only did they work together, but their closeness to Béarn's king had also brought them a friendship.

"Yes," Griff admitted. "Like a sister. Or my mother." Thought of the latter pinched his chest. For months, the *svartalf* had employed Eastern criminals to prevent all travel or trade in the Westlands. Griff could not even send a messenger to assure his mother and stepfather of his well-being. A lump formed in his throat at the thought of his mother's pain. She had lost his elder brother and his father to a plowing accident and overprotected him to the point of paranoia. The last she knew of him, he had disappeared without a trace. "My love for you is special. It's . . . it's . . ." His vocabulary failed him. "I can't explain it. I want this for our child. For you." Shaking back the dark mane, he finally met Tem'aree'-ay's eyes again. "For me."

A light flickered through the canted eyes. Tem'aree'ay would never fully understand the significance; her two hundred years of elfin culture would not allow it. But she did finally realize the importance of her answer to him. "Of course I'll marry you, Sire."

Only at that moment did Griff remember he had no right to ask. The law limited the prospects of all descendants of the king's line, him most of all. He dropped back to his haunches. "Tem'aree'ay, I'm an idiot."

"Sire." The elf's tone chastised his self-deprecation.

Griff sighed. "Here I am talking you into something that doesn't matter to you, and I don't even know if the law allows it."

"It matters to me, Sire," Tem'aree'ay insisted, sliding from the bed to sit beside him, her movements graceful despite her condition. She reached up and placed a gentle hand on his shoulders. "Anything that means so much to you matters to me."

Griff forced a smile, though his heart felt like a stone in his chest. In the moments he had considered it, the marriage had become the central focus of his world. The idea of losing it to formality was painful. He caught Tem'aree'ay into an embrace, reveling in her warmth against him. He clung for a long time, afraid to let go for fear he might lose her forever. He whispered into her ear, "I don't know exactly how the law reads, but it can't say anything about elves. Less than a year ago, we didn't even know you existed. If there's a loophole anywhere, the sage will find it; and we'll marry before our child is born."

Tem'aree'ay squeezed him back, her strength meager compared to his yet more than her usually spare frame suggested possible.

"And Tem'aree'ay?"

"Yes, Sire?"

"Once we're married, you'll have to stop calling me 'sire.' "

A careful tapping at the door interrupted any reply Tem'aree'ay might have given. Reluctantly, Griff released the elfin healer. "Who is it?" he shouted, hoping whichever elf had come to call on Tem'aree'ay would take the hint and leave.

The door muffled the familiar voice. "Your Majesty, it's Darris."

He should be with Matrinka and Marisole. Griff knew Darris felt as strongly about his time with the queen as he did about his with Tem'aree'ay, especially in the days since the birth of the baby. "Is it important, Darris?"

A short pause followed the question. The king placed a hand on Tem'aree'ay's leg and tipped his head toward the door, straining. Just as he thought he had missed Darris' reply, it came. "Very."

Griff lumbered to his feet, not wishing to endure another of Darris' lectures about the floor being too low for his station. "Come in, then."

Tem'aree'ay returned to the bed, smoothing her shift as the door swung open.

Darris peeked inside, mousy curls dangling over thin brows and the large, straight nose that Marisole already showed signs of inheriting. His hazel eyes flitted over the sparse furnishings to land on his king, and the broad lips framed a smile that revealed joy barely contained. "Your Majesty, announcing Lady Helana and her husband, Herwin."

Griff went utterly still; even his heart seemed to stop. He stood staring, unable to speak.

Darris stepped aside, revealing the familiar plump figure of Griff's mother. Though only thirty-three, she harbored wisps of white hair among the black, and a few wrinkles scored her face. She had aged years in the months of their separation. For a moment, their eyes met, exact dark duplicates. Behind her, less than a finger's breadth taller, Griff's stepfather awaited his chance for reunion.

Helana rushed to Griff, silks supplied by the palace fluttering in her wake. She wrapped him in a bear hug; and he clung to her, sobbing. Her warm tears dripped down his collar.

"Mama. Oh, Mama," Griff breathed out at length.

Simultaneously, they said, "I worried so much about you."

Then tears turned to laughter, and Herwin joined the embrace. Though large for a Westerner, he seemed tiny to Griff who had grown substantially in the last year and become accustomed to Béarnides. The sandy hair and gray eyes seemed particularly out of place. A work-hardened hand clutched Griff's arm, calluses rasping against satin. The farm seemed a million years and a trillion miles away.

Mama. Griff closed his eyes, thoughts gliding backward. The odors of fresh-turned earth, damp, and manure filled his nose, accompanied by the snort of the horses, the clank of the plow, and a man's occasional muffled curse. After the accident that had claimed the lives of Griff's father and brother, Helana had refused to allow Griff even to assist with heavy chores, preferring to give up luxuries, even necessities, to pay laborers to tend the farm in Dunwoods. Herwin had been the last of these. Guarded by his mother to the point of suffocation, Griff had found reprieve in a wooded grove near the farm. There, he had spent the happiest times of his childhood listening to the birds and chirruping insects, skipping stones, and exchanging stories with a young blond he had once believed a creation of his own imagination. Only after elves captured him did he finally discover his childhood friend was Ravn Colbeysson, the son of the immortal Renshai and a goddess.

Griff snuggled into the warm security of his parents' arms, and the responsibilities of a kingdom disappeared.

Darris cleared his throat. "Your Majesty, a Northman, a guard in the employ of Pudar accompanied them. We've treated him to a good meal and a warm bath, but he says he can't stay. He has duties in Pudar."

"Give him—" Griff started, then stopped abruptly, embarrassed to order others while in his parents' presence, let alone their embrace. He gently disengaged himself, still trapped in his younger years. Scarlet crept across his cheeks, and the command refused to emerge. He felt like a child caught playing king.

Darris sensed Griff's discomfort. "Majesty, I'll see he gets anything he needs or wants for the trip. And a fresh horse."

"Thank you," Griff said humbly. He returned his attention to mother and stepfather. "Did I mention? I'm king now."

Helana laughed kindly, sharing a wink with the departing bard. "We heard, dear."

The family fell back into another cycle of hugging while Tem'aree'ay looked on happily.

Tae sprawled in the window seat, back against the frame, right leg tucked in front of him, and left leg dangling nearly to the floor. A cross draft from the opposite window sucked in rain that pelted him like grains of ice. Seated on a nearby chest, Kevral clutched her hands in her lap; he had never before seen her so nervous. Ra-khir sat beside her, dressed in his best silk colors. Two chairs occupied the center of the room beneath a candelabra, holding eight burning tapers, that dangled from a ceiling beam by a chain. Occasionally, an unusually heavy gust sent the lamp swinging, and light swirled around the room in erratic ovals.

Tae looked out over the Fields of Wrath from the second floor of the Renshai common house. Cottages scattered without pattern, and occasional paddocks held pigs, horses, goats, or sheep. The clang of steel striking steel rang over the patter of rain against wood and thatch, punctuated by indecipherable commands. Weather made no difference when it came to Renshai sword practices. They preferred to vary sites and conditions, prepared to war under any circumstances. Violence was the very essence of the Renshai, the desperate need to die in glorious combat and find a place in *Valhalla*. Tae, Kevral, and Ra-khir had once visited the haven for the souls of those bravest warriors. He had watched them battle through the day, those slain rising every evening to join the victors in a grand feast until morning brought a new round of warfare. Tae believed he would prefer a more peaceful after-death experience.

The door latch clicked.

Kevral hissed through clenched teeth, "Tae."

He glanced over.

Kevral made a sharp gesture for him to find a more dignified position as the door whipped open and two men entered. The first looked as massive as any Béarnide, middle-aged, broad-boned and -featured with green eyes. He wore his golden hair in braids, the style of Northern warriors. The smaller, younger man who accompanied him kept his dark blond hair clipped as short as Kevral's. Hard blue eyes settled on the bench's occupants. Both sported leather tunics and breeks, a sword thrust through each belt. Their pale skin revealed their once-Northern origins.

Tae shifted from his slouch to a wary crouch. Warriors should appreciate his caution, mannerly or otherwise.

The huge Renshai took the farther chair. "I am Thialnir Thrudazisson."

The second nodded a stiff welcome. "Gareth Lasirsson."

Ra-khir rose and executed a sweeping gesture of greeting that impressed Tae, though neither Renshai seemed affected. "Ra-khir Kedrin's son, Knight to the Erythanian and Béarnian kings: His Grace, King Humfreet, and His Majesty, King Griff." When no one else made a move to take the floor, Ra-khir indicated Kevral with a polite motion. "You know Kevralyn Tainharsdatter."

"Kevral," Kevral interrupted gruffly. She had always despised her full first name. "As you know." She glared pointedly at Ra-khir.

A hint of a smile entered Gareth's expression. "Your peers call you Kevral the Overconfident."

The insult clearly stung. Kevral's hands blanched in her lap, and her face gained the flush her fingers had lost. "My peers choose to ridicule when they cannot compete." Kevral had a right to pride. At fifteen, she had gained her status as a Renshai adult by accomplishing the difficult series of maneuvers rarely mastered before eighteen.

Gareth recoiled, grin disappearing. Tae guessed he had a child or children who would consider themselves among those peers. Thialnir represented the Renshai at meetings of the Béarnian council. He redirected the proceedings back to introductions by turning Tae a stern, questioning look.

Tae did not bother to move, though he did brush away mist that had gathered on his bangs. "Tae," he said simply. In the East, shortening a person's name was grave insult. In the West, people did so routinely.

Kevral gave Tae a squint-eyed stare that held warning. Though she had demonstrated her anger at Ra-khir and Gareth, Tae held initial responsibility for her mood. It seemed he refused to view the proceedings with proper seriousness. "*Prince* Tae Kahn, son of Weile Kahn, ruler of Stalmize, the East's high kingdom, and the East's diplomat to Béarn."

Tae shrugged. *The only person in the world with a title longer than Ra-khir's.* He could not wholly explain his apathy, feeling trapped into an unwinnable situation. Ra-khir's courtly upbringing, classically handsome features, and manners defied competition. Tae never doubted his friend would be found worthy. His own lack of value, to Renshai or others, seemed a foregone conclusion. It did not matter that his father had taken over a kingdom nor how many referred to him as "prince." In his own mind, he would always remain a gang-running, sneak-thieving son of a crime lord. He alone seemed to realize the farce of this testing. Ra-khir's son would join the Renshai and his own would have to deal with the shame of exclusion. Tae did not need to undergo the scrutiny of these two to know he would fail.

Thialnir cleared his throat. "Duly noted." He nodded at Gareth to indicate the younger man should initiate the proceedings.

Gareth obliged. "We've had the children examined. Both healthy. And it does seem as if your claim of different fathers may be correct."

Kevral's scowl deepened. Tae knew she would not allow suspicion about her word or her morals. The process did not require either.

"In that light," Gareth continued, "who would like to go first?"

Ra-khir glanced around Kevral to Tae, offering.

Tae shook his head.

Ra-khir stood, brushing back his tan cape to reveal the Béarnian bear on his blue velvet tunic. "I will, sir." Black breeks and an orange brooch and sash finished his colors. A sword graced his left hip. He adjusted its position from habit, by flicking the edge of the sheath rather than touching the hilt.

"Very well." Gareth also rose, the candles sparking yellow highlights through his darker hair as he moved. He pinned his icy gaze on the Erythanian. "What does your bloodline have to offer the Renshai?"

Ra-khir launched directly into his reasoning, clearly having dedicated much thought to the matter, a preparing Tae did not share. "First, history suggests that red-haired Erythanians descend from Renshai conquerors, so my child may restore some lost blood back to the tribe."

Thialnir nodded thoughtfully. Gareth remained in place, lips pursed, waiting expectantly for more.

Tae settled back into a sitting position, glancing out the window again and seeing nothing through sheets of rain. Droplets bounced from the sill, cold prickles against his cheeks. From habit, he measured the construction of window and building.

"Second, sir," Ra-khir went on, "I offer size and strength."

Renshai maneuvers rely on quickness, not strength. The Colbey quotation came instantly to Tae's mind, though he could not recall whether he had learned it from Kevral or from the biography of Colbey he had stolen from Pudar's castle and gifted to her nearly a year ago. She cited the ancient Renshai often.

"I name patience and determination among my assets. Without them, I could not have become a Knight of—"

Gareth interrupted. "What determination does it take to follow rigid codes? And to expect enemies to do the same?"

Tae jerked his attention back, surprised by Gareth's hostility.

Ra-khir stiffened slightly but otherwise showed no offense. "Sir, there is nothing rigid about morality. And while I do grant all men and women their dignity by assuming they will act with honor, I know how to handle a situation should they choose otherwise. I will always steer friend or opponent toward the reputable path; but I'm not foolish enough to believe they will always take it. I won't apologize for expecting the best from everyone."

Gareth made a wordless, noncommittal grunt. "Determination?" he reminded.

"Sir, the training is years long and grueling. The testing takes an entire day, and any break means instant failure."

"Renshai train from infancy," Gareth snorted. "An entire day of standing in pristine lines is hardly an accomplishment." Turning his back, he headed toward his chair. In most areas of the Westlands, such a gesture indicated trust. From Renshai, it cast profound aspersion, suggesting the other could not muster the competence to prove a threat to an open target.

Ra-khir had spent enough time with Kevral to recognize the insult. His nostrils flared, and his hands tensed. "Sir, you're coming dangerously close to belittling knight's honor."

Gareth spun slowly. "Close?" He took a menacing forward step. "Try this, then." He lowered his voice to a growl. "No self-respecting Renshai would couple with a narrow-minded, inflexible man of pseudo-honor whose only worth is that an ancestor might carry some Renshai blood."

Tae flinched. Even he had never baited Ra-khir so harshly. Kevral's hands leaped to her hilts, and her face purpled. She could not interfere.

The knight maintained his temper admirably. He turned Kevral an apologetic glance before returning his gaze to Gareth. "Sir, I'm going to have to call you out."

Thialnir stood up and moved quietly toward the door. Once there, he did not exit, just leaned against it, watching.

Gareth grinned insolently. "Good."

Ra-khir drew breath. Erythanian law dictated that whoever called the challenge chose time, place, and weapons.

"Don't bother with your details." Gareth deliberately placed a hand on his hilt. "I'm not waiting."

"Proof my patience could serve the tribe." Ra-khir's sword rasped from its sheath.

The Renshai drew quicker, cutting in the same motion.

Anticipating, Ra-khir raised his blade only to block. Sword hammered sword with a clang that echoed through the small room. Both disengaged. Again, the Renshai moved more swiftly, and the knight defended without riposte.

Tae scrambled to a cautious crouch on the sill, prepared to disappear should the battle muddle in his direction. Kevral did not even bother to rise, though her eyes followed every detail of the combat and her hands twitched in her lap, no longer entwined.

Repeatedly, the Renshai's sword slashed, swept, and jabbed. Ra-khir met each attack with a block or parry. Superior size and strength worked to his advantage; he gained no ground but neither did he lose any. Perspiration slicked his hair and beaded the area between nose and upper lip. Every lightning movement flung moisture. In contrast, the Renshai seemed tireless. His slim sword skipped around Ra-khir like a fairy, flashing silver in the candlelight.

Then, suddenly, Kevral sucked in a breath. Ra-khir apparently saw the opening, too. His sword speared through, his first attack. The tip rammed Gareth's crosspiece, and the sword left the Renshai's hand.

He'll try to catch it. Tae wished he could send a mental warning to Ra-khir. The Renshai belief that touching the floor dishonored a sword would make Gareth's next action predictable.

Ra-khir leaped for Gareth as the Renshai sprang for his flying weapon. The knight willfully cast aside his own sword as the two slammed together and his bulk sent the slighter blond rolling. Ra-khir moved with him, grappling for the Renshai's arms and using his weight to pin the other down. Gareth eeled out from under him. Ra-khir followed too slowly. The Renshai pitched, scrambling for his sword. Thialnir clapped his hands. "Enough."

Red-faced, Gareth reclaimed his weapon as Ra-khir climbed to his feet, seeking his own sword. Abruptly, Gareth lunged. Ra-khir recoiled, but not far enough. The flat of the Renshai's sword slammed the side of his head, sprawling him.

Tae winced.

"I said enough!" Thialnir growled.

"Bastard!" Kevral rushed to her husband's defense, placing herself between them and glaring with the ferocity of a wolf guarding cubs. The law that forbade her interference strained her to the limit of endurance.

Ra-khir lay still a moment, then clambered up awkwardly. A reddening bruise marred the perfect curve of his cheek. His green eyes blazed, but he did not translate that anger into action. He recovered his sword, only to sheathe it and battle with words instead. "I'll suffer that for my wife and son. Otherwise, Gareth, I'd have no willing dealings with a group that finds you worthy of membership."

"We had to take *him*. He was born Renshai." The fierce intensity of Thialnir's glower at Kevral stole the humor from his joke. "You taught the knight a Renshai maneuver," he accused.

Ra-khir adjusted his clothing and sword belt.

Kevral's mouth fell open. "I did nothing of the kind."

"Where did he learn *floyetsverd*?"

"Ask him," Kevral suggested. Her gaze followed Gareth as he sheathed his sword and retreated beyond range.

"You mean the disarming, sir?" Ra-khir guessed, touching the wound carefully.

"Yes." Thialnir turned the suspicious stare toward Ra-khir.

"With all respect, sir, the Renshai didn't invent disarming."

Gareth made a noise deep in his throat. Thialnir ignored him. "True. But most others would have left Gareth minus a hand or a few fingers at least." He tossed a braid behind his shoulder, his features placid. "But that was *floyetsverd*, sloppily done but adequate to undo Gareth."

Tae admired how the Renshai's representative managed to offend both parties with a single sentence.

The flush returned to Gareth's features. "He dishonored me and my sword. He deliberately let it touch the ground."

Thialnir raised his brows. "Under the circumstances, I would have done the same."

"But—" Gareth started.

Thialnir silenced him with a gesture, refusing to be sidetracked. "Where did you learn that maneuver, Ra-khir?"

"Sir, I've seen Renshai fight many times." Ra-khir took Kevral's hand, heading back toward his seat. Only a slight stumble revealed his dizziness. "After the nine thousandth time Kevral disarmed me, I figured it out."

Thialnir nodded, accepting the explanation.

Ra-khir looked at Gareth. "Colbey Calistinsson was a Knight of Erythane. Do you doubt his honor, too?"

"Colbey a knight?" Gareth's blue eyes widened. "That's sacrilege."

"It's truth," Kevral defended. "Colbey told us himself."

Tae remembered well. Colbey had first appeared to Kevral and Ra-khir, then the entire party. Later, he had attempted to recruit Kevral to wield the Staff of Chaos against Dh'arlo'mé. Learning it would destroy Kevral, Tae and Ra-khir had argued against Colbey's choice. Whether because of them, or matters Tae did not understand, Colbey had reprieved Kevral and chosen to champion chaos himself. They had not heard from him since.

Thialnir shook his head. "Delusion, Kevral. Colbey died fighting the fires of *Ragnarok* more than three centuries ago."

Kevral abandoned a stale argument. "Believe or not. I know what happened. And I've met with him more than once."

Ra-khir drove for the point. "Sir, it doesn't matter whether you believe we interacted with Colbey. I doubted, too, at first. Research proved me wrong. I can show you documentation that Colbey joined the Knights of Erythane and rode a white charger called Frost Reaver."

Still does. Tae did not add his piece aloud. Whatever divine magic had kept Colbey alive for more than four hundred years did the same for the stallion.

"Sir, whatever you might think of knight's honor, at least we would never blindside an honored foe after the war was declared ended."

"Enough!" Gareth roared.

"Enough," Thialnir agreed, though for different reasons. "No need to drag this out longer. Sir Ra-khir, the Renshai find you worthy of marrying into the tribe and siring warriors. From this moment forth, your son shall bear the name Saviar Rakhirsson, a full-fledged member of the tribe of Renshai."

Gareth presented a grudging nod, Ra-khir a broad but lopsided grin. "Thank you, sir."

"No need for gratitude," Thialnir returned, taking his seat. "You won the honor for your child on your own merits. The Renshai do not bestow charity."

Every eye turned suddenly to Tae where he poised in the window. Pinned, he froze.

"Your turn, Tae," Thialnir said.

My turn. Tae remained in place, ignoring the sting of droplets on the back of his neck. He felt trapped, torn between worrying about his son's self-esteem and his own need to parent. It might hurt the boy to know his brother received an honor refused him; yet turning his child over to Renshai seemed more condemnation than reward. He thought of the life the child would have as a Renshai: unforgiving teachers, daily violence, the eager pursuit of a savage and bloody death not only for enemies but for himself. *I'm not fighting any Renshai.* He had neither the courage nor competence to do so.

Tae shrugged. "I—" he started, catching Kevral's brisk gesture for him to stand from the corner of his eye. With a sigh of resignation, he sprang to the floor. "I have nothing to offer."

"Tae!" Kevral's sharp retort reverberated.

Tae whirled toward her, tiring of the entire situation. Ra-khir had worked so hard yet had still suffered humiliation. Tae knew he had no chance at all. "Damn it, Kevral, it's true. I'm not big. I'm not strong." He outlined a wiry frame little taller than Kevral's. Standing, Ra-khir and Thialnir would tower a head above him, and Gareth half that. "My blood is Eastern farther back than anyone would bother to trace it, and mediocre is a compliment to my sword skill. What do I have to add? Dark eyes? Dark skin? Dark—?"

Gareth's rash draw-cut caught Tae wholly unprepared. The wall prevented retreat, and a dodge forward or to either side would place him squarely in its path. Desperate, Tae dropped and rolled. The blade kissed his scalp, severing strands of hair. A jab followed, foiled by a wild dodge.

Tae scampered to the center of the room. "Why—?"

Gareth's sword whipped for Tae's head again. Tae ducked, deliberately clumsy. As he expected, an instantaneous low attack followed, while he transferred his balance. The sword swept for his legs. Tae jumped to the chair, then to the candelabra as the sword raced for him again. Certain it would not hold his weight long, he scrambled up the chain to the support beam. Swinging his feet onto the beam, Tae crouched and reassessed the situation. Light swept crazily through the room, disrupting every shadow. Gareth leaped to the chair, and the sword stabbed for Tae again. Gauging in an instant, Tae sprang from his beam to the next, then hurled himself through the window. Gareth's boots hammered the floorboards in pursuit.

Catching the sill, Tae flung his body upward. Instead of a two-story fall, he slammed against the wooden construction above the window. Fingers gouging into chinking, he scurried to the roof, rain pounding his back. A moment later, Gareth's head thrust through the opening, naturally looking downward. Tae searched for a rock but immediately discarded that strategy. It would only enrage the Renshai. Instead, he studied the layout of the rooftop. Three rain barrels perched on the thatch, connected to a cistern beneath the common house. *Now what?*

Finding nothing else of use, Tae seized the upper ring of the nearest barrel. Water slicked his hands, and the wind chilled them painfully. The ring would not budge, so he tried another. This one slid free without a struggle. Clutching it in his teeth, Tae clambered down the opposite side of the building, toward his window seat.

Tae entered silently, transferring the ring to his hand. Kevral and Thialnir glanced toward him but said nothing to give him away. Gareth still stood at the opposite window, seeking him through the gloom. Rakhir watched the Renshai, standing, his expression worried.

"Hey!" Tae said, tossing the ring toward Gareth and anticipating the Renshai's movement. Gareth whirled, stepping perfectly. The ring glided over him as if made for that purpose. In the instant it pinned Gareth's sword arm, Tae drew his own blade and charged.

The maneuver gained Tae less time than he expected. His sword barely cleared its sheath when Gareth decreased his girth with breaths and motion. The ring thumped to the floor, clanging, and the Renshai howled toward the challenge.

Tae backpedaled just as Thialnir's voice cleaved the air. "Gareth, enough!"

This time the younger Renshai obeyed, jamming his sword back into place. Familiar with Renshai quickness and with Gareth's temper, Tae bounded to the window seat.

Gareth did not pursue, instead retaking his chair.

Finally, Tae finished his question. "Why in Hel did you do that?" Terror caught him in a rush, and he hid his shaking hands.

Gareth grinned. "Downstairs, Kevral said you were quick. I wanted to see for myself."

Tae's heart thrashed in his chest. "You could have killed me."

"I thought I did with that first strike. A little lower . . ." Gareth shook his head, frustration obvious.

"And killing me would have proved. . . ?" Tae pressed.

"That you don't deserve to father a Renshai's child."

Fear transformed to anger. Tae tipped his head toward Kevral, careful not to take his gaze wholly from Gareth. "Death for failure wasn't part of the deal."

Kevral shrugged helplessly, as ignorant of the process as he.

Thialnir broke in, his features still maddeningly composed. "Tae, until today, I would have said no one could dodge more than one of a Renshai's strokes. If you can teach some of that to us, no doubt you and your son belong among us."

Damn. Tae cursed his misfortune. *Run from people whose ultimate insult is "coward," and it impresses them. To win this one, I'd have had to let him kill me.* "Simple. No teaching needed. The first stroke was the only one that caught me slacking. After that, easy logic. Because of positioning, a jab was the only thing that could get me the second time. After he went high, it only made sense to attack the legs, where'd I placed most of my weight. After that, I was just running."

Thialnir shook his head. "The hoop. How could you possibly know Gareth would swing left when he turned?"

Tae settled deeper into his crouch, heart still racing and guard high. "He had his sword in his right hand. Most warriors would naturally spin right, a stronger defense. I've noticed Renshai tend to turn to weakness." He shrugged. "I took a chance."

Tae's methods obviously did not bother Gareth as Ra-khir's had. He seemed more curious this time. "Why'd you come back at all? You knew I wasn't sparring."

Tae considered the words in a lengthy silence. The answer, when it came to him, both grated on and pleased him. "My best friends were here, including the mother of my son. I wouldn't leave them at the mercy of a Renshai obviously gone deranged."

Kevral and Ra-khir jerked toward Tae simultaneously, both gravely offended, though they surely appreciated his loyalty, too.

Thialnir shook back his war braids. "Kevral also said you're the only person who has ever managed to approach her undetected. Long ago, the Southern barbarians taught us many stealth techniques. Your antics fall into that category. Three hundred years later, we've refined what we've learned, but the barbarians have remained reclusive." He studied Tae gently. "We can teach warriors to anticipate, but not to react to that knowledge so well or so quickly. We have use for your skills, both what you can teach and your natural agility."

Tae scarcely blinked. No one had ever praised him to such a degree before. His father had always proved a harsh guide.

Thialnir continued, grinning, "We have a special name for your son. We have assigned it to no one through the centuries, seeking one worthy of the honor. Named for Colbey's father, we would call him Calistin Taesson."

The compliments made Tae bold. "It would have to be Calistin Kahn Taesson."

Thialnir's smile wilted. "Why?"

"Family tradition," Tae explained. "Tae Kahn. Weile Kahn."

"No." Thialnir shook his head vigorously. "No. No, we can't do that. The child must have a guardian in Valhalla. Same name or no guardian."

Tae looked at Kevral. She stared at him, blank-eyed and disappointed. He sighed, taking another breath to relent.

Before he could, Gareth broke in. "I think I have a solution."

Thialnir looked at him.

"Pseubicon."

Thialnir's lids narrowed, and he seemed about to challenge. Then his lips twitched. The smile returned. "At least a century ago, during a battle in the far south, a Renshai child got lost. Barbarians found and raised her, but she never forgot her roots. Eventually, she found her way back, along with her barbarian husband and son, Pseubicon." Thialnir started to pace. "The boy was three. By Renshai tradition, a child not uniquely named for a warrior in Valhalla by one year of age is considered *uvakt* or 'unguarded.'" Turning, Thialnir headed back toward his chair. "As you can guess, the husband was found worthy. Despite being *uvakt*, Pseubicon became a great warrior and died in glory. However, no one since has cared to take the odd name for a son."

"All right. Pseubi*con*." Tae understood the connection but did not necessarily believe it a solution. "But is it spelled the same? K-A-H-N?"

Gareth laughed. "That's the beauty of it. The barbarians don't have a written language. You can spell it any way you please."

Tae glanced at Kevral. "Do you mind?"

Kevral would not lie. They both knew she preferred Calistin. "I can live with Pseubicon so long as you don't insert a bunch of weird Eastern vowels."

Tae made a throwaway gesture. "I spelled the kahn part. You handle the rest."

Kevral pursed her lips briefly. "Let's make it fair, then. Four letters to four letters. S-U-B-I-K-A-H-N."

Tae turned his attention to Gareth and Thialnir. "And now, if you're done attacking me, I've got a son who's waiting to hear his new name."

Thialnir gestured at the door.

Subikahn Taesson. It was not the name Tae would have chosen, but it suited well enough. He only hoped he could grow as accustomed to his child's tribe. *Father a crime lord, son a Renshai.* Tae groaned. *I'm going to have to learn to sleep with* both *eyes open.*

CHAPTER 2

The Pica Stone

I can't suffer the idea of the Pica in a stranger's hand. If we both claim it for our people, then our peoples must become one and you my brother.
—Colbey Calistinsson to Shadimar

MIDDAY light trickled through a high window, spreading a happy glow through the queen's chambers. Matrinka sat beside Darris on her bed, left hand wrapped around one of the canopy pillars, brown eyes locked on the baby clutched in the bard's arms, and smile permanently pasted on her features. He twined a finger through the wisps of Marisole's dark hair, strands catching on his calluses. Long lashes swept from tiny lids, and the bowlike mouth emitted regular, soft breaths. Matrinka had loved Darris for years, since long before she denied being more than friends, but never more than at this moment.

A firm knock echoed through the chamber. Sighing, Darris rose and passed the baby to Matrinka. Griff's blessing or not, it would not do for Béarn's servants to find him in the queen's bed cuddling the king's baby. "Who is it?" he demanded, his gruffer-than-usual tone his only expression of disappointment.

The answer wafted through the panel. "Prime Minister Davian, Darris. Are His Majesty and Her Ladyship with you?"

Outranked, Darris dropped his brusqueness immediately. "Come in, Lord."

The door edged cautiously open, and the middle-aged prime minister of Béarn looked through the widening crack. Only a year ago, the ex-carver had led a scraggly band of renegades that had, with the help of the Knights of Erythane, ousted the *svartalf* invaders from Béarn and placed Griff upon his throne. His scarred face seemed out of place among the nobility, yet the properly sculpted mane of beard, no-nonsense bearing, and silks made it obvious he took his job seriously and would brook no doubts about his worthiness for the position. Catching a glimpse of Matrinka, he bowed. "Your Ladyship."

Matrinka accepted the formality with only a twinge of displeasure. Over ten months, she had grown accustomed to it. "What can I do for you, Prime Minister?" The warmth of the baby felt comforting against her chest, most of it from Darris.

"There's a meeting of the council about to start, if you wish to attend, Ladyship."

Meetings bored Matrinka. She had already decided to turn down the offer as Davian finished.

"I'm sorry for the lack of notice, Ladyship. Captain has returned, and he called the meeting."

Darris stiffened, obviously eager to attend, though he would have no choice but to stay if she declined.

But the prime minister's words banished that thought from Matrinka's mind. The leader of the light elves, or *lysalf* as they called themselves, Captain had gone to assist those humans harmed by the Easterners' blockade of Westlands travel. Not only had Captain become a trusted adviser and friend, but the oddity of an outworlder convening a meeting suggested matters of great import. A human year passed like days to elves. Most still felt shy and awkward around the conventions of Béarn, alternately forgetting or overplaying decorum. Like deer among the bears, they usually worked with quiet grace, amiable and gracious but socially withdrawn. Having lived among humans millennia longer than his peers, Captain seemed less distressed by human law and custom, but even he had never before called the council.

"Thank you, Davian." Matrinka rose, shifting the baby into a more balanced position against her chest. The tiny eyes opened, then drifted closed again. "I'll be there as soon as I find a nursemaid."

Davian's attention shifted to Darris, and the minister winced obviously enough that the bard clearly noticed. Darris' thick brows arched over hazel eyes, more brown than green in the spare light. "Did I do something to offend you, Lord?"

"No, certainly not." Davian sighed deeply. "I'm only thinking that, if you're here . . ." He drifted off, apparently believing his thought obvious.

Matrinka did not understand.

More familiar with the situation, Darris caught on faster. "If you don't mind, Ladyship, perhaps Davian could find the nursemaid. And we could seek His Majesty."

Matrinka still did not decipher the problem, but she trusted Darris and Davian. "A good idea. Do you mind, Prime Minister?" She offered Marisole.

Davian entered the room and bowed. "An honor, my Lady." He took the baby into his arms with a gentleness that bordered on paranoia, as if he worried he might break her. "The meeting will begin with your arrival." He left, heading down the corridor, eyes locked on the infant princess.

Matrinka dragged down her shawl from a canopy post carved its length with bears. Throwing the garment across her shoulders, she demanded. "Now what was that all about?"

Absently, Darris arranged the fabric for Matrinka, pressing creases from the back. "La—" he started, catching himself. Alone, she discouraged his using titles. "When I'm not guarding King Griff . . ." he offered.

The answer clicked suddenly into place. "Rantire." The Renshai warrior protected the king with the wary savagery of a lioness and an absolute absence of tact. She had won the honor from Ravn with bold words and promises before Griff became king. By convention, Béarn's bard warded the king while Renshai protected the heirs. From the day of Griff's coronation, Rantire grudgingly sacrificed her position; but Griff allowed her at his side while the bard attended other matters.

"Exactly." Darris chuckled. "The prime minister has enough to worry about now. We're used to Rantire and know she means no harm."

"No harm?" Matrinka headed for the door. "Are we talking about the same Rantire?" They had once watched her fling herself, war-howling, onto dozens of Eastern soldiers who posed a danger to Griff. Matrinka had tended the near-fatal wounds afterward, and a still-frenzied Rantire had barely stopped short of attacking her healer. Matrinka grinned broadly to indicate she protested his choice of words, not actions. "Anyway, an excellent idea."

A flurry of white, black, and orange galloped up the corridor toward Matrinka. *Where were you going without me?* Mior complained, accompanied by a demanding, verbal wail.

We're looking for Griff. Then going to a meeting of the council. Matrinka hefted the calico, smoothing the twitching, striped tail. The fur felt warmer than she expected after a venture outside to relieve herself in the gardens.

Darris followed Matrinka into the hallway, closing the door behind them. "Oh, hello, Mior." Then, to Matrinka, "She looks angry."

The cat ignored the bard's greeting. *I go out for a few moments, and you try to disappear.*

Matrinka responded to Darris first, "Mior believes humans exist to serve cats, and the doings in Béarn revolve around her."

Mior purred, tail movements becoming more sinuous. *All true, of course. But you haven't answered me.*

"In her case, she's probably right." Darris winked to show he meant no offense. "The prime minister would have checked the courtroom and knocked on the king's door first, so we can assume Griff's not in either of those places. Tem'aree'ay's quarters?"

You didn't ask a question. And you didn't "go out for a few moments," *either. You were gone an hour. Quit acting like I left the country.* Matrinka addressed Darris. "Likely. Or in the gardens with her." She gestured for him to lead.

Darris obliged, heading toward the stairway. They first passed the door to the king's adjoining room, emblazoned with the royal crest, a rearing bear with ruby eyes. Torches in the corridors struck green highlights from outlining emeralds. Carved and painted scenes filled the walls, brilliantly incorporating real doors and animal-shaped torch brackets into the picture. Despite a lifetime in the castle, the mastery of Béarn's craftsmen still floored Matrinka. She found herself staring, finding details that eluded her even after seventeen years.

Mior clambered to Matrinka's shoulders, waiting until they had descended the entire flight before observing, *You won't find him with the elf* *maiden.*

How do you know that? Matrinka whisked after Darris, toward Tem'-aree'ay's quarters. She stopped suddenly, accusing, *You know where he* *is, don't you, you little demon?*

The tail spiraled into Matrinka's face, tickling. *So what if I happened* *to run into him?*

"Hold up, Darris." *Where is he?*

Darris halted, turning. Brown curls fell into his eyes. "What's the matter?"

With the sage.

With the sage? Shocked, Matrinka needed confirmation, though the method of their communication did not allow for mishearing. The reclusive keeper of all of Béarn's knowledge rarely received visitors, and Griff's flawless ability to rule came of his simple, naturally-neutral naïveté, not wisdom.

Darris came instantly to Matrinka's side. "Is something wrong?"

With the sage, the cat repeated smugly.

"Nothing's wrong. Mior claims Griff's with the sage."

Darris' brow crinkled. "That's odd." A strange light danced through his eyes. The bard's curse, passed always to the oldest child, endowed him with a painful, persistent thirst for knowledge he could only share in song. The sage guarded his scrolls and books with desperate fierceness, and Darris rarely found opportunity even to pass near the twelve-storied tower that housed the sage and a treasure beyond the value of all the kingdom's gold, at least to Darris. He headed back the way they had come. Had Mior chosen to divulge her knowledge sooner, she could have saved them all the steps they had thus far taken.

Matrinka followed. *Just happened to run into him? At the top of the south tower?*

In the main hallway, actually. I followed him there. Is curiosity a crime?

Only when you accuse me of abandoning you. No wonder your fur wasn't cold. You've been running around inside the castle.

Fur brushed Matrinka's cheek, then two huge, yellow eyes appeared in her face. *Excuse me. I found him for you, didn't I? Where's my thank you?*

Oblivious to the mental conversation, Darris tousled Mior's ears. "Thanks, Mior. You saved us a tedious and probably fruitless search. Not to mention an impatient room full of ministers and diplomats."

Matrinka stifled a giggle. *There you are.*

Mior rubbed against Darris' hand. *At least he appreciates me.*

That's because he doesn't know you like I do.

Very funny.

Darris continued talking as they moved quickly past pastoral scenes. The pigs seemed real enough to grunt and the cows to give milk. Occasionally, their own movement transferred to the paintings and tapestries. Matrinka had to stare straight at a grazing horse to convince herself the tail was not twitching. "Knight-Captain Kedrin, the elves, and some of the more seasoned ministers could sit all day, but I sure wouldn't want to face Guard Captain Seiryn or the Renshai's Thialnir after an hour's delay."

Humans are so edgy, Mior inserted.

As opposed to cats.

Missing the sarcasm, Mior settled back into a comfortable position on Matrinka's shoulders. *Right.*

The remainder of the walk continued in a verbal and mental silence that Matrinka appreciated. She wondered about Captain's message, as well as Griff's mission, but focused on neither for long. Time would bring answers, and supposition would add nothing. Pausing only to nod to guards and servants, they continued briskly toward the sage's quarters.

The final flights of the south tower contained portraits of the kings, beginning with a partial work only just beginning to resemble Griff, moving upward to a striking rendition of King Kohleran in his middle years. He had taken the throne at forty, seventeen years before Matrinka's birth. If not for the artwork, she could never have imagined him without white hair; and the commanding presence had disappeared during his slow decline and eventual death after thirty-three years on the throne. Despite Darris' worry about time, Matrinka had to stop and stare. Memories flooded back, and she lost the details to a blurriness that confused her until she realized she was crying.

Darris conveyed his understanding with a touch between her shoulder blades.

Who's that? Mior asked.

That's Grandpapa.

Mior cocked her head, an ear poking into Matrinka's. *Nice. But doesn't look much like him.* The cat had a soft spot for the dying king since he'd rescued her from a rain gutter as a sodden, grimy kitten and given her to Matrinka.

Exactly like him. Before he got old and sick.

Mior's head tipped further. *Are you going to change that much, too?*

The question raised a wave of sadness. Matrinka tried not to think about the difference in life span between cats and humans. *Not that you'll ever see, Dear One.* She kept that thought to herself and tried to hold sadness from her deliberately simple reply, *No, Mior. Not that much.*

Good.

Darris' contact grew more pronounced, a clear but polite request to move on.

Matrinka wiped away the tears with the back of her hand. Of all of Kohleran's line, she alone had continued visiting him after the stench and deterioration from his illness drove the others away. She loved him dearly, missed his firm voice and tender merciful manner, yearned for his fond presence and his stories. He had seemed more parent than grandfather or king in her middle teens, after the death of her father from a peculiar illness later traced to the *svartalf*'s magic. Thoughts of death, past and future, desperately saddened her; and she sought solace in the need to focus on the task at hand.

As Darris and Matrinka continued upward, the faces of past kings and ruling queens spiraled by, all huge and dark. She recognized many from their portraits elsewhere, especially Sterrane, the best known king; modern dating began at zero from the day he took his throne. Statues of him graced the courtyard and the Road of Kings, the legendary route by which the ancient Eastern Wizard, Shadimar, returned him to his throne.

Yet, though modern history considered Sterrane the first king and the forefather of all of Béarn's blooded nobility, the portraits did not end there. Beyond him, a face leered out, crudely interrupted by a twist of parquet like an angry scar. "Morhane," Darris explained as they rushed past. He had a song to cover the situation should Matrinka beg details.

Having heard it several times, Matrinka did not bother. She glanced at the next picture. Though it bore a striking resemblance to Morhane, this one seemed notably gentler-featured. Not an artist, Matrinka could not explain the differences, only marvel at and enjoy them. She knew these two, identical twins. The second, Valar, Sterrane's father had rightfully claimed the throne, only to be betrayed by his brother, Morhane, whose portrait came first.

The rest flashed past quickly, lovingly restored through the years before they could crack beyond recognition. Matrinka's history books contained their names; but she found them impossible to remember, which drove her tutors to distraction. She could recall the designation, description, and use of the rarest herb with an accuracy that defied understanding. Neither she nor they could explain why that talent did not extend to matters in which she had less interest. Matrinka wondered, but dared not ask, if that strange gift bore any relation to her singular ability to communicate with Mior. Since her mother had laughed at her and her closest cousin had teased her for her claim, she had told no one but Darris, Kevral, Ra-khir, and Tae. Even they had forced her to prove it before believing.

Finally, Matrinka and Darris reached the door to the sage's suite, fully outfitted and served so that the old man and his apprentice never needed to leave. Now it was Darris' turn to pause in awe. Sages had chronicled Béarn's history for millennia, the current one for over forty years. The information contained in multimillions of scrolls and books drew Darris with the fatal fascination of a moth to an open fire. The sage's job included rewriting the older texts in more standard language before time and the elements destroyed them.

The door was flung open, and a page several years younger than Matrinka darted through so quickly he nearly crashed headlong into Darris. Both jerked back in time to avoid collision, but the young man attempted a bow simultaneously that his balance could not afford. He tumbled to the ground. "Sorry, Ladyship," he squeaked. "There's a big meeting starting and . . ." He trailed off suddenly. "Oh, but you'd already know that, Ladyship."

Matrinka assisted the young man to stand, though his cheeks flushed bright red at the contact. "No hurry. It won't start without us." *Or without the king.* She realized that either Griff had already left the sage or the page rushed for some other reason than the imminence of the council. The sage's assistants attended both the most minor and the most secret conferences and affairs of state, relaying the details to their master. Béarnian law forbade even the king from excluding them. The sage chose only the most trusted, and falsification or slacking was grounds for far worse than dismissal. "Did you notice His Majesty in there?"

"Oh, yes, Ladyship," the page returned breathlessly. "I always notice King Griff. Everyone does."

"So, he's still there," Darris clarified.

"Yes, sir. He's still there."

"Thank you," Matrinka said, releasing him.

The page charged down the stairs, sandals clomping echoes through the sound-funneling walls of the tower.

As the noise receded enough to talk, Matrinka said, "Do you suppose Griff already knows about the meeting then? And has decided not to go?"

Darris drew a deep breath, hesitating. Matrinka recognized the subtle signs of debate. If he told too much, he would have to resort to song.

Matrinka considered, trying to rescue him from the effort. "Wait. The sage guards his knowledge. He would know about the meeting because Davian would send a message through his pages, but he might not necessarily have told the king."

Darris smiled broadly. "Exactly. But don't judge too harshly. The sage might have assumed the king already knew and had decided not to attend."

"Griff's going to want to hear Captain."

"Of course." Darris seized the latch, drew open the door, and ushered Matrinka through it.

The aromas of ink and old parchment filled the room, accompanied by a faint odor of grease but no hint of mold. Griff perched on one of the two chairs, hands clenched to his head and enormous shoulders hunched over a length of parchment sleeved, top and bottom, over two sanded dowels. Rantire leaned against a table without managing the aura of casual alertness for which she, apparently, strived. She more resembled a coiled spring an instant before breaking. Such an attitude in a place so safe might have seemed odd to Matrinka had she not grown accustomed to Rantire's fanatical dedication. The Renshai's shadow fell directly over Griff's reading material, and she violated his personal space, but he seemed not to notice. Nearly as close, the sage looked up from his own parchment, pen poised in withered but steady hands. Gray curls clung to a veiny scalp, the hair carefully cut away from his eyes. His attempt to work dispassionately seemed as much a desperate act as Rantire's. His attention was fixed on the paper reluctantly surrendered to his king rather than on his own or on the newcomers. His apprentice sorted through a stack of books, glancing up as the door opened.

Rantire crouched, granting Darris and Matrinka a hostile glare. Griff continued reading, oblivious.

You don't suppose she's the reason for the page's hasty exit, Mior surmised.

Wouldn't doubt it.

Darris cleared his throat. "Your Majesty?" His gaze flicked from king to scroll. Then, need won out over politeness, and he locked his attention on the parchment.

Griff almost leaped from his chair. Rantire's scowl intensified, and she moved between them and the king. "I'm sorry, Darris. Matrinka. How long have you been there?"

"Only a moment, Sire." Darris painfully dragged his stare to the king. "Captain's back, and he's called the council. We've come, Sire, to see if you wish to attend."

Griff released the parchment, and it rolled closed. "Of course." He glanced toward the apprentice, who made a nonspecific gesture.

"I'll keep looking, Majesty. And send a message about whatever I find."

"Thank you, Aron." Griff rose, Rantire practically on top of him.

Matrinka did not even know the sage's apprentice had a name. She had never heard them referred to in any manner except as the sage and the sage's apprentice.

"And thank you, Rantire," Darris said firmly. "I'll take things from here."

The guarded relief forming on Griff's features stabbed guilt through Matrinka. The king had done so much for her and Darris, finding a way for them to share a love forbidden by Béarnian law. All three knew he assigned Darris to her for the sole purpose of allowing them time alone together. When he did so, he suffered Rantire. When it came to the job, Matrinka would trust no one to do it more competently. She never doubted Rantire's ability, only Griff's patience for her.

Rantire's gray eyes stared at Darris. Bronze hair lay braided away from her face, styled for war. "You have your charge." She inclined her head toward Matrinka. "And I have mine."

"His Majesty is my charge," Darris reminded.

"But he assigned you to the queen." Rantire drew herself up to her full height, though that left her the shortest in the room by a few fingers' breadth. Despite that, she was, by far, the most menacing.

"And now I'm back with him," Darris insisted as vehemently.

"Who's guarding Her Ladyship, then?"

To reply that he would handle both would not suit Rantire. Like most Renshai, she believed Darris incompetent, along with nearly every other *ganim*, the term they used for non-Renshai. Darris gave the only answer Rantire could accept, "Her Ladyship is not my concern. Or yours. You'll have to take it up with her assigned guardian."

Matrinka winced.

Even without words, Mior seemed to read her mind. *Kevral's not going to like that.*

Distant cousins, the two Renshai had argued frequently over their varied methods of guarding. Kevral trusted her reflexes and sword skill enough to grant Matrinka some freedom. Besides, Kevral's responsibility to Matrinka technically ended when she failed the staff-test. The Renshai were charged with guarding heirs to Béarn's throne and, in peaceful times, usually did so as a group rather than in individual assignments. In Matrinka's youth, often a single Renshai warrior had watched over all of Kohleran's grandchildren and great-grandchildren while they played chase games in the courtyard.

Grudgingly, muttering something Matrinka could not decipher, Rantire stepped aside. Griff, Matrinka, and Darris departed the room with the Renshai at their heels. They headed silently down the stairs, and Rantire took her leave at the bottom. "Let me know the moment you need me again, Sire. I'll come at once."

"Thank you, Rantire," Griff said. "I know you will."

Darris waited until their separate courses took them well apart before asking. "Sire, how did you manage to say that without laughing?"

Griff smiled, then recovered his sober-faced demeanor. "Because I'm serious, Darris."

"You don't have to suffer her, you know," Matrinka reminded the childlike king. "You can pick someone else."

"I couldn't." Griff sounded scandalized. "First, I promised her. She's Darris' official relief."

Matrinka shrugged. "Posts don't have to be lifelong. Things don't always work out."

"But Ravn chose her. And I'd never doubt his judgment. Never."

They both understood Griff's loyalty, and neither would disparage it. Darris stepped in. "She's certainly competent, Majesty. I worry less for your safety in her hands than in my own."

"I'm safe with either," Griff insisted, and could not help adding, "you're just more fun."

Faint praise, Mior inserted.

Hush, Matrinka admonished gently.

The three made their way toward the conference room, murals flowing by them and strings of gems dangling from the torch brackets fluttering in their wake. Occasionally, they nodded, waved at, or called brief greetings to servants and nobles they passed. Darris seemed particularly preoccupied, his salutations little more than wordless grunts and the jerkiness of his slightest movements revealing otherwise well-hidden discomfort.

Just as Matrinka decided to question the bard, Darris addressed his charge. "Your Majesty, at the risk of prying and in the hope you won't find this improper—"

Griff interrupted, "I was looking up old law. Trying to find a loophole that might allow me to marry Tem'aree'ay." He glanced suddenly at Matrinka. "I guess I should have brought that up with you first."

Excitement and concern clutched Matrinka at once. She liked Tem'aree'ay and appreciated the joy that the elf brought Griff. Yet she had suffered the details of castle laws regarding the marriages of Béarnian heirs too long not to know he fought a losing battle. "Oh, Griff." Matrinka placed a comforting arm around him. "You know I'd welcome Tem'aree'ay. She's wonderful."

Before she could add the "but," Darris spoke thoughtfully. "Depends whether the law defines who you can marry or who you can't." He ended, somewhat cryptically, there. Further explanation would require song. "I'll have to check."

Matrinka suspected Darris knew much more than he had revealed. Though he had never mentioned doing so, he had surely sought a loophole for them. She also realized Griff should know. "What have you found out so far?"

The king's massive shoulders rose and fell. "Nothing much yet. We spent most of our time looking for the original wording and later mentions. I was just starting to look things over and . . . well . . ." A touch of color entered his cheeks. "This might not be the best thing for a king to admit." He glanced around the hallway to assure their privacy. "I don't read all that well."

Matrinka doubted that confession would surprise anyone. Through the centuries, the staff-test had chosen simple kings. Her history books claimed Sterrane, himself, had never mastered grammar.

"My parents were first cousins, like us, but close from infancy. Shared cribs, toys, baths. Everyone talked about how they'd certainly marry, so it only seemed natural . . ." Griff's blush deepened. "Anyway, they were only about thirteen when my brother was born and my father banished for it."

Matrinka knew the story. She and her friends had obtained it before charging off to find Griff, but she let him speak. It might embarrass the king to discover that others had learned of his parents' humiliation. He loved his mother and stepfather fiercely.

"My mother went with him; they couldn't stop her, though they tried." Griff looked ahead as they traversed the corridors. "More worried about staying alive, they didn't concern themselves with teaching us to read. Farmers don't much need to, and young teens aren't usually known for liking their studies. After the accident, when Mama didn't let me do any heavy work, I think she realized I'd need to know something. So she finally started working with me on Trading and Béarnese." He lowered his head. "I didn't pay as much attention as I should have." He dropped his voice to a whisper. "I'm a bit slow."

As Matrinka and Darris mouthed the appropriate reassurances about Griff's intellectual function, it finally occurred to her that she had discovered the reason Griff preferred that Darris sire their offspring. He worried that the closeness of his parents' blood had resulted in a dull intellect for him, and a second generation of cousin-spawned offspring might emerge with worse. Yet, though his sluggish speech, guileless conclusions, and childlike manner often made Griff seem dim-witted, she had repeatedly watched him make brilliant decisions and handle impossible logistics with a deftness that made her feel clumsy. Griff was not stupid. He only manifested his intelligence in an unusual manner.

Once the proper, gentle denials had been spoken, Darris pressed the matter beyond the necessary. "Sire, you found a way for Matrinka and me to be together, and I'll always owe you my happiness. I'll find a way for you as well. I promise."

Matrinka hoped her beloved had not just committed himself to the impossible.

Griff's manner changed in an instant. His steps lightened, and a smile touched his features. He trusted his bard implicitly.

Matrinka gave Darris a warning glance. He might have set up more than himself for a fall. If he did not deliver on his promise, he might devastate Griff.

Darris returned a look equally intense. Failure was not an option. "Not only do I have access to the law, but I have information only the bards have gathered. That gives me an advantage even over the sage."

Matrinka wondered whether Darris tried to assure Griff, her, or himself. She had little time to wonder, however, as they reached the conference room. A servant bowed to the king, then the queen, before opening the door for their entrance.

A tumult met Matrinka's ears momentarily, cutting to sudden silence as the door opened, then to the hurried screech and scrape of chair legs against the floor. Those gathered rose and bowed or curtsied with irregular grandeur and timing. Matrinka glanced at their two ranks assembled around the long, rectangular table. Davian had sacrificed his usual place at the far end for Captain. The elf's amber eyes held a glaze of water, and his red-brown hair lay knotted at the nape of his neck. Sunbaked skin, wrinkled into a pattern of smiling, revealed few of his thousands of years of life. Low-set ears and a broad mouth completed the familiar picture.

The usual signs that distinguished human males from females and defined age were absent, as with all elves. Nevertheless, Matrinka somehow always knew their gender, and Captain radiated an indefinable aura of ancientness.

To Captain's right, Prime Minister Davian finished his bow and waited. Beside him, the minister of internal affairs, Aerean, completed a deep curtsy. A past leader of the renegades, like Davian, she tended to irritate the staid, old nobility with a boundless energy and enthusiasm that Matrinka appreciated. Across from her stood her diametric opposite, Saxanar, the minister of courtroom procedure and affairs. Descended from an endless line of titled gentry, he followed rules with the fanaticism of a Knight of Erythane and groused over changes to his carefully measured schedules. Beside him, Minister of Household Affairs Franstaine touched his neatly trimmed beard, expression grim. Only a brightness to his dark brown eyes betrayed his famous patience and strange sense of humor. He was also an in-law uncle of Helana, Griff's mother. Across from Franstaine and beside Aerean stood Zaysharn, who oversaw the caretakers of Béarn's livestock, gardens, and food. Also honorarily titled, he tended toward quiet attentiveness at the meetings, bowing to the superior experiences of the blooded nobility and the renegade leaders. When he did speak, he usually said something of great import.

Matrinka discovered Tae beside Zaysharn, clearly trying and, as usual, succeeding at disappearing into the crowd. She should have noticed a close companion first and immediately. She gave him a deliberate smile, particularly to validate his right, as a foreign diplomat, to attend the council. Despite months in Stalmize's castle, he still seemed uncomfortable and awkward with royal formality. This came, she knew, of his father's relaxed and irregular procedures. Weile Kahn demanded loyalty at the penalty of death, but the toughness of his followers made hierarchies and titles all but impossible. Some called him "Sir," some "Sire," and others chose to avoid any label at all.

Minister of Foreign Affairs Richar rightfully took the position beside Tae, young features glowing with the excitement of a long-term diplomatic charge important enough to attend the council. Usually, he handled visiting Western merchants and disputants in claims too volatile or difficult for local kingdoms. Across from those, tiny Chaveeshia, titled minister of local affairs, tended the relations between Béarn and her close neighbors. Her regular charges were poised at either hand: the Renshai warrior, Thialnir, to her right and Knight-Captain Kedrin nearer the king and queen. The idea of her handling these warriors should problems arise seemed ludicrous. She stood barely to either's chin, and she could wear Thialnir's torque as a girdle. Yet she had a commanding manner for one so small and a sharp-tongued, no-nonsense attitude that gained their respect as well as their trust.

The captain of the Knights of Erythane dragged out his elegant flourish long after the others had already finished. His features closely resembled Ra-khir's, and he sported the same red-blond hair. Age added a mature attractiveness that his son had not yet attained. Every measured movement of the knight seemed as impeccable as his uniform. Only the eyes looked wholly different, blue to Ra-khir's green and so pale they approached white. Rare and captivating, they added an exotic touch to features otherwise classically handsome. The guards' own captain, Seiryn, took the position as close to the open seats as Kedrin, leaving spaces only for Griff, Matrinka, and Darris together. Every member of the council had come . . . and also Tae. The page who had scurried past them in the tower now waited quietly in a far corner.

"Good morning, all," King Griff said mildly, taking his seat at the head of the table. Once he did so, the others also sat, including Matrinka and Darris.

Matrinka could not wait to know about the twins, taking over proceedings properly belonging to Griff or Davian. "Welcome, Tae."

Every eye turned toward the Easterner, which distressed him into wide-eyed fidgeting.

"Do the twins have names now?"

Tae glanced toward Thialnir, whose stony silence threw the question back to him. "Saviar Rakhirsson and Subikahn Taesson, Your Ladyship. Both Renshai."

Matrinka smiled.

You were right. Mior clambered from Matrinka's shoulders to the table, yawning and pulling into a long stretch.

Of course, I was right. I have faith in him.

You might be the only one. Mior casually ambled past warriors and ministers. *And that includes him.*

Obviously not, Matrinka returned with Mior's usual smugness. *The Renshai believed in him, too.*

Griff waited patiently for Matrinka to finish. She nodded once, and he spoke next. "Captain, I understand you have news for us." He executed the arcane gesture that indicated the elf had the floor. Though the formality seemed unnecessary, skipping it would bother the knight and stuffy Saxanar.

Unelflike, Captain went straight to the point. "Your Majesty, we've finally discovered the method for lifting the *svartalf*'s sterility spell."

Excitement thrilled through Matrinka and shone in the eyes of everyone gathered there. Her heart rate seemed to double in an instant.

Captain's words disappeared into a silence even the king seemed too stunned to break, so the elf continued. "It's complicated, and I'll need to describe history that some of you already know. Please bear with me."

Nods circumnavigated the room. Accustomed to human impatience, Captain could not know that understanding the solution would hold the tensest of them for days. Without it, all of humanity faced extinction.

"Millennia ago, after Odin banished the primordial chaos, he created a system to keep the forces in balance. It hinged on four mortals, called the Cardinal Wizards, who became near-immortals once they passed the proper sequence of tests. I say "near" because, although they could not die of disease or starvation and no object of law could harm them, each would choose his or her apprentice and time of passage. Then, in a grand, magical ceremony, the elder would pass all his memories, and those of his predecessors, to this successor. The body he once occupied was utterly destroyed."

Captain glanced around the room, and Matrinka watched the reactions. Most looked back at the elf without judgment, though the stronger-opinioned returned frowns or bobbed their heads thoughtfully. Most considered the tales of humans wielding magic nothing more substantial than mythology, intended to explain the gaps in logical history. Matrinka, however, accepted Captain's words without question. She had always believed in wizardry, even when others dismissed her confidence as silly.

The elf continued, "The Cardinal Wizards lived on Midgard." He made a broad gesture to indicate all of the human lands. "Their job was to keep the world's great forces balanced. The Northern Wizard championed goodness, her charges Northmen and the elves, even when we dwelt on Alfheim."

A snort rumbled through the room, though Matrinka missed the source.

Captain raised a hand for temperance. "Bear with me. Times have changed greatly since then."

A few stern glances silenced the rudeness, though Matrinka still could not place its origin.

Captain lowered his hand to the table, beside the other. "The Southern Wizard represented evil, his charge those humans who lived in the Eastlands."

Several gazes shifted naturally to Tae, who made a show of ignoring them, although his fingers twined in his lap and he slipped further into obscurity in his chair.

"The Eastern and Western Wizards embodied neutrality, speaking for the peoples of the Westlands, such as your own." Captain clarified,

"Most of you." He pressed onward, "It turned out that Odin eventually intended for the Eastern and Western Wizards to champion chaos and law, once they gained enough power through the centuries to handle their charges. Eventually, they did, but it proved the downfall of the Wizards and the Cardinal system. Since then, no human has wielded so much as a modicum of magic."

Richar filled Captain's pause with a question. "How long ago did humans lose all magic?"

"If they ever had any," Saxanar could not help adding. He did not believe.

"First," Captain clarified, "not all of the Cardinal Wizards were human." His features became pensive, especially for an elf. "Well, that's not quite true either. To my knowledge, all of the Cardinal Wizards did start as humans. But Dh'arlo'mé, the leader of the *svartalf*, was the apprentice of the last Northern Sorceress. Had she survived, and had the system continued, he would probably continue to champion goodness to this day."

Chaveeshia made a sound between a laugh and a grunt, a strong noise for one so small. As eyes shifted to her, she explained her lapse. "I just can't fathom Dh'arlo'mé advocating goodness."

Kedrin made a subtle gesture, requesting recognition. Tuned to the knight-captain's value, Griff acknowledged him swiftly. "As Captain said, times change. Those *alive* at the time . . ." he emphasized, reminding the ministers and warriors that the elves had a definite advantage when it came to remembering the past, ". . . understand better than we can. It appears that Colbey shifted the tide of the gods' war, whether you call it the *Ragnarok* or the Great Fire." He tiptoed around the seeds of religious strife. Most believed the enormous fire that had gouged the central areas of the Westlands three centuries past represented a tragic accident. Only the Renshai believed the massive war between the gods, the *Ragnarok* or Great Destruction, had occurred. They explained that the Renshai hero, Colbey Calistinsson, had rescued them all, extinguishing the fire and sacrificing his life to the battle.

With Captain's assistance, and Colbey's, Matrinka now knew both stories were wrong. The *Ragnarok* had occurred, stealing the lives of most of the gods. Colbey's interference had changed the course of events, as Renshai had maintained for centuries. Odin had plotted to coerce Colbey into assisting in his own battle, thereby allowing him to survive. But Colbey had thwarted that plan, instead helping Frey fight the fire giant destined to destroy all the worlds with his conflagration. Against the gods' prophecies, Frey had lived; but the giant had managed to kindle the worlds before he died. Colbey had vanquished the flames from Midgard, as Renshai legend stated, but lived on to become the Keeper of the Balance, replacing the system of the Cardinal Wizards.

Kedrin reminded, "Whatever your proclivities, you have to understand that the Great Fire did destroy the elves' world. Colbey, a human, had a hand in that. Warranted or not, you must understand the elves' . . ." He corrected swiftly, so as not to insult the *lysalf,* ". . . the *svartalf*'s bitterness."

Matrinka cringed at the memory of Captain's previous story. Trapped in flame with no apparent escape, the elves had banded together and directed their magic as never before. They had created a gate to Midgard but not before the vast majority died horribly. The survivors suffered the agony of burns, inside and out, even their magic taking decades or centuries to undo the scarring. Captain had managed to avoid the tragedy, already on Midgard when the *Ragnarok* occurred. Because of that, most of the elves had dismissed his pleas for peace between their kind and humans.

Captain waited only until Kedrin signaled that he had finished before cutting in. "I'm not defending Dh'arlo'mé's actions, only stating facts. I'd like to return to the foreign minister's question, if I may, because it leads into an important detail of lifting the *svartalf*'s spell." He glanced around the room, clearly awaiting more interruptions, which this time did not come. "Nearly anyone could become a Cardinal Wizard, but they chose their successors with caution. Like the heirs to Béarn, the apprentices had to pass a god-mediated test which consisted of seven parts. Failure at any one spelled death. Also, the Cardinal Wizards remained in a constant struggle, each seeking dominance for his or her own charge. To choose a weak successor not only assured rivals' scorn, death at the tasks, and wasted time; but, if he or she somehow managed to survive, an erosion of their own power. It could, ultimately, mean the destruction of their cause or, worse, of the balance and the world itself."

Matrinka did not yet see where Captain's words related to Richar's question about humans losing magic.

As if to answer Matrinka's curiosity, Captain said, "For nearly all of my time here, the Cardinal Four were the only humans capable of magic. Apparently, the mages of Myrcidë lived long before them, and some of the strongest Cardinal Wizards originated from there. Historically, when the Renshai battled their way through the Westlands, they found the Myrcidians an irresistible challenge and massacred the entire line."

Now Thialnir weathered a few hostile stares, but the massive warrior seemed not to notice.

"In the time of the Cardinal Wizards, elfin magic was petty. Carefree and disorganized, we used it only for entertainment. Any Wizard held more mastery in his most meager spell, yet that, in itself, made their use of magic rare. The more powerful the creature, the farther the radiations of its slightest action. That's why the gods do not interfere with our affairs; to do so would cause effects far beyond their intentions. Most times, the Wizards used only tiny fractions of their magic, except when facing one another. And Odin's laws constrained them mightily when it came to casting spells or harming their peers."

Captain shifted forward with tangible excitement. He neared the significant portion of his presentation. Those gathered reacted to his body language with similar motions of their own.

"Magic involves bending chaos to the will and service of law, always dangerous. Elfin structure and nature contains far more natural chaos than mankind's, so our spells rarely backfire. But the Cardinal Wizards often found unintended side effects resulted, especially from the most powerful sorcery. The worst trouble followed the creation of permanent magic."

"Permanent," Captain Seiryn repeated carefully. Then, realizing he had spoken aloud, he added, "What do you mean by permanent?"

"I mean constructed chaos. Structured objects instilled with magic." Captain shook his head, the common tongue failing him. "Examples might prove easier. The gods have a few things you've probably all heard about: Thor's hammer, *Mjollnir*, that only he, while alive, and now only his sons, can lift; Freya's necklace; and the Staves of Law and Chaos, Odin's contribution."

All of these Matrinka knew of from stories.

"Over the millennia, the Wizards created exactly nine 'items' that I know of. Each Wizard had a home or lair with some sort of permanent warding. That's four. Odin dismantled those, and they no longer exist. There were three Swords of Power: the evil, the good, and the neutral. During the fall of the Cardinal Wizards, those became conjoined; and Colbey wields them now as a single weapon. That's seven. The last Eastern Wizard crafted a sword with minor powers that the Renshai keep as a curiosity."

Thialnir made an inquiring noise. "The Sword of Mitrian?"

Captain nodded. "Its powers are likely spent by now, the only magic remaining that which keeps it from corroding."

The ninth is the one that matters, Mior guessed.

Surely.

Captain did not disappoint. "The ninth is the most significant. At only one point in time, all four of the Cardinal Wizards originated in Myrcidë, and they magicked a hand-sized sapphire called the Pica into a scrying stone. They used it to watch apprentices as they struggled through the Tasks of Wizardry. The Pica changed hands many times, and not always among the Wizards. In fact, for centuries after the Renshai destroyed Myrcidë, they kept it as a symbol of their own prowess."

Thialnir frowned, daring anyone to condemn the Renshai's savagery. Wisely, no one did.

"When the Wizards had the Pica, they used it. When they didn't, they simply waited for apprentices to return from the tasks, without knowing details. The last Eastern Wizard, also the last Myrcidian, Shadimar, took the Pica in payment for crafting the Sword of Mitrian. When Colbey underwent the Tasks of Wizardry to become the last Western Wizard, Shadimar had the Pica. The Wizards used it to track Colbey's progress." Captain shook his head, his expression stricken as he considered details that he would not share. "As the result of some action of Colbey's, the Pica shattered. The consequences went far beyond the destruction of the most powerful item currently in existence. Colbey lost the symbol of his people, and Shadimar of his. The blood brotherhood they had entered because of the Pica expired, too; and they eventually became bitter enemies."

Richar lost patience first. "And this affects the sterility spell?"

Captain had a ready answer. "Our research suggests that if we collected every shard of the Pica Stone, we may have the power to lift the *svartalf*'s magic."

"That's it?" Griff asked innocently.

No one challenged the words, though Aerean rolled her eyes and Franstaine's lips framed a careful smile. The latter, the minister of household affairs, said, "How would we go about finding it?"

Saxanar added with narrowed eyes, "Would we need every splinter scattered over centuries? Every speck?"

"Every one," Captain confirmed. "But that's not as impossible as it sounds. I think we can draw them with magic."

Darris visibly trembled with the excitement of participating in something so historical, but he had to ask. "Is it dangerous?"

Captain's gemlike, amber eyes fixed on the bard. "Not per se. What I can't predict is what might happen when the Pica comes together again. Likely, it contains little, if any, magic anymore. But this is unprecedented."

Matrinka looked at Darris who pursed his lips. Finally, he turned his attention to the king. "Sire?"

Griff blinked slowly and deliberately, then fastened his dark gaze back on Darris. "Are you asking me if we should do this thing?"

"Your Majesty, it's your decision."

Griff shook his head, and his coarse hair and beard flew like a lion's mane. "No decision here." He swiveled his head toward the elf. "Captain, what do you need?"

"Not much, Sire." The long-fingered, elfin hands fluttered over the tabletop. "A room no larger than this one. It just needs to fit all the *lysalf*. A flat surface. The floor would do, but I'd find a table more comfortable."

"You'll have those," Griff promised.

Darris contained his agitation admirably. Matrinka suspected she alone noticed him clutching his hands in his lap. "With your permission, Sire. And yours, Captain." He inclined his head toward the opposite end of the table. "I'd like to attend."

Griff gave the floor to Captain with a mild gesture.

The ancient elf obliged. "Spectators would not bother the process."

"I'd like to be there, too," Captain Seiryn stated, though whether to assure Béarn's security or from curiosity, Matrinka could not guess.

"And I," Saxanar asserted.

Several others nodded. Griff raised his hands, and the group dropped to silence. "Who would like to go?" he asked. He flicked the fingers of his right hand and held it out to demonstrate the proper display. Every other person in the room mimicked the motion, including Matrinka. When Griff remained in place while the others revealed their interest, it became clear that the King of Béarn also intended to observe.

Darris' brow furrowed, and sweat beaded the hand still moving nervously in his lap. "I didn't mean to start . . . I mean, maybe . . ." He fell back on a previous question. "Is it safe?"

The king dropped his hand, and the others followed his lead.

Captain tilted his head, lantern light catching white hairs amid the mahogany. The aging little resembled the temple-area graying of humans.

Before Captain could speak, Darris made a throwaway gesture to show he recalled the answer the elf had already given. "Which room shall I have them prepare, Your Majesty?"

"I trust your judgment, Darris," Griff replied.

"Good," Darris muttered so softly that Matrinka believed she alone heard him, "then you'll understand what I'm about to do." Walking to the exit, he opened it suddenly. Torchlight from the corridor funneled in, cutting sharp shadows from the panel that mingled strangely with the ones the lanterns struck inside.

A pair of guards in on-duty leathers and mail stood at rigid attention, heads jerking toward the door. Obviously startled, a young servant scrambled from his chair. "Sir! What can I do for you, sir?" Though he addressed Darris, his wild, dark gaze went beyond to the king and his ministers. "Sir?"

"Fetch Kevral and Rantire to the red strategy room. We'll be moving there shortly, too. See no one bothers us."

Griff closed his eyes at the first command but nodded slightly. Matrinka saw the significance of Darris' decision. If anything dangerous went wrong with the elves' summoning, it would involve chaos. She could think of no warriors she would rather have at her side if threatened than the Renshai. More importantly, only those two had the means to effectively battle chaos. Rantire wielded a sword given to her by Ravn, and Kevral one of Colbey's weapons. Apparently, just being owned by a god at one time granted them some magic, because both had proved effective against demons, the personification of chaos, when all else had failed.

"Yes, sir." The servant bowed, straightening his wrinkled tunic with jerks on the fabric before hurrying away.

Darris returned to Griff's side. "Sorry, Your Majesty."

Griff drew in his features and made a sharp cut with his hand. "Don't apologize for knowing your limits nor assuring my safety. That's your job." He looked out over the group once more. "Captain, gather your elves. We'll reconvene in the red strategy room."

As propriety demanded, Griff, Matrinka, and Darris filed from the meeting room first. The king wore a grin, and excitement lit his face. He trusted the *lysalf* enough to believe the problem already solved. Matrinka knew better, yet she could not keep hope from sparking a fire in her belly. Soon, she hoped, the evil that held the human kingdoms hostage would disappear. And babies younger than her own would fill Béarn again.

CHAPTER 3

The Summoning

I'm no demon. And neither were my people,
so I am no prince among demons.

—Colbey Calistinsson

A sensation of suffocation closed over Kevral as she entered a strategy room packed with more than fifty elves and humans, and the urge to flee rose in ever more troublesome increments. Elves lined the walls, their strangely smooth eyes and array of hair colors odd contrast to the black-haired, swarthy Béarnides who shared the table with Captain. Only a few people stood out as foreigners: Knight-Captain Kedrin with his soft red locks and striking eyes; Darris with his lighter hair and features and the sparer proportions of the civilized plains folk; the Renshai's chieftain, Thialnir; and Rantire crouched like a hungry predator beside the king's chair. Though from the farthest origin, Tae fit in well where the others had not. Despite his smaller size and lack of facial hair, his Eastern coloring matched the Béarnides' perfectly. Mior perched on Matrinka's shoulders.

Kevral also remained standing, though less for purposes of guarding. She trusted herself to rise and strike before anyone or thing could harm Matrinka. Simply, the position eased her tension, reminding her that she could leave at any moment. She had no intention of doing so, at least not without taking her charge; yet the simple knowledge that she could lessened the claustrophobia she had never experienced before the elves had taken her and Ra-khir prisoner. Time locked in Pudar's dungeon had worsened the affliction.

Captain's head sank toward the table, his eyes closed. He raised partially curled fingers above the surface, then sent a mental question, *Ready?*

Kevral heard no reply. The elves' odd form of communication, which they called *khohlar*, allowed them to transfer concepts either to an individual or to everyone in the area. She guessed the others had answered only directly to Captain and, of course, the humans could only respond verbally. None chose to do so, though she detected a few nods. They could not assist in the magic.

Start jovinay arythanik, Captain sent, the elfin term for a shared spell.

A low murmur rose from the elves along the walls, more vibration than sound. Gradually, it increased, and a harmonic emerged. Memory stirred by the familiar sound, Kevral dropped into a crouch as tense as Rantire's. Both Renshai had suffered the elves' *jovinay arythanik* and the sleep spell that had arisen from it. The only survivor of the envoy sent to fetch King Griff, Rantire had spent months as a prisoner of the elves, tortured for information. Kevral had fallen prey to elfin magic three times, the last when the *lysalf* used it against the Easterners who ambushed those on the roads, the second when the *svartalf* used it to capture herself and Ra-khir. The first time she faced it, she and her companions were fighting the then-unified elves to free Rantire and Griff. Then, Darris had played and sang, his loud melodies interfering with the elves' chant. When they silenced him, the elves might have captured and killed them all if not for Captain's call for those elves who also desired peace to withdraw from the magic. The *lysalf* were "born" that day.

Most of the humans in Béarn's strategy room listened with quiet curiosity and interest. Darris strained to catch every nuance, the bardic curse more driving than unpleasant remembrances. Griff rocked, the movement an attempt to relieve the discomfort his gritted teeth revealed. He, too, had endured elfin magic before his capture. Matrinka and her cat seemed wholly unaffected, too busy worrying about the situation and the comfort of her companions, Kevral guessed.

The chant rose and fell in an irregular cadence, the sound as beautiful as studied human song. Suddenly, Captain's head snapped upward. He huffed out harsher syllables that sank like leaden objects amid the golden wave of sound. His fingers undulated, beckoning. Gradually, the air between his hands and the table shimmered with a bluish hue. Sweat wound along a strand of reddish hair, beading the tip into a point. Tension accentuated the high, sharp cheekbones and canted eyes. The color forming between his hands intensified, and Kevral could make out defining cracks and lines. The lopsided object growing between Captain's fingers and the table consisted of pieces, some as large as her elbows and others more like glistening sprinkles of powder. Captain's ample lips bowed, the delighted smile, though commonplace, jarred with the usually hard to read elfin expressions.

"It's working," Matrinka whispered.

Kevral only nodded, desperately concentrating not only on the proceedings but on any movement that seemed out of place. Even more than most, she prayed for an end to the sterilization affecting humankind. She had dwelt in Pudar when the *svartalf* had worked their evil magic; she was fulfilling a promise to the king of the great trading city. She had battled the demon the dark elves had summoned to distract the populace while working their spell, and it had nearly killed her. Only the sword Colbey had given her, now at her left hip, had allowed her to harm the creature that otherwise would have ravaged the world. Soon after, the king had discovered that pregnant women could remain fertile after delivery if bred before their next bleeding cycle. He had imprisoned her and forced her to lie with Prince Leondis, a gentle man nearly as much a victim of the situation as she. Colbey had rescued her the only way he could, by sending another to the prison with whom she willingly lay, a Renshai she now believed was Ravn. Ra-khir had discovered Kevral's predicament and rescued her, but not without cost. They had had to vow never to speak of the situation; and, before knowing the details, Ra-khir had promised to surrender the baby to Pudar upon its birth.

The thought roused a rage that Kevral battered down from need. She had spent many hours raving, wishing she had handled things differently. *King or not, I should have killed the pompous bastard.* Yet the situation had not allowed her to do it. Beaten down by exhaustion, blood loss, and thirst, Kevral had had little choice but to comply. Otherwise, she might still sprawl in chains in Pudar's dungeon, carrying the prince's babies until it killed her or a cycle started, at which point they would have had to take her life. She stood by the vow she had made as she rode back to Béarn with Ra-khir, Mior, the twins, and half a dozen Knights of Erythane: She had agreed that what belonged to Pudar would return there. But Ravn, not Leondis, had sired the child; and she would battle an army rather than turn him or her over to King Cymion of Pudar.

Resolved, Kevral forced her full attention back to the current proceedings. Less than four months along, the baby inside her did not yet show, though she carried more of the weight from the twins than she otherwise would have. Her visual sweep of the room brought her gaze regularly back to Matrinka who, until this day, faced a difficult decision. Before lifting the *svartalf*'s spell became a definite possibility, she confronted the choice of losing her fertility or risking another pregnancy so soon after the first. The queen had an obligation to supply Béarn with heirs; yet, as a healer, she knew the medical perils all too well. Statistics, Kevral now knew, gave her a one-eighth to one-quarter chance of dying during the pregnancy or delivery.

Captain's face contorted. His voice coarsened and increased in volume, and the syllables turned sibilant. His fingers stiffened and gestured fiercely. The disproportionate ball of blue light in front of him remained, ill-balanced and incomplete. His hands dropped to the table with a dull thud. "Damn," he said clearly.

Though soft, the expletive startled Kevral. She had never heard him, or any elf, swear.

The chanting died. The glow dissipated, though the grotesquely shaped sapphire on the table remained, more solid but no more whole.

"Captain?" the king prodded softly.

The elfin ancient shook his head. "The rest won't come, Sire." His regard leaped to a small, ruby-eyed female near the far corner. "Marrih?"

Kevral knew Captain used a shortened form of the elf's name. Until they came to Midgard, the long-lived creatures traditionally used names hopelessly impossible for humans to memorize, usually spanning twelve to twenty syllables Their *khohlar* allowed them to squeeze any name to an instantaneous concept in situations of danger. His own calling, Captain, came of his millennia of piloting the Cardinal Wizards across the sea; and he claimed to have long ago lost any name his parents might have given him. The *lysalf* called him Arak'bar Tulamii Dhor, meaning Elder Who Has Forgotten His Name. The *svartalf* referred to him as Lav'rintir, Destroyer of the Peace and to the *lysalf* as lav'rintii, followers of Lav'rintir. Rather than *svartalf,* they called themselves *dwar'frey'tii* or the chosen of Frey, the god who had created elves.

Marrih's bright red eyes flicked nervously over the crowd. She nodded acknowledgment with a head movement so tiny Kevral wasn't certain she saw it.

Pieces I can't reach. Though surely sent for Marrih, Captain kept his *khohlar* general, to include all in the room. The rest emerged as a concept Kevral could not comprehend in word form. She understood vast frustration, a full-force magical aspiration unrealized, then incomprehensible details communicated in an instant. Captain followed this with a plea for suggestions.

A nonverbal hubbub ensued. Unused to *khohlar,* Kevral could not sort it out. Then, gradually, voices withdrew, leaving only Marrih. *You're using the best way.* She addressed a few details, assigning names to the suggestions, then shooting them down. She clasped her tiny hands in front of her, black hair dribbling down her long forehead.

Captain huffed out a sigh. *You try?*

Marrih's ivory skin paled still more, but she came to Captain without need for further convincing. The ancient moved aside, and the younger elf took his place.

A few mental communications shot through the ranks, none explicable to Kevral, then the throb of the *jovinay arythanik* began again. Marrih leaned over the misshapen stone, thin fingers caressing it. She spoke the words of the spell explicitly, though the syllables resembled no human language. They did not seem elfin either, as the light singsong crispness of their usual speech resembled the Northern tongue, and many words overlapped. Even as the chant swelled to song, Marrih waved them silent. *Unreachable,* she concluded that quickly.

A sense of alarm filled the room, all of it emanating from the humans. Although *khohlar* allowed elves to reveal emotions, they rarely did so.

Betrayed by his own innocent faith, Griff sat utterly still. Matrinka's fingers glided to her mouth, and Mior rubbed reassuring arcs against her sleeves. Prime Minister Davian finally verbalized the concern. "So it's hopeless."

"Not hopeless," Captain returned distractedly, though his tone conveyed no confidence. He explained what Kevral had already inferred. "There're pieces missing. We can't find them with magic and so can't draw them."

That sounded hopeless to Kevral. Along with the others, she silently waited for Captain to finish.

"If we can locate what's missing, we should be able to retrieve it."

Strong but tiny Chaveesia interjected from her seat between Thialnir and Kedrin, "But if you can't find them with magic, how then? We're not likely to stumble upon them."

"Exactly." Captain looked up suddenly. His face gave away nothing, but his eyes refused to focus on anyone in particular. Something troubled him deeply. While he worked toward verbalizing it, the others remained silent. Even the warriors, less used to diplomacy and elves, barely fidgeted. Kedrin, of course, never moved a muscle.

Finally, Captain spoke again. "There's only one way to obtain information beyond magic. To call the last shards of the Pica, we need to summon a . . . demon."

Khohlar suffused the room, contrasting starkly with verbal human comments and the squeak and thump of movement. Rantire glanced at Kevral, cheek twitching. They remembered the demon Dh'arlo'mé had called, swooping down on Captain's ship. Only the *Sea Seraph*'s magical nature had held it together while they fought, and even that did not prove enough. They had slain the demon as the ship shattered. Battered, bruised, nearly broken, Kevral had then wrestled the Southern Sea and barely won. While battling the demon the *svartalf* called against Pudar, she had lost her consciousness and the use of her arm for nearly a week. Without the attendance of a cluster of the best healers in existence, she might have lost her life as well. The idea of deliberately drawing a demon to Béarn Castle, especially in the presence of king and queen, seemed madness beyond contemplation.

"No!" Rantire's voice rose over the assembly, and she shook back her bronze braids with fierce determination. "Too dangerous."

"It is dangerous," Captain admitted. "But I think we can handle it."

"What, exactly, are we risking?" Davian asked.

"Lives," Rantire said, before Captain could answer. "Our king's most of all."

Captain ignored the outburst to address the details beneath Davian's question. "With the help of the other *lysalf,* I'd have to draw the creature here, then bind it according to Odin's law. Once done, it would have to answer questions and, if we wished, perform a service. Then, I'd need to banish it."

Fear entered the elves' sendings, and they quieted. They'd had an experience that Captain and the humans did not share. They had watched Dh'arlo'mé and one of their most magically competent, named Baheth'rin, call the demon sent after the *Sea Seraph,* had seen them lose control. It had shredded Baheth'rin in moments, her screams desperate and haunting, her blood and flesh a warm, pink-red rain. Still tied to its task, the demon had whisked out to sea with the rumbling threat to return for the rest of the elves when it finished.

"Where's the danger?" Richar pressed.

Captain swung his attention to the minister of foreign affairs. "Twofold. I could lose control or fail to gain it in the first place. Then, it would kill me first and move on until someone either killed or banished it."

Shivers traversed the room.

Captain continued, "Second, banishment requires payment, and demons are bound to accept only blood. Depending on their bent and the situation, Wizards have sacrificed everything from followers to self."

"Blood," Griff repeated gently, head shaking. For that reason alone, he might not allow the summoning.

Captain nodded. "Human or elfin. Animal will not suffice. But not necessarily death, although it will ensue if the summoner loses control or takes too long with the banishment spell."

Kedrin demanded the floor. Matrinka recognized him since Griff seemed incapable, too overwhelmed by the horrible details.

The knight-captain rose. "The blood of one willing sacrifice seems to me worth the lives of our unborn through eternity." He performed a mild bow toward Captain, tan cape fluttering back from the royal blue of his tunic. Kevral could not see his lower half but knew he wore Erythane's orange and black somewhere on his person as well. "I volunteer my own."

The words surprised no one but upset many, including Kevral. She would despise losing her father-in-law in such an ignoble way, though she knew him well enough to believe the demon would not take more than a taste without a battle.

"Thank you, Knight-Captain." Captain returned the gesture of respect. "But I can't accept your sacrifice. The claw strikes of a demon claim ten years apiece, and they usually shape four."

Kevral recalled Captain leaping in front of the demon, enduring an arm wound to spare Ra-khir's face. "Ten years each," he had gasped. "I can spare it. You can't."

Apparently locked into the same thought, Captain rubbed his forearm beneath the light linen. "It only makes sense for an elf to accept the risk."

"For the cause of *human* fertility?" Kedrin shook his regal head. "I think not."

"Forty years means nothing to an elf," Captain insisted. "It's barely a sacrifice and the least we can do after our own kind caused the plague."

"The *svartalf* caused the plague," Davian reminded.

Kevral's experience gave her the means to understand Captain's point, even before he spoke it.

"Elves are elves, Prime Minister. We all have the same origins and, until recently, thought with essentially the same mind. Dh'arlo'mé had to borrow words from human language to define my crime. Disloyalty, individuality, betrayal. Those things did not exist in elfin society until we turned against them." Captain glanced around the *lysalf*. "If we stood together, you could not tell us apart. We call them *svartalf* because we find their actions dark, but they call us the destroyers of the peace, the *lav'rintii*. Which side is correct depends on which side you stand."

"I believe," Kedrin finished, "that I humbly speak for all mankind when I state that we prefer the *lysalf's* peaceful coexistence to the *svartalf's* war."

Captain shrugged. His millennia gave him experience and wisdom beyond what any human could ever share. "Most humans still don't know of our existence. Only time will tell whether we chose the right course or they did. I just have to keep reminding myself that Dh'arlo'mé believes in his cause as strongly as I do in mine."

Humans and elves filled the short pause that followed with thought. At length, Captain returned to the practical issues. "I will use myself as sacrifice."

A jumble of *khohlar* met this statement, too many voices for Kevral to sort. A smile again twitched onto Captain's features, wrinkled from sun and sand. "My peers worry that I'm too old to spare forty years either. I

have many willing replacements, all more appropriate than the commander of the Knights of Erythane." He made a genteel motion of dismissal. "Though we all appreciate your offer."

Kedrin returned the gesture with a heartfelt one of his own, though
he did not argue the point. To do so would demean his heroism to stupidity.

Davian cleared his throat loudly. "None of this matters if the king
chooses not to allow the summoning." He pushed for the necessary
knowledge. "So what exactly is the risk? Numerically, I mean. What can
we do to see that things happen smoothly, if they happen at all? Do we
have options should you lose control?"

The entire room tensed for the answers, and Captain addressed each
point in the order asked. "There's one important complication. When
the elfin Council, the Nine, outcast me, they confiscated my library. Including the tomes that described the proper spells. I believe I remember
them, but I have nowhere to turn if I make a mistake. The quieter the
room, the better my concentration. I would request that, if we decide to
perform the summoning, as few humans as possible remain here."

"No problem," Minister Aerean said with clear relief. Several others
nodded or whispered agreement.

Captain continued, "The summoning itself isn't difficult, nor the initial binding. Without distractions and with the *jovinay arythanik* behind
me, I can virtually guarantee no problems there. For simple answers, I
could and would call the least powerful demon possible. They grow in
strength the longer they stay here, while the bindings only weaken.
Though forced to truth while constrained, they tend toward the shortest
possible answers, heavily interspersed with threat. Delay. I'll think out
the phrasing before we summon to minimize the number of questions.
We won't ask it to perform a service, and I'll banish it quickly." He
glanced around the room, then focused in on Davian. "Any numerical
risk would be a guess. Ten percent, perhaps? As far as options if I lose
control, I can attempt to banish it or it can be slain."

Even with weapons capable of harming it, the Renshai women would
suffer a savage and violent battle that Captain's description skirted. Excited by the prospect, Kevral stifled a grin. She would savor the battle
and, if it came, her death in the combat; but more than her own life lay
at stake.

The room fell silent. King Griff should have enough information for
a decision. Further details, if necessary, could wait until he made it.

For several moments, Griff seemed not to realize the next move was
his. He sat in quiet contemplation, meaty hands folded on the tabletop.
In the dim light of the conference room, the seventeen-year-old ruler
looked extremely young and inexperienced.

Darris leaned toward the king and made a gesture unreadable to Kevral, though it mobilized Griff. The Béarnide lifted his face to the ceiling, coarse black hair gliding backward in even layers. He sighed, then turned his cowlike eyes on Captain. "Call the demon." He did not bother with explanation. His absolute trust in Captain, as well as in Kevral and Rantire, came through clearly. "All ministers will have to leave."

Kevral watched as several loosed pent-up breaths, their features lapsing into expressions of clear relief.

"Darris, I'm going to need you with me." Apology entered Griff's tone, strange contrast to its previous gentle command.

Darris closed his eyes and lowered his head, disappointed but resigned. Missing such a grand display clearly tormented his god-compulsed curiosity. "Yes, Sire."

"Thialnir, Kedrin, Seiryn." Griff glanced at the Renshai's spokesman, the knight-captain, and the captain of Béarn's guardsmen in turn. "Your choice. Someone should stay behind in case . . ." He trailed off, clearly unable to state the possibility that Kevral or Rantire might die and someone competent should remain to take up their swords and their battle.

"Staying, Majesty," Thialnir said gruffly. No Renshai would turn away from such an opportunity.

Kedrin made a fluttering maneuver with his hand that dismissed any possibility of leaving. Seiryn looked from the gathered elves to his king. Kevral doubted he could assist much if the demon killed three Renshai and a Knight of Erythane. "I'll attend you, Sire," Seiryn finally said. He glanced at the *lysalf*'s leader. "Captain, give me a few moments to organize defenses, please."

The elf nodded. "Granted, Captain. We'll need that time for strategy ourselves."

"Thank you, Captain."

Kevral bit her lip, glad Kedrin had not joined the conversation. One more person calling the others "Captain" would spark the laughter she had, so far, stifled.

"Best luck," Griff said, rising and heading for the door, his movements revealing no trepidation. His faith would not waver. Darris scrambled after him, throwing only one longing look at those remaining. Matrinka went with Darris, Mior riding her shoulders. Then the others followed, chair legs scraping and footfalls thumping over soft conversation. Rantire's gaze followed the king, twisted features nearly as pained as the bard's. Torn between directly supervising the king's security in a dangerous situation, and joining in the battle itself, she agonized over

Griff's decision. Kevral knew that Rantire believed she belonged at Griff's side, though they needed sword and sword arm more here.

Captain Seiryn hurried after king, queen, and bard, ahead of the dispersing ministers. These last filed out in a leisurely disarray, their conversations crescendoing from whispers into tumultuous speculation. Finally, the door slammed shut behind them, leaving the quiet group of elves, a page, Rantire, taciturn Thialnir, and politely silent Kedrin. Tae slipped into a corner near the door, crouching there. The king had given him no instructions, and he had chosen the role of soundless observer. Kevral nodded once in his direction, acknowledging his presence, then set about measuring the room with her gaze, memorizing the position of every chair and the angle of each corner. Unexpected stumbles had turned the tide of many battles.

Khohlar replaced the ministers' conversations, the bombardment of foreign concept every bit as distracting to Kevral. They discussed magical strategies that mystified her and chose a young male of whose name Kevral caught only In'diago to serve as temporary blood sacrifice until Captain's banishment took effect. Although he had offered himself bravely, his persistent questioning suggested that he later wished he had lost the honor to another volunteer. Kevral remained as aloof from the proceedings as Tae while Kedrin offered himself in the elf's place and was, again, politely refused.

Finally, after what seemed like hours of deliberation, the elves fell into position. Captain finally turned his attention to Kevral and Rantire. *★If I lose control, the demon will kill me before it attacks any other. After that, its actions become predictable only in that it will kill anything of law.★*

Kevral nodded her understanding. The knowledge would help focus attacks, should battle become necessary. Kevral moved between her father-in-law and the Renshai's spokesman. "Sirs, please stay out of combat unless one of us dies." She indicated Rantire with a wave.

Kedrin frowned but nodded in agreement. Thialnir's eyes narrowed. "Kevral," the Renshai warned. "You're overstepping your bounds commanding us."

A flash of angry irritation passed through Kevral.

The knight-captain made a careful gesture of forbearance. "The strategy is valid, and someone needed to raise the point. Only those two have weapons that can strike the creature. If we all naturally leap into war, we're likely to hamper more than help."

"Renshai fight without strategy," Thialnir said gruffly, the words usually true, though unimportant. No tenet of honor held them from it as it did from using shields, armor, or protections of any kind.

Kedrin turned Thialnir a fatherly look, lips pursed and brows arched.

Thialnir cleared his throat, the sound more like an animal's growl. "I'll stay out until I'm needed," he promised. "I just don't need an over-confident, young upstart—"

"Stop," Kedrin said, voice flat and deliberately emotionless. "You're talking about my daughter-in-law. Please don't force me into a challenge we'd both regret."

Thialnir made a brisk, dismissive gesture, dropping his point without apology. He managed to keep the motion just shy of offense and back down without appearing cowardly. Kevral wisely chose distance. She had spoken her piece and did not need to get swept into a war of wills and honor, though she had initiated it.

Everyone ready? Captain sent, all other *khohlar* instantly disappearing.

The humans made various signals of concession, all except Tae, who remained motionless. Apparently, the elves again directed their singular *khohlar* to Captain, because they gave no direct replies Kevral could sense. They spread along the back and side walls again, their eyes like inset gemstones and their angular faces ranging from nearly human to chillingly alien.

The concept of the last sending before the magics commenced accompanied Captain's *khohlar*, *I'll summon it here.* He turned toward the farthest corner from the door. The nearest elves shifted away, leaving sufficient room for the two young Renshai to glide to Captain's either hand. Kevral took up a position to his right, Rantire to his left. Thialnir and Kedrin stood in guard positions near the door.

Captain lowered his head, and Kevral could feel him steeling nerves and self-confidence as he cut off the deliberate contact, reestablishing it a moment later. *Jovinay arythanik.*

The elves began a low chant, like music.

Suddenly, Captain jerked his arms upward. Sounds escaped his lips, a harsh and sibilant contrast to the tranquil chant that fed its power.

Kevral crouched, gaze on the same point as Captain's, though she did not allow her attention to lock fanatically there. To do so might blur her vision and blunt her responses to peripheral dangers.

Gradually, a dark smudge stirred the air in front of Captain, barely visible contrast to the corner's shadows. The tone of the words shifted dramatically, still guttural yet flowing in a more patterned delivery. In response, a silver thread appeared in the area of conjured blackness. Gradually, it twined around the figureless shadow, first in slow loops. Captain's speech quickened into a rush that Kevral could not match, even in her first language, and the bindings whipped into rapid coils as the blackness collected into a shape smaller than either of the demons she had battled.

Attributing the difference in size to the professed weakness of the demon Captain called, Kevral wrapped her left fingers around the hilt of her sword. Renshai training deliberately overcame hand preferences in early childhood, focusing practice always toward weakness. Experience taught her that chaos' demons took form only when summoned, and even that proved fleeting. They changed appearance at will.

Arms and legs, in standard pairs, grew from the darkness, as well as a head scarcely larger than Kevral's own. As the figure became more definingly human, the bindings slipped, dropping abruptly to the floor.

Captain hissed, magical syllables collapsing into a human curse. "Damn!" He flung his arms in savage frustration, summoning more bindings that appeared, entwined, and collapsed in an instant. His amber eyes turned wild.

The demon winked to sudden life, man-shaped with a readied sword that gathered momentum in an arcing blur and sped for Captain's head.

Kevral drew and cut as Captain sprang backward. Even her deadly speed nearly proved too slow. The demon-sword slammed solidly against the one Colbey had given her. Steel chimed, a strange melody against the background chanting, and impact ached through her hand. She started a riposte as the summoned creature lunged a stroke for her gut. Converting the movement to a desperate defense, she managed to batter its sword aside. A moment later Rantire reached Kevral's side, her own attack foiled by a graceful dodge.

Colbey? Captain's startled word barely penetrated Kevral's concentration.

The creature Kevral battled moved with a speed that dazzled, and it managed an attack at each young Renshai before either could gain an opening for offense. Only then, it occurred to Kevral that demons never used objects with form as weapons. She glanced at her opponent, recognizing the feathered golden locks, the familiar Northern features, and the demon-scarred cheek. *It is Colbey!*

The momentary lapse cost Kevral the battle. The tip of Colbey's sword licked under her crossguard, and the blade flew from her hand. He lashed rabidly at Rantire, sending her into startled retreat, and still managed to catch Kevral's hilt.

Kevral back-stepped cautiously, battle wrath dispersing in a sudden rush. More from instinct than threat, she reached for her other hilt.

Captain leaped to the tabletop, scuttling to the opposite end. *Colbey, stop it! What in Hel are you doing?*

"Defending myself." Colbey whipped in on Rantire, elves scattering from the wall behind her. The chanting broke off erratically. Kevral's sword, in Colbey's hand, screamed for Rantire's throat. As she jerked up her blade to parry, Colbey's own carved the grip from her hands as well. Catching Rantire's sword in the same hand as Kevral's, he whirled to face Thialnir who had, apparently, rushed in the moment Kevral lost her weapon. Colbey danced aside, jabbing both of the captured blades through his belt, and Thialnir thundered past him. Kevral never saw the maneuver that claimed the last Renshai's weapon. Colbey pivoted to face Knight-Captain Kedrin and his drawn sword, keeping all of the warriors to his front. "I'm running out of hands."

Kedrin neither sheathed his weapon nor attacked, instead carefully spreading his arms in willing truce. Surely, he realized this also opened his defenses.

Apparently trusting the knight, Colbey turned his attention fully on the three Renshai. Each remained where he had left them. Too little time had passed for other action. He sheathed his sword. "Are we finished?"

Thialnir nodded, studying Colbey's lithe warrior figure. As Colbey's icy blue-gray stare turned to Kevral, she also nodded. Rantire met his scrutiny next, again nodding.

Accepting that, Colbey tossed back the weapons in the same order, each snatching the hilt from the air and returning it to its proper position.

"Who are you?" Thialnir demanded, though Captain had revealed Colbey's name in general *khohlar*. The use of Renshai maneuvers should have clinched the identity, yet Thialnir still refused to believe.

Captain had a more pressing question. "Colbey, are you a demon now?"

Since Captain's query answered Thialnir's, Colbey turned to the elf, still crouched on the tabletop. "You know I'm not."

Kevral sought Tae, no longer in his corner. He had a tendency to appear suddenly in the midst of battle, too often directly in front of her strokes. She found him near the door, stance casual, hands resting lightly on his belt. He acknowledged her only by meeting her eyes.

"Nothing about you is certain anymore." Captain eyed his ancient companion warily. "I know I summoned a demon, and you came."

"I told you I wouldn't bind with the Staff of Chaos." Colbey patted the hilt of his sword, the shape into which he had willed the staff shortly after becoming the Prince of Demons. "Even if you doubt my word, you should realize that your bindings hold creatures of chaos, never of law. Proof enough, I would think."

"I don't know what to think," Captain admitted.

Kevral glanced back and forth between these friends who had supported one another in centuries past, at a time when everyone else had abandoned or turned against Colbey. More than three hundred and twenty years ago, Colbey had completed the task that brought the Staves of Law and Chaos to man's world. Certain only balance could keep the worlds alive, he kept one staff and passed the other to the Wizards who had championed the universe for centuries. Even the gods believed Colbey had chosen chaos, and beings at every level had banded together to destroy him. Only later did they realize he had taken the staff of law. Touched by chaos, the Wizards set the *Ragnarok* in motion, the war that had destroyed most of the gods and elves. Captain alone had refused to judge Colbey, trusting him to follow the course of balance no matter which staff he championed.

This time, Colbey had taken up chaos against law, and even Captain seemed uncertain whether he could keep from fully binding to its cause. Colbey shook his head, a gesture of clear disgust. "Captain, trust me."

The elf jumped down from the table. Kevral moved aside so that he could approach Colbey. "I trust you. You know I do. It's chaos I don't trust."

Colbey's nod defined resignation. He had clearly lost more friends than Captain to his decision. "I'm tired and irritated by the summoning." He looked around the room, apparently weighing the danger of speaking his piece in front of those present. "I walled off all but one opening to chaos' world. I've assured that no amount of chaos sufficient to create a demon escapes at once."

Thialnir sat in the nearest seat, still clearly shocked. Kedrin remained like a statue, accustomed to long, stiffly attentive vigils. Rantire took a defensive position near the door, and Tae returned to his corner. The elves remained near the walls, several gliding to the floor to sit and watch the exchange. The page stayed still.

Captain explained what Colbey surely already knew, "Demons don't just 'escape.' They have to be summoned."

"Indeed."

Captain's eyes narrowed. "Who besides me and Dh'arlo'mé knows how?"

Colbey's look became arch. "Do we need others?"

"You've faced off with Dh'arlo'mé?" The words emerged in a tight squeak.

Colbey's head bobbed once.

Captain back-stepped, his face revealing anxious confusion only to one as skilled in reading elfin expressions as Colbey was. "Doesn't that mean . . ." He trailed off, the rest obvious to only a few. Kevral understood. Colbey had, at first, selected her for the task of wielding chaos. He had explained that the staff would bind with her; she would ultimately become chaos. She would then confront Dh'arlo'mé bound to the Staff of Law. Then they would destroy one another and, with any luck, the extremes of law and chaos.

Colbey waved dismissively. "We fought, but then we separated. And we'll surely fight again." The blue-gray gaze rolled to meet Captain's directly. "But these matters don't concern those gathered here," he said tightly, expression revealing. Kevral guessed he would have told Captain more under other circumstances. It seemed cruel to inform humans and elves of a hovering destruction they could not affect. "What purpose did you have for a demon? Surely, you know better than to try to fight enemies with a summoned abomination."

Thialnir continued to stare. Kevral could almost see the thoughts taking shape in his massive head: Colbey had performed flawless Renshai maneuvers during the combat, yet Thialnir knew all three hundred living tribe members. He still sought some other explanation than that he had confronted a four-centuries-old Renshai out of legend.

Captain shook his head. "I would never do such a thing." His lids clipped the edges of eyes like garnets, the only sign that he had narrowed them. "You know that. I called the least of demons to ask necessary questions, ones that concern the survival of mankind as an entity. Nothing less would have driven me to such desperate action." He added pointedly, "I did not expect to draw the Prince of Demons himself."

Colbey did not deny the title, as he had throughout history. Now that he championed chaos, it held a ring of truth. "Fair enough. What did you need to know?"

Hope spiraled through the room, made tangible by *khohlar*. Captain relaxed visibly, though nothing had revealed his previous tension. "I'm seeking the missing pieces of the Pica."

"The Pica," Colbey repeated, head jerking suddenly to the partially reconstructed sapphire on the meeting room table. He drifted toward it.

"I've gathered as much as possible by magic but can't locate the rest. Restoring it will help break the *svartalf*'s sterility spell. Can you help?"

Colbey circled the mangled stone, as if afraid to touch it. Captain's story explained his reluctance. If he was, indeed, responsible for its destruction, then he might worry about damaging it again.

Several moments passed in silence. Tae remained crouched by the door. Knight-Captain Kedrin held an alert posture wholly lacking threat. Thialnir continued to stare. The elves watched the proceedings through sparkling, homogeneous eyes.

Finally, Colbey spoke, "I can't help you. But I know one who can." He drew his sword with a slow serenity that belied the deadly grace and dispatch that usually characterized the motion. He offered Captain the hilt.

The gesture stunned Kevral. A Renshai would sooner hand over a body part than a sword, even for a moment. Allowing another to touch one's sword conveyed a depth of trust that went far beyond family ties or liege loyalty. Her hand slid naturally to the hilt of the weapon he had given her, with great reluctance, after Dh'arlo'mé's summoned demon had attacked the great trading city of Pudar.

Captain seemed not to understand the profound honor Colbey bestowed upon him. He shied away.

Colbey's mouth formed a crooked grin. "Take it, Captain. The demon you summoned holds the answers you seek."

The elf pursed his lips, turning Colbey an irritated look. "Have your fun with me while you still can, Renshai. I have no mind powers to control the Staff of Chaos. It would ruin me."

Kevral watched the exchange with great interest. Colbey's mind powers, she had learned, came of the succession forced upon him by a desperate Western Wizard. Without foreknowledge, Colbey had inherited the collective consciousness of all of the Western Wizards ahead of him and believed their voices in his head to be his own madness. With the ferocity of a Renshai in wartime, he had battled and destroyed them, in the process sharpening the mental control of the Renshai. It had left him with the ability to read minds, though he never invaded the thoughts of those he cared for or respected uninvited. Strong ideas and emotions, however, radiated to him without intention.

Supporting the sword by the crossguard, Colbey continued to offer it. "The staff and I have an agreement."

"Chaos cannot be bound to promises."

"It needs me as much as I need it," Colbey insisted. "For all its power-mad unpredictability, it would not abandon me for a champion of lesser power." He held the sword at the extent of his reach. "Take it."

Captain's expression never changed, though Colbey's words trapped him. To refuse meant betraying the trust he had earlier sworn, yet to take it might cost him life and sanity. The yellow eyes swiveled to meet Colbey's, and his jaw set in stony determination. The hilt slid into his small, long-fingered hand. No fear flickered through his eyes, nor did his stance reveal any trepidation. Once he had chosen to trust his silent companion, Captain did so implicitly.

Colbey retreated, hands hovering as if he had suddenly become conscious of them and they could find no natural position. A Renshai without a sword might as well remove every scrap of clothing. He felt equally naked.

While Captain communed with the Staff of Chaos, Colbey turned his attention to the others in the room. He approached Thialnir first, tiny compared to the broad-boned and -featured warrior leader, yet far more menacing. "Colbey Calistinsson of the tribe of Renshai." He made a standard gesture of greeting that included displaying both hands to reveal the lack of weaponry.

"I know who you are," Thialnir replied, meeting the icy stare with sharp, green eyes. "No one less skilled could have disarmed me so easily and with a maneuver I don't recognize but still know as Renshai." He made a broad motion of respect. "Thialnir Thrudazisson. Renshai." His face twisted, he shifted restlessly, and his eyes revealed the need Kevral knew well. He wanted to challenge the immortal Renshai, desperately needed to pit his skill against the greatest of all swordsmen and perhaps glean a point of instruction. However, the circumstance did not allow him to ask, and Colbey did not offer.

Acknowledging the introduction with a nod, Colbey moved on to Rantire, placing a hand on her shoulder "Ravn speaks highly of you."

Rantire beamed.

Colbey smiled and nodded to Kedrin as he passed.

"My lord, is it true you were a Knight of Erythane?"

Stopped by the knight-captain's words, Colbey turned. "Were? Was my title revoked?"

"Not by me," Kedrin assured him. "So it's true?"

"Centuries ago, a knight challenged me to fair combat, and I bested him. Later, he attacked me dishonorably, and I was forced to kill him. I took the vow before King Orlis and was awarded my horse, Frost Reaver."

Kedrin executed a respectful bow. "Welcome back, Sir Colbey."

Colbey smiled but, to his credit, did not laugh. It would offend. "Thank you, Captain." Again, he started toward Kevral, this time halted by a thought. "While I'm dealing with the balance, Reaver languishes in a pasture, tended but not properly exercised. Would it burden you too much if I left him in your care?"

Kevral froze, unable even to breathe for a moment. The honor reached nearly the level of sharing a sword and she sensed the truth behind the request. Colbey expected the task he had undertaken to kill him and knew the Knights of Erythane would appreciate the white charger as no others could.

"Not in the least, Sir Colbey." Kedrin bowed again, as grandly. "We would consider it an honor, and he would receive the best of care."

"Thank you, Captain." Colbey finally came to Kevral's side. His gaze fell to her abdomen before meeting her eyes, and he spoke in a low voice that scarcely carried. "Raise my grandchild well, in the best tradition of Renshai."

A wave of excitement swept through Kevral. "I will," she promised.

At least one other heard. Before Kevral could reply further, Kedrin's nostrils flared, and all the joy of Colbey's gift fled in an instant. "Any grandchild borne to Kevral had best be mine." He spoke as softly, but his tone carried clear threat.

Chilled by Kedrin's delivery, Kevral found herself without retort. Memory flooded back: the stench of mold, urine, and unwashed flesh that pervaded Pudar's dungeon; desperation and loathsome weakness inexorably mixed; self-made vows to slaughter King Cymion lost to a promise to Ra-khir. Once again, she would bear a child not her husband's; Ra-khir knew and understood, but others would revile her. The vow of silence to which Pudar had bound them now seemed still more horrible. She had the words to explain but could not, by her own honor and Ra-khir's, speak them.

Colbey rescued Kevral from the need. "It is your grandchild, Captain. In every way that matters." Though barely above a whisper, his voice revealed sorrow. The son of the god Thor by blood, Colbey claimed ties only to his mortal father also.

"Blood matters." Kedrin turned Kevral a withering scrutiny. A fair man, he had accepted Tae's son without comment. This time, he would not prove so forgiving.

Colbey shrugged. "Soon, Captain, the entirety of Béarn will learn otherwise. As will you." Kevral suspected Colbey referred to the baby princess now. His manner stiffened, and he fixed those glacial eyes on Kedrin. "Trust in your son and daughter-in-law. Judging honor in hindsight is only condemnation." He added pointedly, "It's beneath you, Kedrin."

The knight-captain did not argue. Kevral felt certain he would raise the matter again, when she did not have an immortal to defend her. She rolled her glance to Colbey, then looked away. Her hero had betrayed her.

Colbey addressed Kevral's state of mind. "I didn't mean for him to hear, but it's better that he knows."

Kevral did not agree but knew it fruitless to question. She had spent too many years glorifying him to disbelieve his assertions now, even tainted by chaos.

Captain raised his head, then looked at the sword in his hands. His eyes darted restively, seeking some place to set it down that would not offend its champion. He started toward the table.

"Don't," Colbey stopped the elf with a word. "Toss it here." He raised a hand.

Captain hesitated, sword gripped at arm's length. "But I might . . ."

He trailed off, either because he realized Colbey could compensate for any lack of skill on Captain's part or to get rid of it as soon as possible. He hurled it awkwardly toward Colbey.

The sword plummeted a bare arm's length from the *lysalf*'s leader, but Colbey was there, catching the hilt as if it had come to him in a deft and gentle arc. "Did you get your answer?"

"Yes." Captain's tone and expression revealed nothing.

"Very well." Colbey lowered his head, preparing to depart.

"Colbey," Captain said. "Don't turn my work into futile trivia. Keep the balance, and yourself, alive."

"I'll do my best." Colbey winked. "But only because you asked."

Captain did not share the humor. "If it's possible, you'll manage."

A moment later, Colbey disappeared, and a mood hung in the wake of Captain's words. For the first time in over three hundred years, he was clearly worried about Colbey's ability to handle the problem. And, Kevral believed, Colbey shared that concern.

CHAPTER 4

Alone Again

Always the last
Even your die is cast
Your skill at my side in the War.
                              —*Odin to Colbey Calistinsson*

AT the edge of Béarn's woods, Kevral wove and pranced, swords carving crisp arcs and spirals. For nearly an hour, the *svergelse* had occupied every part of her mind and imagination. Her subconscious had registered the movements of Tae and Subikahn nearby but rejected them as harmless. Though she had watched them much of the time, she could not recall anything except the violent prayer she had offered to the god and goddess of Renshai. She launched into a final sequence, a savage flurry of thrust, twist, and charge, ending with a high, spinning kick and slash designed for combat against horsemen. Landing, she ended the session, exertion leaving her panting but enlivening her spirit.

Kevral hauled a rag from her pocket. She wiped cloudy condensation and streaks of splattered sweat from the steel, oiled the blades, soaped the split leather grips, and returned them to their sheaths. Brushing aside strands of hair plastered to her forehead, tugging her plain tan tunic and breeks back into place, she headed toward the spread blanket where she had left the babies and their fathers.

Late-autumn sunlight gleamed from Subikahn's slick, black hair. He sat alone, propped against a twiggy branch, hands pressed together. His dark eyes glimmered, and his lips pursed into pudgy creases.

Finding her not quite four-month-old untended, Kevral suffered a twinge of annoyance that swiftly rose to anger. She hurried toward the child, cheeks hot, red, and slick with sweat.

Before Kevral arrived, Tae emerged from the tree shadows. "So you see, little hunter, darker . . ." He caught sight of Kevral. ". . . *khafarat teh hirot pithrikent.*"

All of the rage rushed from Kevral in an instant, and she smiled. "I wish you'd stop doing that." She wiped moist palms on her breeks.

Tae hefted Subikahn, tickling the tiny belly. The baby giggled, then loosed a high-pitched squeal. "I'm just doing what Thialnir asked. Teaching stealth maneuvers."

"I was talking about the two of you switching into Eastern every time you don't want me to hear." Kevral winked to show she was joking. "It's gotten to the point where I don't understand anything he says."

"Me either." Tae hugged Subikahn, and the baby seized a handful of his father's hair. "I assumed he was speaking Renshai." The speed of his speech increased, revealing excitement. "Do you know there's a Renshai technique called *brunstil*?" The word literally meant "brown and still," and Kevral had learned it years ago. "Learned from barbarians." He attempted to lower the baby. As the tension increased on his hair, he stopped, wincing.

Kevral pulled the rag from her pocket and mopped her face. Dropping it onto the blanket, she unwound Tae's locks from Subikahn's grip. "How do you know that?"

Tae waited until Kevral freed him before skittering beyond sword range. "I could tell you, but you'd probably have to kill me." He tossed Subikahn gently, catching him amid a startled baby laugh.

Kevral worried only a moment for the Renshai's secrets. She recalled the sage's paranoid precautions and the file Tae had stolen from his tower. No information was safe from the Eastern prince. "Climbing Béarn's castle. Endangering my child. Baiting Renshai." She shook her head. "You used to have a survival instinct."

"I still do." Tae shrugged. "I've just learned to ignore it." Holding Subikahn near his face, he added something in Eastern that included a slight incline of his head toward Kevral.

"Hey. Isn't it the parents who're supposed to have a language the children don't understand?" Even as the words left her lips, Kevral wished she had not spoken them, a cruel reminder that Tae did not live with his son.

But Tae took the comment in stride. "Pick one," he said.

Kevral laughed. As a Renshai, she learned her native and the closely related Northern tongue. Like all Westerners, and most Easterners and Northmen, she knew the common trading language. She had deliberately taken up Western, Erythane's native speech, as well. She had met Rakhir while trying to refine the dialectal nuances, a perfectionist at everything she attempted. Aside from Renshai, which the tribe never shared with *ganim*, Tae knew all the languages she did plus Béarnese and his native Eastern. She wondered how long it would be before he picked up enough Renshai from his son to enrage the tribal leaders.

The pounding of hoofbeats interrupted Kevral's thoughts. She glanced up as Tae unconsciously melted back amid the shadows, Subikahn's fusses and coos giving away his position.

A moment later, a massive white stallion galloped into view, hooves drumming the leaf-strewn ground in solid, patterned beats. Its coat gleamed. Spotless blue-and-gold ribbons streamed from mane and tail. A wide bridle with decorative conches set off the wide brow and graceful, triangular head. Ra-khir rode at a dignified crouch that placed his weight solidly over its withers. His hair fluttered, entwined with his cape. As he drew closer, Kevral recognized the red flush of exhilaration on his cheeks and the baby lashed with two blankets to his chest.

Ra-khir reined in the charger a safe distance from Kevral. The animal's powerful legs brought them to a rapid stop; and it stood attentively, ears briskly forward and neck delicately arched. Ra-khir leaped from the saddle, one arm further supporting Saviar. The baby lay limp inside the pack, one arm trailing down the front, head flopped forward, and honey-colored hair with a hint of red dribbling down his forehead.

Flipping the reins over the horse's head, Ra-khir approached Kevral. "I've found the secret to getting the boys to sleep." He waved in the general direction of the stallion. "Works better than ten lullabies."

Kevral smiled. "If only we could get the horse to fit in their cradles." She gave him an affectionate thump on the shoulder.

Ra-khir caught Kevral into an embrace, careful not to crush the baby. "Frost Reaver's unbelievable. I still can't believe Colbey left him with us. Or that my father let me ride him."

Kevral ran her hands along her husband's back, loving the solid feel of him. She did not savor too long, however, worried for Tae's feelings. "Why not? Colbey let you ride him." During their quest to locate and restore Griff, Kevral had suffered a poisoned arrow. Seeking an antidote, Ra-khir had ridden desperately through enemies, and Colbey had provided Frost Reaver for the mission. "The other knights let grooms and stable hands handle their mounts. You rarely do. Who better to exercise an immortal's horse?"

Ra-khir returned to Frost Reaver, rubbing a hand across the sweat-darkened fur of its chest.

"Were we expecting company?" Tae asked from the opposite side of the animal.

Kevral followed Tae's gaze to three dots appearing from the direction of the castle. Her brow furrowed. "Who do you suppose?" Her hands drifted naturally to her hilts, though she anticipated no trouble.

Ra-khir glanced at Saviar, then turned Frost Reaver to face the approaching figures. He remained at the stallion's head, reins loose in his gloved fist. Tae placed Subikahn back into his makeshift chair and returned to join the others. By then, Kevral could make out three horses with riders, two brown and the other as broad and white as Frost Reaver. The rider of the latter wore a plumed hat, and an indigo blanket trimmed with gold tassels fluttered beneath the saddle.

"A knight." Ra-khir absently placed a hand against Saviar's back, attention still fixed on the horsemen.

Recognizing her misplaced caution, Kevral removed her hands from her weapons. Gradually, the riders grew from shapeless blurs to definitive forms. The rigid male on the charger could represent any Knight of Erythane. A Béarnide rode in the center, the lack of a mane revealing her as a female. The last sported the slighter figure of a non-Béarnide Westerner.

"Matrinka." Tae recognized first.

Ra-khir stiffened, shuffling his tangled locks with his fingers and pressing wrinkles from his clothes. It would not do for a knight to appear disheveled in front of his queen.

Once Tae had identified the Béarnide, the others came easily to Kevral. "Darris and your father."

Ra-khir mumbled something incomprehensible, of which Kevral gleaned only the lament that Kedrin appeared whenever Ra-khir became the most unkempt.

For Tae's sake, Kevral resisted jokes about some day discovering her father-in-law in their bed. She glanced at Saviar, sprawled and snoring, and decided not to take him. The movement would awaken the baby, and Ra-khir had a right to relax with his family while off duty. More than once, she had caught Kedrin in compromising positions, entertaining or crooning baby talk to his grandson.

The three horses drew up in front of Kevral, Ra-khir, and Tae, and the men dismounted. Both started toward Matrinka. Kedrin deferred, allowing Darris to assist the queen from her horse while he merely held the reins. Matrinka clambered down, rearranging her skirts and hiding a wince. It took courage for the queen to ride so soon after childbirth.

Ra-khir executed as grand a bow as the tethered baby allowed, ignoring Matrinka's frown. She despised formality, especially from her friends, yet surely understood Ra-khir's dilemma. To treat her with anything but the utmost respect in his father's presence would earn him a severe tongue lashing, possibly suspension or dismissal from the Knights of Erythane.

Everyone yielded to Matrinka to speak first, as convention required. Kedrin's presence demanded manners they would otherwise forgo at Matrinka's insistence.

Matrinka cleared her throat, then gestured toward Kedrin. "Please explain, Captain."

"As you wish, Your Ladyship." Kedrin swept off his hat and also bowed, then looked toward Kevral and Ra-khir without obvious judgment of his son's appearance. In direct contrast, he wore an immaculate tabard and colors. "The nine missing pieces of the Pica have gone to worlds beyond our own. The elves can send a group of up to eight to retrieve them. The council has met, and the constituency of that group was discussed." He looked at each of his companions in turn. "Two elves, a knight, a Renshai and one representative from each of the following areas: Béarn, the East, the North, and the West."

Excitement quickened Kevral's heart rate, and she fought it away. Memories crowded in, of the worrisome days and nights on the road, pursued by Béarn's enemies and Tae's as well. Nothing in her life had seemed more right than her moments in real battle. Yet, she knew better than to hope Kedrin would send his pregnant daughter-in-law on such a mission while still nursing twins.

The knight's captain looked toward Matrinka, but she motioned for him to continue. He did as she bade. "King Griff appreciates the sacrifices you made to return him to his throne. He believes your group, with a few additions, best suited for the job." If Kedrin held any doubts about Griff's decision, he made no sign. It would violate his honor. "He left the choice to you."

Yes. Kevral resisted the urge to shout her answer. To blurt out a commitment without at least a few moments of consideration would make her look unworthy. Besides, she had others to consider, her children as well as her companions.

Finally, Matrinka claimed a floor rightfully hers. "The council refused my participation." She added with a trace of shame, "Had they not, I probably would have withdrawn myself."

Kevral nodded encouragingly. Matrinka had made the right decision for her. Marisole was newly born and Matrinka still recovering. The battles they had fought, against one another and against enemies, had frightened and wounded Matrinka. She could serve Béarn better here. Kevral also realized that the group Kedrin had described did not allow for both Matrinka and Darris. Only one could represent Béarn.

Matrinka smiled at her consort. "But Darris agreed to go."

Like anyone could stop him. Kevral knew the bardic curiosity would drive him every bit as hard as her Renshai lust for battle.

"I'm the only Easterner in Béarn," Tae pointed out, rocking Subikahn.

"And, if you accepted, you'd have to leave before messengers could request and return your father's consent." Kedrin's expression turned more serious, if possible. "That's a lot to ask of a prince." He fidgeted, uncharacteristically. Tae's refusal to respond to titles clearly agitated him, though he duly respected Tae's wishes.

Tae continued swaying. "I'm going."

"Me, too," Kevral said. From the corner of her eye, she could see Ra-khir stiffen. She wondered whether he worried for her or for his honor-bound need to stay with the twins when adventuring would suit him better.

Kedrin did not wait for Ra-khir's reply. "You all worked well without responsibilities to weigh you down. We can't guess the dangers you might face, but they're likely to include battles and magic. Do you believe you can work without distraction?" Although he did not verbally direct the question, his gaze settled on Kevral.

Kevral met the pale eyes steadily. "Renshai have been having babies *and* fighting wars forever." She braced for verbal warfare, unwilling to budge from this position. If the child inside her could not survive the rigors of her life, it would prove too frail for the life of a Renshai. She deliberately pushed away the realization that Pudar would claim the baby as its own.

To Kevral's surprise, Kedrin did not argue. "The queen and Marisole's attendants agreed to watch the boys. Also, your parents will gladly watch them." A smile eased onto otherwise somber features. "They promised to spoil them so rotten you'll never want them back." Turning his attention to Ra-khir, he added carefully, "Assuming you wish to go as well."

Ra-khir made a stiff gesture of respect. "I do. If you can spare me, Captain."

"You're off duty, Ra-khir. 'Father' will do."

Ra-khir arched his brows. "But I know you can spare me as a son. It's as a knight I'm concerned."

"Our king selected you from my men. His judgment is always perfect." Kedrin's grin slipped. "As a son, I can only spare you temporarily."

Ra-khir studied his own child, saying nothing.

"Settled, then." Handing the reins of Matrinka's horse to Darris, Kedrin headed back to his charger. "Any difficulty meeting in the morning in the red strategy room?"

"No, sir," Ra-khir said, while the others quietly shook their heads.

Kedrin replaced his hat and mounted. "We'll have travel gear packed and ready. Bring whatever else you feel you need. If there's anything you don't have, Darris and her Ladyship can see that you get anything within reason." With a brisk wave, he headed off the way he had come, leaving the five friends to converse.

Kevral watched him go, face aglow. The excitement of new worlds and battles beckoned.

Even after three centuries, Colbey admired Asgard's everpresent sunlight and the balmy temperature, maintained by puffs of wind. Sparkling, emerald grasses flattened beneath his feet, then sprang back to attention as he took each next step. He whisked past perfect trees, heading for the monstrous, golden building that represented the gods' meeting hall. The magnificent changelessness of Asgard, once a blessing, now irritated the Lord of Chaos. The staff tapped at his mental barriers. Grudgingly, he winched one down a crack, admitting its counsel.

They won't listen to you, the Staff of Chaos insisted.

They never do. Colbey accepted the assessment without dispute. *But I have to try. I need their assistance.*

If you bind, you'll need nothing but me.

Colbey ignored the tired argument, allowing his mind wall to close without reply. The staff was right. United with the primordial chaos, he could confront the Dh'arlo'mé/Law entity with all the might of a god. Yet then Colbey would cease to exist, a cog in the nearly invincible machinery of chaos. The decision had haunted him since their first meeting. Always before, he had handled even the most formidable of tasks, never worrying for the death in battle he had sought since his childhood mind could conceive of its permanence. This time, so much more lay upon his decision. His enemy far outpowered him, but binding would even their abilities. If he continued to refuse, every world might shatter into oblivion for his mistake and he would lose the very wife and son for whom he had, so far, resisted.

The gods' meeting hall gained proportion as Colbey strode toward it. The sun struck multicolored highlights from myriad gems embedded in the metal walls. Constructed from the sacrifices of worshipers, its gaudiness surpassed any other object on the worlds of gods and men. Always before, Colbey had despised its blazing ostentation. Now, he found beauty in the randomness of its jewelry and the fragments of rainbow reflecting from every nearby tree. He lowered his head. *I've not escaped chaos wholly unchanged.*

The thought brought a cascade of others. Early on, chaos had slowly infused him, attempting to trick him into an insidious and ignorant binding. He had nearly succumbed to its gradual trickle, abandoning ancient honor and nearly alienating his family. Ravn's and Freya's tough stance against him had brought the problem to his attention, and his regained allegiance to them had carried him through a direct confrontation with the primordial chaos. He had triumphed, winning a control that astounded. Once fatal to any creature of law, Chaos World had become his to shape and mold, its reality whatever he chose to make it. The discovery that his work there remained true even on the worlds of law, the gods' Asgard and the humans' Midgard, had shocked him. From that moment, he had deliberately kept his touch light.

Arriving at the Meeting Hall, Colbey loosened his sword in its scabbard before seizing the knob. Braced for hostility, he opened the door. Sunlight flickered over a brace of diamonds in the jamb, shattering shadows through the contrastingly austere interior. A massive, brass-bound table served as the only piece of furniture, surrounded by deities. A candelabra heavier than five humans hung from the ceiling, its many candles lit.

The gods looked toward the interruption. Vidar occupied the head of the table, once Odin's seat. Awe for the AllFather had kept that place empty until Colbey had deliberately taken it a few months earlier. At Vidar's either hand sat his half-brothers, Vali and Baldur. Colbey's half-brothers, Modi and Magni, sat together, Thor's mighty hammer between them on the floor. To Magni's left sat the goddesses Sif, Idunn, and Loki's widow, Sigyn. Blind Hod lounged beside Vali, Honir beside him, then Colbey's brother-in-law, Frey in the next position. Colbey's gaze darted naturally to Freya, his wife; and he went breathless. Months ensconced in chaos had robbed him of the details of beauty so primal it defined the very word. Her golden cascade of hair outlined large blue eyes, a straight, perfectly sculpted nose, and a strong chin. Her every movement bespoke grace. At her side sat their son, Raska "Ravn" Colbeysson.

Every eye swept to Colbey and froze there. Frowns scored many faces. Vali sprang to his feet, yellow braids in disarray and short beard bristling. "You're not welcome here." His voice held deadly warning. "You know that."

Vidar nodded once. This time, not even he would defend the Prince of Demons. "Colbey, you agreed not to return."

Even Ravn's hand stole toward his sword. Colbey noted the various threats but acted upon none of them. If challenged, he would fight, though many gods would die before, and if, they defeated him. "Please. Hear me out."

Vali fairly growled. "We have no time or patience for chaos' lies." He repeated, "You're not welcome here."

Colbey glanced around the room, at the pale Northern faces. Aside from his wife and child, he discovered only hostility in expression and radiated emotion. Freya pursed her lips, uncommitted. Ravn fidgeted. The strongest of the gods had died at the *Ragnarok*, extremes the world no longer needed. "Please."

A lengthy pause followed the request that only Vidar could deny or grant. Colbey still cursed the gods' infernal patience; he did not share it.

"Speak your piece," Vidar said.

Vali whipped his head to his brother so fast his war braids flew. He turned the leader of the gods an expression rife with anger. Nevertheless, he sat.

"Thank you." Colbey shut the door, remaining near it. Too many would read even a cautious approach as attack. He looked directly at Ravn. Blue eyes so like his mother's swiveled to meet Colbey's. The boy licked his lips but said nothing. "You need to know . . ." Colbey started. After taking up chaos, he had passed control of the balance to his son. ". . . that the entity of bound law and Dh'arlo'mé now calls himself Odin."

Modi's fist crashed against the table. His name literally meant "wrath," and Renshai had always called upon him when injured in battle or desperate for a second wind. "Blasphemy!" Rage slashed the room, the other gods less demonstrative but equally bothered.

"No." Colbey kept his voice low and calm. "He calls himself Odin because he *is* Odin."

The goddess the Renshai worshiped, Sif, found her voice first. "The AllFather?"

"Yes."

"The Gray Father?" Baldur queried.

Colbey waved dismissively. "We could list his many names all day, but it won't change anything. My enemy is Odin."

Shock filled the room, accompanied by everything from belligerent doubt to joy. Colbey did not bother to identify which emotion came from whom.

Vidar's eyes flickered in agitation as he, apparently, considered the possibilities. "How can that be? Even the near-infinite powers of the staves should not be able to turn one being into another."

"He's lying," Vali grumbled. "Everything he says is suspect."

Vidar made a curt gesture that silenced his half brother.

Colbey explained, "Odin's contingency plan. He placed a trace of himself in the Staff of Law in case something went wrong at the *Ragnarok*. Which, of course, it did." Colbey fought down a smile. He had bested the AllFather only this once, battling aside Odin's attempts to convince him that he had existed for no other purpose than assisting Odin against the Fenris Wolf at the *Ragnarok*. In the greatest of all wars, physical prowess had played a greater role than magic and mental influence. "It took centuries, but the spark sequestered in the Staff of Law grew. Once Odin became powerful enough to recognize himself, he chose and dominated his champion."

Sigyn's eyes narrowed. "And the Staff of Chaos?"

Colbey swung his attention to her, glad the gods had chosen to listen, no matter how suspiciously. "Grew in opposition, I believe. Even without a champion, the world tends toward balance."

Sif grinned, her obvious delight direct contrast to her squinty-eyed, scowling companions. She shook back metallic gold tresses, replacement for the natural hair stolen by Loki long ago. "This is good news."

"If we believe it," Vali grumped, though a light flickered in his blue eyes, disrupting his otherwise mistrustful glare.

"Odin," Sif said loudly to indicate she had not finished, "can put this all right."

Colbey suffered a brief pang of pain at the intimation that he had badly bungled the balance and championing chaos. Even after centuries among the gods, an insult from the goddess he had worshiped throughout his mortal years stung. Discovering Thor's indiscretion with a mortal Renshai, she had torn Colbey from the dying woman's womb and planted him inside his mother. As Thor's betrayed wife, Sif could have despised Colbey, yet she had watched over him instead. More often than not, she had taken his side in the gods' disputes.

Unconsciously, Colbey executed a gesture of respect, which he had not done for the others. "Under ordinary circumstances, I might agree." He placed a foot on an empty chair and leaned toward Sif. His light tunic and breeks, though simply cut, sported a frenetic panorama of shapes and colors. "But Odin has discovered an ancient prophecy." Colbey cocked his head, warrior-short locks barely slipping with the movement. "It claimed he would survive the *Ragnarok,* as he did, then obliterate all the remaining worlds and creatures to pave the way for a new world devoted entirely to him."

Wordless noises followed, gasps, hisses, and grunts of disbelief. Magni huffed out a coarse laugh. "Madness."

Freya spoke her first words since Colbey's entrance, softening the proceedings, though her expression revealed nothing gentle. At least, his wife did not wear the mask of distrust that most of the others seemed to share. "Colbey, you know better than anyone that the exact wording means more than any interpretation."

Frey added, voice turning singsong as he quoted:

> *"The Eighteenth Dark Lord*
> *Will obtain in his day*
> *A pale-skinned champion*
> *To darken the way.*
> *One destined to betray*

The West and his clan,
A swordsman unmatched
By another mortal man."

Colbey's fists clenched at the words, and he turned Frey a dense glare.

Frey did not heed the obvious warning. "You remember, don't you? The Wizards tried to destroy you for that prophecy, even before the Staves of Law and Chaos came into this world. But you were not mortal then, or now. And the prophecy was not about you."

"Do you think I could forget?" Colbey said, voice turning harsh and stance deadly.

Frey could not miss the obvious and intense irritation. "I'm just agreeing that we need the precise wording of the prophecy to understand it. And even then, we might miss the detail that changes its apparent meaning."

"Lies!" Vali bellowed.

Colbey ignored his blood uncle, tone evening as he cast aside old irritations for new, "You're missing something more important. Prophecies don't just happen. Someone must deliberately fulfill them."

"Odin?" Freya reminded.

"He can't fulfill it if he's dead."

Modi lurched to his feet. Magni slammed the table with Thor's hammer, and several jerked away from the impact aching through their fingers. Usually gracious Idunn spoke the words on many minds, "You arrogant dullard."

Vali intensified. "Bastard."

Colbey glanced at Ravn. His son returned his gaze without judgment, hands idle on his lap.

More accustomed to her husband's boldness, Freya took it in stride. "You wouldn't be the first to attempt to thwart prophecies by slaughtering the subject of them."

Colbey nodded stiffly, lips pursed at another unpleasant memory. Not only had Wizards and friends hunted Colbey for the prediction Frey had cited, but enemies had earlier killed a promising student for a prophecy they had attributed to the younger man rather than properly to Colbey.

Colbey turned his attention to the most rational among the gods. "This is different, Freya. First, even if Odin and I have both misinterpreted the prophecy, he intends to fulfill it that way. And the balance dictates that he die, with or without the prophecy."

"Exact wording would still help."

Colbey tossed up his hands. "I was battling Odin. I had more important things on my mind then memorizing something that, ultimately, matters only in that it's driving Odin to destroy the universe."

Even Freya's features gained a crinkle of skepticism. She did not have to remind him that Odin had crafted the current world as well. "Are you certain he plans to do that?"

Colbey placed both hands along the back of the chair on which he balanced. "I confronted him because he attempted to summon a *kraell*, the most powerful of all demons. He made no attempt to bind it; he intended it to scour the living worlds: men, elves, gods." A thought struck Colbey. "And I might be able to dredge up the exact phrasing you want." Alert for retaliation, he placed a hand on his hilt, deliberately not grasping it.

Chaos filled his head. *Hard-brained idiots.*

Drop the insults. I need—

It interrupted. *I know what you need. I always do.* Colbey could not miss the warning in that statement, an unspoken reminder to bind that, as always, he ignored. Without further prodding, it fed him the words to the prophecy.

Colbey repeated in slow phrases, pausing between them to consult the staff in sword form:

> *"The Father shall avert his fate.*
> *Then the worlds should celebrate.*
> *But far into destruction hurled*
> *Law's vast plan is then unfurled:*
> *A new world to create.*
>
> *All must die to pave the way.*
> *A single god to rule the day.*
> *The only enemy will make*
> *One small lapse; a fatal mistake*
> *Leave the world at the mercy of Gray."*

A prolonged silence, even for gods, trailed the final stanza.

"And before you ask," Colbey added. "Father was capitalized in written form."

"Difficult to misinterpret," Freya admitted.

"Indeed."

Vali fairly exploded. "Am I the only one who can see the obvious?" He rose, joining Modi. "If we dare to believe the Staff of Law and its champion have become Odin, then the Staff of Chaos and Colbey can only be . . ." He paused, allowing the self-evident to glide naturally into every mind.

". . . Loki," Baldur finished. His handsome features thinned, clearly stricken. Of them all, he had most reason to despise the late god of mischief who had tricked blind Hod into slaying him. Though resurrected at the *Ragnarok*, he had suffered millennia in Hel, amplifying that hatred.

Vali continued, "And Loki would say whatever fueled chaos. Truth interspersed with lies, he's trying to turn us against Odin. If he only splits our loyalties, he's done harm enough. Gods against gods. Another *Ragnarok*."

Colbey moved from the chair into a more defensible position, buffeted by waves of others' emotion. Everyone in the room considered Vali's position, though their reactions spanned a gamut. "All reasonable and plausible, Vali. Had I bonded with my charge, I would have essentially become Loki." He added pointedly, "But I didn't bind." Colbey glanced at Ravn then, believing he had proven that well enough at his last visit, at least to his family.

Ravn met his father's gaze, saying nothing.

"I don't believe it," Honir said softly.

Idunn added with more diplomacy, "Colbey, I believe your intentions good, but no one could resist the power of the Staff of Chaos." She lowered her head with clear sympathy. "You may not even realize it yet, but it has you."

Patronized, Colbey fought irritation. "I did not bind." He swept the room for some sign of wavering, one god or goddess who might stand at his side. Everywhere, he found the same stony disbelief, except on the faces of Freya and Ravn. Yet even there he found no true reprieve. Moisture blurred Freya's sky blue eyes, and Ravn's lids closed in sorrow. "I didn't bind!" he shouted, as if sheer volume could convince where words had failed. "That's the 'fatal mistake' of the prophecy—or so Odin believes!"

All believe you bound already. Why not accept the knowledge? The power?

Colbey jerked his hand from the hilt he had forgotten he held, irritation further fueled by Chaos' suggestion. He wrestled desperately with rage; losing control would only harm his point. He needed the assistance of the gods to face Odin again. The father of gods had magic that Colbey had no means to counter, and Odin's mind powers vastly exceeded his own. Only at physical combat did he believe them equally matched. *If the gods refuse me, I'll have little choice but to bind.* The idea grated. He had not won the battle against chaos only to surrender to it for the weakness of his peers. Yet, he realized, if Odin bested him, the world would collapse into ruin. The gods might deserve the doom they courted, but elves and mankind did not. He might have to sacrifice self for immortal fools who blinded themselves to danger. For, once bound, Colbey Calistinsson would no longer exist. Binding would assure the ultimate destruction that he would likely endure anyway when he forced the extremes of law and chaos to shatter one another.

You have nothing to lose by binding and everything to gain. If you don't, you assure total annihilation.

And, if I do, I lose control. Colbey kept the idea to himself, the bare edges of terror clawing at his mind. As a part of chaos, he would become genius and betrayal, fresh idea and patternless lie, wholly bereft of intention. Even in the most frenzied war, he had maintained mastery of every motion. Though he championed balance, he was, in every way, a creature of law. *Silence,* he demanded. *Your distraction will only hinder me. And, ultimately, you.*

The Staff of Chaos obeyed, though not without a wild tremor of irritation that disparaged Colbey's intelligence and sanity.

Vali jabbed a finger toward Colbey. "Be gone, *Second* Father of Lies! You're not welcome here."

Colbey back-stepped, counting silently to contain his anger. Only when he found full composure did he bother to speak aloud again. "I can prove I haven't bound." He freed the chaos sword and slammed it to the tabletop before anyone could think to feel menaced by the draw. Ravn stiffened, and others shocked back from the sudden movement. Baldur and Sif lurched to their feet, bringing the number of standing gods to four. The surprise radiating from his son overpowered other thoughts and emotions bombarding the room. Ravn dared not believe his father, the consummate Renshai, had not only handed over his only weapon but had dishonored it by banging it down on a dirty surface.

Though he felt alarmed and naked without a weapon, Colbey knew no remorse for his action. The honor that governed handling swords was based on a Renshai's respect for his weapon. He only wished the chaos-blade interpreted the gesture as fully as Ravn. He trained his icy gaze fanatically on Vali. "He who doubts my word need only heft the current form of the Staff of Chaos." It was a desperate challenge, the only one left in Colbey's arsenal; and he hoped the gesture alone would regain the gods' trust. Unlike Captain, the gods might prove a worthy substitute for Colbey, and the staff could attempt to bind with any who grasped the hilt. None shared his odd mind powers; they would have to deliberately block its intrusion for as long as it took him to snatch the sword back.

Again, Colbey's gaze circled the room. Movement at the corner of his eye sent him into a startled crouch. Vali plunged over the table. His sword hacked the space where Colbey's neck had been an instant earlier. It spiraled, gathering momentum for a lower strike. "Get Loki while he's still unarmed!"

Dirty coward. Resisting the natural back-step, Colbey sprang forward. Vali's blade skimmed his back, opening his tunic. Cold air kissed the flesh beneath, and Colbey dove for the table. He rolled across the top, seizing his hilt even as Vidar did the same. Strong fingers crushed Colbey's, threatening to steal control of the weapon. Changing his course, Colbey allowed momentum to sweep him into Vidar's lap. The collision sent the gods' leader tumbling. His hand jerked from the hilt with enough force to claim Colbey's grip as well. The sword flew in a wild arc, crashing against the wall behind Idunn. She scrambled aside as it plummeted. Another sword sped for Colbey's face even as Vali's cut a stinging line across his buttocks.

Unable to wholly avoid it, Colbey pitched sideways, dodging the whetted edge. The side of the blade caught him a ringing clout across the ear. He jerked up an arm that hammered its wielder's wrist, parrying the sword harmlessly aside for the moment.

Sif cursed. In the moment it took her to regain control of her weapon, Colbey leaped for his sword again. Snatching up the hilt, he skittered under the table. Air whooshed past him, stealing his balance. Then, Thor's massive hammer smashed a crater into the golden wall where the Sword of Chaos had fallen. The gods' meeting room quaked, and a rain of candles toppled to the tabletop.

"Stop!" Freya screamed, a savage voice of reason that went unheeded.

Colbey rose to meet three swords, wielded by Vali, Sif, and Modi. The great hammer shifted, grinding against metal, then flew over their heads back toward Magni's hand. The blades plunged toward Colbey at once. He evaded Vali's and caught the other two on his own. The combined strength of goddess and god ached through his forearm, yet he still managed a rabid return of weaving metal that gained him moments and space. From the edge of his vision, he could see that Frey had also drawn, though he did not attack. Freya and Ravn avoided the battle, their loyalties clearly torn.

Again, the three lunged simultaneously, a graceful unit. Colbey bobbed, lacing his blade between them, separating. Steel carved deadly patterns through the air around him, two missing cleanly and the third nicking his chest. Even as they condemned him as the bringer of destruction, their strikes definitively lethal, he had, thus far, done nothing but defend. The idea of slaughtering the gods of Renshai, Sif and Modi, never entered his mind; but his strategy would soon unravel. He would have to kill or die.

Colbey scurried toward the door, blocking the lightning attacks of three immortals. Escape would serve better than his usual offense here. The quick, ceaseless movements widened the burning tear in his backside. Blood seeped warmly down the back of his leg, and sweat stung the superficial wound on his chest. Still, he did not slow, zipping in to catch Sif's sword as he ducked beneath Modi's, battering Vali's aside. Luck alone dictated that, eventually, they would coordinate a blitz he could not defend. And Odin's devastating plans would proceed without opposition. *The fatal mistake—requesting assistance from fools.* Colbey shook the thought from his mind, averting another triple attack. He refused to place faith in prophecies, and even that in his religion evaporated. The deities to which he had dedicated his every *svergelse,* spar, and battle since infancy had betrayed him.

The rasp of steel at Colbey's back sent him into a furious, awkward spin. His blade cleaved air, then met resistance, biting through flesh with a force that jarred his hand. True to his training, he completed the maneuver as a scream rang through his ears and hot pinpoints of blood sprayed his naked back. His sword crashed against Sif's. Modi jerked back a lunge. Magni held the hammer in a two-handed grip, fingers white. Vali scurried into wild retreat, eyes round as cut gemstones and pale gaze fastened beyond Colbey. Something slammed the floor at Colbey's back.

Colbey back-stepped, stance low and eyes restlessly seeking every immortal. Two paces brought him far enough to see Baldur lying still in a scarlet puddle, handsome features twisted and wide eyes already beginning to glaze. The god's blood dribbled over Colbey's crossguard, slicking the leather hilt beneath his right palm. Rage and grief hammered him simultaneously. He did not need his talent to read the thoughts taking shape in every head, including his own. *Loki all over again.* It did not matter that the gods had attacked him, nor that he had only defended. He had killed Baldur, just as Loki had centuries before him. And that act had heralded Loki's steadfast devotion to chaos and, ultimately, the *Ragnarok.*

It's over. Colbey backed toward the door, unwilling to sheath the filthy blade yet refusing the insult of cleaning it of Balder's blood in the presence of peers and family. The gods would hear no further arguments from him, and any future forays to Asgard would meet with instant and unified violence. "Damn you." Directed at Vali, words spoken barely above a whisper cut the silence like an explosion.

Take us back to chaos. Colbey sent the sword. *Take us home.*

The sword obeyed, triumph tainting the contact; but it did not gloat. As the wild abandon of Chaos World replaced the solid order of Asgard, Colbey caught a last glimpse of gods rushing, teary-eyed, to the corpse.

The prince of demons found his own vision blurry. *Home.*

CHAPTER 5

The Chosen

*Battles are won by courage, not strength;
by skill, not numbers.*

—Colbey Calistinsson

PINK dawn light trickled through Tae's window in Béarn Castle, casting streaky shadows across the woolen coverlet. Uncertain what other worlds might hold, he folded short-sleeved tunics and blouses into a densely woven cloak, tucking undergarments, breeks, and leather britches into the cracks. He had just reached for his heavy travel blanket when a knock thundered through the room.

Tae abandoned his efforts, trotting to the oaken panel, tripping the latch, and drawing it open. Mior shot through the widening crack, marching back and forth along his legs with purrs loud enough to reach his ears from the floor. Matrinka stood in the hallway. Her dark locks fluttered over her ample bosom, and the slowly dispersing swell of her abdomen enhanced the feminine curves that made Kevral appear boyish in comparison.

Tae bent at the waist, but Matrinka placed a hand on his forehead to stop the movement.

"Bow, and I'll kill you."

Tae froze in mid-movement. Until that moment, he had not realized what he was doing. "And well-deserved punishment that would be."

Matrinka stepped into the room, closing the door behind her. She ushered Tae deeper into the room, and he followed, careful not to trip over the cat still twining around his ankles.

"What can I do for you this morning, Ladyship?"

Matrinka's brows arched, and she turned him a stern look. "You can start by dropping the Ladyship, *Prince* Tae."

"Point taken." Tae sprang to the windowsill, crouching there to leave the choice of bed or chair to Matrinka.

She accepted neither, preferring to stand. Mior's tail lashed as she measured the distance from floor to Tae. Matrinka did not speak for several moments.

Tae broke a hush too awkward for old friends. "Did you come to wish me well, or only to threaten my life?" He added facetiously, "Kevral."

Matrinka smiled. "You know I wouldn't hurt you."

Couldn't, Tae corrected, only to himself. The gentle healer released the occasional spider or beetle found in the hallways, and the idea of her harming a human seemed madness. "I wasn't worried," he said.

Matrinka finally came to the point of her visit, "You've always been the cautious one. The man of reason. Keep the others out of trouble, please."

Matrinka's words stunned Tae, and he could not help laughing, though it clearly distressed her. He explained his cruelty with personal insult. "The cautious, reasonable man is the same lunatic who climbed the castle walls to see a baby."

Mior leaped to the ledge, claws raking the wall as she scrambled into position. Delicately, she hopped onto Tae's knee headed toward a nonexistent lap.

Tae dropped into a less defensive position, providing the cat with a perch against his abdomen and right thigh. "And you're asking me to contain two tornadoes and a hurricane."

Matrinka finally smiled. "Darris is the hurricane?" she guessed.

"Right. Not insane enough to rush, war-screaming, into a battle against thousands . . . and dare to believe he might win." Tae referenced Kevral. "Or to duel a demon who wrinkled his tabard and insulted his mother's footwear." Tae stroked Mior as she settled against him. "But he'd stir up a hornet's nest just to watch the patterns of their flight and experience a quazillion stings for the detail it would add to his songs."

"A quazillion?"

Tae shrugged. "Give or take a few bizillions."

Despite the joke, Matrinka's grin wilted; and she lowered her head.

Tae sighed, hating to make a vow he could not keep, yet knowing how much Matrinka needed it. "I'll do my best." Longer than a year ago, he had escorted Kevral to Pudar amid ambushes and dense patrols of his father's own men charged, not only with preventing travel in the West, but directly with slaughtering him. He had managed to bring Kevral and himself most of the way safely, though it had taken every instinct and wary skill to do so. Kevral would have preferred to attack, killing any who stood in their way, but Tae had managed to convince her of the wisdom of his approach. If necessary, he believed he could do so again.

"I can't ask for more than that."

"You could ask," Tae revised. "But it seems pointless."

The creases in Matrinka's cheeks revealed the smile on her lips, but her position did not allow Tae to see more. The coarse, black hair fell in a wavy curtain, hiding even her eyes.

Guessing Matrinka's other concern, Tae said, "It won't seem the same without you along. We'll miss you." He pitched his voice carefully, so as not to sound disparaging or too wistful. He did not wish to stir any unnecessary guilt. However Matrinka felt about her role in the matter, she did belong in Béarn with Marisole.

"I'll miss all of you, too. And worry for you every day you're gone." Finally, Matrinka raised her head, hair cascading into its proper position against her back. She looked at him from beneath a fringe of straight bangs, her brown eyes enormous and soft as a fawn's. "They've selected your companions." Vacantly, she spread the travel blanket, wrapping his things into a tight bundle worthy of an experienced traveler. "Besides Darris, Kevral, and Ra-khir, there're two elves. There's a Northman called Andvari, an ambassador from Nordmir after the elves recreated peace." Captain and several companions had ended the deadly, *svartalf*-stirred wars in the North with magical illusions. "And there's a Pudarian healer, Perlia. She sells cures in the market." Matrinka added quickly, "Not quackery, known herbs. And her skills."

Mior's weight wore on Tae's leg. The tingling started in his toes, creeping rapidly toward his knee. His petting grew more distracted. He wondered why Matrinka felt it necessary to defend Perlia's practices to a crime lord's son. He attempted to maintain his side of the conversation. "A healer. Good." He gave Mior a long, apologetic caress before shifting her to the sill and dangling his legs to restore blood flow before it became too painful. He added quickly, "Not that we'll need one. I'll be keeping my rasher companions out of trouble."

Mior made a deep sound of protest.

"The hurricane and the tornadoes."

"Right."

"And Perlia?"

Tae jerked his head up, groaning. "She's impulsive, too?"

Mior clambered into Tae's lap, rubbing against his arms as she circled into a comfortable position.

"Oh, no. Not at all." Matrinka finally took a seat on the very edge of the bed. She glanced at the bundled gear in her hands, as if noticing it for the first time, then set it aside. "She's young, gentle, inexperienced. A beautiful woman with a sweet disposition. I thought maybe you could . . . um . . . ." Her chin sank to her chest again, allowing her to hide behind the shielding hair.

Tae rolled his eyes. "Fall madly in love, marry her, and sweep her off to Stalmize as my princess."

Matrinka stiffened, the redness of the skin beneath her hair revealing that he had struck close to home. "I was going to say keep her safe."

Tae stared silently, waiting for Matrinka to meet his gaze, which she finally did.

"Am I that obvious?"

Irritated by the matchmaking, Tae refused to let her off the hook. "Yes."

"I didn't mean . . ." Matrinka stammered. "I only wanted . . . I—I was trying to help."

The reminder brought a fresh rush of grief to a situation he believed he had already accepted. Like his memories of his mother's murder, it swept in to haunt him, usually in the quiet moments when he missed Subikahn and envied Ra-khir's routine nights and evenings with Kevral. To hide welling tears, he turned his gaze out the window, at the leaf and stone gardens that had replaced the multicolored flowers and summer vegetables.

Mior launched into a subdued purr, forgiving his movement with uncharacteristic generosity. The bed creaked as Matrinka rose. A moment later, a gentle hand touched Tae's shoulder. "I'm sorry, Tae. I'm a supreme idiot, and I deserve to freeze in Hel upside down for eternity."

The overstatement allowed Tae to regain his composure. Surreptitiously, he wiped away the tears, though he knew he could not hide his sorrow from Mior and, therefore, from Matrinka. "If that's the punishment for saying stupid things, I don't stand a chance."

Matrinka tousled Tae's hair. "I really am sorry."

Tae made a dismissive gesture. "There's nothing to be sorry about. You just caught me at a weak moment." He wound his fingers through the calico fur. "Actually, things worked out better than I deserved or expected. Not only did I manage to compete with perfection, I have a son to keep me linked to the woman I love forever. Subikahn has a brother and a stepfather who not only adores him but who understands the significance of fathering to me. I never have to worry about him stealing my son." The words came easily. He had considered the matter too long not to have found answers and, at least, a transient peace. "What more could I want?"

"A wife to share your love. A warm presence to cuddle at night and worry for."

Tae shrugged, the romantic image wholly Matrinka's. "My son is enough—I don't want anyone else to worry for." He left a still hand on the cat. "I want to do things right, without repeating my father's mistakes. I don't want eighteen years to pass before my son stops despising and starts loving me." He clamped his lips shut on a bitterness only beginning to disperse. It had taken that long to piece together the memories of stirring in his sleep to find a rough hand replacing slipped blankets and adoring eyes studying him from the darkness. His father had wanted, even believed he needed, Tae tough. He had hidden his affection behind a gruffness that quailed his son, driving him onto the streets at fourteen. Only recently had Tae learned of the myriad invisible safety nets his father had woven to protect a son living alone on the streets. Weile Kahn's words still resounded in Tae's memory: "Return when you're twenty. If you've survived, you'll have proved yourself worthy to succeed me."

Driven West by Weile's enemies, hunted and battered, Tae had sworn never to return. Healing that rift had taken desperate confrontations he would not repeat. Subikahn would not weather Weile Kahn's brutal techniques, ones even the crime-lord-turned-king now realized had unnecessarily traumatized his only child. "Right now, Subikahn is everything. I don't need, or want, the distraction of another woman."

Matrinka studied him through eyes that sympathized without patronizing. "Tae, I don't know if this will help or hurt now. If you were the one who discovered Kevral's plight and declared war on Pudar to rescue her, I'm sure she would have married you."

Tae stared, frozen, the words nonsensical to him. "Plight? War on Pudar? What are you talking about, Matrinka?" He added a hint of warning to his voice. This time, he would not accept that Kevral needed to tell him about it. She had not done so in the week he had thus far spent in Pudar.

"This has to stay between the two of us."

Tae nodded.

Matrinka glanced at Mior. "I'm sorry, the *three* of us."

Reminded of the animal's presence, Tae resumed petting the soft fur.

"Ra-khir and Kevral are sworn to secrecy by King Cymion of Pudar."

At the name, Tae narrowed his eyes. More than a year ago, *svartalf* and enemies of his father had framed him for the murder of crown prince Severin. He had engineered a jail break that had rescued him from a tedious, agonizing execution, but he still harbored resentment against the king who had threatened to draw and quarter him.

"Tae, you have to promise me you won't retaliate for what I tell you. And you'll speak of it to no one."

Tae's gaze swept to Matrinka's eyes. "If I make that vow, I'm going to resent it desperately, aren't I?"

"Yes," Matrinka admitted, returning his look without flinching. "But without the vow, I'm done talking."

Trapped, Tae nodded. He felt certain Matrinka had gotten her information from Mior and wondered at the extent of the cat's intelligence. In the past, she had acted on his simple commands, but the fierce yellow eyes radiated knowledge beyond that of other cats. *As if I have any way to know how smart cats in general are.* "I promise."

"Against what?"

Tae considered briefly. "Against my honor as a Knight of Erythane."

"Funny."

Tae fluttered his fingers in helpless agitation. "What do you want me to swear against?" It all seemed silly to Tae, as if mentioning a value would somehow magically tie it to the vow.

"Your love for your son."

"Fine." Tae scratched beneath Mior's chin, the cat stretching her neck to its limit. "I promise against my love for Subikahn." He appended impatiently, "Tell me already."

Matrinka drew a deep breath. "King Cymion held Kevral prisoner and forced her to lie with Prince Leondis to create a royal heir."

Tae's hands winched around the window sill, and his jaw clenched painfully. The urge to inflict on the king of Pudar every threat lowered against him for the elder prince's death flared suddenly.

"He told Ra-khir she was dead, but Mior helped him find her cell. Even the other knights didn't believe Ra-khir, so he declared war on Pudar."

Tae's eyes grew from slits to wide-eyed disbelief. "By himself?"

"By himself," Matrinka confirmed. "Mior's not good with details, but, apparently, Ra-khir wound up bargaining for Kevral's freedom. No retribution, no mention of the matter, and the prince's baby returns to Pudar at the time of its birth."

"Baby," Tae repeated, rage stoked to a bonfire, violent and barely contained. Splinters from the wooden sill gouged beneath his nails.

Matrinka grimaced. "I forgot to mention she's pregnant, didn't I?"

Information fell into place, and consideration displaced some of Tae's anger. "That explains the heated exchange between Kedrin and Colbey about grandfathering."

"What?"

"I didn't hear the whole thing," Tae admitted. "But I do know Colbey's words to Kevral sparked it."

Matrinka raked back her locks with a hand. "But how could Colbey grandfather . . ." She trailed off, deep contemplation replacing confusion. "You don't think Ravn. . . ?"

Tae made a motion of surrender.

"This complicates things." Matrinka turned away, hands hovering as if on their own. "This complicates things . . . badly."

"I can't rip the bastard's heart out?"

"No."

"I hate you."

Matrinka smoothed her skirts. "You didn't vow against your love for me." She sighed. "Imagine what Kevral wants to do to him."

Tae thought it better to keep that picture from his mind.

"He's the king of Pudar, Tae."

"He's mortal."

"That's not the point." Matrinka whirled back to face Tae. "I chose to tell you because I thought you could handle it without doing something crazy. He's the king, Tae. Well-loved by his people and, other than this extreme lapse of judgment, fair. Assassination would not only create chaos in Pudar at a time when we need order, it would also spark war. If you're caught, against Béarn and the East."

I won't be caught. Tae did not speak the thought aloud. It still did not address Matrinka's first point. "Who else knows about this?"

"I haven't told anyone."

"Not even Darris?"

"No."

Flattered and appalled at once, Tae set Mior on the ledge and stood, brushing hair from his britches. "You have to tell Griff."

Matrinka paced in short, agitated ovals. "No, Tae. I shouldn't even have told you. I violated the sacred oath of a Knight of Erythane."

Tae followed Matrinka's jerky movements with his gaze. "You didn't violate anything, Matrinka." He turned his attention to Mior. Any creature with enough wherewithal to relay such specifics deserved direct acknowledgment. "You didn't take a vow of silence, did you, Mior?"

"Of course not," Matrinka answered for the cat.

"So what's the problem?" Tae could not fathom Matrinka siding with the king of Pudar against Kevral and an unborn baby. Only his experience with her kindness and common sense kept hatred from blunting their long friendship.

"Because no one sane is going to believe I learned that information from a cat."

"Thanks."

Matrinka made a chopping motion. "Present company excepted, of course. They'll all believe Kevral or Ra-khir broke their word."

It still seemed insignificant to Tae compared to the abominable confidence they shared. "All right, Ra-khir and his accursed honor. But Kevral?"

Matrinka spread her hands. "I've gotten enough from Mior to believe Ra-khir vowed for Kevral, too."

"One tornado containing another."

Matrinka shrugged. "Renshai honor's strong as well."

Tae had to agree, though it took a much different form than that of the knights.

"Ra-khir would lose his knighthood, his father's trust, and others' as well."

Tae entwined his fingers, imagining them clamped around Cymion's neck. "Worth the price, in my opinion."

Horror stole over Matrinka's features. "Look, Tae. If Ra-khir wants to sacrifice all that for cheap vengeance and to rescue another man's baby from the life of a prince or princess, it's his decision. I'm not going to be responsible for ruining his life." Her dark eyes turned so fiery with threat, he did not recognize them. "And neither are you."

"Fine," Tae said through gritted teeth. "But now I wish I'd never let you tell me. Had I spied it out on my own, I could have used the information." He looked away, then suddenly back, wondering if he had discovered the reason why Matrinka had taken him into her confidence. He grumbled, "Shackled like a damned prisoner."

The edge left Matrinka's eyes, "And now—"

Tae could not let the matter rest. "So what are we going to do? Let Pudar get away with raping Kevral and stealing a baby that's not even theirs?"

"I don't know, Tae." Matrinka sounded tired. "We'll have to handle it as best we can." She pulled a stylus and paper from her pocket. "We need you to write a note."

"Why?" Despite the simplicity of the request, Tae could not keep sullenness from his tone. He could not let the previous issue rest.

"In case something happens to you or your father calls you back suddenly. One potential war is enough, thank you very much." Matrinka placed the writing implements on his desk and gestured for him to sit. "It'll work best in your own handwriting."

Tae had already handled the matter, but he complied with Matrinka's request. He scrawled in the trading tongue:

> *Went with elves to help lift the sterility plague. I went*
> *voluntarily; don't hold Béarn responsible if I get my fool*
> *self killed.*
> *—Tae Kahn.*

Tae looked up. "How's that?"

Matrinka hesitated, speechless. "Uh . . . a bit blunt. But workable, I suppose." She fidgeted, obviously loath to interfere with Eastern convention. "Don't you think he deserves to know about . . ." She trailed off, her intentions obvious.

"Oh, yeah." Tae added:

By the way, you're a grandfather.

Matrinka turned Tae a stricken look. "You can't do that. You have to give him details."

"Payback," Tae said.

"That's cruel."

He shrugged.

"Oh, Tae." Disappointment tainted Matrinka's voice. "Don't let pettiness spoil your new relationship."

Tae stopped teasing Matrinka. "I'm kidding." He crumpled the parchment and returned her the pen. "Both handled. I've already sent him two notes. He knows Subikahn nearly as well as I do." He grinned. "Did you really think I was going to write the king of the Eastlands in Western trading tongue?"

Matrinka flushed.

Tae headed to the bed. "Now, if you don't mind, I have a council to attend, two tornadoes and a hurricane to tame, and a beautiful Pudarian healer who would laugh in my face if I tried to court her." He hefted his gear.

Matrinka blocked Tae's path to the door. "Tae, that's the third time this conversation I've heard you denigrate yourself."

Clasping the rolled blanket to his chest, Tae shrugged. "Once alley bait, always alley bait."

"What's that supposed to mean?"

"Isn't it obvious?" Tae adjusted his things to a more comfortable position. "I'm a criminal's son, a street tough, a prison escapee, a shamelessly dirty fighter, and a thief—"

"You're not a thief." Matrinka ignored the rest of the list. "You told us that, aside from food, you've only taken things twice. And you gave those back."

"What do you call someone who steals food?"

Matrinka refused to answer.

"Come on, Matrinka. What do you call someone who steals things? Returned or not?"

"A thief," she ventured softly.

"Thank you. And I joined up with the rest of you only so you could fight my enemies for me."

"But after the others killed them, you stayed with us. You made sure we didn't starve, in the woods or in Pudar."

Understanding dawned abruptly. "Mior told you about that, didn't she?" He turned the cat a mock look of disgust. "Filthy spy."

Matrinka laughed. "She called you the same thing."

"Oh, yes," Tae acknowledged. "Forgot that. I'm also a filthy spy."

All mirth left Matrinka. "Béarn's royalty trusts you. The bard trusts you, and the Renshai found you worthy of siring one of their own. Kevral agonized over whether to marry you or a Knight of Erythane. How do you explain that if you're so vile?"

"I've duped you all," Tae tried.

"Uh-huh." Matrinka shook her head, sighing. "All I'm saying is that you're a prince now. An ambassador. And a father. You need to start acting like all of those."

"All right," Tae finally agreed, not wishing to think about such issues now. The distance he had come since childhood frightened him, as if someone had implanted another man's memories in his mind. "I'll use doors instead of windows." He motioned for her to move aside. "Starting now."

Matrinka complied. "You don't have to change your personality, Tae. Nor even your endearing little habits." She intentionally understated the danger of his feats. "Just learn to trust in yourself the way the rest of us do." She added in the tone of a tutor lecturing a student working below his talent. "And not that swaggering, street-born, false bravado either."

Tae had always considered himself a loner, and the realization that Matrinka could read him so well sent a shiver through him. "I'll try to live up to my title." He opened the door, adding pointedly, "Your Ladyship." He skittered through the door, hoping she had no intention of fulfilling her warning.

Neither of them wanted his blood on her hands.

Elves lined the walls of the council room, gemlike eyes gleaming from canted sockets, angular features ranging from nearly human to just as nearly animal. Long limbs and odd muscular attachments gave them a gawky, adolescent look belied by the grace of even their slightest movements. Their hair colors ranged from elder white to inky, inhuman black, spanning every shade of brown and yellow between. Red predominated, from a stawberry blond that perfectly matched Ra-khir and Kedrin to scarlet highlights that graced the palest and the darkest. Captain occupied the farthest corner, deep in conversation with two other elves, a bronze-haired male with amber eyes named Chan'rék'ril and a slight, red-blonde female called El-brinith.

Tae turned his attention to the humans milling in the room's center. Kevral and Ra-khir stood together in conversation. Nearby, Darris studied the room as if to memorize every detail, which seemed likely to Tae. Eventually, the bard would immortalize their journey in song, and the minutiae he captured would bring the images so to life the listeners would feel every bit a part of it. He allowed his eyes to travel briefly over the strange female before alighting on the Northman who Matrinka had called Andvari. An ax girded his waist, and white-blond war braids dangled around a pale face lined with scars. The keen blue eyes slid toward Kevral and Ra-khir, then scurried away with an awkwardness that seemed uncharacteristic. The image otherwise so captured the stereotype of Northmen that Tae would have laughed if not for the perception of another stranger nagging at the edges of his consciousness. His brief glance at the Pudarian had given him only the impression of a child.

Tae cursed the discomfort that would forever taint his dealings with the healer solely because Matrinka had attempted to pair them. It bothered him even to allow his gaze to tarry too long on her, but his learned paranoia would not allow him to leave a companion long unexamined. He forced his attention to Perlia.

The Pudarian huddled in a wary crouch. Light brown eyes skipped restlessly over the elves, never still. Sandy hair hung in irregular clumps around a face that looked barely into its teens. A dirty cloak enwrapped a skinny body lacking curves, and her legs jutted like twigs beneath the hem. As if sensing his attention, her head swung toward him. Her lids narrowed, and she glared a quiet challenge. Full on, her face bore the victim-trying-to-appear-in-control look of a street orphan. He knew it well and also read the dense suspicion of one who had never learned to trust.

Tae glanced casually away, playing a game he had come to hate. Irritation trembled through him, that Matrinka might believe him a match for a filthy, venomous child. He could not fathom how she could expect him to rally his self-esteem while comparing him to such as this. *I was like her once, but no more.* He headed toward his familiar companions, only then noticing the sturdy packs on the floor by their feet. Counting eight, he assumed one belonged to him. Hefting one, he stuffed his few personal items into it, tamping down foodstuffs, a rope, fire-starting materials, and other traveling "essentials." The weight of it bothered him; he had grown accustomed to charging through the Westlands with only a utility knife, a blanket, and his wits.

"Good morning, Tae," Kevral said, an edge in her voice suggesting that she should not have had to prompt him. He had spent longer than he realized getting his bearings.

"Morning, Kevral. Morning, Ra-khir."

Before the knight could respond, Captain's *khohlar* filled Tae's mind. *Ready?*

Chan'rék'ril and El-brinith joined the nodding humans.

Captain explained briefly, *There're a lot of worlds out there. Some we know: Midgard and Asgard. Others, we don't. Most are small, and only magic can get you there and back.*

Tae glanced around his companions. Ra-khir fixed his attention on Captain. Kevral gave Tae an encouraging smile. Chan'rék'ril and El-brinith remained unreadable. Perlia huddled into herself as if to disappear. Andvari's hand sipped to his ax, though his gaze held on Captain. Darris stared at the elves, breathless with expectancy.

Our magic will get you to the proper plane, but we have no idea what you'll find there, other than a piece of the Pica. It'll be up to Chan'rék'ril and El-brinith to bring you back once you've gotten the shard. We'll study it to find the next location, then send you there. Along with the words came a concept of tuning the spell to the eight sent so that the journeying elves could work a transport without a *jovinay arythanik.* *Any questions?*

None followed.

Captain's next communication was clearly directed at the elves, a magical idea that made no sense to Tae. Darris' brow crinkled, and a brown curl slid over one eye as he focused on the *khohlar.* Tae shook his head, glad he did not share the burden of insatiable curiosity. Until now he had never thought much about the suffering such an affliction caused on a daily basis. The inability to teach without singing seemed curse enough.

The elves filled the room with dull and mellow sound, punctuated by Captain's voice raised above the chorus of others. Again, he howled out harsh gutturals worthy of the Eastern language, but so unlike his usual melodic singsong. Tae had already learned much of the spritely elfin tongue just from overhearing conversations between them, its resemblance to Northern rendering it an easy lesson.

The chant swelled, and Captain's words seemed to fade to disjointed roaring. Suddenly, light speared Tae's vision, aching through his retinas. He jerked backward, scuttling into a wary crouch. His eyes burned, utterly blinded, and he snapped his lids closed in delayed reflex. Bright, painful slashes scored the darkness, revealing nothing else. *Something's gone terribly wrong.* He clawed at his lids, worried that he would never see again.

A puff of wind stirring his hair warned Tae he no longer stood in Béarn's council chamber. He forced his lids open, and light funneled in, dull comparison to what he had endured a moment earlier. Gradually,

he made out trees bowing in a gentle breeze and his companions staggering and tearing at their eyes. Perlia clung to a trunk, attempting to hide
terror behind a familiar sham of angry courage. Her broken-nailed fingers clutched as she fought the urge to paw at her face, and the twitchy
movements of head and limbs revealed a lifetime, albeit short, of dodging
predators. *That's no merchant healer.*

Taking advantage of the lost vision, Tae sidled up to Ra-khir and
whispered. "Healer's lying. Hit hard on who and what she really is."

"What?" Ra-khir said, jabbing his fingers into his sockets.

"Quiet," Tae hissed. "Just do it. Explain later." He drifted away from
Ra-khir, crouching at the edge of what he now recognized as a clearing.
Deliberately, he worked his way to a distant position behind the Pud-
arian, careful never to draw within menacing distance.

The youngster watched Tae warily, jerking her attention to Ra-khir
as the knight approached. She took several halting back-steps.

Kevral, Andvari, and Darris explored the edges of the forest, seeking
danger. Trusting the Renshai to recognize and handle any threat, Tae
leaned against a sapling, taking a position that gave Ra-khir a full view
of him and the Pudarian none at all.

Ra-khir cleared his throat. "Excuse me, lady. Who exactly are you?"
He glanced at Tae.

Tae exaggerated his gestures, giving a nod to indicate Ra-khir had the
right idea, followed by a deep frown then several crisp jerks of his arm
to encourage the knight to escalate his questioning.

Ra-khir returned a dangerous look that Tae read easily. The knight
warned that his companion had best have a good explanation once he
finished.

"Pearly," she said in the slushy dialect of Pudar's streets. "Tol' ya that
oncet."

The knight cleared his throat. He towered over the little Pudarian. The
mail he wore beneath his tabard added bulk to an already intimidating mass of muscle. "Ma'am, I don't believe that to be the case."

Tae rolled his eyes, broadening his brisk upward motions. *Don't cod-
dle, grill her.*

"Hain't carin' what ya ba'leev." The Pudarian's chin jutted, and she
started to turn.

Tae feigned engrossment in the brush.

Ra-khir reached out a hand to stop her, and the youngster skittered
away, cringing.

"Doan tech me," she warned, voice unwavering and stance coiled.
"Lessen ya wants a dagger in ya han."

"You're no merchant." Ra-khir's tone finally held the anger Tae sought, though it surely came of the Pudarian's threat, not Tae's request. "And no healer either." He did not approach or try to reach for her again, but he did lower his head nearer to hers. "Who are you?"

Kevral looked over.

"Who are you?" Ra-khir demanded, louder.

"Ra-khir!" Kevral reprimanded. "What are you doing?"

"Git away!" The Pudarian yanked a short-bladed knife from a fold in her stained cloak and waved it wildly. "Git away or I'll cut ya."

"Leave her alone." Kevral hurried toward the confrontation.

Damn. Tae tried to catch the Renshai's attention, without success.

Ra-khir retreated, glancing at Tae for direction.

The Easterner waved his friend away. Though not the hassling he had wanted, it should serve well enough.

"This isn't over," Ra-khir grumbled as he headed to the opposite side of the clearing with Kevral.

"What got into you?" Kevral asked as they walked, then Tae heard nothing more. Shortly, Kevral glanced in his direction.

The Pudarian glowered at their backs, still bristling, like a cat who has managed to bluff an enormous dog from a piece of meat.

Seizing his opportunity, Tae moved in, drawing up beside her. "Let me guess."

The Pudarian stiffened, spinning to face him in a deadly crouch. A moment later, she shook aside the unevenly cut curtain of hair, attempting an air of casual disinterest surely meant to convey she had noted but chosen to ignore his approach.

"When the guards came to get Perlia, you were robbing her stand. They mistook you for her, and you played along to avoid punishment."

Apparently, Tae had struck too close to home for her to deny it. She stuck out her lower lip. "How'sit your bizniss?"

Tae did not bother to address the rhetorical question whose answer they both knew. "What's your *hanno*?" The Pudarian street slang meant the nickname used by gang members. Months in Pudar, outcast by his friends, learning roadways like a map had left Tae with a savvy he never thought he would use.

"Hain't got no *hanno*. Hain't no *ganadan*." She used the word for gang member, sidestepping beyond Tae's reach and still clutching the dagger menacingly.

Assessing the girl's competence by the few movements she had made with the weapon, Tae found her wanting. Though acutely aware of the unpredictability of the untrained, he trusted himself to evade any attack she might make against him. "Only a *streeto*, a street orphan, would know to say *ganadan*."

"Ya hain't no *streeto*," she grabbed a handful of hair to keep it from falling into her eyes. "An' ya knows *ganadan*."

"Eastern *streeto*." Tae indicated himself.

The Pudarian made a sound that resembled spitting, though nothing left her mouth. "Ya *hain't* no *streeto*." She fluttered her fingers through the air to indicate his dress and demeanor, then repeated for the third time. "Ya *hain't no streeto*."

"Used to be." Tae smiled gently. Ra-khir's tough stance may not have driven a frightened girl into Tae's confidence, but he had at least gained Tae a chance to talk. "Things have changed for me. They can for you, too."

The Pudarian snorted. "Maybe I hain't wantin' change."

Tae refused to argue. The gangs considered themselves families, especially in Pudar; but the lone *streetos* universally despised their lives.

"An' my name's Rascal," she added.

"Sounds like a *hanno* to me."

"Hain't. 'S my real name."

Tae doubted it but saw no need to argue. "Look, you're stuck with us for the moment. When we get back to Béarn, I'll explain the mix-up and see that you go free. And get safely back to Pudar."

She glared, the look incongruous with the generous assistance he had just offered. "I hain't sleepin' with ya."

"What?" The word was startled from Tae.

"I ha'dly sleeps, and if'n ya tries to rape me, I'll kill ya."

"We've got a Knight of Erythane in the group. No one's going to rape you."

"Hain't never met a raper who sayed he's goin' ta, least not till he's got ya trapped." She continued fiercely, "An' the ones what try ta ack holy and mighty's the worsest of the bunch. Bin attact by priests, I has." Her scrutiny turned as savage as her tone. "He hain't survive nuther."

Kevral interrupted the discussion. "Tae, there's a path down this way." She made a vague motion toward the opposite end of the clearing. "We're all thinking we should head that way. You want to scout ahead?"

"Sure." Tae sighed, abandoning his new charge for a mission that needed him more. *Barely off the streets, and I'm already trying to save the world.* He trotted off in the indicated direction. "By the way, her name's Rascal, and we'd better curb our tongues and our battles. We hain't got no healer."

"We what?" Kevral's voice trailed Tae into the shadows.

CHAPTER 6

The Price of Understanding

*All the knowledge of the universe is worthless
without the wisdom to wield it.*

—*Colbey Calistinsson*

THE close dampness of the forest dragged sweat from Darris, and he sought to capture every sight and aroma in perfectly remembered detail. Insects buzzed past his ears, occasionally alighting to feast on his blood. Ra-khir seemed to bear the worst of the assault, his leather gloves slapping against flesh with rapid regularity. Surely the layers of clothing, mail, and padding had grown dangerously warm as well, though he suffered without complaint.

Tae disappeared and returned at intervals to lead them in another direction, just as he had when they broke trail through the Westland forests. The elves trailed in silence, though Darris paused to wonder whether they communicated with one another through singular *khohlar*. He tried not to focus on the thought too long. To do so would incite it to an interest that required satisfaction. Too many more significant questions faced them to worry for trivialities that, ultimately, would have no effect upon the mission nor his chronicling of it. He saw no sign of Rascal. No one else appeared to notice, aside from Tae who mumbled something about foolish loners.

Andvari approached Kevral as they walked, his usual warrior composure disappearing, Darris realized now, whenever he drew near the Renshai. His hands twisted together, fingers blanching beneath the pressure, and the smile he assumed seemed strained. For several moments he paced her, until Kevral finally abandoned her search for enemies to glance in his direction.

"I just wanted you to know," the Northman said carefully, "I bear you no ill will for being . . . well, you know."

Kevral's eyes narrowed. "Being what?"

Andvari's fair cheeks showed a scarlet flush quite clearly. "Being . . . well, being of the Renshai . . . type . . . people." He finished lamely, with obvious difficulty.

Darris knew that, historically, the Renshai had once lived among the other nine tribes of the North, hated for their savagery and for dismembering enemies. At the time, Northern religion had supported the notion that a body not brought to pyre intact could never enter Valhalla. Eventually, the Northmen had slaughtered all but a few of the Renshai, and the tribe had taken centuries to recreate itself in the West.

"Ill will?" Kevral blinked with unhurried deliberateness. "I should hope not."

"Of course not," Andvari fidgeted more, if possible.

"Well," Kevral said, surely impatient to continue her vigil. "Did you have something more you wanted to talk about?"

Andvari glanced at the trees that had thinned from towering deciduous varieties to first growth. "No. That was all."

Kevral did not wait for his response before returning her attention to the surroundings. When Andvari wandered to the back of the party, she shared a smile with Darris. "Renshai type people?"

Darris shrugged. "Be gentle with him, Kevral." He broke into song:

> *"The wars in the North have barely ended;*
> Svartalf-*stirred prejudice finally tended.*
> *Their hatred for Renshai much older and stronger—*
> *Getting past that might take a bit longer."*

Apparently, Ra-khir overheard. "It's been *centuries,* Darris."

> *"Time apart can heal the wounds*
> *The pain grows lesser with the moons*
> *But nearness allows the two to learn*
> *The samenesses that take their turn."*

"I think you mean that distance hasn't allowed Northmen and Renshai to work out their differences." Ra-khir gave the bard a sidelong look. "That's about the worst job I've heard from you."

Darris took no offense. "Close enough. You try composing rhymes and tunes instantaneously."

Tae appeared from a copse of trees to their right. "Just don't ask him to interrogate anyone." He spoke directly to Ra-khir now. "You're impressively pathetic."

"Oh, dear," Ra-khir returned in mock self-deprecation. "You've destroyed my long-worked-for dream to become a torturer."

"Sarcasm," Tae said, "doesn't become you."

"My father will be so disappointed." Ra-khir examined Tae through judgmental, green eyes. "Now, explain why you told me to act like a boorish dolt. I trusted you to have a good reason, and you'd best."

Darris winced, worried for the dangerous line Tae paced. Another verbal jab now might turn a playful exchange into warfare.

Apparently, Tae, too, recognized the edge of threat that had entered Ra-khir's tone. He became appropriately serious. "You handle the royalty. Trust me to deal with the underclass."

Ra-khir pursed his lips, nodding at the reasonability of the request. "If it means you'll follow my lead in situations requiring respect and finesse, I can live with challenging strangers now and again."

Darris guessed at Tae's strategy. Street rogues rarely trusted, and then only ones of their ilk. By placing Rascal into apparent jeopardy, Tae had hoped to drive her to confide in him.

Kevral finally joined the conversation, addressing Tae. "So where is she now? Listening to every word?"

Tae shook his head. "She headed west and hasn't circled back. Seems to be trying to put as much distance between us as possible."

Andvari paced the polite boundaries of the discussion, clearly feeling misplaced. The elves waited with their usual silent patience, sun glinting from gemlike eyes.

Kevral shook her head. "How in deepest Hel did Béarn's guards confuse a grubby little sneak-thief with a merchant healer?" Her eyes narrowed thoughtfully, and she shook her head again.

Tae shrugged. "They found her where Perlia should have been, probably taking money. Rascal got desperate. Just because she doesn't speak well doesn't mean she can't. Probably kept her replies brief, went along." He made a gesture of dismissal that implied the details held no significance and would probably never come to light even if they did. "It happened."

Darris could not help surmising: Confronted by burly Béarnide guardsmen, a frightened thief might adopt another's persona to avoid rotting in the dungeon—or worse. Depending on the seriousness of the transgression, or the previous history of the thief, Pudarian law allowed for mutilation or death.

Tae moved on. "None of this matters. We'll ditch her when we get back. Or here."

"She'll have to face Béarn's justice." Ra-khir clung to his honor. "And return anything she's taken."

Tae ignored the knight. Surely he knew arguing would accomplish nothing, so he changed the subject instead. "I doubt we'll find the Pica shard by aimless wandering." He looked at the elves. "Can you find it with magic?"

Chan'rék'ril shook his head, soft hair fluttering around sharp features, then glanced at El-brinith. A single crease appeared around his eyes, and the edges of his lips barely wilted. The female spoke then, "Depending on how tightly Captain wove the Pica and our presences into the sending, we might." Though she had included Chan'rék'ril by using the plural pronoun, she sought no assistance from him, settling amidst the shed needles and moldering leaves on the forest floor. Belatedly, Darris thought to offer his blanket, realizing as the consideration rose that she would refuse it. Centuries on a world without weather or the need for shelter made elves far more comfortable among natural than among man-made constructs.

El-brinith clamped her hands around her thinly hammered leather boots, rocking in a graceful rhythm, eyes closed. For several moments, Darris stared in fascination. After a while, Tae, Ra-khir, and Kevral moved away so that their conversation would not interfere with El-brinith's efforts. Darris found himself incapable of joining them, worried to miss an instant of magic rarely performed in a human's presence. He would not, could not, miss this for anything.

Suddenly, El-brinith belted out several strident gutturals. Though prepared for anything, Darris stiffened, heart rate unstoppably brisk. He drew a deep breath through his nose, loosing it with a slowness designed to calm. The maneuver brought no reprieve. Though the surprise lessened, the excitement of learning kept his heart beat uncomfortably quickened and a tingle dancing through his chest.

Then, as quietly as she had prepared, El-brinith rose. No great flash of light, no illusions, and no sound announced her new knowledge, but she pointed a long finger toward the southeast. "It's about three hundred lengths in that direction."

Darris glanced behind him to alert the others, but they had already come.

Tae went straight to matters of security. "What else is there?"

"No way to know." El-brinith did not bother to look at Tae as she spoke. "Could be nothing or an army of nine hundred. General direction and distance is all I can get, and just once per world. And that's only because Captain bound well."

Darris believed he caught something in her tone or, perhaps, in a mental sending that accompanied the words. It bore the suggestion that the competence of Captain's fusing might prove as much detriment as windfall. He wondered about the details without questioning. Soon enough, he suspected, he would know.

Tae did not await further information, slipping into the brush without a sound, stems bowing and rattling in his wake. Andvari looked after him, massive hand clamped to the haft of his ax. For the moment, his discomfort seemed to have passed.

They headed southeast, guided at intervals by Tae. The Easterner appeared irregularly, without warning; and even knowing that this would happen did not prepare Darris. At every parting, he promised he would not allow Tae to startle him; and, every time, his quiet companion did so. At length, Darris abandoned the game, surrendering to thoughts better left untapped. If Tae could catch him unaware, would-be assassins might also. He worried for his assignment as the high king's guardian and consoled himself with the knowledge that Rantire currently warded Griff. He hunched his pack higher on his left shoulder and adjusted his mandolin more carefully onto his right. His hand fell to his sword easily. He would need to watch that his belongings did not hamper his defenses.

Kevral and Ra-khir talked softly together. Andvari did not join them, though surreptitious glances in their direction suggested that he wished he could. The elves stayed together at the back of the group, no more a true part of it than the middle-aged Northman, though they seemed to take no notice. The elfin individualism often judged by humans as aloofness stemmed more, Darris guessed, from differences in social convention and subtlety of expression.

Tae materialized from a copse behind and to Darris' left. Again, the bard stiffened before turning to meet his companion. Finding his fingers instinctively on his hilt gratified Darris, slightly easing his concerns.

"There's a clearing and a cottage ahead," Tae announced to the group. "A lone old man on the porch." He winked at El-brinith. "Didn't see any armies."

Darris blew out a long breath, muscles uncoiling. This would likely prove as simple as he first believed. Presumably, the Pica had shattered in a random fashion, and they had no reason to believe their mission would involve worst than finding pieces nestled against tree roots or sparkling on a native's windowsill. *Native?* Darris amended his own thought. Captain had warned that creatures outside of human and elfin experience might dwell on these alternate worlds, but they should not find their own kind here. Humans had existed too long without any magic to travel between planes, and the elves knew every individual for as long as their eldest, Captain himself, had lived. All the tension Darris had shed returned in a wild rush. Once more, his hand found his hilt.

Tae broke the ensuing silence. "Do you want me to try to . . . find it?"

The pause brought other words to mind, most notably "steal." Darris suspected Tae had chosen his phrasing to bypass Ra-khir's notice, but it failed.

"No," Ra-khir said emphatically. "Peaceful bargaining first. Violence if unavoidable." He glared at Tae. "Stealing, never."

Tae made a gesture of surrender. "Did I say anything about stealing? I just thought locating it might make bargaining more . . . um . . . effective." His brow knitted tightly, "Taking what we need peacefully should *not* be preferred to bloodshed?"

Darris saw the logic in Tae's words, but Ra-khir's frown only deepened. "Bargain first," the knight said, though Darris read more. Tae's final words could only reaffirm Ra-khir's worry that, upon finding the shard, Tae could not resist taking it.

Kevral added, "We don't even know this old man has it, and you're already arguing over method."

I think we can count on it. Darris kept the thought to himself. He realized now that the Pica likely had a mystical attraction to it, even broken; and the backwash of elfin magic would assure the tasks proved more difficult than the simple gathering of chips of fragmented gemstone he had considered only moments ago. For the first time, he doubted Captain's assurances to the contrary. Lifting a spell of such power as the sterility plague would not happen without sacrifice.

Tae waved to indicate Ra-khir should precede him. His expertise had ended, and he would not take the blame for a failed parley.

Ra-khir took over at once. "We need to look strong, businesslike, and in control; but there's no need to frighten this elder. Please keep hands away from weapons and avoid doing or saying anything menacing unless such becomes necessary." He headed into the brush from which Tae had just emerged, tabard displaying Erythane's orange and black swirling behind him.

Kevral grunted to indicate the painful obviousness of Ra-khir's words, though only loud enough for Darris to hear. They followed him. The elves came next, with Andvari; and Tae vanished again.

Shortly, the forest gave way to stumps, then to a small clearing. A carpet of dull, brown grass spread around a tiny cottage, and a white-haired man sat on a rickety chair on a ground-level deck. Smoke curled from a pipe clutched between his lips. As the party emerged from the woodlands at the side of the house, the old man's head swiveled toward them.

Ra-khir strode the grassland toward the cottage, his posture perfect and his every movement confident. He raised his right hand in a broad, arcing greeting. Darris and Kevral followed, and the bard could hear Andvari at his back. The elves and Tae made no sound.

In reply, the stranger shifted his chair so that it directly faced the group. Wind lifted the hair on the left side of his head. The smoke trailed it, twining like a wraith through a snowy streamer.

As they drew closer, Darris could see the wrinkles that scored the ancient face like parchment. Withered hands clutched the chair sides, the flesh between the fingers sunken into deep crevices. Veins traversed thin skin overlaid with freckles. The cottage listed slightly backward, though it seemed otherwise sturdy, its planks surprisingly uniform and the cracks caulked with a substance resembling ship's tar. The construction of the roof was odd enough to hold Darris' gaze despite the potential danger that might lurk inside the cottage. Scraps of wood about the size of his hand tiled the surface, pitch frozen into oozing patterns beneath them. Darris wondered how it shed rain and if it might not work as well as the regular thatch used by most of the civilized lands.

Ra-khir stopped at a reasonable and nonthreatening distance that would not require shouting for communication. A wooden railing, and the length of two men, separated him from the elder. Ra-khir used the trading tongue, "Hello." He lowered and raised his head in greeting.

The old man watched Ra-khir for several moments in silence.

Only then, it occurred to Darris that they might have no means to communicate with this stranger or any on the other worlds they would soon explore.

Ra-khir filled the awkward hush. "Can you understand me?" He spoke in the slow, loud voice so common to those confronting one who cannot speak their language.

Usually, Darris saw the humor in such an action, but this time he wondered if someone so old might not benefit from such a strategy. Time could have dulled his ears or intellect.

The stranger rose with an unhurried deliberateness that revealed no infirmity. He removed the pipe from his mouth, speaking in a clear voice and at a speed Darris could scarcely follow. "Hello. Good weed, excellent weed." He waved the pipe. "Knights and Renshai and Northmen and elves." Watery, hazel eyes traveled over the party. "Renshai wars weren't enough for Colbey when he was your age. He used to join other Northern tribes on their raids, and once became captain of a ship. Didn't know anything about sailing. Hoho." The sound emerged more as a word than a laugh. "But he got by. That was before the Northmen's attack. Of course, now, there's whole different wars going on in the North . . ." He continued in an endless banter that switched subjects nearly with every sentence.

Ra-khir allowed the elder to ramble, glancing at his companions for suggestions.

El-brinith and Chan-rék'ril listened in polite silence. Andvari looked stunned, even after the topic of Northmen grew distant.

Kevral fidgeted like a child at a ceremony led by knights. Before anyone could think to suggest anything, she interrupted the swift and belabored litany. "Excuse me, but have you seen a fragment of blue gemstone?"

If the elder noticed Kevral's rudeness, he showed no sign. "Blue, yes."

Hope bubbled to life, quickly squelched as the man continued.

"Blue, aquamarine, indigo, sea, sky, steel, beryl, sapphire—"

"Sapphire," Kevral jumped in. "That's what we're looking for. A shard of a sapphire. Have you seen such a thing?"

"Sapphire," the man repeated. "A particularly pretty color. A gem, too, I'm sure you know. The most magical stone ever was a sapphire. The Pica—"

Darris stiffened, along with Ra-khir.

"That's it!" Kevral shouted. "The Pica. A piece of the Pica!"

"It broke, you know," the man continued, his patter directed somewhat by Kevral. "Lost its magic. But once no item rivaled it. Of course there was Shadimar's permanent storm. And Trilless' . . ."

Kevral threw up her hands in disgust. She turned and headed back toward the edge of the woods, gesturing for the others to follow.

Ra-khir, Andvari, and the elves obeyed immediately. Tae slithered from a shadow of the cottage to join them. Darris hesitated. The more he heard of the old man's random babbling, the more he felt certain of its extent and accuracy. He could learn much from this stranger, if the method of teaching did not drive him fully insane. Reluctantly, he joined the others, studying the man over his shoulder as he walked.

The elder watched them leave, his voice wafting after them, ". . . as compared with insects with four wings who hover . . ." As they reached the edge of the woodlands, the pipe returned to his teeth, and he retook the chair as if they had never come.

They stopped at the forest's boundary, within sight but beyond earshot. "This is pointless," Kevral said with clear contempt. "We can't bargain with a nonsensical moron."

"He's no moron." Darris insisted. "Everything historical sounded right to me, and the rest seemed plausible enough."

Tae agreed with Darris. "He slipped in some foreign words now and again—used correctly and in places where it would have taken whole phrases in trading to say the same thing."

El-brinith turned Chan'rék'ril a smug look. "I thought I heard elfin once or twice." The male elf returned nothing.

"Semantics." Kevral waved an arm wildly. "Brilliant or stupid, he's insane. We're not going to get straight answers."

Ra-khir glanced toward the cottage. "What are you suggesting? We attack him? Break into his home?" He did not wait for a reply; an affirmative would only enrage him. "We can't do either."

"Violence," Chan'rék'ril said, "would be unwise"

"Unnecessary, perhaps," Tae corrected. "And maybe dishonorable. But unwise?"

El-brinith's emerald eyes snapped to Tae, and she switched to *khohlar*. Her sending brought a concept of ambient magic, ancient and sourceless. She believed the old man was warded in an inexplicable fashion, by something larger and older than any elf.

Ra-khir shivered. "Kevral's questions seemed to divert him somewhat. Maybe if we work together, we can corral him into answers."

"Maybe." Darris hoped his eagerness came through plainly. He wanted a part of it, to hear enough of the elder's ravings to learn things he never knew, including the identity of this stranger. No mythology explained the presence of an aged human possessed of lunacy and lore alone on a wooded world. Yet, to trust El-brinith's *khohlar* meant considering that gods had placed and sanctioned this madman. To justify his interest, however, would require song.

Kevral said, "And just in case, I suggest Tae searches the house for entrances and the obvious presence of the Pica shard while we talk."

Ra-khir whirled on his wife. "No, Kevral. I won't be a party to theft." He added more gently, "I *can't* be a party to it. You know that."

Tae's depthless eyes flashed. "I'm not a thief, Ra-khir, and I'm getting a bit tired of you suggesting otherwise."

Ra-khir lowered his head, his look conciliatory. "I'm sorry. I'm not trying to offend. I know you're not a thief. I'd trust you with anything mine, even my family."

Darris tried not to smile. He realized the significance of Ra-khir's words, a verbalization of ultimate faith in their friendship. The knight intended to express that he would turn over his prize possessions to Tae and never worry for them, though Tae openly coveted his wife. Yet, Darris could not help noting that Ra-khir risked little by handing over his family to Tae since it would take an army to harm Kevral.

Ra-khir continued, "It's just that I know you'd do whatever you felt necessary to rescue fertility, especially if Kevral asked you. And your methods don't always jibe with mine."

Kevral took Ra-khir's hand. "I'm not suggesting he steal. I just believe it best to know whether or not this man even has the shard. Otherwise, we're wasting our time."

Tae dropped his argument and his look of offense. A moment later, he glided into the woods mumbling, "Why is it more noble to kill than to steal? I'll never understand . . ."

"Strategy," Ra-khir said, watching after Tae with a bemused expression that bordered on guilt. His brows dipped low across his forehead. "We need a plan."

"I'm not sure one's possible." Kevral looked toward the cottage with an intensity she usually reserved for battle. "Let's just say what seems right and model the victories."

Andvari stood aside, listening but not joining the discussion.

Darris shrugged. Hearing a Renshai say they could not devise tactics convinced little; they exulted in battle without pattern or tactics. Yet this time, he had to agree. Rigid plans seemed unlikely to succeed when it came to directing insanity.

"Let's go, then." Ra-khir again headed boldly for the cottage, Darris, Kevral, Andvari, El-brinith, and Chan'rék'ril trailing.

As before, the old man arose as they drew nearer, removing the pipe when Ra-khir opened his mouth to speak. "Good day, sir."

"Day," the elder repeated. "One light cycle and one dark. The time it takes for a world to pass around its sun . . ."

Darris considered the first wholly nonsensical words the stranger had spoken. *Worlds going around suns?* He shook his head.

Ra-khir chimed in as the old man switched to tedious and nebulous definitions of the word "good." "Have you seen a fragment of blue gemstone?"

"Gemstones: minerals cut, polished, and used in jewelry. Sometimes petrified . . . why I remember one—"

Kevral interrupted next, "A blue gemstone fragment."

The elder barely wavered, eyes wandering to the Renshai in her turn. "—topaz that caused a war between Pudar and Corpa Bickat in the era of King Horatiannon. And an uncut diamond once caught the eye of Queen Cenna. Lovely lady. Not unlike the East's—"

And so it went, with even the elves verbally nudging the native and Darris entering now and again. For the most part, his curse allowed questions, since they left him the recipient, rather than the purveyor, of knowledge. Snippets of understanding: lore, mythology, methodology, and language colored the elder's ramblings. Darris found himself captivated, nearly as fascinated as frustrated. For all the elder's inability to focus, his green-brown eyes retained an alert brightness that belied the obvious madness.

Hours of guiding and questioning gleaned no information about the Pica shard, and his companions' vocalizations grew more tense and terse. At length, even the elves grew twitchy, and Ra-khir threw up his hands. "Regroup."

Humans and elves retreated back to the edge of the woods, and the man calmly returned to his chair. Ra-khir ran a gloved hand through hair slick with sweat. "Did anyone notice anything useful? A method? Something he said that might give us a clue?"

Kevral shook her head, the blonde feathers falling into wild disarray. "Nothing we didn't already attempt to use. It's hopeless." She sighed. "Look, maybe if we leave a suitable amount of money in its place it wouldn't be stealing. How much could a chip of sapphire be worth? If Tae—"

Darris cringed, awaiting a fierce reaction from Ra-khir. But, before the knight could speak, Tae's voice wafted from the brush. "Won't work. Couldn't tell it from here, but there's glass in those windows and it won't budge. There's no chimney, and the door's locked." He turned Ra-khir a painless glare. "Despite what our redheaded man of honor thinks, locks and bolts thwart even me."

Ra-khir executed a gesture of respect, an obvious apology. "I'm sorry, Tae. I didn't mean insult."

Darris deliberately hid his amusement. The two had come a long way since their months of bickering that had, more than once, nearly led to violence. For whatever reason, Tae was playing victim amid friends who knew him too well. Ra-khir had not misread Tae's intentions; thief or not, he had planned to steal the Pica shard. And his years of running from predators and existing on Stalmize's streets had taught him skills with little other practical use.

Kevral ignored the exchange for the more important matter. "You can't get in?" She addressed Tae, incredulity tainting her tone.

Tae shrugged. "The glass is sturdy. *I'm* not strong enough to break it." The words left a clear opening, which Ra-khir ignored. After a brief pause, Tae continued. "And I do think it's in there. There's a mug resting on an irregular blue disk that sheds light brilliantly."

Kevral loosed a snorting laugh, then clamped her hand over her face. "A Pica shard coaster. Now there's a good use."

El-brinith watched Kevral, clearly missing the humor. "Maybe Tae can get the key from the man?"

"He doesn't keep it in any of his pockets." Tae returned instantly.

Ra-khir's openmouthed expression swiveled to Tae, who quickly stopped speaking and retreated a few steps.

Darris clamped his lips closed around a chuckle, thoughts returning to the tiresome and redundant exchange between the old man and their party. Only once had the elder maintained a thought longer than two to three sentences; he had sung two verses of a song about the gods without missing a single word. At the time, Darris had focused on the need to steer the old man toward the entreaties of his companions to let them search for the sapphire fragment in his cottage. Now, Darris realized, the man had sung with a pitch as perfect as his own. The voice had risen with an astounding resonance, free from the grating that tainted his speech. Darris would have believed such talent beyond the ability of one so frail from age. Only now, another thought struggled to consciousness. During the song, Darris had felt an odd kinship with this elusive stranger that seemed more driving than just a talent shared. "May I try something?"

Ra-khir abandoned his exchange with Tae. "What are you thinking, Darris?"

"I'm thinking," Darris started, then broke off with a sigh. He shrugged the mandolin from his shoulder to his hands.

Ra-khir raised a hand to stop him. "Does it involve violence or stealing?"

Darris shook his head.

"That's all I need to know." Ra-khir saved Darris the need for song. He glanced around to ascertain none of their companions felt differently. Finding no sign, he said, "Carry on."

Darris knelt with the instrument on his lap, tuning the eight strings in moments to the remembered proper tone.

"Darris," Ra-khir said gently, careful not to interfere with the process. "You know we always love to hear you sing, but you really don't have to explain."

"I'm not explaining." Darris frowned. The need to justify his lack of explanation might prove more difficult and dreary than the explanation itself. "You'll see." He appreciated Ra-khir's diplomacy as well. Throughout Béarn, citizens begged him for songs but when forced to ad lib rhymes, his talents proved barely tolerable. Rising, instrument still in hand, he headed toward the porch once more. This time, the others trailed him.

As before, the ancient met them at the railing, pipe balanced in his hand.

Having seen the uselessness of salutations on the last two visits, Darris did not bother with one. Instead, he launched into a song the instant he reached conversational distance. Sound flowed from the strings in a mellow wave, interspersed with notes that fluttered crisply from beneath each stroke. After a short introduction, Darris added his voice to a shocking cacophony of chaotic, four-note chords. The music perfectly simulated madness, plunging listeners into a frightening world that only psychotics knew at other times. His words held a balanced edge of sanity, at times wavering enough to threaten a plunge into depthless insanity from which there was no escape.

Gradually, the music gained pattern, weaving toward balance and beyond. Then, another voice joined Darris': the old man's, remarkable in its beauty. It added happy discovery to every word, and its notes blended smooth harmonies that complemented music and pitch in a way even Darris could not anticipate. The tone flickered gradually from tumult to tranquillity, then slid beyond to a joy Darris could not help but share. When the song ended, he glided immediately into another, this one a complicated, exuberant dance that promised to tax self and companion to a level beyond the last. The old man kept pace with barely a waver as one tune turned to the next. Darris did not attempt to guess how his partner knew the words to a song he had written as a young man; exhilaration did not allow for consideration.

The melodious voice followed Darris' through jumps of more than an octave, pitch never wavering from perfection. The speed of the chord changes wore even on Darris' trained fingers, but the old man found the speed no barrier. His harmonies blended into sweet precision, steady even as he clambered down from the porch and groped beneath it. A moment later, he emerged with a case embroidered with intricate designs. Though his efforts scarcely allowed for observation, Darris could tell that the case had once been expensive. A loving hand had soaped and oiled it, unable to wholly block the ravages of time.

Gradually, the song wound to a quiet close, little resembling the jerky, jabbing sounds that had characterized the opening. Darris lowered his mandolin, finally turning his attention to his companions. They stood, spellbound, even the elves; and a familiar disappointment scored their features. They wanted more.

Darris watched as the old man laid the case on the porch's planks. The native hesitated as the sounds of Darris' music died away, head cocked as if to catch the last faint echoes. He flipped open the case, revealing a lute, affectionately and artistically crafted into a droplet with the slender grace of a deer. The rare scratches and warping scarcely detracted from the beauty of an instrument that looked nearly as old as its owner, though far more appreciated. "Jahiran," he said, poking his own chest with a withered finger. He froze in place then, trenches creeping across his brow, as if he had forgotten his intention. Nestled in cloth surrounding the instrument, something brass caught the light for an instant.

Jahiran. The name paralyzed Darris, even as his companions broke from their trances. *Jahiran? Impossible.*

Kevral prodded Darris. "Play something else," she hissed. "Before he reverts back."

Jahiran. Darris scrambled to obey, his mind suddenly emptied of the

usually endless parade of ideas. One song filled his head, viciously holding all others at bay. And he sang it with question that all but pleaded,
his need to understand growing desperate:

> *"Jahiran was born on a warm Western day.*
> *The babe looked at his father, and then he did say:*
> *Father, why is the way of the world the way?*
> *Why does the hen, not the rooster, lay,*
> *While our men, not our women, enter the fray?*
> *And why do the gods rule us all?"*

Reoriented, the elder plucked his instrument from its rest, its lines
and curves defining acoustics the most skilled craftsmen might envy
with the same hot intensity that enveloped Darris at the sight. He had
coveted nothing in his life but Griff's marriage to Matrinka, yet now he
cavorted with the emotion as if it had served as a longtime companion.
He continued to sing as the old man added not only voice, but music, to
a song that had earned its place as one of Darris' least favorite:

> *"Jahiran turned ten on a spring day so cold,*
> *And vowed to learn all by the time he grew old.*
> *That night he learned every use for mined gold*
> *Why the* wisule *is timid, the* aristiri *bold.*
> *But he understood naught of laws Wizards uphold.*
> *And why the gods rule us all."*

The gentle braid of harmonics added a lyrical quality the melody had
lacked through the ages. Darris knew he would no longer despise the
song, though it would leave him longing for this placid interweave of
sound he might never find again. For now, he blessed the final seven
verses, wishing for twice as many.

> *"When Jahiran turned twenty, he had to know why*
> *The stars took the patterns they did in the sky.*
> *Why* aristiri *hawks sing as well as fly,*
> *Why the fox slinks from brush to rock on the sly,*
> *The messages hidden in a baby's cry,*
> *And why the gods rule us all.*
>
> *At thirty, he knocked on the West Sorceress' door*
> *Said "Natalia, please," and he knelt to implore.*
> *"There's a fire inside me that burns to my core*

It feeds, not on air, but on knowledge and lore.
I will die if some power won't help me learn more.
And I must know why gods rule us all.

Natalia fixed him with an ancient's knowing eye.
"You cannot learn all, and you shouldn't even try.
There is danger in knowledge," and her look went wry.
"Understanding cost even the AllFather an eye."
But the pain on his face almost made her cry,
Though she knew why the gods rule us all.

So Natalia, she gave him aristiri's *shape,*
And he saw things that men and gods usually drape;
Saw the passion of love and the violence of rape,
Saw upstanding men fall prey to wine's grape,
Saw Thor coit with a mortal, and that made him gape,
But he still knew not why gods reign over all.

The first bard learned much of the gods and their rule,
But facts don't bring wisdom unto a fool.
Jahiran used singing hawk form as a tool,
And he crooned to Thor's wife of his tryst by a pool.
Though Jahiran's purpose was stupid, not cruel,
Thor showed him why gods rule us all.

Odin stepped in before Jahiran was flayed.
"I realize your need, but this can't go unpaid."
Then the One-Eyed One grasped the hawk by its head
And cut out half its tongue with a razor sharp blade.
Then, where once perched a hawk, now a wounded man lay
Who wished he knew less of the gods.

Then Odin spoke, and his voice it did ring,
"You can no longer speak, but you can still sing,
And your fingers will keep the grace of hawk's wings;
They will dance across any instrument's strings.
Yet your quest to know all will continue to sting.
Mortal life is too short to know gods."

The last mordant line rang from mandolin and lute while the others stood like statues, straining for the final notes as if loath to lose even the last, dying vibration. Darris shared their yearning, wishing the ensemble would never end. He had played duets with his mother, the previous bard, the only one he met who dared try to match his talent. She had exceeded him, as the man who had called himself Jahiran would put even her abilities to shame. Yet, no matter the old man's talent, he could not be Jahiran.

Not for the first time, Darris despised the curse that forced him to impart knowledge only in song. Swiftly, he composed, the precision of the previous piece making his impromptu creation sound even more awkward:

"*Natalia passed 2500 years before*
History was set to zero.
If you're Jahiran, you must be
A 2800-year-old hero."

The elder strummed his ornate lute and sang his answer in a voice as clear and competent as Darris' own. Yet, though he also rhymed, he put forth his points with a competence that made it seem more concept than words. By the time they reached Darris' ears, he could not have recreated the constructs. Like *khohlar*, only the ideas remained: [*I am no hero. But I am Jahiran.*]

Darris glanced at his companions. They stood waiting but did not interfere. He alone had the old man speaking coherently, if not wholly sensibly. Tae had, once again, disappeared:

"*Please tell me how such can be*
It makes no sense at all.
You've got your life, your tongue and speech,
After such an enormous fall."

The elder responded with the same smoothness, and Darris found himself, once again, ensconced in awed jealousy: [*When I neared the end of my life, the gods took pity on me and my line. They offered me a wish. I'm afraid I proved no wiser than before. I asked for all the knowledge of the universe.*] He lowered his head, thin white locks falling like water to his shoulders. Guilt radiated from him like a mantle.

Darris stared, the enormity of meeting an ancestor stunning him beyond the ability to comfort:

"*Please, forefather, no need for shame.*
No bardic heir could find you to blame."

Darris shook his head. *None of us would have done any differently.*
[*I had the chance to save my son and my descendants through eternity, but I*

chose selfishly. I've suffered for my wish. The gods decreed I will not die until I've learned what I requested.]

The knowledge of the universe. Just the thought sent Darris' heart into excited pounding. *No wonder so much of what he said made sense.* A thought nearly staggered him. *All of it. What doesn't concur is my misconception, not his.*

Oblivious to Darris' thoughts, Jahiran continued. [*When the Wizards died and magic left man's world, Odin took pity and returned my tongue. He removed the curse from my line.*]

Or maybe not my *misconception,* Darris amended. Only now, he noticed the massive scar that split the old man's tongue. He cleared his throat and played again:

> *"The curse remains on Jahiran's line*
> *Believe me, I've suffered it in my time."*

[*By your choice, hundredth grandson. From the time of my restoration, your predecessors and yourself may speak freely, as I can.*]

Darris stared, wondering if Jahiran had any clue how he sounded when he spoke.

[*And, when the day comes that I know all, it'll also free my line of the infernal quest for understanding.*]

Hope flared, instantly replaced by realization. *Still the fool, Jahiran.* Darris heaved an enormous sigh. *So long as the world has a future, you'll never know all. And, by then, the curse will have no meaning.* Despite that, Darris could only begin to imagine the information Jahiran could impart, whether singing or through his chaotic ramblings. "Teach me," he said.

Jahiran studied Darris several moments in silence. Then, suddenly, he loosed a series of sounds from the lute strings that exactly simulated laughter. [*Do you have 2800 years to spare, youngling?*]

Images of Matrinka and Marisole filled Darris' mind's eye. Griff would see that they wanted for nothing, yet there was one thing Griff could never supply. *Matrinka needs me.* Yet the idea of learning from the master of all knowledge, of spending his years in endless duet with a musician of unmatched skill enticed with a bonfire of need. He glanced toward his companions again. Ra-khir wore a look of impatience. The whole thing seemed ludicrous to him. Kevral turned Darris a wide-eyed, bemused expression. She understood as few others could. She would follow Colbey Calistinsson to her death and revel in the opportunity; nothing and no one could stand in the way of her learning should he agree to teach.

Darris gritted his teeth. *I'm not a Renshai or a fool.* "No," he admitted. "No, I haven't."

[*What did you come for?*] Jahiran sang with a secret smile that he did not explain, nor did he need to. [*If it is in my possession, you may have it.*]

Kevral spoke for the first time since the singing started. "A shard from a broken sapphire."

Jahiran granted the Rensai a single nod. He set the lute on his knee, reaching into the case toward the glint of brass Darris had noticed when the ancient had first opened it. His face lapsed further into wrinkles.

Tae emerged from the far side of the porch. "It's in your back pocket."

Jahiran's lips pursed in clear doubt, but his hand went to the indicated place, as much from instinct as any belief he would find it there. He made a sudden noise of discovery, drawing key and Pica shard from his britches together. He smiled, passing the sapphire chip to Darris and tossing the key back into the case.

Darris gave Tae a withering look, but the Easterner dodged it with a sudden, intense interest in studying the further horizon.

Jahiran placed his lute back into its case even as Darris requested one more song.

"Song," Jahiran repeated. "Why I once knew lots of songs. Did you know that there's a tribe of barbarians in the southwest that worships music as a god? And speaking of gods . . ."

Kevral seized Darris' hand and led him toward the woodlands.

My life and loyalties belong to my world, not my curse. Darris could not help looking back, even as Jahiran returned to his chair and his pipe. It was a lesson the first bard had learned too late.

CHAPTER 7

Return of the Father

The difference between a blood-sire and a father is the differ-
ence between having the flesh to hold a sword and learning
the competence to wield it. I may be the Child of Thunder
you name me. I may carry the blood of Thor; but I am always
first Calistin's son.

—Colbey Calistinsson

A whiff of grease from the kitchen twined beneath the study room door
in Pudar Castle, strange contrast to the flower-petal incense. Wide-open
shutters emitted afternoon sunlight that sheened from off-white walls,
striped the bare wood floor, and glared from parchments on the tabletop.
King Cymion pinned one of these with a thick, callused hand, auburn
hair flecked with gray curling across his forehead. He indicated a passage
scrawled on the paper with a brisk tap of one meaty finger. "See there.
History never lies."

Prince Leondis nodded with an abstraction that seemed more politeness than interest. Dark brown locks bobbed around his shoulders, and
he glanced at his father with the king's own blue eyes.

With a sigh, Cymion let his hand flop to the page. *Severin would have*
devoured this. He banished the thought before the tears could rise. Longer
than a year had passed since the death of the elder prince, but Leondis'
every failing still raised memories of his favorite.

A firm knock on the door wrenched the king from somber thoughts.
"Who is it?" he demanded gruffly.

No answer followed. The thick panel muffled sound, and the other
could not have heard him.

Leondis rose with a swift grace that suggested he appreciated the interruption, though he said nothing to confirm the impression. He trotted
to the door.

Cymion judged the prince's every movement. There, he admitted grudgingly, Leondis bested his late brother. What Leondis lacked in wisdom, judgment, and political savvy, he gained in grace and strength. Expecting to become a military officer in his brother's employ, he had trained to war from an early age. Honed muscles, pleasant features, and charming manners had made him the favorite of Pudar's females, if not of his father. At least, his recent marriage to one of New Loven's princesses seemed to have curtailed his appetite for women.

The new train of thought wrenched another sigh from King Cymion. He had long hoped to bypass the need for Leondis to rule Pudar by holding the crown until age addled him, then passing it to the prince's child. Yet, despite Leondis' well-known indiscretions, he had never sired offspring, even before the sterility plague. Except once.

As Cymion's considerations turned bitterly toward Kevral, the door eased open to reveal Javonzir, his most trusted adviser. Executing a flourishing bow, he kept his hazel eyes low, nearly hidden beneath straight, dark bangs.

"Get in here, Javon," Cymion fairly growled. The dense propriety was unnecessary. Cousins, they had played together as children, and Javonzir only became this rigid about protocol when he disapproved of something the king had said or done. The formality had grown aggravatingly thick in the last several months.

Leondis stepped aside, and Javonzir complied. The door clicked shut behind him.

Cymion pursed his lips, and they disappeared into his beard. "What have I done this time?"

Leondis placed a hand over his own mouth, but his eyes betrayed the smile he hid. He could not help finding amusement in the rarity of his leonine father's defensiveness.

"Done?" Javonzir repeated, shaking his head. "Many wonderful things, Your Majesty. At a time of crisis, you've kept the populace content, especially with your policies, Sire."

"But. . . ?" Cymion inserted.

Leondis reclaimed his seat, watching but graciously keeping his inspection moderate and nonjudgmental.

"But nothing, Sire. You've done nothing that concerns me." Javonzir bowed once more before stepping closer. "I only came to bring you this." He held out a thin scroll of parchment tied with a ribbon and secured with a wax imprint of Béarn's bear. "A messenger brought it moments ago."

Cymion studied his adviser's familiar eyes, a muddled mix of green and brown with unusually thick folds at the inner corners. Although Javonzir had not unrolled the parchment, he surely worried for the contents, which made little sense. Béarn and Pudar had been comfortably allied for centuries. Taking the tube, he assembled the logical pieces of information. "The messenger told you its contents."

Javonzir gave no reply. In his stodgy moods, he responded only to the king's questions.

Cymion did not press. He held the answers in his hand. Snapping the seal, he slid the ribbon off one end and opened the message, reading:

> *To: His Highness, King Cymion of Pudar*
> *From: Griff, High King of the West in Béarn*
>
> *Your Majesty,*
> *This note is to inform you that the* lysalf *have*
> *discovered a method likely to lift the sterility plague, and*
> *we have embarked on the course posthaste. It requires the*
> *time and effort of eight heroes who have volunteered for a*
> *mission that might prove dangerous or even fatal. We do not*
> *know for certain if they will meet with success, but we hope*
> *your best wishes attend them as well as our own . . .*

Excitement wound through Cymion's chest, and a grin twitched across his thin lips. He continued reading:

> *. . . Acknowledging the multicultural nature of this*
> *problem, we have assembled: two elves, Béarn's own bard, a*
> *Knight of Erythane, a Northern warrior, a Renshai, and a*
> *Pudarian healer. The East's only prince has honored us with*
> *his presence as well. I regret that time did not permit us*
> *to consult you prior to the selection process, but we*
> *believed it best for all to start, and thus complete, this*
> *business as swiftly as possible. We hope we have not*
> *offended you or any other with this method and that you are*
> *as excited as us by the prospect of forcing this damnable*
> *plague to its conclusion.*
>
> *With all best wishes of the High Kingdom*
> *I remain your ally and friend:*
> *King Griff*

Cymion's mouth parted, enhancing his smile. He let out an undignified whoop of joy, passing the parchment to Leondis so the prince could share his enthusiasm. "At last, a cure. At last, peace and an end to the worry that mankind as a whole might perish. At last . . ." He broke off, realizing that Javonzir remained still, expression unrevealing when he should have been grinning and dancing like a fool. "Damn it, what am I missing, Javon?" He tensed for an evasive answer that would only fuel his anger. Javonzir knew him too well to misunderstand the question, no matter how vague.

The adviser knew when not to enrage his king. He ran slender fingers through hair that did not need the combing. Oil and sticky perfume held the pole-straight locks in perfect order. "Sire, the specifics of those chosen for the task."

Cymion jerked the parchment from the prince's hand. He had focused in on the one Pudarian, an unknown healer, likely not the one he would have selected. But he understood, even appreciated, Béarn's expediency. He glanced over the list again. The elves only made sense; Béarn would need them to work the magic. He considered the others: the bard, a knight, a Northman, a Renshai, and the Eastern prince. Memory descended on Cymion, accompanied by a dark rush of discomfort. Kind-hearted Severin, a prince of the people, had died attempting to rescue a grimy Eastern street thief getting pounded by more of his own. Every witness had fingered the victim's wild slashes as the cause of Severin's death. *Tae.*

Hatred flared, as hot as the white center of a fire. Cymion had captured the weasely Easterner, but Tae had escaped the impossible, taking the worst of Pudar's criminals with him. The guards had killed all but Tae and a locksmith turned thief. A legal technicality spared Tae from the slow, agonizing drawing-and-quartering he deserved, but not from King Cymion's unremitting hatred. Even the letter he had received from Tae's father, who had claimed the throne of the East's high kingdom, asserting Tae's innocence and presenting the "real" murderer in his place, scarcely dented Cymion's rage. Surely, Weile Kahn had coerced the confession; Cymion would have done the same for Severin, even for Leondis. He would tolerate the East's prince and remain allied with the East for the good of the West and Pudar, but no one could make him like Tae Kahn.

Leondis and Javonzir remained respectfully silent, though the set of the prince's face revealed sufficient joy to show he had read enough of the letter before Cymion had reclaimed it.

Gradually, Cymion's mind bullied past growing sullenness to pluck out the significant. *A knight and a Renshai.* He whipped his head to Javonzir, auburn-and-white curls flying in a wild mane. "It's Kevral, isn't it? And that irritating knight who fathered her bastards."

"Husband, now, Sire," Javonzir corrected.

"Of course." Cymion waved an irritated backhand. "His honor would force that." He squinted, allowing his anger to carry him to details that did not matter. "Though it didn't keep him from sleeping with her in the first place."

Leondis shifted uncomfortably, gaze darting to Javonzir. Cymion had attempted to wed Kevral to the prince in payment for battling a demon that nearly destroyed the West's largest city, mostly an attempt to keep her, and her offspring, in Pudar teaching his guards. The prince had charmed her with wit and warrior competence as well as looks, but she had refused his offer of marriage. Leondis had expressed his aversion for the nightly passionless sex his father had forced him to inflict on a woman he cherished and admired, but the king's desire for her to bear his grandchild knew no boundary. Leondis still bore the scars from the beating he had suffered from initially refusing his father's demand. In the end, it was the king's threat to rape Kevral in the prince's place that convinced him to comply.

King Cymion's fist crashed to the tabletop, and several parchments washed to the floor. "Has Griff lost the wits of his line? How could he send her into danger in her condition?"

"Now, Sire," Javonzir said sternly. "It hardly seems fair to attribute Kevral's actions to His Highness. She's only three and a half months past conception, your Majesty. Surely, her condition hasn't become visible yet."

Cymion's hand slammed the table again, with enough force to make it jump and to send pain lancing through his wrist. The shock further stoked his anger, and he leapt to his feet, powerful frame towering over his adviser. Though both had trained as warriors in their youths, Cymion had had the vast advantage in size. And he had kept up his practices even as he entered his sixth decade. "That bitch! She's trying to kill the baby."

Leondis scurried into retreat as the table lurched abruptly toward him.

Javonzir did not await a question. "Sire, I was afraid you'd react like this."

"Afraid," King Cymion roared. "Afraid! She's trying to murder the only heir to Pudar's throne, and you would accuse me of overreacting?"

Javonzir lowered his head with stiff respect. "Your Majesty," he said clearly. "I would never presume to accuse the throne of anything."

Cymion paced, expending the energy he needed to lose before he could attempt to regain control.

Leondis added his piece in quiet tones that jarred in the wake of Cymion's screaming, "To quote Kevral, 'Renshai have been waging wars *and* having babies for centuries.' I got to know her better than anyone over the months she stayed here. I don't think she's deliberately placing the baby in jeopardy."

Cymion loosed a deep, wordless noise.

Javonzir cleared his throat. "Your Majesty, if I may speak freely."

Still pacing, Cymion made a dismissing gesture. Not long ago, Javonzir always spoke his mind, and the king had all but begged for the forthright cousin he had known in his youth.

Javonzir complied, "Your Majesty is the finest king Pudar has ever served. The citizens adore you, and the nobles are content. We're allied with the North and every country in the West. Trade is flourishing, and we're richer than ever."

Cymion made a another snappy gesture, encouraging Javonzir to cut through the complimentary crap to the meat of his point.

"Sire, it's hard to blame Kevral for despising a baby forced upon her, even if it is the future king or queen of Pudar." Javonzir stiffened, as if worried he might have to run from Cymion's sudden, uncontrollable wrath.

Bothered that his beloved adviser would fear him, Cymion lost the raw edge of his anger. "We should not have had to force her. She should have done, willing, what was in the best interests of Pudar."

Leondis added carefully, "Father, she is not Pudarian."

Cymion rounded on his son. *Fool.* "What is in the best interests of Pudar is in the best interests of the West. She is a Westerner. All Renshai are."

Javonzir rescued the prince from his father's rage. "That aside, Your Majesty, I've spoken to women with child who lack the time or money to care for them. And those without husbands to assist them. Their stories are similar."

Uncertain where his adviser was headed, Cymion remained attentive, an eyebrow cocked. The story had best prove germane.

"Sire, even those who most fervently wished their babies would die often changed their minds about the fourth month."

Cymion tossed his head. "Why?" he growled.

"Because, Sire," Javonzir's expression remained steadfast. "That's when they feel the baby move."

The king's mood shifted to quiet contemplation in an instant, though the unreasoning ire remained only shallowly buried. "So you're saying that we only have to suffer two more weeks of that woman attempting to murder Pudar's only heir." His hands balled to fists, and his next words turned the previous to sarcasm. "The baby may not make it that long, Javon."

Javonzir retained his usual placid dignity. "Then, Majesty, we draft a letter to King Griff politely urging him to remove Kevral from activities that might endanger the baby."

Cymion flopped back into his seat. *Tell him we imprisoned the woman and forced Leondis upon her to create an heir?* He shook his head, images of gentle, innocent King Kohleran filling his mind. Passages of his childhood studies returned verbatim, detailing the naive neutrality of all of Béarn's kings. The uplifted Dunwoodian farm boy seemed more so even than his ancestors. Yet, another thought came to soothe the first. Bound by oath, Ra-khir and Kevral could never speak of the atrocity. Though several Knights of Erythane knew he had held Kevral prisoner, also bound by vows to silence, they did not know about the pregnancy. A handful of elves knew of the baby, but not the circumstances of its conception. Only the five of them and Pudar's general, Markanyin, had the entire story. Many of Pudar's citizens had witnessed Leondis and Kevral deliberately and willingly courting, and several healers had overheard his proposal of marriage. Kevral had already borne illegitimate twins. No one would question that she willfully coupled with the prince.

Javonzir awaited words from his king, a formal instruction.

Cymion finally abandoned thought for speech. "We will draft a letter. You and I." He studied his adviser for some sign that he had made a mistake or that the man he so trusted did not approve of his next words. "King Griff will have to do as we ask." Seeking support from Javonzir, he framed a question, trying not to sound weak or uncertain. "Won't he?"

Javonzir avoided the obvious trap of reminding his liege that the high king in Béarn could do as he pleased. "Sire, a reasonable, *neutral* man could do nothing else." He emphasized the proper word, reminding Cymion of Griff's natural bent. "And, Your Majesty, I'm sure he will see to it that the baby comes to Pudar immediately after its birth. By law, royal blood takes precedence over any other. Leondis, Sire, not Kevral, will raise this baby."

Suddenly the focus of king and adviser, Leondis stiffened. A flicker of pain flashed through his eyes, tainted with guilt. It disappeared as swiftly as it had come, Cymion noted with satisfaction. He understood Leondis' discomfort, but he appreciated the wisdom that had followed. The deed was done. Now, no other course of action served logic or the West. The only heir to Pudar's throne had to come home.

King Cymion would see to it. Even if it meant a war.

A chill wind whipped across Asgard, bowing the emerald grassland in a sweeping wave and sending seed pods skittering across the practice field. Ravn froze in position, long sword held in angled defense, scimitar raised for attack. The cold air racing over sweat-dampened skin made the sparse, blond hair on his arms stand on end. His gaze swept the clearing, seeking a source for weather that had never before plagued the world of gods—and finding nothing. Logic goaded him to return to the daily sword work that had been the most important part of his life for as long as he could remember, yet something unnamed held him back.

Again, an icy wind shot across the sunlit grasses, dappled by the shadows of straight, perfect trees. Ravn spun, still seeking a physical enemy for his sword. The gale seemed to carry a presence, a driving call that dragged his senses toward the Meeting Hall. He answered with a resistance dredged from the core of his being, the adolescent reaction natural and instantaneous. As the summons died, he gained a moment to analyze its frail ephemerality, its dense and unspoken need for him, and its alien nature that fueled his suspicions. He lowered his swords but raised his guard. His thoughts sailed to Colbey and the trouble he had stirred since agreeing to wield the Staff of Chaos. Hostility rose up in Ravn, a burning in his chest. *What's he up to this time?*

Sheathing the scimitar, Ravn walked sedately in the direction of the wind. He refused to hurry; blundering into a creature battling for control with chaos would prove sure suicide. Colbey's mastery over his charge had already proven desperately tenuous. *He agreed to, then refused to allow others to touch the Staff . . .* he amended . . . *the Sword of Chaos. He killed Baldur.* Grief and rage intensified the fire in Ravn's heart. He needed to keep his attention high, to judge every moment on its own merits, to keep his trust as liquid and malleable as the chaos his father championed.

Once more, the wind thrashed past Ravn, ruffling grasses, bowing trees, and slapping coldly at the wet, golden hair at the nape of his neck. He knew it wiser to ignore Colbey's summons, better still to warn the others. Yet Colbey Calistinsson was his beloved father. If the elder Renshai risked slow torture and death for this visit, Ravn could not bear to deny him. He followed the wind, only to find it still drawing him inexorably toward the Meeting Hall.

Pinpoints of light in rainbow hues danced amid the trees, reflections from the gem-studded Meeting Hall. Ravn paused, fascinated. The shy puffs of breeze that occasionally twined across Asgard barely stirred the leaves, and it took a wind of these proportions to reveal the true magnificence of the structure. He paused in wonder, only then noticing larger shapes shifting amid the lights, other gods drawn by vicious gusts rattling across an otherwise flawless world. They whispered among themselves as they funneled through the great doorway, the glimmer of the doorjamb's diamonds adding a vast array of hues to an already sweeping spectacle.

Freya drew up beside her son and laid a hand upon his shoulder. "There you are."

Ravn looked up into his mother's familiar features and felt a measure of discomfort dissolve. Though he would never admit it to her, he appreciated her presence beside him. "What's going on?"

Freya stared toward the hall. "It can only be Odin."

"Odin," Ravn repeated, an uneasy half-smile touching his features. Guilt flared, replaced almost immediately by a vicarious smugness. "Father was right."

Freya pursed her lips, her uneasiness obvious. "He usually is, Ravn."

Ravn walked around the goddess to regain the full attention of those sapphire eyes. "So Odin is our enemy?"

Freya's focus snapped fully to her son. "Your father is *usually* right. Odin *always* has been." Her eyes blazed with raw anger. "And it never ceases to infuriate me." Without further word, she strode toward the Meeting Hall.

Ravn edged after his mother, still pulled even without the wind. Thoughts thundered through his head, unsorted and disquieting. He could not forget that, early on, chaos had trickled into his father, twisting his will. Murder had tinged the blue-gray eyes, threatening death and dishonor, slaughtering long-held trust. Yet, Colbey had overcome that burden and others equally horrible. *He killed Baldur.* That crime barred Colbey eternally from Asgard, but not from his own son's mind and heart.

As the last trees brushed aside, Ravn confronted the gods' Meeting Hall in all its jeweled glory. His every movement brought new sparkles to life, colors flickering in random patternlessness across his retinas. He watched his mother disappear through the doors, the white spray of diamond reflections flickering across walls, trees, and the god-shaped shadows within the confines. Hurrying, Ravn caught the panel before it closed, then surrendered it to Sigyn, who entered just behind him.

The candelabra swayed, set in motion by the currents of gods' movement, the opening and closing door, and wind that rushed through the portal. Though candles no longer littered the tabletop, several gaps in the candelabra above revealed their previous locations. Light winked and sparked in lopsided sweeps across the golden walls. The crater left by Modi's thrown hammer remained, polished but still marred by scratches. The urge to prostrate himself seized Ravn with such sudden violence, he barely controlled his body's obsession. Fear jabbed through him, stealing thought. A trickle of urine warmed his thigh in a line. Flushing crimson, he caught and stopped the stream, but the shift of focus lost him other restraint. He glided to his knees, head bowed, before he could think to prevent the motion.

Freya seized her son's arm, tugging him up and to a place at the table. He moved dazedly, managing only a dizzy glimpse of the others staring at him, some with evident surprise and others with bemused smirks. Vali's soft comment reached his ears, but his mind could not process the words: "It's the human blood in him."

Freya's harsh glance kept Vali from further disparagement.

"I—I'm sorry," Ravn stammered, more confused than embarrassed.

Freya waved off his apology, silently nonjudgmental.

Reprieved, Ravn looked around the table. Frey and Idunn sat across from him, Sigyn taking a seat to Idunn's left, toward the head of the table. Vali held the position beside Freya, unusual for one who usually sat at Vidar's hand. Blind Hod sat by Sigyn, and Thor's sons occupied the chairs directly across from them. Honir perched directly across from Vali. The chair to the left of the head lay empty.

Only then, Ravn realized a figure occupied the head chair, as if some force had kept him from turning his gaze there until he had had his fill of lesser details. A massive god seemed to glut that entire half of the room. Red-blond hair fell to stately shoulders. A gray robe and cape flowed over an elegant figure that mandated respect. A broad-brimmed hat left the forehead shadowed, emphasizing sharp cheekbones. The set of the features struck Ravn's mind as perfect, and the single green eye blazed like a beacon, replete with ancient knowledge. Ravn stared, unable to look away. The eye seemed to flay him like a fish, extracting every thought and intention.

The door slammed open one more time, admitting Vidar amidst a blast of wind that sent his white cape into a flapping dance. "What's the meaning of this?" he demanded, blue eyes narrowing. "And who are you in my seat?"

The accusation broke the spell. Only then, Ravn realized the creature in the high seat was shorter than himself and half again as light. The figure that had once appeared massive now looked delicate, and he recognized the other as Dh'arlo'mé the elf. Yet, even Vidar's verbal attack could not wholly detract from the almighty charisma of this newcomer in the head chair.

The voice that emerged from the elfin figure, though soft, filled the Meeting Hall like a clarion. "My name is Hooded, also Wayweary. I am the Ruler and the Helmet-bearer. I am called Much-loved. I am called Third. I am Pudr and Udr, Hel-blinder and the High One. I am Host Glad and the Overthrower, Flaming-eyed and Law Bearer. I am called Wide in Wisdom, Broad Hat, and Long Beard. The Father of Victory. The AllFather. I am Shouter and the Gray God. The Terrible One. The Lord of Men. I have used no single name since I first graced Midgard with my presence. To you, I am Odin—know me! And challenge, my son, if you dare."

Vidar fell silent, hands balled to tense fists and pale eyes narrowed to slits. The hall seemed to quake in the aftermath of the AllFather's words.

For several moments, no one spoke. The eyes of the gods remained fixed on Vidar, awaiting his reaction before implementing their own.

Gradually, Vidar's fingers fell open, and his palms dropped to his sides. Without a word, he circled the opposite side of the table and took his seat at Dharlo'mé/Odin's left hand.

Odin's features remained blank, a featureless mask that went beyond the elves' natural propensity toward minimizing emotion. "Good day, my peers."

The neutral tone, the well-chosen words could not hide the truth. Ravn heard the word "peers" yet could not help processing it as "inferiors." He drew his eyes away, casting his glance at his own hands on the table. To his surprise, he found them trembling. He drew them into his lap where no one else would see his trepidation, though none of the deities seemed to notice anything past Odin.

No one dared demand proof, though Vidar managed the question on every mind. "How is it that you are my father yet you little resemble the one you claim to be?"

The lid glided slowly over the eye and returned, a fraction of a second's reprieve during which every god and goddess but Odin took a deep breath. "My body was destroyed at the *Ragnarok,* as you know. I have claimed this one." Odin's head made a gentle arc, gaze passing over each in turn. "And my rightful place in Asgard." His brow jerked suddenly upward, an unusual gesture in an otherwise subtle repertoire. "Any who wish to challenge should do so now."

Several of the gods shifted anxiously in their chairs, but no one rallied to his or her feet.

Ravn glanced around the gathering, their sheepish acceptance of one unproven grating at his sensibilities. No matter his awesome personality, no one should rule deities without some demonstration of his worth. Not even the First Father of the gods, if, indeed, this force of law in elfin form was Odin. Against every rational fiber of his being, Ravn forced himself to stand.

The edges of Odin's lips twitched upward, thinning the heart-shaped lips, the first hint of expression. "I would expect nothing less from the Son of Chaos."

Murmurs traversed the room. Freya closed her fingers over Ravn's wrist. "Odin is who he claims. He could be no other."

Odin's grin broadened. "Come." He spread his arms to Ravn in wide welcome. "Approach me."

The need to obey nearly overpowered Ravn, but he managed a soft reply to his mother. "I'm not challenging his identity. It's his right to rule I question."

Freya stiffened, eyes twitching wide in disbelief. Apparently overhearing, Frey also turned his head toward his nephew. Ravn had never seen either caught off-guard before.

"Ravn," Freya hissed. "You've never seen—"

"Come," Odin said again, his tone still friendly. "Come to me, Raska Colbeysson."

Ravn took two steps in the indicated direction before he realized he had moved. He forced himself to stop. "If we're going to fight, it seems best to do so outside."

Odin leaned forward, dropping all of his features into the hat brim's shadow. "First," he said. "We talk." He raised a hand, palm up, then beckoned with his index finger.

This time, Ravn went. To fight further would have required too much strength to bother, especially in the moments before battle. As he rounded the table and started past his uncle, however, he came to another halt. Unclipping the long sword, Harval, from his belt, he set the sheathed weapon on the table in front of Frey. "If I die, the balance is yours to uphold."

Frey darted a glance from weapon to nephew to Odin. He opened his mouth, surely to refuse. His commitment to the elves whom he had created made neutrality impossible. Returning his gaze to Ravn, he placed a hand upon the stained leather sheath. His handsome features crinkled, and a light kindled in the depths of his eyes. Ravn could imagine the thoughts taking shape behind the sculpted cheeks and broad, sky blue eyes they shared. Frey had denounced Dh'arlo'mé as bitterness transformed his jovial elfin innocence into a cruel and desperate vengeance aimed at mankind. Either his rage against the elf whose body Odin had claimed, or Ravn's own courage, allowed the god of elves and sunshine to accept his nephew's gift. "I prefer that you wield it and believe you most suited for the job. But if the need arises, I will do my best to see it done right."

"Come," Odin said, more firmly.

As Ravn scrambled to obey, Frey pressed his own sword into his nephew's hand to replace the one he now guarded.

Warmth suffused Ravn. To trust another with one's sword was the highest compliment among all of Northern background, not just Renshai. He had had little choice but to keep the Sword of Balance from one pledged to an extreme, such as law. But nothing had forced Frey to hand his personal weapon to his nephew, not even the possibility of leaving

Ravn undefended since the youngest among the gods always carried a second sword.

At last, Ravn came before Odin, meeting the green eye with the defiance adolescents perfected. A moment later, the orb seemed to penetrate him, not simply reading his mind but tearing directly into his system. The Meeting Room faded around him. The quiet exchanges of his peers became the occasional stiff song of a distant bird and the rattle of leaves and branches in a familiar, cold wind. Knobby gray-and-brown trunks of varying widths towered over his head, their waving leaves resplendent in shades of green, indigo, and orange. Carpeted in mulch, the ground lay speckled with crisp, dying foliage that crunched beneath his boots.

It never occurred to Ravn to wonder how he came here. It seemed perfectly natural to find himself suddenly thrown into woodlands, without purpose or memory of how he came there. His hands went naturally to his hilts. The left latched onto the scimitar and the right stroked the frigid metal pommel of Frey's broadsword.

A sound from behind sent Ravn spinning into a crouch. A man swung gracefully from a tree branch, landing on the ground at what was no longer Ravn's back. "Looking for me?"

Ravn studied the lithe, tall figure and a handsome face halfway between round and oval in shape. Blond hair fluttered in the breeze. Eyes not-quite blue, green, or gray danced with mischief, seeming to change color with the light. Though a stranger, he had an odd familiarity about him, and the sword at his right hip bore the split leather grip, S-shaped guard, and simple pommel that Colbey preferred. Ravn did not believe he now faced the one he sought. "No," he said. "Not you."

The other laughed. "You don't recognize me." It was a statement not a question, so he added, "Do you, child of wrath?"

"Child of wrath?" Ravn's eyes narrowed, contemplating nonsensical words. "I'm not Modi's son. You've mistaken me for someone else." He shook his head at another realization. "In fact, Modi has no offspring, so you've mistaken me for nobody."

The stranger back-stepped with a dexterous hop that seemed more elflike than human. "Don't take me literally, Raska Colbeysson. The Renshai are the followers of Modi, hence the children of wrath—by word, by law, by nature." He made a grand flourish, as if to royalty, adding agile sweeps that belittled his own gesture of respect. "Child of chaos, if you prefer. Do you recognize me now?" The eyes mutated through a wild spectrum of colors.

That, and the habit of immortals to use titles in place of names, allowed understanding a slow dawning. Ravn took a wary back-step. "Loki."

"Indeed. Are you ready?"

Ravn could not imagine a Northman born who did not relish the chance to rid the world of the First Father of Lies, he who had dedicated himself to the ruination of all things living. For now, it did not occur to Ravn that the Lord of Chaos had died at the *Ragnarok* centuries past. He drew his swords.

Loki unsheathed and cut faster. Even as Ravn jerked backward, the tip of the blade slashed skin and sleeve from his wrist. Renshai training overrode his natural inclination to let go of the hilt in the injured hand. Instead, he used the blade to block, charging in low with the scimitar. Loki skipped aside, trailing mocking laughter. His blade launched in, met a block or parry, and retreated three times before Ravn found an opening. He lunged in, only to find it closed.

"Got you." Loki's blade slashed for Ravn's face. The Renshai ducked, throwing up a defensive block. Loki's blade skipped past his own, plowing a line of skin from his scalp.

Searing pain grappled for Ravn's concentration, and lost. Renshai fought, not through pain, but because of it. "Modi," he hissed, using the second wind the cry brought to leap upon his opponent.

But Loki slithered aside with lithe, animal grace. His sword cut the air with a swiftness that revealed only starry flashes of silver. Even so, Ravn recognized it. *Chaos. But that's Father's sword. How?* The need for defense usurped further thought. As he whirled back toward his dodging opponent, he barely avoided a lightning-quick attack then parried another before he could manage a riposte. *Renshai maneuvers*, he realized, at the same time knowing that only one immortal besides himself had learned them. "Father?"

The chaos-sword blazed toward Ravn again. He spun aside, brisk defense stealing his memory for location. His foot slammed down on a root, bruising his instep through the boot sole. He rocked backward, catching balance too late. Loki's leg jammed behind his ankle, and an elbow crashed into his face. Ravn toppled. He tensed to roll, only to find the chaos sword at his throat. He went still.

Fear spread through Ravn like a net. His mouth went dry, his heart pounded, and tremors wound beneath his skin. He clamped down on the emotion, refusing to reveal it to his enemy. If not truly, he would at least appear to die bravely.

When, after several seconds, the death blow did not fall, Ravn raised his gaze to his opponent, meeting the other's gaze with square courage. The eyes now held Colbey's familiar blue-gray coloring, and the chiseled features lapsed into the familiar blunt cheekbones, gently-arched chin, and average nose of his father. The four straight scars in front of one ear completed the picture, left from a long-ago battle with a demon. Three things jarred: disheveled golden hair usually worn too short for knots, a wild sparkle in his icy stare, and an expression of twisted cruelty Ravn had never before seen upon Colbey's face.

"Father," Ravn said with relief. His heart slowed, and he wet his lips with returning saliva. "Let me up. Please."

The creature towering over Ravn did not move the blade from his throat. "I am . . ." he said carefully. ". . .not your father . . . any more." He studied Ravn intently, clearly seeking movement. "I am . . . the Father of Lies. Of the Fenris Wolf. Of the Midgard Serpent. Of Hel and of Odin's steed." He lowered his head but not his guard. "I'm sorry, Ravn. I tried to resist. Chaos was stronger." The blade retreated, but only to gather momentum.

Ravn seized the only moment he had, eeling aside though he knew it futile. Colbey's practiced speed made his turtlelike in comparison. Ravn anticipated the sharp sting of steel through his vitals, the instant of agonized understanding before death claimed him.

Ravn's vision filled with the light of myriad candles, reflections swaying through a hall of gods and goddesses. He met Odin's green eye and found it brighter than sunlight. Burned by its intensity, he looked away. He could still feel the pressure of a sword tip against his neck, his sleeve flapped open, and a droplet wound down his forehead from the stinging injury across his scalp. He rubbed at the trickle with the back of his hand, surprised by a smear of scarlet. The line between illusion and reality blurred; fact lost logic and relevance.

Ravn drew breath to ask what had happened, but Odin answered before the words emerged.

"The truth is self-explanatory."

Certain he would receive nothing more, Ravn did not bother to question. With the eye of every god upon him, he headed back around the table to his seat, pausing only to exchange swords with Frey.

Unlike her son, who still labored to separate actuality from inflicted fantasy, Freya kept the presence of mind to ask the question Ravn had abandoned. "What did you do to him?"

The Great One's head swiveled toward Colbey's family, the elfin features a sharp contrast to the demeanor of a god. "Only showed him his folly." His gaze shifted directly to Ravn. "Revealed the future to him."

Ravn searched for his tongue, but words continued to fail him. Uncontrollable trembling seized his hands first, then traveled through his body in a violent wave.

An awed murmur swept through the meeting room, but it did not affect Freya. "That's bluff, Gray Father. Your wisdom spans all, but the future has always defied your knowledge."

Though slight, the smile that touched Odin's lips held a perfect measure of defiance. "Not anymore. Rebirth restructured my mastery, and the youth of my new body adds strength as well. Nothing limits me now."

Ravn knotted the tatters of his shirt into a wrist bandage, then pressed a fist to his head to stop the bleeding there. The wound gradually dulled into an ache that throbbed deep within his skull. He clung to his faith. "Illusion," he insisted. "Not future."

Odin's grin wilted to neutrality and barely beyond to a frown. "Your loyalty is touching, understandable, and also foolish. I can prove that Colbey exists only as an entity bound to chaos."

"Not necessary," Vali said, earning a glare from his brother.

"I would see this proof," Vidar countered, and others nodded to indicate their interest. Even Loki's widow, Sigyn, who had suffered enough insults toward her late husband, made a gesture to indicate Odin should proceed.

Odin's gaze speared Frey, Freya, and Idunn in turn, the three most magical left among the gods. "Summon a demon."

Alarmed glances and bits of conversation followed the order. Ravn understood their reluctance. Like ripples on a pond, even the smallest magics of gods tended to result in massive unintended consequences. The act of calling a demon would result in repercussions that went far beyond their ability to control and banish it.

Odin accurately read the problem. "You cannot damage the balance any more than the one you call already has. Trust me, no harm will come to the world's equilibrium as the result of this action, and you will learn whom to trust and whom to destroy."

Even Ravn could see the need to give Odin the chance to prove himself, though he worried for the cost.

A long time passed in silence before Vidar said quietly, "Do it."

Freya, Frey, and Idunn came together in whispered discussion. By mutual consent, they could call forth the least powerful of the creatures.

"You need not bother with bindings," the AllFather said. "You cannot contain it."

Alarm sent Ravn surging to his feet, memories in Colbey's voice filling his mind: "I confronted [Odin] because he attempted to summon a *kraell*, the most powerful of all demons. He made no attempt to bind it; he intended for it to scour the living worlds: men, elves, gods." Ravn warned softly, "Mother."

Freya excused herself from the group to come to him.

Ravn whispered fiercely. "Remember what Father said. Demon. No bindings. He's trying to trick you into destroying us all."

Freya heaved a deep sigh. "Ravn, your father . . ." She broke off, onto another track. "We've considered it. We won't summon anything we can't handle even without bindings."

Ravn had anticipated that but still worried. "What if he interferes?" He indicated Odin with a slight movement of his head.

"We'll detect it and break the spell."

Odin's easy ability to manipulate his mind kept Ravn skeptical. "What if he does it without your knowledge?"

Freya turned her son a reassuring smile. "Ravn, he could have called a demon himself and sent it against us. I do believe he's trying to show us something we need to understand. Trust me. I've known Odin millennia longer than you."

Ravn nodded erratically. He no longer felt certain who or what to trust. He still saw gaps in the explanation: Colbey had claimed to have stopped Odin's summoning earlier. Perhaps the grim gray father of gods believed Colbey would not interfere with Freya's summoning as with his own. Or, perhaps, he intended to confuse Colbey by having others do the summoning. Frustrated by his own ignorance of situation and magic, Ravn found himself incapable of constructing answers. He had to believe that, if Colbey could tell when and the type of demons Odin called upon, he would surely know when and how Freya, Frey, and Idunn did so as well.

This time, Frey proved the voice of reason. "You say our bindings cannot hold this demon, nor apparently do you intend to direct which one we summon. How can this be?"

Odin said only, "You will see." He folded delicate arms across his chest in a gesture more suited to one of great musculature and power.

Vidar fidgeted in his chair, only his stint as leader overcoming his fearful reverence for his father. "I can't allow them to bring a creature beyond their ability to contain here, at least not without a full explanation. It would place too many gods and worlds in jeopardy."

"Very well." Odin leaned across the table, gaze fastening and releasing each deity in turn. "No matter what you call, the Prince of Demons himself will answer the summons. We all know nothing of law can survive on chaos world. If Colbey comes from there, you must agree he could only have bound to his charge."

Again, nods circled the group, some reluctant, others thoughtful, and most eager. Some, like Vali and Sigyn, sought any excuse to condemn Baldur's murderer.

Odin's glittering eye pinned Freya once more. "Will that convince you?"

The goddess lowered her head. "I'm afraid it'll have to."

CHAPTER 8

All For One

Loyalty cannot be bought or sold.

—Colbey Calistinsson

A breeze twined through the alien forest of the first bard's world, sending high weeds bobbing, spilling seeds, and setting branches clicking in the trees. A steady rain of dry leaves pattered to the forest floor and onto the heads of the two elves and five humans gathered beneath it. Apart from the others, Tae stood with a cold hand pressed to the bark of an unfamiliar tree, watching and listening for danger. Darris perched on a weathered gray boulder, observing in a thoughtful hush, his mind likely occupied with Jahiran. Ra-khir and Kevral were poised near the elves, awaiting requests and occasionally exchanging soft comments that Tae could not hear. Andvari sat cross-legged on the ground, dragging a whetstone across a dagger blade that had seen no use since its last sharpening.

At length, El-brinith looked up from her crouch, head barely moving. The flat sapphire eyes held a gleam of sincere sorrow. "I can't get us back to Béarn until we all come together."

Darris raised his head. Chan'rék'ril nodded gentle agreement. Ra-khir paced two steps from the others, his expression unaccountably relieved. Kevral spoke the question on every mind, "What do you mean?"

"The spell's keyed specifically to us. All *eight* of us."

Ra-khir said more with a single word, "Rascal." He had never felt comfortable abandoning her here, though her own unsociability condemned her.

Tae sighed, stirring strands of hair that had fallen into his eyes.

Kevral looked at her husband, then back to El-brinith. "Is that right? We need her to travel?"

"I'm afraid so," the elf said in her high, musical voice.

Andvari lowered knife and stone to his lap, shaking back war braids that had fallen over his shoulders. "Fool," he grumbled. "Best off rid of her—"

Kevral could not resist baiting him. "Why? You don't like *Westerners* either?"

"No!" Andvari stiffened, stone dropping from his fingers. "I just meant . . . I mean I only . . ." He gathered his thoughts with a deep breath and a moment's pause. "I'd feel the same way about her if she came from my own tribe."

Kevral grunted. "Uh-huh."

"I'm not a bigot, if that's what you're trying to say."

Kevral pursued as savagely as she would in battle. "If you weren't, you wouldn't have to say it."

Ra-khir leaped in before Kevral could escalate the arguing to violence. "Enough!"

Tae smiled. The knight had weathered similar attacks from Kevral against his honor in the first several months they had traveled together. At first, Tae had deliberately fueled those attacks. Later, as he came to know and care for both, he forced a change. Without his interference, bloodshed would surely have resulted and their mission would likely have failed. Now Ra-khir's turn as mediator had come.

Ra-khir continued, "We're stuck together until we find Rascal and convince her to return with us. When we get back to Béarn, we can regroup. Fighting won't change any of that."

Chan'rék'ril made a sound in his throat, higher-pitched and more polite than a clearing, yet with the same effect. "I'm afraid El-brinith and I didn't make the situation fully clear to you." He repeated the sound, returning the scrutiny of his human companions without obvious discomfort. "The magic of Arak'bar Tulamii Dhor, Captain, is cast and tuned specifically to the eight of us. Spells this focused cannot be easily recast, if at all."

Andvari froze in a half-crouch. Kevral and Ra-khir exchanged glances. Darris rolled his eyes in the thoughtful manner that revealed he was busily memorizing. Tae needed clarification. "You mean we can't change the makeup of the group?"

"Correct." Chan'rék'ril seemed pleased with his ability to communicate a difficult point.

"At all?"

"Correct."

Tae smacked the heel of his hand to his forehead, imaging them chasing a paranoid, antisocial street orphan through seven more worlds. Kevral's and Andvari's bickering would limit them enough when it came to dealing with situations as delicate, or worse, than the one they had faced.

Andvari still questioned the details. "We're stuck with that . . ." He closed his eyes, choosing his words with extreme care. ". . . disagreeable girl until this is finished?"

Kevral spoke through clenched teeth, "You'd best be referring to Rascal."

"Huh?" Apparently only then realizing the description could pass for Kevral as well, Andvari winced. "Of course I mean Rascal. I'm not—" He broke off, features painfully clenched. "I'm just not." He rose, standing as tall and broad as Ra-khir. "Let's go find her."

The casualness of the final suggestion amused Tae, and he watched with arched brows as Andvari stomped past him. "Where do you propose to look, Northman?"

Andvari whirled, faced flushed around the scars. Tae read more curiosity than anger, and he suspected it came of his tendency to use descriptions in place of names. Surely, Andvari wondered how Tae got away with emphasizing racial differences while his every subtle comment was met with an accusation of bigotry.

Exactly why, but you wouldn't understand. Tae turned the huge Northman an interested look. Beneath the Easterner's placid exterior dwelt a hunted boy ready to dart into shadowed forest at the first sign of challenge.

All trace of red drained from Andvari's features. "We'll search the whole world, if necessary. What choice do we have?"

"Well," Tae kept his tone light; Kevral had hassled the warrior enough. "We could sit here the rest of our natural lives and achieve the same results."

"Meaning," Andvari snapped, patience used up by Kevral.

"If a child of the streets doesn't want to be found, she won't be." Tae kept his tone conversational. "In an area this big, we'll only find her if we give her reason to want to be found."

Kevral gnawed at her lower lip, clearly worried. Likely, she had expected Tae to locate the Pudarian.

True to his training, Ra-khir set straight to strategy. "We could spread out and promise her something at the top of our lungs."

"I could sing," Darris suggested. He ran a loving hand across the mandolin. "My voice carries."

El-brinith added something Tae found more useful. "I could locate her. As I did the Pica shard."

⋆What do we have that she might want?⋆ Chan'rék'ril wondered in general *khohlar.*

"Easy." Tae took over his area of expertise. "She's a product of the West's biggest city. She's no more comfortable here than I am." It had taken Tae months to understand woodlands, longer than a year to find the quiet solace that Matrinka and Darris described. The Eastlands had sacrificed their forests for necessary dwelling space and farmland long before his birth, and the cities had sprawled into one another until many of the old names disappeared. "She wants to go back to Béarn nearly as much as we do and may agree for that reason alone."

"If we can get her to listen," Ra-khir reminded.

Tae nodded. "Our biggest hurdle. She's not likely to stay in one place long, especially if she hears one or more of us coming toward her." He brushed back strands of hair nearly blue in the sunlight. "If El-brinith gives me a direction, I can try to sneak close enough to talk before she runs."

Ra-khir shuffled his feet, frowning. "If we try to trap her, we'll lose her trust. Basically, it would come down to which of you is more wary."

We never had her trust. Tae saw no reason to argue the point. "If she catches me creeping up on her, we might die here before we find her again. But—"

"I don't like that possibility." Kevral shook her head, slight and slow at first, then quickening. "Better to openly shout for her first. If that fails, then we'll try your idea, Tae."

Tae made no reply. Arguing would never convince people who did not have the street mentality. He forced himself to think the way he had as a young teen, though ugly memories he would rather have avoided accompanied the exercise. *Flee the danger. Locate or create safe places to hide. Secure basic necessities. Then, work on the problem: in this case, how to get home without winding up jailed for theft.*

El-brinith knelt, Chan'rék'ril and Darris hovering. Tae glanced over. In a moment, the elf would cast away their only chance to locate the street thief. *Rascal's not going to stay in one place, and she's not likely to be close by—flee the danger.* Though driven to stop El-brinith, Tae remained in place. Kevral and Ra-khir had made their strategy clear, and the silence of every other companion on the matter suggested tacit agreement. Instead of interfering, he kept his attention on the woodlands, seeking signs of movement that might herald unknown or unexpected dangers on this alien world.

"Three hundred and twenty lengths due west," El-brinith announced at length.

Tae's eyes narrowed in consideration, the number far lower than he expected. He turned to question, but someone apparently beat him to it because El-brinith repeated distance and direction. *Rascal has to know where we are. I would in her place. She fled long ago enough to put a lot more distance between us. She's had time to locate a sanctuary. Is it there? An abandoned burrow? A cave? Something that makes it worth the risk of remaining close to people considered enemies?*

Kevral knelt, etching diagrams in the dirt with a stick. "All right. I'll circle around here. Ra-khir, you go straight this way. Darris . . ." She waved him closer. ". . . like this. Andvari, stay in this area here. Tae . . ." She looked up. "Tae? Where the. . . ?"

Tae stepped into plain sight. "Here."

"I wish you'd stop doing that." Kevral's complaint emerged half-heartedly. More often than not, she appreciated his subtlety. Besides, he had not actually hidden, simply stood still in a location beyond her linear sight. "I need you to curve around her and approach from the back." She carved a broad loop in the dirt.

Tae nodded.

"You can't possibly see the diagram from there," Andvari accused, some of his irritation likely stemming from Kevral's harassment and the fact that she appeared to let Tae get away with words and actions for which she would fry him. He had no way to know the conflicts and heart-to-hearts that had led to that understanding.

"He's right," Ra-khir said.

Tae shuffled forward, his thoughts still on Rascal's motivation. Kevral's words had defined his responsibilities well enough, and he held little enough faith in the plan not to concern himself with details. Nevertheless, he approached and looked over his crouched and kneeling companions to the scratches Kevral had constructed. *Secure basic necessities.* He stiffened. *Basic necessities. Rascal's probably never hunted a rabbit or eaten a berry in her life.*

Apparently trusting Tae to unscramble the lines, arcs, and circles without her assistance, Kevral continued. "The elves can stay with our things."

"No," Tae said.

Every head swiveled toward Tae.

Worried that the others might interfere with his plan again, Tae sought unrelated explanations for his contradiction. "The elves can use that mind call of theirs. It carries farther and doesn't strain their voices." He anticipated the objection. "It's gentle and nonhurtful, so it's more likely to make her curious than afraid."

Kevral turned her attention to the elves. Chan'rék'ril replied, "We're here for more than transportation. We have no problem with assisting."

"I was thinking of your safety," Ra-khir explained.

Chan'rék'ril shrugged off the concern. "Don't worry for us. We're good at avoiding violence."

El-brinith added, "Our magic can assure that."

"All right." Kevral returned her attention to her diagram. "Then Darris will stay."

Tae cleared his throat loudly.

Again, Kevral looked at him, getting his point without further need for words. "Tae, you can't stay. No one else could get behind her."

"Trust me," Tae said.

"I do. I trust you to circle around—"

"Trust me," Tae said again.

"All . . . right . . ." Kevral turned him a questioning stare that he did not address. Finally, she again joined those low in the huddle. "Tae stays behind. Chan'rék'ril and El-brinith keep together just in case, and go this way."

Tae did not bother to watch where Kevral sent various companions. He doubted it would matter. Instead, he headed back to the clearing, rearranging packs and personal items, the others' as well as his own. He concentrated on burying the food deep within the packs.

While Tae worked, the others formulated the best approach: the words they would shout to get Rascal's attention, the course they would take if she came to one of them, and how soon they should return if their piece of the mission proved unsuccessful. Finally, as the others broke ranks, Tae joined them. Each headed in the appointed direction, and Tae pretended to leave also. Though it seemed unlikely that Rascal had reached their camp yet, appearances could count for something. Sticking to the shadowed areas of the woodlands, Tae swung back toward the camp as nearby shouts for Rascal permeated the forest.

Moving as cautiously and quietly as possible, Tae worked his way back to the packs and the clearing. Seizing the trunk of a thick, heavily barked deciduous tree, he scrambled onto the branches to a position directly above the camp. Hidden amid curling, brown leaves, he found a comfortable position that he knew he could maintain long-term. Concealment hinged more upon his remaining as motionless as possible than what he chose to hide behind.

Tae remained in place long after the shouts of his companions became swallowed by the density of woodlands and only the elves' *khohlar* reached him. Gradually, even that passed beyond range. Then, he focused on the damp odors of mulching leaves and rotting bark, the crick of swaying branches and the crackle of tousled leaves, and the cold wash of the wind across his limbs and face. Though accustomed to long vigils, his crouched legs eventually surrendered to cramps, and his fingers grew frigid from lack of movement. Mentally seeking a new position that would handle all of his discomforts, require minimal change, and still allow lengthy maintenance, he noticed a movement at the edge of his vision.

Cursing the timing, Tae ignored his body's protests. His legs tingled, warning of impending loss of blood flow. His fingers turned numb on the branches. His neck and upper back developed a deep ache, and his eyes stung. He blinked rapidly, lulling his parts with that one relieving action. His vision cleared, revealing the slow, steady progress of one attempting to remain unseen. He gradually carved out details: the uneven sandy hair, the skinny limbs jutting from contrastingly well-made clothes given to her at the start of their mission. Rascal's attention glided toward the clearing and the temptation of its many packs, then swept the surrounding forest. Her eyes flickered like an animal's, never in one position longer than an instant. She did not look upward.

Tae forced his muscles to uncoil; tension would only worsen the pain and stilt his actions. Even unnoticed and this close, he did not definitively have the upper hand. He would get one chance to sway her. If he failed, negotiations would become ten times trickier the next time. He banished thoughts about consequences that would follow. Not only did they distract him, they caused him to worry over things he felt ignorant to answer. If one of the eight died, would it leave them stranded? Could Captain craft another spell to rescue them? For now those details did not matter. He still had a chance to confront Rascal and bargain, coerce, or force compliance.

Rascal stepped into the clearing. Even from his distance, Tae recognized the tautness of her stance, the wariness that would send her skittering like a hunted deer at the slightest hint of danger.

Tae cringed. She would not stay to listen to words. He had little choice but to confine her until he made his points, yet that action itself would assure hostility. *Damn.* His mind raised a dozen options in the moments it took her to finally drift beneath him. Then, all time for consideration disappeared. If he did not act immediately, he might not gain another chance. Gauging distances with experienced care, he leaped from the branch.

A wash of leaves accompanied the movement. Cued by sound, Rascal jerked her head upward as Tae plummeted. She lurched sideways, screaming, but not far enough. Tae seized an arm and a handful of hair, dragging her into a roll to diminish the momentum of his landing. He scrambled for a better hold.

Rascal scratched, clawed, and bit like an animal. Guarding his eyes, wrenching to protect his genitals, Tae weathered the agony of her fingernails along his cheek. Her teeth gouged his arm, and a knee slammed into the side of his thigh. Blinded by his own actions, he cursed. Kinked fingers betrayed him, and he lost his grip on her hair. She twisted, gathering the momentum to kick him in the face. Tae's neck jerked backward, spearing his head with a white bolt of agony. Pain exploded through his nose. Rascal jerked free.

Swearing viciously, Tae hurled himself at the girl's legs. His shoulder slammed the back of one knee, toppling her again. She rolled. Anticipating the movement, he veered with her. His fingers closed over an ankle as the heel sped toward his groin. Pinning it with a leg, he grasped one flailing arm, then the other. Spread-eagled on the ground, Rascal did not surrender. She struggled wildly, snapping like a rabid animal for any part in reach.

Tae's arm throbbed, and his nose felt on fire. Something liquid trickled along his elbow. He tasted blood. He swallowed anger and the desire for revenge, concentrating only on increasing his physical control of Rascal without falling victim to her panicked and savage defense. Painstakingly, he moved until his heavier body tacked hers to the forest floor, his legs pinned hers in place, and his hands bound her wrists like shackles.

For several moments, the Pudarian's teeth clicked on empty air, and she snarled out curses that might make a foot soldier blush.

A drop of scarlet pattered to her cheek, then a second fell on her nose. Tae cursed his inability to check and repair the damage, yet the warm blood seemed to draw her to rationality. Fixing Tae with brown eyes glazed with defiance and hatred, she went still. Words followed immediately, "Go 'head an' rape me. I's gonna hurt ya worser 'an ya hurt me."

Tae suppressed an irritated response beneath a deep sigh. "I'm not going to rape you, damn it. I just want to talk." His voice emerged annoyingly nasal. *If she broke my nose, I'll . . .* No course of action followed; even his anger could not conjure up suitable punishment. After all, he had instigated the attack. He had fought as hard and as desperately fiercely in similar situations.

"Jumpin' me hain't talkin'."

"I was just trying to make you listen. To keep you from running."

Rascal spit at Tae, but it did not reach him. Instead, it plummeted to her own face, bubbles of saliva diluting the blood. Another drop dribbled to her face. "Ditty bastard." She enunciated that word clearly enough, as if insults alone were worthy of her attention. "Ya bleedin' on me."

"Prolonging this won't make it easier." Tae guessed his own eyes, though darker, echoed hers like a mirror. "Until you're ready to listen, I'm not moving. I'll bleed all over you if I have to."

"Hain't 'fraid of ditt. Blood nuther. Bleed to death, Eastin bastard. Hain't lissnin'."

Tae raised one eyebrow but otherwise made no reply.

For several moments they glared at one another in silence, during which only a single drop of blood trickled from Tae's nose onto hers.

"Talk," Rascal finally said.

Tae saw no long-term solution but the truth. A lie would only gain temporary cooperation. "Unfortunately, we need you with us to get back to Béarn. And to complete the mission."

Rascal's eyes narrowed. "Why?"

"Effect of the elves' magic."

"Meant why shud I do whatcha wants?"

"Because," Tae explained carefully, keeping his gaze glaring fully into hers to demonstrate that he was not bluffing. He deliberately held pain from his expression, a weakness he could not afford. "If you don't, you're stuck here, too. Forever."

"So."

"So," Tae repeated, but did not bother with further explanation. He knew enough about street orphans to feel confident that she would not wish to stay in strange circumstances any longer than necessary. Control meant everything; without it, violation or death would swiftly ensue. He only needed to watch that he did not force her to choose between the control that came of familiar circumstances and control of the situation. That she had gotten into her current situation suggested that she had not yet learned to buy future security with present discomfort.

Three more drops of blood fell on her face, one rolling into an eye. "Ya not lettin' me up tills I agrees, is ya?"

"I can't afford to," Tae admitted, fighting a well-ingrained need to win at her expense. If he negotiated right, they could both get what they wanted.

"If'n I's go back ta B'yarn, they's gonna toss me."

Tae recognized the slang. "They can't lock you up. We need you to complete the mission. That's seven more trips to other worlds."

The pale brown eyes widened. "Y'expectin' me ta do this 'gain an' 'gain?" She slithered her left foot experimentally.

Tae gave no ground, certain he could outlast her in one position, especially when he held the top. "Seven more times."

"Hain't doin' it."

Tae did not allow the refusal to upset him; he had expected no other answer. "Fine. When the others get back, I'll have enough hands to tie you." He only hoped he could stifle the discomfort that long. Exploited, his injuries could steal his consciousness or his power over her.

Rascal seemed to shrink into herself, and her eyes betrayed a flash of fear. "Ya'd tie me?"

Tae realized he had uncovered her failing, his only true negotiating point. "If you leave me no choice. We need you to complete a mission of ultimate importance to the world and its future."

"Ul'ament impotens." Rascal made a disapproving noise. "Ya hain't no streeto."

"Kin tahk like ya, if'n I wants." Tae simulated Pudarian street speech with only a hint of his Eastern accent. "I was a streeto *and* a ganadan. You don't survive either without smarts or the ability to imitate high-borns when the need arises." He added emphatically, "Perlia."

Rascal grunted again. "Yeah. But which one's yo im'tayshin?"

Tae gave a shrug so small it did not grant Rascal any openings for escape. "Doesn't matter, does it? I didn't get where I am without sacrifice, hard work, and a lot of soul searching." He did not add that his father's toil had also played a role. He would have come to the same place with or without Weile Kahn's bid for Stalmize's throne, and mentioning it would dilute his point.

Rascal rocked her head back and forth, apparently seeking space. "Ya don' b'come a prins like that."

Tae smiled. "Sometimes, Rascal, you do."

"Gots ta be born ta da king."

"Not always." Tae waxed philosophical. "They'll always be high-born who think of me as slime and low-born who think I'm too big for my station. But all that really matters is what I think." Memory stirred. *Damn. Isn't that essentially what Matrinka said to me?*

Rascal rolled her eyes. "Lek' shur done?"

"Yeah." Tae wondered if he could ever break through her walls. "Listen. If we're unsuccessful, there'll never be another baby born. Never. Humans will eventually cease to exist."

Rascal slowly closed and opened her lids, in lieu of a shrug. "Hain't wantin' no babies."

"Rascal, I'm talking about the complete extinction of mankind."

"Hain't my problim."

Was I ever that stupid and self-absorbed? Tae tried not to contemplate. To believe it so might destroy the fragile self-esteem he had managed to build. To deny it might damage his will to assist her. Further proselytizing would gain him nothing. "Let's bargain."

Rascal came instantly to life. "Wants full freedom. Kin do's I want w'out no one's buggin' me. Room in da cassil. B'come a prinsis."

Tae bit back a laugh. "The high king himself doesn't have that much independence." He presented a more than reasonable alternative. "You stay with us through all eight tasks, and I'll keep you out of the dungeon for any crimes you've already committed." Tae knew Ra-khir would despise the concession, but he felt certain Rascal would never agree to anything lesser. "You haven't killed anyone, have you?"

"Not yet," Rascal hissed.

Tae's grin returned.

"I's still lissnin'."

Tae continued, "A cottage in Pudar, or Béarn if you prefer. Enough gold to start a legitimate business of your choice . . ."

"Gold?" For the first time, Rascal's fierce facade slipped.

". . . and the advice to get it started."

"How mich gold?"

Tae schooled his expression to utter sincerity. "Imagine all the gold you've seen in your entire life. Pretend all the silver you've seen is gold and add that."

Rascal nodded eagerly.

"More than that."

"Deal." Likely, Rascal could not have stopped herself from saying it. "But I gits the gold fust."

Tae knew better than to agree. Even a quarter up front would probably prove enough to send her running with it. "After."

Sounds in the brush sent both heads flicking toward it. The first of Tae's companions had returned. He eased his hold slightly, knowing her cooperation would require threat as well as promises. "And one more thing. I've got connections even a streeto couldn't fathom. You run, you will be found. Some of the people I know don't share my morals. I'll get you back alive; but short of that, I won't guarantee anything." He gave her his best "I'm-not-bluffing" glare. "Then we drag you, bound, through seven worlds, after which you get nothing but a long stay in Béarn's dungeon." He let her up, anticipating an attempt at escape despite bargains and warnings. As excitement diminished, the pain in his nose grew in increments.

Rascal scrambled to a crouch, but she did not flee.

The brush parted to reveal Kevral and both elves. The Renshai's eyes went to Rascal, and she shook her head evenly. Her attention flitted to Tae. "How?" she started, then her expression went soft as she apparently noticed his injury.

"Scum knows scum," Tae said, suffering roughening his self-respect as well as his answer.

El-brinith glided toward them. "Let me take care of that injury."

Tae placed himself in her care, hoping her elfin magic could take the place of the healer they did not have, now or, he realized suddenly, over the course of the next seven tasks.

Asgard's golden walls sparked a million bright reflections, the familiar patterns blunted by the candles not yet replaced after the battle that had resulted in Baldur's death. The gaps shadowed Odin where he sat in the high seat, adding an aura of mystery and power that he scarcely needed. Ravn could not fully shake the awe that no longer drove him to acts of obeisance but still suffused his judgment of every action of the AllFather.

Odin seemed bothered by the missing candles, frowning at intervals at the odd array of glimmers and glancing at the candelabra more often than his otherwise casual movements warranted. Near the door of the Meeting Hall, Freya, Frey, and Idunn crafted their spell with a few graceful gestures and huffed gutturals. No great flash of light or magnificent gesture announced their conclusion. Only a dark shape forming between them revealed their magic and a single silver spiral that wound from its top, defining a human form before slithering to the floor.

A frown scored Odin's elfin features, though whether because of the newcomer or the extra trickle of magic, Ravn did not know enough to guess. The AllFather had proclaimed wards useless and unnecessary, yet someone had doubted enough to try.

In a moment, the conjured shape became more distinct, a lean sinewy man who, even in stillness, showed astounding grace. Colors shimmered through otherwise simple linens, flickering oddly in the irregular candlelight. Golden locks a bit longer than usual feathered from defining features.

Vali, Sif, Modi, and Vidar glided around the table, weapons readied. Magni wrapped his fists around the haft of Thor's hammer.

"It is as I said." Despite impending violence, Odin remained placidly in his seat. "From the plane of chaos. The Prince of Demons himself."

Despite the bared steel, Colbey did not draw his chaos sword.

To Ravn's mind, the truth became irrefutable. Memories of his confrontation out-of-time rushed back to the forefront of his thoughts, its reality certain. Absently, he rubbed the knot at his injured wrist. *My father is a demon. Colbey is chaos incarnate.* The ideas materialized from nowhere, yet disputing them never occurred to Ravn. He simply stared, stunned into immobility.

A foreign presence touched his mind suddenly, a gentle request for entry. Enraged beyond reason by the intrusion, Ravn found his hand on his sword. Then, the contact turned apologetic and angry at once. Pain stabbed his head as thoughts that had felt integrally his moments before peeled away, leaving the doubt and confusion that now seemed as right as his condemnation of the father he loved had moments earlier. He staggered to his feet, his chair crashing to the floor behind him.

Colbey's features twisted, eyes locked on Odin despite the threat at every side. He raised a hand toward the AllFather, as swift and cutting as a Renshai maneuver. The irregularity of the light intensified, shot through with a spectrum of color so divided and intense it defied Ravn's ability to define it.

Raw chaos, Ravn realized, even as Odin dodged aside, looking astounded for the first time in Ravn's experience. The gray god's hands wove furiously through the air, restructuring the format of the room: first the air, then the candelabra, then the table. Deities leaped aside as objects swirled, fragmented, and reformed, the wind of creation a frigid swirl that muted light to darkness and upended reason.

Then, as suddenly as it began, it ended. Odin stood in his place. The sixteen remaining candles, positioned in perfect groupings of four, whirled and flashed highlights from the gold. The table had vanished, a black circle hovering in its place. In the confusion, Colbey had slipped nearer the door, no longer directly threatened by the gods' weapons.

All eyes zipped to the ball of darkness. *A gate*, Ravn realized, and the explanation followed. Colbey had attacked Odin with chaos, and the AllFather had fashioned it into a brand-new world. *Creation*. Ravn's short lifetime, though all of it spent among gods, had not prepared him for this. All of the worlds had existed since long before his birth. *I've witnessed creation*. The awe that had originally assailed him in Odin's presence returned.

Colbey's steady voice broke the silence, effective for its deadly quiet. "He killed Honir."

Only then, Ravn realized the long-legged indecisive god had disappeared.

"And he will kill the rest—"

"He did it!" Odin roared over Colbey's warning. "He tried to destroy us all. His chaos—"

"Could have harmed only him!" Colbey shouted over the AllFather, the loss of composure uncharacteristic. "He sacrificed Honir to the creation process . . . but he didn't need to—"

Odin interrupted again. "Lies!"

"From the new Father of Lies!" Vali added, brandishing his sword.

Odin finished, "His chaos killed Honir. Just as it did Baldur." The reference to the murder of the most beloved of the gods filled nearly every eye with burning rage. "Get him."

Vali, Sif, and Modi lunged for Colbey, swords leading. Uncertain of his next action, Ravn started toward the conflict. His foot came down on the edge of his fallen chair. The wood flipped, slamming his shin. Agony shot through his leg, and he backpedaled for balance. Misjudging the chair's position, he brought his other foot down along a leg. Skin tore in a line across ankle and calf, dotting his breeks with scarlet. A door banged against its lintel. Ravn toppled to the floor, rolling to rescue his hip from a bruising. By the time he scrambled to his feet once more, Colbey had vanished, leaving only a jumble of words in his head: "Cowardice is always wrong, but it is acceptable to abandon a battle if it can only result in killing friends." A strange emphasis on the last word gave it the connotation of "fools."

Only my father would pause to teach in a situation like this.

Vali fumbled with the door Colbey had apparently slammed as he departed. "Get him."

"Stay," Odin commanded.

Vali's free hand balled, but he obeyed.

"He's long gone." Odin's voice dripped distaste. "Back to chaos world with the other demons."

Idunn moved from her corner, speaking her first words since the spell. "Wouldn't he need banishing?"

Vali snarled, "Did Loki need banishing? He's not really a demon, just an entity bound to the Staff of Chaos."

"Honir," Sigyn whispered, the first to go teary-eyed. "First Baldur, now Honir."

Vali still stood at the door, as if debating whether to violate Odin's request. "He's working to destroy us."

Ravn said nothing, needing time to process all the events. The battle had begun in his head, he felt certain. If Colbey had bound with chaos, if he no longer held loyalty toward family, why would he single out his son for such a thing?

Though Ravn had not spoken, he received an answer: *Because chaos can manipulate your loyalty to one no longer your father. Until you detach yourself from a love now misplaced, you remain vulnerable.* A wash of certainty accompanied the words, this time too weak to penetrate the depths of his doubts.

Deliberately, Ravn shoved the train of thought aside, his mind no longer safe from intrusion. For all he worried about his father, he worried for Odin's influence as much. Experience told him no one was solely right or wrong, good or bad. And Odin had much of evil in him.

Odin addressed the group. If, as Ravn believed, the AllFather was the one who had spoken to his thoughts, he gave no sign of it now. "Mourn your loss as per tradition. Then disperse to your homes. I will contact each of you about your part in dispatching this threat to our worlds. We defeated chaos once at the *Ragnarok*. Handled properly, we can do so again."

To Ravn's relief, not all of the deities let Odin's plan go unchallenged. Frey tugged at the sleeve of his own cloak and met Odin's single eye. "You will inform us of our roles? It seems wiser for the greatest minds in existence to work together on this problem."

Vidar chose to answer before Odin could. The soft, commanding voice soothed, taking its rightful place at the meeting. "Colbey reads, even manipulates, minds. Binding with the staff could only have made that power stronger."

Nods followed the point. Though not the explanation Frey sought, it made the answer clear enough. If they all knew the plan, Colbey shortly would also. Only Odin had the power to detect and dispel Colbey's mental probes, so he alone could have access to the entirety of the strategy.

Though it bothered Ravn to place his trust in what little Odin decided to reveal to him, he had no choice in the matter. None of the others seemed to harbor his doubts and concerns.

Odin strode for the door. Vali stepped aside, and the AllFather exited into the daylight, trailed by a mental warning: *You are the weak link, Ravn. I cannot allow your foolish, young doubts to destroy us all.*

Uncertain whether he had received a threat or a warning, Ravn forced his attention to Vidar and the beginning funeral service.

CHAPTER 9

A Hero's Welcome

When love and kindness fail, there's always violence.
—Colbey Calistinsson

HEALING bag dangling from a shoulder strap, Matrinka tapped on the door to Tae's room, warned to tread lightly by descriptions of his appearance and demeanor. When the adventurers had returned from the first leg of their mission, Tae had reportedly thundered from the room without a word to anyone. The servants stationed to watch for them had mentioned two black eyes and a swollen nose purple with clotted blood. The child who had replaced the healer Perlia had acted sullen and suspicious, but the others seemed in high spirits. Kevral and Ra-khir had headed off to wash before their requested audience with her and King Griff. After a brief exchange of hugs and hurried promises to meet later, Matrinka and Darris had separated. With Andvari, the bard had left to take the Pica shard to Captain and discuss the details with the elf and the sage. She looked forward to hearing them as well, once she assisted Tae and the uglier business with Ra-khir and Kevral had finished.

Matrinka hitched her kit higher onto her shoulder, then knocked on the panel again, this time rewarded by a loud, gruff answer.

"Who is it?"

"It's Matrinka, Tae."

Several moments passed in silence while the Eastern prince debated his options. "It's not locked."

Matrinka suspected that was the closest she would get to an invitation. Tripping the latch, she eased the door open.

Tae sat on his bed, knees tucked to his chest, still wearing the rumpled, bloodstained tunic and britches from the journey. Black hair fell in tangled, matted clumps to his shoulders. Between errant strands, partially healed scratches marred his cheeks, and the swarthy skin darkened in circles around his eyes. The bloated nose displayed every shade of purple, brown, and red. He did not look at her, though he had surely heard her enter. Ingrained wariness would not let otherwise be the case.

Matrinka closed the door with a quiet click, then walked to stand directly in front of Tae. She placed a hand over the hanging pouch of herbs, salves, and bandages.

Tae did not move.

Matrinka placed a hand on a shoulder as hard and tense as stone. The urge to question him burned strong, but her healing instincts nudged her toward matters less likely to fuel anger. "Let me see to those wounds."

"I don't think there's anything you can do," Tae mumbled. "El-brin-ith tried."

Is that what's bothering him? Matrinka studied the damage, doubting the thought as it arose. Tae had gotten hurt many times in his life, often without anyone to tend him. He knew such a wound would eventually heal, even without the assistance of healers. "Captain says neither El-brinith nor Chan'rék'ril have much healing ability." Actually, Captain had claimed they lacked the fine finesse of the best elfin healers, though they could perform the gross necessities in life-threatening situations. She doubted such specifics would interest Tae, however, especially now. She ran gentle fingers along his scratches. At least the elf's magic had initiated the healing process, making the wounds appear several days old. She had not done as thorough a job on Tae's nose, probably flustered when the eye changes occurred.

"Perfect," Tae said bitterly. "No healers at all."

"I know about Perlia." Matrinka set to work with a soothing balm that would take away the sting and ward against infection. She could do little for Tae's nose, but she believed Captain's or Tem'aree'ay's magic might prove more useful, if she could convince Tae to allow their ministrations. "The real Perlia showed up shortly after you left. I'm not sure why the girl impersonated her, but there's not much we can do about it now."

Tae muttered something that Matrinka felt certain she would feel better never deciphering. He added, more directly. "Anyone here had better guard their gold. If Rascal gets any, she's gone and the mission ruined."

"Tae!" Matrinka reprimanded. "That's not nice."

"It's true." Tae finally rolled his dark gaze to Matrinka. "You'd best make damn certain she doesn't leave the castle between tasks."

"Tae . . ." Matrinka started again.

"I'm not kidding."

Finished with the salve, Matrinka replaced it with a damp bandage. She started cleaning the dried blood from his nose with subtle pressure so as not to hurt him more than necessary. Now that she had him talking, the time seemed right. "What happened, Tae?"

"Had a run-in with a demon."

Matrinka's head jerked up. "Really?"

"No," Tae said. "Not really. At least not in the way you think I mean."

"So what do you mean?"

Tae sighed, barely wincing, hiding the pain. "You wouldn't understand."

The words were insult. "This is Matrinka you're talking to."

Tae closed his eyes, clearly fighting the need to pull away from her hands. "You wouldn't understand. Just leave it at that."

For the moment, Matrinka did. Wading up a bandage smeared with old blood, she sat on her haunches. "I can't do much more there, though Captain might. Any other injuries?"

Tae rolled up his sleeve to reveal a circular bruise, darker at the periphery. There, too, the skin lay broken in several places, ridged with clotted blood.

Matrinka studied it, recognizing it as a human bite. She turned Tae a measuring gaze. "What makes you so sure I wouldn't understand?" She rooted through the pack for the anti-infection salve and a fresh bandage.

Tae watched Matrinka's every movement. "It involves street mentality. Stubbornness. Stupidity. Frustration."

"Three out of four," Matrinka returned. "Give me a chance." She scrubbed at the injury.

Tae tensed, barely stopping himself from jerking free. "You wouldn't understand." His tone turned sullen. "You've never known disappointment."

Matrinka froze. Slowly, her gaze swept along Tae's arm, to his shoulder, then across his ruined face to his eyes. "Excuse me?"

Tae loosed a wordless noise of frustration. "I didn't mean that the way it sounded. You don't know what it's like to have nothing, to steal what you need, and to have to fight to keep what little you gain. You don't know what it's like to want something desperately and know you'll never have it."

"Don't I?" Matrinka caught a trickle of blood from a reopened wound with the bandage. Human bites notoriously became infected, and she would have to open and clean out each healing area. "Is that really what you think?"

"Well . . ." Tae started. "You were always a princess."

"So you think I got everything, and it was slathered in silver and accompanied by fanfares?"

Tae's silence spoke louder than an answer.

Matrinka stopped working to emphasize her point. "You know, Tae, for someone who worries that I can't understand his outlook, you sure don't notice mine."

Tae scrambled for diplomacy. "I'm sorry. I'm not trying to say there's anything wrong with being born royal. Hel, I'd have done it if I could have."

"I'm going to assume irritation has blunted your ability to think." Matrinka set back to work, ignoring the pain she caused Tae. "You've got a country to satisfy, knowing that doing or saying the wrong thing could spark a war that sees thousands killed. You've got a son whose childhood you can't enjoy because you spend every moment examining every action or utterance to make certain you're doing everything right— and you spend more time beating yourself up for making mistakes. You're trapped, forever tied to a woman you want but can't ever have. You're torn in ten million directions, and in the need to handle others, you've lost yourself." Matrinka stared fiercely. "Has your life really gotten that much simpler since you've become royalty?"

"Infinitely more complicated," Tae admitted, appearing clearly impressed with Matrinka's ability to read his situation.

"I wanted to be queen," Matrinka said softly, mind returning to the staff-test. Sometimes, late at night, she could still feel doubts hemming her and the condemnation of a god-mediated test that had deemed her unworthy.

"You *are* queen," Tae reminded.

"Not the way I wanted to be." Matrinka scrubbed at the bite. "I wanted to earn the title on my own merits, to feel comfortable knowing that my decisions, my very morality, would benefit Béarn and the world."

Tae's opposite hand drifted toward the bite, though he did not interfere with Matrinka's work. "You're still upset about the staff-test?"

"Tae, think about what happened to the others who failed it." Matrinka's thoughts went immediately to her cousin Xyxthris who had betrayed Béarn to the *svartalf*, was imprisoned, then hanged himself in the cell with his own twisted clothing. Other cousins had suicided, murdered one another, or became hopelessly dependent on mind-numbing medicines or alcohol. "Do you think I'm different?"

"Clearly," Tae said carefully, "you are."

"It didn't come without a struggle every bit as difficult and life-threatening as weathering winter nights in makeshift shelters." Matrinka cracked another scabbing hole. "And my own demons still haunt me late at night or whenever Griff leaves a decision to me."

Tae nodded.

Matrinka continued, "Look, I'm not belittling starvation, exposure, or getting raped and brutally murdered by predators on the street."

Tae looked at Matrinka as if he never expected her to know the details of a street orphan's life.

"I'm just saying that different lifestyles come with different troubles. Having gold doesn't make a person happy." Matrinka turned Tae a lopsided grin. "In fact, having a single gold piece could make a street thief ecstatic where a roomful might not budge the mood of a lonely king." Bittersweet memories indulged the smile. "I would trade my title and all my wealth to have married Darris."

Tae whirled toward Matrinka, arm jerking from her grip and splashing blood on the coverlet. "I've never understood why you didn't."

That being her early point, Matrinka raised her brows. Tae's origin would never allow him to comprehend the pain she would have caused her grandfather and family by renouncing her blood ties. That they had died did not matter; she could not dishonor the memory of those she loved, not even for one she loved as much. And the populace had made their wishes as well. To rescue the diminishing bloodline, the only one that spawned the innocent neutral kings that the high position required, they had insisted upon her marriage to Griff. It went against both of their wishes, yet they could have done nothing else. *The lowest born will never know how little joy, how little freedom that wealth and status confer. How many of them would choose to buy such imprisonment if they truly understood the details.* "Tae, let's agree that neither of us will ever wholly understand the other, but that all people share the same emotions. And assist one another so far as that weakness allows."

The angry lines disappeared from around Tae's mouth, though he did not smile. "All right," he agreed.

"The problem?" Matrinka reminded.

"It's that little street thief. Rascal."

Matrinka could have guessed that easily enough. "She's the one who caused this?" She indicated the bite and the facial injuries with a single gesture.

"Yeah." Tae lowered his head but not before Matrinka thought she detected a hint of smile.

Matrinka worked on another break in his skin. "I had thought you beyond worrying about getting the best of every battle."

"I got hammered by a little girl."

"Tae," Matrinka let a tinge of reproach slip into her tone. "You won that battle by staying cool and resisting the urge to hurt her as badly as she hurt you. Did you get what you wanted?"

"Needed," Tae corrected. "And it remains to be seen."

Matrinka put the pieces together easily. "So, you're upset because you—" Wild scratching at the door interrupted Matrinka's question. "Mior." She glanced at Tae. "Do you mind if I let her in?"

Tae waved toward the door, indicating Matrinka should do as she requested. He and the cat had always managed a close relationship, though they could not communicate.

Matrinka opened the door, and the calico squeezed through the smallest crack. Mior complained even as she rubbed across Matrinka's calves. *Why did you leave me?*

I didn't leave you, Matrinka reminded fruitlessly. *You wanted to nap with Marisole. Remember?*

You said you were going to do boring kingdom stuff. You didn't mention Tae.

I didn't realize he needed me then.

You should have come got me.

Knowing Mior would never drop the matter, and Tae waited while they conversed, Matrinka made no reply. Mior would insist on the last word anyway. The queen moved back into position to work on Tae's arm. She searched for the thread of the conversation, only to get struck with sudden worry. *Who's with Marisole?*

Her papa. They're having a great time. Same mental level.

Mior!

Dropping the sidetrack, Mior returned to the original matter, *Tae needs me, too. You know, petting cats has healing properties.*

Uh-huh.

"You're right," Tae said. "I'm not really upset about the fight. It's Rascal."

It does, Mior insisted. *It makes people feel better. And that makes them heal better.*

It makes them feel better? Or you?

What's wrong with mutual benefit? Mior hopped into Tae's lap.

Tae ran his good hand over the colorful patches of fur. "Are you listening to me? Or to Mior?"

"Both," Matrinka admitted, giving the cat a warning glare. "But Mior is going to shut up now so I can give you my full attention."

Only for Tae, Mior returned, implying not only that she would not do so in other situations, but also that she did not quiet for her mistress.

"If not the . . . cosmetic changes . . . what about Rascal is troubling you?" Matrinka seized the conversation to prove she had not let the animal fully distract her.

"I can't get through to her." Tae threw up his free hand. "She's on the fast track to misery and death, and nothing of reason works."

"Well," Matrinka said, emphasizing each word. "I couldn't possibly understand what it feels like to try to get through to a stubborn, irritating street thief too stupid to realize where his actions and attitude are leading him."

"Touché." Tae chuckled. "So give me some advice. How did you get through to me?"

Matrinka considered. "Time, Tae. And seizing teaching opportunities when they arose." Finished, she tied a bandage to the wound and released his arm. "Mostly, I didn't have to do anything. Your underlying goodness shone through all the bluster the streets taught you. You still hide behind it sometimes, but less and less often."

Tae started to speak, then stopped. He opened his mouth again, then closed it. A long hush followed, during which Mior's loud purring filled the air and the cat sent a nonverbal message glorifying her own patience. Finally, Tae spoke, displaying the disillusioned weakness he had repressed until that moment. "But what if the other person doesn't have any underlying goodness?" He cringed, lids gliding over his dark eyes.

"What's wrong?" Matrinka ignored the chance to preach. She had come to help Tae, not to force her opinions upon him.

"Dumb question. You're just going to say there's good in everyone."

Matrinka stepped back, placing her hands on her hips. "Give me some credit."

You were *going to say that,* Mior accused.

Mior had a point Matrinka could not deny, so she ignored the cat. The queen's healing studies had progressed to the workings of the mind, probably Mior's basis for the 'mental levels' crack; and her tutor had discussed a situation just that morning that had definite applications to this situation.

"I'm sorry," Tae examined the bandage on his arm. "I shouldn't assume."

Matrinka forced a smile. "Mior pointed out with her usual eloquence that I might have done exactly as you accused. There is good in everyone, though it's buried deeper in some."

"Mmmm."

"Tae?"

He looked at her.

"Why is this so important to you?"

Tae shook his head. "I don't know," he said, shaking his head again. "I really don't."

Matrinka believed she did. Tae saw the girl as his project, perhaps his way to pay the others back for teaching him to trust and care. His every success and failure had become bound to his self-worth.

"Maybe if *you* spent some time with her," Tae said with uncharacteristic meekness. "You're good at this. You could get through to her."

Now, Matrinka shook her head. "The stress of the mission, the life-and-death situations you might face, these provide the background for teaching. I would have no luck at all trying to train her here, even if Captain's magic could spare her."

Besides, Mior added, *she's his project, not yours.*

Mior's insight never ceased to amaze Matrinka. *I just hope there's a chance.*

Meaning? Mior's tail twitched wildly.

Tutor says there's evidence that children whose basic needs aren't met by someone in the first few years of life never learn to trust. They can't ever fathom how others feel, so they hurt people without guilt.

Tae sucked in a huge mouthful of air, releasing it slowly. "Then I'll have to do the best I can."

Tell him what you told me.

Matrinka suffered her own twinge of guilt. *No.*

Mior circled agitatedly. *He needs to know he has no chance for success.*

There's always a chance. We don't know Rascal's early history. If I give Tae a reason to give up on her, he will. And no one else can or will help her.

Who's more important, Tae or a stranger?

Matrinka saw the point, knew a disastrous finish could devastate Tae, yet the thought of the girl losing her only opportunity for salvation ached, the stronger burden. If Tae triumphed, it would work wonders on his spirit. *Tae, you don't know how much I wish I* could *take this obligation onto myself.* Keeping the thought to herself, she told Mior, *We learn as much from our failures as our successes.* Hard thoughts of her own struggle against the aftereffects of the staff-test surfaced, and she cast them aside. She addressed her final words to Tae. "The best you can, indeed." She turned him a solemn and affirming expression. "No one could do more."

Dismissing the guards, the king and queen of Béarn took audience with Kevral and Ra-khir in only the presences of Mior and the sage's recording servant. It would have pleased Matrinka more to send the page away as well, but Béarnian law commanded his attendance as well as forbade him speaking the details to anyone but his master. Through history, no page had ever violated that sacred trust.

The moment the last inner guardsmen filed from the court and the door swung shut, Griff clambered from his throne to sit on the edge of the dais. He gestured for the others to join him.

Matrinka took a seat beside him, Mior curling up on the soft cushion of the queen's chair. The queen pitied the poor servant who had to brush cat hairs from the red velvet.

Dressed in her customary linens and leathers, a sword at each hip, Kevral approached with the wariness that defined Renshai. She barely curtsied to the king and not at all to the queen, who appreciated the lack of formality. Ra-khir, in contrast, wore the entire knight uniform: the blue-and-gold Béarnian tabard with its rearing bear over a wrinkle-free, black silk shirt. The wide belt held a broad sword at the properly raked angle. As he walked toward the dais, he swept the hat from his head, sending its feather bobbing in a gentle dance and spilling groomed and perfumed red locks.

Ra-khir bowed fully to each of them in turn, a graceful flourish accompanying every movement. He ended in a kneeling position, head low and hat over his heart.

Certain nothing else would suffice, Griff reverted to protocol. "Rise, Sir Ra-khir, and at ease. This is important, but informal."

Ra-khir stood, revealing the breathtaking features that kept him the focus of female attention even long after his marriage. Women throughout Béarn studied him surreptitiously, but Matrinka had witnessed only an occasional wary flirtation since the wedding. Most feared Kevral too much to incur her wrath.

You're staring. Mior teased.

Matrinka jerked her eyes away, suddenly self-conscious. *He's just a friend,* she reminded. *And another friend's husband, at that.*

My point exactly.

Last I checked, looking's not a crime.

For once, Mior dropped the point first, the strategy more effective. Matrinka's own guilt would taunt her more than the cat ever could.

"Please sit," Griff said, indicating a pair of chairs in front of the dais. Matrinka knew he would have preferred that the two sit beside them, but that would have made conversation difficult.

Kevral and Ra-khir took their places. Matrinka found the location of her own eyes the sudden focus of her full attention. *Damn it, Mior. Why'd you have to do that?* She ran her gaze around the room, attending to the familiar high ceiling, the rearing bear banner behind the thrones, and the golden carpet scrolling down the aisle between rows of chairs.

Griff cleared his throat, then went right to the point. Directness would work better than vague tedium, at least for Kevral. "While you were gone, we received a message from King Cymion in Pudar."

Kevral stiffened visibly, flicking her gaze to Ra-khir. The knight showed nothing, keeping his regard directly on his king.

"He requested that we remove Kevral from the mission, stating that she is carrying the heir to Pudar's throne."

Kevral jumped to her feet. "No!" she said emphatically.

The tension in the room rose tangibly. Matrinka swallowed, eyes skipping from Kevral to Ra-khir and back, unable to meet anyone's gaze.

In his usual simplistic manner, Griff stayed on the topic. "Are you pregnant, Kevral?"

Kevral's hands went defensively to her abdomen, but she did not answer.

Ra-khir did so for her. "Yes, Sire. She is."

One thick, dark eyebrow rose. "And is the father Pudar's prince?" Griff asked in an effective monotone, without judgment. Kevral's indiscretions did not concern him, only the politics that accompanied them.

"No!" Kevral's right hand slid to a sword hilt.

If the guards had remained, Matrinka knew that they would have positioned themselves between her and their king, their hands twitchy on their own weapons. The acceleration that might have caused made her glad Griff had dismissed them. No matter the situation, Kevral would not harm them.

Griff's other eyebrow joined the first, and both rose another increment. "So, the prince of Pudar could not have sired the infant?"

"He didn't," Kevral said sullenly.

Ra-khir cleared his throat. "It is not impossible, Your Majesty."

Kevral whirled on her husband. "I'm telling them."

"No." Though stated softly and with manners, the word held an edge of threat. Ra-khir gave his wife a hard look that spoke volumes.

"They need to know," Kevral insisted, surprisingly choosing words over action.

"We swore a vow, Kevral." Ra-khir reached for her, his motion loving. "Without loyalty to his word, a man cannot earn even his own respect."

Kevral allowed Ra-khir to hold her, burying her face in his shoulder.

Matrinka had never before seen Kevral vulnerable. Her heart felt like a warm puddle in her chest, and she wished she could do something, anything, to help.

You're staring again.

I can't help it. All I can think of is strangers taking Marisole. Matrinka gritted her teeth against the agony the thought inspired. Tears pooled in her eyes. *Poor Kevral.*

Poor Ra-khir, Mior added. *Don't think Griff would be any less upset to see Marisole taken.*

Griff watched the two for several moments before looking to his queen for assistance.

Matrinka shrugged, helpless to add more.

Griff turned back to the couple on the floor. "What's going on, Ra-khir? Without details, I can't help you."

"Your Majesty." Ra-khir released Kevral to perform another bow. His hat remained in his hand, partially crushed. "If I could tell you, I would. But, Majesty, we're bound to secrecy."

No longer held, Kevral turned, pounding a fist on her chair with such ferocity she sent it skittering toward the others, feet scraping the floor.

Griff sighed. "I understand, and I won't command you to violate your oath."

Matrinka appreciated the king's leniency nearly as much as Ra-khir. Torn between a personal promise and his king's command, he would battle his conscience for eternity. In the end, loyalty to the oath would have to take precedence, and Griff would be forced to imprison a beloved and faithful companion.

". . . but," Griff continued, "I have to act on the information I have. If there's any chance that baby carries the royal blood of Pudar's line, I have to order its surrender to King Cymion."

"It doesn't," Kevral growled. "I know it doesn't. Colbey said—"

Ra-khir caught Kevral's arm, earning a glare.

"Is it possible, Ra-khir?" Griff asked.

Ra-khir had already answered the question once. He would not lie. "It *is* possible, Your Majesty." He turned to Kevral. "I'm sorry."

"Colbey says it's not." Kevral fairly hissed. Rage burned in her blue eyes, and Matrinka knew her well enough to tell she perched on the edge of violence.

"Darling." Ra-khir managed the pet name without sounding patronizing. "Colbey's the greatest swordsman in existence, but he's not all knowing. Just because he chooses to believe otherwise doesn't make it truth." His timbre managed to make the gentle point that the last applied to Kevral as well.

A blur of silver cut the air, mangled the chair, and returned to Kevral's sheath so swiftly that Matrinka never had the chance to feel menaced. Hunks of wood sailed across the audience chamber, clattering and skidding across the tile.

A dense silence followed.

For once unable to dispel a problem with violence, Kevral attacked Ra-khir with words. "You smug, rigid bastard! Just because it isn't yours doesn't mean you can destroy my baby's life!"

Matrinka winced.

She didn't mean that.

No, Matrinka agreed. *Ra-khir gets the honor of suffering anger she can't vent on King Cymion or Griff.*

Clearly stunned, Ra-khir swallowed hard. "Kevral, we'll discuss this later." He bowed apologetically. "Forgive the outburst, please, Your Majesty. She's under a lot of stress."

"Understandably," Griff gave each of them a nod. Having already explained his obligation to the matter, he returned to the other detail of

Cymion's request. "Captain said he might manage to key his spell down to seven of the original eight, though not without the risk of losing it altogether."

Matrinka simplified, "We might be able to take Kevral out, but we couldn't replace her."

Every eye roved to the seething Renshai. Unless Griff forced the issue, which he would not, only she could make that decision.

"I'm not pulling out," Kevral said categorically, adding almost too late, "Sire." Her knuckles blanched, fingers screwed to fists. "If it's what that fool in king's guise wants, I'll do the opposite every time."

Ra-khir softened the reason. "Your Majesty, we can't risk the mission."

Griff studied his silk shoes, and Matrinka tensed in anticipation. "Sir Ra-khir, in this instance, we can. The heir to a throne actually does take precedence over the fertility of the rest of the world. If I had no heirs, or the Eastlands, or the North, we could argue otherwise."

Kevral broke into agitated pacing. "I'd plunge a knife through my womb before I'd let that pompous dullard decide my life."

She'd do it, too. Mior sat up on the cushion.

"Kevral," Ra-khir hissed. "Control." He addressed the king next. "Sire, we need Kevral's swordarm. And we need to save the option of keying to seven in case Rascal runs or, gods will it, someone dies."

Matrinka looked to her husband. Though he had not taken the staff-test, the world still believed him the ultimate creature of justice. If anyone could find the right answer, he could.

"I'll apologize to King Cymion for placing his heir at risk. I'll inform him that removing Kevral from the mission would doom it to failure and promise that she will use appropriate caution to see that the baby survives." He leaned forward. "That means no plunging of knives. Agreed?"

Kevral gave a sullen nod. Then, at Ra-khir's pleading glare added, "Agreed, Your Majesty."

"Dismissed." King Griff said.

Ra-khir and Kevral turned, heading up the golden carpet. They would have a lot to discuss that night.

It's not over. Mior raised a hind leg, cleaning it with delicate strokes of her tongue.

Not, Matrinka answered, *by a long shot.*

Griff flopped his head to his hands.

In the royal suite, Darris sat with his back pressed to the wall, Marisole balanced against his drawn-up knees. For the moment, innocent joy usurped all other emotion. He found his gaze singularly locked on the infant, incapable of distraction. Softened by baby roundness, the coarse, Béarnian features seemed a living perfection that even his oversized nose could not ruin. Brown eyes with barely a hint of residual blue examined him with the same intensity as he did her. Wholly captivated, the bard smiled.

The baby's tiny lips bowed upward in response, and Darris' smile muted into an all-encompassing and silly grin. He laughed, stroking the fine wisps of dark hair. *I love you, little princess.* For now, his devotion to the fragile life in his hands distracted him from the driving need to accompany and guard the king. Safe in Kevral's and Ra-khir's presence, Griff had little use for his bodyguard, and Darris knew worry for his charge played no part in his desire. Bard curiosity alone goaded him to take part in that meeting. The idea that his friends shared a secret he could not distressed him beyond all reason.

As the familiar yearning prickled through Darris' chest, his thoughts slipped for the millionth time to Jahiran. The idea of sharing his ancestor's fate, the raving loneliness and madness, was repulsive; yet two details clung resolutely. *The knowledge of the universe.* Darris shook his head in awe, the thought finally tearing his attention from the infant he had sired. *All of it.* The same bard-driven wonder that caused him so much pain allowed him to revel in the understanding, forever riveted and longing. That same knowledge, without the obsessive need to seek it or the accompanying eternal life, could finally free his mind of the agonizing quest that had haunted his line since Jahiran's original mistake. Darris could not help considering that his ancestor should not have abandoned his wish, simply phrased it more clearly.

Marisole's face screwed into wrinkles, and her mouth opened to emit a deep noise, a prelude to crying.

"What's wrong, pretty girl?" Darris gathered the baby into his arms, and she snuggled against his chest without another sound. For an instant, Darris felt trapped in a cycle far beyond human control. Grandparents generations removed had passed Jahiran's curse to their firstborn sons and daughters for centuries. *Beyond human control.* Darris shook his head at the thought. Surely, any of his ancestors could have put an end to the bardic curse simply by choosing a life of celibacy. For the first time, he wondered why not one of them had considered doing so. Clutching Marisole tighter, he dared not imagine the world without her, the consummate testament to love defined. And believed he understood.

The second detail haunted Darris next. Jahiran claimed Odin had lifted part of the curse from the bard's line, that Darris suffered it only because he chose to do so. *He said I can speak openly, without fear of gods' reprisal.* The freedom those words inspired held him in quiet awe, wings that could carry him to a once-forbidden world others took for granted. He hugged Marisole. She would benefit at least as much if he proved the original bard right, but the cost might prove too high. If Jahiran was wrong, if Darris incurred the wrath of gods, he might place not just himself but his companions, his blood-daughter, and the city of Béarn at stake. Even if they chose to punish him alone, or if he plunged into the same madness as Jahiran, it would leave Marisole without a kindred soul to guide her through the realities of the curse, to teach her to embrace rather than despair over her affliction.

Marisole grumbled again, this time followed by a steady rush of crying.

Darris cradled the baby in his arms, rocking gently, beginning the soft lullaby sung by loving parents to all Béarnian children. Its simplicity required little attention from Béarn's bard, unable to fully distract him from the worry racing through his mind. *A baby. The next bard.* Darris had never in his life felt so overwhelmed and incompetent. Tears burned his eyes, and he realized he desperately missed his mother. *What do I do? How do I do it? Why couldn't you be here to help me?* His agitation grew as Marisole's faded. Her cries stopped, and her eyes drifted slowly closed.

Once again, Darris studied Griff's daughter. She needed more than just a father. Perhaps some day he would test Jahiran's claim but not until he had guided the princess through the frightening maze of a childhood damned by firstborn bardic blood. One day, when she no longer needed him, he would teach without song and, perhaps, win his successors their freedom. Marisole might not benefit from his sacrifice, but her eldest child and subsequent generations might.

As the baby glided into sleep, Darris found his thoughts wholly on his mother.

CHAPTER 10

The Collector

Renshai place their trust in circumstances, not plans.
—Colbey Calistinsson

ASSISTED by elfin magic, Tae's injuries fully healed by the time the chosen eight gathered to seek the second Pica shard. With renewed enthusiasm, he set to the task of overseeing Rascal, preparing for situations that would afford him the opportunity to teach. The Pudarian did not make it easy for him, avoiding conversation, even direct questions; when she did respond, she did so in surly monosyllables meant to incite. Distracting himself from these small failures became tenfold more difficult because Kevral and Ra-khir clung to one another in a way that only making up after a cruel fight could explain. The intensity of their concentration on one another made Tae marvel that Ra-khir had not lost a major body part prior to reconciliation. *Or maybe it's just not one I can see.* Tae entertained himself with that thought for several moments.

Once again, elves filled the strategy room, remaining near the walls to allow the voyagers ample space in the center. Captain stood upon a table where all of the participants could see his every gesture. Servants collected Saviar and Subikahn from Ra-khir and Kevral, and Matrinka held up Marisole so that Darris could get one last glimpse. Pain tingled through Tae's chest, and he watched the servants' disappearing backs through stinging eyes. Though he had spent the last several days with his son, he already missed Subikahn. He worried for the amount of time he might lose should it pass differently on other worlds. He had asked Captain about that possibility and received only a vague and barely sensible answer. Either the elf did not know, or he preferred that Tae did not.

Ra-khir and Kevral also watched after the babies as they departed, her right hand enclosed in his enormous left. Tae doubted they had chosen the position accidentally; Ra-khir would want to keep his dominant hand free for combat while Kevral, like all Renshai, favored neither.

Darris rubbed at bloodshot eyes. He had spent most of his free time poring over books in the library and the sage's tower when Griff could obtain consent. The king's protectiveness of Darris' abstraction, relieving the bard from his entertainment, as well as his guarding, responsibilities suggested that Darris' pursuit held a personal interest for the king. Even Griff would not deliberately tether himself on a whim to someone as irritating as Rantire.

Chan'rék'ril and El-brinith stood quietly in the center of the throng, likely communicating their "good-byes" in *khohlar*. Andvari kept a hand near the haft of his ax, and Rascal crouched in the pose of feigned disinterest that street gangs had perfected. He knew she would face any threat with equally-contrived bravado or, if possible, a hasty exit. Only then, Tae realized his demeanor mimicked Rascal's closely, though he sought anonymity rather than the appearance of control.

Ready? Captain sent.

Ready, Chan'rék'ril and El-brinith returned simultaneously. Rakhir, Darris, and Kevral nodded without cadence. Andvari lowered his head once. Tae and Rascal gave back nothing, another affectation that Tae doubted he would ever lose. Matrinka had pegged him right when she said he still hid behind street-learned defenses, but many of those served him well, both now and then.

Too late, Tae remembered the vision-shattering flash that accompanied jumping worlds. Light stabbed his eyes, raw agony. He slammed his lids closed with a curse at his own stupidity. Colors striped his retinas, and he blinked repeatedly, uncontrollably. Gradually, his sight cleared to reveal every one of his companions staggering. They had all forgotten, too. Beyond them, rare trees, each a different type, shaded patches of grassland holding mounds of desks, weapons, jewels, cloth, foodstuffs, artwork, and every other thing Tae could conceive of. A cow and a chicken milled through the piles, and a cage holding a large, pacing creature stood at the farthest edge of Tae's vision.

"Wow." Darris expressed the stunned thought on every mind.

Overwhelmed, Tae found himself focusing on the expression. *An oddly short word to represent the concept of infinite wonder.* His eyes flitted between objects, incapable of settling. He found simple beds and a wardrobe of intricate design. Toys lay carelessly heaped upon delicate sculptures. Capes, blankets, and tunics of myriad designs fluttered over devices unlike anything Tae had ever seen. Flags of every obscure city flapped in an intermittent breeze, and he could not identify the origins of several. Writing implements, furniture, and iceboxes dotted every tiny portion of ground, grass, dirt, and rocks jutting through the gaps. Quills and waterclocks, plates and polearms, curtains and horseshoes, jewelry and parchments spread across the plane, stretching to each horizon. It seemed only logical that a shard of the Pica existed amidst such plenty, but he dreaded the need to dig through even a single stack to find it.

Ra-khir made an expansive gesture toward the elves. "I believe it's in your hands, El-brinith, if you don't mind."

"Not at all." The elf began delicately clearing away a site large enough to sit. Chan'rék'ril joined her, his long, narrow hands gliding like scoops through the heap.

Rascal said nothing, but her eyes measured every item. Tae sighed, watching her closely, worried as much for the possible consequences of stealing from a magical place as that she might find something of sufficient worth to drive her to break their alliance.

While Ra-khir and Darris assisted the elves, Andvari approached Kevral once again. Though his eyes remained on Rascal, Tae tuned an ear toward the Northman. He would surely embarrass himself again; Kevral would likely see to it.

Keeping his hands well away from his belt and the ax, Andvari trained his blue eyes on Kevral. He used a gentle voice, clearly pitched to compromise, "I'm truly sorry about how my ancestors treated yours. I apologize deeply for the wars that saw your people . . . well . . ."

"Dead," Kevral supplied bluntly.

"Well . . . yes." Andvari's cheeks developed the flush that Kevral always inspired in him, a flaming red compared with his usual sallow coloring.

"Is that what your history teaches?" Kevral attacked like an enraged mother bear. "That the Renshai were nearly obliterated in a war?"

As Rascal settled into a quiet crouch, hands unmoving in her lap, Tae turned his full attention to the conversation. He kept Rascal always between himself and them.

Andvari blinked. "Well . . . I mean . . ."

Kevral did not wait for an answer. "A war is when one group announces its intentions of violence against the other. They battle fairly, sword to sword, and the most capable side wins."

Andvari fell silent, blue eyes flitting in all directions.

"Sneaking to an island in the middle of the night, cutting down sleeping men, women, and children, and mutilating them in an attempt to block their souls from Valhalla is not a war." Kevral's expression turned predatory, and Tae sensed real anger. Andvari had raised a bitterness probably buried somewhere in every Renshai's psyche. "It's a coward's slaughter."

A hint of indignation entered Andvari's tone as well. "I said I was sorry."

"Sorry?" Kevral turned him a withering look. "Oh, all right. Sorry. That'll make up for hundreds of years of inbreeding just to maintain some of the original Renshai blood." She did not mention her own deliberate "contamination" of the line, Tae's only clue that at least some of her wrath was feigned.

Andvari retreated between the stacks and beyond Kevral's sight. Her gaze followed him only a few steps, then gradually turned in Tae's direction. He greeted her with raised brows and arms folded across his chest, judgmental and questioning.

"What?" Kevral groused.

Apparently believing the word aimed at her, Rascal stared back. The portion of her expression that Tae could see carried its usual dour grimace.

Good job putting this group together. Tae tipped his head reproachfully.

"What?" Kevral repeated.

Tae approached so that he would not have to include others in the conversation, but not far enough that he could not keep Rascal in his sight. "Ease off him, Kevral."

The familiar bright eyes that had come to define beauty burned with a far deeper anger than the one vented against Andvari. "I didn't start it. Either time. He keeps coming to me with those stupid . . . those stupid . . ." At a clear loss for words, she shook her head.

Tae had spent years keeping his speech simple, direct, and always tough, but the same adroitness that allowed him to pick up five languages in childhood also supplied him verbal eloquence when the mood struck. ". . . conciliatory gestures?"

"Yeah."

"Attempts to make peace." Tae gasped in a high-pitched lungful of air. "How *evil* of him."

Kevral hit him. With her hand, he appreciated. "Stop it, Tae."

"Well?" Tae put the onus back on Kevral, still eyeing Rascal from the corner of his vision.

"It's the way he phrases things." Kevral looked away. "I don't know. He infuriates me."

Tae sought the cause, though he believed it had more to do with King Cymion. *Why did I ever let Matrinka bind me to silence?* "Maybe it's because he's the first Northman you've ever met. Maybe you harbor more resentment than you knew."

"He's not the first." Kevral looked back at Tae. "I spent a year training a Northman in Pudar's guard force." She spat out the country name like poison.

"And you got along all right?"

"Not at first," Kevral admitted. "Tyrion hated Renshai and didn't hesitate to say so. Caused me more than a bit of trouble before I put him in his place."

Tae recognized the name. Tyrion had convinced Captain and his elves to travel to the North and create peace between tribes stirred by the *svartalf* to genocidal wars. Tae had learned from the elves' oldest that Tyrion's sincere apology for his actions against Kevral had convinced Captain to perform the favor and, ultimately, driven the resultant harmony between Northmen. Tyrion had also escorted Griff's parents to Béarn. Now, Tae considered Kevral's words, believing them truth. Her frame of mind caused some of their strife, but Andvari's style needed work as well. "Just don't let your hostility harm the mission."

"You know I won't." Kevral struggled with the insult inherent in the warning but suffered Tae's affront as she never would Andvari's.

Beyond the elves, a sudden flash splattered across an already bright sky. El-brinith sat in wonder, Chan'rék'ril crouched beside her. Darris rose. Ra-khir spun toward the new threat, hand on his sword hilt, though he did not draw. Kevral glided closer, working her way in front of the others. Andvari did likewise, the action so similar it might have amused Tae under other circumstances. He faded into still silence as Rascal scrambled behind a pile of fabric.

A moment later, a man appeared. Hair as blond as Kevral's fell to shoulders like boulders, and he towered over even Andvari and Ra-khir. Eyes gray as cliff stone flickered over them in turn. He wore a spiked whip mace and a hammer at his belt, but his beefy hands neither touched them nor hovered as if they might. Tae believed the stranger could cup Rascal's entire head in one palm.

"Greetings," Ra-khir said. "I am—"

The newcomer laughed sharply. "Little man, are you welcoming me to my own home?"

Momentarily stunned by a designation he had surely never heard applied to him in his entire life, Ra-khir hesitated. "I—I . . ." he finally stammered, ". . . didn't intend rudeness. It's just that you had only arrived, and welcoming in any case seemed appropriate."

"Where did you come from?" the giant asked bluntly.

The others let Ra-khir speak for them, as usual. He had the most training and experience in diplomacy. "Another world. The gods call it Midgard."

"Hmmm." The massive stranger scratched at his head. "You came by magic?"

"Yes."

Brusqueness again: "What do you want?"

Ra-khir politely kept his attention on the other's face, while Andvari and Kevral studied his hands. The elves remained in place, Darris attentive in front of them. "We're looking for a shard of a broken gemstone."

" 'Zat right?" The large man cocked his head to one side. "Any shard in particular? Or just your generic shard?"

Tae smiled. Kevral shifted from one foot to the other. Ra-khir mimicked none of her impatience. "It's a piece from a sapphire."

The giant's eyes narrowed, fine-lashed lids gliding downward. "Got one. From a great magical stone called the Pica."

Ra-khir glanced toward the others. "That's it!" he said excitedly. "That's what we're looking for."

"Why?" the stranger asked with obvious suspicion.

Tae winced. The huge man's tone suggested he had no intention of parting with it. *Kevral, don't let Ra-khir tell him. Kevral, stop him. Kevral . . .*

"We need it . . ."

Want it, Tae corrected in his head.

". . . to work some magic." Ra-khir added carefully, "Good magic that will help the entire world."

Tae hissed through his teeth as the price soared.

"*Your* world," the giant corrected.

"Well, yes." Ra-khir admitted. "But it certainly won't harm yours. We're willing to pay, of course."

"Payment," the massive man said, "is not the problem."

Tae froze.

"I'm a collector." The stranger amended. "*The* Collector. I own at least one of everything in existence on any world. If you want this shard, you'll have to trade it for another from the Pica."

If he had not dedicated himself to stillness, Tae would have smacked a hand over his face.

Ra-khir shook his head slightly. "No, sir. You don't understand. To work the magic, we need all of the shards. To trade one would defeat our very purpose for coming."

The Collector shrugged. "Sorry you bothered."

Kevral could hold her tongue no longer. "You're still missing the point."

Ra-khir raised a hand for temperance, but he might as well have tried to stop Tae's proverbial tornado.

"We're not leaving without that shard. We'd prefer to bargain for it." Kevral dropped her voice almost beyond hearing "Most of us would, anyway." Her tone returned to its previous strength. "But we'll kill you and take it if you leave us no choice."

Ra-khir did not attempt to soften the pronouncement. Even if it were not too late to manage it, Kevral had spoken the truth.

The Collector ran his gaze over the group again. "Too bad such a fine young group would have to die."

Kevral smiled, probably at the stranger's confidence, which she shared. "Even were there as many of you as us, even twice as many, you would all die, not us."

"Is that right?" The giant leaned toward Kevral.

Ra-khir intervened. "That's how important this is to us. Skill aside, our desperation would make us undefeatable."

"Skill," Kevral grumbled, "is enough."

The Collector rose to his full height again, taller even than Tae had first realized, towering over the biggest of them by more than a head. "That important, hmm?"

"That important," Ra-khir repeated, sincerity clear.

"Here's my deal, then," the Collector said. "It is the only one you'll get. First, you must locate the shard yourselves."

El-brinith nodded to indicate the success of her spell. They would likely have to dig through a stack or two, but they would surely find it.

"Second, in exchange, you must bring me something unique, the like of which I do not own." The Collector added swiftly, "And, unique as it must be, sketching or building something with your own hand will not do. I own paintings and sculptures a-plenty by artists of true talent."

"That is your bargain?" Ra-khir reiterated. "We locate the shard and exchange it for something you do not own?"

"I do not own one *like* it," the Collector corrected, then supplied an example. "I own leather tunics, though I don't own yours." He shook back the thin locks. "For your part, if you cannot meet those terms, you must leave without violence."

"I will need to discuss it with my companions." Ra-khir glanced at those nearest.

"Swiftly, then," the Collector said. "I have better things to do than wait around here. Know this: I will offer no other deal but one unique item for another. Also, I am not alone here."

Ra-khir gathered the others while Kevral stood woodenly, refusing to take her eyes from the Collector. Rascal remained aloof, and Tae did not bother to join the group either. The agreement seemed reasonable on the Collector's part, and no one could have one of everything. At worst, they could return to Midgard and snatch up the latest invention of the king's most creative.

The elves, Andvari, Darris, and Ra-khir huddled for a few moments. When they broke, Ra-khir looked uncomfortable. He gave Tae a cautious glance, clearly eliciting his opinion. Tae gave back a single, bright nod, accompanied by a wink to indicate he had the problem in hand. It surprised Tae that Darris, Ra-khir, or the elves had not surmised the same easy solution he had.

Ra-khir returned to confront the Collector. "We'll take your offer."

"Fine," the giant said.

"How will we let you know we're ready."

"Come back to this same spot," the Collector suggested. "I'll know by that." He started to turn, then pirouetted on his heel back to face them. An evil grin lit his massive features, granting them an alien cast. "By the way, your agreement to the terms sealed my spell. Don't try to transport off this world until the agreement's complete, or you'll fly into nil space." He lowered his head to Ra-khir's level, snakelike. "And no one can save you." With that, he whirled again, striding off across heaps of junk and treasures.

Ra-khir spoke through clenched teeth, green eyes flashing. "How dare he!"

Tae knew the mistrust, not the magic, bothered the honest Knight of Erythane. He left Ra-khir's consolation to Kevral, as concern for his own idea banished concern for Ra-khir in an instant. He consulted Chan'rék'-ril. "Is that possible?" He jerked a thumb after the disappearing figure.

"You mean, can he endanger a transport?"

"Yes."

"I don't know." Chan'rék'ril rubbed at his amber eyes as if they hurt him. "I've never heard of such a thing."

Having overheard, Darris added his piece, "I don't care to challenge it."

Probably his intention. Tae already knew the Collector possessed magical powers; he simply doubted one creature's ability to bind them to something so severe. However, they dared not risk the possibility that he spoke truth, given the unpredictability of magic and their own ignorance.

"Doesn't matter." Ra-khir's hand on Kevral's showed blanched knuckles, and he turned Tae a steady glower. "I wouldn't violate an agreement. And I wouldn't let you do so either."

Next time, I do the bargaining. Tae knew he could only blame not having done so this time on himself. He pointed out what Ra-khir clearly missed. "I wasn't thinking of cheating. I just thought we could go to the castle for something to trade."

"Impossible," El-brinith said quietly as she rose from her position. "Remember, if we leave here without the shard, we can't find the others. Captain's and Marrih's study of the last shard suggested we couldn't return here if we left."

Realization struck Ra-khir suddenly. His scrutiny of Tae intensified. "Was that your plan?"

Uh-oh. Tae changed the subject before anyone else made the connection that Ra-khir had agreed based on a hopeless idea that would have come to light had Tae joined the discussion process. "We'd better get the shard before the Collector deliberately moves it."

The understanding that El-brinith could only locate an object once per world sent the attention of everyone swinging to her. Though surely uncomfortable under the scrutiny, she hid her discomfort beneath elfin subtlety. "This way." She pointed opposite the way the Collector had taken. "Two hundred ninety lengths."

The eight lumbered in the indicated direction, hampered by stacks, mounds, and heaps of collected things. An occasional animal twined through the mess, glancing in their direction, then trotting onward. Nothing dangerous wandered toward them, though Tae did discover an enormous striped wild cat penned into a solid cage. As they walked, he wondered how the Collector kept track of his things. Would he knew whether or not he already had something they offered? Would he even tell the truth? What could they possibly have brought on their journey that could fulfill the description? Tae shook his head doubtfully. Likely, the Collector did not even know the location of the Pica shard, but his hurried suggestion had distracted Ra-khir from the same questions that plagued Tae now. *I made him believe I had a foolproof plan. Now it's up to me to find another.*

At length, they came to the appropriate place and searched systematically through the collection for a glimpse of the Pica shard. At first, they carefully displaced objects, the pursuit growing more desperate and less gentle with each passing moment. Kevral paused to examine a brooch in the shape of a horse, studded with diamonds of enough colors to separate mane, tail, ear leathers, and eyes from the sparkling, white body. Tae looked at it over her shoulder, admiring a craftsmanship few could come close to matching. The materials themselves were worth a small fortune, but surely no one would dismantle it. Its value as art far exceeded its components.

Tae glanced up in time to see Rascal's quick movement, a sure sign she tried to hide her own interest in the jewel. As Kevral reached to place it on another pile, Tae caught her hand. "Hold onto it."

Kevral's expression held warning. "Tae, that's very generous, but . . ." Her pale eyes bore into his nearly black ones. ". . . it's not yours to give me."

Tae dropped his hands onto a hide drum. "Not you, too, Kevral. Don't always assume I have the worst in mind."

Kevral's look hardened, if possible. "So giving it to me would be the *worst*."

Tae refused the trap. "You assumed I planned to take it when I really just wanted to protect it from . . ." More subtle than an elf, he tipped his head toward Rascal.

Given an explanation, Kevral grew more defensive. "Well, it's tough to resist. Even for me."

Tae hoped he had misinterpreted her intention, and he gave her a way out. "Are you saying you would understand if Rascal took it?"

"No, I'm saying I would understand if you—" Kevral broke off, the realization of her own cruel near-mistake striking her. "I mean . . ." She dropped the point. "I'll hold it."

"Don't become high and mighty with me just because you're married to a knight." Even as he spoke, Tae wished he had not. No matter how valid the point, it could only come across as petty bitterness. Without a further word, he moved to a different searching place. To his relief, Kevral did not follow. To continue the conversation, even just to clarify it, could only worsen the situation.

"Found it." Andvari's exclamation rescued Tae from further embarrassment. They all trotted over to look at a jagged chip of sapphire scarcely larger than the first joint of Tae's finger. It seemed amazing that a small, irregular fragment could represent so much. Yet, the future of all mankind rested upon this shard—and seven like it. He watched as the Northman handed the piece to Darris, who cradled it in his palm as if it might break.

Ra-khir approached Tae. "All right. Now, what's your idea?"

Trapped, Tae shook his head and told the truth. "I'm still working on it."

A look of horror stole over Ra-khir's face. "You mean I made a vow against a plan that doesn't exist?"

"I had one at the time. Problems arose."

"Tae, this isn't funny."

"For me either." Tae glanced at the others. Rascal seemed to have taken an interest in something in one of the stacks. "We'll just have to pool everything we have and find or build something unique."

Skepticism burned clearly in the knight's green eyes, but he did not challenge. No other course of action existed. He headed back to the others to relay the need while Tae sat pawing through his own pack. Clothing, toiletries, and foodstuffs spilled onto the ground, none remarkable on its own merits. The Collector had already made it clear he would not accept something simply because of belonging to, or becoming altered by, a certain individual made it singular. He doubted tying his clothing together in patterns and using it to carry other things or fashioning it into a different look or use would impress the giant. They might try resewing things to form one-legged pants for amputees or four-legged sweaters for cats, but Tae doubted even those would prove unique amid the Collector's things. *Three-legged tunic for amputee cats?* Tae shrugged. *Why not?* He walked over to join the others, hoping they had come up with something less desperate.

Ra-khir rose as Tae approached. "Any luck?"

"Just silly things."

"You didn't happen to bring any of those hand-made climbing tools with you . . . or anything . . . similar." Ra-khir cautiously probed for objects Tae might have used during his days on the streets, indicating that he would not condemn.

Tae shook his head. Even if he had brought his claws, it would not have mattered. He had seen similar ones amid the collection. Other than those, he used only his wits and practiced agility to obtain food and escape predators. "Nothing like that."

Darris reviewed their possessions aloud, "Clothes, bandages, food, waterskins, combs, brushes, weapons, mandolin, and herbs." He flapped closed his pack. "Nothing I haven't seen here."

Andvari confronted El-brinith. "Can you create something?"

"Create?" El-brinith repeated.

"From magic."

El-brinith's gemlike eyes glittered in the sunlight. "Not all the elves together can do that. Ordering chaos with law is magic. Transforming chaos *into* law is just impossible."

Chan'rék'ril explained further, "Even the Cardinal Wizards together only managed to instill chaos into items of law a few times. That's why those things are so valuable. It took all of them to magic the Pica Stone, but the four most powerful together could not make objects from chaos."

Tae recalled the creation stories. Odin himself had not manufactured creatures and places from disorder. Instead, he reportedly banished the primordial chaos to its plane and fashioned the world from law. "What about just summoning raw chaos?"

Darris looked about to explode from the need to address the question, though he would have to sing to do so.

Chan'rék'ril saved the bard. "All worlds have some free chaos; it's leaked from its plane almost since the moment Odin banished it. The Collector could not contain it, but neither could we. And if we summoned it, unbound chaos would have to come in demon form."

"I'll bet that's something he doesn't have," Kevral said.

Chan'rék'ril's head swiveled to the Renshai, eyes wide enough to reveal surprise. "Even if the two of us could summon one, we would not have the strength to contain it."

"Without a *jovinay arythanik*, we do not have the power to call a demon," El-brinith moved to stand directly beside her fellow elf. "Besides, we already know summoning would only bring Colbey."

"Certainly unique," Kevral grumbled.

Tae could not resist responding, "I don't think the Collector could control him any more than raw chaos."

Kevral responded to a clearly rhetorical statement, tossing the diamond brooch, then catching it without needing to follow its course with her gaze. "Keeping him isn't our problem, just delivering something unique."

Ra-khir cut through brainstorming that had gone far beyond worthy discussion. "Once El-brinith informed us she hadn't the power, everything after became moot. No matter how unusual, a human only works as an item of barter if the Collector does not already have one."

Darris spoke softly and hesitantly, treading the lines of teaching. "He did say he doesn't live on this world alone."

Tae turned his attention to Rascal once more, studying the set of her clothing for any sign that she had added items belonging to the Collector.

"So we can't surrender a human," Kevral guessed. "What about an unborn child? I'll bet he doesn't have one of those."

"Kevral," Ra-khir said gruffly.

The cause of Kevral's mood came out in an instant. "I'd rather leave it here in a jar of hard wine than turn it over to that bastard Cymion."

"Kevral." Ra-khir's warning became unmistakable. "That's a king you're talking about."

"Fine. That bastard *King* Cymion."

"Kevral!"

Tae made the necessary interruption. "Anyone sew?"

"A bit," almost everyone mumbled.

Believing El-brinith the most likely to prove capable, Tae turned to her. "I doubt the Collector has a three-legged tunic for crippled animals. Perhaps we could fashion one from our clothing."

"I could do that." El-brinith smiled, probably more for the humans than as a natural expression.

The faces around Tae registered everything from consideration to dense skepticism.

"I suppose it's worth a try," Darris said.

Rascal snorted. A hint of silver glinted from her palm so swiftly Tae would not have believed he saw it if not for his own anticipation and suspicion. He glided toward her.

El-brinith set to work while the others milled and talked, still seeking other answers to a difficult problem. Rascal deliberately avoided Tae, so he discarded the direct approach, allowing normal movement to bring him occasionally into her vicinity.

Light flared as El-brinith fashioned the last line of stitches, and the Collector stood again in front of them. Tae backpedaled, bringing himself even nearer to his target. If the Collector had come because of Rascal's impropriety, she would need all the protection he could supply. And probably more.

"So," the giant said, blond bangs stirring to his breaths. "Did you find it?"

"Yes," Darris replied, without bothering to display the shard.

"And my trade?"

Kevral glanced from the Collector toward where they had first arrived on his world. "I thought you wouldn't come until we went over there." She pointed to the place they had originally gathered.

The huge man shrugged. "You spent so much time here, I thought I'd see how you were getting along."

"Done," El-brinith said. She displayed the tunic.

The Collector looked only a moment, then laughed. Without another word, he strode across the plane, his long strides taking him to the edge of vision within a few steps. As Tae edged casually toward Rascal, the Collector returned, a sweater dangling from his grip. Dog hairs peppered the wool, and he opened it to reveal it had only three holes.

El-brinith lowered the garment.

The giant laughed again, the sound rumbling across the plane like thunder. "Don't bother with five legs, three for humans, or any other permutation. I have them all." His stony gaze pinned Darris. "Now, my shard, please."

"Wait!" Tae said, thoughts racing.

The giant rolled those hard eyes to the Easterner.

"Where did you get that sweater?"

"From Midgard." The lids squeezed into a squint. "Why?"

"You took it from a cold, three-legged dog?"

"No." The Collector crouched to Tae's level. "The dog eventually died, and the owner threw the sweater away."

Damn. Tae tried another tack. He placed a hand on a dusty desk. "And this? Where did you get it?"

"Midgard. I bought it. Why does any of this concern—?"

Tae walked to where Kevral stood, tossing and catching the brooch. He snatched it from midair. "This?"

"All right," the giant snarled. "I took it from a king's cache. What of it?"

Tae examined the pin as if for the first time. "This belongs to you, right?"

The Collector returned to his full height, deliberately towering. "Of course it's mine."

"Of course," Tae said. "You stole it, but it's in your possession now." He flicked his gaze upward. "Right?"

"Give it to me," the Collector demanded.

Tae complied, tossing the jewelry to the Collector. Light struck the diamonds, flashing in a dozen directions before it disappeared into a beefy hand.

"Because," Tae continued, "just because you stole it doesn't make it any less yours. Right?"

The Collector considered a long time.

"Because," Tae pressed, not daring to look at Ra-khir to see if the knight disapproved of his methods. If he violated Ra-khir's honor, it would invalidate everything he had done since the vow had been made by the knight. "If you don't own it, or anything else that came to you through theft . . ." He left the understanding hang, boxing the Collector into the answer he wanted.

The Collector's hand tightened around the brooch. "Of course it's mine." He struggled for damage control. "And nothing currently in my possession will qualify as yours, even if you steal it, you obnoxious little thief."

Tae raised his hands as much as a gesture of peace as to prove them empty. "I'm no thief." He glided back to Rascal, fanning a glimpse at a flawless pearl marbled with scarlet and an emerald-encrusted trinket in her pocket. "But I'd venture to guess you don't own a red pearl."

"Of course I do!"

"Of course you did." Tae slipped the items from Rascal's pocket, holding up the pearl to the light. "But by your own rules it ceased to be yours the moment she took it."

The Collector roared. "I said you couldn't steal . . ."

"You said," Tae countered, "that nothing currently in your possession could be stolen. First, that was not a provision of your initial bargain. Second, it was taken before—"

"Why you. . . !" The Collector lunged toward Tae.

Swords rasped from sheaths, and Andvari's ax rose. Tae skittered aside, and Ra-khir took over the negotiations. "We've met your conditions. If you violate your promise, you've left us the right to violence."

The Collector grasped his whip mace, mouth pursed into a white line and gaze tearing into each of the travelers in turn.

While the others prepared for battle, Darris readied his mandolin. A sweet song of peace peeled from voice and strings, carrying Tae's worry on a tender wave of sound. Darris sang of bargains kept, of desperate need, and of reveling in shrewdness, even when it works to one's own detriment. Mellow harmonies enwrapped Tae, erasing rage and despair, begging understanding. When at last the music ended, he felt refreshed, cleansed of the darkness of his tactic and prepared for diplomacy, not war.

The Collector's attention swung from Kevral to Darris. "That song. It will stay with me always." The corners of his mouth twitched grudgingly, almost into a smile. "Had you requested trading that, I would have been satisfied."

Tae winced, feeling as foolish as he had clever moments before. *Why didn't I think of that?*

The grimaces on Kevral's and Darris' faces suggested that they suffered equally from their own lapses in judgment.

As the effects of the song disappeared, the Collector glared again at Rascal. "Everything she has taken must be returned."

"Of course." Ra-khir would have it no other way. He gestured for Tae to see to Rascal.

Moments later, the party was on its way back to Béarn.

CHAPTER 11

Plans Awry

Details turn the tide of wars.

—*Colbey Calistinsson*

WINTER cold seeped through the cracks of Béarn Castle, and Ra-khir snuggled deep within the heavy blankets, attuned to the quiet music of Kevral's breaths. Worried for her comfort, he curled around her, contributing his warmth to hers. His right hand rested lightly against the dainty mound of her abdomen, his left pillowing her head. The fine gold tresses tickled his arm, and he reveled in the early morning stillness, her presence, the few days or weeks of peace before leaping to the next task. So far, they had managed to avoid battles; wits alone had bought the first two Pica shards. *Darris' wits,* he corrected himself. *And Tae's.* Although the knight wished he had played a greater role, he did not begrudge the two their successes. Darris had learned a lesson from an ancient ancestor that Ra-khir could never fully comprehend, and Tae needed anything to boost his confidence. In the heat of the moments following their return to Béarn, Ra-khir only hoped he had thanked his wary companion enough.

A light, brisk movement snapped against Ra-khir's palm. Kevral tensed, abruptly awake, though she remained in place, unspeaking.

Again, Ra-khir felt a slight, sharp kick. Excitement, joy, and horror rushed down on him at once. In that moment, the baby turned from concept to extraordinarily complicated reality. *My wife. My baby.* Before he could suppress it, selfish need seized him, supported by Béarn's law. *My baby.* The unborn drew him with the intensity that training to become a knight once did. He clutched Kevral tighter, possessively.

The Renshai shuddered against him.

Crying. Instantly, Ra-khir's touch went gentle. He stroked her hair and her side, desperate to whisper reassurances he dared not offer. Powerless to protect either of them, he struggled against impotent anger that could only turn to depression. In return for Kevral's freedom, they had promised the baby to Pudar. Breaking his oath could prove far worse than shattering his honor and his knighthood; it could spark a war. The baby would become the prince or princess of Pudar, the heir to a throne, a life anyone might envy. He or she would never know about their loss or, perhaps, even of their existence. Only he and Kevral would suffer, and the security of Béarn and of Pudar seemed worth that sacrifice.

Logically.

But, at the moment, with the one Ra-khir loved most in the world sobbing in his arms, his vow and his honor seemed distant concepts barely worthy of his attention. In the depths of his being, he knew he would never go against either; but he did not need to think about that now. For the moment, he made the silent consolation of his wife the sole focus of his universe.

Gradually, Kevral calmed and again found sleep, helped along by the fatigue that always accompanied pregnancy. Once certain of her comfort, Ra-khir clambered from the bed, ignoring the chill. The dread that clutched his own heart refused to leave, and he could not sleep again until he felt the living warmth of his child in his arms. Quietly, he crept toward the crib where Saviar slept, glad that Tae had the solace of Subikahn tonight as well. Though those two surely rested without the burdens and dilemmas that wrested sleep from Ra-khir, they could still draw comfort from one another.

Ra-khir hefted the baby, cradling him in his arms. The tiny lips smacked several times. The blue eyes fell sleepily open, met his gaze, then collapsed closed again. For longer than an hour, Ra-khir rocked his baby son, allowing joy and innocence to wash away his troubles. In the morning, the problem would return to haunt him. But, for now, he found sleep.

As the rising sun finally funneled through Tae Kahn's south- and west-facing windows, it found him stalking around his bed on hands and knees. Silently, he peeked around the end, confronted by a tiny face studying him from the opposite side. Subikahn's lips bowed into a delighted grin, and he bounced excitedly, the movement jostling hair as black as his father's own. Double time, he crawled to Tae, who ducked back beyond the edge too late. Wee fingers curled around his hand, and high-pitched, hissing laughter filled his ears with joy. Soon, he knew, giggles would turn to cries as hunger displaced even the thrill of play. Until Subikahn definitively needed his mother's breast, Tae would wring out the last few moments of fun with his son.

Eyes shining, smile turning to a grimace of determination, Subikahn tugged his way up Tae's sleeve to his head. A handful of his father's hair in each hand, Subikahn steadied himself to stand. Ignoring the pain, Tae clapped at his son's achievement, and the baby let out a loud squeal of self-delight. *Standing already.* Proud of his child's remarkably early development, Tae did not brood over the fact that he and Kevral had missed the first time. Larger, heavier Saviar had only just begun to manage sitting without assistance, and Matrinka had made it clear that babies develop at different rates—all normal. Tae only hoped that Subikahn's early physical development boded well for his agility. Bombarded by languages: common trading, Western, Eastern, Renshai, Northern and even, occasionally, Béarnian, he seemed unlikely to ever learn to talk.

A knock sounded on the door. Guessing a servant had come to collect Subikahn for his breakfast, Tae sighed. "Just a moment." He unwound pudgy fingers from his hair and caught the baby into his arms. Hoping for as much playtime as possible, he still wore his nightshirt.

Tae placed Subikahn on the floor, where the baby immediately pulled himself up using the coverlet, earning another round of applause. Quickly, Tae hauled britches and a tunic from his wardrobe. Doffing and donning in record time, he ignored his disheveled locks, worsened by Subikahn. As he hurried to the door, he remembered the minute wooden sword on the night stand. Thrusting the hilt into Subikahn's waiting hand, Tae continued his walk to the door. It seemed unlikely a Renshai would have come for him at this hour, but Kevral might; and the baby's training required that he keep hold of the weapon as much as possible. He could not fathom what the *torke* taught a six-month-old; but he had noticed that Subikahn tended to hit more often than he believed one so young should.

Finally, Tae opened the door to a middle-aged Béarnide wearing servant's livery and an apron. Liberally flecked with gray, her coarse black locks flowed to her shoulders, lacking the bronze bear threaded onto a thong that should be a part of her uniform. She curtsied at the sight of him.

Tae barely resisted the urge to turn to see who she honored in this manner. "Good morning," he sang out, happy times with his son making him giddy.

"Good morning, Sire," the woman said. "Her Majesty has requested your presence at the court this morning."

The court? Terror displaced joy momentarily. Unable to fully escape his past, Tae still feared summoning to a king's hall of justice, even when he knew he had done nothing wrong. His mind raised and discarded a number of possibilities, all bad, before he considered that Matrinka simply wanted him to witness an interesting case. Weile Kahn had sent Tae here to observe the details of rulership, especially the techniques that made the high Western kingdom so celebrated and successful. Dutifully, he had attended several sessions of the court, the tax negotiations, treaty refinements, and petty squabbles that defined a king's life so dreadfully boring he had pitied Griff and any ruler who chose to pattern his court the same. Occasionally, more significant or interesting matters confronted King Griff. Tae found himself at a loss to handle these, though the king's simple justice made the answers so clear moments later that Tae could not help believing he would have found the same ones in short time.

When Tae stood several moments without speaking, the servant shifted nervously. The apron suggested that she did not deliver messages often, her proper place in the kitchen.

Subikahn wailed, suddenly aware of his empty belly.

Relieved to find a new topic of conversation, the servant spoke again. "Oh, how sweet. May I hold him?"

Tae nodded, but the servant flounced past him before she could possibly have seen his answer. She gathered Subikahn into her arms, gently removing the sword from his hand and setting it on the bed. "Goodness, child. You shouldn't have that," she addressed the baby, though Tae guessed the admonishment was aimed at him. "You could hurt yourself . . . or someone else." She continued, her voice dropping into incomprehensible cooing lost beneath the baby's screams. She rocked Subikahn, the movement helping little. Finally, she looked at Tae. "I think he's hungry, Sire."

"You can be certain of it," Tae responded, combing his hair with his fingers, barely rearranging the tangles.

"May I feed him?"

Tae snatched up the little practice sword, too light and dull to damage anything. "He's just started on ground-up foods. And he'll need his mother's milk." He handed over the weapon. "And speaking of ground-up foods, you'd better make certain he's got this, or his Renshai mother may dice both of us." He passed over the sword.

"Oh," she said carefully. Then her eyes widened as she finally put together the details of who the child must be. "Oh! Yes, of course, Sire." She tucked the practice sword under her arm while Subikahn continued to shriek in her arms. "I'll see him to Lady Kevral." She made a gesture at the hallway. "You should get going as well, Sire."

Tae swept his arm to indicate the servant should precede him, which she did. He watched her waddle toward the kitchen for a moment before he turned in the opposite direction. He crept through the familiar corridors and trotted down stairways, suffused with the lingering warmth of a night and a morning with Subikahn. Gradually, adult concerns replaced his memories. His demeanor changed to the wary stiffness that came as much from concern as formality. His walk brought him to the king's court, on the lowest level of the west wing. There, a pair of guardsmen clutching polearms stepped aside to let him enter, without passing a word to him or between them.

Tae opened the rightmost of the double doors. Warm dampness flowed from the interior, mingling the scents of spices and cleaners with nervous perspiration. Rows of chairs flanked a carpet of woven gold wool, nearly all of them empty. The carpetway led to the dais where King Griff sat, surrounded by his inner court guards. Darris perched on a chair at his right hand, and the guard's captain, Seiryn, at his left. In front of him, the head gardener spoke too softly for Tae to hear, sharp hand gestures that had become his trademark punctuating the conversation at irregular intervals. The guards jerked every time one of those movements flew in the king's direction, though at least a length separated them.

The handful of spectators included Griff's parents and also Matrinka, who sat on the side the scattered nobles had chosen. Servants occupied chairs to the right of the carpetway, most kitchen staff. Cued by the aproned woman's loose hair, he noticed that the evening chef did not wear the silver badge Griff had awarded him for excellence, and another of the serving girls had replaced the bronze bear thong with a plain piece of string.

It felt odd to Tae that shifting into the leftward chairs seemed more natural now than the right, though surely he looked out-of-place. The simple tunic and breeks he had chosen for swift comfort rather than appearance jarred, especially the hole in his right knee. He glided into the seat beside Matrinka. "What's going on?" he whispered.

Matrinka kept her eyes on the proceedings as Mior rose and stepped from her lap to Tae's, purring. "Discussing the designs for the spring flower beds." She glanced at Tae suddenly, probably cued by the calico, and frowned with clear disapproval. "Tae, I had the maid bring a comb to your room yesterday."

"A comb?" Tae furrowed his brow, pretending to consider deeply. "Oh," he said as if with great wisdom. "I've been using it to strain tea."

"Very funny," the queen hissed at her guest. Mior batted at the strings of fabric still barely connecting the sides of his britches' knee. "And what are you doing crawling around?"

"Seems fairer than expecting Subikahn to walk."

Matrinka grunted. The hole had surely gotten worn long before the baby became mobile.

Tae returned to the point. "I'm not worried about the gardens. I meant why did you call me here?" Seeing the opportunity, he returned to the admonishments. "With a little more warning, I could have dressed properly." He ran his hands over Mior from neck to tail, forcing the cat to rise and press against his hands in ecstasy. Multicolored hairs flew, clinging to Matrinka's velvet dress.

Matrinka plucked fur from her bodice, her lap already hopelessly speckled. "You're a prince, remember? You should dress properly all the time."

"So I'm supposed to restrain tornadoes and hurricanes in my temple best?" Tae removed his hand from the cat to gesture at his exposed knee, and Mior toppled to his lap. "All my clothes would look like this. The ones not already stained with baby drool."

"I'm not wholly unfamiliar with baby drool," Matrinka reminded, smoothing her dress over hips only just returning to their normal contour. As the head gardener bowed and passed back up the golden carpet, Matrinka inclined her head toward the double doors. "I thought you should hear what's coming next."

Tae nodded. As realization struck, he frozen in mid-movement. "This has something to do with Rascal, doesn't it?"

Matrinka made a noncommittal gesture that all but confirmed his concern.

The door opened to release the gardener, and the supervisor of the kitchen staff, Walfron, took his place. Enormously wide, even for a Béarnide, Walfron's every step thundered through the courtroom. He walked with the wide-based gait forced by the size of his thighs and approached a king who stood taller but whom he significantly outweighed. Only Tae's previous discoveries allowed him to notice three brass studs missing from near the cuffs of Walfron's britches. The doors banged shut as the supervisor marched halfway down the carpetway. He finished his trek in silence, stopping in front of the dais and bowing as low as his gut allowed.

"Rise, Walfron," Griff said. "And state your complaint."

Walfron straightened, joints creaking. "It's about the Pudarian girl, Your Majesty. The one who calls herself Rascal."

Tae groaned.

Matrinka silenced him with a look emphasized by a casual tightening of Mior's claws through the fabric of his britches.

"What's the problem, Walfron?" Griff coaxed.

"She's stealing food, Your Majesty."

Tae's cheeks warmed, and the urge to confront Rascal became nearly impossible to suppress.

"Food." Griff blinked several times, brow creasing. "You are to be supplying her as much as she chooses to eat."

Walfron fidgeted, flesh jiggling and hands wringing as the king's judgment turned on him. "Well, yes, Sire. And we do, Sire. I mean, we invite her to all the meals. She doesn't come, Sire. Then she steals it."

Tae's fingers winched into fists. *When I get my hands on her, she'll wish I was Kevral.*

Griff studied the kitchen supervisor several moments in silence, then spoke in a gentle tone. "Walfron, she's a child of the streets. Crowds and nobles surely make her uncomfortable. It's not surprising she would choose to avoid the regular meals."

"B—but, Sire, Walfron stammered, occasionally glancing back the way he had come. "We've offered to feed her alone. She's stealing the food, Your Majesty."

"It's all right," the king soothed. "She's used to taking her food that way. It doesn't hurt anyone."

Wrong! Mior's claws gouging deeper into his leg warned Tae that he had started to rise. *So long as people keep justifying her bad behavior, it'll only worsen. And that'll hurt everyone.* For the first time in Tae's experience, Griff had made a clearly poor decision. He realized something else, the source of the missing hair ties, studs, and badge. Clearly, the staff had not yet pieced that bit of information to the rest, or Walfron would have mentioned it.

"From the kitchen, Your Majesty," Walfron said incredulously. "She's stealing from the kitchen."

"Walfron," Griff said.

The supervisor acknowledged the king with another bow.

Griff continued softly, "That's where the food is."

"Yes, Sire." Walfron mumbled, now looking openly toward the exit.

"Anything else?"

"No, Sire."

"Dismissed, then."

Walfron breathed a "Thank you, Sire," though speaking it aloud might have appeared disrespectful. He hurried back up the carpetway as fast as his thick legs could carry him without breaking into a run.

King Griff's gaze alighted on Tae, lingering there several moments before turning to the silk-swathed merchant advancing confidently down the aisle. Tae had never wished so fervently for the elves' ability at *khohlar.* Suppressed rage had him quaking.

Matrinka took Tae's arm. "You will handle this problem, won't you?"

Tae gritted his teeth, forcing a calm reply. "I—" he started, thoughts racing. "Damn it, Matrinka." He managed to convey strength in a whisper. "I'm not her father. Despite the rumors, I didn't start siring children at six, which is the oldest I could have been for her."

"Think of yourself as her brother," Matrinka gave back.

"I'd rather think of myself as the one who beat some sense into her."
Matrinka glared. "Tae, stop thinking like a Renshai. You know violence doesn't solve anything."

Centuries of history would prove you wrong. Tae dropped the argument. It would only dilute his point. "Matrinka, a miserable childhood doesn't entitle a person to a happy adulthood, especially at the expense of others. It's people dismissing her petty crimes that will eventually drive her to murder and mayhem. Now, the high king lets her off because she's a poor, orphaned, child. Soon, it'll be because she's a penniless mother with sick babies to feed—who, by the way, will be lucky to take third place to her own selfish cravings. Whether they survive their own battered childhoods will depend on how well they serve: first as objects of upper-class pity, then as thieves for their mother." Tae's argument succumbed to the logic of the sterility plague, but only in detail. His point was still valid. "Assuming our mission is successful, tossing out miserable brats in her own image could support her through her old age. Eventually, the bitter, frail old woman can say and do as she pleases."

Matrinka winced at the image. "Do you really believe that?"

"I've seen it a dozen times." Tae fought the images of ragged, dirty children used, as their parents had been, more familiar with thrashings than love. He recalled his father's stories of the men and women who joined his underground. "Heard about it a hundred more."

"Then, Tae, you'll have to handle the problem."

I have a child who needs my time and effort, who deserves it. Tae lowered his head, knowing argument would prove futile. For better or worse, he had taken this project upon himself, and he would see it through. "I'll handle it," he promised, despising every moment the effort took from his own child. Yet he knew his conscience would force him to try.

Tae ignored the aroma of lamb stew, mushroom gravy, crusty bread, and sweet spices that perfumed the hallways leading to Béarn's kitchen, attention focused on other matters. Shortly after dinner, Rascal had spent far longer than necessary selecting foodstuffs and munching them down in front of the busy kitchen staff. Forced to work around the king-sanctioned thief in their midst, the servants had bustled about her, storing leftovers, replacing items she repeatedly left lying out, and sweeping crumbs that pattered to the floor at her feet. Her grinning insolence made it clear that she would work the king's decree to its limit, reveling in the control it granted her and the trouble it inflicted on the help. More importantly, their irritation and grand displays of cleaning around her kept them near enough for her to plunder insignias, badges, and other displays of rank, likely her real reason for preferring to take her meals in the kitchen. She barely seemed to notice when Walfron locked the gold torque Tae had given him for this purpose into a drawer.

Unseen, Tae had watched, rage growing blacker by the moment. Bad enough Rascal chose to continue actions she knew bothered the staff; she did not need to taunt them. Her thefts only fueled his anger. He had stolen his share of food in his time, but never valuables and always from those who could afford much more. Nobles saw all of the poor the same, rabble to disdain or pity depending upon proclivity and conscience. But the underclass ranked itself with the distinction of royalty. The lowest of the low were the bullies who targeted those weaker: murdering street orphans for their meager possessions, victimizing children of the streets for sexual pleasure, or stealing food from the mouths of those already starving. Thwarted by defenses or, more likely, fearing the consequences, Rascal avoided the valuables of a castle full of nobles, instead robbing those who could least afford it. That action alone had turned Tae's dislike for the child to revulsion.

Eventually, Rascal had leaped from the table on which she had perched, stretched casually, and headed from the room. As soon as she departed, a server rushed to wash the table, scrubbing vigorously with the strongest cleaners of the castle. The whispered comments about Rascal's gall and lack of hygiene lasted until the last crumb was swept. Then the kitchen staff put out the lights, heading to bed for the night.

Tae waited several moments to assure no one would return before creeping into the darkened room, sword knife tapping at his thigh. A cook stove black with ash filled one wall, pots dangling from myriad hooks. A glassless window vented the room, shuttered for the night. Cupboards and drawers lined every other part of the kitchen, stuffed with tableware and utensils of sundry types, all of the same bear design. Tae wondered if Rascal had purloined any of them, though they would prove difficult to fence. She might find no one willing to touch items so obviously taken from the high king.

Discovering a dark corner between a low chopping block and a solid cabinet, Tae settled into the most comfortable position he could devise, the long knife proving his biggest impediment. During his wait, he thought of Subikahn, hoping Rascal would arrive early enough for him to claim his son for the night. He did not wish to bother Ra-khir and Kevral too late. *If she makes me lose a night with my baby . . .* He did not bother to complete the threat, even for his own peace of mind. Rascal would choose her time for her own convenience and safety, not to deliberately ruin Tae's plans.

Rascal did not make Tae wait as long as he expected. Pink bands of sunset still sifted through cracks in the shutters when the whisking noise of fabric scraping wood touched his ears. No further sounds followed, but a shadow shifted through irregular patches of gray and black. Tae remained as still as stone, keeping his breaths shallow and silent. Pausing several times to scan the room for danger, Rascal sprang onto a working surface and reached for an upper cabinet.

Diversion, Tae guessed. She had permission to come here. In the case of a trap, kitchen staff would likely confront her as swiftly as possible . . . and find her reaching innocently for food.

Armed with a bowl of raisins, Rascal clambered from the countertop. Her head swiveled as she studied the room once more. Trusting his choice of hiding place, Tae concentrated solely on remaining motionless. Apparently comfortable, Rascal headed for Walfron's drawer. For several moments, she hunched over the simple lock, an occasional muffled click or scratch of metal against metal reaching Tae's ears. He frowned. He had examined the device, a simple rusty affair that could not have thwarted the most ignorant of people who lived by their wits. Even his minuscule experience with locks and robbery would have allowed him to handle it more quickly than Rascal already had.

Then, suddenly, came the definitive snap of corroded metal breaking. Rascal spun to a crouch. Though tiny, the sound would seem thunderous to one in a room so unremittingly quiet and worried about getting caught. Clutching the bin of raisins, she dropped to the floor, munching with a young guilelessness that might have fooled even the most hardened. She waited for repercussions several moments. Had someone heard her, they would surely have come to investigate by now.

Left arm clamping the bowl to her chest, Rascal tugged at the drawer with her right. At her back, Tae assumed a readied crouch. The drawer slid open with a barely audible hiss, and Rascal reached her hand inside.

Tae lunged for her, extracting his sword knife and slamming the drawer shut. The wood crashed against Rascal's wrist, bouncing open. She jerked backward with a gasp. The bowl slammed the floor, flinging raisins in a wild spray. Rascal spun to face him, then pressed her back against the cabinet at the sight of readied steel.

"Ya spooked me," Rascal said, her tone containing just the right combination of innocent shock, fear, and outrage. "Juss comed for a snack."

"Spare me," Tae said, dark eyes glaring into hers. "I know what you 'comed' for."

"Snack." Rascal clung hopelessly to her story. "Gots the king's pramisshun. Hain't nothin' ya kin do 'bout dat." Brown hair lay in a wild mane, giving her a feral animal look.

"King Griff didn't give you permission to steal from the staff." Tae kept the knife at Rascal's chest, far enough to maintain the distance needed for momentum and to keep it from any tricks of her own. "I know about the hair bindings and the badges. I even know about the studs."

"Not knowin' what ya's talkin' 'bout."

"You're going to return them," Tae said evenly. "With apologies. You can do it by yourself, or I can announce it in front of everyone and let the king dispense the justice."

Rascal's attention turned fully to the blade.

Tae read the thought attached to the look. "No, I'm not bluffing," he lied. "I'll run you through if you give me no other choice."

"An' lose ya misshun?" Rascal's smile went positively evil. "Hain't thinkin' so." She ducked suddenly, but the knife followed her.

Tae fought the dense fog of rage that threatened to overtake him. "Just give the things back. And don't take anything else while you're here."

Rascal's pinch-faced look and sullen silence promised grudging obedience. She rose, Tae trailing with the weapon. Unable to win that point, she switched to one she could. Her hand floated nonthreateningly to her throat, and she unfastened the topmost stay.

"What are you doing?" Tae demanded.

"Doin' what ya wants," Rascal snapped, opening another catch. "Ya gots me alone at knife point." She unloosened another, revealing undeveloped breasts. "Hain't no one gonna proteck one like me." She pulled the shirt apart, fully revealing herself. "Ya knows ya want me."

Tae banged the knife back into his sheath. "Don't flatter yourself." Without another word, he turned and left the room, anger fleeing with every step. He still had more than enough time to collect Subikahn for the night.

Rascal burned with all the rage Tae no longer suffered. Still flattened against the cabinets, she whipped the shirt back into place, fingers fumbling to restore the stays. Quaking anger ruined her usual dexterity. At length, she managed to fully close her clothing; but the time it took only stoked the fire in her veins. Cheeks blazing, she stomped the spilled raisins into the floor, twisting her foot to grind the stains deep. She had no choice but to return the kitchen help's property, but she could still make them miserable in return. *Them . . . and HIM.* The desperate need for revenge flared into a bonfire. Tae's prize possession could not defend himself, and babies brought more gold than trinkets on the current market. Eventually, Tae would likely get Subikahn back, but not before he suffered the worry and shame he had inflicted on her.

Once conjured, the idea would not leave Rascal's mind. Straying from its image resulted in a restless discomfort that drove her relentlessly back to the thought. She knew she could never snatch the baby from Tae, nor from his savage Renshai mother. Ra-khir might fall victim to trickery, though unlikely to her own. But none of that mattered. Rascal had seen Kevral turn the babies over to a servant who had rolled their cribs to a grizzled old woman in the play room. From the brief conversation that had accompanied the exchange, Rascal believed the elder a great-grand-parent. She would fall easy prey to youthful strength and quickness.

Rascal raced through the castle hallways, worried that Tae might beat her to the infant. She arrived shortly, catching her breath for several moments before knocking on the door. She would have to gauge the situation swiftly and plan accordingly. If anyone other than babies and grandmother occupied the room, she would run. Otherwise, she would snatch up Subikahn and race for the window. She would attempt to climb; but a two-story fall into gardens should not harm her. She would protect the baby as best as she could or lose the money it represented. But if the gods willed the baby dead, she would escape without it and consider her vengeance complete.

Heart pounding, Rascal watched the door ease open, prepared to dash into the shadows in an instant. Tae might threaten, but he could never prove she meant the child harm.

A weathered arm, flesh sagging, appeared through the crack, then Rascal faced a woman easily approaching seventy. Hair white as milk curved around a wrinkled face, and watery blue eyes studied Rascal without presumption. She wore a V-necked tunic and tan linen britches instead of the house dress Rascal expected. Focused on the lack of other occupants, the two full cribs, and the window on the opposite side of the room, Rascal did not notice the sword belt fastened to the old woman's waist. Two chairs, a table, and a chest filled with toys completed the furnishings.

Shoving the elder aside, Rascal made a dash for the cribs. Intent on the dark-haired one, she barely heard the door slam closed and the bolt clack into place. She grabbed Subikahn, whirling toward the window. Now she could see the glass that framed it top to bottom, a detail she had never considered. Tae worried too much about Rascal escaping to allow her a room with a window, and her experience never placed her in a location rich enough to afford such luxuries.

Rascal's instant of hesitation gave the old woman the time she needed. A silver streak hammered the baby from Rascal's grip. The child sailed, shrieking, snatched from the air by a great-grandmother accustomed to catching flying swords. Still clutching a wailing Subikahn, the old woman struck directly for Rascal.

Unable to suppress a scream, Rascal threw herself sideways. The sword stung against her arm, and she crashed into a chair. Momentum flung her over it. It slammed to the ground at her back, even as her shoulder struck the floor with bruising force. She rolled over a shard, struggling to her feet, only to see the sword speeding toward her again. . . .

Tae forced himself to amble through the corridors from Kevral and Ra-khir's room, eager for Subikahn yet wanting Kevral's kindly old grandmother to have as much time with the twins as he could spare her. The exercise proved harder than he expected. He understood Kevral and Ra-khir's need for a night of privacy they rarely had, especially while searching for the pieces of Pica. But surely the great-grandmother would understand Tae's own need to see his child during their recoveries between worlds. She had the opportunity to play with the boys while they stayed with Kevral's parents.

A scream, followed by a solid crash interrupted Tae's train of thought. Though accustomed to approaching conflict cautiously, he ran toward it. The noises came from the direction of the toy room, and he could not risk the chance that it threatened his son.

A series of thuds followed, then another scream. A baby sobbed. As Tae rounded the corner, he lost all doubt. Panic hammered him as he careened through the corridor. He seized the door latch and yanked. It did not yield. Frustration emerged in a desperate screech. "Let me in!" He pounded hard enough to bruise his fists. "Damn it, open this door!"

"Please, no. No!" someone shouted. The baby continued to cry. Something heavy struck the door.

Tae abandoned his efforts, charging to the nearest stairway and barreling to the upper stories. Dashing through the first open door, he found an unpaned window, jerked the bolt, and slapped open the shutters. Moonlight funneled through the opening, reflecting from an ice-covered pond several stories below. Tae scrambled to the ledge. Seizing it, he swung his legs downward, barely bothering to catch toeholds before beginning his sideways descent. Terror usurped caution. His fingernails cracked against stone, tearing the tender pads of his fingers. He dashed from hold to hold like a hunted insect, at dangerous speed. He had scarcely reached the third story when his boot toe skidded from a bulge. His leg plummeted suddenly, jarring loose the other foot and a hand hold. He clung by three fingers, toes squabbling wildly at stone. Then that, too, failed, and he plunged from the castle wall.

Tae barely had a chance to tuck before he slammed into ice that shattered beneath him. Impact shocked through him, eroding consciousness.

He gasped in a mouthful of water that spasmed his windpipe closed. A deadly chill washed over him, and he struggled to sort direction in the dense, black water. Moonlight mirrored oddly from the ice, stealing all sense of bearings. He flattened his body, allowing the water to buoy him upward, sacrificing necessary speed for direction. All the swimming in the world could not save him if he shoved himself deeper.

Tae drifted upward, lungs bucking against his control, desperately seeking air. As he became certain of his course, he kicked his legs, propelling himself upward. At last he reached the top, surging toward the surface with a sudden second wind. His head crashed into ice so hard it drove him back under. The understanding of certain death reached him, accompanied by panic. He had lost the hole of his entry. Without it, he could not escape. Already, the coldness of the water seeped into his body, threatening to finish him before the search. He pounded against the ice, but without the momentum of a fall, he could not break it.

No. Tae bucked against a death so unlike what he had expected. Gathering his wits, he turned his face toward the ice, exploring it for a weakness. Water trickled across his forehead. *Movement.* Tae leaped for this new savior. A tiny pocket of air had layered between the water and the ice. He plunged his nose into the space, just as his windpipe surrendered to his lungs' demands. Screwing his mouth tight, he sucked blessed air through his nostrils. Its coldness, and the dribble of icy water that accompanied it, cut his insides like knives. He ignored the pain, propelling himself along the underside of the ice, forcing composure. The air could not last long with no way to replenish, and the cold already made every movement stiff and painful. He could feel his thoughts slowing along with his mind, and the urge to give up to the frigid waters seemed nearly overwhelming.

Subikahn. Tae roused himself with thoughts of his son in danger. Faster, he pushed himself along the ice, his nose now pressed against it and guzzling in nearly as much water as air. At length, he had no choice but to hold his breath again, knowing he had brief moments before death claimed him. His hands banged solid ice twice more. As he wrestled down the impulse to pound the ice in frenzied, hopeless hysteria, an edge of ice sliced open his smallest finger. Tae gathered his all for one last surge, and emerged, sputtering, from the pond. Catching an edge of the ice, Tae levered himself over, keeping his weight evenly distributed so as not to break the surface and send himself under again. Using the patience that might have prevented the fall in the first place, he crawled across the frozen pond to shore.

A shiver wracked Tae, straining muscles with its abrupt ferocity. *Subikahn.* He staggered across the ground, seizing handholds immediately beneath the proper window, studying the shadow of its deep shutter ledges. Upward he climbed, every motion more instinct than intention. The winter wind stabbed through his sodden clothing, numbing his fingers until he no longer knew where they were. Somehow, they continued to draw him upward and to the proper ledge. Balanced there barely long enough to recognize Rascal shrieking and dodging the old woman's sword, he hurled himself through the window. The glass shattered, raining over the floor in a high-pitched sprinkle, accompanied by droplets of blood. Without bothering to assess the damage, Tae collapsed between Rascal and the blade. "No. Stop," he managed. *What the hell is going on?*

Only then Tae managed to drag the details together. The Renshai grandmother could not have chosen to kill Rascal, or she would already lie dead. The flat of the sword that sheered away in time to miss him demonstrated that as well. She had chosen only to beat at Rascal, presumably to hurt her. But there could be only one reason Rascal had come here, one that made him wish the grandmother had intended to kill. *Subikahn.* Tae tried to ask about the baby's well-being aloud, but even the name refused to emerge. Soaked from head to toe, buffeted by chills, he finally managed to clamber to his feet.

Rascal cowered behind the toy chest.

The Renshai stood with her hands on her hips, sword sheathed. The babies lay safely in their cribs, Subikahn's breaths shuddering and tears clinging to his lashes. "Give me one reason not to batter her senseless."

You're asking the wrong person. Tae kept that thought deliberately silent. "What happened?"

Rascal puffed out a breathless answer. "I comed lookin' for ya. Crazy ol' hag 'tacked me."

The Renshai jerked warningly, which sent Rascal ducking back behind the chest.

"She grabbed Subikahn," the elder explained calmly. "Should I kill her?"

It was an idle threat, Tae knew. The Renshai would not murder an unarmed adversary in an unfair fight. "No." Fatigue crushed in on him. No longer in desperate danger, his son safe with his great-grandmother, Tae saw no reason to fight any longer. "I'll handle her." He limped toward the door, tossing a gesture to Rascal over his shoulder.

For once, Rascal's bravado disappeared. She scurried after Tae, keeping him between herself and the Renshai at all times.

Tae hoped with all his heart she had finally learned her lesson.

CHAPTER 12

A Deeper Chill

Fire warms the body;
Exertion warms the spirit.

—*Colbey Calistinsson*

THE hearth fire in the queen's chamber dispelled Tae's chill, chased the numbness from fingers and toes, and dried his wet clothing. Huddled on the floor as close as safety allowed, he watched the flames flicker and snap while Matrinka tended his cuts, scrapes, and bruises. Laughter occasionally wafted from the room next door, the king's deep rumble accompanied by the higher-pitched sounds of his mother and the lighter, more disjointed chuckles of his stepfather. Though less frequent, Tem'-aree'ay's giggles emerged as sweet as bell-song, and the perfect chords of Darris' lute broke the quieter moments at intervals.

Tae watched the color gradually return to his fingers. "I'm sorry I pulled you away from the celebration." Exhaustion made thought difficult; he felt broken and guilty, hating that he had torn Matrinka from a last night of private revelry before the travelers set out after the third Pica shard. Between their mission and Darris' dedication to Griff's task, she rarely found time to spend with her beloved.

"Not at all." Matrinka sat back on her haunches. "I don't mind, Tae. Really."

The door connecting the king's and queen's rooms creaked, and a furry head poked through the widening crack. Mior sat in the opening, cleaning her neck with long strokes of her tongue.

Tae grinned. "That must be torture for a cat. Choosing between so many laps and a fire."

Mior stopped licking to look at Tae, and Matrinka laughed. "That's uncanny."

"What?"

"You called it exactly. She's whining about the temptation I created by not closing the door."

Still in cat mode, Tae guessed. "She would have complained at least as much if you had shut her out there."

"No doubt."

Mior rose haughtily, raised her head and tail, and trotted back into the king's room.

"I'm sorry." Tae watched after the disappearing cat. "Did I offend her?"

"You just struck a little too close to home." Matrinka smoothed her skirt, skillfully embroidered with dancing bears. "When she stops feeling huffy, she'll be impressed by your insight. You've got a real gift."

A gift for thinking like a cat. Great. How useful. Tae held the thought. To express it might offend, Mior if not Matrinka. And the queen would chide him for denigrating himself again. "I wish it extended to Rascal."

"You mean you wish you could read her intentions?" Finished with her ministrations, Matrinka rocked to her feet, disappearing behind her bed. A drawer rattled open.

"Right," Tae said, lowering his head. A damp clump of hair fell into his face with the movement.

The bed muffled Matrinka's question, "Are you sure you can't?" The drawer clapped closed.

Tae shrugged, though Matrinka could not see the motion. She had a point. Nothing Rascal had done so far surprised him, only enraged and disappointed. "I hope I can't. I expect nothing but the worst from her." He mumbled, "And so far, I haven't been proved wrong."

"Excuse me?" Matrinka came back around the bed, clutching a comb and a shearing knife. "I missed the last part."

Not wishing to repeat the concluding line, Tae hedged. "I said I expect nothing but the worst from her." He watched Matrinka take a new position beside him. "What are you doing? I don't need anything amputated, do I?" The lack of concern in his voice should have made it clear he did not really worry for that possibility.

"You mean aside from a heavy dose of cynicism?" Matrinka started the comb through Tae's hair, stopped immediately by a snarl. "No." She added with a solemnity she rarely displayed, "Truthfully, though, I think this is one situation where preparation for the worst might work to your advantage. And maybe even Rascal's."

Another wave of laughter seeped through the partially opened door.

Tae scanned the room with overplayed movements of head and eyes.

Matrinka removed the comb before it became hopelessly tangled. "What are you doing?"

"Looking for the trusting optimist Matrinka I know, you stranger."

Matrinka whopped Tae with the comb. Without reply, she stood, closing the door between the rooms fully, as much to keep their conversation private as to escape the distraction.

"Mior will make you pay for that."

"Don't I know it." Matrinka returned to Tae's side. "But you deserve my full attention; and Griff doesn't need to hear me say that he's the naive, innocent ruler, not me. Your explanation in the courtroom made sense to me, though I would never have thought of it on my own." She sighed, returning her focus to Tae's hair. "I've become a lot more interested in handling children since Marisole's birth. She's not going to get any discipline from Griff. Darris can only teach with song, and a disobedient child won't have patience for that. It's up to me, and I don't want to make too many mistakes."

Tae swallowed hard, only then realizing how close Matrinka had come to concerns he had not, until that moment, recognized. He had considered Rascal an annoying distraction from Subikahn. Now, he realized, Subikahn actually propelled his need to rescue Rascal. If he could handle the nasty little hoodlum, he could face any problem that came with fatherhood. "Well, don't look to me for the answers. I don't even have a positive parental model. My mother died when . . ." Sorrow snapped into position despite his best effort to keep it at bay. He knew he would never forget the day that his father's enemies killed his mother and left him, stabbed multiple times, for dead. He managed to finish with only a catch in his voice to reveal how near he had come to crying. ". . . I was ten. And my father made every possible mistake."

"You do so well with Subikahn." Matrinka plucked at the knot in Tae's hair. "Better, I hate to admit, than the rest of us with our babies."

Tae screwed up his face. "That's ludicrous."

"Oh, Ra-khir and Kevral, me and Griff and Darris. We all love the babies." Matrinka struggled with the comb. "But we're more the holding and rocking types. You actually get down on the floor and roughhouse. There's something special about people who can do that."

It surprised Tae to learn that not everyone could do something that came so naturally to him. "You're all capable of rollicking around like maniacs."

"Physically," Matrinka admitted. "But we don't know what to do, what to say. In front of others we're embarrassed. It just doesn't feel right."

Considering the situation in this new light, Tae realized most parents behaved as Matrinka did. Perhaps his play was already a mistake, but he could not bear to stop it. Besides, Matrinka seemed to believe it a good thing, even enviable. As the comb jerked at his roots, he winced. "Matrinka, isn't it beneath your station to groom . . ." He stopped himself from saying something personally derogatory which, while funnier, would upset his companion. ". . . me?"

"Not at all," Matrinka worked harder on the tangle. "Emotional healing is as important as physical. If you look more like a prince, you'll feel more like one."

Tae believed he had now heard himself called a prince more than a hundred times, and it still sounded ridiculous.

Matrinka set to work with the shearing knife as well as the comb. "But you've gotten me way off the subject. Now, I know you fell in a pond, and the guards tell me you climbed the wall and broke a window. I don't doubt you have an excellent explanation."

Appreciating Matrinka's trust, Tae launched into his story, describing the events of the evening with detailed accuracy. As he talked, she combed and cut. Black locks tumbled to the floor, gleaming blue and scarlet in the firelight. He finished by describing the events in the toy room. ". . . so I probably saved her life, or at least from an extraordinary beating. And, for all I know, she came to kill my baby." He gave Matrinka a raised-brow look to indicate he had finished.

Only then, Matrinka added her piece, "You did well, Tae."

Tae blinked several times. "The kitchen staff still has to contend with her, and she has their possessions. Subikahn got menaced. I nearly died. Where's the 'well' part of all that?"

"You let Rascal know what you expected of her and that you would see right done. You showed her that she can't get her way with negativity or with sex. And she got punished for attempting vengeance." Matrinka smiled at an image that had already amused Tae: Rascal believing she could bully an old woman who turned out to be a Renshai. "Most importantly, you got the opportunity to show her that you've done all of this from love."

No word could have surprised Tae more. "Love?" he repeated warningly. If Matrinka had a match between Tae and Rascal in mind, he would storm from the room without a backward look.

"Caring, if you prefer." Matrinka ran the comb easily through Tae's hair now, a pleasant sensation that reminded him of the time Kevral had done it, a turning point in their relationship. He tried not to enjoy the queen's touch too much. "You saved her when allowing her to die would have served you better. And she knows it's not because you want something from her since you already refused the chance to sleep with her."

"Rape her," Tae reminded, using Rascal's own words.

Though two years younger than Tae, Matrinka patted him like an older sister. "Oh, Tae. A woman fearing assault doesn't willingly open her clothing. She wants you."

Tae recoiled as if struck, shocked the thought had never occurred to him. He did not share the affection; he felt certain of that. "Maybe," he conceded. "But not because she loves me romantically. It's probably the only type of relationship she ever had with a father or a brother."

Having finished with his hair, Matrinka settled cross-legged in front of Tae. "So she sees you in that role now. That's a good thing."

"Because . . ." Tae pressed.

"Because you can do it right this time. Show her the true role of a brother. Firm but merciful guidance. No sex."

The very idea of coupling with Rascal turned Tae's stomach.

"You did well," Matrinka repeated. "I guarantee you'll see a positive change in her behavior."

Tae stood, exhaustion like a lead weight across his shoulders. "And if I don't?"

Matrinka's features went stricken, but she did not answer. "Almost forgot. Package came from your father. It's by your door."

"Thanks." Tae headed toward the door, appreciating the change of subject, despite its abruptness. He doubted resteering Matrinka to the topic would gain him an answer. So instead he wondered about a package important enough to send a party through months of travel. *Months of travel.* Tae rolled his eyes, blaming tiredness for his lack of thought. Surely, Weile Kahn had utilized a messenger line. Easterners would only have to have gone to the edge of the first Westland or Northern town and paid for others to pass it along. Yet, even that would have required a month and a significant amount of gold. Had it held political significance, it would have gone to the king. More likely, his father had sent him a gift on a whim. Tae managed a weak smile. Soon enough, he would know.

Fatigue and curiosity drew Tae toward his room, but he forced himself to the kitchen instead. Worried for the damage Rascal might have inflicted prior to going after Subikahn, he thought it best to spare the already burdened staff. As he stumbled toward it, glad he had left the infant in Kevral's capable care for the night, he realized that he had seen no weapons in Rascal's hand. Coming from the kitchen, she had had plenty of opportunity to seize a knife. That suggested that her intentions in the toy room fell short of murder and eased some of his tension. For the first time, he dared to consider Matrinka's optimism a possibility. The scene he discovered in the kitchen might tell him more. Seizing the door, he opened it.

Moonlight funneled through the only window, playing over quiet utensils, counter tops, and cooking areas. The raisins lay spread across the floor, many deliberately ground into the stone. That small act of defiance seemed like nothing in the wake of the carnage Tae had expected. A glint of bronze from a carving block caught his eye, and he moved to inspect it. Hair ties, studs, badges, and copper instruments lay spread across its surface. A smile eased onto Tae's face. Though not the direct confrontation he had demanded, and unaccompanied by apology, at least Rascal had returned the objects she had stolen. He dashed to the once-locked drawer, trampling more raisins in his haste. The torque lay where Walfron had left it. Smiling, Tae shoved in the drawer and twisted the broken lock back into reasonable shape.

With the exhilaration that came of unexpected success, Tae gathered the raisins and scrubbed at the stains. Though not a thorough job, it might at least ease some of the tension the following day if the spill looked accidental. With renewed enthusiasm, he headed upstairs and through the corridors to his bedroom. He waved at a guard he passed, pleased with himself for the first time in as long as he could remember, scarcely believing that, not long ago, he had battled for his life. Only the residual exhaustion paid any credence to that struggle, and the thought of collapsing into bed made even that a pleasure. Finally, he had succeeded at a task that had seemed impossible. Perhaps, this once, his parenting instincts had overcome his lack of experience. Always before he had worried he would freeze in front of his child, running possibilities through his mind in a desperate race and still choosing wrongly. Now, he allowed himself to consider the possibility that he might truly make a competent father.

Tae's door came into view, a pile of something unidentifiable beside it. *The package.* He stared at it as he approached, gradually making out rumpled leather, cloth, and unraveled rope. *Someone opened it?* He blinked, trying to make sense of what he saw. The closer he got, the more he realized that someone had definitely tampered with the contents. Quickening his pace, he arrived at his door and crouched in front of the package. The rope lay, cut. Wadded vellum perched atop a shredded pile of velvet, silk, and gingham. He snatched up the supple parchment, opening it to reveal the writing: "Prince Tae Kahn at Béarn Castle." He flipped it over. Eastern runes scrawled across it in his father's neat handwriting: "Knew this would take months to get to you, so I had them made big. As handsome as Subikahn will look in these, don't let any Béarnian princesses steal his heart. My son refuses to take my place, and I need an heir." There followed a string of symbols that represented laughter.

Tae's lips twitched upward, immediately stopped by remembrance of the carnage that lay beneath the message. Scooping up a pile of fabric, he let the torn scraps flutter back to the floor. Here and there, a swatch revealed its original purpose: a sleeve here, a laced collar there. The whole blurred to a multicolored smear that glided through his fingers, as soft as down. *Rascal did this.* Tae buried his face in the silk. The loss of the clothing did not bother him; Subikahn would never go naked. The gift from his father had meant so much more: an end to the bitterness and cruelty that had tainted their relationship, a promise of closeness between an elder who had only just learned to love and a grandson as yet too young to understand.

Newly found confidence crumbled, replaced by the wary walls the difficulties of Tae's childhood had crafted. Too tired to fight them, he let the tears glide where they would.

The shapeless soup of chaos, with its flickering array of colors and everchanging densities had long ago faded to insignificant background to Colbey Calistinsson. He had found a bittersweet irony that the demons could never fathom: the unpredictable inconsistency of chaos had, itself, become a stability in a life torn apart by his commitment to the cause of balance. He thought back to the day he had nearly handed over the Staff of Chaos to Kevral, knowing that she would bind and believing that the only way to oppose Dh'arlo'mé's subjugation to the Staff of Law. Then, Ra-khir's impassioned pleas and Tae's attempt to sacrifice himself had changed Colbey's mind. Had he known then about Odin, he would never have considered handing the task to another.

Willing the plane of chaos to a dirt pathway, Colbey paced. So much had changed since the day he demanded that the staff bring him here. Shreds of law became the seeds for demons, but nothing else living had ever survived on chaos' world. History and logic had deemed that Colbey should have fragmented the instant of his arrival, adding a new mass of demons to chaos' horde. The power of mind and body had rescued him. Slaughtering demons had won his place as their prince, though even that gained him only their fear and individual obeisance. The creatures of chaos could never, by nature, organize.

Gradually, Colbey's mastery over chaos had grown. When he willed it, objects and boundaries came into existence on a world once lacking such concepts. Experimentation had revealed that, aside from self and staff/sword, anything he took from this world ceased to exist on the others, except as raw chaos. Objects brought here shattered or became as mutable as everything else. Colbey paused at the end of his track, then spun on a heel to travel the other direction. A path that had closed behind him reappeared, and he trod the length, continuing his thoughts. If he could draw Odin to chaos' world, he would gain the upper hand, even without the assistance of the other gods. Short of that, he had little hope of besting the AllFather. He believed he might prove the better swordsman, but Odin had the stronger mind powers. And Odin had magic.

You could have magic, too, the staff/sword reminded, dismissed by a brisk chop of Colbey's hand. *You know you'll have to bond eventually. If you wait too long, you may lose that chance.*

Hush! Colbey's command left no space for further argument. He would never admit that the staff was probably right. Once linked to chaos, he lost control; and without control, he could not regulate the outcome of the battle. The entity he became would no longer care about balance. It would battle law until nothing remained. With any luck, the forces would destroy one another; but, if either the bound-Colbey or Odin triumphed, all of humanity would succumb. Whether to chaos or to Odin's self-centered annihilation did not matter. *If you can't suggest something useful, don't bother me.*

Binding at least gives you a chance for what you seek. Without it, you can only die—and bring chaos down with you.

Colbey wondered if he could ever get the staff to understand that becoming part of the primordial chaos was worse than dying. *At least against Odin I have a chance to die in battle.*

Moot, at best. Do you think Odin would leave Valhalla intact? Even if he did, he would banish you from it.

Colbey did not bother to argue. His need for an honorable death no longer held any basis in Valhalla. Thoughts of Odin brought him back to his first battle with the arisen god. Then, he had noticed two things. When the Staff of Chaos had carved through the entity bound to law, parts of both had canceled one another, the backlash a blast that had blown him back to chaos' world and nearly taken his life. Second, bits of Odin's mental attack that he had walled away and brought back with him had fizzled into nothingness against chaos. Realization struck with painful clarity. *If Odin came here, it would not just even the battle. It would destroy him.*

Chaos leaped to its own defense. *The resultant explosion would kill you, too.* It did not speak the obvious, clear enough to Colbey. It would also destroy chaos' world. Colbey froze in mid-step, astounded by his new discovery. Devastation of the largest entities of law and of chaos would accomplish precisely what he had intended. His own death did not matter. He had anticipated nothing different.

No! the staff's voice echoed emphatically through Colbey's mind. *I won't allow it.*

Colbey watched colors ooze and twine around him, without reply. He already knew the practicalities would prove far more difficult than the conception. Odin would never come of his own will. *Try and stop me.*

Colbey vowed to relish his final battle.

This time, Kevral remembered to squeeze her eyes shut as Captain's magic transported her and her seven companions to a world of unknown perils or tedium. The familiar tingle rippled through her, and she clutched the hilts at each hip. So far, they had obtained Pica fragments without violence; and logic suggested they would procure the others at least as easily. Even she would not quibble over a worthless shard of sapphire, though she secretly hoped someone would. The urge to wield her swords in something other than spar or practice itched, her reason for joining the expedition in the first place. It seemed nonsensical to drag a Renshai along without a need for combat, yet she knew they had chosen her because no one could predict the occupants of unknown worlds.

Kevral opened her eyes, blinking against dull light diffused by a blanket of silver fog. She stood on an indistinct mulch of leaves and ancient bark, surrounded by her companions. Ra-khir gazed about in wonder. Tae crouched, almost invisible in the haze. Darris' hand rested on his sword hilt also, and his eyes darted to all corners of the mist. Andvari stood tall, the muscles in his arms tense balls but his stance otherwise revealing no trace of discomfort. Rascal hunched into herself, on the exact opposite side of the party from Tae. El-brinith showed an agitation uncharacteristic for elves, shuffling from position to position with an attentiveness Kevral had never seen from her before. Chan'rék'ril remained still beside her, his face tipped toward her, though he did not speak. Likely, they discussed her discomfort in singular *khohlar*.

Kevral approached El-brinith. "What's the matter?"

El-brinith turned her eyes to Kevral, though not for long. Even as she answered, her gaze flitted around the area again. "Strange magic. Nothing I've encountered before."

Anxiety balled in the pit of Kevral's stomach. Danger never frightened Renshai, but sorcery could prove a threat she had no means to analyze or counter. "What is it?"

El-brinith shrugged.

Chan'rék'ril addressed Kevral's need. "I don't even notice it." He indicated El-brinith by inclining his head toward her. "She's working on it."

"She'd better work quickly," Tae said. "We've got company."

Kevral jerked around, eyes scanning the silver. She saw nothing out of place, just a few shadows pressing dark against the fog. "Where?"

"Ahead." Tae's direction meant little since it varied by position and he did not point. Kevral studied the mist, orienting herself by Tae. Gradually, she noticed that some of the dark splotches appeared to be moving toward them.

Hands glided back to hilts and hafts, except Kevral's and the elves'. The latter had too little training to perform an act so instinctively warlike, and Kevral avoided doing so as a matter of pride. Renshai training should make her capable of drawing and cutting faster than even the most readied soldier could strike with a weapon in hand.

But the three figures who materialized from the fog carried no obvious weaponry and took no notice of their visitors' preparedness. All female, they sported long, silver hair so silky it reflected rainbow colors from the damp. Dark, slitted eyes more pupil than white peered out from heart-shaped faces that resembled elves more than humans. Slender arms and legs jutted from torsos shorter than, but nearly as bulky as, Béarnides'. Despite lumpish bodies carried on wiry legs, they moved with the grace of dancers. Expertly woven from material that shimmered in the gloom, their dresses swirled around their ankles with every movement.

Andvari's fingers slid from his ax, and the others followed in subtle motions. As usual, Ra-khir accepted the position as negotiator, challenged by no one. Like herself, Kevral guessed, most felt relieved that he willingly took this responsibility.

"Hello," Ra-khir said, avoiding the "greetings" salutation that had so irritated the Collector. "I am Sir Ra-khir Kedrin's son, knight to the Erythanian and Béarnian kings: His Grace, King Humfreet and His Majesty, King Griff." He bowed graciously.

The women glanced at one another. Then, they mimicked Ra-khir's bow. The middle one spoke, her voice tinny and inflection as Western as his own. "Hello Ra-khir Kedrin's son, knight to the Airyth . . . the Eryth . . ."

Kevral suspected the woman believed the entire title Ra-khir's name. Recalling her own attempts to learn elfin names, she had to admit the woman had done better than she could have under the same circumstances.

"Ra-khir will do," the knight interrupted hurriedly.

"Hello, Ra-khir." The one to the right turned her stammering companion a glare. "I'm Lissa." She gestured at her associates with a stiff-fingered hand. "These are Sassar." The middle one nodded. "And Phis-lah."

Ra-khir indicated each of the rest of the party, limiting himself to personal names without parentage or titles. And he did so, Kevral marveled at how strange it seemed that people from another world who appeared so alien spoke human trading tongue at all, let alone fluently.

Communication had not bothered her during the previous two trials: it made sense that a former bard would speak trading, and the well-traveled Collector probably used many languages. Only now, she realized another reason why the Council had insisted on such a diverse party, beyond diplomacy. Among them, they spoke the languages of every known intelligent creatures, save only barbarian. *Of course, they only needed Tae, an elf, and me for that.* Tae's natural verbal propensity and his experience also made him competent to pick up new forms of communication rapidly.

Introductions finished, Ra-khir continued. "We apologize for barging in on your world, but we're looking for something."

"What are you looking for?" Sassar questioned. "Perhaps we can help you."

Kevral smiled. It seemed this would prove the easiest shard of all to obtain. As much as she appreciated a rousing battle, had even hoped for one when they started, she knew it best to gather the shards with as little bloodshed as possible, especially of their own. She turned her attention to El-brinith as Ra-khir described the Pica shard. The elf had settled to a cross-legged position in the detritus, her head bowed and a hand gripping each knee. Blonde hair, with barely a trace of red, dangled like a curtain. Worried for her, Kevral looked at Chan'rék'ril.

The male elf sent Kevral a directed *khohlar*, *She's locating the shard.* He raised one brow over a gemlike yellow eye. *And she's fascinated by this magic she's discovered. Apparently, it's extensive. She thinks the mist is related.*

Phislah spoke her first words, her voice flighty and higher-pitched than the others. "I've seen nothing like that."

"Me neither," Sassar added.

Lissa only shook her head.

"But you're welcome to look for it," Sassar continued. "We'll even assist."

"Thank you," Ra-khir showed his grin through the party. "I think we can find it. And you will be compensated." He, too, studied El-brinith now. Beads of moisture rolled from the elf's hairline, an oddity Kevral could not miss. She had never noticed elves sweating and wondered whether it came of intense effort or the fog.

Apparently recognizing every gaze on her, El-brinith raised her face, revealing a frown, and shook her head ever so slightly. "Can't locate it."

"Why not?" Darris piped in, needing the information for reasons beyond just finding a means around the problem.

"Interference." El-brinith's head shaking grew more fervent. "This whole world is vibrant with magic, and I can't get past it to cast my own."

Kevral turned the strangers a look that demanded explanation, but they seemed to take no notice of it.

"We'll bring you back to our village," Lissa suggested. "Let everyone know you're here and your purpose. If no one else knows where to find this sapphire fragment, we'll help you look."

Ra-khir glanced around, seeking dissenters. When no one spoke up against the plan, he told Lissa. "That sounds fine. Thank you for your assistance."

"Perhaps," Tae suggested, "we should know what we might run into here."

The strange women turned toward him. A light breeze that barely stirred Kevral's bangs tugged their fine hair into streamers, and their light garments billowed around them. Again, Kevral marveled at the craftsmanship and fabric. Even in Béarn's castle, she had never seen material both so gossamer and so sturdy nor one that seemed to glimmer from the spectrum of color that natural humidity evinced. The tailor had woven it in stitches so tight that Kevral could elicit no seams or flaws.

Tae clarified. "Other people less friendly than you. Perhaps enemies of your village or those among you who don't like outworlders." He used the term usually applied to elves but which seemed apt here. "Large or ferocious animals."

Sassar laughed, the sound pitched almost beyond the range of Kevral's hearing. "Nothing like that. You'll find our people hospitable and the only intelligent creatures here. The few animals left won't harm you."

Phislah gave Sassar a look Kevral could not read.

Tae asked the question on every mind. "Left?"

Lissa explained. "We've not had a good year for our animals. Some years are like that, no?"

"Unfortunately," Darris confirmed, more attentive than most to the cycles of nature as well as livestock. "Shall we go?"

Kevral added her nod to the others shifting erratically through the group. Only El-brinith gave no sign, having returned to her slumped position. As he often did, Chan'rék'ril spoke for her. "She wants to stay." He did not explain, though Kevral guessed it had to do with her fascination with the odd magic and her need to unravel it. The Renshai had found herself as fanatically devoted to war maneuvers whose fundamental purpose, use, or execution eluded her at first.

Ra-khir opened his mouth to question, silenced by a poke in the ribs from Kevral's elbow. She would explain later. Darris' unsolicited nod suggested Chan'rék'ril had explained the situation to him in *khohlar,* wisely understanding that the bard would most require an immediate justification. Tae's nostrils flared, but he chose silence. Familiar with subterfuge, he probably understood that the reasons might not please their hostesses and better remained with the party, even if only a few members knew.

"I'll stay with her," Chan'rék'ril volunteered.

Ra-khir acknowledged the elf's words, and the sense of his decision, with a nod. Kevral knew a warrior should remain behind as well, in case El-brinith encountered resistance or open hostility. However, she worried more for danger at the village. To leave their only Renshai here seemed foolishness of the basest sort. They needed Ra-khir's diplomacy, and neither Tae nor Rascal would prove much assistance in a face-to-face confrontation.

Kevral glanced toward Darris, but the bard had followed the logic as swiftly. "I'll stay, too," he said with a hesitancy that suggested he might have made a bad decision. Kevral suspected that had more to do with worrying that the more interesting material for song would occur at the village, though the need to understand El-brinith's interest had to fascinate him as well.

"Do you think they're safe?" Kevral whispered to Ra-khir.

"We trust him with the king's life," Ra-khir reminded.

Kevral had little choice but to accept the answer. Though Darris' sword skills had never particularly impressed her, she had had few chances to evaluate them. Embroiled in her own battles, protecting Matrinka concurrently, she had rarely watched him fight, though he seemed to hold his own. Others described him as more than capable. Accustomed to Renshai, she rarely considered any other better than barely adequate. The elves' *khohlar*, when distilled into a cry for help, carried reasonably far. She trusted Darris to hold off enemies long enough for Chan'rék'ril or El-brinith to call for them. "Let's go, then."

Kevral and Ra-khir, Andvari, Rascal, and Tae followed Lissa and Sassar, while Phislah dashed ahead to warn the village of their arrival. The women moved with a graceful quiet amid the leaves, gliding through the roiling mist. As Kevral's eyes grew more accustomed to light glazed into patches by fog, she believed she could see further. Dark shapes sharpened into trees, deadfalls, and a lake long before she worried for running into them. Fog seemed to billow from the water, like smoke from a steaming pot. Yet the coolness of the air around them defied the image.

Gradually, straight lines appeared at the edge of Kevral's vision, and movement became discernible. The shadows resolved into a series of cottages with walls constructed from woven thatch. Massive looms filled the spaces between cottages, partially crafted clothing stretched across the frames. Figures drifted toward them, all similar to those of Lissa, Sassar, and Phislah. As they stepped into view, Kevral recognized Phislah at the head of a group of strangers. None carried weapons, and they all wore somber expressions, difficult to read. Kevral sensed no tenseness or hostility, so she offered them a smile.

Several grinned back at her. They appeared of like breeding: all silver-haired, dark-eyed, and female. Kevral wondered for their reproductive capacities, though she felt it impolite to ask. She noticed no children among them either. All appeared to be in their late teens to early thirties. Nearly all sported the rounded abdomen that seemed so out of place for their spindly limbs, and she wondered if they might all be pregnant. Her thoughts channeled in odd directions, and she wondered if a lone man existed somewhere. Perhaps he slaughtered the boy babies to avoid competition, which would explain why these women appeared so kindred. Kevral frowned at an idea so repugnant it bothered her long after she realized she was only guessing. Surely a group that appeared to consist of about twenty-five women, no matter how peaceful, would band together against such a heinous dullard.

As if in reminder, the baby kicked, drawing Kevral from her thoughts. A flash of rage accompanied the movement, and she wondered how much her ideas, and her disgust, stemmed from King Cymion's dastardly and craven actions. She abandoned the train of thought for now, but moved nearer to Ra-khir. If such a system existed, it might endanger their men.

Phislah addressed Ra-khir. "I'm afraid no one's seen or heard of this sapphire shard, but you're welcome to look for it."

Ra-khir's expression went stricken, likely at the thought of combing an entire world for a tiny piece of gemstone that might turn up anywhere.

Apparently noticing Ra-khir's discomfort, Sassar suggested, "We will help you, but we'll need direction. Perhaps some of you could lead groups to look in the forest and others could stay and search amid our homes."

The idea of further splitting the group jangled at Kevral's nerves, but she trusted Tae and Rascal to evade trouble. She worried little for Andvari, and she would keep Ra-khir at her side.

"I'll lead a group out," Tae said, his intentions obvious to Kevral. He knew the woodlands best, and they would give him plenty of places to hide should danger appear.

Andvari's gaze rolled to Kevral's expanding abdomen. "I'll head out, too." He gave no reason; it would only incite a new wave of argument between them, but he clearly believed it best that she stay in the village.

"I goes wit' him." Rascal jabbed a finger at Andvari. Deliberately avoiding Tae, she clearly saw Andvari as the most reasonable alternative.

Kevral would have preferred that the three stay together, but she knew that would double the time it took them to find the shard.

"How big is this place anyway?" Tae shook back locks that barely fell past his ears, Matrinka's handiwork. His tone contained clear doubt.

"Not too," an unnamed woman said.

"You've traveled across most of it," Lissa said. "We'll find it."

Kevral found the words reassuring for more reasons than that it would make searching simpler. It became much less likely that they would stray beyond *khohlar* range. "Whoever finds the shard should go to El-brinith. She should be able to call the rest."

"Good idea." Ra-khir took Kevral's hand. "I guess that leaves the two of us to check the village."

Believing her husband spoke to the strangers, not her, Kevral gave no answer. She watched Tae head out, trailed by a dozen of the women. Guided by Lissa, Andvari and Rascal set off in the opposite direction, another dozen women scuttling after them. Soon, the fog swallowed both groups, leaving Ra-khir, Kevral, Sassar, and at least twenty more of the strangers at the village. Kevral revised her count, guessing as many as sixty might live here, though that would mean at least four bodies to any one cottage.

"You make your own clothing." Ra-khir stated the obvious, gaze traveling to the top of a broad, upright loom, attempting to elicit an explanation without directly questioning.

"We're weavers," Sassar explained. She made an arching gesture that included every woman. "All of us. That's how we make our living." Her words explained the perfect stitches of their clothing as well as the massive looms around the cottages. The skinny arms and long, narrow fingers would make their chosen profession a natural one. Kevral concentrated on a way to ask about the missing males, the train of her thoughts taking her away from the salient question of where they sold their goods and how they survived on a world with a single occupation.

As Ra-khir headed toward the first cottage, a woman tapped Kevral on the shoulder. "Would you like to start at opposite ends?"

Despite the helpful friendliness of all of the women thus far, something felt ominously out of place. Though Kevral could not direct or quantitate her discomfort, she refused to part from Ra-khir. As the sensation of misplaced uneasiness stole over her, she suddenly wished she had not allowed Tae to go off alone. In fact, the idea of splitting the party at all seemed stupid beyond consideration. "No, thank you. We'll stay together." She hurried to Ra-khir's side, alert for hostile movement, as they headed to the first cottage. She used the sudden fluid motion to cover her whisper to Ra-khir. "Stay alert. They make me uncomfortable."

Ra-khir turned Kevral a bewildered look and hissed back as one of the strangers opened the door. "Why?"

"Doesn't it strike you as weird that they're all female?"

"What makes you think they're female?"

Ra-khir's words struck Kevral momentarily dumb. She watched the natives sort themselves, a few funneling into the cottage, others hanging back to leave room for the Outworlders. "What?"

Surely Ra-khir knew Kevral had heard him, yet he dutifully repeated. "What makes you think they're female?"

Kevral continued to stare, still getting that impression from every one. "Their features?" she tried.

"Flat-chested, round-bellied, thin-limbed, long-haired." Ra-khir shrugged. "That could pass for either."

"But they all look the same."

"I have trouble distinguishing elves."

They edged toward the opening, ushered by slender arms that seemed to sway in the wind like weed stalks. Kevral attempted one last communication. "They look mostly all . . . well . . . pregnant."

The sorrowful look Ra-khir turned Kevral discomfited her nearly as much as this world. Not another word passed between them, yet Kevral understood her husband's point, even grudgingly agreed. *Am I projecting my condition, and the frenzy it's causing, onto them?*

Kevral barely had time to wonder before she and Ra-khir stepped across the threshold into a cottage filled with smaller looms holding a dozen partially finished projects. Kevral stopped, looking at one parallel to the floor that held a colorful garment studded with twigs and leaves in intricate patterns. A perpendicular loom nearly too large for the room held a gossamer blanket that shimmered in the light admitted through the doorway. A door at the far end led to a second room that Kevral estimated by the outside dimensions could only contain half the space of the main room, barely enough for a pantry, let alone cooking and sleeping space. "Make sense of this," she said to Ra-khir, not caring that two women had gotten between them and heard her. These gave her curious looks far gentler than Ra-khir's warning glare.

Phislah appeared suddenly at the threshold. "We think we've found it!" She gestured excitedly in no particular direction. "Come on."

Those inside the cottage with Ra-khir and Kevral scooted for the door, their guests scrambling after. The knight stole the moment to say, "I've seen people this dedicated to their craft. Artists are an unusual lot."

"They all look nearly alike," Kevral reminded. "Female."

"They're not human," Ra-khir returned. He rolled his eyes heavenward, as if beseeching the gods to forgive the comparison. "If animals wore clothes, I couldn't tell the genders of most." He managed nothing more before his exit from the cottage placed him in the middle of a throng of strangers, all tugging him toward a central cottage.

Kevral hurried to interpose herself between her husband and the weavers she still could only see as women, then found herself as much an object of their attention. They stumbled through fog and dirt to a wide open door that led to a room with a maze of looms. Beyond them, the inner door also stood open, revealing a storage room filled with woven clothing. *No food. No utensils. No pallets.* Kevral turned a triumphantly wide-eyed look at Ra-khir that said "I told you so" better than words ever could. *Weird.*

Ra-khir returned a barely satisfying nod. Surely he realized that an entire cottage filled only with craft left no space for necessities, let alone luxuries. He allowed Sassar to lead him toward a pile of fabric. She and two others raised a blanket with bits of colored glass and gemstone woven into the pattern. Ra-khir's gaze traveled over the fragments, scanning the blue ones for the sapphire shard they sought. Kevral started toward him, stopped by a smaller, apparently younger woman who held up a gauzy, beautifully patterned dress, perfect for romantic nights. From the look of it, it would fit Kevral exactly.

Trusting Ra-khir to handle barter for the blanket or, at least, for the shard, Kevral turned her attention to the dress. "Very pretty."

"Try it on." The youngster rolled the garment and lifted it over Kevral's head. "It was supposed to fit me before . . ." She ran a hand over her abdomen, confirming Kevral's suspicion. "But by the time I'm back to normal shape, I'll have grown too tall for it."

"Pity to have it go to waste," another said as the youngster slipped the neck over Kevral's head.

The fine-drawn fabric fluttered over Kevral, glittering through an array of colors in the light the door admitted. Still wary, she placed her hands on her hilts, working for an arrangement that did not compromise her guard.

"There," Ra-khir said. "In the center. It looks like the other Pica—"

A shrill mental scream cut over Ra-khir's words, accompanied by a sensation of triumph tempered by raw terror. The weavers froze in place, several clamping their hands over their ears, though that could have no effect on *khohlar.*

El-brinith. The identification came instantly. Lightning slashed the skies, accompanied by a rumble that shook the world. Kevral attempted to draw as the ground seemed to crumble beneath her. She could not move. Enwrapped in suffocating gossamer webbing that no longer resembled clothing, she found herself incapable of motion, other than her eyes. Those registered an abrupt change in their hosts. The skinny arms and legs doubled. Fingers and toes fused to points, and necks dissolved. *Spiders. Gods above, they're spiders.* Kevral's mind continued to work, though her limbs remained pinned.

Chan'rék'ril's panic stabbed hotly through Kevral's thoughts. Then, several things happened at once. Something sharp jabbed through her cocoon and into her flesh. She saw the woven blanket, still studded with gemstones, fly toward Ra-khir. He dodged it, sword whipping free in an instant. Spiders scuttled from this sudden menace, leaving Ra-khir the opening he needed. Snatching the blanket, he lurched toward Kevral, even as the creatures recovered, plastering themselves across the exit. Kevral counted a dozen and more clambering outside.

Two skittered into Ra-khir's path. His sword sliced through one, flinging gore in an arc across the wall. The other back-stepped, shooting webbing. As Ra-khir ducked, it flew over his head, flopping to the ground like a misshapen tapestry. His blade leaped for the webs holding Kevral, even as the spider jumped at him, snapping its mandibles. The bite in Kevral's side gouged deeper.

Ra-khir sidestepped, but not far enough. The bulbous body crashed against his shoulder, spinning him. As his weakness became apparent, the others surged toward him. He whipped his sword in a wild arc, sending them into an equally wild retreat, then shoved the blade through the one scrambling over him. Its mandibles snapped shut, short of its target. Unopposed, Ra-khir made a desperate slash for Kevral's cocoon that opened the fabric of web and clothing and a line of flesh as well. She toppled free, pain searing her upper abdomen and the back of her left hand. Ignoring it, she drew and cut, severing the one still attached to her hip. The head flopped to the ground, the mandibles tearing from her skin.

El-brinith's warning came as a distant shout. *Spirit spiders. Avoid their weavings. Don't let them bite you!*

Chan'rék'ril screamed again, with a paralyzing agony.

Rage surged through Kevral, accompanied by a battle wrath that stole all reason. Ignoring the elf's pain as well as her own, she charged the mass of spiders at the door. Two fell dead before the others could scuttle beyond range. She followed them, swords cleaving in silver blurs.

"Watch the webs," Ra-khir shouted, his words meaningless to the frenzied Renshai. Behind her, he could not attack without harming her worse than he already had.

Sticky threads shot toward the door in a concerted wave, a clear attempt to block the opening. Kevral howled toward them like a rabid wolf, chopping a head from a body, then sweeping off a series of legs from another. Webbing brushed her cheek and tangled around one arm, but the abrupt destruction of their pattern did not give the construction enough solidity to trap Kevral. She bounded through the doorway and sprang into the largest grouping, barely bothering to dodge the biting mandibles. Her swords ripped through them, leaving a trail of massive arachnoid bodies and still-twitching legs.

Ra-khir joined her, his larger sword hacking spiders into splotches. The woven blanket dangled from his fist, gingerly carried so as not to cover his body. Light spun and danced from the gemstones. The fog lifted as fully as the spiders' illusions.

Morale shattered as twenty spiders fell dead. The few remaining scattered, bolting desperately for the safety of the forest. "Modi!" Kevral shrieked, pursuing relentlessly. She hacked one from a trunk, running through a second that tried to escape past her. Ra-khir chopped down one more. The others disappeared amid the trees.

Only then, pain and dizziness rushed down on Kevral. Blood soaked her breeks, and cold air kissed the flesh of her stomach except where blood trickled in warm lines. She sank to one knee, swords sagging in her grip. War fury dispersed, leaving her feeling shaky and desperately cold.

Dropping the gem-studded blanket, Ra-khir doffed his cloak, then his tunic, tearing the fine cloth. He wrapped Kevral's hip with these crude bandages, watching with dismay as blood soaked through his handiwork. He applied another layer, tighter, then wrapped his cloak around her.

Shivering beneath the fabric, Kevral used the bandages that she would have offered, given the chance, to instead clean her blades before sheathing them. She glanced at Ra-khir. He stood beside her, sword still drawn and filthy, watching for signs of further danger. The broad, defined muscles of his chest heaved, the movement stirring the fine growth of red hair that had only appeared that year. Abdominal muscles disappeared into his britches in perfect lines. Spider gore and bits of web spotted his arms.

Kevral rose to wobbly legs with Ra-khir's assistance, snuggling into his enormous cloak. "We need to check on the others." Her own words lanced painful realization through her. *If we still have others.* She worried most for Tae, alone among a dozen. *Wary as he is, he wouldn't know to avoid their clothing. Any more than I did.*

"I'm sorry." Ra-khir knew better than to steady Kevral's walk, instead remaining alert for ambush. He folded the blanket, using only the tips of thumb and first finger, then tucked it under his arm. "I should have trusted your instincts."

"It's all right." Kevral remained attentive for sounds of movement as well. As they hurried back toward where they had left El-brinith, she scanned the treetops as well as the woodlands around them. Spiders could climb and would think nothing of leaping upon a victim from above. "It wouldn't have changed anything."

"Might have kept you from getting bitten," Ra-khir said softly. Though he also watched around them, his gaze frequently returned to her hip.

Surely, he worried for the possibility of poison, but Kevral felt none of the burning and spreading she would have expected from such a thing. She had suffered poisoning once, laced onto an arrow fired by one of Weile Kahn's men in the days when he and his criminal gang had worked in the *svartalf*'s employ. This resembled that incident no more than any other wound. "I doubt it," she reassured, but Ra-khir was not listening.

"I kept thinking of Béarn. If a bunch of friendly outworlders came there seeking something, the Béarnides would prove just as helpful.

"Ra-khir, it's not your fault." Kevral strived for a tone of finality. Whatever came of the bite, she would handle it. Allowing the knight to beat himself up over it would accomplish nothing. She worried more for the fate of El-brinith and Chan'rék'ril. If the elves did not exist to transport them back to Midgard, they would remain trapped until Captain found another way. No healer would exist to assist the wound, and she might not find a means to die in battle.

"It didn't seem so unlikely . . ." Ra-khir continued, unswayed by Kevral's forgiveness.

Then, a ring of ten to twenty spiders came into view over a rise, precisely where they had left the elves, Darris, and their belongings.

"Demons!" Ra-khir swore, sword leaping from its sheath as he ran.

Battle wrath flared like fire in Kevral's veins, instantly usurping pain and exhaustion. She charged, war screaming, into the fray. The spiders whirled toward their attackers, their hairy bodies and weaving legs the only things Kevral's vision allowed. She cut through three.

Khohlar shot through Kevral's head. **Danger ahead!** Before El-brinith could elicit the details, Kevral's momentum swept her into an invisible barrier. She slammed against it, shoulder first, sparks flying from the contact. A jolt shuddered through her, stinging. She flung herself backward, unable to save balance, and toppled to the ground. Spiders swarmed over her, filling her vision with snapping mandibles. She threw up an arm to protect her face, slamming the hilt into one's head. That one flew sideways. Another collapsed, severed by Ra-khir's sword. The wet body flopped across Kevral, its gore bitter on her tongue. She heaved, rolling, catching sight of something springing from a tree above. Anticipating its heavy landing, she spiraled further, suddenly free of spiders. Only then, she recognized the newcomer as Tae, dashing in to assist Ra-khir. Aligning back to back, the men hacked and jabbed at the creatures.

Hip aching, milder pains spasming through her lower abdomen, Kevral lurched to her feet, slipping on spider guts. The awkward movement rescued her from one that launched itself at her. She cleaved it as it flew past, slashing aside two more to take a position at Tae's side. Ra-khir could hold his own, but the smaller, less well-trained Easterner could not. He jerked from a bite, the sudden movement knocking Ra-khir's equilibrium. The knight's sword skimmed a spider he had intended to skewer, and it returned with a wild snap that he barely dodged.

Kevral hacked down a spider whose mandibles had already pierced Tae's tunic, and it dropped before they could close over flesh. The last two attempted flight, hammered into bloody smears by Kevral's sword. Long after she had battered them beyond death, she finally regained enough control to turn. Both elves sat, Chan'rék'ril clutching his left arm, his fingers striped with pink-red, elven blood. A shredded cocoon lay beside him. Darris stood with his hand on his hilt, though the magical barrier prevented him from assisting the battle.

El-brinith communicated through the magic. *Chan'rék'ril got bit. The rest of us are fine. I put up the shield to protect us. Thanks for helping.*

The choppy information assured Kevral that speech would not penetrate the barrier as *khohlar* had.

Ra-khir opened his mouth, but Tae spoke first, confirming what Kevral suspected. "Don't bother. They can't hear you."

"Where did *you* come from?" Ra-khir questioned the only one he could.

Tae pointed upward. "When I found the elves protected by magic, I hid in the trees. Waited there till you came. The spiders were so busy with the barrier, they didn't notice me." He studied Kevral. "Are you all right?" He winced. "Doesn't look good."

"Bit, too," Kevral said succinctly. Only then she recognized the cramps fluttering through her lower abdomen, light background to the pain of her wounds. *The baby.* Terror ground through her, dragging a lead weight of emotion she deliberately shoved to the back of her mind. Her people remained strong because only infants who could withstand the rigors of a Renshai womb survived. Her hopes and misgivings over its birth played no role here. *It will live, or it will die.* Kevral deliberately rationalized herself into apathy, knowing worry would catch up to her in the quiet moments preceding sleep.

Ra-khir placed a protective arm around Kevral. "Did El-brinith mention the . . ." He swallowed hard. ". . . consequences?"

Tae shook his head.

Kevral distracted herself from the discomfort in her uterus with a plaguing question, "What happened to the spiders with you, Tae?"

"Lost them."

"So they're still out there?"

Tae made a vague gesture. "Maybe. Unless these are them." He gestured at the bodies, glancing about nervously for more. "Have you seen Andvari and Rascal?"

"No," Darris answered, revealing that El-brinith had lowered the barrier. "Are you all right?"

Prepared to repeat the entire conversation, Kevral sighed.

"Kevral's bit," Tae explained quickly. "We're fine." He indicated Ra-khir and himself.

Ra-khir had to know. "What's going to happen to Kevral?"

Chan'rék'ril moaned. El-brinith glanced about, as if physically seeking another topic of conversation, and finding it. "There they are!"

Kevral had noticed Andvari limping from the brush simultaneously, Rascal clinging to him like a frightened toddler. The Northman's shirt hung in filthy tatters, and gore speckled every part of him. His cheeks flushed with exertion, and a rabid spark in his eyes revealed the diminishment of a battle rage as frenzied as Kevral's own.

Ra-khir dashed over to assist Andvari. Rascal released her hold on the Northman, feigning disinterest in the proceedings. Unfooled, Kevral read fear in her trembling hands and the eyes that dodged hers. The Pudarian fast-walked to the group, her attempt at composure only partially successful.

"No solid bites," Andvari replied to a question Kevral had not heard Ra-khir ask. "Got slashed by those mouth pieces of theirs a couple times and buffeted about a lot by legs." He joined the rest. "Did anyone get the shard?" Worried for injuries, no one had thought to ask the all-important question.

El-brinith's *khohlar* beat Ra-khir's response. *Someone did. It's with us.*

Ra-khir held up the folded blanket without bothering with speech.

Guard me, El-brinith sent unnecessarily. *We're leaving.*

"So what's the effect of the bite?" Kevral demanded again, though she knew the elves would prove too preoccupied to answer. She turned her gaze pointedly at Darris. If the information existed, he would have it.

The bard caught her hands. "Apparently, spirit spiders feed on souls."

Then light slashed painfully through Kevral's vision as the elves triggered the transport.

CHAPTER 13

Preparing for the Worst

When you hear hoofbeats, expect horses but prepare for elephants.

—*Colbey Calistinsson*

RA-KHIR ducked beneath a broad sweep of Harritin's ax, then lunged in with a jab that drove Knight-Captain Kedrin, on the sidelines, to wild waving. The sparring partners disengaged, Ra-khir immediately taken aside by his father. "What weapon do you hold in your hand, Sir Ra-khir?"

Ra-khir ran his gaze to his practice ax.

Kedrin's brows rose over the blue-white eyes in increments. "You have to look?"

"An ax, Captain." Ra-khir ignored the second question for the first, only then realizing it was probably equally rhetorical. "It's an ax." He knew what had to come next.

"Can we stab with axes, Sir Ra-khir?"

"No, Captain." Ra-khir lowered his attention to his father's boots, the polish marred by stripes of dirt. "I'm sorry. I'm a bit distracted." *My wife may have lost her soul.* For the hundredth time, he contemplated the significance of the thought. Until that moment, he had focused on Kevral's fanatical quest for Valhalla, the one that had consumed her, as all Renshai, since infancy. The enormity of her pain possessed him, all encompassing. His love for her compelled him to draw all of her torment upon himself and to solve all of her problems. Kevral's strength and unholy independence had made that impossible most times; and now that she faced an enemy she could not fight, he found himself equally crippled. A new thought trickled into Ra-khir's mind: *Soul or no soul, it will affect her life with us only so much as we allow it.* Mortified that such a thing could even present itself to him, Ra-khir clamped down on his considerations. Selfishness belonged nowhere in the repertoire of a Knight of Erythane.

Only then, Ra-khir realized Kedrin was speaking to him and had been for at least the last several moments.

". . . with a Renshai has definitely improved your sword work, never your best weapon. But you must see that it doesn't overtake your other training."

Ra-khir's face flushed past his ears, and his cheeks felt on fire. He could not tolerate his own disrespect for his commander and his father. "Yes, Captain." He acknowledged what he had heard and hoped he had not missed much.

The knight captain made a dismissing gesture toward Harritin, and the spar commenced in a blur that Ra-khir could barely recall scant moments later. The morning stretched into an afternoon of protocol and drill, even the jousts unable to drag Ra-khir from the density of his contemplation. He had hoped that the normalcy of knight's exercises, the mock battles if not the tedium of manners and rites, would draw him from the worry that plagued him. He contributed little to the discussions of ethical dilemmas, glad so many of his peers chose to voice their opinions; and only the need to concentrate on pike, shield, and horse brought him any reprieve. To atone for slighting his captain father, Ra-khir deliberately practiced through his lunch break, though his heart did not accompany his actions and Kedrin had clearly taken no notice of the affront.

By the time Kedrin broke the off-duty ranks for time out, exhaustion lead-weighted Ra-khir. The need to return to home and family pressed him, but he ignored the call. The timing of his arrival would not change the elves' findings, and the idea of coming to the room before Kevral and waiting in suspense for answers became unbearable. Instead, he turned his attention to his horse, Silver Warrior, brushing aside stable hands to tend to the animal himself. Only after he had groomed the white coat until it shimmered all over and plucked the mane until every coarse hair fell to exactly the same length did he turn his attention to his other charge.

Frost Reaver stood with his head across the stall partition, as if measuring Ra-khir's every action with his own stallion; yet the dark eyes remained soft and nonjudgmental. The head formed a gentle triangle, the nostrils broad, and the ears pricked forward to catch every sound. The graceful neck arched over the barrier, and the mane fell in tangleless clumps across both sides. Ra-khir turned toward Colbey's stallion once more as he scrubbed every speck of dirt and manure from Warrior's white hooves. As he rose, his hat bumped Silver Warrior's chin, sending the calm animal a single step backward with a sharp whinny that seemed more irritated than alarmed. The hat tumbled into the straw.

Ra-khir hefted it before he or the stallion accidentally stepped on it. Usually, he removed as much of his uniform as the weather and propriety allowed while grooming his mount, but his current abstraction usurped even that usual action. He brushed seeds and flecks from the hat with even strokes of his hand, then looked for a place to put it while he finished. The consistent walls of the stalls provided nothing. He glanced at Frost Reaver, who seemed to return his gaze, and smiled. "Would you hold this for me a moment, my friend?"

Frost Reaver bobbed his head, as if in answer.

Finally, Ra-khir managed a smile, carefully balancing the hat over Frost Reaver's ears and crown. Like most knight's horses, the ageless stallion tolerated the indignity without attempts to dislodge it. The brim settled across the broad nose, tipping the whole into a jaunty angle. Wisps of forelock escaped from beneath it, like errant strands of unkempt hair. Ra-khir laughed aloud at the image, then continued with his work. Likely, the hat would slide from Frost Reaver's head, but he trusted the horse not to deliberately trample it when that happened. He would wash it, along with his cape and silks, that evening.

Kedrin's voice wafted to him. "Ah, Ra-khir. You've changed."

Ra-khir leaped up so fast he slammed his head against the door latch. Fighting through the pain that followed, he belted out a clenched-toothed, "Captain!" Vision unfocused, he reached for his hat to deliver a respectful salute, only then remembering it sat on another's head. He staggered to Frost Reaver.

"Relax," Kedrin said. "It's 'Father.' You're off-duty."

Ra-khir clapped a hand to his headache. "I'm sorry. I still shouldn't have . . ." He reached for the hat.

Leaning across the stall door, Kedrin stopped Ra-khir with a motion. "I haven't known a knight yet who didn't try that at least once." He pointed at Frost Reaver with a wink of understanding. "Including me." He added without malice, "Though I have to admit you're the first to humiliate a god's own horse."

Apparently guessing himself the center of attention, Frost Reaver raised his head and trotted around his stall, the hat proudly aloft.

"He doesn't look too shamed to me." Ra-khir watched Frost Reaver prance with amusement. "Being trusted with a knight's paraphernalia hardly seems a dishonor."

"That's because . . ." Kedrin snatched the hat with a single graceful movement, flourished it, and placed it over his own red-blond locks. ". . . *you're* not a horse."

The implication seemed obvious. Ra-khir gave his father a mock-stern look. "And you?"

"Also am not." Kedrin removed the hat, absently plucking lint from the brim and unwittingly leaving a straw in his hair. Muscles bunched, visible as thick knots even beneath the layers of clothing. His cape flowed fluidly over broad shoulders, and even familiarity with similar features in his room's mirror could not keep Ra-khir from noticing his father's striking handsomeness. The knight's captain had always seen his beauty as more handicap than boon, tainting his dealings with all but the blind.

Ra-khir tested the water he had filled for Silver Warrior moments before, finding it still comfortably lukewarm. He gathered curries, brushes, picks, and combs. Taking that as a finished cue, Silver Warrior turned his attention to his hay. Ra-khir placed most of the tools into their bucket. Still clutching a brush, he approached his father, leaned on the partition, and asked casually. "What do you think happens to us when we die?"

A brief pause followed. Kedrin shrugged. "It's not a matter of thought, Ra-khir. We slump to the ground and never move again. Depending on situation, religion, family, and colleagues, we're disposed of in one form or another and return to the earth as dirt."

Ra-khir had grown accustomed to his father's dodges on the matter during his adolescence and had avoided the topic for years. "I meant to our souls."

"Only the gods know that for sure."

Before the religions had banded together, the Easterners had followed a single all-powerful deity, the Northmen their pantheon, and the Westerners an unrelated one. The old religions still existed in small pockets throughout the world, but most now acknowledged the Northern gods as the viable ones. Even within the religion once considered Northern, major differences existed, not the least of which was the Renshai's and the Northmen's staunch belief in the dichotomy of Valhalla, the haven for warriors who died bravely in combat, and Hel, the icy and miserable end that awaited cowards or those who succumbed to illness. The remainder of the West still subscribed to the theory of the Yonderworld, trusting either that all souls found the same resting place or that only strivers toward Valhalla faced the possibility of Hel. Ra-khir had seen Valhalla. Kevral had insisted on visiting it once before taking up Colbey's cause of chaos, and he had granted that wish. Tae and Ra-khir had accompanied her.

Yet even that glimpse left Ra-khir in doubt. Did Valhalla exist for all or only for believers? And what role did his own, Kevral's own, and even Colbey's own faith play in the situation? Ra-khir abandoned answerless questions to press his father. "You still haven't addressed my question. I asked what *you* personally believe happens to our souls after death."

Kedrin shook back his head, dislodging the straw enough to send it drifting toward his eyes. He removed it, bending the golden strand between his fingers. "It doesn't matter what I think."

"It does to me."

Kedrin shifted, one hand still on the partition, eyes distant. "Ra-khir, it's not my place to speculate, nor to judge. I've seen men murder, sometimes en masse, for details of doctrine whose difference I can't fathom." He dropped the straw, watching it flutter to the ground to join more. "Whenever faith is involved, whenever men believe something so intensely that they know in their hearts the gods share their convictions, they lose their compassion for disparity and grow blind and deaf to others. When so many conflicting people clash, each believing themselves utterly correct, I don't see how any of them possibly could be."

Ra-khir refused to release his point. "And you believe?"

Kedrin sighed deeply. "I believe, Ra-khir, that ultimately it doesn't matter what happens to our souls after death. I'll attempt to handle whatever comes with my honor intact." The pale eyes met Ra-khir's. "In reality, the truth matters far less than what men believe is truth. And how they handle the dissent that constitutes others' outlooks."

Ra-khir had learned to find lessons in his father's riddles, though understanding never struck without thorough contemplation. He changed his tack. "So, if a god came to you and offered the truth, you wouldn't take it?"

Kedrin remained silent several moments, before a grin worked its way across his lips. "Once I would have dismissed the question as ludicrous. Times have certainly changed."

"Evasive again," Ra-khir noted.

Kedrin responded with the directness he usually reserved for his knights. "Knowing the truth would change nothing. My actions vary with circumstances, but honor itself is not situational."

Ra-khir dove for the loophole, "Unless you discovered that some action before death affected your circumstances after death."

Kedrin placed the hat on Ra-khir's head, adjusting it to the proper pitch. "I don't believe that would happen."

The response confused Ra-khir. Almost every religion, no matter how defunct, had based itself on such a point. "Why not?"

"Because, if the gods wanted us to act in a certain way, supplying afterlife rewards and punishments for doing so, they would have let us know. Unequivocally."

"The faithful of most religions and variations would say the gods already have."

"A sure violation of the word 'unequivocally.'"

Ra-khir could not argue that. He only knew that the discussion that had begun as a concern for Kevral could never wholly pull him from that worry. Like the rest of Béarn, the knight's captain knew nothing of the spirit spiders. Until the elves determined their effects on Kevral, Andvari, and Chan'rék'ril, he could not speak of them. It would become the council's responsibility, with the input of those affected, to determine what, if anything, to tell the populace. As a member of that group, Kedrin would soon have the details, yet Ra-khir did not have the right to reveal the problem in advance. Just asking the question came dangerously near to violating confidentiality and his honor.

When Ra-khir said no more, Kedrin continued. "Ra-khir, as knights, we're called to handle missions of ultimate diplomacy. Fixed or— hopefully—open, you have your religious beliefs. Keep them to yourself as much as possible, and don't let them taint your dealings with strangers."

Ra-khir nodded, understanding that simply voicing his opinions could interfere with negotiations, now or in the future. "You can't even tell your son?"

Kedrin stared. "You're still after my beliefs?"

Ra-khir nodded.

"I believe," Kedrin said carefully, "that no one religion or individual has exclusive access to truth."

A non-answer. Ra-khir grinned weakly, expecting nothing different from his father. It seemed barely possible that Kedrin truly held no personal opinion on the matter, which allowed him to look at situations from anyone else's point of view as the need arose. Yet, Ra-khir realized, his mother's and stepfather's ideas had long ago lost meaning for him; and his experiences changed his own thoughts and approaches, even ones he once staunchly protected, daily. He let his father off the hook. "Good enough."

"Glad to hear it," Kedrin replied. "That's all you get."

Silver Warrior stomped away a fly.

An ominous sense of discomfort suffused Ra-khir suddenly, and the need to change the topic swept through him. If he did not, his mind would cling to the image of Kevral lost to Valhalla and mourning an afterlife that must have some significance, whether or not any specific religion had fathomed it. "Is it all right if I take Frost Reaver for a ride?"

Kedrin made a broad gesture toward Colbey's stallion, the expression suitable for royalty. "He's your charge." He backed away from the door.

Tripping the latch, Ra-khir swung open the stall door, stepped onto the walkway, and closed the door. "Who's been taking care of him while I'm gone?"

Frost Reaver removed his head from over Silver Warrior's partition. Ra-khir's horse followed the movement with ears and, presumably, eyes then returned to his eating.

"Stable hands, mostly. One's taken a particular liking to him. Various knights have volunteered to ride him." Kedrin gave Ra-khir an easy smile. "I've taken him out once or twice. It's not too hard to find people who want to exercise him."

Finding common ground excited Ra-khir. "Isn't he the smoothest animal you've ever ridden?"

"Snow Stormer's no slouch." Kedrin defended the animal he had ridden for longer than a decade, a magnificent stallion with a conformation at least as impressive as Frost Reaver's. "But Reaver's marvelously gaited. And responsive."

Ra-khir agreed. "Practically reads your mind." He heaved his saddle from its shelf just outside Silver Warrior's stall, then dangled Frost Reaver's nonceremonial bridle across the seat.

"Practically." Kedrin's tone implied it might not be as unlikely a possibility as it seemed. Centuries in Asgard had surely formed Reaver into something more than an ordinary horse, even had he not received training from a superior horseman who also happened to be immortal. He opened Frost Reaver's stall for Ra-khir, then took off the hat again as he went past. "You won't be needing this."

Sliding the bridle over his wrist, Ra-khir placed the saddle onto Frost Reaver's back. The stallion stood statue still as Ra-khir reached for the cinch.

"Or this." Kedrin reached across his son's shoulder as he bent, unfastened the pin, and took Ra-khir's cape.

As Ra-khir tightened the leathers, he quipped, "Didn't know you were training to become a maid."

"Valet," Kedrin returned easily, folding the cape. "No more odd than my son becoming a groomsman."

Ra-khir would have begged to differ had the entire point not been absurd.

"Actually, I'm rescuing the launderer and the seamstress. You go through more clothing than any other knight." Kedrin added, anticipating, "And no. You do enough of your own laundry already. In all seriousness, I really am proud of the way you insist on handling your own mount. The bond you forge with the animal could save your life one day."

Ra-khir did not know enough to deny it, even if he had wished to contradict his father. He tacked and groomed his own mount for other reasons, the least generous of which was that he trusted no one to do a better job. "My horse deserves at least as much of my attention as my armor."

"Indeed." Kedrin left the stall, boots crunching over straw and oat hulls.

Finishing the saddle work and placing the bridle in its proper position, Ra-khir led Frost Reaver toward the exit, his father moving aside to let him pass.

"You think you and Kevral could bring the boys by to see me tonight?" Kedrin's voice turned wistful. While Ra-khir and Kevral fulfilled their mission, Subikahn and Saviar stayed with Kevral's parents. Most of Kedrin's time with Ra-khir consisted of directing and admonishing him within the framework of the knights.

Though he hated to disappoint his father, Ra-khir doubted Kevral or himself would feel much like socializing no matter what the elves discovered. "Tomorrow," Ra-khir promised. By then, the council would know as much as he did about Kevral's future.

"Tomorrow." Kedrin accepted the change without challenge or obvious disappointment. "I'll look forward to it."

Ra-khir quashed the natural urge to say the same. Though he coveted his time with the father from whom he had been estranged through most of his childhood, he would not risk a lie. This night might herald misery that a single day could not disperse. Without a reply, he gave Frost Reaver gentle kicks to the flanks that sent him across dead grasses at a rolling lope. Ra-khir reined toward the open farms.

The effortless flow of Frost Reaver's movement lulled Ra-khir as nothing else had managed. He watched ground scroll beneath each hooffall and the pleasant bob of the landscape growing ever closer, then disappearing behind him. A cluster of Béarnian children cleared a barren field of debris, tossing stones, stems, and sticks onto a hay rack pulled by a drooping, sway-backed bay. A hand jerked up toward him, and the children looked in his direction in an undirected mass. Several leaped onto the hay rack, following his progress with awed interest.

Ra-khir gave them a cheery wave before they passed from his sight. The legends of the knights spanned centuries and all corners of the world. Awe and trust swathed them like a mantle, their very word law in the outlying areas of the world. Accustomed to remaining at the castle or among friends, where familiarity usurped reverence, Ra-khir had nearly forgotten the respect knights commanded elsewhere. He kicked Frost Reaver into a canter.

The white charger sprang into ice-grained winds, the momentum sweeping Ra-khir's hair into a fiery mane. His cloak flapped like a flag, and cold air shot through the sleeves. It felt surprisingly invigorating.

Concerns finally disappeared, replaced by a raw joy that made even the physical discomforts of winter bearable. Reaver eased into a gallop, without Ra-khir's command, clearly delighting in the run every bit as much as his rider. Although a knight's horse should remain as rigidly attentive and controlled as his person, Ra-khir did not reprimand. The wind tearing past him, the rushing scenery, the mellow sensation of lightning movement culminated in a sensation eerily akin to flight. Like some massive and magnificent bird, he soared through late afternoon's chill, and the boundaries of world and worry disappeared far beneath him.

Ra-khir did not know how long he remained, suspended in the world Frost Reaver created. As they crested a rise, the horse's hooves clattered on stone. Ra-khir drew rein, as much to sit and enjoy the sunset as to rescue Reaver from a potential fall. The horse responded reluctantly, slowing in a graceful arc that defied increments and gaits. He went still, coat silver against the grayness of dusk. Ra-khir swung down, snapping the reins into loops against the bridle but not bothering to secure the horse. He trusted Frost Reaver not to stray, and he only wished to keep him from tangling a leg in the leathers.

Patches of snow decorated the highlands. Breath steaming, Ra-khir found a boulder jutting like a chair from the main rock of the mountain. Perching on it, he studied the horizon where the sun sank below the world's edge. Like a diver plunging into ink, it left a wake of color splashed across the sky. Bands of purple and aqua, pale greens, yellows, and oranges gave way to a vast expanse of scarlet. Red-pink slashed through the others, like the blood of some sacrificial elf splattered in battle. With the vision came happy memories, snuggled against Kevral beneath travel blankets, talking about trivialities deep into the night. Even the remembrances of her taunts and threats against his honor, in the days when they could all have benefited from lessons in tolerance, returned to him in a sweet rush. He smiled. They had all come so far, suffered so much, and survived it. The experiences had made every one of them stronger.

A tug at Ra-khir's belt jerked him from reverie. A fuzzy head butted the hand that fell naturally toward his sword hilt, then vanished. His fingers fell on empty leather. "Hey!" Ra-khir sprang to his feet, balanced on the rock. Frost Reaver capered like a puppy, the hilt of Ra-khir's sword clamped in his mouth. The blade jutted sideways, gleaming red in the fading light.

"Hey!" Ra-khir repeated, too concerned about the horse cutting his lips to see the humor in the situation. "What are you doing?" He lunged for Frost Reaver. "Give me that."

The horse waited until Ra-khir had nearly reached him, then spiraled away, trotting just beyond reach. Two blasts of gray steam emerged suddenly from his nostrils, accompanied by a snort.

"Reaver, come on. Give me the sword." Ra-khir approached more slowly this time, hand extended as if offering a treat. Again, Frost Reaver allowed him almost within reach before veering. Ra-khir dodged the clumsy blade sweep that accompanied the movement.

Frost Reaver's circular run brought him within a length of Ra-khir again.

"Reaver, stop it." The exertion warmed Ra-khir, even as the coldness of winter evening drove him to pull on his gloves. "If you misstep, you might stab yourself."

The horse snorted again, this time retreating as Ra-khir advanced.

"This is not funny." Ra-khir tried to keep his tone stern, even as it occurred to him that he was wrong. He could not help finding humor in it.

Apparently another did also. A musical voice with a Northern accent touched his ears. "Actually, it's hilarious."

The sword clattered to the stones, and Frost Reaver trumpeted a series of low-pitched twisted whinnies that Ra-khir had only before heard in response to the oat bin opening. The horse trotted to his side, ears pricked in opposite directions.

Ra-khir retrieved his sword as he scanned the dusk. The sun had nearly disappeared, making vision difficult. The voice had not sounded threatening, but the ability of the other to catch him off-guard made him wary. "Show yourself, please."

A figure appeared amidst gray air and stone. Shorter and narrower than Ra-khir, the other moved with a familiar grace. Blond hair topped the head, remarkably visible through the gloom.

Frost Reaver darted forward, nuzzling the newcomer hard enough to off-balance him. Staggering a step backward, the man caught his equilibrium swiftly, dropping to a crouch to save his dignity. That allowed the horse the opportunity to lip saliva through the golden hair.

"Colbey?" Ra-khir guessed, wondering what Kevral would think if she saw her hero roughed about by a horse.

The blond responded to the thought rather than the words, clinching his identity. "Nothing like a happy horse to destroy all semblance of composure." He shoved Frost Reaver's muzzle away. "Stop that."

Ra-khir resisted the urge to laugh, instead executing a formal bow. "Greetings, lord."

"I stand corrected, Ra-khir. It's only hilarious when it's happening to someone else." Colbey rose, ignoring the knight's formality. "Good to see you, too." He caught Frost Reaver around the neck, hugging, this time deliberately sacrificing dignity.

Ra-khir gave the two a few moments before walking to the horse's side. "Would you like to return for some grooming and feed first or just take him from here?" He patted the silky side, noticing frost clinging to the animal's whiskers. A wisp of longing glided through him, swiftly staunched. Ra-khir could not tolerate envy in himself. He would miss Frost Reaver, but the horse had never belonged to him. He considered himself lucky to have ridden the stallion once, let alone the dozen or more times he had gotten.

Colbey smoothed back the white forelock. "He's yours, Ra-khir."

The words made no sense. "Excuse me, Lord?"

"I want you to keep him."

"You mean Reaver?"

"Yes."

Ra-khir scarcely dared to breathe, let alone believe. "Keep Frost Reaver? Me?"

"This isn't high strategy, Ra-khir." Colbey spoke the insult with such gentleness, it did not offend. "I want you to keep Frost Reaver forever." Though he addressed the knight, he studied the horse, as if reading the animal's reaction to his decision. "Think about it a while. It's a long-term commitment. He's likely to outlive you, having eaten his share of Idunn's golden apples of youth." He grinned, slapping Frost Reaver's neck. "Maybe more than his share. He's frisky as a colt." He gave the stallion a mock stern look. "A very bad colt."

Keep Frost Reaver. Ra-khir wondered if he would ever wade past the shock of Colbey's suggestion. "Of course, I'll keep him. I'd be honored. And, certainly, I'll return him to you if you change your mind."

Colbey shook his head with a slow sadness. "There's no turning back for me. I want Reaver happy, and he clearly is with you."

"Th–thank you," Ra-khir stammered, endless thoughts of soaring over snow and grasslands filling his vision. A thought stepped in to ruin the image. *What about Silver Warrior?*

"What *about* Silver Warrior?" Colbey voiced the concern aloud.

Apparently, Ra-khir's worry had emerged strongly enough to drift to the immortal; he trusted Colbey not to invade his mind. Ra-khir flushed, sorry to have brought up an issue that might prove no problem at all. "He was my assignment when I earned my knighthood. It's only been a few months. I don't think my father will mind assigning him to the next apprentice who passes the tests. In the meantime, I can exercise him when I'm home." He would miss the horse, yet no knight charger would ever go uncared for or even unassigned.

"It'll work out." Colbey's tone revealed no doubt. "And now—"

Worried that Colbey might leave without addressing significant concerns, Ra-khir said, "Sorry, lord, for interrupting. I have questions that I could not forgive myself forgetting to ask one who lived among gods."

Colbey stiffened, and his expression hardened. "If it's the answers of the universe you seek, I have no knowledge—" This time he broke off himself. "What's happened to Kevral?"

Ra-khir shuddered, glad he did not need to converse with the old Renshai often. He wondered if Colbey's tendency to jump past words to thoughts bothered his family as much as it did Ra-khir.

"Ravn despises it," Colbey confirmed. "Now, what's happened to Kevral?"

"She got bitten by a spirit spider."

Colbey shook his head to indicate he had no experience with such things.

"Chan'rék'ril also got bit, and he's certain his soul can no longer pass into the body of a newborn elf." Ra-khir winced at a tragedy that his concern for Kevral only now allowed him to contemplate. One less soul among the elves meant one less elf for all eternity and that all the memories and experiences of the elves who had shared that soul through millennia had died. Now, more than ever, the fate of the elves clearly rested on Tem'aree'ay's mixed baby. "The *lysalf* are determining whether or not Kevral lost her spirit as well."

"Her soul," Colbey corrected.

Ra-khir blinked. "I wasn't aware of a difference."

The last edge of sun tumbled over the horizon, leaving them at the mercy of half-moon and stars. Colbey explained, "The soul is a spark of life that remains after the body ceases to function. Spirit is the way that same creature handles life, his internal courage and daring." Darkness hid the intensity of his features as well as the scars and gentled blue-gray eyes as icy as a winter gale. "Kevral's spirit, her *fortitude*, if you will, should bring her through whatever the elves discover. She's too strong to let it crush her."

Ra-khir said nothing. He trusted Kevral's resilience and stamina also, yet this went beyond a disappointment, an injury, even beyond death. It threatened to topple the core of her beliefs, the very epitome of her existence.

Colbey clamped a hand to Ra-khir's arm, its cold seeping through layers of linen and silk. "I'm not saying it won't take time, soul-searching if you'll pardon the pun. And pain." He released his grip. "But I know she'll come through it. You must believe in her, too."

"I do," Ra-khir said, defensively. "I do," he repeated with sincerity. "I just hoped you could give me some information that might help."

Colbey had heard enough to anticipate the question. "You want to know what happens to souls after bodies die."

"Is there . . . ? Is there . . . ?" Startled by the directness of the question, Ra-khir lost the means to diplomatically couch his query. He wondered how long it would take to achieve the complete imperturbability of his father. Kedrin never stammered. ". . . some vow that gods take not to reveal such information?"

Colbey ruffled the feathers of his hair with a hand small compared to Ra-khir's. Even in the darkness, the knight could make out the white disarray of calluses against the Renshai's palm. "Not to my knowledge, though such would not affect me. I'm not a god, just an immortal. That, by the way, comes as much from my time as a Wizard as my blood parentage." He waved the same hand. "I don't believe I know any more on the matter than you and Kevral, though you're welcome to the information. I have discovered only warrior souls in Valhalla, including a few who doubted its existence. Before the *Ragnarok*, Hel contained its share also; but those were destroyed during the battle, along with their keeper. I don't know whether Hel still exists or if souls still go there; and I have no experience with other places souls might or might not find."

Ra-khir nodded his understanding and appreciation. Other than the mention of Hel, Colbey had revealed nothing he did not already know. Despite disappointment, he still appreciated the effort and candor. "Thank you."

"Don't thank me," Colbey insisted. "Rather, pay me back with a favor."

Ra-khir dodged the trap that had nearly claimed Kevral, responding "anything" to a similar request from Colbey. "Do you have a specific favor in mind?"

"You'll see the Captain tonight?"

"My father?"

"I meant the elf."

The winter chill cut through Ra-khir, no longer partially negated by the sun. "Yes. I'll need to talk to him about what he found." He knew he could simply ask Kevral, but he worried that concern might make her information less complete. He had watched Matrinka repeatedly and patiently describe the same details of a child's illness to her distraught mother.

"Could you please tell him that the leader has abandoned Nualfheim for Asgard?"

"Certainly." Ra-khir breathed a mental sigh at the simplicity of the assignment, hoping Colbey could not read the reaction. The words themselves meant little yet, without definition of the clearly Northern term, *Nualfheim,* but surely would with the clarity the Captain would add. For now, he had other matters nipping at his mind. Likely, any message from Colbey would bode more danger than he currently wanted to know.

"And please tell Kevral . . ."

Ra-khir naturally completed the sentence with "Good-bye," so it took him several moments to realize Colbey had not done so. The words "don't you think it would be better if you told her yourself" died on his tongue.

"Tell her to never surrender. And neither, I promise, will I."

Ra-khir looked pointedly at Frost Reaver.

Colbey shrugged. "But it doesn't mean I can't prepare for the worst."

CHAPTER 14

Brothers

*A pact of brotherhood is stronger than any ties to family.
Trust, honor and loyalty are sweeter and stouter than bonds
of blood.*

—Colbey Calistinsson

COLBEY watched the white charger gallop toward its destiny, the cloak
of its regal passenger flapping like a linen mane. He felt no guilt—Ra-
khir would treat the stallion well and Frost Reaver had indicated his
own comfort with the arrangement—but he still suffered a dense sorrow,
as if a hole replaced his heart. Long after his friends and companions
had succumbed to their mortality, the horse had remained with him.
More recently, he discovered many of his bravest friends and relatives in
Valhalla; but circumstances had stolen his contact with them as well.
Permanently, it seemed.

Movement flashed at the corner of Colbey's vision. Instinctively, he
ducked and turned. A massive hammer whooshed through the air above
his head, slamming the rocks just beyond him. Thunder slammed
through his ears, and a tremor shook the mountain. The staff/sword
screamed, *Watch out!*

Colbey lowered his center of gravity, weathering the quake. *Thanks,*
he returned with obvious sarcasm. Had he waited for the alarm, he would
have become a bloody smear on rock. He sought the source of the attack,
even as the hammer eased from its crater and sailed back over his head.

Colbey discovered Thor's sons before the hammer returned to them.
Magni snatched its short haft from the air, and Modi's fingers winched
closed around the sword at his hip. Thirty lengths beyond Colbey's
sword range, he did not bother to draw. Orange war braids fell around
somber faces and eyes that held a hint of premature triumph. Their
stances contained no trace of the nervousness that had kept gods from
challenging Colbey in Asgard. They clearly believed every deity stood at
their backs, and Colbey had no choice but to assume them right.

Magni hurled the hammer again, its lightning quickness a match for Colbey's own. Again, he jerked aside, barely far enough. Its head grazed his shoulder, that meager touch enough to bruise. He staggered two steps sideways, grace stolen by the impact as well as the slam of *Mjollnir* against stone. Another thunderclap shattered his hearing. Once more, the hammer disengaged, darting back toward its wielder.

Colbey leaped for the hammer. Experience and legend warned him he could not lift it, let alone catch it in flight. Frustration drove him to strike the flat of his sword against it instead. The collision jolted through his hands, raw agony.

The sword thrummed, voicing its outrage. *Ow! Why in Hel would you do that!*

Colbey had no reply. The hammer tumbled as it zipped toward Magni, and Colbey's sharp eye detected imperfections in its course. If his maneuver made its landing unpredictable, it served a purpose beyond venting a bit of fury. He charged the divine brothers.

Magni reached for his father's hammer casually, with the ease of long practice. But instead of the hilt, he found his fingers wrapped around the head. It plowed through his catch, slamming his chest with enough force to hurl him backward. He lay still beneath the weapon.

Modi howled with the familiar war rage Renshai called upon in times of need, granted by this very god. He lunged across his limp brother for the hammer.

Colbey skidded to a stop just within sword range. Before Modi's fingers closed around the hammer's haft, the tip of Renshai's blade flicked across the sword at the god's hip. The blade flicked free of its sheath, and Colbey snatched the hilt in midair. "If it's a fight you want, make it fair, you *coward!*" He tossed the sword back to Modi.

Twisting to face Colbey, Modi caught the weapon. Scarlet streaked his features. His eyes seemed to burn with real fire. He pitched toward Colbey, sword sweeping in a wild cross-stroke that Colbey barely caught on his own. The crash of steel rang as loudly as the hammer's fall, and pain lanced through his right arm.

Dodge left! chaos screamed in Colbey's head.

Worried for his grip, Colbey dove rightward, against the natural movement. Instead of sliding, pitting strength against strength, the blades disengaged, freeing a hand rapidly growing numb. As he rolled to his feet to face the next attack, Colbey changed the hilt to his left fist. *Stay out of this!*

Without words, chaos radiated a sincere desire to help, not hinder. *You try saying nothing when it's the only control you've got.*

Modi's next roaring attack precluded an answer. The god swept in with a gut level cut that combined all the strength of the ages. Unwilling to risk his other hand, Colbey ducked, forced to a low crouch by the height of the strike. At the end of his cut, Modi immediately reversed direction even as Colbey surged to stand. The Renshai caught the blow on his hilt, the area diffusing the impact, though it still hammered his wrist. Driven back to his crouch, he struggled against Modi's wrath-driven power, clutching his hilt with both hands.

Magni groaned.

Modi stiffened, and the anger receded slightly. "I was going to torture you to death slowly; but if he's alive, I'll only torture you to death."

Colbey could not afford to let Modi gain control, to add strategy to mindless rage. "Is that any way to treat your brother, Brother?"

Modi shrieked. "You're *not* my brother." His foot lashed toward Colbey.

Releasing his right hand from his hilt, Colbey seized the leg and twisted. He lost the hilt lock instantly, but the jerk sent Modi flopping to the ground. His blade scratched harmlessly down Colbey's. Instantly, Colbey executed a deft backswing that slammed the flat against Modi's head.

Stumbling to safety, Modi shrieked, "You are *not* my brother." The argument was wasted breath. Despite their shared blood, Colbey had always denied their relationship, the mortal Renshai who had raised and trained him the only parents he needed. Abruptly, the god of wrath howled down on Colbey, sword raised.

A simple stop-thrust sent Modi dodging aside, not quite battle-crazed enough to skewer himself. Colbey slashed as the god raced past, opening a line across Modi's forehead. Only then, he wondered how much of Modi's tactics were delay and why it was taking so long for the backup he clearly expected. Colbey shoved the thought aside to face another bull rush from Modi. Blinded by blood and rage, the god flung his sword in desperate figure eights, a wild attack/defense sequence. Colbey retreated, biding his time. As the pattern of Modi's sword became clear, he cut his own weapon through the sequence. The blades capered over and around one another like deadly silver dancers. Then Colbey spiraled through an opening. His sword sped for Modi's head, even as the god cut for Colbey.

A fiery line of pain tore the muscle of Colbey's back, and cold air kissed through the slice in his tunic. The flat of his sword smacked Modi's temple. The god crumpled, Colbey catching the falling sword but not bothering to assist Modi. High on a rush of action, Colbey recognized an irony that had eluded him for centuries. Renshai would not allow a respected enemy's sword to touch the ground, but the man himself could flounder in mud without concern for his dignity.

The idea flashed through Colbey's mind in an instant, not worthy of consideration when lives might lie at stake. Although Magni and Modi had attacked him and deserved whatever end resulted from a bad decision, he knew Odin's influence underlay the assault. He understood their trust. Even he had feared the father of gods the vast majority of his life, respecting him for all of it. The eerie, evil charisma of the one-eyed god defied human logic or even, it appeared, that of deities. If anyone could turn his own family against him, Odin could; and Colbey suffered a frenzied flash of anger at the realization that he had already said his good-byes. To even attempt contact with Ravn and Freya might mean losing the battle he had sacrificed himself to win.

Colbey pressed his fingers to Modi's neck. Warmth accompanied the touch, and a pulse throbbed against his fingers. Trickles of blood rolled down his own back. As the sweat of exertion waned, winter cold chilled him to the bone. He sheathed the chaos sword. Seizing Modi by the shoulders, he pulled. Pain throbbed through both hands, and the tendons of his wrists sent flashes of sharp agony with even slight tension. Unable to drag the massive god, Colbey addressed the sword. *Take us home. Both of us.*

The sword hesitated only a moment, as if to remind Colbey how dangerous such an action would prove to Modi. Apparently placing the chance to destroy a powerful creature of law over loyalty to its champion, chaos did as instructed.

The swirling colors of chaos' world appeared suddenly, immediately formed by Colbey into a stone box with walls thick enough to prevent escape and the penetration of sound. Transported inside his creation, still clutching Modi, he let the god flop to the floor.

Now what? the sword asked with clear sullenness.

Back to where we were.

Can't.

Colbey gripped the hilt, prepared to bash the sword to pieces against the walls if it deliberately refused to cooperate.

But imprisonment suited the Staff of Chaos even less than Colbey. *Walls constructed of chaos. No magic born of chaos can escape this.*

All magic is born of chaos. Colbey reminded.

Exactly.

Colbey smiled at the unexpected boon. *Excellent.*

The staff/sword sent a splash of surprise to Colbey. *Our definitions of "excellent" don't seem to jibe.*

For a force that believes itself the source of all imagination, you lack one, my friend. Colbey created a door from chaos soup, exiting into the main part of chaos' world before disposing of the opening. *Apparently, only *creation-magic defies the rules, and I can perform that here. More importantly, it means only Odin or I can free them from the box, and if I can draw Odin here, I'm already the winner.* ★

   ★*By winner, of course, you mean loser.* ★

   ★*It's all a matter of perspective.* ★ Colbey touched the hilt of his sword.
★*Now, back to the mountains. Before Magni awakens.* ★

   With a flicker of warning, the staff/sword did as Colbey commanded.

Ra-khir recognized his ride as delay only after he started on the homeward leg. Suffering the guilt of leaving Kevral with problems better handled in her husband's arms, he found no joy at all in this journey. Even pride of ownership of Frost Reaver could not penetrate the shame seeping through his every part and deep into his soul. It became a guilty cycle; the simple realization that he still had a soul to harbor the shame became as painful as the shame itself.

Only the hope that Matrinka, and perhaps Tae, consoled Kevral soothed the fires of Ra-khir's self-condemnation. The queen always seemed to know what to say, with an easy understanding that bordered on instinct. Ra-khir knew better. His manners and strict adherence to honor probably seemed as natural, though it came only of daily hours of practice and constant self-judgment. Like a protective older brother hovering over a dying sister, he wished some surgeon could slice away what Kevral needed from him and somehow graft it onto her. Even guided by father, mother, and Colbey, he still had no particular beliefs about the afterlife. Knights of Erythane, he finally decided, needed no life but the blessed one they found here. If he could have, he would have given his own soul to Kevral.

Though he hated to do so, Ra-khir left Frost Reaver in the care of a competent stable hand before sprinting to the castle. Later tonight, if Kevral could spare him, he would check on the stallion and tend to any needs not already met. When he saw his father the following day, he would discuss the disposition of Silver Warrior. Those things, though important, could wait.

Ra-khir ignored the courtyard gardens and the occasional noble lovers who braved the cold and thunder to find some moments alone. He strode past statuary and earth beds that had been raked into rows before the dirt froze beyond manipulation. He passed the pond into which Tae had fallen, frozen into irregular bulges as nature repaired the gaps, holes, and jutting hunks of ice. The walk to the entrance seemed to span an eternity; though, once there, he was little delayed by the guards. All of them knew him, respecting the elite Knights of Erythane. And they surely wanted the door shut, the winter air closed from the corridors, as he did.

Ra-khir dashed first to his room, finding no one there. Though driven to run, he forced himself to change clothes before traversing the stairways and corridors to tap gently on the queen's door. It opened to reveal Darris pointing out objects through the window, clutching Saviar to the sill with his other hand. Seated on her bed, Matrinka looked toward Ra-khir, Marisole supported in her lap. Subikahn sat in front of the younger baby, touching her nose, her hands, her hair while the girl stared curiously back. Mior curled beside them, just beyond reach. A twist in her fur suggested she had once served as the baby's source of entertainment, though probably not for long. To Ra-khir's surprise, it was Captain who held the panel open.

Without thought, Ra-khir performed a flourishing bow that earned him Matrinka's angry glare. "Forgive me . . ." he choked off the title, only then remembering Matrinka's discomfort with formality from friends.

"Matrinka," she supplied.

"Yes, My Lady," Ra-khir responded from habit, catching himself again, this time too late.

Matrinka's tone went flat. "Glad I could be of assistance, *Sir* Ra-khir."

Ra-khir flushed, her use of titles only reminding him of his informal orange tunic, blue-and-tan cloak, and black britches. Even at their most casual, the knights wore these colors. Kevral had even teasingly accused him of tying on painted head sashes while they made love.

Darris turned from the window with a bemused smile. Tae appeared suddenly, closer than Ra-khir would have believed it possible for him to miss. Startled, he leaped backward and into a crouch. "How do you do that?"

"Emerge from the shadows?" Tae guessed.

"Exactly." Ra-khir regained his composure, entering the room and allowing Captain to close the door behind him.

Tae explained with a twinge of mockery, "I stand in the shadows. Then I step out of them."

Despite his anxiety, Ra-khir managed a smile. "Thanks. That clears it."

"Glad I could be of assistance, *Sir* Ra-khir." Tae deliberately mimicked Matrinka's words, with an apologetic wink toward the queen.

Reassured by his companions' teasing, Ra-khir managed to keep most of the worry from his question, "Where's Kevral?"

Tae answered, "Headed toward the practice room last I saw." He gave Ra-khir a look of mild disdain. Usually, the knight knew enough to check there first.

Ra-khir dismissed the insult, more excited by the hope that choice of location inspired. "So she's . . . I mean she's not . . ." He looked expectantly at Captain.

The elf did not crack a smile through the friends' jabs, nor now, unusual for one with wrinkles set into grin lines. "Her injuries were tended. The cramps have stopped, and she's not going to lose the baby."

Ra-khir relaxed only slightly, gaze still fanatically trained on the elf. Kevral had survived worse injuries. She had never mentioned the cramps to him, and he had not thought to worry for the baby. "Her soul?" he pressed.

"Can't tell," Captain admitted.

Ra-khir winced, awaiting more.

"We've definitely lost Chan'rék'ril's. Andvari, it seems, is fine. With Kevral . . ." Captain shook his head, bothered by the failure. "I can tell there's something missing, but I catch a sense of *ejenlyàndel.*"

Ra-khir blinked. "A sense of what?"

Captain did not bother to repeat the strange word. "It's an elfin concept. Essentially, an immortality echo. The sense of infinality that's a normal part of every human and, more so, of elves. From our *ejenlyàndel,* we can read details of past lives and . . ." He struggled for words, then gave up with another toss of mahogany locks. ". . . magical things." He waved a hand. "Things that don't matter here."

"Kevral," Ra-khir reminded, trying to pull the whole together and losing track of the significance beneath the details.

"I'm not sure," Captain reminded. "There's something not right but also something there." He shrugged helplessly. "I've never examined a human without a soul before." He delivered the blow in a careful monotone. "It's possible it feels like this. All I have is speculation, not truth."

"The truth," Ra-khir returned as carefully, essentially quoting his father, "matters far less than what Kevral believes." Words that had confused him earlier suddenly made perfect sense.

Riddles bothered Captain less. "For that, you'll have to go to Kevral."

With a stiff gesture of farewell, Ra-khir started for the door, then stopped with his hand on the knob. He met Captain's amber gaze again. "Colbey gave me a message for you."

Captain's features paled. "You saw Colbey?"

"He came to ask me to keep his horse." Ra-khir tried to remember Colbey's exact words, certain that would prove important. "He said to tell you 'the leader has abandoned Nualfheim for Asgard.' "

Captain waited with his head tipped, clearly expecting more.

"That's it," Ra-khir said, watching the color return to Captain's high cheeks.

The once everpresent smile stretched the elf's broad lips. "Good news from Colbey Calistinsson. Who could expect such a thing?"

"Good news?" Ra-khir pressed, looking around at his companions to see if the phrase meant more to them than him. Tae chewed his lower lip. Matrinka watched the babies, but her brows slid toward her eyes. Darris nodded thoughtfully. Only he had fathomed the message, which soothed Ra-khir. Darris had information the rest of them did not, which made Ra-khir feel less stupid.

"Dh'arlo'mé's gone to Asgard to take his place as Odin," Captain clarified.

"Oh." *Of course.* As Ra-khir realized that he did have the knowledge to decipher Colbey's words, he felt foolish once again. Realization struck harder. "Oh!"

Tae put the last together as Ra-khir did the same. "He's left the *svart-alf* leaderless."

"Not leaderless," Captain corrected, the gem-like eyes swinging to Tae. "There's still the Nine, the elfin council. But without Dh'arlo'mé's impatience to guide them, they won't decide anything swiftly. Weeks or months to realize he's not returning. Another month to decide who will take his place on the council—and that short only because it's the oldest one not already part of the Nine who takes the empty slot, by unbroken convention."

"It certainly explains why we've had no more trouble from them . . . don't do that please, honey." Matrinka caught Subikahn's hand as a finger jabbed toward Marisole's eye. Mior rubbed against the infant, distracting him.

Captain made a gesture of agreement. "It's a chance for someone else to take over, one with a vision of peace or one who follows Dh'arlo'mé's bitter course. Elves have a long history of rarely changing, even over millenia. The *Ragnarok* and Dh'arlo'mé affected a change. His wake seems the right place to affect another." Realizing he mostly addressed himself, Captain bowed in Matrinka's direction. "Ladyship, will you please inform His Majesty that I must leave Béarn? I don't know how long I'll be gone."

Ra-khir deliberately blocked Captain's way. "You can't leave now. We haven't finished gathering the shards."

"I'll send you toward the next one. Then, Marrih can take over my part in the *jovinay arythanik.*" Captain paused in front of Ra-khir, gaze on the door. "It won't harm your mission. If I can rescue my people, I can't abandon that chance."

Ra-khir marveled at the arbitrariness of magic, that it mattered if one of them left the quest, but the one who had controlled and managed the whole operation could pass his role to another without price.

Darris finally spoke his piece. "You just said elves do nothing fast. Can't you wait until we're finished so we can assist you?"

Captain paused, rubbing his hands together in a nervous gesture nearly unheard of among elves. He had spent the longest on man's world and picked up more of their habits. "No. I can't afford the possibility that Dh'arlo'mé's impatience has affected them or that he left a successor. This is something I have to do now." He anticipated the possibility that one might suggest placing the fertility mission on hold. "With only other elves to help me."

Ra-khir opened the door and stepped aside, offering a knight-sign of fidelity. "If you change your mind, you know where to find us."

"Exactly where," Captain reminded before exiting into the hallway.

Ra-khir followed him through.

On the first floor of Béarn Castle, not far from the main entrance, the practice room enclosed as much space as the king's and queen's bedroom suites together. Ra-khir had collected his sword on the way back past his room, knowing Kevral would expect it. He had long ago discovered that the only safe way to interrupt a Renshai's practice was with an attack. That strategy held additional advantages: it showed an interest in working his own swordarm, which Kevral appreciated, and it gained him a workout with a competent, if somewhat brutal, teacher. *And it's taught me to stab with an ax.* Ra-khir remembered his session that morning with mild chagrin.

Ra-khir edged open the door, marveling, as always, that a small war could take place in a room so large. At times, he had discovered every Renshai in Béarn training there, their swords slashing and weaving like a silver forest of weeds in chaotic winds. This time, however, he found only Kevral. She capered and leaped, more graceful than the kingdom's finest dancers. She had laid out terrain carved from wood for this purpose: several deadfalls, trunks, and rocks. Straw-filled burlap bags that represented bodies lay strewn around the room. Ra-khir could not help wondering if they represented Kevral's suppressed wrath, the corpses a warrior of lesser morality might leave in a wild and violent rush of despair.

Ra-khir shook his head. *Stop guessing. Let her tell you how she feels.* Stepping inside, he closed the door. For several moments, he could only watch, absorbed by the deadly beauty of her sword work. The blade skipped around her so quickly he could not have seen it save for the occasional flash of highlight from torches scattered on the periphery. Her limbs moved with silken smoothness, her clothing close-fitting so as not to entangle the weapon. Her hair feathered tightly around fierce features softened by youth, the locks deliberately too short to fall into her eyes. Sweat sheened her Northern-pale skin.

Certain his staring would agitate Kevral if it lasted too long, Ra-khir drew his sword and charged his wife. Kevral rushed to meet him halfway, lunging in with a ferocious zigzag that parried his attack and slapped his cheek with the flat in the same sequence. The blow stung, as much for its humiliation as its force. Ra-khir retreated, but Kevral followed his movement, boring in with a wild flurry that touched right shoulder, left hip, and forehead in turn. He managed to dodge the last by enough to make it unlikely a mediator would have called it a hit, though it hardly mattered. The other two would have proved fatal enough outside of spar.

"Damn." Ra-khir spun aside, managing to avoid Kevral's next frenzied assault and even jabbing through an opening. Kevral parried the attempt, stabbing for his face with enough vigor to cause real damage. Ra-khir leaped backward, sweeping low as she went high. The maneuver might have gained him a hit had his foot not mired on one of Kevral's placed "corpses." He tumbled too quickly to attempt catching his balance, sprawling into an awkward heap. Pain shot through the back of his head, and a wooden rock bruised his spine. Kevral's sword descended toward his chest. He managed a desperate roll that saved him only because she did not pursue.

"Ow, ow, ow." Ra-khir skittered to the far side of the room. "Time!" He called an end to the match.

But Kevral refused to accept the halt. Raging toward him like a wounded bear, she cut the air in front of him with agile sweeps, then jabbed for his midsection. Ra-khir redirected her attack, but another followed before his riposte. Again, he managed a parry, only to have her cut back in without following the natural extension of the stroke. Faster and faster she fought, her sword disappearing into the same blur as during her practice. Less acquainted with the Renshai practice of sparring with live steel, Ra-khir dared not trust his own control. Worried about accidentally harming her with a desperate defense, he kept his movements short and crisp. He tipped aside a dozen strokes before her blitz overwhelmed him. Her blade sliced through his defenses more than a dozen times, slamming him with the flat, nicking him with the tip, leaving tiny rents in his clothing. Scarlet splotches blazed across her cheeks, and her eyes seemed on fire with madness.

"Kevral!" Ra-khir shouted, stung by a myriad of tiny cuts. He said nothing more, nearly breathless from protecting himself. He withdrew continuously, Kevral bearing in and shadowing his every movement. Only her continued use of flat and tip demonstrated that she still maintained some control. Soon, Ra-khir began to worry that, too, would break and the battle would begin in earnest. Even if he found an opening, he could not kill Kevral; he could only die at her hand.

Ra-khir's back slammed the wall, stealing the last of his air. He ducked a slash that tore a line of paint from the wall. His sword cut shielding arcs in front of him, ringing against the steel of Kevral's blade, rapid and musical. Then her sword tip carved the hilt from his hand. The weapon flew toward Kevral, who snatched it from the air. He stood still, the stone cold against his tunic, bravely facing mercy or death, whatever she chose to deal.

For an instant, Kevral stood with a weapon in each hand, staring at the man she loved. The fire disappeared from her eyes, quenched by a moisture that welled into tears. She returned his sword, then hurled her own to the floor. It was a clear gesture of disdain, not for him but for herself. Then she collapsed into his arms, sobbing.

Still clutching his hilt, Ra-khir wrapped his arms around Kevral. Nearly paralyzed by propriety, he worried about his actions even as he comforted. Nothing in his honor forbade dropping his sword on the floor, yet doing so might offend Kevral since she had gone to the trouble of handing it to him. Ordinarily, he would not have let such an issue bother him; but it might prove highly significant to Kevral. For now, he continued to hold the sword and her, careful to keep the sharpened edges turned from her back.

For a long time, they stood locked together, Kevral crying and Ra-khir remaining quietly steadfast. He fought the sensual excitement that accompanied her closeness, resigned to the adolescent body that would betray him despite his best efforts. Experience taught him to worry only for her; she would likely notice nothing but words and gestures that caring and honor would keep wholly focused on her needs. He tried to think of words to question her tears without sounding ignorantly oblivious or stupidly obvious. It seemed prudent to let Kevral broach the subject and console in silence until she felt ready to talk.

Finally, Kevral did so. "I'm sorry I hurt you. I shouldn't have done that."

Reminded of his bruises, Ra-khir suffered their dull aches and the sharper twinges of the scratches. "I'm fine. Nothing Captain can't handle." He deliberately used the elder's name rather than simply saying "elves." It might stimulate her to discuss her real concern.

The baby kicked, abrupt movement against Ra-khir's upper thigh. "Nevertheless, I shouldn't have taken out my anger on you."

"Better me than anyone else." Ra-khir tightened his hold. "I love you. I always will."

Kevral raised blue eyes that glimmered like diamonds in the torchlight. Ra-khir had never seen the self-assured Renshai look vulnerable before, and it awakened protective urges he had long suppressed. "Captain said I probably lost my soul." She repeated, "My *soul*."

"I just left Captain. He seemed uncertain."

"He said something was missing." Kevral turned away, and Ra-khir seized the opening to sheathe his sword.

"And something was there," Ra-khir reminded. He sought the best possibility. "Spiders on our world feed on blood, draining it bit by bit. The loss of a soul might work the same. We interrupted the spider's meal, and it took only part of your soul. Like blood, your body will create more until it's back to its normal strength."

Kevral considered the words, her back to Ra-khir. "Perhaps," she said at length. She turned. "If that's right, we'll know over time."

Ra-khir nodded encouragingly, wondering if would not prove better if they could never confirm his notion. So long as it remained a possibility, he could keep hope alive for both of them.

Kevral raised less optimistic ideas. "Or perhaps what they sensed is the normal feel of a soul-emptied human."

Ra-khir wished he had knowledge to argue.

"Or they even created that 'something there' sensation to make me feel better."

"Lie?" Ra-khir gave his head a hard toss, though it awakened a deep ache where his skull had struck the floor. "The *lysalf?* I don't think they're capable."

"Or," Kevral said carefully, "it could be the baby."

Ra-khir cocked his head, red hair slithering over his ear. "I hadn't thought of that," he admitted. "Its presence might interfere with their search."

"You're spending too much time with Matrinka, finding the best in everything." Kevral looked down at the sword near her feet, cringing. Renshai law deemed her unworthy of wielding it unless she performed a complicated ceremony of apology. Only now, he noticed she had not wielded the weapon that Colbey had given her. Dropping that would have disparaged the old Renshai as well as herself. "I meant the spirit echo they're finding is the baby's. Or it's mine and the lost soul is the baby's."

Kevral's interpretation made so much sense, Ra-khir found no grounds to contradict. He made a mental note to ask Captain before he left for the *svartalf*'s island. Ra-khir appealed to Kevral's strength, her spirit as Colbey called it. "We can only speculate, so we might as well believe the best. Colbey told me to tell you never to surrender."

"Colbey?" A light of determination entered Kevral's eyes at the mention of her hero. "You saw Colbey?"

"I'll discuss the details later," Ra-khir promised, knowing she would want to hear direct quotations and descriptions of his every movement. "The important thing is the message he asked me to pass along to you."

"Never surrender," Kevral repeated.

"That's right."

"Did he know—?"

"Only what I did." Ra-khir took Kevral's hand. "Not much at the time. And little more now."

Kevral lowered her head. The blonde locks sagged across her brow, the features limp from sweat. She had more to think about, Ra-khir knew. She had to come to grips with the possible loss of Valhalla, the trivialization of all she had sought that formed the basis of her culture and religion. Yet she would not listen to lectures from him. Not here. Not now. Over time, he would chip away at those insecurities, find other reasons for her to live and to care, build a new future as vast and significant as the first.

When Kevral was ready, Ra-khir would be there.

C H A P T E R 15

Law's Reach

With Law's reach long
And new grip strong
The world could little change.
Is as it was
Was as it is
For none to rearrange.
　　　　　—The Guardian of the Tasks of Wizardry
　　　　　　　　　　　　　　　　(Odin)

AS the shard-questing party gathered in a strategy room filled with elves, Kevral suffered the awesome afterimages of a dream unlike any she had ever known. Chased by faceless enemies, she had drawn her sword to battle, only to have it disappear in her hands. She had run, a terror beyond reality washing through every part. It gripped her, inescapable, for what seemed like hours before it finally occurred to her that she always carried a second weapon. Again, she had whirled, finding the creatures so near she could feel their warmth and gag on pants of putrid breath. Yet they remained blurry and indistinct. She had dismissed this as normal in a way only dreamers can, though frustration added its fire to the mix. She raised the sword that Colbey had gifted her, drawing strength from the control and security battle offered. It rattled free, growing unbearably heavy in her hands. Its weight bore her to the ground, and the nameless things that sought her sprang upon her.

Kevral had awakened then, dread a bonded part of her. Her heart hammered as hard and fast as it did in war. The baby thrashed, as restless as she. It took a long time, eyes pried wide open, to convince herself of the unreality of the nightmare. Vestiges of it had colored the remainder of her sleep. Now, the vividness of the images finally faded, but memory of the stark fright remained. For the first time in her life, she felt out of control. Even the duties of her waking life became too much: the loss of her baby seemed inevitable, and she had even lost the distant promise of Valhalla.

". . . Valhalla," Captain said, as if in echo.

The word jerked Kevral instantly from her thoughts. "What?"

Captain's amber eyes swung to the Renshai. "The next shard. The Asgard shard."

Kevral nodded, suddenly intensely interested. "What about it?"

Rascal made a loud sound filled with disdain.

Ra-khir placed a protective arm on Kevral's shoulder. "Because it's on a known plane, a close one, they localized it for us." His expression questioned her comfort and whether or not she felt prepared for chasing after another shard.

Had Ra-khir asked her moments before, Kevral might have leaped on the opportunity for delay. "Valhalla?" She could scarcely believe it. "The shard is in Valhalla?"

Concern creased the old elf's features, and the others remained solemnly silent in deference. "It may well prove the most difficult of your tasks. The gods may take exception to humans on their world, and their whims dispose them to slaughter as often as mercy. Also," he looked directly at Ra-khir. "We have reason to believe Odin has returned there, in the guise of Dh'arlo'mé. We already know that elf's opinion of humans, and he'll have essentially limitless power."

Even the normally unshakable El-brinith shivered at Captain's words. Darris clasped his hands. Rascal sidled toward the exit, halted by Tae's deliberate step into her path. Under ordinary circumstances, they would grant anyone's wish to refuse; but the magic and the urgency of their mission did not allow it this time.

"I can't transport you inside Valhalla, because there's surely magic warding it. It's traditionally exclusive about who gets in." Captain studied the group. "I'd worry for your safety if we attempted to thwart gods' magic. Do you want some time for strategy?"

"Will you be all right?" Ra-khir whispered in Kevral's ear.

"May be my last chance to see Valhalla," Kevral returned nearly as softly, delight pounding through her previous dense sorrow. "Nothing could keep me away."

When no one else answered Captain's question, Tae spoke. "Send us just outside the fence, if you can. We'll handle it from there."

Captain switched to *khohlar*, *Ready?*

A chorus of mental reassurances followed. Captain looked toward the humans, but none of them bothered to speak. The chant of the *jovinay arythanik* swelled, filling the room with the familiar rumble of sound. Captain's staccato syllables chopped through the chorus of steady elfin voices. Eagerness lengthened the preparations. A queasy sensation seeped through Kevral, its source contained pleasure. Circumstance had granted her one more opportunity to see Valhalla, and she would savor every moment of the experience, no matter how horrible the end result.

Light exploded through the room, raw agony against Kevral's retinas. Anticipation had, once again, stolen remembrance of the need to close her eyes. Desperately, she blinked away long slashes of white that destroyed her vision and remained even when she screwed shut her lids. Gradually, her vision returned, showing her a wonderland still vivid in her every memory. Her companions seemed to disappear around her; she could spare attention only for the wrought-iron fence and the brisk movement taking place within it. A massive war erupted in every corner, the maneuvers of the participants honed over years, decades, or centuries. Swords, spears, axes, and hammers caught the light of Asgard's eternal sun, flinging silver glimmers in a million directions. Men and women, rewarded for their valor, locked in a conflict that sent them lunging and surging, charging and retreating, battle cries and horn blasts reverberating. Bodies lay strewn across the ground, blood mingling with ankle-length grasses that never needed cutting. At the end of the day, survivors and dead alike would rise and retire to the feasting hall for the night, only to battle again the following day. Dense longing filled Kevral, and the idea that she might lose all this slid from concept to bitter reality. Eyes burning, she drifted closer, hands reaching for the bars.

A woman appeared suddenly between Kevral and the fence. Blonde hair flowed from beneath a winged helmet. Blue eyes as hard as diamond chips glared into Kevral's face. The fine construction of her armor might make even a Knight of Erythane suffer a moment's jealousy. She clutched a spear in a tight diagonal across her body, and a sword swung at her hip. "Living mortals may not enter."

Kevral gave only a single step of ground, assuming an offensive stance. "Who are you?" They had met no opposition the last time they had come to Valhalla.

"I am called Skögul, Raging to the most common human tongue." Only her mouth moved. "My twelve sisters and I choose who passes through the gates called Valgrind." She lowered her head to glare into Kevral's face. "And we have not chosen you."

Rage flared up in Kevral, and her hand fell to her hilt. Ra-khir seized her wrist, never knowing how near he came to losing his hand; and Tae moved to Kevral's other side.

Darris sang softly:

> *"Across the vast heavens*
> *Valkyries ride proud,*

The manes of their horses
Like ink stripe the cloud.

The host of thirteen,
Always shunning the meek,
Fly over the battle:
The brave dead they seek.

Whisked home to Valhalla,
Battle rage reigniting,
Blessed forever—
Their souls ever fighting."

Kevral stiffened, never having heard the familiar Northern war song in the trading tongue. The translation remained remarkably true, if somewhat forced by the rhyme scheme; and it reminded Kevral that she faced a creature she had worshiped since infancy. Hostility receded, and she managed a stiff curtsy, though her gaze remained locked on Skögul's sculpted face. She did not recall any gates at her last visit and had assumed the valiant dead entered by magic. Or, as she once had, by a challenging climb.

Releasing Kevral, Ra-khir bowed, demonstrating none of Kevral's caution. Kevral could not help wondering whether he trusted Skögul not to attack or his Renshai wife to protect him against such uncordialness. "Please forgive my wife's impertinence. She meant no disrespect. It's just that we've come here before, and no one stopped us then."

Andvari added a more relevant detail. "She's Renshai."

Barring Rascal and the elves, the entire party turned to glare at the Northman, who became visibly self-conscious beneath their scrutiny. The others had learned long ago not to mention Kevral's heritage to strangers. Even so many centuries after the Renshai's falling out with the North and their reign of terror across the West, prejudice remained. The mere mention of the guardians of Béarn's heirs sent some townsfolk fleeing and others tiptoeing around offense as if facing angered royalty. Kevral made a mental note to kill her irritating companion the moment the mission ended, even as Ra-khir surely reminded himself to warn Andvari not to announce her heritage again.

As Andvari slunk as far into the shadows as Tae, Kevral turned back to the Valkyrie.

"Ah," Skögul said, nodding thoughtfully and seeming to take no notice of the humans' chagrin. "That explains it."

"My Lady," Ra-khir continued, as if Andvari had not interrupted.

"Our world requires a broken bit of something that happens to have come to rest in Valhalla. If we could just retrieve it—"

"No!" The spear butt slammed the ground. "No mortal will enter Valhalla."

Kevral grinned, about to reveal that she already had once before, but Ra-khir anticipated the gloating and forestalled it with a warning tap of his boot against her ankle. "My Lady, perhaps you would consent to relay our need to those inside. Or allow us to speak with them through the fence."

Kevral lowered her head. The disappointment of remaining outside overpowered the joy that should have followed such a reasonable suggestion. She could already feel the slam of swords against her own, the music of clattering steel, the sweet perfume of exertion. Desperate craving exploded into need. The spirit spiders had stolen her chance to arrive here by merit. She gritted her teeth as the rest of her body seemed to lapse into boneless weakness, unable to bear her own weight, let alone the sacrifice. In a moment, her last chance to enter Valhalla would disappear. She found herself hoping the Valkyrie would refuse, shocked when Skögul did exactly that.

"Impossible." Fine gold ringlets slid across the Valkyrie's forehead. "No sound can penetrate that." She gestured over her shoulder toward the fence, without bothering to look where she indicated.

Immediately in control of her muscles again, Kevral glanced toward the never-ending war within Valhalla's wrought-iron barrier. She had had no difficulty hearing the clash of weapons, the clatter of a hard blow fended by armor, and the glorious shouts of victory. When she and Colbey had climbed inside, they had easily communicated with Ra-khir and Tae on the outside. "That's not right!" Kevral shouted before Ra-khir could stop her. She waved rapidly, indicating the broad spaces between the bars. Although they would not admit even a toddler, sound could pass freely through such an opening.

El-brinith saved Skögul the need to explain. "There's an unseen barrier. It seems to me it would prevent physical and magical entrance in addition to sound."

Kevral's hands fell to her sides, balled into fists. "But I hear the war cries. The screams. Threats and howls of victory. The chime of . . ." She trailed off, recognizing every eye curiously upon her. Cocking her head, she listened again, shocked to discover only a dense and eerie silence issuing from beyond the fence. Imagination, not reality, had added sound to a spectacular war.

"My Lady." Ra-khir tore concerned attention from his wife to address Skögul again. "Could we then impose upon some servant of yours to communicate our need to the warriors?"

"Einherjar," Skögul corrected, smiling fiercely. "The warriors of Valhalla are called *Einherjar*. And I'll think about it." She turned her back on the gathering.

Incited by a gesture Renshai deemed insult, Kevral clamped a hand to the hilt of one sword. Battling a Valkyrie would prove as exciting as satisfying, especially when she sliced that irritating grin from the woman's face.

Ra-khir shook his head in warning, a clear plea for tolerance. The party studied Skögul with an intensity she could not ignore. Even the patience of an immortal must wither under such long scrutiny.

Finally, Skögul rolled her eyes. An ululating cry broke from her lips so suddenly that Kevral assumed a defensive posture. Even Ra-khir's steady hand wrapped around his hilt. The Valkyrie fell silent almost immediately. Moments later, another appeared, alike enough to pass for a twin. She, too, wore armor that shimmered in the sunlight and clutched a spear in a battle-scarred fist. Savagely beautiful features peered out from waves of wheaten hair.

Skögul stepped back to speak with her sister. The newcomer's eyes found the party and remained there throughout their discussion. Finally, Skögul addressed Ra-khir. "What is it you seek?"

Ra-khir described the Pica shard, aside from the specifics of its shape. They would not know that until they found it.

The second Valkyrie nodded once, then headed around the fence once more.

"Herfjötur will perform as you have asked." Skögul seemed to find it necessary to add, "Not because it's your bidding, but because it is mine. In this way, I hope to dismiss you from my notice." She executed a back-handed wave clearly meant to indicate they lay beneath her regard, though she had spent much time in conversation with them.

Darris had slipped back with Tae and Andvari. He made a motion for Ra-khir and Kevral to join him, which they did. It seemed reasonable to give the Valkyrie some space after she had granted them a favor. Kevral went only reluctantly. The urge to match her skill against one of Odin's chosen became a red-hot ball of need burning in her chest. Alone, she would have accepted any excuse for a fight. Now she forced her attention to the need of mankind and her promises to Béarn's queen to heed the mission first.

They had barely drawn beyond hearing range when Kevral grumped, "What happened? No magical barriers and Valkyries last time we came. Why aren't they out picking up warriors from the battlefield where they belong?"

"What battlefield?" Andvari supplied. "The North is finally at peace, and I don't know of any current danger to Béarn."

Just Andvari's voice irritated Kevral, and she turned her suppressed irritation on him. "You stay out of this!" she shouted, not caring if Skögul heard. "Are you just stupid? Or are you trying to incite people against me?"

"I—I wasn't—" Andvari started.

Kevral leaped in again. "Just answer the question."

"Kevral," Ra-khir said with a hint of patronage. "There's really no safe or correct way to answer that question, the way you phrased it."

Kevral whirled on her husband. "He didn't have to reveal me. You know how dangerous that can be to the mission."

Tae summoned Andvari with a subtle jerk of his chin.

Ra-khir soothed, voice approaching a whisper. "Actually, Kevral, it's not a danger here. Valkyries obviously love Renshai. In fact, that might be the real reason Raging did us the favor."

Kevral could only concede the argument, though she credited it to Ra-khir, not Andvari.

Darris seized upon Kevral's silence with the answer she had sought before the simple act of Andvari speaking had goaded her to fight instead. This time, he unslung his lute to accompany the singing of another translation, this time a piece of a Northern prayer:

> *"Chosen by the Valkyries,*
> Einherjar *war the day,*
> *Then retire to* Odin's *barracks;*
> *The feast is underway."*

Darris paused, fingers still on the strings to ascertain whether or not he had made his point. Kevral caught it at once, nodding briskly while others without her religious background considered moments longer.

"Odin controls the Valkyries and the wars," Kevral said thoughtfully, suddenly certain whom Odin intended his new security to ban from Valhalla. *Colbey.* Faith instilled since birth clashed with a frenzy that required time and deep-searching to become realization. The very foundation of Northern religion had been built on respect, awe, and fear for the AllFather. Yet Kevral could not help holding Colbey in equal esteem; the once-mortal Renshai turned god had become an object of worship among her own people and her own personal hero. She already knew the two worked against one another, yet the actual understanding failed to penetrate until that moment.

Before Kevral could consider longer, the one known as Host-fetter, Herfjötur, again appeared around the fence. She took a position beside her sister, standing as tall and with the same uncompromising posture.

Highlights more like sparks seemed to emerge, rather than glimmer, from the spear points. "A Northman called Mundilnarvi states he has the thing you seek. He will not surrender it to a Renshai . . ." Her gaze swung to Kevral whose sudden, intense rage at Andvari rekindled. ". . . unless you agree to battle him to the death."

"Coward," Kevral spit. She could not help adding, "Like all Northmen," for the sole purpose of insulting Andvari.

"Kevral . . ." Ra-khir warned.

Kevral justified her words, "He knows he can't really die. And I can."

Tae gave Andvari an encouraging nod, but the Northman backed down from the argument with a hopeless shake of his head. Ra-khir fought the battle for him. "Fine. Then this Mundil . . ." he strived for the ancient, Northern name. "Mundil . . ." When the correct syllables did not come, he used others. ". . . this *Einherjar* is a coward." The words clashed absolutely. "There's no reason to drag friends and strangers down with the same label."

"What do you call people who attack others at night, asleep, unannounced, and in numbers of ten to one?"

When Ra-khir did not answer swiftly enough, Kevral jerked toward Andvari. "What do you call Northmen who set out to deliberately destroy a single tribe, butchering honored warriors, once slain, to bar them from Valhalla?"

"I chose many of those Renshai," Skögul reminded, speaking easy memory of a battle more than three centuries old. "Take the news back to your kin: dismemberment cannot bar a brave fighter from Valhalla. Perhaps where ignorance fosters bitterness, knowledge can overcome it."

The words stunned all of the anger from Kevral. She had not expected the Valkyrie to speak freely on such matters. Colbey had already informed her of the error of a belief most Renshai and Northmen had surrendered centuries past. Yet, though most vocalized the understanding, many still superstitiously believed and worried desperately over injuries the way Kevral now did for her soul.

"Now," Skögul continued, jabbing a finger toward distant parts of Asgard. "Go."

"My Lady," Ra-khir started. "Could you not grant us the right to further bargaining?"

Herfjötur's eyebrows glided upward even as Skögul's pressed inward, expressing irritation. "We've wasted as much time on you as we will. Mundilnarvi cannot leave. You cannot enter." Skögul made a dismissive gesture.

Kevral swung around to argue, this time stopped by Ra-khir's gentle head shake. For the second time, the humans retreated to discuss their options and Darris chose to continue his song:

"Through the battle undisturbed,
The Valkyries come raging.
Shields and byrnies striped with blood
The worth of corpses gauging.

But Freya comes to claim her half
Of casualties most worthy.
Odin's choosers take the rest
Of those whom they deem . . ."

Darris broke off with an apologetic smile, speaking the last word: "nerve-y. Sorry. Rhymes in translation don't always work. Either the meaning gets distorted, sentence structure becomes impossible, or . . ." He grinned again. ". . . you stretch a bit."

Ra-khir tried to rescue the struggling bard. "Not all songs have to rhyme."

"The teaching ones do. Otherwise, we could just say whatever we wanted to a tune, without effort. Not much of a curse."

"Odin's curse," El-brinith reminded, their current feelings about the AllFather unpleasant.

Darris shrugged. "A permanent and unremitting curse, nonetheless. Jahiran may claim otherwise, but look what happened to him." He shivered at the memory of the crazed bard on the first shard world. "I don't care to personally suffer the result of attempting to break a centuries' old decree by the most powerful of gods, thank you very much."

Kevral gleaned the information inherent in the song. "Freya claims half the *Einherjar*." She brightened, repeating with a measure of understanding, "*Freya* claims half the *Einherjar*." Kevral looked at Darris to ascertain she had taken home the right message. "She should have some say in who enters Valhalla."

Darris nodded broadly.

"And Freya is Colbey's wife," Tae reminded. "Surely she'll at least listen."

"Maybe we shouldn't all go," Chan'rék'ril finally added his piece, leaving Rascal as the only one who had not yet spoken. The Pudarian spent most of her time avoiding Tae and keeping her mouth shut. "A bit intimidating." He made a circular motion with one finger to indicate the size and oddness of their group.

"To a goddess?" Andvari said.

Mind gliding back to the spirit spiders, Kevral stiffened; and Ra-khir spoke the thought aloud. "I don't like the thought of splitting up. Especially when we have Odin to worry about."

"Bigger problem." Tae spoke from his haunches, peering out over the vast emerald grassland. "How do we find her? I don't suggest wandering around till it happens. And I doubt they're going to help us." He fluttered his fingers toward Skögul.

"Practice field," Ra-khir said suddenly.

Kevral smiled. When Colbey had brought them to Valhalla, he had paused long enough to show them one of his favorite skill-honing areas. Freya might not prove as obsessive about going there, but Ravn probably would. "Perfect." Kevral started off before anyone could recommend another course of action, and the others scrambled after her without protest.

They trotted across meadowlands filled with symmetrical, uniform grass spears and interrupted by wildflowers. At first, worries about addressing a goddess captured Kevral's thoughts, but, at length, an oddity claimed her attention. Asgard's patterned routine, its lack of weather, and its steady temperature had added to its alien and special feel the first time she had come here. She knew the grasses remained always at human ankle length, but she did not recall the clover, yellow *chrishius,* and amethyst-weed seeming so patterned. The breeze that added a touch of reality to a world that seemed more like perfectly painted play backdrops had disappeared. Every green blade pointed toward the sky, without a stir of air to bow it.

As the group followed the pathway into forest, Kevral's gaze traced lines of evergreen, constructed of ever smaller triangles. At her last visit, these had seemed perfect. Now, they seemed *too* perfect, every angle alike and every side matching. Each towered nearly to the same height, unmoving beneath the golden ball of sunlight. The sky resembled a sapphire shroud, the sun gleaming through a precisely cut circle and fluffy clouds stable amidst the blue, like statues of sheep. She recalled other trees the last time they had come, hardy deciduous types unlike anything on Midgard, with seed pods spinning like tops in gentle currents.

The forest broke upon another meadow, like a vast ocean of green water. The evergreens apparently blotted sound, for the instant they stepped from the trees' shelter, sounds wafted to them. The flawless chime of a well-timed block preceded a flurry of chinging sword clashes. Then the sound of combat stopped, replaced by a voice whose words could not quite reach Kevral. She froze, the others stilling behind her. Scanning the field, she discovered two figures, the smaller one demonstrating something from behind the other. She watched as they disengaged, and the teacher began a kata with a sweep that seemed endless, the blade tossing highlights like tiny suns. His sword cut back suddenly, direction reversing impossibly fast, and a second leaped out to join it.

These spun and wove together in chaotic movements too fast to follow. At times, it seemed as if the swords cut through their wielder and one another.

Kevral recognized the method, if not the details. *Renshai maneuvers.* Then the lithe wielder added his own movements to the drill. Slender and sinewy, he moved with a grace and speed that held Kevral spellbound. Threading through the motion of his swords, he sprang and spun and capered like some new type of faery. The swords seemed a part of him, their movement never slowing, even when he shoulder-rolled or barrelled across the grass. He launched into a wild series of high maneuvers, leaping, spinning, and kicking in midair, without ever losing the track of the thrashing swords. Then a hand closed around Kevral's arm. She whirled to Ra-khir, drawn from the scene long enough to realize she had drifted dangerously near it. The man's *svergelse* had enthralled her, hauling her with the inexorability of undertow.

"Ow! Damn it!" the man's musical curses broke the last traces of his spell.

A female voice followed. "That's what you get for showing off."

"Ow! Ow!" The male grumbled breathlessly, "Your sympathy is greatly appreciated, Mother."

Kevral glanced back at the combatants. The fiery beauty of the man's movements had kept her focused on them, and only now she recognized Ravn rocking on the ground, clutching his left foot. His boot lay beside him. Ash-blond hair hung nearly to his shoulders, tangled from his wild *svergelse,* and a single lock curled between his eyes. Though not classically handsome, like Ra-khir, his features held enough of Colbey's likeness to fascinate her and enough of Freya's to make him striking. Kevral caught herself staring, unable to turn her gaze to the perfect loveliness of the woman who stood over him.

"Cut all my stupid toes off, and all you can say is I deserve it."

"Not enough blood for that." Freya's stance radiated more caring than her words. She headed toward him, then stopped suddenly and looked toward the woods. Noticing the audience, she froze in place.

Still oblivious, Ravn continued wistfully, "If Father hadn't left, I'd have had that thing perfected by now."

Freya said something too soft for Kevral to hear, then Ravn stopped complaining and looked up suddenly. His hand fell from his foot, and he reached for his boot, eyes locked on her and Ra-khir.

Freya stepped protectively in front of her son. Now, Kevral managed a good look at her: the mild, flawless oval of her face, the billowing cascade of golden hair, and a body whose curves defined the female ideal. She glanced toward Ra-khir, only to find him shielding his eyes with a hand. He performed a bow that lasted longer than she would have believed possible, containing every possible flourish, then dropped to one knee, head bowed.

Stunned, Kevral took several moments to realize she should also demonstrate some grand display of respect. As the understanding that she faced a deity finally struck, she found herself incapable of remembering even the protocol for royalty. For the first time ever, she wished Matrinka allowed her the practice. Capable of nothing grander, she lowered herself to one knee beside her husband.

Ravn stepped around his mother. "Kevral," he said, cheeks scarlet against ivory. He limped to her, taking her hands, and assisting her to her feet.

His touch felt electric. Memories flooded Kevral suddenly, a dreamlike picture in which the participants seemed ghostly and faded: the strange, golden figure with the sword maneuvers of a Renshai; the single night of quiet passion amidst Leondis' wooden and teary-eyed rape during which the prince, not she, had cried; and the Renshai's apologetic and gentle ministrations. More than once, she had wondered if any of it had truly occurred or if her own desperation had created all of it. Colbey's words had added the truth intellectually, but only now did she finally know in her heart. Ravn Colbeysson had likely sired the baby stirring inside her.

Under his mother's curious scrutiny, Ravn pulled Kevral aside. "I'm sorry," he said. "I—Father said—I didn't want. . ." Running out of words, he shook his head.

Kevral found herself equally incapable of speech. The being in front of her looked as nervous and abashed as any teenager caught in a desperately compromising situation. She could scarcely believe she stood in the presence of divinity. Equally to her surprise, she found her tongue first. "Please don't apologize, my lord. You did me a favor and an honor. I begged your father's assistance, and he helped the only way he could." She closed her fingers around his scarred and callused hands. "I . . . did so willingly. If not for you, I would be carrying Pudar's baby." She demonstrated her revulsion with tone and expression.

The word "baby" turned his face a deeper red, and she noticed he avoided his mother's gaze at least as fanatically as Ra-khir did. "It's possible . . ." he finally managed, though he got no further.

Kevral reassured with the best smile she could muster, "I know. But I can allow myself to believe it a certainty." *At least I know it's not twins with different fathers this time.* The elves had detected only one, though they could tell her nothing about gender or parentage.

"Tell Ra-khir . . ." Ravn swallowed hard and glanced at the knight, whom he could tell himself if he wished to do so. The two had never met face-to-face, but the god had likely seen the young knight through whatever magical means deities used. "Tell him I won't interfere. I couldn't if I wanted to. It's a lot like my father's situation. Love and nurturing matters more than blood."

Kevral tried to grin again as his face blurred through welling tears. "Thank you," she managed, fighting for control. "But it won't matter." She gulped several breaths of air while he watched her with wonder. She called upon the Renshai mind-over-body techniques to steel herself. Ravn did need to know. "Pudar has claimed the baby, and it looks like they'll get it." She rolled her eyes up to his, gentle blue compared with his father's icy blue-gray. "Can you help?"

Ravn closed his eyes and shook his head. "I'm sorry." He winced as he choked out the necessary words. "Even for that, I cannot interfere on Midgard." He released Kevral's hands.

"I understand," Kevral said. And did.

Ra-khir and Freya had entered their own conversation, punctuated by the knight's bows. His eyes flitted from the woods, to the field, to the sky, averted from Freya's enthralling beauty and the private conversation between Kevral and Ravn. As that came to an end, Kevral rejoined her husband in time to hear him remark: "I spoke with Colbey only a few days ago."

A light flickered through Freya's eyes. Kevral thought she saw a hint of innocent worry and need before the blue orbs turned cold. "Indeed? Where?"

Guilty for her time with Ravn, Kevral linked her arm through Ra-khir's. He gave her hand an encouraging squeeze but otherwise showed no notice of the gesture. "On a mountain in the outlying region of Béarn. He gave me his horse." He glanced at Kevral, guarding his tongue. "He seemed resigned to the possibility he might die, but he promised not to surrender."

Freya nodded, her response surprisingly restrained.

Ra-khir seemed not to know where to go from that point. "If I . . . if I see him again, My Lady, would you like me to tell him anything?"

"No." Freya swallowed hard, but her words emerged with a frigid calculation that revealed no hesitation. "It's best if you have nothing to do with him, either. He's . . . dangerous."

"Dangerous, My Lady?" Ra-khir pressed gently, while Kevral stifled the urge to mention how ridiculously self-evident that was, now and in the past.

Ravn came over to stand beside his mother. His choice of position seemed every bit as supportive as Kevral's for Ra-khir.

"It's not something with which mortals need to concern themselves." Freya's tone held a warning that quelled the possibility of further questions. "Now, I will allow Kevral access to Valhalla for the purpose of retrieving this shard with the understanding that the rest of you will wait outside. And none of you will interfere with the system Odin created there."

Ra-khir paled. "But, My Lady, I was hoping you would allow us, please, to speak with this warrior. See if we can't convince him to help without bloodshed."

The skin around Freya's eyes flickered, the last vestige of a stifled wince. "That's all I can offer. Anything more would require Odin's approval, and I prefer not to disturb him for mortal matters."

Kevral read the implied warning. Involving Odin might well prove fatal. "Thank you, Lady." She finally remembered a curtsy. "And you." She performed another for Ravn, who returned a stiff and stony-faced nod.

"Likely, he's watching us now," Ravn said. "If he sees the need to step in, he will."

Freya shook her head slightly and frowned at her son, but Kevral appreciated the candor, suspecting their expressed attitudes toward Colbey probably had a basis in Odin's spying. It surprised her that Ravn had dared to discuss the baby, and she suspected that his surprise at seeing her and his need to place her at ease had overridden memory or common sense. She only hoped Odin would not see the similarity between her baby and Colbey's origins as a threat.

Ra-khir executed one more flowery bow. "Thank you, My Lady." He turned Ravn a direct and knowing stare. "And thank you, too, My Lord."

Ravn smiled, clearly realizing that Ra-khir had not thanked him for the same reason and appreciative of the knight's understanding. "You're welcome," he said. "And good luck."

Kevral cherished the god's blessing. They would surely need it.

CHAPTER 16

The Ultimate Sacrifice

Never surrender.

—Colbey Calistinsson

SKÖGUL and three of her sisters revealed a massive gate, by magic, in the fence around Valhalla. Dressed in golden armor that shimmered like fire in the sunlight, the Valkyries all clutched spears, points angled toward the heavens. Though hard, Skögul's expression suggested no particular malice, despite Freya overruling her command; and she opened the gate a crack for Kevral's entrance. The other three muscled in to assure that no one attempted to accompany the Renshai, though none of her companions showed any inclination to violate their oath to the goddess. Ra-khir did, however, catch Kevral's hand as she started to move. "Careful, my love. Try to avoid a battle if you can." His eyes beseeched a promise she could not give him.

Acid seemed to scald Kevral's veins, the desperate need for battle irresistible. On the walk over, she had finally considered Mundilnarvi's odd name. Andvari had added the final clue by stating that it sounded like the ancient form of Mundinari. Surely, she would face a warrior with centuries in Valhalla to learn his craft. In that time, he had surely fought many Renshai. Her tricks and swift maneuvers would not catch him off-guard. This would surely prove the greatest battle of her existence, her final opportunity to fight *Einherjar*. If she survived, she accomplished a worthy feat; and, if she died, she would do so with honor. No matter how competent, this *Einherjar* would earn himself an admirable battle.

"Kevral." Tae tugged at her other sleeve. "See if you can work a deal that he gives us the shard even if you lose."

Ra-khir turned his Eastern companion a grim-lipped glare that Tae deliberately ignored.

"You may have to do better than your best," the Easterner reminded. "The future of all children depends on you."

Kevral fixed her gaze on the swarming chaos of battle. The urge seized her to dart to the center of the conflict, joining ancestors and bygone enemies in a wild flurry of thrust and dodge. Their war howls stoked her excitement, melody to the underplay of thumping hammers and clashing steel.

Giving up on the possibility of peaceful diplomacy, Ra-khir spoke the best words he could have chosen, Colbey's own. "Never surrender, Kevral. Never surrender."

Kevral stepped through the gates at Skögul's side. As the metal snapped closed, cutting off the sounds of her companions' concerns and encouragements, Skögul pointed. "That's Mundilnarvi."

Kevral followed the gesture to a massive Northman leaning against the fence, apart from the battles. A knotted, dark green scarf covered the top of a head that seemed too large even for his massive torso. Sandy war braids hung past shoulders that bunched like boulders beneath a bulky leather tunic. He wore a massive, broad-bladed sword at his right hip, and a hand ax graced a loop at his left. Green eyes studied her hungrily, like prey. The warrior belted out a laugh. He spoke in a thickly accented bass, his structure archaic: "The contaminated bloodline grows puny—weaker with each generation." He held up an irregular shard of sapphire, then flipped it into an inner pocket beneath his tunic. "Let us not tarry. A real battle awaits." He jerked his head toward an armored Northman, as sizable as himself, standing nearby. "Be at you in trifling time."

The waiting Northman gave no response, features screwed in condemnation.

Kevral's heart beat a slow, heavy cadence in her chest, the calm anticipation of war. She returned a wry, verbal shrug in the form of a Renshai proverb, "The larger the enemy, the larger the victory."

Mundilnarvi smiled. "Slaughtered my fully shareness of Renshai at the magnificent battle which as much as ended your bloodline. Defiled at fully every corpse." He took a menacing step closer, his eyes narrowing to animal slits. "Everyway I could." He made an unrecognizable gesture she guessed was once obscene. "And at yours, too."

Kevral felt her insides boil with revulsion and need, but she forced calm. Her rage would instantly gain him the upper hand. "If you fight half as much as you yammer, your friend will wait a long time."

Mundilnarvi clapped his left hand to his hand ax, Kevral's eyes naturally following the movement. Too late, she recognized the feint. His sword jerked free first, thrust at her face. Her swords glided out and up as swiftly as a blink, yet almost not fast enough. She caught his blade on a crossblock, the force of the blow aching through her arms. She riposted immediately with both blades, only to meet low blocks by sword and hand ax. *Strong, arrogant, and fast.* Kevral faced the challenge bravely. He might well prove more than she could handle.

The battle erupted into a riot of attack, dodge, and parry. His sword came at her nearly as quickly as she could return, his speed incalculable for one without Renshai maneuvers. Her preference for evasion over block, further evened their speed. She could not afford to parry too many of his power strokes. If they did not snap her blades, they might shatter her arms. Repeatedly, she bore in, forced to pirouette beneath his longer reach, only to find herself foiled by his hand ax and sword defense. Like every non-Renshai she had ever met, he used his second weapon only for protection, but he would take an occasional swipe when he found her too near for a full force attack of his blade. He relied heavily on thrust, aware as she that he did not need much momentum to power it through her small form.

For longer than any spar, Kevral exchanged jabs, sweeps, and deflections with her massive foe. Breath rattled in her throat, and the air seemed unusually thin. Fatigue weighted her arms, as much from the force of his attacks as the lengthy duration of the battle. Then she managed a weaving sweep and spin that opened the fabric of his tunic and rang against a band of steel. As she rolled past, swinging back to catch a sure riposte, his laughter rumbled through her ears. "Hidden armor befuddles Renshai every time."

"Coward," Kevral growled, bounding in for an attack before reining anger. He hooked her gut thrust with the hand ax and hammered down her sword with a directed head strike. A Renshai twist saved her from his assault, but his blade slammed her own down on her head. Pain shocked through Kevral, dropping her to one knee. His sword screamed toward her, and she spiraled awkwardly away. "Modi!" she screamed, which kindled his laughter anew.

"Hurt?" Mundilnarvi back-stepped, as if in sympathy though she knew he only gathered momentum to run her through.

Kevral lunged into a crossblock, needing both arms to redirect a mighty thrust that would strain her sinews. Even as his sword sped toward her, she sighted another movement at the edge of her vision. She barely managed to jerk sideways before his ax flew true. Only the abruptness of her movement saved her chest from the blade. Instead, the pole crashed against her right shoulder. Her arm flopped to her side, Colbey's sword lost to her fingers.

"No!" The need to rescue the weapon from disrespect stole all focus on pain. Kevral dove for the sword, driven backward by a sudden flurry of attack from Mundilnarvi. The sword tumbled, plowing up a furrow of dirt. Pain receded, leaving her right arm desperately numb. She raised the other sword bravely, the fight essentially over.

But Mundilnarvi did not press his advantage. Leaning deliberately over Colbey's sword, he spat upon the blade.

Nothing could have enraged Kevral more. With a screech of frenzy, she launched herself at Mundilnarvi with a savagery he barely defended. The swords sliced and hewed in a wild death dance that neither dared to slow. When they finally disengaged, air-hunger burned Kevral's lungs. Her head throbbed, holding thought and strategy at bay. She surged in with a dangerous in-and-out maneuver she had learned from watching Colbey, though not yet perfected. None of her blows landed, but the last left her an opening. Even as Mundilnarvi closed his defenses, her blade licked through, whipping across his head.

Contact thrummed against Kevral's hand, and triumph surged through her. She completed her follow-through from practice rather than any belief she needed to do so. His scarf slid down her blade. No one could have survived that cut. Yet, miraculously, he had, his secret the same that had fended her last successful hit. A dented helm protected his skull, well-hidden beneath the scarf. Mundilnarvi seized her moment of surprise to snatch up his hand ax, and Kevral chose to grab Colbey's sword rather than press. Stinging fingers scarcely managed the task, and an arm that felt like a boiled noodle seemed incapable of raising the blade. Yet somehow she met his next attack with a double defense, careful to take the blow mostly with her good left arm.

Kevral switched to a defensive strategy, blocking strikes as strong as any blacksmith's hammer. Even the small amount of force she allowed against her right sword seemed too much. The thunder strikes drove her into desperate retreat. Finally, one pounded hard enough to plunge her to her knees, strength failing. Howling his triumph, Mundilnarvi slammed his blade down on Kevral for the last time. She caught it on an unequal cross, then dropped her weakened right hand, guiding his blade downward. Both saw the opening at the same time. Kevral jerked her left arm upward, dropping her notched and battered blade to his shoulder. He jolted backward as she sliced, his ax whipping up to defend. Like a saw, the damaged blade chewed through the flesh where neck met shoulder. Blood geysered from the wound, hot against Kevral's face. As he fell, she struggled to her feet, skewering his abdomen with Colbey's sword. Too late, she remembered the armor, but it did not matter. The blade glided through the steel, and she buried it to the hilt inside him.

Not a single word escaped Mundilnarvi as he collapsed, though his eyes contained none of the terror death usually inspired and his lips held a slight smile. That night, he would rise to feast among his fellows once more, suffering only the teasing that must follow fairly losing a battle to a young mortal.

Sensation fully returned to Kevral's arm in a white hot surge. She planted a foot against Mundilnarvi's massive chest, bracing as she jerked on her sword. For a moment, it foiled her efforts. Then, gradually, the blade glided from flesh and armor, followed by a rush of dark blood. Drawing a rag, she set to cleaning gore from the steel, unable to keep herself from pitying him. The wild rush of battle had to lose some of its joy when a warrior no longer risked the ultimate sacrifice.

The ultimate sacrifice. Kevral shook her head, only now coming far enough out of her battle rage to realize that several of the *Einherjar* remained to watch her. Though great, death did not meet that definition; but she already had. To surrender one's life to a cause required the bravery that resulted in Valhalla; yet it could not compare to giving up a soul. Colbey had chosen to do so for the good of the world. Kevral shook her head again, harder, inciting a wave of dizziness. She had lost that opportunity to a spider. Only now, she realized that bothered her as much as losing Valhalla.

Ignoring her audience, Kevral cleaned, rising rage making her movements nearly as violent as combat. For longer than necessary, she worked on Colbey's sword, refusing to leave an invisible dot of grime on a blade dishonored by an enemy so abhorrent. No matter how many times she scrubbed, she could still imagine the filth he had spat onto it, evading her every effort. So she polished while anger burned and gradually receded, leaving her feeling spent and the steel gleaming like quicksilver in the regular sunlight. Sheathing it, she raised the second sword for a similar workout, only to find the blade notched even beyond safe sheathing. Holding it across her arms, she lowered her head and muttered a prayer, as if over a fallen comrade. It felt odd to evoke the names of gods while on Asgard; yet she could not bear to do otherwise, especially when it involved a sword she had only recently suffered through a lengthy ritual to regain the honor to wield.

Finally, Kevral set to the task for which she had come. Laying the damaged sword across her vanquished foe, she rummaged through his pocket for the Pica shard. Finding it, she headed toward the gate, only then realizing she had never addressed, or even looked at, the *Einherjar*. Realization brought heat to her cheeks; and, though she still evaded their eyes, she became self-conscious for it. Not long ago, she had desperately wanted to find herself in this position. Now that she had, she could not stand to examine it too closely. Doing so might make living without it impossible.

Kevral carried her prize to the gates, where Tae, Ra-khir, the elves, and Darris watched her with joy and relief etched clearly on their faces. The four Valkyries guarded them vigilantly. Rascal crouched among the grasses, seeming to take no notice of the activity inside Valhalla's fence.

"Are you well?" Ra-khir asked, his voice carrying easily through the bars.

Still in the mind-set that no sound could reach her companions, Kevral did not answer immediately. She realized the Valkyries must have dismantled their spell in the area of the gate in order to admit her. Apparently, they saw no reason to replace it until the time came for her to leave. "I'm fine," Kevral finally answered distractedly, passing the shard through the opening.

Ra-khir accepted it, squeezing her hand. Skögul headed for the gate, and Kevral backed away to allow it space to swing open.

"Wait," a male voice called from behind her, the accent indecipherable.

Skögul's head swung upward and beyond Kevral. The Renshai spun to face a wall of *Einherjar*, including the Northman who had so casually watched her battle with Mundilnarvi.

A handsome, slender blond in a light leather tunic and breeks spoke, his voice matching the previous command. "We want her to stay."

The spears of the Valkyries rattled downward, menacing the mortals outside the gate more than those they intended to intimidate. Herfjötur stepped forward. "We choose who stays."

Kevral recognized the next *Einherjar*, a sinewy woman with long, golden hair knotted at the back. Ranilda Battlemad was Colbey's mother. "No, you choose who enters." She whipped her sword out in a single swirling kata that Kevral scarcely had time to admire before it returned to its sheath. "We decide who stays." She smiled sweetly at Kevral. "And you may stay, young Renshai."

Kevral could not control the grin that all but wrapped itself around her face. She pictured herself exchanging graceful Renshai maneuvers with their inventors, learning age-old tactics lost to time and obscurity, forever locked in combat with the greatest swordmasters of every era. Though she had pictured the scene a million times, since her mind could first grasp the idea of such a place, the scene gained a perfection and beauty that the certainty of losing her soul had stolen these last several days. Like a man burdened by months of pain finding pleasure in the simple cessation, she reveled in the possibility of regaining the ultimate reward, so recently lost to her.

A massive warrior with dark blond hair and piercing green eyes studied her from amidst the others. Though similar to the first man's accent, his tone contained a heavy solidity the other's had lacked. Likely, they had lived in the same time, but the first tainted his speech with a musical touch of Northern while the second did not. "You can refuse, of course, Kevral." He turned his companions warning looks. "Your competence and courage will surely bring you here eventually anyway." Now his attention rolled to the Valkyries, as if to warn them not to discriminate against her in the future because of this incident.

Ra-khir made a pained noise, but he did not speak. He would not attempt to influence a decision wholly Kevral's, though she knew he had more than his love for her at stake. Her children had the support of many, but they would still suffer for her absence. Her companions might find a way to finish the mission without her. If she turned down the *Einherjar,* she felt certain the Valkyries would not allow her back in Valhalla while alive. Dead, she did not have the means to return.

Kevral sucked in a deep breath and let it out slowly. Finally, she allowed herself a view of the world every Renshai sought. Beyond the group in front of her, warriors battled with a skill and speed only the most practiced and gifted accomplished on Midgard. War cries drifted, and the patternless chime of steel filled her ears. She looked out over a massive battlefield interrupted only by the barracks where they partied through the night and the wrought-iron fence that enclosed the area. Every eye held a permanent spark of excitement or blazing battle joy. No man or woman of courage could tire of such a place. The decision should prove easy: a few more years or decades on Midgard versus an eternity in the haven for the bravest warriors. Yet, the best course of action eluded Kevral. Never before would she have believed she could allow anything to get between herself and Valhalla, yet the love of her family mattered at least as much.

Kevral chose to explain her hesitation. "I have no soul." She had intended the words to emerge in a matter-of-fact tone, but she choked on them. "I can't return." Angrily, she fought rising tears. One more question begged answering. "If I die here . . . ?"

Brows knit and heads swayed. A few whispered exchanges resulted before the massive, green-eyed man spoke again. "We don't know. It's never come up. But we can keep it under consideration."

The first speaker said, "Without weakening your battles, of course. Your wounds would still heal by nightfall. We'd just have to pull the killing strokes." He grinned. "If any."

"Rache," someone challenged down the line. "You insolent son of a bitch, you'll get yours today."

"Promises. Promises." Rache clarified, "Colbey's the only one to kill me in over a hundred years, but every day someone swears they'll take me out."

Kevral glanced at her companions. Ra-khir had steeled his expression, but his teeth gnawing his lower lip revealed the discomfort he otherwise hid. Tae shook his head, dark eyes locked on Kevral. The elves seemed more curious than concerned, and Darris kept his hands wrapped around the bars, committed to documenting, not influencing, history. Again, Kevral looked at the *Einherjar*, plucking Renshai from their midst by their lack of armor, their grace, and their swords. She had never heard of Renshai using other weapons, though she recognized Rache by his name and he carried a small flail as well as two long swords thrust through his belt.

"Leave!" a Valkyrie roared. "The living do not belong here!"

The words all but clinched Kevral's decision to stay, but she refused to bow, even to her own defiance. She dared not complicate the situation by mentioning the baby. Born here, it could surely stay; and she would prefer that over surrendering it to Pudar.

Finally, the Northman who had waited for a turn against Mundilnarvi spoke. "Kevral." His blue eyes glimmered with the usual zeal, but they also held a deep intelligence and sorrow. The hawklike nose gave him a predatory look, and broad lips diminished the size of his cheeks. Straw-colored hair hung in war braids tied with ribbons more appropriate for women, yet they did not diminish his masculinity. Apparently, in his day, men wore them in this fashion, too. "May I tell you a story?"

Kevral discarded a dislike that stemmed wholly from Mundilnarvi's association with him. "All right," she said carefully.

"Centuries ago, I lived in Nordmir. And I, too, participated in the battle that ended the Renshai bloodline in the North."

Unlike with Andvari, Kevral did not quibble over the word "battle."

Rache cleared his throat. "Kirin . . . ?"

The Northman dutifully amended, "Aside from Rache, whose line, unfortunately, did not survive either. For other reasons." He confronted Rache with raised brows over a friendly expression. Clearly, his original assertion had not required contradiction. The end result was the same.

But the detail explained much to Kevral. Renshai named their children after warriors believed to have earned Valhalla, and the Renshai tribe of Rache descended from a man who had lived in King Sterrane's era. This could only be the namesake of that Rache. She listened with guarded interest to a self-confessed enemy of her people.

"At the time, it seemed right to devastate those enemies to the North who slaughtered our kin and damaged their bodies to bar them from Valhalla."

"But . . ." Kevral interrupted, only to find her own words suspended by Rache's.

"Renshai were a tribe of Northmen, like the others, but we did deliberately hew off body parts." Rache pursed his lips, dismayed by that aspect of his heritage. "Though never from our most worthy opponents.

It broke the morale of those who dared to attack us and eventually led to the tribe's banishment." He oriented Kevral to the proper time. "Colbey was twenty-nine when the Renshai returned to the North. The attack occurred twenty years later, when I was ten."

Only at that moment, it struck Kevral that she faced ancestors so distant who had participated in making the history they now studied. She had known it intellectually of course, but true understanding struck with gale force.

"The current Renshai descend from two sources: Those few of our people who remained in the West when the others returned North." Rache glanced through the ranks, apparently seeking anyone he might offend, then added, "Whom the returning Renshai viewed as traitors. And those trained into the tribe." He gestured toward the dark-blond. "Santagithi's daughter, Mitrian, who married a Western Renshai named Tannin."

Tannin. Kevral recognized the name of the second tribe of Renshai.

"And her son from her first marriage, named for me."

The tribe of Rache. Kevral finally put the last detail into place, already knowing that her tribe, that of Modrey, descended from full-blooded Western Renshai.

Kirin cleared his throat. "If you're finished with the lesson, my brother, I'd like to finish my story."

The words stunned Kevral even more than the realization of their beginnings. She knew the two could share no heredity, but a pact of brotherhood between a Renshai and a slayer of Renshai seemed nearly as inconceivable.

Rache laughed. "Sorry."

Kirin paused a moment longer, apparently seeking the lost thread of his tale. "I earned the name Valr, Slayer, during that war. I killed my share of Renshai in the most glorious battle of my mortal existence." His expression went pensive, never shameful. "For that, my greatest honor, I am also remorseful." He gave Kevral a sincere nod.

Rache could not help interjecting, "You will notice that I, not Mundilnarvi, am his chosen brother. Valr Kirin and Colbey negotiated the peace between Renshai and the other Northmen."

Kevral could not recall Renshai ever being referred to as Northmen, though most knew of their Northern origins.

"Kirin's all right," Rache finished.

Valr Kirin turned Rache a stare that contained barely the tolerance the Renshai *Einherjar* had attributed to him.

Kevral tried to help. "But missing a body part doesn't bar a warrior from Valhalla, so the whole reason for banishing Renshai and, later, obliterating them from the North loses any merit it might have had."

Kirin swung his hard gaze to Kevral. "Exactly . . . *not* my point."

Kevral tried to return a stare as fierce.

"It's easy to judge centuries after the fact. And difficult to account for disparity in knowledge and societal morals." Valr Kirin caught and held Kevral's gaze without malice or regret. "We all believed absolutely that a missing body part barred even the most courageous warrior from Valhalla."

Every Northman in the group, Renshai or otherwise, nodded. Kevral expected Kirin to next defend the Northmen's actions or Rache to explain the Renshai's version, so the Slayer's next words caught her off guard.

"Which placed any living warrior who lost a major body part into your exact situation."

Kevral's first instinct, to deny the analogy, passed quickly. Valr Kirin's point remained valid. Amputees once believed, with the same certainty she did, that they could never reach Valhalla.

Kirin waited for understanding to sink deep within Kevral, while those around him remained deferentially silent. Finally, he said, "My brother was a high-ranking officer in the army of the Northern high king. He lost a hand in the Renshai War."

Kevral froze, suddenly feeling a kinship with a Northern warrior centuries her senior. "What did he do?" she asked, surprised to find her mouth dry. The answer mattered more than she would have imagined.

"He learned to live with it." Valr Kirin gave the simple answer first. "He remained the bravest warrior I've ever known." Kirin made a subtle gesture to remind her of the comparison, scores of *Einherjar*. "Those who had once hailed him as the greatest of leaders refused to follow a man the Valkyries would spurn. Even that didn't stop him. He changed his style of combat and remained a competent warrior. Eventually, he became a general in the Great War between the East and the West, fighting and strategizing alongside Colbey in what remains history's most magnificent war. He died a hero, maintaining to his grave that courage was its own reward, that dying with honor mattered more than Valhalla."

Kevral caught herself about to ask if the brother did find Valhalla. The whole point of the story was that it did not matter.

Courage is its own reward. The words seemed to echo through Kevral's head. *Dying with honor matters more than Valhalla.* The words seemed sacrilege, yet the immortal she had worshiped since infancy personified them every bit as much as the unnamed brother. Colbey planned to surrender his soul to rescue the world from Odin's destruction. For her, the ultimate sacrifice was neither death nor the loss of her soul, which had occurred without her choice or knowledge. The ultimate sacrifice was losing Valhalla. She only needed to decide whether her children, her husband, and her friends were worth that price.

Kevral looked back at Ra-khir. He held his head low, the disarray of his red-blond locks out of character yet strangely attractive. All their arguments over honor seemed to culminate in that moment, and for the first time she understood. Knights of Erythane rarely spoke of the afterlife. Like Renshai, their valor and bravery remained absolute; but the knights dedicated themselves solely to personal honor. They required no eternal reward, finding their peace in the morality they displayed during their lifetimes. *When a man believes he lives only once,* Kedrin had once said in a quiet moment, *he becomes obligated to make that one life virtuous.* At that time, Kevral had paid little heed. Now, she thought she had discovered the source of the knight's integrity. Not only did it prove their only means of immortality, but they wished for everyone's single chance at life to be happy.

Ra-khir glanced up, meeting Kevral's sapphire eyes. "I love you," he said, his soft voice miraculously reaching her through the clamor of war and the murmurs of the *Einherjar.* "Do what's best for you. I'll learn to understand, and the boys will, too."

Tae opened his mouth to speak, then turned away, shaking his head. He would never fully comprehend warriors and their ways.

"Thank you," Kevral said to the *Einherjar.* "It's an honor I'll never forget. But my friends and family need me." She managed only a slight smile, certain regret would ebb and flow over time. "And I need them, too."

Gradually, the *Einherjar* dispersed back to their skirmishes and battles, until only Rache remained. He unsheathed one of his swords, a slender blade tempered to demanding Renshai specifications. Kevral found a defensive stance, certain he sought one last battle with her before she left Valhalla forever. But though Rache approached, he did not attack. He offered the hilt.

Kevral stared, uncertain of the *Einherjar*'s intentions. A Renshai would not willingly sacrifice his sword. Even Colbey had surrendered the one she now carried reluctantly; though, without it, mankind could not hope to battle the demons the *svartalf* had called against them.

Yet a moment later Rache stated the impossible. "I called it Tisis." Kevral recognized the Renshai word for retaliation. "I don't need it any more, and you can rename it."

Most people, Renshai or otherwise, did not name their swords, and Kevral was unfamiliar with the concept of requiring a new owner for a renaming. Likely, the practice had ended long before her birth, its significance lost on later generations. "This is a great honor. Are you sure . . . ?"

Rache pressed the hilt into Kevral's hand. "I'm sure." He gave the oiled blade a gentle kiss, speaking a version of Renshai little changed over the centuries. "I'll call you Motfrabelonning." Literally it meant Reward of Courage. "And I expect you to return it when you're finished."

"Return it?" Kevral's shoulders slumped even as she accepted the weapon. "I can't—"

Rache made a brisk, silencing gesture. "Never surrender," he said.

Rache's words startled Kevral, leaving her to wonder whether Colbey had defied Odin and braved Valhalla once more. It never occurred to her that he had simply overheard Ra-khir, seen the significance of the catch phrase to Kevral, and repeated it at the opportune moment.

As Kevral turned her back toward him, Ra-khir and the ancient Renshai *Einherjar* exchanged careful smiles.

CHAPTER 17

Unbelonging

Many mortals preferred to shun me as demon-spawned than believe my skill born of a daily effort they were too lazy to spare. To the gods, I am simply and forever human.
—Colbey Calistinsson

THE instant the shard-seekers returned from Valhalla, servants rushed Kevral and Ra-khir away to prepare, while Darris and the elves handled the shard. Rascal trotted off to her own business, trailed by two stewards who, experience taught, she would soon exhaust or lose. Discovering Mior in the corridors, Tae followed the cat to Matrinka, seeking details of the business that demanded Kevral and Ra-khir so swiftly, without even the time to rest.

Swept to a tub room, Kevral suffered women stripping off the sweat- and blood-soaked clothing and easing her into the bath. The warmth of the water eased the deep ache of her arms, especially the right shoulder, but accomplished nothing for her headache. A healer arrived before it became clear that little of the blood had come from her, and that only from cuts so tiny she had not noticed them. The healer handled those with a cloying salve that stung worse than the injuries ever could. By the time Kevral managed a protest, they had bustled her into an overlong tunic that flared enough at the thighs to pass for a dress, her arm in a high sling.

"My swords," Kevral insisted as the maids whisked her toward the door.

"No swords, Lady Kevral," said a rotund woman nearly as tall as Ra-khir. "Not politic."

Kevral dug her heels into the floor, only then realizing she wore fancy slippers. "Not possible." Before anyone could stop her, she jerked free of her many assistants to grab her sword belt.

"My Lady," the huge Béarnide pleaded as another whipped a comb through Kevral's wet hair. "Please don't. There's no danger. It could cause trouble—"

Kevral ignored the warning. "Let's go." She paused to allow the servant to sweep her short locks into proper feathers. "Where are we going anyway?"

"Nowhere with those weapons, Lady," the speaker insisted, even as two of the women ushered Kevral to the door. Her voice escalated as she addressed her companions. "Did you hear me? Those swords do not leave this room."

One of the two, a short grizzled Erythanian turned on the leader. "The day my job includes disarming Renshai, I quit."

The leader wrung her hands, appealing to Kevral. "Visiting royalty will take offense, my Lady."

The other escort, a plumply curvaceous Béarnian female, placed a guiding hand on Kevral's injured shoulder. "Let His Majesty's guards handle that problem, Zelshia." She released Kevral to open the door.

Kevral finished buckling her belt, the weight of a sword at each hip finally dispelling the discomfort that had assailed her from the moment the other woman had removed it. Her time in the bath had revealed a definite swelling where the baby floated quietly, exhausted by its mother's battle. Her abdomen seemed to have grown visibly since that morning.

"Come, please, Lady Kevral." The women led Kevral into the hallway toward the stairs. As they walked with a quiet dignity that little resembled the scramble to ready her, Kevral finally considered the details. She hoped but doubted the "visiting royalty" referred to Tae's father or emissaries from some small Western kingdom that needed the assistance of Ra-khir and herself. Yet, logic led her to the proper conclusion. *Pudar.* The word had become a curse the equal of coward. For the first time, she considered Zelshia's request. If King Cymion had come, all of Béarn's and Pudar's guards together, even the vows of self and Ra-khir, might not keep her from killing him.

The servants led Kevral through Béarn's straight corridors, down a series of stairs and toward the main court. But, instead of taking her there as she expected, they stopped in front of a smaller suite nestled among strategy rooms, studies, and libraries. Ra-khir awaited Kevral there, surrounded by milling male servants and straight ranks of stony-faced guards. Some wore Béarn's blue and gold or tan, while others sported Pudar's brown tunics over armor graced, front and back, with silver wolves. Ra-khir had dressed in his best knight silks, black shirt and britches under a blue tabard emblazoned with Béarn's golden bear. A deep saffron cape covered the orange circle and black sword of Erythane on the back of the tabard, and a gold brooch clasped it into place. A pristine hat with a delicately veined feather perched on his head. Strawberry-blond hair cascaded from beneath it only in the back, combed to a sheen.

Kevral's mind refused to focus on the coming events; they could only enrage her. She allowed her mind to wander off on minutiae, identifying which Pudarian guardsmen she had trained. She also wondered, for the first time, why Erythane and Béarn insisted on maintaining clashing color schemes, then expecting their most elite and gallant warriors to wear both. She marveled at how the knights managed to arrange those colors without looking tawdry. Though always handsome, Ra-khir appeared positively breathtaking in his knightly proper garb. The uniform accentuated the chiseled refinement of his features, and the multicolored silks heightened the emerald-green of his eyes.

Ra-khir maneuvered through the crowd with a dignified smoothness that barely revealed movement. Drawing to Kevral's side, he placed an arm around her waist. Having done their work, the servants disappeared, leaving knight and Renshai to face the guards alone. Ra-khir deliberately avoided resting his fingers on Kevral's hilt. His presence hampered her draw enough, and touching another's sword without permission was insult. He did whisper a reminder, "We're under oath to personal honor."

"I haven't forgotten," Kevral spat back, most of her irritation stemming from the need to focus on the proceedings again. Staring at Ra-khir pleased her more.

"They're not going to let you take those swords in."

"Anyone who tries to stop me had better get used to fighting left-handed."

Ra-khir's brows rose, but he gave no other response to the threat. "Even me?"

Kevral did not hesitate. "Even you."

"Ahh," Ra-khir quipped. "So it's negotiable."

Kevral did not bother with a reply. She watched the guards ready themselves into two ranks: the Béarnian and the Pudarian.

Ra-khir tried again. "It's difficult enough for them to allow us to meet with the prince alone. They can't permit weapons."

Kevral stiffened, returning her gaze to her husband. "We're meeting Le alone?"

"Prince Leondis," Ra-khir reminded. "He can't very well discuss the details in front of others."

No, I suppose he can't. Kevral fought rising memories and the rage that had to accompany them. Her fingers banged Ra-khir's arm, the first indication she had reached for her swords. "Bad enough I'm fat. I'm not facing an enemy naked."

"You're not fat, you're pregnant." Ra-khir continued to speak in a low voice that the guards could not hear. "He's not an enemy. And you're certainly not naked." He studied her outfit. "That just might be the most feminine thing I've ever seen you wear."

Kevral ignored the final comment for the more important issue. "Without my swords, I *am* naked."

Ra-khir did not bother to argue. "I vowed to keep you from revenge. You'll have to kill me to get to the prince."

"I'm not going to kill you," Kevral assured. "Or the snake's damned son."

"Good," Ra-khir returned. "I'll talk with the guards—make sure they understand that you need those swords but won't use them." His subtle head shake made it clear he expected more difficulty than his words conveyed. "If I get them to agree to the weapons, could you do me one favor?"

Kevral nodded.

"Could you please not address the crown prince of Pudar as 'the snake's damned son?' "

Kevral smiled. "I'll be polite. And I won't kill anyone who doesn't try to kill one of us first."

"Deal." Ra-khir approached a Pudarian whose reversed colors revealed him as a leader. For several moments, guard and knight engaged in animated discussion, Ra-khir's every movement fluid and dignified, the Pudarian's brisk and jabbing. Finally, the captain threw up his hands and opened the door. He disappeared into the room, and the door clicked shut behind him. Shortly after, he emerged, his lips pursed to white lines and his dark eyes bright with irritation. He said something to Ra-khir, punctuated by a raised fist that made a heavy point without threatening.

Ra-khir returned to Kevral, suppressing a smile until he reached her. "The prince agreed to let you bring your swords, and he still wants us alone."

Though Kevral had hoped for no other outcome, the ease of the victory bothered her. She wondered whether she should take offense that the prince did not worry for the threat of an armed Renshai.

Apparently reading something in her face, Ra-khir addressed the concern. "Can't have it all ways, Kevral. I'm sure he wanted to avoid an argument he couldn't win, and he trusts our promises."

Kevral suspected Leondis trusted Ra-khir's promise, not hers; but it did not matter. As much as she would have enjoyed quibbling with Leondis and his entourage, it seemed prudent to conclude their business as soon as possible. The longer she faced them, the more likely she lost control and caused an international incident.

A guard whisked open the door, and four others ushered Kevral and Ra-khir through it. The one at the portal announced, "His majesty, Prince Leondis. Sir Ra-khir and the Renshai, Kevral."

The windowless room contained a table ringed by a dozen wooden chairs. Bookshelves held maps, rolled parchments, and books in a neat, dustless array. Leondis sat in the head seat, dressed in fur-trimmed satin. Dark brown hair with just a hint of curl tumbled to his shoulders, and long lashes striped his blue eyes. Kevral could not help seeing him as the charming young warrior who had wooed her and offered to legitimize the twins by marrying her moments before their birth. The man who had tearfully forced himself upon her while she lay, chained and helpless, seemed like a distant nightmare, wholly unrelated.

A movement at Kevral's back sent her scurrying sideways. A guard's kick, intended to remind her to kneel, brushed by her right calf instead. Had it connected, Kevral could not have stopped herself from inflicting a painful warning. As it happened, she gave him a sour look, then curt-sied with a brevity that barely detracted from Ra-khir's stiff formality. Though the knight performed the proper sequence for royalty, he omit-ted the respectful and highly personal flourishes that would have brought the gesture to life. The hat ended in his hands and remained there.

The four guards filed out. The last gave Leondis a look every bit as pleading as Zelshia's had been.

In response, Leondis pointed to the hallway, and the guard closed the door with obvious reluctance.

Kevral waited only until the door clicked closed before asking gruffly, "What do you want?"

Ra-khir nudged his wife to remind her of her promise. "Your Grace, what she means is that we would like very much to know the reason for our summoning."

Leondis tented callused fingers on the table. "Sir Knight, I know *exactly* what she meant." He gestured at the chairs. "Please sit."

"No," Kevral said as Ra-khir moved to obey.

The knight paused, glaring at his wife. "Kevral, what happened to 'polite'?"

It vanished when he raped me. Kevral forced control. She *had* promised. "No, *Sire*," she amended.

Leondis tolerated the disrespect as his father never would. "Suit your-self."

Ra-khir continued to a chair but hovered over it, likely torn between following orders and remaining close enough to maintain the shred of influence he might hold over his wife. He set the hat on the table.

"I see no reason to drag this out," Leondis continued. "We came for the baby."

"Baby, Your Majesty?"

Even Kevral looked at Ra-khir, who seemed to have suddenly become stupid.

"My baby," Leondis prompted.

"Your baby, Your Majesty. Of course." Ra-khir lowered his bottom to the chair but remained facing Kevral. "I apologize for my confusion, but Béarn has been recently blessed with babies. And the one you speak of, Sire, hasn't been born."

"Due in less than three months." Leondis shook back his thick mane of hair, and perfume wafted briefly from the locks. "And her last babies were early."

Kevral bit her lip, allowing Ra-khir to speak. All of the positive feelings reawakened by seeing Leondis became crushed beneath the understanding of what he had come to accomplish.

"Twins, Sire," Ra-khir reminded. "Always early."

Leondis sucked air through his nose and looked at Kevral. As his gaze slid from her face to her abdomen, the soft regret in his expression gave way to a sparkle of innocent excitement.

Kevral could not hold her tongue. "It's *my* baby, Leondis."

"Your Majesty, Prince Leondis," Ra-khir corrected with a deferential nod.

"Let's not make this more difficult than it already is." The prince dropped the formality that had never suited him. "Kevral, I hate the circumstances surrounding the baby's conception. My father had a desperate decision to make and no time to consider it. Never before or since has a woman had a child forced upon her. But that baby, and no other baby, carries the royal bloodline of Pudar."

Ra-khir went silent, unaccustomed to nobles departing so abruptly from convention, especially in the presence of a knight. Nothing in his training prepared him for this.

Where Leondis' straightforward approach befuddled Ra-khir, it slightly diminished Kevral's anger. "Why can't you lay with other women who have just given birth? Or the young ones with cycles just starting?" She named the only two conditions that allowed women to remain fertile since the *svartalf*'s spell. "Surely more than one would couple willingly with a prince and joyfully carry Pudar's heir."

Leondis flushed at Kevral's open discussion of sexuality, but he did address her questions. "Don't think I haven't tried. Yours was the only successful . . ." The word came with more difficulty from him. ". . . coupling."

Ra-khir cringed, knowing what had to follow, and Kevral did not disappoint. "That, Your Majesty, is because it's not your baby." She clamped a hand to the bulge beneath her tunic.

Leondis rolled his pale eyes. "Kevral, you came to Pudar rather . . . uneducated on the matter. But surely you know now how conception occurs."

Kevral glanced at her husband, worried that her choice of words, intended to hurt the prince, might fall hard on Ra-khir's ears as well. He avoided her eyes, running a finger along the brim of his hat. "While your father held me prisoner, I coupled with another man."

Leondis jerked backward, shocked only a moment by her revelation before he laughed. "Impossible."

"It happened."

Leondis leaned onto the table. "Kevral, you were chained in an underground dungeon under guard. No one could have slipped past without their knowledge."

"A god came to me and offered his son. I accepted."

"A god." Leondis blinked, his expression going from challenging to pitying in that instant. His tone softened to the ginger caution usually reserved for the dangerously insane. "All right, then. A god." He glanced at Ra-khir who returned the look with earnest silence.

An intense hush followed, broken by Leondis. "Well then. When this god comes to claim his child, we'll have no choice but to surrender it, will we?"

Kevral glared. "Stop speaking to me like a puppy." She bit her lower lip with a fierceness that drew blood. "He's not coming."

"Of course not." Leondis again focused on Ra-khir, demanding his interference.

Ra-khir winced but complied. "Your Majesty, she did sleep with an immortal's son." He chose the term that Colbey preferred. "But there's no way to know which of you conceived that baby."

Leondis stared fanatically at Ra-khir. Knights of Erythane did not lie, and it seemed unlikely that Kevral's madness had become contagious. His tone turned patronizing again. "Love can make a man accept the impossible."

Ra-khir made a noncommittal motion. "Your Majesty, I can tell you only that, if it's his conception, the immortal wants me to be the child's father."

"He told you this?"

"He told Kevral, Sire."

"Ah." Leondis' earlier comment covered the situation. "Enough of this." Though he surely did not believe them, he gave them the benefit of his doubts verbally. "There's at least a high likelihood this baby is mine. The other possible father is willing to allow others to raise the baby. I'm not."

Possessed of a sudden urge to bite the insolent expression from the prince's face, Kevral spoke before thinking. "Neither am I."

"You made a vow," Leondis reminded.

"I retract it!"

Ra-khir swung toward Kevral. "You can't do that." His tone revealed sorrow, not anger.

Leondis tore his blue gaze from Kevral to lay it solidly upon Ra-khir. "And you, Sir? Do you retract your vow as well?"

Kevral thought she saw rising tears, though Ra-khir's voice did not crack. "No, Sire. I can't do that."

All the seriousness returned to Leondis' features, and a flame sprang to light in his eyes. Kevral had never before seen him angry. "Kevral Tainharsdatter, know this. Pudar will not leave without its heir. If it means directing your own husband to tear it from your arms, that will happen." He rose from his chair, emphasizing his points with a stab of his index finger. Never before had he so resembled his father. "If it means declaring war against Béarn, it will happen. Even if it means cutting you open and tearing the infant from your bleeding womb!"

Ra-khir leaped to his feet. "Your Majesty, I draw the line there." Necessary decorum stole the warning from his words, especially in the wake of the other's anger.

At least, it claimed Leondis' attention momentarily. He gave the knight a measuring look, wholly lacking bluff. "Sir Ra-khir, you *will* follow the letter of your vow, no matter what it entails."

The hand on Ra-khir's hat band shook, and scarlet crept across his cheeks. Rage otherwise fully hidden, he spoke with impossible composure. "Your Majesty, I only mean it will not come to measures so desperate."

Oh, it can. And it will. Kevral narrowed her eyes and bared her teeth, counting on Leondis' pique to assure that he surmised her thought.

The prince did not look in Kevral's direction, likely anticipating an impertinent expression that could only further claim his control. "My father insisted that we either pull Kevral from the mission or that my entourage and I join you to keep her from doing anything that might harm the heir. King Griff convinced us not to risk it. He claimed you would act reasonably." He shook his head and finally met Kevral's eyes. "I should have known better than to trust a Renshai."

Enraged beyond worry for consequence, Kevral drew and charged. Ra-khir scrambled between Renshai and prince. Only Kevral's abrupt check deterred a collision. She came to her senses then, calling up Renshai mind training to douse the fire in her veins. Suppressing the urge to hack down Ra-khir and the prince a moment later, she resheathed her weapon with a violence that accidentally slammed the hilt across her husband's shoulder. His eyes revealed an instant of pain but none of the fear any other who had barely escaped a Renshai's attack would display.

Realization of how near she had come to slaying a loved one sapped the rest of Kevral's rage, though not the hatred. Without another word, she stormed from the conference room, leaving Ra-khir to handle parting amenities and ruffled feathers. Not for the first time, she would have to apologize to a loving husband whose loyalty and gentleness made him the obvious, but undeserving, target of her rage and mood swings.

The baby fluttered and kicked inside her.

Tae huddled in the dense shadows of the conference room bookcase, bombarded by an oppressive silence that followed Kevral's tempestuous exit. A cautious peek revealed Prince Leondis' back, muscles balled beneath satin and fists clenched at his sides. Ra-khir knelt in front of him, head bowed, waiting patiently for a formal dismissal. His hair dangled in even red curtains, and he clutched his hat to his heart. Nothing about him revealed the anger that had to seethe within him. Tae could picture him pinning the prince with green eyes full of the promise of murder, spitting the words Tae so wished he would say: "I surrendered my knighthood once for Kevral and declared war on Pudar. Do not think I would not do so again."

But Ra-khir said nothing. Like a statue, he maintained his respectful attitude, performing no action to enhance or dispel the fiery hush filling the room.

Leondis broke first, as he must. Tone still tinged with rage, he managed a reasonably civil, "You're dismissed, Ra-khir."

Ra-khir rose with an appropriate, if not fervent, bow, turned, and replaced his hat. Walking to the door, he tripped the latch. As he exited, Tae caught sight of milling guards, several surreptitiously attempting to glance through the crack. After Kevral's wild departure, they surely worried for the fate of their prince. Then, the door snapped closed. Leondis heaved an enormous sigh, collapsing his upper body to the table.

Tae stepped out from the shadows. For several moments, he watched the prince run tense hands through the dark curls at the back of his hair. The regal shoulders slumped, and his face lay hidden against the wood. Tae weighed his options as he stood behind the prince. He had to speak first; to allow the prince to discover him might well lead to the accusation of intended assassination. He had left his weapons in his room, including his utility dagger; but that precaution would prove little use if prince or guards slaughtered him before he had a chance to assert his innocent intentions.

Sudden regret for his actions assailed Tae. He had come from curiosity, wondering what event of significance caused Béarn to summon Kevral and Ra-khir immediately from the task. Once Tae had slipped past the inspection of Pudar's guards, wedged behind the bookshelf, he had lost any chance of avoiding the transaction. The room's lack of a window made him claustrophobic, and he had wished himself anywhere else more than once until the discussion had started. Then, the proceedings had kept him enthralled until this moment. Certain things required saying, and no one other than Tae would speak them. Clinging to the description Kevral had given—she had once described the crown prince of Pudar as reasonable and charming—he finally gathered the courage to speak. "Joining the quest for the Pica shards would not be a good idea."

Leondis rose and whirled with a speed that startled Tae into a wary back-step. Only one trained to war could move so swiftly.

Swallowing his terror, Tae continued. "Yesterday, Kevral faced the choice of staying on another world or returning. As you can see, she came back. Had you been there to demand it, she would have stayed. And the baby with her."

Deep blue eyes studied Tae like prey. Leondis pursed his lips. "Who are you? How did you get past my guards?"

Tae thought it best to avoid both questions. "I'm only trying to help." He finally remembered to add, "Your Majesty. The more you pressure Kevral, the more she will rebel. It becomes a challenge, and I've never seen a Renshai back down from a challenge."

Leondis continued his scrutiny. Tae recognized the muscles bunched onto an otherwise slender frame. The prince's expression had glided from surprised to confused. Now, a taint of pink drifted from the edges of his lips toward eyes that narrowed slightly. "Tae Kahn."

Tae did not deny the identification. "Sire—"

The prince's color deepened to scarlet, spreading to his forehead. "You killed my brother." He jabbed a finger at Tae, even as his other hand clasped the hilt of his sword. "You murdered Severin."

Tae barely stopped himself from losing control of his bladder. Terror lurched through him, driving him to flee. Like a caged animal, he retreated toward the back wall, lowering his center of gravity. "I didn't kill Prince Severin." His voice emerged steady despite his fear. "Did you not receive the confession—"

"—coerced from some innocent by your father." Leondis advanced as slowly and resolutely as Tae withdrew. "My father would have done the same for . . ." He paused long enough for Tae to mentally fill in "me" before finishing with, "Severin." He stopped moving when Tae's heel touched the wall. "I've also managed to uncover some interesting details:

Your father is a base and heinous criminal who won over the Eastern populace with lies and masterminded the blockade to Western travel that caused many small towns to literally starve to death."

Tae mustered his courage, without bothering to correct trivia. The prince had struck close enough to truth. "This isn't about my ancestors." He had not anticipated this reaction from Leondis and vowed to teach Kevral the meaning of "reasonable and charming" if he survived this encounter. "I'm trying to help you."

"Like you 'helped' Severin?"

"The same enemies of my father who are feeding you information killed your brother and set me up to take the blame." Anger fueled Tae's boldness. "I didn't kill Prince Severin."

"Prove it."

Tae heaved a sigh, cut short by the realization that the prince had resumed his forward movement. "Interesting suggestion. You try proving you *didn't* do something."

Abruptly drawn, a knife chinged against Leondis' belt buckle. The blade glimmered silver in dim light.

Tae's heart hammered in his ears. He tried to keep his voice calm, soothing. "I'm not armed."

"Good. That should make it easy." Nevertheless, Leondis did not attack. The maneuver seemed clearly designed to intimidate, not kill. "And you will address me as proper for a prince."

Tae noted, with alarm, it had its intended effect. His tone contained an unexpected squeak, "I could demand the same."

"Never." Leondis stepped to within weapon's range, then stopped, stance offensive. He lowered his head, teeth in perfect repair, breath minty and sweet. Tae could smell the perfumed oils in his hair. "The blood of a hundred kings runs through my veins, and that of my unborn child. You're thieving scum, bastard-born to blackguards, whores, and filth. The only difference between you and feces: I wouldn't trouble myself to step on the shit."

The words struck Tae like a sledgehammer in the belly. The need to attack evaded his control, but he maintained enough self-preservation instinct to choose words instead of actions. "At least I don't have to rape women to get them to sleep with me."

The fire in Prince Leondis' cheeks fled, and he stared into Tae's dark face. "What do you know?" he demanded.

"All of it." Tae chose this time to add snidely, "Your Majesty. I know that your father kept Kevral prisoner and that you forced yourself upon her. I know that the baby you claim has the blood of a hundred kings might not contain any at all." His own words fueled his anger. "And the only blood known for certain is that of a Renshai you dismissed as untrustworthy."

Leondis' fist tightened around his knife, and he raised it threateningly. "Who broke their solemn vow?" He amended to the actual question, "Who told you this?"

Tae smiled. Earlier that day, his promise to Matrinka would have held him silent, but circumstances had changed. "You did, Sire."

Leondis' eyes widened as he apparently considered the incriminating words Tae had overheard. Panic flashed through the blue orbs, but only for an instant. The prince's gaze turned intense, and Tae could not help believing the young heir truly felt sorry about what had to follow. Situations and pressures had battered the rationality from a prince forced to a crown that rightly belonged to his brother. "Tae, if you were anyone but the murderer of my brother, I could never bring myself to do this." The knife jerked.

Tae dove and rolled, spinning back to face Leondis. Only then, he realized the attack was not against him. The satin at the prince's right shoulder blade gaped, and blood spilled through the opening. Tossed from Leondis' hand, the unadorned knife spun across the floor, slammed the wall, and bounced to the ground, splashing drops of scarlet. The prince heaved his chair over, bellowing in pain and anger as he did so.

The door crashed open as Leondis lurched toward Tae, and guards streamed inside. Several hustled Leondis to a safe corner. The others rushed Tae, who dropped to a desperate crouch. He dodged the first set of hands, scrambling between two guards to emerge into a swarm. Fingers grabbed at his tunic. He evaded them with a spinning maneuver that carried him past the bulk of them. Then, a hand snagged his tunic, wrenching him backward with a suddenness that jabbed his collar against his throat. Breath disappeared. He sucked raggedly for air, his struggle becoming frantically undirected. Cloth tore, momentum throwing him, shirtless, into a sea of Pudarian and Béarnian guardsmen. Only then, logic penetrated. *Don't fight, you fool. Makes you look guilty.* He stilled, allowing a Pudarian to wrench his arms behind his back so hard he worried for the bones of his wrists.

"Careful," a heavily-accented Béarnian voice declared over the hubbub. "That's a prince you're manhandling."

"Whoever he is, he stabbed me in the back." Leondis spoke in pained grunts Tae doubted he had to feign. Though worried for his own situation, he marveled at Leondis' ability not only to tolerate, but to self-inflict, such a wound. "Lock him in his room and let Béarn deal with him."

The Pudarian who held Tae's arms clamped tighter, gouging his fingers painfully into the Easterner's flesh. Another pinioned his shoulders from the front. When that guard believed no Béarnian could see, he rammed his knee into Tae's groin. Agony shot through his gut, and he went limp. Only the guards' support kept him standing, but he found himself wholly incapable of speech. The man's words hissed hotly into Tae's ear. "Give me any excuse to kill you. Please."

Tae had no intention of doing so. He allowed the guards to half-brace, half-drag him through Béarn's hallways. Servants, courtiers, and sentries stepped aside to let the contingent pass, watching Tae with looks that ranged from startled to patronizing to wise understanding. He listened as a captain delegated a group in the courtyard to "kill anything that comes out of his window." And he gained a series of "accidental" bruises and abrasions during the walk any of which, he felt certain, they could explain away as his uncooperativeness.

They passed Mior in a fourth floor corridor, the cat pausing to watch the procession, then running ahead of it in bursts. As the guards stopped in front of Tae's door to trip the latch, the cat drew up as if to sniff the prisoner. He mouthed the words, "Get Matrinka," and hoped the animal was smart enough to read lips. In truth, it surely did not matter. The queen would know of the event soon enough, albeit with details skewed. As he watched the calico scamper off, Tae had too much on his mind to wonder why the guards did not struggle with his lock. A moment later, the panel swung open, and three massive Pudarians launched him inside. The slam of the closing door cut off a Béarnian's protest.

Unable to maneuver in midair, Tae slammed headfirst against his bed. He collapsed on the floor, his roll awkward and far too late. Pain hammered through his head, ached across his abdomen, and screamed from myriad bruises. He staggered to his feet, only to discover a surprised Rascal crouched by the chest that held his personal belongings.

The sight proved too much for Tae. Seizing his sword, he smashed the blade down on the chest's wooden lid. Rascal skittered aside, loosing a high-pitched scream. Wood shattered beneath the blow, and an arc of splinters trailed Tae's follow-through. He struck the chest again, then a third time, until the contents lay fully exposed and remnants of the chest littered his floor. Only then, he threw the sword. It skidded across the floorboards to snarl in a woven carpet. Tae glared at Rascal.

The girl crouched in a far corner, attempting to look as fierce. When it became clear Tae had no intention of hurting her, she finally demanded, "Why ya done that?"

"You were going to do it anyway." Tae found himself surprisingly near tears. *I brought this all upon myself.* The prince's use of the word "whore" to describe his mother struck particularly hard. "I figured I'd save you the trouble."

"S'not what I uz gonna done." Rascal edged toward the broken chest, like she worried the shards might attack her.

Tae did not believe the denial. "What *were* you going to do?"

"This." Eyes glued to Tae, Rascal opened a drawer in a wardrobe beside the chest and hauled out one of the neatly tailored shirts Matrinka had given him that he had never worn. "An' this." Carefully displaying her utility knife, she dragged a hole into the fabric.

Tae did not have the strength to stop her. "Oh," he managed.

Rascal dropped the shirt. "What happen ta ya?"

Tae shook his head, not wanting to explain. He looked at his dirt-rimed, callused hands and hated himself for attempting to help. They were the hands of street scum.

When Tae did not answer, Rascal shrugged. "Guess I hain't goin' out there." She jerked a thumb toward the door.

"Guess you hain't," Tae confirmed.

Rascal drifted toward the window.

For a brief, cruel moment, Tae considered letting her go. "I wouldn't do that either, if I were you."

Rascal turned her head toward him, measuring him. For the first time, Tae realized she had difficulty reading expressions and understanding meanings beneath words, not because she was stupid but because she lacked empathy.

Tae helped her. "It's not a challenge. The guards have orders to kill anything that leaves."

Rascal sat sullenly. "Hain't done nothin' wrong."

Tae sighed, seeing no reason not to share. Emotional discussions had broken the walls between himself and Ra-khir, turning hatred to friendship. Perhaps it would work for Rascal as well. "The Prince of Pudar called me 'thieving scum bastard-born to blackguards, whores, and filth.'"

Rascal mulled the words for several moments before returning, "Royal-types hain't never knowin' how ta swear. Where I comed from, that'd be a complimint."

"Where you come from," Tae corrected, "I come from. Our beginnings aren't as different as you believe."

"Ya beginnins letted ya becomed a prince." Rascal's look remained defiant. "Hain't never gonna happint ta me."

"You're right." Tae rose, inciting a riot of aches. He had not realized how hard the journey had been on him until that moment. "But it has nothing to do with origins. It has to do with attitude." Tae could not help seeing the irony. "Of course, attitude is what got me here, too. They're going to lock me up for attacking a prince, and I didn't even do it."

"They'd a kilt the likes o' me."

Tae stiffened at the realization Rascal's comment raised. "If I'm tried in Pudar, they'll do worse than that." Memories flooded back, of his days in the lifer's cell watching the most hardened of Pudar's criminals scrapping over food and water. Only the knowledge that more prisoners meant more sustenance kept them from slaughtering one another. He had heard the pronouncement of his punishment: only a slow and public drawing and quartering could appease King Cymion then. Now, he doubted even that torture would suffice.

Rascal jarred Tae back to reality. "Hain't never gonna happint ta no prins."

Griff and Matrinka would never turn me over to Pudar. The thought soothed only momentarily as another came to replace it. *They're turning over Kevral's baby.* Tae would never have expected such a thing from them either. The strange honor and conventions of nobility confused him, and he had little basis on which to surmise. Tae could think of no better answer for Rascal. "I'm afraid I actually hope you're right."

"Ya hain't one o' us," Rascal said firmly.

Tae knew she was as right about that as Prince Leondis. He felt an odd kinship with the Pica stone, his pieces scattered to many different worlds. And he truly belonged to none of them.

CHAPTER 18

When Honors Clash

When a man believes he lives only once, he becomes obligated to make that one life virtuous.
                                                    —*Knight-Captain Kedrin*

A breeze thick with damp and hinting of spring fluttered the curtains of Prince Leondis' window. The gauzy fabric swirled around him, alternately covering and revealing the bandage on his right shoulder. His loyal steward, Boshkin, sat politely at a desk chair, attentive to the prince's silence. Guards filled the hallway outside his door, the occasional clank of metal reminding him of their presences and of his own status. Though he stared over Béarn's tended gardens that lay poised for the new growth of vegetables and flowers, his thoughts remained with his own country, the one to which he had eternally pledged his loyalty.

The loosely woven curtain fluttered across Leondis' cheek, like a woman's gentle touch. He imagined his new, young wife, Princess Alenna of Corpa Bickat, the dewy blush of youth still tinting her cheeks. Though not classically pretty, the castle's best women worked her hair, cosmetics, and dresses into a finery all Western women envied. Her innocent naïveté in the bedroom pleased him, cheerful contrast to the usual moon-eyed lovers clambering for the ministrations of a prince. He had worried that a princess might prove giddy and spoiled, so her strength of character and intelligence first surprised, and later pleased, him. Severin's death had forced Leondis to give up his wanton ways for the responsibilities befitting the heir, but he would have done so anyway out of respect for his wife. Aside from the newly-delivered mothers and the girls maturing into their womanhood who consented to share his bed for the kingdom's need, he had slept with no one but his wife in the months since their marriage. He had come to hate even those necessary dalliances, desperately relishing the time when he could commit himself fully to his wife.

Leondis turned to face his steward. "I hate this, Bosh. All of it."

Boshkin immediately sprang to attention. He lowered and raised his balding head before allowing his brown eyes to meet his charge's face. "It'll be over soon, Sire."

"No. It won't." Leondis smoothed back his dark locks, anticipating a tearing agony through his injured shoulder that did not come. The elves had healed the wound so that it seemed several days old, aching only minimally. Rage had caused him to sink the blade deeper than necessary; Leondis suspected it would scar. That thought brought the image of Tae's bared torso to his mind. Scars had riddled the small, taut muscles, brown against his swarthy skin. An unmistakable knife wound marred Tae's ribs, directly over his heart.

Leondis banished the vision with grim memories of Severin's corpse. Beloved by the people, admired by his younger brother, all but worshiped by King Cymion, Severin had died needlessly at that murderer's hand. Tae had barely survived a life of violence, but the prince refused to pity it. No matter how the Easterner's beginnings had inured him to killing, no matter how many times Tae's tragic existence caused others to bury knives into his body, he had had no right to inflict the same on innocent Severin.

Boshkin sought the source of Leondis' pain. "Does your shoulder hurt, Sire?"

Absently, Leondis shook his head, placing a hand over his chest to indicate the location of the pain. "If I ruin this, my father will have my head."

"Sire!" Boshkin's voice held a derogatory tone few others would dare. Their long association and confidences allowed it. "Don't talk that way. Your father would never harm you."

Leondis shrugged, not so sure. "He's never really considered me worthy. Not like Severin." No bitterness entered thought or tone. The elder prince had been groomed for the kingship since birth, and his natural kindness and intelligence made him the obvious choice. Since his midteens, Severin had walked the streets of Pudar with the town watch, learning the details of street life and his populace. In the end, the very action that made him so popular had cost him his life. Leondis had planned to become an officer in his brother's army, taking advantage of the freedoms that came with royal lineage and no claim to the throne: the parties; the entertainment of foreign dignitaries, especially the women; and the recreation his generous allowance could supply. Tae Kahn had changed all of that. And now a second time. "I'm not stupid, Boshkin. I know Father's planning to pass the crown to this baby when it comes of age. He's plotted out its life, boy or girl, to the end of its years. It means everything to him. He would sacrifice me for it in an instant if such a situation arose."

Boshkin cocked his head, trying to reconcile tone and words. "Sire, are you jealous of your own child?"

Though wrong, the steward's guess did not offend. "Not at all." Leondis recalled the pride that had swept through him at the sight of Kevral's bulging abdomen. At that moment, the truth of the baby's existence had become real. Propriety, and the realization that Kevral would not tolerate it, had held him back from the exuberant embrace he had wanted to deliver. A smile eased onto his features. "I'm excited. A papa at last, and Alenna will make a radiant mother." The point that had to follow stole his grin. "The only thing worse than worrying over losing our child is the realization that Father might kill me, and others, if I do."

"That won't happen, Sire," Boshkin soothed. "It can't."

Leondis returned to the window. "It can. If Kevral breaks her vow . . ." He trailed off, allowing Boshkin to interrupt without offense.

"The knight will keep her silent."

Leondis made a subtle gesture of uncertainty. "His love for her and his own desire for the baby might make him sloppy." He drummed his fingers on the sill. "And I'm not sure anyone can control that demon in woman's guise."

"The king made that arrangement, Sire," Boshkin reminded. "He can't hold you responsible if it falls through."

Leondis' hand stilled. "But Tae is *my* problem. If Béarn believes him . . ." He shook his head at the enormity of the dilemma.

Boshkin moved to the prince's side. "He gave up all credibility when he attacked you." He indicated the bandage without touching it. "No one could deny he meant to kill you, and the fact that he crept up from behind makes it clear he did not deliver the blow in defense."

Leondis stomped on rising guilt, too shamed to even admit the truth to his faithful retainer. Yet he believed he had acted for the greater good, not only of Pudar but of Béarn. A technicality kept King Cymion from punishing Tae for Severin's murder, and it seemed fitting that a falsehood would correct that injustice. Furthermore, they needed a capital crime to silence the spy who had discovered what no one outside the king's inner circle must know. *First rape, then false accusations and lies.* All of Leondis' reprehensible actions had occurred in the last year, too common and easy. *Is this the price for the crown?* He shook his head. *I don't want it.* "Kevral might find a way to confirm Tae's claims." He turned, lips pursed. "We can't let that happen. Tae has to be permanently . . . hushed."

Finding the prince suddenly too close for protocol, Boshkin retreated. "He hushed himself when he attacked a prince."

The steward's optimistic certainty fell prey to complications. "He's considered a prince, too. He helped rescue the king of Béarn," Leondis reminded. "And he's become a confidante of Queen Matrinka. It won't prove as simple as you believe."

A sudden rapping on the door interrupted any reply Boshkin might have given. The latch rattled, then the door glided open a crack. Leondis could see a hint of Pudarian brown uniform. "Your Majesty, Béarn is ready to see you now."

Leondis closed his eyes and siphoned a slow stream of air through his nose. Calmed by the maneuver, he released the breath through his mouth. He sought a demeanor of ruffled dignity and the composure to remind the king and queen that their alliance had spanned more centuries than anyone could remember. In contrast, Béarn's relationship with the East had wavered from desperate hostility to wary unity over the ages.

"Good luck, Sire," Boshkin said, joining Prince Leondis as the guard opened the door more widely.

The dozen guardsmen assembled in a tight rank in the hallway bowed as their prince emerged. In front of them, a young page in Béarn's blue and gold rubbed his hands nervously together. Though only three quarters grown, he stood as tall and broad as many of Pudar's soldiers. His bow swept him nearly to the floor, the coarse black hair barely moving even with so enthusiastic a motion. "Your Majesty, King Griff and Queen Matrinka asked if you would prefer to present yourself and your case before the council or them alone."

Leondis considered this turn of affairs. Unlike the seventeen-year-old rulers, the members of the council would have history and age's wisdom to guide them in such matters. Also, none of them would have a close personal relationship with his enemy.

Apparently having drawn the same conclusions, Boshkin spoke his piece in the gentle whisper he had perfected through the years. Even in quiet situations, he could advise the prince without others hearing, so long as he dropped as many words as possible, including titles. "Council."

Experience prevented Boshkin's approach from feeling offensive. Leondis mentally filled in the "Sire, I believe it would be best if we appeared before the . . ." Both knew the steward only intended to suggest, never mandate.

"I would like very much to address the council," Prince Leondis said in a mannerly fashion. "I thank His Majesty and Her Grace for the opportunity." Words and attitude scarcely conveyed his joy at the opportunity. "Should we wait for them to gather?"

The page flushed, as if he worried Leondis might misinterpret what followed. "They're gathered, Sire." He added hurriedly, "Just in case you chose that option, Sire. Not because anyone *assumed* . . ." Seeing the understanding half-smile on Leondis' face, he broke off. "Follow me, Sire."

The guards fell into formation, trooping through the hallway with Leondis and Boshkin at their center. Leondis passed through the grand corridors without noticing any of the tapestries and art. He kept his thoughts trained on the coming discussion, seeking words that might convince the council, if not the king and queen. Certain thoughts kept reoccurring: to handle this well or suffer the worst wrath of King Cymion, the absolute need to silence Tae Kahn, the loss Pudar would endure should he fail. He discovered his hands shaking and forced himself to focus on the necessary amenities, proprieties, and composure. He had never taken those details as seriously as he should have, trusting his brother to forgive him. Until her death, Leondis' mother had made excuses for his wildness; and his father had centered his attention on Severin. The last year had proven a trial for both survivors.

Prince Leondis scarcely noticed as the page led them past the courtroom where he had expected his audience and to the regular meeting room of Béarn's council. Boshkin slipped through the ranks of soldiers to announce the prince's arrival. The door flew open, and the guards ushered him to it.

Prince Leondis found every person in the room standing respectfully around a rectangular table, Griff and Matrinka conspicuously absent. Likely, those two had awaited him in the courtroom in case he chose not to meet with the entire council. Two empty chairs at the far head of the table assured that they intended to join the others soon, and the seat nearest the door remained for Leondis himself. As the prince came to the entrance, all of the assembled bowed or curtsied in grand fashion. Another page identified the members of the council quietly for Leondis' benefit, beginning at the left-hand corner and continuing down the long side toward Leondis. "Prime Minister Davian." A middle-aged man with the proper Béarnian darkness and beard bowed at the sound of his name, an awkwardness to his motion suggesting that he had not grown up around nobility. The scars on his face also fit that image. Having performed his individual act of obeisance, he sat.

The page indicated the next man in line, a dour-faced elder who executed his bow with meticulous formality. "Minister of Courtroom Procedure and Affairs Saxanar." More white than ebony, every portion of his neatly trimmed beard touched his neck at the same level, and the thick hair on his head matched its length exactly. He also sat without speaking, as convention demanded.

"Minister of Household Affairs Franstaine." The younger man attempted a flourish that seemed more dance than courtesy. His dark eyes held a sparkle of mischief, and Leondis took an immediate liking to him. Under other circumstances, he seemed exactly the sort who would enjoy a good joke, drink, or party. Probably, he was a blood relation to the king, a cousin or uncle. Had life dealt Severin a different hand, Leondis could have become the equivalent of Franstaine had his military career not come to fruition.

As Franstaine sat, Leondis politely turned his attention to the familiar man beside him. Richar, the minister of foreign affairs, had attended to the prince's needs more than once since his arrival. He had also traveled to Pudar to discuss diplomatic situations, including the unborn heir, with King Cymion. Exuberance, an ingrained fairness, and a natural tact made him ideal for the position, despite his youth. Surely, he, too, carried the blood of Béarn's kings, known for their instinctive flare for justice.

Also male, the last minister on that side of the table bowed graciously, if a bit nervously. Taking his cues from those who had gone before him, he imitated their demonstrations of respect and sat before the page could speak his name. "Zaysharn, overseer of the caretakers of Béarn's livestock, gardens, and food."

Leondis smiled reassuringly, understanding that the rapidity of Zaysharn's greeting stemmed from discomfort, not disrespect. His gaze traveled from his own seat, which he had not yet accepted, to the opposite side of the table where the members of the council still stood.

Directly across from Zaysharn sat a burly guardsman dressed in Béarn's colors and decked with symbols of office. "Captain Seiryn," the page said as the highest leader of Béarn's military executed an easy gesture of dispensation that he had clearly made thousands of times before. He sat at wary attention, and it seemed clear that he had come to secure Leondis, not his king and queen.

"Local Affairs Minister Chaveeshia." The page indicated a tiny woman, invisible until the captain had taken his seat. Leondis' smile increased at the thought that they had chosen her to handle problems with Béarn's Renshai neighbors, like the massive blond to her right. She also would have to coordinate relations between Erythane and the kingdom, which might explain her size. Her lighter hair, slightness, and the tinge of green in her brown eyes suggested a mixed heritage, probably Erythanian. She curtsied pleasantly, then sat.

The blond finally turned his head, giving Leondis a sharp look. "This is Thialnir," the page said, substituting extra words for the missing title. Thialnir plopped his bottom to the chair with barely a nod, and the page explained apologetically. "He represents the Renshai."

The next man could not have proven more opposite. Though also powerfully built and red-blond, he added every rich, archaic flourish to his bow, as if to make up for the Renshai's lack. He wore the unmistakable uniform and colors of the Knights of Erythane, pristine in every aspect. *Ra-khir's father.* Caught up in the situation, Leondis had forgotten that Ra-khir descended from the captain of the knights, but the uncanny resemblance brought remembrance to the fore. Blue-white eyes that he did not share with his son expertly kept below Leondis' own. *Probably shouldn't be here. He has a vested interest.* Leondis chose not to mention the impropriety. They had come to discuss Tae, not the baby; and he trusted the knight to remain impartial no matter how closely the judgment impacted him. His training demanded it.

The page cleared his throat to recite the long title that Kedrin's etiquette would not allow him to shorten: "Knight-Captain Kedrin, Ramytan's son, knight to the Erythanian and Béarnian kings: His Grace, King Humfreet, and His Majesty, King Griff." Kedrin finally took his seat, leaving only one last woman to introduce.

Dutifully, the page gestured at an energetic young Béarnide whose fidgeting clearly irritated the oldest of the ministers, Saxanar. "Internal Affairs Minister, Aerean." He leaped to sudden attention as she sat. Leondis turned to his guards as they stepped aside, allowing a lane for the king and queen of Béarn, accompanied by the king's bodyguard/bard.

The entire room rose again. Leondis nearly groaned. As impatient as Aerean, he hoped they would not have to suffer an exact repeat of the formality. Dutifully, he stepped to his seat, joining the others in animated gestures of esteem. Griff and Matrinka bowed to Leondis as he did to them, then the king's gruff bass echoed across room and corridor simultaneously. "Sit, everyone, please."

Thialnir obeyed at once, the others doing so in ragged singles and pairs. Convention dictated that royalty find the position of comfort first, reigning monarchs before heirs. Torn between the strict discipline beaten into him by his father and tutors and placing the courtiers at ease, Leondis took his seat swiftly. Boshkin followed. That allowed the ministers the security of maintaining their manners for the foreign prince, if not for the king who had commanded his own indignity.

Only Kedrin remained standing by the time King Griff and Queen Matrinka reached their seats at the far end of the room, his loyalty to convention taking precedence over the king's informality. As king and queen settled into position, even the knight finally joined the others. Darris remained standing just behind and to the right of the king. Hyperalert, Leondis did not miss the high eyebrow the knight turned the bard. Darris gave back a helpless shrug. He could advise the farm-raised king on formality for decades and still not convince him of the necessity for the knights' immaculate devotion to procedure.

King Griff did follow the rule that he must speak first, though more likely from simple exigency than decorum. No minister would break the silence, and Leondis knew better than to do so also. "Prince Leondis, all of Béarn apologizes for any wrong that was inflicted upon you while under our protection."

Leondis acknowledged the king's regret with a deep nod. "No one holds you or yours responsible, Your Majesty." He made a motion toward Seiryn to personally absolve him. "My own guards are at least as much to blame for missing the assassin during their inspection of the room." He chose the worst possible word for Tae without lowering himself to cursing. "Your Majesty, no one could have predicted his presence."

King Griff continued, "At your request, Prince Leondis, we have allowed Tae no contact until you have spoken your piece."

Leondis plucked the significant from the king's comment. Clear convention dictated that the king and queen hear royalty speak before any other. In this case, they could have chosen to let Tae speak first, since he also qualified as a visiting prince. Three details worked in Leondis' favor, however. First, his father had already announced him as the crown prince whereas Tae's had not yet publicly named his successor. Second, at least by appearances, Leondis was the wronged party in the dispute. Third, Pudar's long association with Béarn should also give him precedence. Only after these thoughts sped through Leondis' mind did he recognize a lengthy silence.

At Leondis' side, Boshkin nudged him gently.

Leondis cleared his throat. "Your Majesties. Representatives of Béarn's council. I apologize for providing a temptation, my presence in your castle, that one man could not resist. Tae Kahn—" Catching Kedrin's frown from the corner of his eye, he amended, "Prince Tae Kahn has reason to dislike the royal family of Pudar, but I never expected him to resort to violence. Otherwise, I would have warned my guards to watch for him."

Foreign Minister Richar bounced slightly in his chair. He knew history that others did not and Saxanar sought to elucidate. The elder executed the gesture requesting clarification that Leondis nearly missed. Pudar had long ago discarded such archaic formality.

In case others had not seen the motion, Leondis turned toward the aging minister of court procedure. "Minister Saxanar, it was this same man who assassinated my brother, Prince Severin."

Several ministers recoiled from this information. The queen opened her mouth as if to correct the accusation, then closed it without speaking.

Her bias as Tae's close friend would force her to vindicate him and also render her excuses meaningless. The Easterner's defense came instead from an unexpected source. The knight-captain gestured for an acknowledgment granted by his king. "Prince Tae Kahn's version of those events differs, Your Grace."

Leondis accepted the nonjudgmental information without malice, suppressing the heat that came naturally to his face. "Understandably, Captain. Who would confess to such evil?" Diplomacy dictated that the prince remain at least apparently equitable. "Let's set aside the certainty of his guilt or innocence in that matter." He deliberately looked at Matrinka. "Right or wrong, he spent time in Pudar's worst dungeon under sentence of slow execution." Leondis reminded the ministers, who would expect better treatment of royalty no matter the crime, "At that time, his father had no claim upon Stalmize's throne and was, in fact, commanding the band of Eastern murderers who obstructed all travel in the West." Leondis glanced around to assure everyone had garnered his point but saw consideration on more than one face. "Give Prince Tae the benefit of our doubts and call him innocent. I could see where he might feel justified to commit the crime for which he had already suffered, the assassination of Pudar's crown prince." Leondis paused, allowing his words to fully penetrate. "If he is guilty of Severin's murder, as several witnesses confirm, then he has obvious and clear intention of destroying Pudar's line."

"But why?" Aerean asked. Though Leondis had finished his thought, Saxanar, Davian, and Kedrin all turned her nonverbal warnings for skipping formalities in the presence of visiting royalty.

Prince Leondis chose to answer the question despite other's discomfort. "Only Prince Tae could answer that." He wished he could kick himself. Preventing a meeting with Tae was the foremost issue on his agenda. "I can't help speculating that it bears some relation to his father's purge in Stalmize. King Weile Kahn ascended from beginnings less than humble to the Eastlands' throne." Again, Leondis paused for effect. "Tae wouldn't be the first son to shadow, even to best, his father." Indirectly, he hoped, these Béarnides would recognize the threat of Tae to their own security as well.

"Tae would never do that," Matrinka blurted out of turn, though no one dared chastise her with words or stares.

Leondis bowed and lifted his head before looking directly at the queen. "If I may quote the captain of our prison guards, Your Ladyship?"

Clearly humbled by her own outburst, Matrinka returned the gesture of respect. "Of course, Prince Leondis. Please."

Though Leondis could not quote directly, he remembered well

enough to pretend. "The difference between a habitual liar and an honest man is that the liar's story sounds more credible."

Strained chuckles followed.

The prince finished strongly. "Your Ladyship, the successful coup begins by lulling those in charge. History reveals many examples where kings lost their lives and power to their most trusted advisers or their own brothers." Béarn had fallen twice: once to a king's own twin; and, most recently, to the *svartalf* with the assistance of a long-respected prime minister and a disgruntled prince.

A stunned hush followed those words. No one could forget the invasion that had seen the demise of the entire previous council. The current prime minister had earned his position by leading the assault that had restored the proper king. With such clear and recent evidence in front of them, even Matrinka had to see the possibility that Tae had crafted their friendship for his own dark purposes.

Davian finally broke the silence. "So, Sire, you believe the Eastern prince's motive is a grasp for power?"

Leondis met the scarred face evenly. "Partially, perhaps, Prime Minister. At least initially. I believe revenge played a role. And then, there's Kevral's defense."

Several ministers vied for acknowledgment, but Thialnir leapt in first, without formality. "Kevral needs no defending. She's Renshai."

Chaveeshia smoothed over her charge's outburst, as her job required. "I don't believe His Highness meant a physical defense, Thialnir." She turned Prince Leondis an apologetic look. "If I may be so bold as to assume."

Leondis accepted Chaveeshia's temerity without offense. "When Prince Tae stabbed me . . ." His hand wandered to the wound. ". . . he made some ludicrous accusations against me and Pudar in regard to the heir. Said he'd see to it the baby stayed with Kevral, whatever it took." The prince shook his head. "At the time, I was too stunned and pained to think about his words; but I've had plenty of time since. I'm concerned that his lies might harm Pudar." His gaze swept the assembly, steadily meeting gazes. The appearance of honest suffering would go a long way toward getting his concessions.

A pained look crossed Matrinka's features, and she squirmed in her chair. Griff had discarded his usual smile outside the room and appeared grim. The ministers returned the prince's scrutiny in turn. Minister of Household Affairs Franstaine asked softly, "Why do you think he would do such a thing, Sire?"

"He loves her," Aerean piped in before the prince could answer, earning her another round of glares.

Leondis conceded the point he was about to make with a gesture toward the minister of internal affairs and a nod. Even he had learned that Tae fathered one of the twins and proposed to Kevral before she married Ra-khir. Every other in the room surely already knew. The time seemed right to make his demands. "Pudar wants those lies fully suppressed. And we want the assassin extradited."

Several of those assembled physically jerked at the suggestion. Mouths glided open. Eyes rounded. The king finally spoke again, "Prince Leondis, I . . ." He assumed court mode, reaching for words he used there and probably nowhere else in his life. ". . .understand and sympathize with your situation. But the lowest of my citizens has the right to trial. I could no more deny him that than I could yourself."

"Understood, Your Majesty." Leondis had predicted opposition. "And he will get a fair trial in Pudar." He glanced at Boshkin who gave him a sign of strength beneath the table. *A fair trial. And a fair execution.*

"Prince Leondis, I would never presume anything less from Pudar . . ."

Unable to contain herself, the queen broke in, "But the crime occurred here."

Griff swung his head to Matrinka, clearly startled. Born, bred, and trained to royalty, she usually followed protocol diligently in such affairs. Only among personal friends did she disdain it.

The queen flushed, finishing her issue in a low voice approaching a whisper. "He should be tried here."

"Your Ladyship." Prince Leondis maintained his composure even after Matrinka lost hers. Such a stance, his father taught, gave him power. "I'm not asking you to forgo his rights. In fact, I could not allow it. I'm simply asking that the council consider extradition as its verdict. And that the trial occur there rather than in front of nobles and peasants who might become . . ." He sought a word that would not insult the citizenry, ". . . influenced by his lies. Your Majesty, every country has some who enjoy scandal or who seek excuses to dislike other kingdoms."

Boshkin whispered, "Best for him, too. Fewer knowing what he did."

Leondis liked the detail. It added equity. "Besides, Your Majesty, it's safer for Tae and the East if the whole kingdom doesn't know he attempted to assassinate a prince."

Boshkin made a positive signal in his lap.

"Ah," Griff said. "Well, if it works in his favor as well, I should think Prince Tae would agree to speak his piece to the council."

Though Leondis did not feel as certain, his manners did not allow him to contradict. Doing so would only spoil his argument. "Thank you, Your Majesty."

Griff drew breath as Matrinka leaned toward him. He closed his mouth, listening for several moments. Then, he nodded and said something equally soft in return. Matrinka rose from the assemblage and headed for the door. Turning his attention to his bodyguard, the king spoke loud enough for all to hear. "If everyone has spoken their piece. . . ?" He paused long enough for contradictions, which did not come. "Darris, sing for us, please. Something appropriate."

Darris shrugged a pack from his shoulders. Removing a flat, curvy instrument, he strummed out gentle harmonics in a rhythm as billowy as its silhouette. After a long introduction, he began to sing.

CHAPTER 19

Turmoil

Strange how some of the same people who place so much emphasis on ancestry dare to brag about their methods of child-rearing. If bloodline is everything, then parenting is nothing.
—Colbey Calistinsson

DICE tumbled across the floor, bone clicking against wood. The first settled on one. The second skittered a moment longer, then fell showing a five. Tae settled back on his haunches. "Damn. You win again." He tossed a copper at Rascal. "You're cheating, aren't you?"

The girl took the insult in stride, regarding Tae around brown bangs that fell into her eyes. Gathering darkness softened her features, and the glow of a single lamp barely reflected from dusty hair that had surely gone unwashed for weeks. "Your dice," she reminded.

"You're throwing them."

Rascal gathered the dice, then dropped back into a crouch. "Hain't how ya cheats. Lessen I'm changin' nature-laws, hain't barely no ways I kin cheat thataway."

Tae did not pursue. He had made the accusation without thought or any true condemnation. Of all his contacts, he had known only one who could consistently manipulate properly made dice. Even if Rascal had had that man's agility, it did not matter. Tae could afford the coppers, and he only played for distraction. Waiting in stoic silence left him brooding over his fate, and conversation with Rascal required intense effort. He could not concentrate enough to assure that he did not destroy the progress, minimal as it was, that he had made with her so far.

The dice clattered across the floorboards. A momentary hush followed, then Rascal scrambled after them. "Winned agin."

"Hmmm?" Tae looked down just in time to see a single-throw winning combination—for himself. Not until Rascal had them securely back in her hands did he realize he had won the toss. "Wait, that . . ." Arguing seemed too tiresome. He tossed her another copper, now clear on how Rascal kept besting him. She simply capitalized on his inattentiveness.

A solid knock resounded through the room, then the door whipped open before Tae could respond. Tensed for another round of ill-treatment, he stiffened without bothering to look toward the entrance. A moment later, the door slammed closed; and he heard an offended meow.

Matrinka's voice boomed, "What in Hel is going on, Tae Kahn?"

Tae rose and whirled. Rascal answered first. "We's playin' dice."

Apparently startled by Rascal's presence, Matrinka went silent. Mior leaped onto the bed, then sprang off the end toward Tae. Though worried for her claws, Tae caught the cat, snuggling her against his chest while she purred evenly.

Matrinka rolled her dark eyes toward Rascal in question.

"Here when I got here," Tae explained. He inclined his head toward the door and the array of guardsmen that Matrinka had surely negotiated. "Can't leave."

Matrinka heaved a sigh. "Come with me." She gestured at Rascal who dropped the dice, snatched up the copper, and did as Matrinka bade.

Tae sat on the edge of the bed, his back to the proceedings. He did not want to see any of the Pudarian guards' insolent expressions nor engage in a war of wills. He stroked Mior's soft fur while she pressed herself against him as if to become a part of him. "Thanks for your help, honey." He doubted the calico had anything to do with Matrinka's arrival; too much time had passed for that. *But Mior will take the credit.*

Shortly, the door closed again, with a quiet click this time. Tae looked over his shoulder to Béarn's queen. "I'm in big trouble, aren't I?"

"You've been in worse," Matrinka said, the words barely encouraging given his history. "What happened?"

Tae told his version of the events with as few words as possible, petting the cat the entire time.

When he finished, Matrinka remained silent several moments. Finally, she said, "Leondis stabbed himself?"

Tae looked up fiercely, worried that his own friend might challenge his claim. "Yes," he said through gritted teeth, prepared for a battle Matrinka did not give him.

"What were you doing in that room?" Arranging her skirts with proper modesty, Matrinka perched on the side of the bed.

Tae lowered his head. "Eavesdropping. I know I shouldn't have, but I didn't mean any harm."

"He said you accused him of . . . things." Matrinka's bright gaze held Tae's.

"I did," Tae admitted.

Matrinka's eyes went moist. Her fingers plucked at her skirts, and her scrutiny followed them. "You promised me you wouldn't do that."

"I promised not to use the information *you* gave me." Tae studied the side of Matrinka's head, the thick, black curls that tumbled over her ear. If a man could choose his own siblings, she would already be his sister. "I only threw back his own words."

"You shouldn't have done that, Tae."

"Someone had to."

"You shouldn't have done it." Matrinka was right.

"I know."

Finally, Matrinka glanced at Tae, though only briefly and sidelong. "You went there to hear him confirm what I told you."

"No."

"So you could get around your vow."

"No," Tae insisted. "I didn't. I went from curiosity. I wanted to know why Kevral and Ra-khir got summoned so suddenly. I worried—"

"I told you Pudar summoned them." Matrinka interrupted. "You had to know why."

"But I didn't know just . . ." Tae started, suddenly intensely uncomfortable. "Gods, Matrinka. Maybe I did go to hear the prince speak those words." He clenched his hands over the cat. "Keeping that vow about killed me, but I'd never knowingly break it."

Now it was Matrinka's turn to say, "I know."

"I didn't think I . . ." Tae began, then stopped. "Leave it at 'I didn't think.'" He shook back locks with barely a tangle since their cutting. "But I didn't bring any weapons with me. And I didn't attack anyone."

Matrinka caught Tae's arm, and sudden pain flashed from the contact. Before he could decide to hide it, he flinched, and whatever words the queen intended to speak disappeared. "You're hurt?" She slid her hand to his, turned the palm up, and drew back his sleeve.

"The guards already judged and convicted me."

Matrinka's attention jerked suddenly to Tae's face, and he read anger in her eyes. "The guards mishandled you?"

Only then, Tae realized the trouble he could create. "Pudar's, not Béarn's."

"Béarn's should have stopped them." Matrinka's gaze rolled to a series of finger-shaped bruises. "Oh, Tae. I'm sorry."

Mior half rose, sniffing delicately at Tae's arm.

Tickled by Mior's whiskers, Tae pushed her head away gently with his other hand. "It's not their fault. Really. Once they warned the prince's men, most of this happened . . . um . . . covertly."

"They should have stopped it." Unable to minister to bruising, Matrinka replaced Tae's sleeve, though she still held his arm.

"I don't think they could have." Tae continued to defend Béarn's guardsmen, though it seemed ludicrous when his own life might lie at stake. "And I don't blame Pudar's guards either. They had reason to believe I tried to kill their prince." Still needing confirmation from Matrinka, he added sharply, "Though I didn't."

"I believe you, Tae." Matrinka sounded almost defensive. "But not everyone will. Prince Leondis' wound was . . . significant."

"Yes." Tae refused to repeat the events or to assert his innocence again. "So, what happens now?"

"You come before the council." Matrinka lowered her hands to the bedspread. "Or you can undergo a public trial, if you prefer."

Tae shivered at the thought. Years of living on the edge had made him leery of crowds, especially ones that might condemn him. "I'll brave the council, thank you."

"Good. That's what the prince requested."

"Then I'll take the trial."

"Tae."

"Kidding." Tae returned to stroking the cat, and she assisted by walking back and forth across his lap, pressing her body against his hand.

Matrinka sucked in a deep lungful of air, staring at the opposite wall for several moments. Whatever came next would surely carry great significance. "Tae, maybe I've become too much a queen, but I truly see two sides to the matter of Kevral's baby."

Shocked silent, Tae stared.

"Spying has consequences."

Ire rising, Tae whirled on Matrinka, nearly dumping Mior. "Don't patronize me. I started spying while you were still in your crib. Nobody expects a four-year-old to understand three languages, and I was always small enough to pass as years younger than my age." Tae halted abruptly, surprised by his own words. He had forgotten about that part of his life until that moment. At the time, he had not understood the implications of the conversations he passed along to his father. "Get caught spying on criminals, and it's a death sentence without trial."

Matrinka accepted the attack good-naturedly, as she did nearly everything. "That explains a lot, Tae."

Tae shrugged. He imagined it truly did, from his ability to notice and negotiate alternate ways into and out of rooms to the quiet stealth of his movements. Even his decision to listen in on Prince Leondis' meeting with Ra-khir and Kevral.

Matrinka gathered a protesting Mior from Tae's lap and placed the cat in her own. "When you corner a lion, expect a war to the death."

The analogy worked well. Even the prince's name meant "royal lion of the gods." "He's not exactly cornered," Tae protested. "I clearly am."

"No, Tae." Mior clambered from Matrinka's lap with an overplayed casualness that did not fool the queen. She caught the animal halfway to Tae, earning a yellow-eyed glare and a yowl of protest. "When you revealed what you overheard, you cornered him. If it becomes common knowledge, it could cause unrest in Pudar. It could strain relationships with every other kingdom. It could foster war with Renshai. Leondis can't let that happen." Her hands quickened across Mior. "I don't want it to happen either."

Tae appreciated that she did not say she could not allow it to happen, which would imply that she intended to work against him. He had not thought of the situation in that light. Though it pained him, he spoke the necessary words, "What if I promise not to speak of it? Again?"

Matrinka scratched beneath Mior's chin, and the cat threw her head backward as far as it could go. "If you were Ra-khir, I think that would satisfy Pudar enough that they might not insist on your execution."

Trapped, Tae demanded, "So what am I supposed to do?"

Matrinka gave no immediate reply.

"Become a Knight of Erythane, then make the vow?"

Matrinka adopted a sarcasm that ill-suited her. "That could happen." Mior twisted her head back to give Matrinka a withering look, and the queen continued in her normal tone. "Perhaps if you made a remarkable conciliatory gesture with clear good faith, Prince Leondis might trust your intentions enough to accept your promise."

Tae did not like the sound of that. At all. "Like admit to a crime I didn't commit."

"And apologize. And throw yourself on Griff's mercy."

Responding to a sudden surge of anger, Tae slammed his fist into the bedspread. It left a harmless indentation that barely diffused his rage. "What's the punishment for stabbing a prince?"

Matrinka answered only indirectly. "Your surrender would put you solely under Griff's authority. He couldn't extradite you, and he would never order your execution."

Tae had other concerns. "He might imprison me for life."

"He won't."

"How do you know?"

"Trust me."

Tae lowered his face to his hands, anger waning, leaving terror in its place. "I didn't do it."

Matrinka's silken arm settled across Tae's shoulders. "I know that. And so does Prince Leondis. It's unfair, but few others will believe it. And, if you force them to convict you, it'll go much harder."

A long pause followed, during which Tae realized he had nothing to consider. "When do we do this?"

Matrinka's touch conveyed tender consolation. "As soon as you get composure."

Composure. Tae shook his head. *That should only take a decade or two.*

Fingertips tented against the window, Ra-khir watched clouds bunch over Béarn's courtyard, bundling gardens, whitestone benches, and ponds into a gloom beyond evening. For more than two hours, his thoughts had followed as many pathways as he could see from his bedroom, yet always they spiraled back to the same answers. Only one course remained true to his honor. That he did not like it did not matter. Ethics and preferences rarely overlapped. Honest men, knights and others of virtue, followed their principles. Evil chose the selfish route.

The door clicked open, and Ra-khir froze. The glass pressed coldly against the ends of his fingers, twisting a chill through him. The first of the feared moments had arrived, and he had no choice but to face it bravely, no matter the cost. He waited for the crash of the slamming door, but it did not come. The panel hit the jamb with little more force than usual, and the clack of the latch echoed only because of his own intense silence.

Ra-khir turned to look at his wife. Her hair lay in sweaty disarray. Her cheeks bore the glow of a grueling practice, and the blue eyes glimmered with new-found purpose. The split leather hilt of her nearer sword lay dark with moisture, the other hilt hidden by the bulge of her abdomen. "I'm keeping my baby," she announced defiantly.

Kevral's tone proved the final, overwhelming burden for Ra-khir. "It's not *your* baby, Kevral. It's *our* baby."

The blonde brows lowered, too wispy to form an effective glare. "You, too, Ra-khir?"

"Me, too," Ra-khir admitted. "You did not, cannot, make a baby by yourself." He added pointedly, "Neither could you rear one alone. Three parents for the twins, and we're still relying heavily on nursemaids and grandparents."

"You're not blaming me for the mission."

Ra-khir shrugged. "If not this mission, another one. Renshai have always shared the trials of raising children within the tribe. According to Thialnir, it's not unusual to leave every child under ten with a few adults while the rest ride off to war."

Kevral ran her fingers through her hair, raking it back into untidy feathers. "Your point?" she demanded.

"I have a say in this matter, too."

Love should have granted him at least that much, but Kevral already knew which side he would take. And she refused to hear it. "I'm the one who's carried it for longer than six months. And nearly three more to come. I'm the one who thrills to its movements. No one could ever care for him or her as I do."

Kevral's words cut Ra-khir to the heart. For an instant he stood on the verge of tears before will bubbled up like anger. "How dare you!" For the first time in his life, he felt a slash of hatred for the woman he would have sacrificed his knighthood to marry.

"It's true."

"That a couple of months of feeling movement before birth takes precedence over a lifetime of love and caring? You know better." Ra-khir took a menacing step toward Kevral, though he would not have harmed her even if he could have. "You've reduced fatherhood to a silly charade and parenting to insignificant parody. Dare tell me that months in your womb makes you the better parent to Subikahn than Tae. Dare tell me that you love either of those boys more than I do. Dare it, and our marriage can go the way of my parents'." Ra-khir could no longer hold back the hot tears that blurred his vision. He could not bear to live with anyone who would denigrate a love so expansive and inexorably real. "My mother said that I was 'more hers than my father's because she carried me inside her.' I don't remember my time in the womb, but what came after remains vivid. Note well: I'm with my father now. By choice."

Kevral turned away, though the wilting of her stance cued Ra-khir that she did not plan to fight. All of the confidence she had gained by violence seemed to disappear in that moment.

Ra-khir found his hands trembling. The memories that had accompanied his own words returned to haunt him, raw wounds incapable of healing. Worried he might lose control, he forced himself back to the genuine issue at hand. "Kevral, we have to surrender the baby to Pudar."

Kevral snapped back to attention. "No!" Desperate beyond worry for consequences, she jabbed for the open sores. "You're only saying that because it's not really your child."

Ra-khir exploded into a fury that seemed depthless. Red scored his vision, stealing sight of the familiar furnishings. He struggled against a hatred that threatened to ruin his devotion to Kevral irrevocably. The intensity sucked in all focus, making it seem too permanent to deny. He soothed himself with quiet determination: *This, too, will pass;* but the words contained a hope that seemed meaningless and foolish. He managed to hide his rage beneath a flat tone that could ignite at any moment. "That baby is real, Kevral. And so am I. Your words are not only gross effrontery, they're cruelty. And I expect better from you."

Kevral opened her mouth, but Ra-khir lunged back in. Anything she said could only loosen his tenuous hold on composure.

"Tell Griff that he's not Marisole's real father. Or that his love is lesser for the blood they don't share. Tell every man or woman who has taken in an orphan, a half orphan, or an abandoned child."

Again Kevral tried to speak, and Ra-khir did not allow it.

"Tell every man who has succored the children of a friend or brother, every woman who has wet nursed the baby of a sister killed by childbirth." Ra-khir added the coup de grace. "Tell Colbey himself." Colbey had shared the dense suffering his infertility had wrought, his love for the orphaned Renshai he had raised strengthened by an appreciation for children that the fertile took for granted. Even centuries after Calistin's death, Colbey still considered himself the son of the mortal who loved and raised him, not of the immortal who sired him. Only then, Ra-khir let Kevral say her piece, bracing for the worst.

Kevral sat heavily on the bed, wrapping her arms around her abdomen. "You're right."

Expecting other words, Ra-khir took an unreasonable amount of time to absorb them. The surges of emotion became as exhausting as physical effort. "I just realized I may owe Khirwith an apology."

Kevral swiveled her head to look at her husband, her face still pudgy with youth. She seemed far too young to have given birth to children. "Your stepfather?"

Ra-khir nodded. "I've always blamed him equally for lying to me about my father. Though wrong in our case, Prince Leondis had a point about men loving their women enough to believe things that would otherwise seem outlandish." He took a seat beside Kevral, still thoughtful. "Like that my knight father treated her harshly. And that he wanted no part of raising me." Ra-khir did not know whether he had assessed the situation correctly after so long, having never before considered it in this light. "Too much a child himself, Khirwith never made a good father, but I do believe he loved me as much as he could any child."

Kevral sat quietly.

Ra-khir winced at the need to tack again. Though emotionally wracking for him, the turn of the conversation to his past reprieved Kevral. Discussion of the baby had to happen now, while she remained willing to listen. "Kevral, it's not as if we'd be turning the baby over to a pack of wolves to devour. He or she would have a better life than we could offer: an adoring father dedicated to warcraft, a doting grandfather, a mother who appreciates him as only one who has known the pain of a barren womb can."

"No," Kevral said, softly this time.

"Three babies," Ra-khir reminded. "Even with three parents, I feel overwhelmed by two."

"Some women have eight or nine," Kevral reminded.

"Over a lifetime." Ra-khir smoothed Kevral's hair with gentle affection. "I don't know anyone with three under a year old. Can they all get the time and attention they deserve?"

"We have plenty of help." Kevral's volume started to rise again, the defensiveness returning to her tone, though she resisted the accusations that had so angered him before.

Ra-khir slid his arm down the back of Kevral's neck to shoulders tensed like rocks. "I'm not saying we can't handle it, only that the baby's best interests might lie with Pudar."

"Never."

"Kevral." Ra-khir kept his touch light, knowing his next words might anger her as much as hers had him, but needing to speak them anyway. "You're still thinking of this baby like an organ. A kidney, perhaps. Or a heart. A part of you. But that ends the day it leaves the birth tract. Babies are born innocent, without preconceived notions or prejudice. They have only needs. They love the ones who satisfy those needs, their parents. Blood does not become significant until their minds become warped by societal bigotry."

"You've already made that point," Kevral sulked.

"New point." Ra-khir raised his free hand. "Relies partially on the old. The truest, purest gesture of love: sacrificing one's own happiness for the other."

Kevral jerked her head to Ra-khir. Only the suddenness of her gesture made him realize the significance of his words to his own decision to surrender his knighthood and life to rescue her from King Cymion.

"Set aside your desires. Set aside pride of ownership. Set aside your anger and your hatred, no matter how burning or significant. For the moment, set aside even Béarn's security. Now, decide what is best for our baby."

Kevral closed her eyes. "Not Cymion. That cannot be the answer."

Ra-khir lowered the hand, placing it firmly on Kevral's abdomen. Tiny flickers of movement drummed against his palm, and a warm rush of affection for that baby nearly overwhelmed him. His honor committed him to a cause that made his decision more certain than Kevral's, though no easier. He abandoned opinion and lecture for the words he had to say. "Kevral, I'm bound by the vows we made, but I'll always love you and respect your decision." Fresh tears sprang to his eyes, these cold pinpricks that washed away the old. "Even if I have to oppose it."

"I understand," Kevral said with unexpected tranquillity. She entwined her fingers with his.

They spent a long time in silence.

* * *

Asgard's sky stretched above Ravn's head, as smooth and changeless as a massive sapphire and interrupted only by the perfect, yellow circle of sun. Limbs bathed with perspiration, he longed for the whisper of breeze that had once wound through the otherwise still air, keeping the temperature just a hair cooler than perfection. With it had gone the gentle rattle of leaves and branches, leaving a dead silence that emphasized his every breath. He had practiced the Renshai maneuvers since awakening that morning, yet mastery still eluded him and frustration became a constant, irritating companion.

Again, Ravn launched into the sequence, sword sweeping in blurry loops as quick as lightning, legs pumping their graceful rhythm. His father's words rose to his mind as they often did: "Skill has no limits, and anything will come with practice. If it does not, look to your own dedication and will." *Focus!* Ravn tossed his all into the next sequence, the one that had tripped him up at the time of Kevral's visit. At that moment, his father's voice became a shout that foiled his concentration. *How can you focus when you're torn? Like skill, chaos has no limits.*

Startled by the sudden intensity of the thought, Ravn lost control. His left-hand sword clipped his knee with a pain that made him howl. He dropped to his opposite side, rolling to draw attention from the agony.

The voice in his head assisted. *Betray the gods and join me. Father and son. Together, we have the power to rule the universe.*

Something ignited in Ravn's thoughts, feeding on a stress that transcended the morning and the anguish hammering through his leg. Fueled by the frenzy, he leaped to his feet despite the injury, glaring around for the source of the intrusion. A uniform plain of green carpeted the ground. Trees sat motionless, branches sagging with heavy bubbles of fruit. Paranoid that the other poised behind him, Ravn whirled, momentarily inciting an injury whose pain had already diminished to a dull, aching reminder of his own incompetence.

Strength beyond Modi's. Battle wrath sweeter than any candy. Knowledge that Odin himself cannot comprehend. The source of creation. Genius. The sustenance of magic.

"Show yourself!" Ravn screamed. "Show yourself, you coward." His words shattered the stillness and seemed to linger endlessly before the world returned a soft echo.

A second challenge followed, making his sound puny in comparison. *Coward, indeed! Rescue your own, or I will destroy him. Utterly.*

Before Ravn could make sense of the words, before the bonfire that had sparked inside him could recede, the words disappeared as completely as his memory of their speaking. Only his own voice returned to him, unheeded.

A figure appeared at the edge of Ravn's vision as he suffered a fiery need for violence that erupted from some place he could not name. He charged it, stopped short by the recognition of his mother. He spun the other way, his wound no longer bothering him, though the wrath it had spurred remained.

And the voice returned to his head: *Ravn, I fought what I should have embraced. Forsake the balance. Forsake the gods. You owe them nothing.*

"Where are you?" Ravn growled, brandishing his swords. "Show yourself."

Again, the intruder transcended Ravn's thoughts. *Last chance before I scramble his brains like a shattered melon!* Then, as before, the call melted into obscurity, a nonentity that, to Ravn's ability to remember had never happened.

Words seemed to glide into Ravn's head, gentle as his mother's kiss. *Things are not as they seem.* Then Colbey appeared at the edge of the practice grounds.

The sight of him lit something primal inside Ravn. All rationality fled, burned away by the fire, and he attacked with a madman's fury.

One sword to two, Colbey blocked the attack, driven three steps backward by its ferocity. He managed only a single riposte before the sword of balance and its partner careened for him again. Colbey dodged a low strike, cutting and ducking simultaneously. Steel cut coldly along Ravn's rib cage. Then Colbey spun free, leaving a gap that could have allowed for talk.

For an instant, Ravn felt nothing. Abruptly, pain enveloped him, all consuming. He glanced at the wound, finding the gap in his tunic and the sticky scarlet stream gushing through the opening. *Fatal.* Ravn assessed in an instant, surprised to find himself standing and coherent. Then rage and desperation stole the last of his logical reserves. "Modi!" he screamed, charging his father like a rabid bull. Nothing mattered anymore but dying in glory. And taking the traitor with him.

Steel rang like a clarion symphony as Ravn hacked and slashed with a speed and strength borne of urgency. True to his teachings, Colbey did not speak or invade Ravn's mind again. The old Renshai simply met each thrust with a parry, each feint with a spinning redirection, each sweep with a dodge. Trapped in a crimson world devoid of deliberation, Ravn fought tirelessly and with a ferocity beyond the ability of his own mind to conjure.

Even Freya's voice barely penetrated. "No! Stop! Leave him alone!" A stone flew from the sidelines and crashed against Colbey's ear. Sparks flew from a contact enhanced by magic.

The old Renshai staggered, losing his attack. Ravn bore toward the opening this created. Only a wild leap rescued Colbey from a sword blow powerful enough to fracture his skull. Something akin to sorrow flashed through his blue-gray eyes, yet surely not for himself.

Ravn hesitated for a moment, needing to understand. Then, a flood of power crushed that tiny spark, and he launched himself at Colbey again.

More rocks flew. This time, Colbey avoided them, even as he wove in and out of Ravn's deadly attacks. A string of mental insults berated Ravn's mind, scarcely penetrating the fog and out of synchrony with Colbey's actions. Ravn noticed none of it, battling to his last breath to take the chaos-bound abomination with him; though, from the moment of death, they would part. Ravn hoped he would live on in Valhalla while the creature in front of him, and the chaos it represented, simply ceased to exist.

Logic should have told Ravn otherwise, if only through Harval's willingness to fight. The sword of balance should have recognized the danger of siding against a force of such power, should have realized that destroying such a mass of chaos would tip the world irrevocably toward law. Yet, it performed smoothly in Ravn's hands, its balance ever more flawless.

For an instant, understanding seeped through, and Ravn paused. That split second proved his undoing. Colbey's sword sprang through the opening, catching Ravn a head blow that toppled him and sent his consciousness swimming. Then, Freya stormed in to take his place, thrusting herself between her son and any death blow Colbey might deal.

Ravn's awareness faded into darkness.

C H A P T E R 20

Justice

In this new age, no man chooses the path of evil; he only confuses personal happiness with goodness.
                                    —*Colbey Calistinsson*

RAVN awakened with a headache that pounded to every heartbeat, his world a gray blur that bore no relation to the defining, uniform colors of Asgard. Ingrained habit sent him skittering to a defensive crouch, a hand falling to each hilt. The abrupt movement slammed pain through his skull, reducing vision to a thick, swirling curtain of dull spots. Detached from control, he felt himself vomiting and falling. He managed to maintain balance by dropping his center of gravity, but his lunch did not fare as well. The indefinable sixth sense of a warrior suggested no immediate danger. He lowered his head, attempting thought that remained just beyond comprehension.

Ravn managed thought before sight, recalling the unreasoning rage that had driven him to a crazed assault upon his father. His mind sorted the tangible battle into the reality column and the fury into dream. It seemed ludicrous, a turnabout of possibility; yet, as he considered the whole in more detail, the division made more sense. The agony in his head and the lesser aches of his muscles confirmed the truth of physical conflict. The emotion, however, left no impression, its source outside him. Someone had manipulated him.

That idea raised an anger all its own. Ravn recalled the voice in his head, beckoning him to abandon balance and the gods to join the cause of chaos. Then, he had believed that mind-voice Colbey's without question. Now, that unconsidered certainty, in and of itself, grew suspect. *Things are not as they seem.* At the time, that gentle warning had disappeared beneath the demanding avalanche in his head. He now focused on this piece that jarred, though only for a moment. Another thought took sudden precedence: *Fatally wounded.* He clamped both hands to his ribs. His fingers wormed through a tear in the fabric, touching bruised flesh but no crusted blood or flaps of skin.

Gradually, the spiraling shroud that ruined Ravn's vision receded, and strength seeped into his limbs. He noticed his mother leaning against a gray expanse of wall, watching him. The room contained no furnishings, only four unadorned stone walls and a matching ceiling and floor. He saw no doors or entryways. He stared at his side, surprised to find exactly what his fingers already told him. He forced his memory back one more time, now realizing that the wound he had visualized never existed. Its foreignness now seemed as clear as the voice that had once filled his head.

Freya walked to Ravn and crouched in front of him. "Are you well?"

Ravn rose cautiously, prepared for a second round of vomiting or for pain to drop him again. This time, he managed to stand, moving away from his sickness with his mother at his side. "I'm all right. What happened?"

Freya knew better than to assist too much. Like mortal adolescents, Ravn became annoyed by anything he perceived as parenting, though right now he would have secretly enjoyed a bit of worried mothering. "I'd like to hear your version."

Ravn understood. If Freya had suffered anything close to the war that had taken place in his head, sifting truth from illusion would require the input of everyone involved. He described the events from the moment of the first voice until he lost consciousness, to the best of his recollection.

Freya listened to the entire story without comment. Only after he stated "and then I woke up . . . wherever we are . . ." did she finally comment. "Apparently, we're on chaos' world."

A gasp escaped Ravn before he could think or speak. He jerked backward, glad his headache had lessened enough to allow the swift movement. "I thought things of law could not exist here." Realization struck a mighty blow. "Are we dead?"

Freya smiled, though it looked strained. "No." She moved her right leg in a circular motion before pacing a double step. The familiar habit soothed Ravn at time when separating reality from fantasy had become difficult and he could no longer trust even his own thoughts and emotions. "I didn't see the wound you spoke of, but your reaction at the time convinced me Colbey had attempted to kill you. That's when I joined in."

"The rocks?"

"Right." Freya turned back, pink circles etched against alabaster cheeks. "Didn't have a weapon with me, and I didn't want to waste time getting it."

Ravn shivered at the family transgression. "Father would have lectured you into eternity."

"He did."

"You talked to him?" Ravn settled back to his haunches. "Perhaps you'd better tell me your version."

Freya hunkered down beside Ravn. "That's about it. After you went down, I attacked your father."

Ravn stared. "Without a sword?"

Freya placed an arm defensively around Ravn. "Mothers protecting sons aren't always thinking clearly. I was trying to prevent a killing blow."

In the privacy of this simple room, Ravn allowed, even cherished, his mother's contact. "Why didn't you use magic?"

"Against chaos?" Freya shook her head. "It would be like battling the sea with spit."

Ravn knew too little of magic to comment.

"Of course, I could never have arrived in time to save you if he truly wanted you dead, but I ran and hoped for the best. When I reached you, I glided into the edge of a mental battle. Caught a glimpse of the Odin-creature. Felt magic prickling toward us. Put up a shield, mostly from instinct." Freya shook her head, golden locks gliding across her head like foam. "The backlash of that magic was massive. Whatever Odin's spell, it might have killed all three of us. Then Colbey brought us here."

"To chaos' world," Ravn reminded, still wondering how they managed to remain whole.

Freya's blue eyes glimmered with concern. "As I understand it, we're within a construct that protects us."

"A construct." Ravn looked at his mother, trusting her knowledge of magic and trying not to consider the possibility that her presence, too, was merely illusion. "On chaos' world?"

Freya cleared her throat. "He says he can build anything he wishes here." She returned Ravn's stare deeply, as if to dredge the next question from him. She wanted his opinion, not merely to have him mull her own.

Ravn did not miss the significance. "Creation magic." He tried to imagine himself advancing from no magical knowledge to the most powerful of all. "Is that possible?"

"Apparently."

Ravn slumped. "So he *has* bound himself to chaos."

"He claims he hasn't."

Ravn tried not to hope. He turned his gaze to Freya's once more. "And you believe him?"

"After what I saw earlier, I'm inclined to."

Ravn said nothing.

"And you?" Freya pressed.

"I don't know." Now, Ravn rose. "I don't know what to believe anymore." He sighed. "I once believed my faith in my father unshakable."

Freya laughed.

Ravn smiled. "All right. I didn't always listen to him. I challenged him. I'm an adolescent; it's my job. But . . ." He worked to place the paradox into words. "Against anyone but me, I'd battle to the death on his side."

"But things have changed since Odin came."

Ravn wiggled a finger at Freya. "Yes, that's right."

"You find yourself doubting things that once seemed indisputable."

"Yes."

"You're uncertain what's truth and what lie. What's reality and what's fantasy."

"Yes and yes." Suspicion ground through Ravn, and he worried at the accuracy of his mother's suggestions. "How do you know that?"

Freya ignored the question for another. "Since Odin returned."

"Right." Ravn deliberated. "He's been messing with my mind a lot longer than I realize. Hasn't he?"

"Mine, too." Freya finally addressed the original question. "I actually came to believe Colbey was the enemy. That he bound himself to chaos. That he wanted to destroy us. And that Odin organized all of us to kill Colbey."

Ravn paused longer than necessary, waiting for Freya to finish the sentence with ". . . because it was right" or ". . . because it was necessary." But she did not. Only then, he realized she had completely changed her point. "Surely, you're not doubting that Odin intended all of us to band together and kill Father."

"Surely," Freya corrected, "I am."

Ravn could not believe he heard accurately. "Are you saying Odin doesn't want Colbey dead?"

"I'm not saying that at all." Apparently tiring of talking up to her son, Freya also rose, immediately launching into the habitual pacing mode. "I believe he wants Colbey dead. But he organized that so-called plan of his to destroy us, not Colbey."

Ravn still did not understand. " 'Us' meaning. . . ?"

"The gods."

Suddenly, things clicked into place. "You mean, the pieces of his plan don't fit together, as he claimed?"

Freya continued pacing. "I mean that he's coaching us to face Colbey in groups of two and three, knowing that's about how many Colbey can handle." Her words tumbled over one another as she spoke her recent discoveries aloud. "Fewer than two or three might mean Colbey takes them alive, like us. More would result in Colbey's death and leave the rest of us for Odin to handle."

Father was right. Odin does plan to destroy the worlds and create a new one devoted entirely to himself. Ravn finally joined in, "Which would put Odin in the position of facing all of us at once. Which he couldn't win." He stomped his foot, irritated that he had not come up with the idea first. "How did you figure that out?"

Having reached a wall, Freya turned, easily reading the true intention behind her son's question. "I had access to information that you didn't. I know your father already captured Modi and Magni."

Ravn shook his head, marveling at the genius of Odin's plan. He remembered the desperate outrage that had followed Baldur's slaying. Each subsequent death would get blamed on Colbey, fueling the attacks against him and further securing the gods' loyalty to Odin and, simultaneously, assuring their own demise.

A knock sounded through the confines. Wondering at its source, Ravn spun, finding nothing. Colbey's voice followed, gentle and contrite. "Is it safe?"

Freya looked at Ravn. "It's safe," the boy called to the ceiling.

A moment later, seams appeared in the far corner of one wall, muting into an opening beyond which lay a dizzying array of moving color. Rainbows leaped through one another like fish sluicing through particolored waterfalls, endlessly changing. Then the entryway dissolved, leaving only the slight, sinewy figure of his father. After Ravn's glimpse of chaos' splendor, Colbey appeared insignificant. The scarred face looked tired, the limbs powerless and quiet. Only the blue-gray eyes still held a spark of determination, and they studied Ravn quizzically.

A rush of love struck Ravn's heart, and the wish to embrace his father sped through him. Suspicious of abrupt and powerful emotions, he did not act upon the desire. Instead, he analyzed it, exploring its source, its nourishment, and its very existence.

A smile crept onto Colbey's face. Surely, he read Ravn's internal battle, though he said nothing to indicate his knowledge.

Soothed by his ability to contemplate his feelings, Ravn finally acted upon them. He approached Colbey. The two men stood, studying one another, for several moments.

Finally, Freya devastated the hush and also the moment. "Now you sniff each other, piss on each other's territory, and decide if you want to wag your tails or fight."

Ravn lost a nervous giggle he immediately wished he could have stifled. Undeterred, Colbey caught the young man in his arms and hugged him exuberantly. Ravn clung.

"Even better," Freya proclaimed.

"I'm sorry," Ravn sobbed.

The smaller of the two, Colbey spoke into his son's neck. "Sorry for what?"

"Doubting you. Attacking you."

"You're Renshai," Colbey returned, daring to teach even in such a situation. "Don't ever apologize for attacking."

Freya added, "You're a thinking being. Don't ever apologize for doubting."

Trapped, Ravn chuckled. "I'm sorry I apologized." He slapped a hand to his mouth in mock horror. "Don't tell me. I'm a god. Don't ever apologize."

Colbey released Ravn. "I thought it was an *adolescent* rule: never apologize to *parents*."

"Another good reason." Ravn sobered abruptly. "We'd better get back and warn the others."

Colbey straightened a tunic nearly as colorful as chaos. "No. Odin'll invade your minds the instant you get back, if he even bothers. He chose you to die near the first for a reason. He doesn't trust your loyalty to him nor his ability to turn you against me.

Ravn considered that, not liking the options.

"What do you suggest?" Freya asked.

"You're safe here."

Ravn shook his head. "We can't help you caged like prisoners."

Colbey reached over and fingered the hole the chaos sword had sliced in Ravn's shirt. "If you leave, Odin will destroy you. Or he'll find a way to make me destroy you. Either way you're lost. Either way you can't help me; and your deaths will devastate me."

Though Ravn saw the wisdom in Colbey's words, he still hated the options. "I want to fight at your side."

"Of course you do." Not a shred of doubt entered Colbey's words or tone. No Renshai would wish otherwise. "But you can't."

Freya found a more practical problem. "You're the only one who can manipulate this chaos' world construct. If you're killed, we're trapped forever."

"I thought of that." Colbey grinned at a detail his singly focused warrior mentality might once have made him miss. "I've crafted a new material for the walls that will still protect you from chaos but will allow formed magic to penetrate." The smile wilted. "There're at least two flaws. First, I can't trust Modi and Magni, so they *will* remain trapped. I'm not sure that's a huge problem anyway. If Odin destroys me, he'd find a way to kill them, too. Second, if formed magic can penetrate it, then you're no longer wholly safe." Colbey did not elaborate, deliberately, Ravn suspected. Given Odin's ability to exploit thoughts, it seemed better for Ravn not to question, though he could not completely suppress his own speculation. Apparently, if Freya could get them out, others with magic could get inside with them.

Freya asked the necessary question. "Any chance you'll link with chaos?"

Colbey's gaze jerked to his hilt, likely in response to the chaos sword. "I can't say it's impossible, but only if I can find no other way. If I don't warn you first, it could only be because I chose to do so at the time of my own destruction. In that case, a warning won't matter."

"Can it. . . ?" Freya started, then swallowed, her gaze following Colbey's. She obliquely requested his input on whether to speak freely in the mutated Staff of Chaos' presence.

Colbey anticipated the question or, more likely, read it from Freya's unwitting projection. "I don't believe it can overtake me unwilling, though it grows stronger daily. I'll let you know before it becomes too formidable an enemy." Freya gave Colbey a hard look that prompted him to add, "By *your* standards." They all knew he never seemed to see anything as too powerful a threat. He looked at Ravn. "I wouldn't have hurt you."

"I know that now," Ravn assured. "But Odin kept me from thinking things through. He's already too formidable an enemy for me." A flash of anger made him toss his head. "I'm sorry I let him . . ." He broke off as both parents gave him admonishing looks. "Yeah, I know. Don't apologize."

Colbey moved to Freya, taking her hands. "The sooner I face the remaining gods, the less time passes and the smaller chaos' power when I battle Odin." Ravn realized Colbey would have the choice of joining with chaos or warring against it and Odin/law in the end. Oddly, timing seemed the one thing on which the AllFather and Colbey would agree. Each must believe a prompt clash better for his own cause: Colbey because he would struggle against a weaker chaos and Odin because he stood a better chance against Colbey if the Renshai remained unbound or, if bound, to a feebler enemy.

"Be careful," Ravn said, the words a contradiction to Renshai training that he hoped his father would forgive. The end result of this battle allowed it since it encompassed more than just triumph or death in glorious combat.

"Wait," Freya said, sweeping an arm to indicate the barren room. "How about some furnishings?"

Hiding his face from Freya, Colbey rolled his eyes to his son, a gesture that bespoke a single word: "women." "At once, dear." He could not resist adding mentally to Ravn, *If Odin had married before the worlds' creation, we'd wait for it still.*

Ravn forced a smile. And hoped he would see his father again.

Accompanied by six of Béarn's guards and four of Pudar's, Tae's trek through the castle corridors occurred at a far more leisurely and peaceful pace than it had earlier that day. The Béarnides at his either hand walked at a steady clip, but their furrowed brows belied the worry their stances did not. Clearly Matrinka's doing, they handled Tae as gently as a royal infant, keeping themselves between him and Pudar's men at all times.

Another guard in Béarn's colors opened the council room door as they arrived, gesturing for Tae to enter. All ten of his escorts retreated then, leaving him in Captain Seiryn's capable hands. As the door clicked closed, every man and woman in the room stood, except for the king, the queen, and Pudar's prince. Discomforted by the sudden attention, Tae skittered to the only empty chair, away from the already overcrowded table and against one of the side walls. He tried to maintain an aura of dignity but suspected he more closely resembled a frightened rat.

Tae settled into his chair, and the members of the Council took their seats as well. Only the knights' captain executed a formal bow, and Tae forced himself to meet Kedrin's eyes squarely. Refusing to do so would make him look guilty; and, though he planned to confess to being so, he was not. The blue-white eyes seemed to probe Tae, questioning without condemnation. Suddenly, Tae felt an unlikely kinship. Kedrin had innocently faced the court for a similar crime and had also chosen to accept a punishment he did not deserve. Tae hated that he had played a role in that deception and only hoped it would go easier on him than it had on the Knight of Erythane.

King Griff spoke first, as he must. "Prince Tae Kahn, do you know why we brought you here?"

Tae turned his head to the king, unable to reconcile the deep voice and formal words to the childlike Béarnide he had rescued from the elves' prison, though he had sat in on Béarn's court many times. "Yes, Sire. I know."

"What do you have to say for yourself?" Griff's tone gentled in direct contrast to his demand. The soft brown eyes sought logic in the unthinkable.

"I made a mistake, Sire." Tae referred to his decision to eavesdrop, though he knew the Council would draw other conclusions. Deliberately, he swung his attention to Pudar's prince. Leondis sat stiffly, expression unrevealing. "And give myself over to Béarn's mercy."

If possible, the room went more silent. Tae's explanation should have filled the hush, but he said nothing more.

Leondis' brows slid upward, widening his eyes until white showed nearly all around them. Though he surely anticipated a denial, he revealed no other evidence of surprise.

Worried hatred might drive him to say something he regretted, Tae cast his gaze back to the only man who could truly understand: Knight-Captain Kedrin. Tae hoped his eyes sent a clear message of blamelessness. For reasons he could not explain, he wanted Ra-khir's father to believe him.

Copper-blond locks slid rightward as Kedrin cocked his head in consideration. He fingered the hat perched jauntily in his lap.

Griff seemed not to realize that Tae had finished, and it took him inordinately long to speak. "Is that all you have to say on your behalf, Prince Tae?"

"That's all, Sire," Tae acknowledged. He shifted in his chair, balancing on the ball of one foot with his knee bent, the other leg straight out in front of him. He assumed the position from habit, one he had shared with his mother, when she lived. He kept his eyes averted from King Griff; Eastern tradition dictated holding one's gaze below that of the king and it did not matter that Béarn did not demand the same. The formality of the proceedings brought back lessons well-learned in childhood, though he had never actually met the king who had preceded his father. Eastern doctrine did not demand the same for the queen, however, so he met Matrinka's gaze levelly. And trusted her advice.

"Very well." Griff addressed the entire company. "Apparently, the law is quite clear on this situation." He glanced at Darris, who had surely informed him of such a thing. The bard had done little but pore over kingdom law between searches for Pica shards. In a clear attempt to spare the Council another serenade, this one unrehearsed, Griff nodded toward the knight. "Please elaborate, Sir Kedrin."

Kedrin rose to the occasion, clearly having prepared himself for this eventuality. He stood to deliver the oration. "I believe two statutes apply to this matter, Your Majesty." His gaze shifted ever so slightly to include Darris, who nodded. "One states that in the event of major conflict between visiting dignitaries, the rulers of the respective countries shall be contacted and given the opportunity to express their opinions on the matter." He added carefully, "Not in those exact words, of course, Your Majesty."

Griff gave a single, encouraging gesture.

"The second, Your Majesty," Kedrin continued, "grants immunity from prosecution to visiting royalty, or its representative, in any situation short of murder." He sat to indicate he had finished.

"Immunity!" Boshkin shouted, instantly waved silent by Prince Leondis. Murmurs traversed the room.

"Sire," Leondis said with all the composure his servant lacked. He scratched at his injured shoulder. "Surely, this would qualify as an act of murder."

Tae looked directly at Matrinka now, deliberate accusation in his expression. If Darris had known the immunity law, then she had also. She could have placed Tae totally at ease and told him he risked nothing by arguing his innocence.

The king's face crinkled in response to the Pudarian's words. "Prince Leondis, your being here . . ." He paused, clearly struggling for words. Then, Darris whispered something, and Griff continued, ". . . denies that qualification. Without a corpse, there's been no murder."

"An obvious attempt, Your Majesty."

"Perhaps so, Prince Leondis." Griff balanced delivery against content to avoid offending either party. His "so" emerged definitive enough to draw attention from the "perhaps" that suggested doubt, yet not so much as to verbally convict Tae. "But I'm afraid it still clearly falls into the 'situation short of murder' category."

Leondis avoided staring, though he still managed to broadcast disbelief. "Your Majesty, you're saying you'll mete no punishment at all for the attempted assassination of a royal visitor?"

"I'm saying, Prince Leondis, that Béarnian law directly forbids it."

Leondis managed to keep his tone civil, though it surely took great effort. Beneath the table, his hands twitched in his lap, more nervous to Tae's assessment than angry. "Sire, sometimes old laws outlive their purpose. Perchance the time has come to change it."

"Maybe." Griff easily accepted the possibility. "But even if we did so, only the law in effect at the time of the incident matters."

Leondis sucked in a deep breath but did not argue that point. "Sire, there is the assassination of my brother to consider. Clear murder there, Your Majesty."

Matrinka chose to answer while Griff mulled his reply. "Prince Leondis, I believe a sentence was carried out for that crime, and Pudarian law does not allow two." She looked at Tae. "Nevertheless, the guilty party was rooted out, tried, and executed in another kingdom."

Tae nodded.

Leondis dropped an argument he could not win. "Please, Your Majesty, Your Ladyship. I'm not asking you to pronounce punishment against your law. I merely beg extradition, so Pudar can exact discipline consistent with its own law."

Griff's massive, leonine head waved slowly back and forth. "Extradition, Prince Leondis, is a form of punishment. It is also out of the question." Darris nudged his king, who ignored the warning. "Let's imagine for the moment that the situation were reversed. Would you wish extradition to Stalmize?"

"No, Sire," Leondis admitted. "But what criminal would wish to face justice?" He looked pointedly at Tae.

Tae resisted the urge to glare, instead attempting to inspire guilt with a look of innocent pity. They both knew he was blameless, not of wrongdoing, but of the crime the prince had claimed.

Richar leaped in. "Prince Tae doesn't seem particularly concerned about facing justice." The young minister of foreign affairs had grown close to Tae in the months the Easterner had served as his only charge. He did not voice the obvious, if erroneous converse, that an innocent man would not worry.

"With all respect due," Leondis countered. "He had reason and means to know Béarn's law." He stopped short of accusing Darris or Matrinka of informing Tae. No convention forbade them from doing so. "A man who cannot be prosecuted for his crimes has no reason to fear the law. Or to temper his actions."

Tae did not bother to proclaim his ignorance. Anyone who needed convincing would not believe him, and the truth did not matter to Leondis.

Darris cleared his throat, redirecting the proceedings from conversation inspired by the king's rhetorical question.

Attentive to his bard/bodyguard, King Griff returned to protocol. "Any further discussion on the matter?"

Prime Minister Davian seized the floor. "I believe the law is clear. We send messages to Pudar and Stalmize detailing the situation as we know it." He glanced at Tae, as if to remind the Eastern prince that he had not actually given his account. "While we're awaiting their replies, Prince Tae receives full immunity as per the law."

Stodgy Saxanar claimed the floor next, his glance at Leondis apologetic. "I would add only that we enhance the security of Prince Leondis to his satisfaction and within our capabilities."

"Thank you," Pudar's prince replied. "But I'm quite satisfied with Béarn's security." Though his tone sounded sincere, he clipped his words from an irritation that had nothing to do with Saxanar's suggestion and everything to do with Davian's.

Tae relaxed. Those not already swayed to his side by friendship rigidly followed the course of law or of their more experienced peers. Impossible as it had seemed when he waited in his room anticipating the worst, it appeared he would receive no punishment at all.

The king would not conclude without the knight-captain's direct opinion. He motioned for Kedrin to speak his piece, though the knight had not requested it.

Kedrin rose and bowed. "I suggest we leave things as they are and reconvene when we have heard from the countries involved. Until then, Stalmize's crown prince must go free."

Tae suspected Kedrin had deliberately chosen the title to remind the others of Tae's status, but it caught him more off-guard than them. Since his father had not announced him the successor, no one had ever referred to him as the crown prince before. Yet, he suspected, Kedrin assumed the right to do so because Weile Kahn had no other children and had not specifically denounced Tae.

No one challenged the assertion, though Leondis frowned and others seemed lost in thought.

Kedrin continued, "I believe the parties involved should approve the messages before they're sent and, as always, have the right to send one of their own separately to clarify." He added, clearly for Leondis' satisfaction, "I do not believe we should consider the matter wholly ended until such time as we have reviewed any reply." He made a flourishing gesture to denote his conclusion.

Griff acknowledged it, and the knight retook his seat while the king glanced around the gathering. "Does anyone oppose the plan as outlined by the prime minister, the minister of courtroom procedure and affairs, and the captain of Erythane's knights?"

Thialnir grumbled something unintelligible but did not seek recognition. Likely, he would have preferred something on the order of trial by combat, but he had to stand behind the father of a Renshai. No one else spoke, though several shook their heads. Every eye shifted to Prince Leondis.

Responding to the attention, Leondis spoke his piece. "I believe I've made it clear I don't agree with immunity in this case, but I accept the suggestion of the council to grant the kings their say. I will, of course, allow my father to fully speak for me."

At that point, the gazes shifted to Tae, who quailed. Even if he could speak so eloquently, he could barely stand the attention. Unlike Leondis, he would never place his fate solely in his father's hands. Weile Kahn had made many bad decisions in the name of teaching, including sending Tae away at fourteen with the intention of reclaiming him at twenty if he survived the crime lord's many enemies. Nevertheless, Tae held one advantage over Leondis. Weile Kahn would not care whether or not the event had occurred. He would take his son's side over the prince of Pudar for reasons that had nothing to do with justice. "I've already placed my fate in Béarn's hands."

"Done, then," Griff declared. He dismissed the council with a series of movements of his right hand. Tae watched the ministers file out, little more at ease than at his entrance. Crafty King Cymion would not accept the council's answer as easily as his son, and Tae suspected the worst of the battle was yet to come.

CHAPTER 21

Devils' Play

The years of wandering that honed our skills and defined the tribe of Renshai, during which we slaughtered our way across every land of Midgard, have turned, in time, from greatest glory to vastest shame.
—*Colbey Calistinsson*

ELFIN magic sent Tae and his companions to a plane of desolation. While El-brinith crouched, working her locating spell, Tae surveyed this new world to which the search for Pica shards had brought them. The week since his ordeal had passed more like a month. He had spent most of it cooped up in his room with Subikahn, avoiding all visitors except Matrinka, Mior, and the servants who claimed the baby for feedings. Now he stared out over a brown wasteland beneath a gray shroud of clouds and believed this place perfectly defined his mood.

Ra-khir came toward him as Tae knew he would. He had denied the knight audience on more than one occasion with shallow excuses that likely caused his friend pain. He had let the guilt for that fester with the anger, self-pity and disappointment, attending only to the joy his son brought to a life otherwise dark. The solitude had bought him too much time to brood over events he could not affect; and the gentle press of wind against his face seemed a comfortable change despite the landscape, though it brought a faint odor of smoke. He both welcomed and dreaded his friend's approach, glad to return to familiar events yet not wanting a reminder of that which he had tried so hard to escape considering.

Tae deliberately wandered several steps away from the party, as much from delay as to keep any conversation private. Ra-khir quickened his pace, catching the Easterner's shoulder. "Tae."

Tae stopped, not bothering to feign surprise. They both knew even the depths of despair could not keep him from noticing another's presence. "What can I do for you, Ra-khir?"

"Tae." Now Ra-khir looked back to the others. Chan'rék'ril knelt beside El-brinith, while Kevral, Andvari, and Darris stood over them. Not far from the group, Rascal crouched, watching. Ra-khir kept his voice pitched low so only Tae could hear. "Kevral and I appreciate your concern and your assistance." He sounded upbeat, sincere, yet Tae sensed a coming "but."

Tae made no comment, but he did continue to return Ra-khir's regard.

"I know you did what you did because you care about us—"

Tae felt the need to interrupt. "I didn't stab the prince of Pudar."

Ra-khir stared. "Neither did I," he finally managed.

Confused, Tae insisted, "You were going to ask me that, weren't you?"

"No. Why would I?"

Tae met Ra-khir's green eyes, finding honest bewilderment. "He accused me of it."

"I know."

"Then why . . . ?" Tae started and stopped. "Don't you want to know the truth?"

"I know the truth," Ra-khir said matter-of-factly. "Matrinka told me. Why would I doubt my queen?"

"Maybe because she got her version of the events from me."

"Why would I doubt you?"

Tae blinked several times in succession. "Is this the same young man who claimed he would never travel with me? Who called me a thief, a traitor, and a liar and tried to get me to battle him to the death? Twice?"

Ra-khir smiled. "The one and, I hope, the only."

"You don't doubt me?"

"Not any more." The knight shrugged. "When circumstances change, I change my mind. What do you do?"

Tae ignored the rhetorical question, too shocked to accept Ra-khir's trust. "You don't doubt me at all. Not even a little?"

Ra-khir rolled his eyes. "Tae, is this incessant repetition relevant?"

"I don't know," Tae admitted, not the one who had initiated the conversation. "You tell me."

"It's not." Ra-khir glanced across the plain of dark earth, then back at Tae. "I just wanted to ask you not to interfere. Please leave the matter of the coming baby to Kevral and me. We can handle it." He added more emphatically, "In fact, we're the only ones who can or should. Your involvement is only going to get you in trouble."

Tae found irony in the understatement. "You mean *more* trouble."

"If you like."

Tae nodded sagely. "Matrinka put you up to this, didn't she?"

"She expressed her concern," Ra-khir admitted. "But, no, she didn't ask me to say this if that's what you mean." He returned doggedly to his point. "So do you think you can stay out of it?"

Tae thought about Ra-khir's words longer than should have seemed necessary. His friends deserved the truth. "I honestly don't know," he finally said. "I didn't go there to meddle—at least, I don't think I did. But when the opportunity came up, I just couldn't resist."

"Tae."

"Yeah."

"In the future." Ra-khir gave Tae a look of earnest reproach. "Resist."

"Yeah."

Ra-khir sighed deeply, not liking the answer. "We've come a long way since I wanted to kill you. If you put me in a position where I have to, I'll do what I have to do. Even if I hate it."

Tae's eyes narrowed, and he sought clarification. "You'd kill me over this baby?"

"Only if I had to." Ra-khir sighed again. "I might have to stand against Kevral, too. That's bad enough."

Tae could not help noticing Ra-khir did not assume he could kill Kevral. She was, after all, the superior swordsman.

"Please don't make me have to."

"I'll try," Tae said.

Unconvinced, Ra-khir lowered his head, cupping his face between his palms. "Tae, there's more to this than just a kingdom trying to steal a baby from people you love."

The comment seemed bare insult. Tae turned Ra-khir a sidelong glare. "I think I've had ample chance to learn that."

Ra-khir did not back down or apologize. "I'm just trying to spare you learning the hardest way again."

The knight had an undeniable point, and it left Tae to wonder whether his father's conviction, building toughness with life-risking trials, played a role in his own choices. "I said I'll try. I'll do my best to stay out of the way, but I'm not going to make some wholehearted, unbreakable promise. That's what got me into trouble in the first place." He added, his tone razor sharp, "And you, too, Ra-khir."

Ra-khir had little choice but to accept that; they both knew he would get nothing more. "Thank you." He raised his head. "I appreciate your concern and your honesty. And I'm sorry about what happened." He took a step toward the group, then stopped and turned back to Tae. "If it's any consolation, my father also believes you're innocent." Without awaiting a reply, he headed back toward Kevral.

Tae grinned, surprised to find himself feeling better than he had since the whole incident started. Kedrin's trust meant more than he would have guessed. He had come a long way, finally recognizing what his years of bluffing among the gangs had nearly destroyed. Ultimately, truth would win more respect than lies.

The dankness of the landscape stole nothing from Kevral's happy mood. Away from Béarn's court and the inescapable presence of Pudarian guards in the hallways, she frolicked like a colt in the cool breezes. The baby slept, the only reminder of its presence, and the controversy of its existence, the bulge that had become familiar over the last year. Anticipation of a battle filled Kevral's blood with a comfortable warmth, and she clung to that notion as a shield against logic. Though they had found none of the shards easy to obtain, most of the tasks had not involved physical combat. Still, the last one remained vivid in her memory, her opponent irritating but worthy in his skill. Concentration on warfare could fully distract her thoughts from the politics and diplomacy she hated. She envied Ra-khir's maturity, wondering whether the two years of age between them made the difference. Though she desperately wanted to place the best interests of the child first, possessiveness always interfered with the decision.

El-brinith stood. "It's that way." She pointed in a direction Kevral randomly labeled west. Even the intermittent appearance of the sun from behind the clouds gave her scant information. She had no way to know if it rose and set the same directions as in their world, though there seemed no harm in defining bearings with that assumption.

Kevral scanned the area for the rest of the group. Tae and Rascal remained separately apart. Ra-khir headed toward where the others gathered. As they walked in the indicated direction, Tae shifted to the front, though it seemed ludicrous to scout ahead. The flat, brown terrain offered little concealment. To Kevral's surprise, Rascal joined Tae. Apparently, they had discovered a truce of sorts, her deliberate avoidance of him finished, at least for the moment.

Gradually, the new world gained landscape. They spotted patches of forest to the left, then the right. A copse opened in front of them, charred deadfalls flopped randomly around piled ashes, and greenery struggled from one side of a blackened, listing tree.

"*Djevskulka,*" Andvari breathed.

The common Northern expression irritated Kevral. "Do you know where that comes from?"

Andvari surveyed the ash. "No, but I'm guessing a campfire got out of control."

Darris agreed, "Certainly looks like it."

Kevral refused to get sidetracked. "I mean the term. *Djevskulka.*"

Surely recognizing the all-too-familiar disdain in Kevral's tone, Andvari winced. "It's an innocent word we say in the North when we come upon destruction unexpectedly. *Djevskulka.* More appropriately, *skulka i djevlir.* Devils' play." He shook his head, war braids flying. "Not play, exactly. More like . . ." He struggled for the translation. ". . . brutal fun."

Kevral elaborated, easily shifting between trading and Northern, dialectically as well as verbally. "Shortened from *skulkë i djevgullenhåri.*"

"Golden-haired devils'—" Andvari started to translate, then broke off. "Thor's thunder, Kevral. You can't believe I knew it once referred to Renshai."

"I did."

"Maybe that's because you're a—"

"Renshai?" Kevral cut in. "So I'm oversensitive? So I care too much about what insults my people?"

Andvari's gait turned rigid, and his eyes restlessly sought escape. "I was going to say 'student of languages.' "

"Rabbit," Tae called suddenly, using a loud voice wholly out-of-character, especially when scouting. Rascal skittered aside.

Alarmed by Tae's manner, Kevral darted toward him. Ra-khir did the same thing simultaneously, drawing his sword as he moved. "What is it?" the knight said.

Tae turned, then recoiled from the bared steel. "Easy, Red. Do you always hunt rabbits with a sword?"

"Rabbits," Ra-khir repeated, sheathing his weapon. "You mean it's really a rabbit?"

Sarcasm tinged Tae's voice. "No. It's really an army. I just called it a rabbit to annoy you."

The distraction allowed Andvari ample time for escape, a purpose Kevral did not divine. "Why did you shout about a rabbit?"

"First living thing I saw here besides us," Tae explained. "Thought you all should know about it."

"Thanks," Ra-khir said, the word emerging more befuddled than grateful. He returned to Darris and the elves, Kevral trailing. "Now what were we talking about?"

Again rescuing Andvari, Tae broke in, "We were talking about what might have caused that fire. And this one up ahead."

This time, all of the others hurried to Tae's position. An irregular circle of trees leaned away from a core of charred undergrowth, their trunks fouled by ash.

"Another campfire?" Chan'rék'ril ventured doubtfully.

Kevral recalled a story from her childhood. "Renshai legend tells of a demon that terrorized a Western farming town until Colbey destroyed it." She glared at Andvari. "The demon, not the town."

The Northman raised his hands in a gesture of surrender, which did not raise her opinion of him. Renshai had no corresponding signal; their culture scorned it.

Kevral continued, "The version my grandmother tells starts with farmers finding burnt circles in their fields." Her blood warmed. If a demon lived here, she would face a battle whose proportions might match the one in Valhalla. She alone carried a magical weapon, and nothing of law could harm a demon. Her gaze went naturally to the swords at her belt, Colbey's on the left and Rache's *Motfrabelonning* on the right.

The party exchanged looks. Tae encouraged, "And the burnt circles were. . . ?"

The question surprised Kevral who had heard the tale often enough for it to seem obvious. "The demon's doing. Its breath."

More glances passed between them. This time, Ra-khir questioned. "The demon that attacked the boat didn't breathe fire." He rolled his eyes toward the heavens in silent gratitude.

"Nor the one I fought in Pudar," Kevral admitted. "But apparently some can. At least according to legend." She considered longer. Though not her favorite Colbey story, she had heard it often enough to remember details. It had never occurred to her to compare tales she had not even believed as a child to fantastical creatures that had become all too real over the past year. "In the story, the demon keeps its shape, too. Until the end. Then it's not really clear if it deliberately changes or only because of the magic of a Wizard assisting Colbey."

Darris sat on a blackened deadfall, ignoring the soot this smeared across his britches. Wind tossed brown curls into his eyes, and his broad lips pursed in consideration. While he searched for alternate explanations, Rascal spoke the thought on every mind. "Hain't this Colbey like some sorter god but better with'n a sword?" She placed small, grimy hands on her waist. "An' he been needin' a Wizard ta hep him? Hain't we gots no chance."

Ra-khir had the answer. "Kevral, Darris, Andvari, and I could give Colbey a good fight. At the risk of belittling, I'd say we could best him together. And we've got elves for magic."

"Not that kind of magic." Chan'rék'ril brought Ra-khir back to reality. "I'm decent with shields and enhancements, and I can heal a bit. Elbrinith's good at tracking, sensing, travel. Those sorts of things." He turned the knight an apologetic look. "Fighting?" He shook his head in an awkward and deliberately human gesture. "I'm afraid any elf with a tendency toward violence would more likely have remained among the *svartalf.*"

Kevral's pulse hammered through her ears. "Colbey vanquished that creature with a sword that couldn't strike it. I have one that can." She patted the hilt Colbey had given her.

The logical extension, that no one else could fight a demon, did not occur to Kevral at that moment. Her mind clung to the excitement of the war.

Ra-khir addressed the lack that Kevral did not. "Perhaps two swords that can." She followed his gaze to *Motfrabelonning.* "We know a sword merely used by an immortal can strike a demon: Colbey's for you and Ravn's for Rantire. Perhaps an *Einherjar's* sword can work as well."

Kevral grinned. She had not considered that benefit when Rache had honored her with his weapon. Her mind filled with images of a demon's dark bulk hewed by a flying double web of silver. She could deal it death with either hand or both at once. Then, the image faded beyond the reality of the entire party staring directly at her, their expressions demanding.

Only then, Kevral understood the suggestion behind Ra-khir's explanation. The idea of turning over one of her swords to anyone seemed as ugly and horrible as the soulless death she faced. Jolted fully back to reality, she reveled in the excitement battle had managed to kindle despite the loss of the greatest of all rewards: death in glory, her place in Valhalla. With Valr Kirin's help, she had managed to discover the joy of war itself, to see death as the ultimate reward for courage, to find her immortality in the model she left for future warriors. She also realized the unfairness of leaving all of her companions cowering behind magical barriers while she wrung all of the pleasure from the battle. She had no choice but to share, no matter the discomfort of it. "Here." Lovingly, she unclipped *Motfrabelonning* and offered it to Ra-khir.

The knight bowed deeply, sweeping his hat from his head to acknowledge understanding of her sacrifice. "I won't take it now. Only if it's needed."

Nodding once, Kevral replaced the weapon. It felt secure and right at her side, and she could not banish the idea that she had dodged disaster.

Darris watched the sequence without comment. His sword skill probably matched Ra-khir's, but it made more sense for her to trust the weapon to her husband and allow Darris his watchful chronicling. Kevral supposed that Tae might make good use of the weapon, yet he would fare just as well by creating distractions. In a face-to-face conflict, he would only get in her way. Not until that moment did she realize she had not seen their swarthy companion or his living shadow since shortly after she had mentioned the possibility of a demon.

As if on cue, Rascal blundered from the foliage. Tae emerged immediately behind her. "Good guess, Kevral. There's a cave ahead with a massive creature I couldn't identify in the dark. Bigger than any bear, though. I saw an occasional smoky huff come out, like breath in winter."

"I'll take that sword now." Ra-khir unfastened his own weapon to make an exchange.

Kevral appreciated the gesture though she refused it. His broad and heavy sword might hamper the delicate balance Renshai maneuvers required. Besides, it could not cut the demon. "Let's go." She dashed off in the direction from which Tae had come.

The Easterner's voice chased her. "Wait!"

Battle-starved, Kevral could not have heeded him if she had wanted to do so. A moment later, Ra-khir's heavy bootfalls crashed through the brush, drowning out any warnings Tae might have spoken. The lighter tromp of feet sounded behind them, the others joining at a safe distance. They could not assist, except to keep themselves secure.

A sudden gust of wind bowed the weeds and sent tree branches into wild dances. Leaves and twigs washed over Kevral, accompanied by a repetitive slapping sound that echoed through the forest. Darkness blotted the patches of sunlight leeching through the umbrella of foliage.

Ra-khir shouted, "Kevral, move!"

Understanding finally trickled through the blur of joyous anticipation. *It flies.* Kevral sprang sideways as Ra-khir dashed forward and her other companions retreated. Fire slashed through the treetops, stabbing the spot where she and Ra-khir had stood. Flaming debris showered to the ground. A branch slammed Kevral's shoulder with bruising force, and heat seared her cheek. Smoke sputtered from the contact. Then a red-orange blaze leaped to life on her sleeve. *Damn!* Kevral dropped to the ground, rolling. Contact with the ground provoked more pain than the burn itself, crushing grit into a raw wound. Battering sparks that threatened her hair, Kevral spun to a crouch as the creature's bulk darkened intermittent openings in the overgrowth. It clearly banked for another attack.

Ra-khir rushed to Kevral's side. "Are you all right?"

"Fine," Kevral said, distracted by her need to watch the demon's every movement. "We need a better battle ground. One that's not flammable."

"What we need," Ra-khir corrected, flipping his gaze back and forth between Kevral's partially charred tunic and the banking creature, "is wings."

"Now!" El-brinith shouted, magic or elfin vision granting her a better view of the creature.

Kevral and Ra-khir scattered. Another gout of flame splashed the ground where they had stood, igniting nearby trees and brush, striking hot pinpoints against the Renshai's legs and cheeks. Mammoth wing beats fanned the flames above, and they crackled across green leaves, spreading from tree to tree.

Chan'rék'ril dashed to Kevral's side, mumbling unintelligible syllables in none of the many languages Kevral knew. Harsh and dense, the words sounded odd in the musical elfin accent. Cued by El-brinith's gentle chanting that fell like back-beat to Chan'rék'ril's melody, Kevral knew he worked magic. And cursed. If the elf intended to shield her, he wasted his breath. She would force him to remove anything that might protect her from flames or direct attack. Renshai shunned unnatural defenses. Hiding behind magic would brand her a coward, in her own mind most of all.

The elf back-pedaled, returning to a light version of the trading tongue. "Think 'up.'" Bronze hair curved across his cheeks, shrouding his face like a hood. The canted amber eyes reflected leaping flames like mirrors.

"Up?" Uncertain how to follow Chan'rék'ril's command, Kevral concentrated on the letters forming the word. Nothing happened. She looked toward the elf, intending to question but saw only Chan'rék'ril's retreating back as he headed to assist Ra-khir.

"Up," Kevral repeated, this time focusing on the concept. She felt herself rise, feet hovering, the ground growing smaller beneath her.

"Kevral, watch out!" Darris screamed.

Heat prickled Kevral's scalp. She jerked her attention upward, only to find her vision obscured in a red blur of flame. Smoke stung her eyes and choked her lungs. Throat spasming, she hacked out a shriek as the treetop fire enveloped her.

"Up," Chan'rék'ril shouted. "Think 'up!'"

Kevral thrashed, trying to escape the flames. She felt herself plummeting, the whipping wind soothing against blistering flesh. Survival instinct barely kicked in in time. She envisioned herself floating, and her headlong fall ceased. Vision blurred by water, she saw a hazy image of dark ground. Now she allowed herself to drop to it, pitching to quench the last of the fire. Pained in every part, she watched Ra-khir glide upward, avoiding the blazing treetops that had proven her own downfall. The elves sprinted toward her.

Kevral did not wait for their arrival. She would not leave Ra-khir to battle the demon alone. Even as they reached her, she flew, the abrupt movement tearing agony through patches of burned flesh. This time, she followed Ra-khir's path, soaring through foliage that the demon's breath had not yet set aflame. She hurtled upward, speed responding to desperation, flying past Ra-khir and intercepting the demon as it rocketed toward him. She got her first full glimpse of the creature at that moment. Red eyes glared out from a ratlike, hairless head. The body appeared sleek and sinuous, as large as two cottages together and as black as moonless night. Four legs ended in leonine claws, and two lizard tails swept from its hindquarters. As Kevral zipped past, unable to stop her headlong rush quickly enough, it opened its mouth to reveal a scarlet cavern and teeth as silver, long, and sharp as daggers.

"Go for the wings!" Kevral shouted as she struggled to turn. Despite years of converting thought into instant and graceful movement, she found herself helpless to fathom the proper sequence of commands to control flight. Awkwardness became desperate frustration. She watched as Ra-khir engaged the creature, the sword in his hand flailing to strike any part of it. The blade sliced harmlessly through the demon's dark bulk, and it howled in triumph. Rache's sword did not contain the chaos needed to cut it.

The creature moved with catlike grace. Its claws raked toward Ra-khir.

Every nail that struck flesh would claim ten years of Ra-khir's life, and each paw held six. Horrified, Kevral sped toward them, sword drawn, aiming directly for the demon's back.

Ra-khir managed an awkward, weaving dodge that spared him both claw strokes. Then the rodent head dipped forward, fast as a snake striking. The jaws closed around his torso, and red droplets pattered toward the forest. The knight screamed, the sound rending Kevral's heart yet oddly reassuring. At least the bite had not instantly killed him.

The lizard tails whipped out, Kevral barreling between them. Redirected by the need for evasion, she lost the positioning of her sword. She managed only to slash a tail as she crashed against the beast with enough force to jar Ra-khir free. The knight tumbled. Kevral slid across the smooth bulk, momentum spilling her over its haunches. Tossed back into open air, she willed herself upward, only then realizing that Ra-khir's fall remained uncontrolled. The demon plunged toward the smoking forest, no active flames remaining from its previous attacks.

Panic tore through Kevral, concern for Ra-khir stealing all joy from the battle. If he still lived, impact with the ground would surely kill him. She turned her fall into a deliberate dive, forcing herself to greater and greater speed. In less than a second, she reached the demon and the treetops. The ground seemed to bound upward to catch her.

Chan'rék'ril's panicked *khohlar* reached Kevral, sending full concept faster than he could speak a single word: *I can handle Ra-khir. Save yourself.*

Kevral attempted a frantic rise, too late. She plummeted helplessly, unable to overcome inertia and air currents. The death she had envisioned for Ra-khir had become her own. She struggled hopelessly, refusing to surrender. A moment later, she slammed, shoulder leading, against something solid. Agony rocked through her. Her breath dashed from her chest in a rush. She felt herself tumbling as blackness overtook her. She awakened almost immediately, flopping limply from the demon's bulk, air wheezing back into her battered lungs.

"Kevral!" Darris shouted. She saw him running toward her before the demon interposed itself between them. Understanding seeped slowly to the fore. The demon had broken her fall, its softer body and its own downward motion rescuing her from an impact that should have killed her. Its claws sped toward her. She gathered all of her strength into a roll that barely saved her. Her fist ached, impressions of the sword's knurling tattooed against the palm. True to her Renshai instincts, she had clung to it even through her brief spell of unconsciousness. She slashed for the only part of the demon she could reach, and whetted steel carved a line of blood across its chest.

The creature bellowed, recoiling. Likely, it expected her sword to accomplish nothing more than Ra-khir's. Its head reared back, preparing to strike or breathe fire. Bruised, burned, and battered, Kevral found her feet unsteady. She could dodge its bite, but she could not escape a blast of fire.

Clambering to the demon's back, Darris grabbed its head and clamped his fingers over its eyes. Seizing the moment of blindness, Kevral dashed forward, slashing the fine membranes of its right wing.

The demon roared. The mangled wing flashed downward. The tails lashed for Kevral, and its head flailed. Hurled to the ground, Darris stumbled to his feet. A claw thrashed toward him. Tangled into the silken wing, the tails missed Kevral. She struggled to its back, veering from the whipping opposite wing and the tails that beat the air in a wild assault. She plunged her sword as deep as her strength allowed into the creature's spine.

The demon stiffened, a single spasm, then flopped to the forest floor. Its red eyes opened widely, like coals pressed into shadow. Pained bleats emerged in bursts from its jaws. Kevral collapsed to its bulk, too weak even to remove her sword and finish the suffering beast.

El-brinith approached Kevral, nervously watching the limp creature. Her hands felt soothing as ice against Kevral's burns, and the gentle elfin touch channeled back a bit of her wrung-out reserves. The repetitive howls of the demon ached through her ears, stealing concentration. As soon as the Renshai could walk, she jerked her sword from its wedge between the demon's vertebrae, splattering them both with blood. Reluctantly, she abandoned El-brinith's ministrations to jab the blade through the demon's eye. Scarlet welled around the wound. The mouth remained open, drooling a red froth that rekindled Kevral's terror. She had done no injury to internal organs, so the blood was likely Ra-khir's, not the beast's.

Again, Kevral ripped the sword from her enemy. Though it came free much easier, the effort proved too much. She stumbled two steps backward, then collapsed on the ground. Her consciousness swam but did not recede. El-brinith set to work again. Unlike Matrinka, she did not chastise. Kevral forced a smile. "Will I live?"

Yes. El-brinith did not bother with words. *And the baby, too.*

For the first time, Kevral found herself actually glad of that assessment. So many times before she thought of the baby as a real entity, she had hoped it would simply die within her. "What's the damage?" She both hoped and dreaded that El-brinith would read her need to know about Ra-khir's condition as well. She could not bring herself to ask directly yet. Renshai mind techniques included assessing the details of one's own wounds, but Kevral could not yet spare the energy for a search.

Snapped the left collarbone. And a rib. The rest is bruising and burns. Healers back home can handle it all, so long as it doesn't get . . . Kevral inserted the word "infected" for the vast concept that followed. Elves did not suffer from illnesses or the decay that afflicted dirty human wounds. Kevral refused to contemplate the eventuality now. Burns, especially ones as extensive as she had suffered, became infected more easily than any other kind of wound. She would place her trust in Matrinka's capable hands and hope her worst concern was scarring.

Kevral cleared her throat, forced to ask what El-brinith had not addressed. "Ra-khir? Is he. . . ?"

El-brinith sent general *khohlar,* her obvious target her elfin companion. *She wants to know about your charge.*

Punctured spleen, Chan'rék'ril returned.

Kevral's heart froze. A splenic injury could bleed a man out in less time than it took to find the wound. She had never heard of anyone surviving such a thing.

Lost a lot of blood, but I got it staunched. Nothing else inside. Lots of external punctures.

Kevral thanked every god for elfin magic. Nothing human could have saved Ra-khir. "He's going to live?"

El-brinith remained as elusive as most healers. "Captain and the others should be able to handle it."

"Jealous of my scars, huh?" Tae spoke from so close, it startled Kevral. "Had to get a few of his own."

"I'm all right, too." Darris limped to a rock near Kevral and sat. Dirt streaked his whole body, and twigs lay entangled in his curls. "If anyone wanted to know." No malice entered his tone. He, too, simply intended to lighten the mood.

"Hey," Tae said. "Aren't you supposed to sing that?"

Darris complied:

> *"I fell on my head.*
> *The demon was dread.*
> *Now please take me*
> *Home to bed."*

Tae tried one of his own to the same simple tune:

> *"You fell on your brain.*
> *The demon's now tame.*
> *That verse you sang*
> *Was remarkably lame."*

Now strong enough to clean her sword, Kevral set to work, smiling at her friends' efforts to cheer her. "Tae, singing may not be your best skill."

Tae feigned a pout. "Well, then. Perhaps I'm better at this." He extended a hand to reveal a ragged chunk of blue stone.

Kevral stared at the Pica shard, then at Tae. "Where did you get that?"

"Rascal and I sneaked in the back of the cave and took it."

Kevral glanced in Ra-khir's direction. "How long have you had it?"

Tae followed Kevral's gaze, and all humor vanished.

Rascal stepped from the brush, ignoring Tae's brisk, silencing gestures. "Long 'nuff ta git back an' watch mosta the fight."

Kevral swallowed hard.

"What!" Darris glared at their Eastern companion. "You mean we could have avoided most of this?"

Kevral cringed. She understood Darris' rage. She and Ra-khir might still succumb to infection. Any of them could have been killed outright. But now was not a good time to question Tae's judgment, especially when the blame better lay on herself. "No, Darris, we couldn't have. I wouldn't have left the battle. And Ra-khir would have worried for others this abomination might have harmed." She waved at the massive corpse. "Tae knew that."

Tae shrugged, nodding. "I did try to suggest it before the two of you went charging in, but you didn't listen then. And you wouldn't have in the middle of combat."

"You're right," Darris said, calm now. "I'm sorry I got angry."

"I understand." Tae beckoned Rascal.

With clear reluctance, the girl plucked a whole, small ruby from her pocket and passed it to him. "We found this. Amid some quartz, pyrite, and scraps of steel. A collector, too, though more in the sense of a crow." He pocketed the ruby. "I promised Rascal she could have it after we completed the last task, if you don't think that's a problem."

Kevral shook her head. "Not for me."

The Pudarian's gaze followed the trinket from Tae's hand to a pocket or pouch inside his vest. A look of determination filled her brown eyes. Kevral did not envy Tae's need to keep it from its eventual owner until the right time, but she understood it. Once Rascal had the gemstone, she would disappear to spend it, risking the entire mission.

Let's go, Chan'rék'ril sent. *Sooner is better for Ra-khir.*

Kevral rose, finally daring to look closely in that direction. The elf crouched over Ra-khir's still form whose head lay cradled in Andvari's lap. The Northman tended the wounded warrior like a brother. Apparently noticing Kevral's attention, Andvari rose, lowering Ra-khir gently to the ground. To her relief, the Knight of Erythane stirred at the motion, her first objective sign that he still lived. Only then, she realized Andvari held Rache's sword, the blade freshly oiled and the sheath well-soaped. Hilt leading in the proper gesture of peace, he offered it to Kevral.

As Kevral accepted the sword, her mind flashed back to the time of its giving and the blood brotherhood that had developed between a Renshai who had lost all his kin and a Northman who had participated in the slaughter.

"I'm afraid it touched the ground," Andvari said, deferring to a Renshai doctrine that the other Northern tribes had never shared.

Atoning for dishonoring swords has become a familiar pastime. Kevral did not have the opportunity to speak the words aloud before elfin magic opened the way to Béarn.

Threats and Decisions

Like ripples on a pond, fame spreads until its own vastness leads to its demise. Lasting glory is achieved by heroism day to day.

—Colbey Calistinsson

COLBEY walled his worry for his family into the furthest reaches of his consciousness, safe from exploitation. Odin must not know of the one place on chaos' world that he could access and the treasure trove he would find there. The old Renshai would have preferred to lock those he loved into a stronghold more secure than the impenetrable one he had crafted for Modi and Magni, but that would leave Freya and Ravn wholly dependent on him. His worry seemed ludicrous. The fate of every world lay in his hands, yet he refused to trust the lives of wife and son there. They deserved the chance to rescue themselves when the masses of power destroyed one another, paving the way for a newer, more stable balance. And as the Keeper of the Balance, Ravn would have time to hone his abilities, to gain wisdom, to achieve the necessary strength to prevent such a thing from happening again.

To Asgard, Colbey told the Staff of Chaos. *The practice field.*

Hungry for the battle that it hoped would destroy law utterly, leaving itself in control, chaos triggered the proper transport. Colbey derived no satisfaction from its dutiful response. Their association lasted only so long as their goals overlapped.

The familiar tingle of magic surrounded Colbey, captured in one of the darkest songs of Béarn's bards. An ancestor of Darris' who had lived during Colbey's mortal years had found the sensation so hideous and invasive, he had compared it to rape and never allowed the Wizards to transport him again. Yet, Colbey found comfort in the prickle that enveloped him like a second skin. The sudden blast of chaos-stuff in a contained area made even the ceaseless parade of colors on its world seem dim. The new and vibrant shades defied Colbey's description, unlike anything within the constraints of Midgard's rainbow. Ideas usually whirled through the soup of chaos' world, hopelessly ungraspable. Here they found fruition, shaped by the modicum of law necessary to direct chaos into magic. Every time Colbey transported, he learned something new about the world's composition, its science, its mathematics, the concepts of its past and future genius.

This time something felt different to Colbey. The use of magic always required restraint, but this time it seemed more like bondage. The dribble of law that usually shaped the spell grew into a dangerous torrent that beckoned with surprising gentleness. Chaos channeled him toward Asgard, but it labored too hard for the location of his landing. The brilliance that chaos sparked allowed him to divine the answer within the seconds of the spell's existence. Other magic had acted upon his, guiding him toward a defined destination.

Too late to cancel the transport, Colbey attempted one of his lightning retreats. His body could not physically affect the formless, but his mind might. He concentrated on the mental aspects of movement, galloping from the landing point the outside force had chosen.

The invader proved stronger. Like a whirlwind, it dragged him into a disorienting spiral. Colbey fought for reason. He pictured the second magic as an enemy, hewing at it with an imagined sword. The blade carved through, with no more effect than it would have on wind. He struggled against the inexorable pulling, allowing himself to spin in dazzling revolutions, more concerned with movement in the opposite direction of its vacuum. The combined strength of two magic sources defeated him. The spell he had requested and the meddler he believed was Odin both hauled him toward Asgard.

The tremor of chaos subsided, and the colors dulled as the spell drew toward conclusion. Worried for his landing, Colbey attempted one last evasion, this time sideways. He plowed through the weakening forces, his body responding as well as his mind. He dodged, missing the destination the other intended by scant fingers' breadths. A magical force as heavy as a hewn-stone rooftop crashed against his trailing foot, then hammered the ground hard enough to quake it. Agony shot through his leg, and he worried for the bone. Asgard's blue-green grasses jabbed his face and neck. Exhaustion gripped his head like a vice. He had not realized just how hard he had labored against the magics, stealing the energy of body and mind.

Get him, someone unseen instructed.

A sword whipped toward Colbey. He rolled, feeling the cold passage of the strike. He gained his feet, relieved that both sustained his weight.

The pain in his ankle faded slightly, a sure sign he had suffered no long-term damage there. When the blade sped toward him again, he drew-cut and met it, prepared for a power that would strain his arms. But the wielder proved no stronger than himself. The other disengaged from the block with a quickness that betrayed expertise. For a moment, Colbey worried that he battled a Renshai at a time when mental warfare had exhausted him beyond ethical considerations or, possibly, even a good fight.

Colbey's own speed, which usually granted him three strikes to any opponent's one, succumbed to fatigue. He sacrificed his attack for a glance at his opponent. Blue eyes shone rabidly from the familiar face of the Renshai's patron goddess, Sif. Tresses crafted from metallic gold flowed around features he had worshiped since childhood, and the excitement that should have accompanied a battle with an able foe turned cold. He had escaped one trap only to blunder into another. The struggle against his own weariness stole the bulk of his concentration. He did not wish to kill Sif, but he would do so if she forced his hand.

Colbey mulled the best strategy as he met another thunderous rush. *Grab her and transport.* He started a complicated Renshai maneuver, ending with an in-and-out weave intended to bypass her defenses and disarm. But mind combat drained him worse than anything physical could. His movements turned sloppy, lacking power. She drove aside his assault with a deft flipflop that bared his head to her next stroke. He evaded it with a desperate spinning retreat that she trailed. Her sword skimmed an arm throw out further than usual for balance.

"I got a better fight from you centuries ago," Sif sneered, ignoring a high feint for the low maneuver that followed.

Colbey remembered. In his mortal years, she had appeared to him, sanctioning his decision to change the dedication of the Renshai from gleeful slaughter to hired swords in ethical causes. Renshai still sought Valhalla; but their glories, triumphs, and deaths came now at the price of enemies not innocents. Their current confrontation seemed to undermine the very principle that had brought them together.

Steel flashed beneath Asgard's perfect sun, highlights of gold and silver flickering over the uniform grasses. Colbey blocked, parried, or dodged all of Sif's brutal assaults. More saddened than angered by her attack, emotions blunted by lassitude, Colbey's only offense consisted of complex maneuvers intended to gingerly disarm. His own tired sloppiness, or her brilliant defenses, thwarted half a hundred opportunities. Doggedly, Colbey awaited more.

Sif's assault seemed to gain power, even as Colbey's lost it. "If not for me, you wouldn't exist." She reminded him that she had discovered her husband's tryst with a mortal Renshai that resulted in his conception. When that warrior had died with Colbey barely formed in her womb, Sif had transferred him inside his barren mother. Thus, she had dealt him mercy twice; once by this rescue and also by refraining from destroying him out of jealous anger. "I would never have spared you had I known . . ." Her voice caught, and her sword wavered before driving in for a neck strike that nearly landed for its unexpected hesitancy. Thoughts jumping, Colbey passed the insignificant thought that beginning students often proved most dangerous for that reason. Their inexperience made them difficult to defend against, though they always fell to competent offense. ". . . you would kill my sons!" She hammered his next attack with newfound rage.

The blades scratched down one another with a painful shrillness, locking at the crossguards. Colbey allowed Sif to break the maneuver with a sudden thrust that sent him into graceful retreat. She charged him like a hungry predator.

Colbey did not waste his energy on explanation, though she deserved it. His mind barely managed to find meaning in her outburst. His arms felt like lead weights, his legs like pliant twigs. Unable to concentrate, he abandoned his intricate disarming maneuvers for crude offense. As she rushed him, he cut for her legs. She thrust her blade down to block; and he reversed, aiming for her head.

Sif jerked her sword upward, too slow. The flat of Colbey's blade slapped across her right eye, upper nose, and forehead. The force jerked her head backward, and she tumbled into a heap on the grass. Colbey collapsed with her, a controlled fall that left him kneeling. Afraid he might have killed her, as worried he might not have hit hard enough, he struggled toward her.

He's in the zone! Odin's mental voice touched the bare edge of Colbey's perception, clearly not intended for him. It held a force just shy of compulsion. *Drop it now!*

But Sif's in there, came the desperate reply, Frey's mind-voice equally identifiable. *It'll kill her, too.*

Colbey struggled toward Sif, his vision disappearing as he battered all remaining energy to his limbs.

Faster! the Staff of Chaos beseeched him. *If they destroy us, it's over.*

Colbey's only answer was an urgent leap toward Sif.

Bind! I can give you the strength you need.

Colbey gritted his teeth, without strength to reply. Blindly he groped, catching Sif's still legs. He let the staff/sword know he had her, without squandering energy for mental command.

The staff flashed an emotion akin to human panic. *Can't transport. Encased in law.*

Though mental, Odin's command felt like a shout. *Do it!*
I can't kill Sif.

Bind! the Staff of Chaos shrieked. *Can't fight it this time. If you don't bind, we're dead. You, me, and the worlds!*

Odin lectured Frey, *Sif is dead. And Modi and Magni, Baldur, Honir, Hod, and Sigyn. Would you let him murder us all to rescue a goddess already lost?*

Hod? Sigyn? Realization spiked through Colbey. He's killing deities and blaming me. Rage lent a second wind that the uneven battle had not. Ignoring the staff/sword's pleas, he staggered to his feet. *Where's the barrier?*

Surely you're not—

You're wasting precious time! Show me! Colbey released a trickle of his remaining energy to his senses. Sight returned, revealing the flawless, stagnant colors of Asgard. It occurred to him that the world of gods had changed, veering toward the law that Odin claimed to control. Colbey wondered if the gray god even realized that the force influenced him as well.

Highlighted by the Staff of Chaos, an electric yellow wall sputtered to life, forming a perfect square around Colbey. He vented his anger in a wild attack, sword against obstacle. Chaos steel slammed the barrier. Sparks cascaded from the contact, flickering through a wild spectrum. The wall shook visibly, then a wave of agony crashed against Colbey, from sword and Odin alike. Rejuvenated by this small victory, he raised the sword to strike again.

It fought him. *Have you gone mad? That's almost pure law! Every bit of it I conquer, I lose the same of myself.*

Odin's voice: *Do it, Frey! Now. Or, so help me, I'll slaughter you myself.*

Colbey maintained his position, not daring to struggle. *Stop fighting me. You're fully lost if Frey drops that spell.*

If you just bind—

I'd let us die before I did that. Colbey blessed the strangeness of his mind barriers that made their natural position up. Opening, not closing, them proved difficult. Had his functioned like every other he had encountered, chaos would already have him in his weakened state. He swung for Odin's construct again, and chaos reluctantly allowed it. Again, he smashed the sword against the barrier. For an instant, nothing happened. Then, the wall exploded with a report louder than any thunder. The force hurled Colbey backward, chips of matter slashing through his clothes and flesh. The sword thrummed, vibrating at a painful frequency that sent his arm quivering beyond his control. He flailed for Sif, catching a still leg as the sword triggered a transport.

The tingle of magic became lost in the numbness that followed the discharge. Odin's scream of rage and anguish was the last thing Colbey heard on Asgard.

Perched upon Tem'aree'ay's bed, King Griff deliberately lost himself in the whirling radiance of her dance. No problem seemed too difficult in her presence, no threat a danger. Her delicate, almost fragile-appearing frame little resembled the Béarnian concept of beauty; yet he could not force his eyes from her. Her golden curls flew like living things. Her oval face, her high cheekbones, her heart-shaped lips no longer seemed the least bit alien. Even the canted eyes that had once appeared more like stones than reflectors of emotion became familiar perfection. Though as far along in her pregnancy as Kevral, it did not show as much. Elfin infants grew more slowly in the womb, and Captain had assured him that the baby seemed normal to his magical sight.

Thoughts of the elfin leader raised other concerns to Griff's mind. Captain had remained to tend Ra-khir's wounds. As one week, then two, had passed, he had yielded that responsibility to other elfin and human healers. Once again, Captain expressed his too-long delayed need to confront the *svartalf* whom Dh'arlo'mé had abandoned. Though Griff worried that he would never see the oldest of the elves again, he had had little choice but to assent. Already, servants equipped a small ship for Captain and his chosen companions, all elves; and the Captain had not left the deck in the two days since preparations began.

Tem'aree'ay fluttered through a sequence that made her body appear bonelessly supple. Her arms drifted on waves, and her feet pranced over the floorboards in patterns as airy as sunlight. Though proud joy filled Griff's mind, his heart felt squeezed. Darris still had not found a loophole that would allow the king and his elfin lover to marry, to legitimize their child.

Apparently sensing Griff's discomfort, Tem'aree'ay joined him on the coverlet. Her dainty hand spread only halfway across his scarred and massive fist. "What's wrong, my love?"

Not wanting to burden Tem'aree'ay, Griff shook his head.

Tem'aree'ay knew Griff too well. "You know it's you I love, not your kingdom. Father your heirs from Queen Matrinka and your bastards from me." Tem'aree'ay's musical accent and tender delivery rendered the birth circumstances equal, if different. "I have no designs on the throne, and I'll love you with or without an official decree."

The king clamped his other hand over Tem'aree'ay's, pinning hers between his own. "I'm not worried for that. Darris will find a way." He did not allow doubt to enter his voice, more for himself than her. He knew she spoke the truth; she was incapable of bitterness or petty jealousies. "It's courtroom matters troubling me."

"How so?"

Griff shook his head again. "Not worth bothering you, my love. Matrinka and I, with the Council. We can handle it."

"You can handle it with them." Tem'aree'ay added her last hand to the stack. "But with me, you can unburden."

"I love you," Griff said, glad for her presence. She would listen without judgment or the distancing deference that made it almost impossible to elicit opinion of his decisions. "It's about Tae."

"The answers have come," Tem'aree'ay guessed correctly.

"The answers have come," Griff confirmed, wincing at his memory of them. "At nearly the same time, which suggests King Cymion took much longer to consider his reply." Releasing Tem'aree'ay's hands, he scooted across the bed to support his back against the wall, though it left his legs sticking straight out in front of him. "Knowing what it says, I'm glad he didn't consider it lightly, though that also suggests he's not likely to change his mind." Realizing he had become too cryptic for the elf to follow, Griff turned to more comfortable, direct tactics. "King Weile Kahn of Stalmize sent only his greetings and stated he trusts his son to handle the situation. King Cymion of Pudar demanded Tae's extradition and Kevral's baby, making it very clear that he would consider withholding either an act of war."

"War?" Tem'aree'ay shivered, withdrawing into the fine velvet, lace, and silk of her dress. "People killing other people?"

Griff hated seeing his loved one so desperately uncomfortable. He leaned forward, reaching for her. "I'm sorry I told you."

Tem'aree'ay slid into his arms. "No, I asked to know. It's just so strange. So uniquely *human*."

Griff held her tightly, her dainty form weightless in his grip. He did not bother to remind her that the uniqueness had disappeared when Dh'arlo'mé led the elves against Béarn. Though rarely direct conflict, the *svartalf*'s mayhem, murders, and even the sterility spell passed for acts of war.

Tem'aree'ay looked up at Griff, her eyes glittering like sapphires in the lamplight. "If not so tragic, it would all seem wonderfully ironic."

Griff turned the elfin maiden a sidelong glance.

Tem'aree'ay explained her strange statement. "The inexperienced prince has the solid support of his kingdom. The one with a lifetime of royal exposure has the whole matter wrenched from his control, despite the fact that he appears to be the wronged party and has had the most say."

Tem'aree'ay's observation demanded thought. "A difference between cultures," the king explained, though he could not stop his mind from zipping beyond that superficial answer. At seventeen, he had become the king of the West's highest kingdom. Though he respected mother and stepfather, still uncomfortable commanding others in their presences, the idea of Herwin speaking for him at Tae's nineteen or Leondis' twenty-five seemed ludicrous and insulting.

"What are you going to do?" Tem'aree'ay asked the all-important question.

Griff heaved an enormous sigh. "I don't know." The Council had sat in a deep and lengthy silence following the reading of the messages. "No one wants to go to war." He amended, "Except the Renshai, Thialnir, of course."

Tem'aree'ay's curls tickled Griff's lips, remarkably soft amid the wiry coarseness of his beard. She relaxed noticeably. At one time, Dh'arlo'mé had all of the elves convinced that humans delighted in slaughter.

Griff kept the details to himself. Bad enough to lose a longtime supporter, but Pudar's population was quadruple Béarn's and they tended to share allies. Though all of the West swore its ultimate allegiance to Béarn, a civil war could place them on either side. Pudar held the advantage of supplies and money, the main market for each industrial town, every tiny farming hamlet, even for Béarn's own stone masons. It would only make sense for the East to assist Béarn, given the nature of the dispute; but the warrior tribes of the North might side with Pudar not only because of trade, but simply to oppose the East. Or the Renshai.

Tem'aree'ay sat up, pulling far enough away to allow an earnest look. "You'll do whatever you must to avoid a war, won't you, my love?"

It's not that simple. Always before, the right answers had come to Griff with little need for consideration. This time, he struggled desperately, enough to make him wonder whether or not he truly would have passed the staff-test. "I'll do my best to avoid war." Griff tried to reassure, yet he would not lie. "But not at the cost of allowing any country with an army to dictate policy with threats." Realizing he had slipped into court talk, he changed his approach. "I'm not going to do as King Cymion demands just because he threatens war if I don't. That would only encourage him to do it every time he wants something from us."

Tem'aree'ay found a position beside Griff, her back also pressed to the wall. She loosed a pent-up breath. "So it's just a threat. He's not serious."

"I'm sure he's serious." Griff stared at the far wall, painted with a forest mural that he had commissioned. He hoped it made her feel more at home. "Otherwise, he would not have sent the crown prince. Or threatened us with war for the first time in history."

Tem'aree'ay fidgeted. "People will die if war happens." She stated the obvious as if it were a great revelation.

"Many people, my love," Griff admitted. "And at a time we can ill afford it. The sterility spell already plagues our survival as humans."

"Is it not worth surrendering one man and one baby to prevent that?"

The question had basic merit, and Griff reminded himself that elves had no experience with such situations. "There are other things to consider, Tem'aree'ay. This time, Pudar wants Kevral's baby and Tae. Next time, they might want Matrinka and Marisole. Or the kingdom itself." He tried not to contemplate the freedom that would give him. He had never wished to rule Béarn, would love to shed the lead weight of burdens doing so had dumped upon his shoulders. Yet Griff had come to understand the need for the neutral kings sanctioned by the gods. "If King Cymion takes control of Béarn, the future toll in lives might go far beyond those lost in a war. It might destroy the balance . . . and the world."

Having explained it in a way no one could question, Griff backtracked to ethics. "My people have obligations to the kingdom, but I at least have as many obligations to them as well. Not the least of those is protecting them from injustice, not just as a group but as individuals. I cannot abandon that obligation, even facing the threat of war."

"Tae," Tem'aree'ay reminded, "is not a citizen of Béarn. And neither is the baby."

Griff lowered his head. He had spent hours explaining many human conventions, and she had done the same for elfin ways. Always before, she had displayed the innocence of an infant; it hurt to have her suggest that he abandon his morals, even for so great a threat as war. "But they are under my protection."

Tem'aree'ay studied her lover, easily reading his discomfort. "Griff, I'm not giving advice, only trying to think out this problem from all directions, even those that seem disagreeable. And helping you to do the same."

The king nodded, understanding. "It's not as simple as I'm making it sound."

"I know," Tem'aree'ay said softly. "You're not withholding an innocent Béarnian citizen demanded by an unreasoning king. And the baby—"

"—belongs in Pudar," Griff could not resist finishing. "That part, at least, is clear. Pudar has a right to demand that child, and I have no right to deny them. I will order Kevral to turn over the baby, but she is Renshai. She'll do as she pleases and suffer the consequences gladly."

"So you can meet at least one of Pudar's demands without doing it *because* they threatened."

Griff returned his lover's stare. "Prime Minister Davian said the exact same thing at the council."

Tem'aree'ay smiled. "Obviously a great mind."

"Exactly why I chose him." Griff ran his finger's along Tem'aree'ay's. "And you." He shrugged, thick, black locks slipping from his right shoulder. "He's working on the wording for that in the reply now. But there's still the matter of Tae."

"Sire." Tem'aree'ay caught herself, grinning briefly. "My love, he saved your life."

Griff flinched. He could not forget the sacrifices Tae had made, leaping from a boat, wounded and in the dead of night, to slip past the elves' defenses. Even locating Griff had proven an effort that cost Tae his dignity, more scars, and nearly his life. He had fallen through a roof poorly designed by elves copying the appearance, but not the structure, of mankind's buildings. The elves had captured and tortured him before he managed to obtain the key to release himself, Griff, and Rantire. "He risked everything for me. He deserves better than to suffer Cymion's vengeance. And yet . . ." Griff lowered his head, hating to continue. He often deliberately broke his thoughts at this same place.

Tem'aree'ay pressed. "And yet, what?"

"Prince Leondis describes an assassination attempt that Tae does not deny. And the evidence cannot be argued."

"If someone who had not saved your life had committed such a crime, would you deliver him to King Cymion?"

Griff did not hesitate, "Probably. But it's not just the rescue that has me baffled. He's a visiting prince, exempt from our law by our law." He raised his hand, anticipating the argument Saxanar had spoken. "Admittedly, there's that other law that gives us leeway, the one that states the kingdoms should have a say in all this. But there's more here. King Weile placed Tae's fate in his own hands, and Tae placed it into mine. That gives me the legal right to extradite him." He shook his head, frowning. "But not the ethical right. My heart tells me that I should reward Stalmize's trust, not Pudar's threats. And that there's more to this incident than the obvious." Griff did not bother to mention that he was not alone in his suspicions. Knight-Captain Kedrin had confessed his support for Tae at a time when impartiality seemed essential, though the knight would obey Griff's decision, no matter how unfair he believed it. Matrinka, too, had asserted Tae's innocence.

Tem'aree'ay stared at the woodland mural, as if losing herself among the trees. "My love, I've heard many humans proclaim it best in affairs of state to follow one's head and never one's heart." She tapped a long, delicate finger on Griff's chest. "I have the bias of knowing that, when elves switched from play to logic, we nearly destroyed ourselves."

Griff nodded, wishing he could commiserate. If not for the change in elfin character, he would never have found Tem'aree'ay.

"According to what I've read, Béarn's kings have followed their hearts through eternity and are acclaimed for their natural wisdom."

Only then, Griff realized how Tem'aree'ay had manipulated him, dragging his considerations in a direction he dreaded only to return him to what he already knew. He had always loved her beauty and her gentleness. Now, he discovered an intelligence nearly as candid, though without the guilelessness. And it made him love her all the more.

CHAPTER 23

Desperation

When you corner a lion, expect a war to the death.
—*Queen Matrinka of Béarn*

FLYING Béarn's colors, a small ship wound through the currents of the Southern Sea. Wind tugged Captain's hair, floating strands that escaped the knot at the nape of his neck. The blue sail stretched taut, occasional gusts fluttering its tan bear, making it appear to dance. Droplets pattered from the hull, their circular splashes accentuating the cutting line of the rudder. Captain sucked salt air deep into his lungs. It tasted different than it did when he perched upon the beach staring out over the pounding waves, a thousand times better. The sun beat down on his scalp, but he did not seek cover below deck or beneath the shade of drawn tarps as his elfin crew of six had done. Even this blinding warmth seemed a welcome and long-awaited friend. It would bleach his mahogany hair to a pale brown, flecked with gold and white, and bake his skin to its familiar brown.

Kholar reached Captain in bursts, none of it intended directly for him. Coached by human sailors, and by himself, the crew struggled with lines and bearings. They need not have bothered. After millennia alone upon the sea, Captain could have steered the simple craft with his eyes closed, one leg lamed, and manacles locked to his wrists. Nevertheless, he allowed them to struggle without direction. He could fix anything short of a massive hole in the hull, and he knew this portion of the sea contained no shoals. Few seafarers would have agreed with his methods. Most human captains maintained their commands and their ships by demanding perfection, but Captain preferred that his shipmates learn the joy of sailing by experimentation and error. His memory carried him back to his own early years: the ships that seemed to buck against his every desire, the unexpected jerks that burned ropes across his palms, and the gales that had swallowed him, threatening to lay him forever in a watery grave. Captain smiled, cracking a glaze of crusted salt. He had not known to fear those things then, death a far distant construct without meaning.

The ship yawed, thrown broadside into the wind. The sail flapped wildly, spilling its cargo. Captain skipped over the gunwale, catching a loose line whose clamp rattled desperately. He called a few commands, glad for *khohlar.* A human captain would have had to shout over the crackling dance of the sail, alarming the crew with volume. His elves would never know how close they had come to scuttling the ship and losing their lives, and those of their successors, to the sea.

For several moments, elves hauled and cleated lines, wrestled the pitching tiller, and transported ballast, engaged in one of the great battles that Captain relished. Finally, damp and exhausted, they fought the ship back into full submission. Light wind puffed into the mainsail. The ship scudded eastward, bobbing gently in the swells. Panic disappeared from the edges of shared *khohlar,* and an all-too-human triumph gradually replaced it. Captain sat back in the hot sun, basking in the excitement of the crew. He had risked the ship but accomplished so much. And many more battles lay ahead. Each success would fuel confidence for the task of bargaining with *svartalf,* and it might even make sailors of his crew.

Atonement for a grounded sword required weeks of prayer, verbal and in the form of rabid practices beyond the point of pain. Kevral found the latter easy to inspire. Bruises ached through days and nights, the broken rib stabbed her lungs with every deep breath, and movement tore at healing burns. Every touch become an agony. The human healers smeared on salves that kept infection at bay, and a parade of elves attended her. The skill they had acquired from mending the aftereffects of the *Ragnarok* on their own people helped immensely. They had learned that preventing the scars worked better and, ultimately, more quickly than fixing them. Though this meant suffering with open wounds far longer, Kevral appreciated their method. Recalling a conversation with Matrinka shortly after Béarn had assigned her to the princess, she quoted Colbey to Ra-khir during a joint healing session: "Scars are a warrior's badge of honor . . ." Kevral finished by paraphrasing Matrinka's response, ". . . but there's no reason to work toward the worst possible outcome."

Though Ra-khir had sustained the more dangerous wound, he recovered more swiftly, regaining his strength as his body replaced the lost blood. The punctures of the demon's teeth required less attention and allowed faster healing than Kevral's extensive burns. The worst injury, the gash in his spleen had been appropriately handled by Chan'rék'ril at the time. Had the elf not diagnosed and magically staunched it immediately, Ra-khir would have escaped fatal impact only to bleed to death an instant later.

Now the two sat holding hands in their quarters while the healers packed up their salves and creams. Saviar slumbered quietly in his crib, eyes closed, tiny lips pursed, arms thrown wide. The agony of the healers' ministrations still ached through Kevral, but she preferred the discomfort to dulling her senses with painkillers. The collarbone break no longer bothered her at all, but the figure-of-eight bandage that allowed for its proper healing grated against the burns. Even the light touch of cool linens irritated those, and she had just considered shedding her clothing when a knock sounded.

Ra-khir tensed to rise, but a young male healer waved him down. "We're leaving now anyway, sir." He opened the door to reveal Andvari waiting on the other side. The Northman back-stepped, allowing the healers to escape out into the hallway. Only when the last had filed from the room did he glance toward Kevral and Ra-khir. He wore casual clothes, and their Béarnian cut seemed ill-suited to his pale coloring, braids, and warrior build.

Kevral looked away.

Ra-khir gave Andvari a friendly, beckoning wave. "Come in. Come in."

Andvari did as Ra-khir bade, closing the door behind him. Pain and aversion made Kevral irascible. She glowered at Ra-khir, disdaining his invitation, though they both knew politeness dictated no other action. He squeezed her hand, a plea for tolerance.

Andvari turned back to his hosts, having missed the exchange. "How are you?"

Kevral deliberately said nothing, leaving Ra-khir to respond for both of them.

"I'm fine," the knight reassured. "Kevral's coming along more slowly, but the healers are pleased. We're past the worst. They're not likely to fester now."

"Good." Andvari's gaze dropped. Avoiding his eyes, Kevral took inordinately long to realize he looked at the sword near her left hip: Rache's sword. The one he had tended after Ra-khir's fall. Finding it in place, he smiled slightly. "Well." He cleared his throat. "That's all. I just wanted to make sure you're all right."

Ra-khir nudged Kevral, the touch of his elbow raw pain against freshly reopened wounds. It raised another wave of anger, inappropriately directed toward the Northman. She knew what Ra-khir wanted and dutifully gave it. "Thanks for tending the sword." She spoke in a flat tone, with none of the gratitude the words implied, though she meant them.

"You're welcome." Andvari's grin widened, now obvious. "Perhaps now you realize I'm not along to vilify . . . your people."

"My people," Kevral repeated, fists clinching.

"Yes."

"You mean Renshai."

"Y-yes." The grin wilted, along with the aura of confident camaraderie.

"You can't say it, can you?"

"Kevral," Ra-khir warned, placing a hand over one fist.

"Of course, I can," Andvari insisted. He forced out the word, his pronunciation careful and his manner nervous, "Renshai."

Kevral had already leaped to another cause for dispute, "Do you think oiling one sword will erase centuries of persecution?"

"Kevral!" Ra-khir's cautioning turned sharp. His hand enclosed hers.

Andvari cringed. Red slashed briefly across his cheeks, then disappeared as he controlled his rage and returned to his usual conciliatory tactics. "That's not why I did it." He glanced at Ra-khir, who made an encouraging gesture. "As you know, I'm Nordmirian. One of our great historical heroes is the Slayer, Valr Kirin. He formed a blood brotherhood with a . . ." The pause was shorter-lived this time, ". . . Renshai. And legends claim he sealed the pact by giving Rache a sword." His eyes glided to the weapon again.

Kevral opened her free hand to touch the hilt with a finger. "You believe this is that sword?"

"It could be. *Tisis*, Rache called it. Vengeance." Andvari shrugged. "At the time of the blood brotherhood, Rache was surrounded by enemies, hiding his tribe. It's said he entered the relationship unwillingly, worried for what others would assume if he refused." He shrugged again. "If Rache intended to eventually kill Nordmirians with the blade, I could think of no better name to give it."

Kevral could not wholly dispute the history. Rache and Kirin had personally confirmed much of it. She knew nothing about the Nordmirian giving Rache a sword, yet such a gesture would suggest that Valr Kirin considered himself the greater-honored party, so it made no sense for her to argue in that vein. However, to satisfy her irritation, she found another. "I should have known you didn't honor the sword because it belonged to a respected companion but only because it might have belonged to a Nordmirian." Kevral withdrew from the weapon as if it had suddenly become soiled. "Now I've got another month of atonement before I'd dare to wield it."

Ra-khir's grip tightened painfully around her knuckles, and he turned her a withering look. He had spent enough time among Renshai to understand the depth of such an insult.

"But I . . ." Andvari stammered. "I mean, I would have . . ." He tried again. "If it had come down to—" He broke off, shaking his head. "Forget it, Kevral. Just forget it." With that, he stormed from the room, flipping the door shut behind him. The panel struck the jamb, then bounced back open. Andvari's bootfalls thundered down the hall.

Ra-khir released Kevral's fist, rose, and shut the door. Only then, he rounded on her. "Kevral, give him a chance."

Kevral studied her fingernails, chipped by sword work, grooves from base to tip testimony to intermittent, minor damages to the nail bed. "I've given him lots of chances. More than I should have."

Ra-khir glared. "There's only one person I've ever seen you treat this badly. Do you know who that was?"

Kevral did not have to think long. Tae's chastisement came easily to memory: *You're being too damned hard on Ra-khir.* "You?"

"Right." Ra-khir's look turned piercing. "Are you in love with *him,* too?"

Kevral's mood turned the words from humor to sniping. "I hate him. And it's time you knew. When I treated you like that, I hated you, too."

"Matrinka says love and hate are closely related." Ra-khir refused to let go of a point that had started as a joke. "That's why my mother treated my father so badly after their marriage failed. Her feelings for him turned from intense love to equally intense hatred."

Though Kevral knew the words difficult for Ra-khir to speak, she refused to let go of anger fueled as much by constant physical discomfort as by Andvari. "Sometimes, Ra-khir, hatred is just hatred."

"And sometimes, Kevral . . ." Ra-khir returned to the bedside, but he did not sit. ". . . hatred is just prejudice."

"Exactly," Kevral fairly crowed. Ra-khir had struck to the heart of the matter. "He's prejudiced. He can't even say 'Renshai,' let alone learn to work with one."

Ra-khir placed both hands on the coverlet and leaned toward his wife. "I meant *you,* Kevral."

"Me?" Kevral did not understand. "Me, what?"

"You're the one showing prejudice."

"Huh?" Now, Kevral understood, but the words made no sense. "That's impossible. Renshai aren't the ones who tried to annihilate Northmen. Renshai aren't the ones who forbade a tribe of their own from returning to their homeland in the North."

"So you think prejudice is limited to the winners of a conflict?"

It seemed so clear to Kevral, she wondered how Ra-khir could miss it. "To the ones who inflicted the evil."

Ra-khir stared, brows high. "If caravans could travel only west, we'd have no trade."

"Your point?"

"Roads carry people in both directions. Prejudice is the same."

Kevral did not agree. "Victims have legitimate right and reason to hate. It's not prejudice."

Ra-khir looked away. "Prejudice, Kevral, is when you punish every member of a group for the actions of a few. Even those members who condemn the few." He paced a couple steps, then whirled back in Kevral's direction. "If a Béarnian highwayman waylaid my father, no one would denounce me for hunting the thief down. But if I used the incident to torment a Béarnian woman in the marketplace, it would be prejudice."

The example insulted Kevral's intelligence. "Clearly."

"But I'd be a victim."

"It's not the same." Kevral waved her hands, desperate to make her point. "If the Béarnian army destroyed Erythane and killed everyone you knew . . ." She nodded, having restored the seriousness of the Northmen's crime."

". . . then I would have the right to torment a woman in the marketplace?"

Kevral's triumph withered. "It would be more understandable."

"But still prejudice. And beneath my honor." Ra-khir's green eyes bored into Kevral, past simple discussion. "Kevral, neither you nor Andvari was born when the Northmen clashed with the Renshai. You blaming the annihilation of Renshai on him would be like Béarn executing the highwayman's infant son for the father's crime. The baby would be innocent. Andvari is also." He added with emphasis. "And you are not a victim."

Kevral had to concede his point about prejudice, but she would still argue the latter. "If not for the slaughter, Renshai would still live in the North, and in far greater numbers."

"Maybe." Ra-khir refused to surrender that argument either. "Or perhaps the Renshai would have died out for their own aggression. According to my books, the tribe was dwindling. Because of constant war, only the rare member lived to thirty. Their rugged life made childbearing difficult. Women came into their cycles later, if at all; and most died in battle before they could give birth even once."

Kevral folded her arms gently across her chest, the huffy gesture foiled by the need to keep every touch careful. "When did you become the expert on Renshai?"

"Since I married one. And fathered another." Ra-khir perched on the edge of the bed, his demeanor relaxing. "Kevral, bad things happen. As long as there have been humans, there's been war: honorable and dishonorable. The conquerors do as they will with the spoils of their victory, including the people. Assimilation, slavery, torture, extermination." He shook his head sadly. "There's no way to know where history would have eventually taken anyone's people had any specific event not occurred, and hating the descendants of the strong accomplishes nothing good. You need only look to the examples of the *svartalf* and *lysalf* for proof. By your definition, the *svartalf*'s hatred for humans is justified by the *Ragnarok*. And not prejudice."

Kevral considered. "When did you get so smart?"

Ra-khir smiled. There seemed no modest way to answer that question without belittling himself, but he found it. "It doesn't take intelligence to figure that out, only perspective. Biases are always justifiable when they're yours. The only logical way to break through the delusion is to find common ground, someone prejudiced against us both. My mistake was turning to analogy before real life events. Comparisons are never perfect. They always leave an out for people who want to cling to their bigotry." Apparently realizing he had turned clinical, Ra-khir switched to lighter matters. "If the Renshai still lived in the North, I would never have met you. If you had even been born, your life would have been different. Not necessarily better." Ra-khir teased, "In your case, definitely worse. You wouldn't have had my handsome face and enormous intellect."

"And ego," Kevral could not help adding. She hugged her husband, not caring about the physical pain it caused. For now, the warm glow of their love meant more. "I still don't understand why I found peace with a Northern soldier in Pudar who attacked me, but I can't find it with a companion."

Ra-khir kept a careful touch around Kevral. "Think about it. The answer will come."

Kevral did not feel as certain. "I'll try." So many other problems had confronted her recently, and she found few solutions. For now, thoughts about the baby had to take precedence.

King Cymion paced Pudar's Great Hall like a caged lion, his tread as heavy as his thoughts. The four-tiered candelabra overhead struck brass highlights through a room that contained only a lengthy table with a spotless white tablecloth. Gauzy curtains embroidered with flowers haloed thick glass that overlooked blurry gardens and masons toiling to reconstruct the courtyard wall. Cymion clutched a rolled parchment in his right hand, Béarn's blue ribbon crushed beneath his fingers.

A knock echoed through the massive chamber. Cymion turned on his boot heel, only then realizing he had paced himself to the far end. No servant or guard remained to open the door; he had sent them away while he considered King Griff's answer. It would take him inordinately long to cross back to the door, and he doubted even his commanding voice would carry to the person on the opposite side.

Fortunately, the other did not wait. Summoned to the king's presence, Javonzir paused only a moment before tapping open the door and peering inside. His hazel eyes flickered around the room, clearly seeking his king. He wore a tunic of Pudarian brown tied with a silver sash that perfectly matched the wolf embroidered across the chest. Dark brown hair fell straight to his shoulders, properly oiled. Distance made his medium build appear slight, especially compared with Cymion's robust, warrior frame. Though first cousins on his mother's side, they little resembled one another.

Finally, Javonzir's gaze found the king, and he performed a careful bow without pretension. Cymion let out a pent-up breath he did not even realize he held. Javonzir displayed his disagreement with his king's policies by becoming irritatingly formal. Cymion craved one of the intimate discussions he could get only from this man with whom he had shared a childhood. For the next hour or so, he wanted a friend, not a subordinate.

"Thanks for coming," Cymion said, the boom necessary to carry his voice across the broad room echoing.

Javonzir avoided speaking what they both knew. When the king requested a person's presence, the summoned one dared not refuse. "My pleasure, Sire." He closed and latched the door behind him, the click lost to distance. His softer voice barely reached the king's ears. "May I approach?"

"Please do." Cymion wished they could dispense with even this formality, but it served an important purpose. If Javonzir dropped all of his pretenses, others might, too. It also denoted respect and reminded them both whose word must always carry the most authority.

Javonzir headed past the table, meeting Cymion near a window. Reading something on the king's face, he pursed his thin lips until they nearly disappeared. "Is it your adviser that you need, Your Majesty? Or a friend?"

"Both," Cymion admitted.

Javonzir shuffled one step nearer. For an instant, Cymion thought the smaller man might hug him. He stiffened, only then realizing that he would appreciate an affectionate gesture he had not experienced since his wife died and his sons had grown. Then, the cousin-turned-adviser glanced through the glass at the workers. Apparently worried about appearances, he did not complete the embrace. Instead, he indicated a chair at the table. "Would you like to sit, Your Majesty?"

Having never considered the obvious position, Cymion stared stupidly at the myriad chairs, "Thank you, Javon. A good idea."

Javonzir pulled out one near the head, and Cymion perched on the edge. He motioned for his adviser to join him. Pulling out a second chair to comfortable speaking distance, Javonzir also sat.

Cymion did not wait for him to settle into place before clapping the parchment to the table. "What did you think of this?"

"I . . ." Javonzir spoke very slowly, ". . . found some parts pleasing, Sire. King Griff plans to turn over Pudar's heir. He's appropriately sympathetic about the . . . incident."

"The incident." Cymion raised and lowered the parchment again. "That so-called 'incident' was an attempt on my son's life."

Javonzir acknowledged the words with a sideways tilt of his head. "Indeed, Your Majesty."

"By the same ignominious bastard who murdered Severin."

"Apparently, Sire," Javonzir said carefully. "Tae denies—"

Cymion's hand struck the table again, this time with venom. "Don't ever use that name in my castle. Not even in my kingdom!"

Javonzir shifted his chair further from the table. "Sire." He emphasized each word, "He Who Shall Not Be Named denies killing Severin."

The point seemed as unnecessary as the title. "Did you think he would confess?"

"He confessed to the attack against Leondis easily enough, Your Majesty. If we take his word for one, why not the other? It could have occurred as his father said. The dark elves could have played a part."

Cymion did not see it the same way. "He's just becoming more cocky, throwing it in our faces. Now that he's a prince and—apparently— immune to justice, he's saying he can do as he pleases."

Javonzir cleared his throat. His muddy eyes measured his king. "Sire, once Kevral accepted his punishment, he was immune for the first crime also. No reason for him not to admit to Severin's assassination, especially if he's 'throwing it in our faces.' "

Cymion calmed, considering the familiar wisdom of his adviser's words. Possibilities remained to explain Tae's behavior, but they did not matter. The crime to which Tae had confessed was enough. "He may need to maintain his innocence, or his so-called integrity, to keep the goodwill of Béarn. Caught in the act, he could not deny the attack on Leondis."

As usual, Javonzir read a lot from a single comment. "You think it's an Eastern plot to win over Béarn, Your Majesty?"

Cymion trusted his adviser's opinion more. "What do you think?"

"The first step to successful invasion is cutting off a kingdom from its strongest allies."

Cymion studied Javonzir. The words made sense but did not directly address his question. He guessed at the point, "You think the East is deliberately stirring war between us? That I'm playing into their hands?"

Javonzir shook his head, well-oiled locks barely moving. "I doubt they assumed we'd go to war, Sire. In fact, that might foil their plan since Pudar is the stronger kingdom. And likely to win, Sire."

A rush of uncertainty kept Cymion silent several moments. He did not even challenge the word 'likely,' though it expressed inappropriate doubt about Pudar's power. "Am I doing the right thing?"

Javonzir said nothing.

Cymion lowered his head, gray-flecked auburn curls dipping into his eyes, his beard like wire against his throat. "I never used to wonder, Javon."

Javonzir attempted to console, "Aside from Kevral, Sire, no one has ever questioned."

The words raised unexpected anger. Cymion's fingers closed over the parchment. "I was *not* wrong about Kevral."

Javonzir developed a sudden, intense interest in the hem of his tunic, a sure sign of nervousness. He had tried to warn Cymion of the danger of his preoccupation with keeping the Renshai, without success. The king had executed the capture and impregnation of Kevral without his adviser's knowledge, and Javonzir had deftly handled the Renshai and her consort when the plan broke down. It was one of the few times they had differed on major policy matters, and Cymion still struggled to make his cousin understand.

"I was trying to forestall a war of succession." Cymion lifted his head. "Some three centuries ago, such a thing destroyed the royal line that preceded our own. Baronies were laid to waste. A quarter of Pudar's citizens died of violence, disease, and subsequent famine."

Javonzir's interest in his hem grew fanatical. The same tutors had taught him history.

Driven to justify actions he had already believed well-understood by his cousin, Cymion continued, "The discomfort of one Renshai in my employ seemed worth avoiding a repeat of that tragedy. It still does." He softened his tone. "I regret only that it had to be accomplished through physical restraint and forced intimacy." His fingers winched tighter, crushing Béarn's message. "She made those things necessary. And they *were* necessary. I will take it to my grave that I did the right thing."

Javonzir remained silently in place, plucking agitatedly at his garment. His upbringing would never allow him to admit that his king had erred.

Guilty for his outburst, and the discomfort it caused one he so fully trusted, King Cymion sighed and released the parchment. "Javon, I asked you a question."

Javonzir acknowledged the statement with a nod. "Yes, Sire, forgive me." Even through the king's tirade, he had not forgotten. He proved his attentiveness by repeating the query, "Are you doing the right thing now?"

Cymion's heart rate settled back to normal, and he shed defensiveness like a mantle. "Yes."

Javonzir released his hem. "Sire, I can only give you my opinion on the matter."

Cymion dismissed the comment with a brisk gesture. "As always."

Javonzir cleared his throat. "I believe, Your Majesty, that King Griff's cooperation attests to the rightness of your decision about Kevral and the heir." He measured Cymion's reaction to each word now. "Whatever my previous, personal concerns about the circumstances of the conception, the gods must have sanctioned it, Sire. No other union of Leondis' resulted in pregnancy."

Cymion sucked in a deep breath, loosing it slowly. "Javonzir, I've told no one this, and you must never mention it." He did not wait for a vow from his adviser; none was necessary. "Kevral claims the baby isn't Leondis'. That some deity impregnated her to rescue her from repeated couplings with the prince."

Javonzir's thick brows lifted. "A deity, Sire?"

"A desperate story." Cymion shrugged. "An attempt to hurt him. A dream."

Emboldened by Cymion's acceptance of even his most indelicate utterance, Javonzir continued to speak openly, "Sire, I would say the same if Leondis had fathered one other child before or after the sterility plague. He's never been particularly . . ." He clearly searched for the most diplomatic word.

". . . celibate," Cymion supplied, not wanting ginger politics to interfere with an opinion he desperately needed. "So you believe a deity sired Kevral's baby?"

"Your Majesty, I believe . . ." Javonzir hesitated, considering. ". . . I believe it's not wholly impossible that another man sneaked into Kevral's cell and fathered that baby. She was helpless, weakened by childbirth, emotionally distraught. Sire, the mind can do wondrous things in bad situations. She might convince herself that a guard was a deity come to rescue her from misery."

"A guard," Cymion repeated, dispelled anger returning in a cold rush. "One of my guards?"

"Who else would have had a key, Your Majesty?"

Cymion struck the table again, this time so hard the boards squeaked a protest. "I'll kill the bastard."

Javonzir skittered beyond reach. He used his most soothing tone. "Your Majesty, with a request for forbearance if you find the words treasonous, he may have done you a favor."

Cymion rose, whirling on his adviser. "How so?"

"You have an heir who, for all appearances, is Leondis'. Does the bloodline really matter?"

The question struck King Cymion dumb. He blinked several times, seeking to clear his head. "Yes," he admitted grudgingly.

"Enough, Sire, to leave the throne of Pudar open for dispute?"

"No," Cymion admitted. "Not enough for that." He resumed pacing, faced with a new problem. "Kevral is already committed to silence. We would need only to find the guilty party and quiet him as well. The child and the citizenry would never know there was a possibility he or she did not carry Pudar's royal blood."

"We would know, Sire."

"Yes." Cymion knew his cousin well enough to feel certain he did not face a threat. Javonzir would never give away a secret of the king, and the lack of royal blood would not bother Javonzir at all. His rare and special personality allowed for no prejudice. Less impartial, Cymion would see the possibility of tainted blood in the child's every failing. Yet he believed time and his training could overcome even that. "But that baby is Pudar's only hope. Of royal lineage or not, it is Leondis' only heir." Another thought struck with gale force. *If the truth comes out, we could embellish the deity claim of Kevral's. It could only work to Pudar's advantage to exaggerate the already common belief that the kings carry divine blood. Most would never doubt that a god took possession of Leondis' body to refresh the lordliness of our line.*

Javonzir fell into another hush.

Cymion spun about to look at his cousin. The adviser's expression would explain why he chose quiet contemplation over response. He discovered peaceful, nonjudgmental features, lacking the formality that would suggest disagreement with his king. Relieved, Cymion managed a tight smile. The other matter still confronted him, the one for which he had believed he actually needed insight. Until Javonzir had raised the possibility that Kevral's claim about the baby could hold some merit, he had thought his handling of the attack against Leondis his only possibility for error. Now, he realized, he had harbored residual doubt about the heir, fully dispelled by their discussion. "What about the assassin? Do *you* believe I have a right to demand extradition?"

Javonzir stared. "Your Majesty, you have the right to demand anything."

The hint of formality in Javonzir's answer troubled Cymion. The stuffiness only appeared when he disagreed with his king. "Of course. But am I making a mistake in this matter?" He forestalled the obvious answer, "And, yes, I know the king never makes a mistake."

Javonzir followed the careful tacks of a king who clearly needed his advice. "Sire, I believe you have every right to demand T—" He caught himself. ". . . the assassin's extradition."

"Really?" The confirmation on the heels of rigid propriety surprised Cymion.

"Really," Javonzir confirmed. "I don't believe any loving father who happens to be a king would demand anything else. If Leondis had stabbed . . . the assassin, King Weile would surely insist on Leondis' extradition there."

"Kahn," Cymion corrected.

"What?"

"King Weile *Kahn*. Easterners consider shortening names a grave insult."

"I know, Sire," Javonzir said, hazel eyes twinkling. "Under the circumstances, it seemed appropriate."

Cymion's grin grew, almost to normal size. "I get it."

"I'm not sure you do, Sire," Javonzir's comment bordered on insubordination, not for the first time. "Would you allow your prince's extradition?"

"If he tried to kill another prince? Yes."

Javonzir stroked his chin, clearly not getting the answer he sought. "What if it were Severin instead of Leondis?"

Even after so long, a pang of regret struck Cymion at the mention of his elder son. His smile disappeared. "Severin would not do such a thing."

Javonzir sucked air through his teeth. "For the sake of the discussion, Sire. Imagine it."

Finally, Cymion considered Javonzir's point and the difficulties it raised. "I would attempt to bargain with the other king. At least assure a fair trial. And that the punishment of a prince, not a commoner, was forthcoming."

Javonzir made no comment, allowing time for the king to infer what had to follow.

"I understand, Javon. I need to push for extradition. And, once I win it, the trial must be fair. The punishment appropriate."

Again seizing on Cymion's willingness to listen, Javonzir spoke freely, "We can't try him for Severin's murder, only Leondis' wounding, Your Majesty. We can consider imprisonment, exile, a whipping. But not execution. Never execution."

Cymion clenched his fingers. Nothing could have pleased him more than throttling Tae with his own hands, yet he knew Javonzir spoke wisely.

"And King Weile Kahn should have a say in the matter."

Cymion kept his fingers laced. "He'd tie our hands."

Javonzir did not agree. "From what I've heard of Weile Kahn, Sire, he might encourage a few lashes to teach his son a lesson."

The words did not surprise Cymion. He might do the same for Leondis. Then reality intruded. "That's assuming the king's not a part of whatever plan Tae has to turn Béarn against Pudar." He spoke the name easily this time, a sure sign discussion had dispelled much of the bitterness and anger that had plagued him for so long.

"That's the best part of the whole thing, Your Majesty," Javonzir insisted. "It doesn't matter. The fastest and most secure alliances are usually born of hardship. Sire, if you handle this right, you could gain an ally of tremendous power."

"The East?" It seemed an impossible suggestion. The West and East had remained enemies for so long. When the chance for unity opened to Cymion, it brought the promise of so much more. Joined to the high kingdoms of North and East, Pudar would become all-powerful, virtually invincible.

"Sire, you can address the best interests of Pudar and still satisfy the vengeance of every man, woman, and child who loved Severin." Javonzir found a diplomatic way to address Cymion's rage, which always slipped beyond the reasonable when it came to Tae. "But it all hinges on convincing Béarn to extradite."

Cymion sat, staring at the crumpled parchment. "King Griff won't surrender him."

Javonzir settled back into his own chair. "Perhaps, Sire, if you explained to King Griff that you intend to prosecute . . ." He met Cymion's cold blue gaze, ". . . Tae as a prince. That you'll confine him without resorting to the dungeons. That you'll consult Stalmize and rule out the possibility of execution. He might prove more willing, less apt to see it as sending his own savior to slaughter."

"Maybe." That information might ease Griff's concerns, but it would not change Béarnian law. He wished the naive adolescent who perched upon Béarn's throne could recognize the threat that Leondis had elicited. If Stalmize continued to work its way into the graces of Béarn, at the expense of Pudar, the East would rule the world. "And if he continues to refuse?"

"Then, Sire," Javonzir said carefully. "There is still war."

CHAPTER 24

Loki's Citadel

Loki means "fire" in the Northern tongue. Grand, glorious, beautiful. Necessary for security and warmth, when controlled. Searing to the touch. Freed, it becomes mischievous, evil, and devastating. As unpredictable as chaos itself.
— *Colbey Calistinsson*

MAGIC tugged at Colbey through the single remaining gap in the boundaries he had formed to separate his chaos' realm from the other worlds. He recognized the signature of the caster, Idunn, which surprised him. Before Colbey had become the literal Prince of Demons, magic had fully lacked understanding and logic. The Cardinal Wizards, and the few gods who dabbled in it, rarely dared its use for the danger of its unintended side effects. Now, the magic sought him amid the ever-changing soup that only his will held to patterns. It called to him as it would to a demon; but, where those before had summoned the regular denizens of chaos, this one clearly demanded him.

Colbey sighed. His leg had fully healed, a minor injury; and he always spoiled for a battle. Yet the conflicts the gods offered had turned from joyous challenge to bother. Hampered by the understanding that they attacked him out of ignorance, he dedicated himself to transporting rather than killing them. Their magic baffled him, threatening to destroy him unexpectedly and without glory. They had become annoying obstacles in a dilemma that now involved them only as they could become Odin's directed toys. He suspected that one of these times the AllFather would back them. Already grossly unfair, the battle would tip wholly into law's favor.

The magic swirled around Colbey, tingling incessantly. He could continue to ignore the summons, but doing so would gain him nothing. The sooner he finished these nuisance battles, the quicker he faced Odin and the less likely he would lose his own struggle to burgeoning chaos. With a touch to his hilt to assure the chaos sword remained in place, he surrendered to Idunn's call.

Magic surrounded Colbey, the prickling barely more insistent than the constant tide on chaos' world. Stagnant trees took shape on the horizon, followed by a blurry stretch of aqua. While he materialized, Colbey knew, nothing could strike him, not even the weapons of gods. But the instant the smear of color revealed itself as grassland, he dove sideways. Two swords sliced the spot where he had appeared, and he rolled to face Vidar and Vali at once.

Fierce, hot joy charged through Colbey as he realized he faced a "real" battle. He howled a challenge, lunging toward the half-brothers even as they cut for him. He glided around Vidar's blade to slam his sword against Vali's. They crashed together, ringing tinny echoes across Asgard's plain. He shouldered toward Vidar to disrupt a stab, only to slam against an invisible barrier.

Magic shield! the sword/staff sent.

Air whistled through Colbey's teeth, and he eeled just far enough to turn Vidar's death thrust into a painful skim across his right hip. *Thanks for the warning.* Keeping his shoulder against the barrier, Colbey rolled around it. A cut at Vidar sent the god leaping backward, and the support of the shield disappeared. Colbey turned a stumble into a graceful dodge that rescued him from a whipping slash of Vali's blade for his head. Colbey riposted with a wild flurry of attack that sent Vali into a scurrying retreat. Then Vidar leaped in to seize Colbey's attention.

Magic wielder's two lengths off your left flank.

Colbey launched into a spiraling attack/defense combination that confounded direction. His sword belled against Vidar's and Vali's in rapid sequence, then he bore in on Vali. His sword slammed another solid, invisible barrier, jarring his arm to the elbow. He cursed. Vidar slashed for the opening, even as Colbey deliberately bounced from the shield. He parried the attack, gouging for Vidar's wrist. The tip of his sword licked across the pommel stone, a perfect disarming maneuver.

Before Colbey could savor his triumph, fiery pain pierced his chest, shocking through his entire body. Thunder hammered his ears, deafening. He collapsed. Vali charged him with sword raised in victory. Colbey's nostrils were thick with the odor of ozone. He choked, forcing a roll from a body that obeyed sluggishly. Ringing filled his hearing.

It was the magic-wielder who hit you.

Damn. Colbey managed to wriggle around Vali's strike, catching Vidar's reclaimed weapon on a sword barely supported by a tingling arm. The force drove his own hilt into his face, and he barely managed to find his feet. *Can't take another.*

Then move! the sword screamed.

Light slashed the corner of Colbey's vision. He lurched forward, the movement more desperate crawl than evasion. Lightning stabbed the place he had lain, raising every hair. A painful tremor jarred through every part that touched the ground. He forced himself to his feet, his body nearly defying his will.

I'm transporting us back.

"No!" Colbey croaked aloud, surprised at the rasp of his own voice. He had never run from a fight. Never would. He managed an awkward parry of Vidar's strike that weakened his grip. Then Vidar's sword slammed Colbey's, knocking the hilt from his hand. Colbey scrambled for it, only to find two blades in his face. He jerked backward, saving himself from one. The other sliced his forehead. Blood oozed, warm and stinging, into his eyes. For the first time ever, Colbey's sword struck the ground. Without the contact of his hand, it could not force a transport.

Though Colbey's consciousness swam, he remained acutely aware of the position of all three of his enemies. He recognized an unformed spell at his back as he managed a defensive crouch. "I killed only Baldur. Odin—"

"Save your last breath." Vali rocketed in for the kill, Vidar joining him. Idunn's spell rushed for Colbey simultaneously.

Exhausted, Colbey measured the three, preparing his evasions in an instant. All possibilities fell short. He could dodge two attacks, but the third would surely claim him. Unwilling to surrender, he launched into a nimble sequence. He saw magic shatter the stillness, brilliant and wild. The swords sped toward him, their wielders' speed more like flight.

Though Colbey had sought this end since childhood, an honor to die at the hand of three gods, sadness tainted the glory of his moment. His doom would drag the world down with it. He whipped into a shimmering spin, his usually deadly speed ruined by pain. Then, suddenly, a burst of chaos cut the air around him. Idunn's spell channeled directly to this interference. Vidar and Vali reached it nearly simultaneously. Light exploded through a savage spectrum, bolts shooting between them like javelins. The gods dropped silently to the ground.

Jerking free of his frenzied diversion, Colbey whirled to face this new threat. His spiral revealed Idunn, too, lying still, facedown in Asgard's grassland. He used mental communication, which allowed for more in less time. *Odin, you coward! Wiser to wait until they killed me, too. Or do you believe the one who's figured out your game easier to handle?*

The being who stepped around a sculpted copse of trees sported golden hair in seven war braids, handsome features, and eyes too much like Freya's own. Suddenly, Colbey wished he'd chosen speech. He could have bitten off words, but he could not stop his sending in time. "Frey? You did this?" He made a broad gesture to indicate the fallen gods, using it also as an excuse to search for Odin and to locate his sword. "Why?"

"I wanted to hear what you had to say."

Colbey blinked, still awaiting a trap. Odin had to stand behind anything that made absolutely no sense. "Enough to kill your own peers?"

Frey circled Colbey without evident weaponry. "They're not dead, Colbey. Is my sister?"

"No." The Renshai swiveled, following Frey's movement without a step in any direction. "Nor Ravn, Modi, Sif, or Magni. You would have to ask Odin about the others."

Frey stopped at Colbey's sword and bent to heft it.

"Don't," Colbey warned.

Gracefully stooped, Frey looked askance at Colbey.

"The Staff of Chaos would love another wielder." Colbey tried not to offend. "You're likely strong enough to repel it, but why take the chance?"

Frey rose. "I was going to toss it back to you. A show of trust."

Colbey read the situation accurately. "Your previous display was more than enough." Again, he indicated Vidar, Vali, and Idunn. "And I don't believe you're the one who needs to win trust." He did not disparage the gesture by pointing out that he could have Vidar's or Vali's sword in his hand faster than Frey would think to stop him.

Frey retreated with a grand gesture intended to indicate Colbey should collect his own sword. A mild wave of uncertainty and need wafted from him. Frey worried that he had made a mistake, and he needed reassurance.

Colbey had little to give. He had already attempted to win the gods' trust, without success. Few moves remained to him. "It's safer not to talk here. I could take you where Odin can't overhear."

Frey shook his head. "I'm not ready for that yet. Convince me, and I'll trust you enough to go where you ask. Otherwise, I risk nothing by staying here."

The argument made sense. Colbey glanced about to make certain the others did not move. He collected his sword so as not to belittle Frey's gesture, sheathing it immediately as an equally strong signal. "It's as I said before. Odin plans to destroy us all to pave the way for a new world created by and devoted wholly to him. What he doesn't seem to realize is the hold law gained over him." Colbey pointed at an Asgard gone dormant, sprinkled with identical trees and grasses all exactly the same height and missing the once-intermittent breeze. "He will destroy our worlds for a new one that cannot sustain itself, devoid of newness and wonder, of creation and genius."

Frey shuffled a foot. "Is that Colbey talking? Or chaos?"

"I'm not denying chaos has had an effect on me as well. The difference is, I didn't bind. Dh'arlo'mé clearly did."

Frey could hardly deny the last statement. "Prove you haven't."

Colbey sighed. Doing so would require Frey to grasp the Staff of Chaos, too dangerous to allow. "I can't."

"Come here." Frey beckoned with a toss of his head.

Colbey obeyed, limping toward Frey with more difficulty than he expected. His insides felt charred, his consciousness tenuous.

Suddenly, Frey lashed a hand for Colbey's face. He jerked backward, too slow. The blow landed, leaving stinging, finger-shaped blotches of redness against the pale skin.

"Ow!" Colbey stumbled but did not draw his sword. "Why in coldest, darkest Hel did you do that?"

Frey massaged the offending hand with the other. "Because I just proved your point."

Colbey stared.

"Nothing of law can strike pure chaos. I am a being of law. If you had bound . . ."

Colbey finished, ". . . you couldn't have hit me." The simplicity of the affirmation floored him. "Why didn't I think of that before?" His tone turned accusing, "Why didn't *you?*"

"I don't know," Frey admitted. "High emotions, perhaps. More likely, Odin masked it, like a lot of things. You and I seem less susceptible to his mind-powers. I can't explain why for certain, but I believe defying him once breeds the skepticism to challenge again. I cheated him at the creation and gained life for the elves; you stress him daily."

Though Colbey wanted to hear the story of the elves' beginning, especially the part where Frey bested Odin, he allowed his only ally on Asgard to finish.

"I got suspicious when gods kept disappearing, but Odin's brilliant plan never came to fruition. Then he wanted me to kill Sif with you when calling others in to help would have worked better. You saved me at the *Ragnarok*. Though you doomed the elves in order to rescue mankind, I owe you my life. And, given how the elves have forsaken me, I can't help wondering if you didn't push me into the better choice." He lowered his head, deliberately and awkwardly changing tactics. "The others are alive?"

"The ones I named. The ones Odin 'handled' in my name are likely dead."

Frey ignored the latter statement for the former. "Safe?"

"Yes."

"Take these there, then." Frey indicated the fallen gods. "And count me on your side. The survivors can take care of Odin together."

Colbey pursed his lips. "No."

"No?"

"It would be too easy for Odin to turn them against me again during battle. He's already an enemy too strong for me. Better I destroy him—or die alone."

"Now that's chaos talking."

"No." Colbey shook his head, wondering if Frey and his sister would ever understand. "It's a matter of security and survival. Are you coming?"

"No," Frey said.

Disappointment rocked Colbey. He had fully expected the opposite answer. "Then I'll take these three. For their own protection."

Frey nodded. "Take them."

"And you?"

Frey met Colbey's eyes. "I can't let you lock me up to save me any more than you would let me do so for you."

"Even I'm not insane enough to stay here. Odin surely saw every action, heard every word. It's a wonder he's not here now, attacking while I'm weak. Frey, he will kill you."

"He can try," Frey said crisply, eyes betraying no fear.

Colbey smiled. "You would have made a good Renshai."

Frey laughed at the sacrilege.

Clouds gathered over the Ífing River, smearing sunlight into a dense glaze. On its opposite bank, the eternal beauty of Asgard stood in splendid contrast to the bleary reality of Jötunheim, the world of giants. Centuries earlier, Surtr's fire had scoured the land, leaving only a vast wasteland. Now fertile soil awaited the landing of a single seed to repopulate the shattered lands, without success. The river that separated the worlds allowed nothing to cross it; the gentle breezes that had once played across Asgard did not have the power to breach it.

Standing on a barren delta with his companions, Tae studied a citadel that perched on neither plane, a crumbling edifice of stone that defined a world between the two. In Captain's place, Marrih's magic had brought the shard-seekers here, and El-brinith's spell located the Pica fragment inside the only building of this tiny world. "What is this place?" he wondered aloud.

To his surprise, Andvari had an answer; and he delivered it in song:

> *"Between the arms of Ífing bright*
> *Lies Ugagnevangar,*
> *Dark Plain of Misfortune,*
> *And perched on it Loki's estate*
> *Brysombolig."*

Tae glanced at Darris. "Don't tell me it's contagious."

"Brysombolig," Kevral translated, "means 'Troublesome House'. It's supposedly where Loki lived until the gods punished his deadly mischief by binding him to a stone in Hel beneath the dripping venom of a snake."

Though Tae had heard the myth before, he could not suppress a shiver at the image. "So, it's long abandoned." He ignored Rascal at his side.

Ra-khir nodded. "It would certainly seem so. Though, if such a place existed on Midgard, I doubt it would stay empty long."

Chan'rék'ril studied the terrain. "No giants left to move in, and the gods have halls of their own. Even if they didn't, I would think they would rather build one than use the outcast's."

"I wonder," El-brinith said, leaving the statement unfinished.

Politely, everyone awaited more. When nothing came for several moments, Kevral asked, "Wonder what, El-brinith?"

Though the elf had clearly intended to keep the rest of the thought to herself, when Kevral pressed, she continued. "I wonder if Alfheim looks like this." She made a short, brisk gesture toward the ruins of Jötunheim.

"Very likely," Chan'rék'ril supplied. He turned El-brinith a sad look. "Do not entertain thoughts of recreating it. The plant life there was unique and its balance the reason for its lack of weather and its unparalleled cycles of nature. At best, we could turn Alfheim into a smaller version of Midgard." He shook his head at the image, and his left cheek twitched. "Then would come the problems with portals, the need for transport . . ."

Tae forestalled a long discussion on the relative merits of elves living among or separate from humans. It seemed equally likely that Alfheim had exploded into pieces as minute as the Pica shards. "So, nothing lives in Troublesome House. That should make things simple."

"That should make things simple," Ra-khir repeated. "The last words of many men." He smiled at Tae to show he meant no offense. "Much of this task seemed easy at first glance, but none of it has turned out that way."

Andvari took Tae's side. "But this time we have an estate abandoned for centuries and nothing living anywhere nearby."

"Let's go." Kevral charged forward boldly. Within two strides, the ground collapsed beneath her, and she disappeared into a hole that widened before their startled eyes. An instant later, Darris and El-brinith disappeared. The others managed to scramble backward fast enough to avoid the expanding edge. As Tae gathered his wits, Chan'rék'ril dove purposefully after the others.

The hole stopped growing, and Tae crept cautiously to the edge. The sides swiftly fell away into a darkness as black as pitch. No sound escaped the opening, nothing to indicate that anything heavy had struck a solid bottom. "Gods," he breathed, terror creeping over him. More than enough time had passed for his companions to have plummeted to their deaths or found a steady surface from which to shout or climb. Gingerly, he poked the side, worried about restarting the dilation. Clay crumbled beneath his touch, swallowed by the gloom. He did not bother to shout. The vibrations of his call could trigger an avalanche. He hoped that was what kept the others quiet as well.

Ra-khir drew to Tae's side. "What do you see?" Worry tainted his tone.

Tae shook his head, saying nothing.

"No," Ra-khir whispered, adding nothing more. They all knew they could die on this quest, even as suddenly as this had occurred.

Andvari joined them. "I've seen earthquakes, but never so quiet. Nothing like this."

Tae lowered himself to his haunches. "This wasn't an earthquake."

Before he could explain further, El-brinith flew from the opening, clutching Darris against her smaller body. She panted, and sweat plastered her red-blond hair to her cheeks. Landing on the far side of the men, she dumped Darris unceremoniously to the ground.

Tae, Ra-khir, and Andvari rushed to attend. "Are you all right?" they asked, nearly simultaneously.

Neither El-brinith nor Darris answered, each assuming the three had addressed the other. El-brinith darted back into the hole, leaving them with only a haunting *khohlar:* *Have to try.*

Darris finally replied, "I'm fine." To demonstrate, he rose to legs shaky from shock, not injury. "If there's a bottom to that hole, we never found it. I believe Chan'rék'ril went after Kevral." He stopped at description; any speculation would require song, which seemed inappropriate at the moment.

Tae's thoughts raced, seeking anything that might aid the situation. His mind brought no answers but a comfort born of an eerie idea. If the Chaos Lord's magic indeed rendered the fall infinite, Kevral and Chan'rék'ril could never strike a bottom. The elf might manage to rescue Kevral. Logic intervened. The two would eventually reach a depth that Chan'rék'ril's strength could not overcome, and an eternity spent falling would prove no kindness. The longer they remained in the hole, the less likely they would ever return.

Ra-khir started stripping off armor he had donned in case this task proved as much a battle as the last. "I'm going after her."

Tae interposed himself between the knight and the hole, though he did not turn.

Andvari seized Ra-khir's arm. "There's nothing you can do." The Northman spoke the simple truth.

Tae nodded, staring into the darkness. He had come to the conclusion that the hole had to have a bottom, no matter its depth. Memories surfaced of his plunge from the side of Béarn Castle, the instant dragged to eternity by terror while air shrieked past his ears, then the bruising slam of his body against ice that mercifully gave beneath him. If it hadn't, he would have died there. Finally, he swiveled his head to Ra-khir. The knight's green eyes glazed with agony. Tae supposed he relived his own, more recent, fall, assuming unconsciousness had not stolen the recollection. It only remained to discover whether Chan'rék'ril caught Kevral before the bottom, without crashing into it himself in his rush to dive below her. And whether he had the power to haul her back to the top.

Tae glanced back into the hole and saw movement. A rush of excitement warmed him before he could think to keep it guarded. He stiffened, a clear signal that sent the other three rushing to his side. A moment later, Kevral's head emerged from the hole, El-brinith and Chan'rék'ril struggling to support her. Ra-khir reached dangerously far out over the chasm, Tae, Darris, and Andvari scrambling to steady him. Kevral leaned, managing to catch Ra-khir's wrists as he caught hers. Chan'rék'ril faltered, scrabbling for a hold. Tae loosed Ra-khir as Darris and Andvari dragged the knight and his new burden from the edge. Tae grabbed for Chan'rék'ril, guiding the elf's small hands to the lip. With El-brinith's assistance, he managed to lug Chan'rék'ril partway across the verge. While he lay there, panting, El-brinith struggled over the edge as well.

Tae let them rest, though he worried for the stability of the ground beneath them. At any moment, it could collapse, pitching them back into a fall they no longer had the strength to battle. He clung to Chan'rék'ril's hands, doubting his grip could manage much more than assuring he fell with the elf. Then, suddenly, Ra-khir clasped Chan'rék'ril's forearms. Andvari and Darris held El-brinith. The three hauled the elves to safety.

"I'm fine," Kevral said, anticipating the question. "I'd always heard that when you're falling, a few stories feels like a million lengths. It seemed like we fell forever, and the way back up didn't seem any shorter."

Darris' eyes widened, and he tipped his head, pleading for someone to rescue him from the need to sing.

Tae tried, "As long as you were down there, it almost had to be a million lengths for you not to strike bottom." He glanced at Darris to see if he had handled it all, but the bard still wanted more. "If there even is a bottom."

"They's allus a bottom." Rascal spoke her first words since their arrival, sitting well beyond the danger. She had not assisted.

"I believe I saw it, too." Kevral glanced at Chan'rék'ril for confirmation. "The air grew suddenly, intensely cold. The darkness opened to a dull gray, and I thought I saw a cavern. Some movement, maybe. Then, the elf caught up with me."

Chan'rék'ril sucked air in gasps. He could not have spoken, but his *khohlar* reached them clearly. *It was Hel. Had we reached it, we could not have returned.*

El-brinith rolled her head toward her fellow. *Elves don't wind up there.*

I would have been the first. I had to fight its pull even as close as I came. I don't think I could have escaped.

"Elves don't go to Hel when they die?" Tae studied the breathless outworlders. "What happens to them?"

Kevral changed the subject awkwardly. "How twistedly ironic. Dying a death without glory and winding up in Hel, body as well as soul. I wonder what would have happened to me?"

"Let's not find out, all right?" Ra-khir followed Kevral's tack rather than press Tae's question, to the Easterner's surprise. Of them all, Ra-khir most wanted to understand the afterlife.

Tae glanced at each of his human companions in turn. Darris, Kevral, and Ra-khir all returned cautioning looks. They knew something about elfin afterlife that they did not want to become common knowledge. He only hoped they could read his own silent communication. He would drop the subject for now but expected a full explanation when Andvari and Rascal were not among them.

Tae suspected Chan'rék'ril had evaded a worse fate. He also lacked a soul. Since he had flown down, he might not have died on impact. A living creature trapped for eternity in Hel seemed the worst possible fate.

Andvari smoothed his tunic and shook dirt from his braids. Wound through with trinkets and feathers, they clicked together with the movement. "Tae, earlier you said you didn't believe this was an earthquake. What did you mean by that?"

Andvari's memory of an offhand comment in such a tense situation surprised Tae, but he knew his reply would shock his companions more. "I believe this was a deliberate trap."

Every eye found its way to Tae. Rascal questioned first. "Ya thinks some 'un dugged a pit alla way ta Hel so's we ud not git a piecea stone?"

"Not necessarily us," Ra-khir corrected. "Nor to protect the Pica shard." His eyes narrowed as he considered the unlikeliness of even a general trap. "It seems awfully dangerous to protect a citadel in such a way. Come home late one night. Tired. In the dark." He made a falling motion with his hand. "Not to mention the danger to legitimate guests."

"I doubt the Father of Lies had a lot of legitimate guests," Andvari pointed out. "By legend, Loki led the hordes of Hel at the *Ragnarok*. It probably didn't pose any particular danger to him."

"Poison's dangerous to the bearer, too," Tae said, certain his companions would remember how Kevral had nearly died from a superficial wound because of a toxic arrow. "But it doesn't stop some people from painting it on their weapons."

"It would fit Loki's humor to make a pitfall that drops you to Hel." Kevral walked kinks from muscles surely knotted in fright during her lengthy fall. She stopped at Tae's side. "What makes you so sure it's unnatural?"

Tae hated to admit he had expertise in the matter. His father's myriad enemies had made hiding a priority, and Weile had sometimes warded his secret refuges with the most devious traps his followers could design. Tae had also learned much from the thieves in his father's employ who bragged about evading the best tricks of kings and rivals. His own experiences came mostly from avoiding the snares his father's enemies set for him as he fled from Eastlands to Westlands, and the sweeps of soldiers attempting to eliminate the gangs with which he had run in his teens. "The speed of its fall and the regularity of its spread suggested an unstable surface bridging a predug hole. Also, the soil on the lips isn't fresh."

Darris still seemed unconvinced. "No one could dig a hole that deep. Where would he put all the dirt?"

"Magic could." Chan'rék'ril finally returned to normal speech. Tae noticed the elves seemed to prefer it, apparently because they could more easily control how far their speaking voice carried. They mostly used *khohlar* when engaged in singular conversation when they did not wish others to overhear.

"But he wouldn't trap the *inside* of his home," Kevral tried, attention fully on Tae. "Would he?"

"Troublesome House." Tae despised his answer. "I think we can count on it." He noticed that most of his companions studied the hole to Hel warily. "Once you get used to walking in certain ways, to avoiding certain areas, to unlatching in certain sequences, you can learn to live with a house full of traps."

Ra-khir rescued the shed pieces of armor. "Not lethal ones, though. Why would anyone risk dying in his own home?"

Andvari said, "What's lethal to us might not be to a god."

Tae had another answer. "If your system for avoiding your own traps is strong enough, the danger is immaterial."

Ra-khir looked up from his work. "Not really."

Tae shrugged. "Really enough. From what I understand of Northern/ Western religion, Loki started out mischievous and became more evil over time. Opposing the gods and working toward world destruction does not strike me as particularly self-preserving. Or merciful."

El-brinith found a sitting position, her voice soft and weak. "Are you suggesting we give up now?" She rolled her eyes toward the pit. "I don't think I could do that again."

"I know I couldn't," Chan'rék'ril added. "Not without a long rest first." He paused, before inserting, "Probably not even then."

Tae had to explain, though he knew his words would not comfort. "Surely Loki had more imagination than to use the same trick repeatedly. Each one will likely pose a unique challenge."

"Tae," Ra-khir said in a teasing singsong. "You sound almost excited."

Tae snorted. "You're mistaking me for your wife, Red. Only a Renshai could find entertainment in charging toward death. If we didn't have so much at stake, I'd suggest we turn back."

"Ev'n if'n there'd be piles o' gold inside?"

"Even if'n," Tae responded to Rascal's query. "My life's worth more, thank you. And you can bet anything valuable is surrounded by the worst Loki has to offer."

"Like the Pica shard?" Kevral offered.

Tae doubted it. "A chip of sapphire without magic? A curiosity at best. It's surprising enough that any god would place enough value on it to bother keeping it in his home."

"So." Darris summarized, sticking with information already divulged by his companions to rescue them from an aria. "We've got the shard in a house probably full of lethal traps. Unless you're wrong, Tae, it sounds hopeless."

Tae hated to play both sides, but he saw no recourse. "I'd venture to guess that every trap in that house can either be dodged, easily dismantled, or avoided. Otherwise, Loki could not have lived there."

Darris rocked his head from side to side. "That seems logical. But how can you possibly know Loki's method for skirting every one?"

"We can't," Tae admitted, only then realizing another among them might have some experience with locks, snares, and pits. "But we can apply logic. Something has to trigger a trap, or it would activate at random. Trips, no matter how well camouflaged, can be found. Unstable surfaces leave cracks and often don't lie flush. If we move slowly, stay alert . . ." He shrugged. "We have a reasonable chance of finding the dangers before we trigger them. Ninety percent of an effective trap is surprise, and we've already negated that by realizing they probably exist.

"Once we find the mechanisms, we should be able to figure out the essence of the trap. And dismantle or avoid it." Tae glanced about to find every eye intent on him. He realized they expected him to bring them all safely through the Trickster's deadly pranks, a trust he seemed likely to betray. The hunting snares of Weile Kahn's enemies could not compare to a god's complexity, and he had never had to locate or to evade the deterrents constructed for his father.

Tae sighed, accepting the responsibility. "No one likes splitting the group, but it might prove best this time." When no one questioned his reason, Tae explained anyway. "The fewer who go, the less area we cover and the less we weigh as a group. Gives us a better chance to randomly avoid trouble."

Ra-khir folded his arms over his chest, apparently willing to listen but not wholly convinced about the need to separate. Tae guessed the particulars of his division would sway the knight one way or the other.

"I'll go, of course." The complete lack of reaction made it clear Tae had read their attention properly. "Only an elf could find something activated in a magical fashion."

"I'm best," El-brinith said. "Feeling magic. Separating and defining it. I'm good at that."

Tae knew that from their encounter with the spirit spiders.

Chan'rék'ril made a gentle gesture with his fingers that meant nothing to Tae. "You should have me, too. In case El-brinith misses something. I'm an artist, so I might have a better eye for determining detail. And I've got more healing practice should something go wrong."

Tae did not voice the opinion that, if something went wrong, healing would likely not suffice. "Thank you. I'm certain we all have talents to add, but we can't afford duplication. In this case, avoiding danger seems more important than coping with the aftermath. El-brinith could serve the cause better, if she's willing."

"I am," the female elf assured.

Tae continued his list, "I'll need someone with an excellent grasp of the religion."

"That's me." Andvari volunteered enthusiastically, cut short by a withering glare from Kevral.

"Or me," she said. "Did you think living in the North gives you more knowledge?"

"No, I didn't." Andvari backed down, not for the first time. "I just, I mean I thought—"

Tae had tired of the bickering. He knew Kevral's bullheaded loyalty to her people caused most of the problem, but Andvari's lackluster attempts to tiptoe around offense played a role as well. "Don't let her get away with that."

Andvari and Kevral both jerked toward Tae.

"You're not going to get respect from Kevral, or any Renshai, unless you fight back."

"What?" Andvari managed.

"Look, you both know she's Renshai and you're Nordmirian." Tae gestured at each in turn. "Stop worrying that you might commit the sin of saying the wrong thing. Just say what you mean."

Andvari considered the words several moments, studying Tae. His expression fairly pleaded with the Easterner not to trick him into worsening the situation.

Kevral's look turned hard, but she no longer faced off with Andvari. Now Tae weathered her glare, a much safer target. Strong, like everything about her, her derision could wound as deeply as her sword. He had suffered it, too, but never as severely as Ra-khir. It had taken him embarrassingly long to finally realize that those whose pride stemmed from their sword work became the casualties of her contempt. Andvari could redeem himself by demonstrating warrior competence, but he had not had the opportunity to do so. Strength in words might, at least, lighten her attitude. "Do it," Tae said.

Andvari turned his gaze to Kevral. For once, his blue eyes did not dodge hers. "Stop treating me like something you clean from your sword after a battle. I volunteered to accompany Tae and El-brinith because I've got a good grasp of Northern religion and a good fighting arm, not because I believe you don't have those things. Not everything I say or do has anything to do with you."

The hostility vanished from Kevral's face, leaving something akin to appreciation. She glanced from Tae to Ra-khir, who nodded. Finally, she turned her attention to Andvari. "Accepted. I offer myself for the position as well."

Tae sighed, hating the dilemma he had created. He could not afford to take them both, and he knew which one he most trusted at his side. He gestured to the pit. "Easily triggered, but only in the center. Inside,

Loki wouldn't have had the luxury of space. Poking ahead should reveal anything likely to disappear beneath our feet, unless it requires more weight. I'd prefer taking only companions lighter than me, though I'll defer to the group's decisions."

Kevral saw through to the significant. "That's me."

Tae nodded. "And El-brinith." He searched for the quietest of their companions, finding her standing apart and well away from the edge of the chasm. "And Rascal, if she wishes to come."

The girl looked up through a ratty snarl of brown bangs. "Oh, yeah. I's be wantin' ta git misself killed."

"Might learn something useful." Tae tried to entice. Ordinarily, he would have preferred to leave the babysitting to others, but he suspected Rascal could prove more useful than any of them believed. Her thieving surely gave her some experience, and she could fit into small places that Kevral could ordinarily handle, if not for her grossly swollen abdomen.

Rascal said nothing.

Tae gave her a furtive look, brows highly arched. "Think about it." He had the words to convince her, a simple description of the wealth of the robbery victims who could afford such protections. Learning to dodge or disarm the simplest of Loki's traps could get her past the defenses of the most paranoid noble. He did not dare speak the idea aloud, knowing Ra-khir would not approve.

Rascal's hazel eyes narrowed, then widened. Her fingers twitched at her side. "I'll go." She made it sound as if she did Tae a reluctant favor, fooling no one. They all knew her well enough to realize she would perform no action that did not directly benefit herself.

Ra-khir sighed, but he did not pry or chastise. "You'll need at least one more sword."

Tae shook his head. "It's not going to be that kind of fight."

"How do you know?" Andvari asked.

In truth, Tae had no way to know what they would face. It would not surprise him to find no traps or tricks at all. "We know Loki's dead some three hundred years, and his house lay vacant for several centuries prior even to that. Anything alive inside would have succumbed long ago. No one's come by here, or they would have triggered that pit before us."

"Magic," Kevral tried.

"Cannot create," El-brinith reminded. "Especially living things. Anything onto which he placed transport magic would also have died long ago."

Ra-khir found the loophole. "Gods create."

Andvari had the answer to that concern. "Not Loki. He represented fire, destruction. He dedicated himself exclusively to ruining what the others made."

"Let's go." Tae looked at the citadel, training mind and eyes toward details. "Safety requires we work very slowly."

"How slowly?" Ra-khir reached for Kevral.

Tae found a suitable example. "Remember when Darris led you through the catacombs to release your father from the dungeon?"

Ra-khir paled. Ancient builders had designed the dark, twisted maze to assure that escaped prisoners died rather than found their way out. Only the bard and his or her heir memorized the proper route, and any deviation spelled death in aimless wandering. Then, Tae had followed Ra-khir and Darris, placing markers so that he could find his own way out as well. Groping for slashes in moss and dropped possessions had nearly driven Tae to madness when circumstance forced him to free the knights' captain by himself. Now, he suspected, this task would prove nearly as difficult. He consoled himself with the realization that, if he failed, death would at least come swiftly. "That slow?"

"Slower."

"Slower?" Ra-khir rolled his eyes from Kevral to Tae, the signal clear. Kevral might not have the patience to accompany him.

Tae shrugged. He could not help agreeing, but his need for lighter weight companions, though true, told only half the story. If combat did occur, a Renshai of Kevral's competence, even nearly eight months pregnant, was worth any three Northmen or Knights of Erythane. Soon enough, he would find himself embroiled in minutiae. For now, he needed to lighten the mood. "Let's put it this way. If we're not back in two months, consider us lost forever."

Kevral rubbed her abdomen. "If we're not back in a month or so, look for five of us."

Darris winked. "Admit it, Tae. You just like being surrounded by women." He made a motion to indicate Tae had chosen only female companions.

"An elf, a child, and a pregnant, married Renshai who could kill me anytime she wanted." Tae smiled tolerantly. "Aren't I clever?" It surprised him how easily the words emerged. Any bitterness he harbored against Ra-khir had disappeared, and he found himself in no particular hurry for a family. If he discovered the right woman, he would treasure her. If not, he had Subikahn and his friends to fill the emotional void; and he doubted a prince would have difficulty with the physical one either. Realizing he had become the one stalling, Tae went serious. "If we get into trouble, El-brinith will signal."

Andvari, Darris, and Ra-khir nodded.

Tae detailed his strategy. "No matter how slow I'm moving, let me have the front unless I ask for help. Follow in my footsteps, exactly if you can." Realizing he would probably spend most of his time low, the logical location of most triggers, he amended, "Or hand and knee prints as the case may be. El-brinith, I'd like you directly behind me. Sing out if any magic looks suspicious, preferably before I blunder into it. Any questions?"

"Is I gonna git to see nothin'?"

Tae glanced back at Rascal. "I'll make sure you know whenever I find something interesting."

Kevral piped in, "Constant description might keep me from dying of boredom, too."

Tae flinched. Sound might trigger traps, though not as easily as touch or weight. "I'll let you know what I'm doing. Otherwise keep quiet as much as you can. Please. And pay attention to the route. We'll need to find our way back, and it can happen much more quickly if I don't have to find the exact same things I did on the way in." This time, he did not solicit opinions, worried that they might never get started.

Center of gravity low, Tae hunched around the pit, across the stretch of grass leading to Loki's estate. Eyes and ears tuned to breaking, he explored each upcoming step with a cautious placement of part of his weight upon it, tensed to spring in any direction. By the time he safely reached the doorway, his eyes burned, tearing. His shoulders ached from his position, and he worried about the sanity of continuing the search. He could not help wondering if the immortal Trickster hoped unexpected visitors would kill themselves with their own caution. He edged toward the door to examine it more closely.

A thin wire jutting near the knob caught Tae's attention almost immediately. He headed toward it for a better look.

As he moved, El-brinith cautioned. *There's a concentrated band of magic near your feet.*

Tae froze, then carefully back-stepped. "Where?"

There. El-brinith pointed, the gesture too vague for Tae's liking. She spoke a word outside Tae's understanding, then spread her hands, fingers wide apart. Dust rose from the ground, swimming around a bar of dense light that hovered just off the ground in front of him. Though easily avoided by a high step, it first required seeing. Focused on the wire, he would likely have missed the magic, even if he had El-brinith's talent.

Expect a lot of this, Tae warned himself. The strategy of placing an obvious trap just beyond a subtle one made sense. Attention locked on the second, the best would-be thief would likely trip the first. Tae amended the thought. Loki probably did not worry about robbers but for neighboring giants and gods. *Traps in twos and threes designed to stop massive creatures and deities. Great.* Now, more than before, he appreciated the relative slightness of his companions. And the need to find snares without activating them.

"Rascal."

The Pudarian approached Tae hesitantly.

"Help me figure this out."

For longer than an hour, the two followed angles and speculated about the nature of the trap. At first, the girl contributed little. Over time, she discovered the mechanical portion of her mind, a marvelously complicated area that she clearly had used only intuitively in the past. A half hour brought the realization that Loki had interwoven the two traps, assuring that those who made it past the magical trigger fell prey to the solid reality of the second.

Kevral attempted to practice sword forms, stopped by a vicious shake of Tae's head. Conversely, the elf seemed unbothered by the delay, patience the virtue of the near immortal. Kevral found a position hunkered in the grass that did not appease her long. She paced; but, as she managed to keep her movements confined to areas already explored, Tae did not attempt to stop her. "Why don't you just take the door off its hinges. Loki wouldn't have expected that."

Rascal snorted and rolled her eyes which, luckily, Kevral did not see. Near an answer, Tae shook his head without turning from his scrutiny. "Remember, Kevral. Loki would set things up so that those ignorant, reckless, or sneaky would suffer. He'd go insane living in a home that he couldn't enter and leave swiftly."

"Insane is precisely how most would describe the creature who started the *Ragnarok,* then opposed the gods, all the while knowing they would kill him."

Tae had to concede the point, though he did so without looking from the magical and mechanical devices and the inferences that had to take the place of what lay hidden behind the door. "Even the insane tolerate only so much inconvenience." He looked at Rascal. "What do you think? Press the wire against the door and trip the latch at the same time?"

Rascal smiled, for the first time not accompanied by a smirk. "That'd be my guess." She could not help adding, "Ya goes first."

Eyes open, Tae did as he had suggested, poised for danger. When nothing untoward happened, he eased open the panel to reveal a room caked with dust. Every wall held an entryway. Lumps that represented rotted objects, possibly furniture, lay strewn around the room, the only identifiable object a filthy scaffolding that held a massive spear pointed directly at him. The wire branched, one part leading to the device, the other running along the jamb to the floor near his feet. Tae froze, afraid to let go.

El-brinith came to his side.

"Careful," Tae whispered.

El-brinith did not acknowledge the cautioning. *Two disturbances.* She spoke the same word as out on the porch, made a similar gesture. Copious dust flashed upward to highlight a narrow strip spanning the center of the room at about the height of his forehead. Another set criss-crossed madly in the exit to the right of the door.

"Don't stand in line with the door," Tae instructed. "And don't come any closer." Easing his thumb from the wire, he dove sideways. An ancient rug disintegrated, and his shoulder slammed the stone floor. Rolling to his feet, he studied the spear. It looked no different than before. Nothing had changed where the wire stabbed into the floor either. Apparently, he had found the sequence that temporarily disarmed the traps and made entry safe. Now, he could see that the open panel kept the wires lax.

Rising, Tae sighed. Their time away might seem long to those waiting, but to him it would stretch into infinity. He peered back outside. El-brinith waited near the entryway. The others dutifully hung back, and he could see Darris, Ra-khir, Andvari, and Chan'rék'ril watching him also. He made a crisp, sideways motion of his open palm, a curt greeting. Then he turned his attention fully to Kevral and Rascal. "Step over the bar without touching it." He jabbed a finger toward the magic El-brinith had detected in front of the door. "Then it seems safe to come in. Best to leave the door open."

Without waiting to see if they complied, Tae ducked under the magical trigger in the room. He gestured for El-brinith to accompany him. "I assume we need to go that way." He pointed to the web of magic.

El-brinith followed Tae's finger with her gaze. "I'd guess straight ahead. But I don't have a whole lot of experience with buildings."

Tae turned his attention to the indicated exit, filled with spear and scaffolding that could hide any number of tiny devices, wires, magics, and springs. Until he saw the moldering, dust-caked furniture, it had not occurred to him that the decay of time might not only have harmlessly triggered some of the Trickster's traps but might have ruined some of the built-in safety features that kept their creator from falling prey to his own inventions. Tae groaned. "That exit would have been my second guess." He glanced at Rascal, who came forward eagerly. As she approached the hovering magic, he shouted, "Duck!"

Rascal laughed, passing harmlessly under the bar. "Hain't thinkin' I knows where my head ends?"

Keep taking chances like that, and your head will "ends" up in pieces on the floor. Tae glanced at Kevral. "This will take a while."

Kevral met his gaze with pleading eyes. A finger traced the hilt of one sword.

"No, Kevral. Not here. El-brinith or I could have missed something. We can't take that chance."

Kevral let her hand sag. "Is it going to be like this the whole way?"

Tae nodded apologetically.

Kevral sucked in a deep breath, releasing it slowly. "Why don't I just save time and plunge into madness now?"

Tae turned back to the job, but not before turning her a cock-eyed smile. "As you please."

Béarn numbered rather than named its sea craft, yet Ship 90 morphed to *Sea Knighty* within a week of travel. During one of the ocean's calmest days, the elves pooled agility and magic to emblazon the name across the prow. Béarn might see it as vandalism, but Captain did not discourage the action. To him, it demonstrated respect for the most valuable tool of a sailor. They could always clean it when they returned.

CHAPTER 25

Relative Morality

When a force kills one's friends, it is evil. When the same force kills one's enemies, it becomes the blessed will of gods.
— *Colbey Calistinsson*

MORNING dragged into night. Black with dirt and mold, Tae's hands felt like ground sausages, raw with rub burns, scratches, and abrasions. He had worn holes into the knees of his britches, leaving nothing to protect bruised flesh. Sweat glued his hair to cheeks and forehead. His eyes burned, meaningless sound buzzed in his ears, and he had strained his mental powers past their breaking point. Rascal's enthusiasm had died to a spark. Increasingly more often, she simply shrugged or nodded to confirm his suspicions, rather than offer any suggestions of her own. Tae had successfully brought them past more than a hundred of Loki's tricks, though only time's ravages had rescued him from several. He had evaded his one failure with a quick jumping roll that had saved him from a pit filled with brackish water that had probably once held carnivorous fish or reptiles. Now it might have caused nothing worse than making him wet and foul-smelling, one more discomfort to weather with the others.

Tae lowered his head, shoulders aching. He had not taken them by a direct route, deliberately bypassing some of Loki's magical creations. These would most likely remain the most lethal, often inscrutable. In some instances, Tae found no means to avoid a touch. In others, he saw no connection between the trips and mechanical processes. A word or gesture probably rendered them passable, but Loki would not have posted those details for strangers to find. Surely, they had died with him. Tae only hoped their power had also diminished with time. Eventually, he worried, they could not avoid all of these.

"The shard should be near here." El-brinith's voice broke a long silence, and Tae stiffened, sending a jolt of pain through aching muscles. "Look carefully. If not in this room, it's close."

Tae blinked rapidly several times. His tear ducts seemed empty, and his too-dry eyes gave back blurry pictures. Hours ago, he had given up on chastising Kevral's fidgeting or silencing Rascal's complaints. Exhaustion plagued him, but boredom might prove the heavier burden for the others. Kevral had probably not gone without a practice this long before in her life. He dropped to a sitting position, too tired to bother with the others. He and El-brinith had studied the room with a caution that surely seemed like paranoia to the others. Even after so many victories, he still expected the immortal schemer to trip him up with something unforeseen. Tae did not even voice his discomfort when the others left formation to search, diligently stepping around or over the magical snarl El-brinith had revealed near an exit to the west.

"Here it is!" Kevral shouted suddenly. Her boot scraped over stone as she moved.

The call mobilized Tae, and he leaped to his feet faster than his cramped muscles preferred. Pain exploded through him, even as his eyes registered the scene. Kevral headed east, lunging leftward toward a staircase he had examined only cursorily. He had confined his scrutiny to the top step, otherwise he probably would have found the shard himself.

A click reached Tae's ears, barely differentiable from the constant ringing. He caught movement from an upper corner of his vision, above Kevral's head. "No!" He sprang at Kevral, slamming her safely aside. Ceiling stones collapsed around him as he toppled down the staircase. One crashed against his hand with an agony that wrenched out a scream. Then, the edge of a step smashed Tae's forehead, and he knew nothing more.

Once the traps had been disarmed or delineated, it did not take El-brinith long to guide Ra-khir, Andvari, Darris, and Chan'rék'ril through them. The five arrived to find Kevral pawing furiously through rubble. Feverish digging accomplished little, but she did not stop until Ra-khir took her in his arms and physically dragged her from the pile. Only then, she allowed the tears to flow. "I killed him," she croaked, voice muffled into Ra-khir's tunic. "It's all my fault."

"Stuppid ta cry," Rascal said without sympathy. "He knowed the danger when he comed. All us did."

Kevral would have throttled the ragged Pudarian had Ra-khir's strong arms not held her in place. "Frustrated. Impatient. Not thinking straight."

Chan'rék'ril knelt beside them. "Even with magic, it'll take at least a couple days to move all this."

Kevral rolled her eyes to Ra-khir, and he cringed. "Then we work for a couple of days."

The elf guarded his tongue. "Tae might need . . . attention. Two days might be . . . too long. More likely, it's already . . ."

Kevral gave him a fierce look.

"I'll do my best," Chan'rék'ril said. "I just don't want to raise unrealistic hopes."

El-brinith called Chan'rék'ril with a subtle gesture likely intended to silence him.

Andvari studied the situation. "It's a staircase, you say?" Tears filled his eyes as well. It seemed odd that the two trained to war fell prey to sorrow first.

Kevral nodded.

Andvari finished, "If he slid down far enough, it's possible he missed the worst of the debris."

Chan'rék'ril ran with the suggestion. "I could clear a space at the top. Someone small could climb through and assess the situation below. If we know where Tae is, it'll change the way we move the stones."

All eyes went naturally to Rascal, who scowled. "Hain't volunteerin'."

The urge to kill Rascal flared again. Kevral looked at the urchin from over Ra-khir's shoulder. "After all Tae's done for you, you won't scout for him? With his life at stake?"

Rascal balled her fists. "I seed what happent when he tried ta save ya. Now, he's daid an' ya's 'live." She turned away. "Hain't no one's life worth more'n mine."

Kevral gritted her teeth. *Yours isn't worth anything right now.*

Ra-khir tightened his grip. "It's her decision, Kevral."

Arguing the point would only waste valuable time. "I'll go," Kevral said. "It's only right."

"Begging your pardon, Lady." Chan'rék'ril shook his head. "If I clear a space large enough for you in your current state, I risk crushing Tae with shifting stone."

"Please, Rascal," Darris said. "You're the only one—"

"No." Rascal kept her back to the others, slamming her crossed arms to her chest emphatically. "Hain't riskin' misself for one what's alriddy daid."

Kevral spoke through gritted teeth, her tears turning hot. "Please, let me kill her."

Ra-khir shook his head with the expression of a teacher disciplining an inattentive student. "She has a point, Kevral. And a right to preserve her own life."

"What about me?" El-brinith said.

Kevral appreciated the sacrifice. "You're no smaller than me."

"True." El-brinith sized the young Renshai with her gaze. "But I'm a bit more . . . um . . . streamlined at the moment."

Chan'rék'ril looked worried, though Kevral could not define the subtle changes in expression that gave her that impression. "More risk than with her." His head barely moved in Rascal's direction. "But we'll have to make do with what we have."

They all glanced once more at Rascal, who turned toward them, still with arms doubled over her chest and her lower lip jutting.

Chan'rék'ril delegated swiftly, using *khohlar* concept to send Ra-khir, Darris, and Andvari to specific places to help move and steady rock. Every step onto the piled rubble sent pieces shifting dangerously, usually toward unseen portions of the mound. Every click, grind, or scrape made Kevral cringe as she imagined rock tumbling onto Tae's helplessly pinned face. She also worried for the men, pitched headlong to their own demises. Once in place, however, they fell into a cooperative rhythm, Chan'rék'ril cautiously easing free the top layers of rock and the men guiding the boulders harmlessly aside.

Kevral suffered a new hatred for the bulge that hampered her ability to rescue a trapped friend. Though not clumsy, El-brinith lacked the experience to handle the situation as deftly as a daily-trained warrior or a sneak thief. Rascal's size gave her all the advantages, yet there seemed no way to convince her of their need. Kevral had to try one last time, before Chan'rék'ril widened the hole that last dangerous notch, before El-brinith desperately risked her own life and Tae's to squeeze through it. She walked toward Rascal, the Pudarian back-stepping warily at her approach.

"Hold still," Kevral instructed.

"Hain't lettin' ya kill me."

The words sounded ludicrous to the Renshai warrior. "If I planned to kill you, you'd already be dead."

"Ya hain't that fast."

"Yes," Kevral said, eyes trained on Rascal's. "I am. Don't force me to show you."

Rascal only glared with clear defiance. "Killin' me hain't makin' Tae 'live."

No, but it'll give me satisfaction. Threat did not seem like the best approach. "If El-brinith is killed, we're trapped here. We need both elves for the transport."

"Hain't askin' her ta risk it." Rascal's shoulders zipped upward, then lowered with slow insolence. "'Sides, we's trapped here anyways. Thought we's needin' all us ta go. We's loss't Tae."

Kevral pursed her lips. She had nearly forgotten that the focused transport spell required all members of the group. She verbalized the loophole, "Captain said he might make it work without one of us. But we can't even trigger it without El-brinith."

"If'n ya loss't Tae an' me, loss't two. Cain't work either."

Kevral glanced behind her at the working men, then back to Rascal. She huffed out a frustrated breath. "Rascal, Tae's done so much for you. He's practically fathered you since you joined us: helping, teaching, supporting. If not for him, one of us would have killed you by now. Don't you feel any loyalty at all?"

Light brown eyes sparkled between narrowing lids. "Lo'lty?" she repeated. "I seed what lo'lty gets ya." She whipped an arm toward the rubble. "Tae's lo'lty ta ya gotted him kilt."

A painful flare of guilt saved Rascal's life. Kevral could not deny that her impulsiveness had caused Tae's predicament. Had she heeded his many warnings, she would not have triggered the trap and he would not lie buried beneath tons of rubble. "I made a mistake, Rascal. A big one. But that doesn't mean you should compound it."

"Which's cum'poundin' it? Not goin' affer him? Or gettin' misself kilt, too?" Rascal's hands became white fists at her sides, and she balanced on the balls of her feet, prepared for a swift escape. "Hain't gettin' ya people. Ya 'grees ta try this quess thin' knowin' least one a ya's goin' ta die. Ya's all fightin' types." She flicked a wrist toward Darris. "Ev'n body guarders what's trained ta die for others. Gettin' daid hain't no big deal for types like ya. You's got close youself lass time. Why's ya gettin' so fussled now?"

The clatter of falling stone jerked Kevral's attention behind her. The men stopped working, all staring at the same spot near Darris' left foot. A hole had opened between the pile and the ceiling that seemed barely big enough for a cat. "Most soldiers don't go to war because they want to, but because they have to. Reluctantly. In defense of cities or countries. At their king's command. Others dedicate themselves to their rulers with more enthusiasm. They're not seeking death but fulfilling honor or moral need."

Rascal did not blink. "Hain't explain' ya."

Chan'rék'ril stepped back. "Can't risk anything more. Any luck, Kevral?"

Kevral studied Rascal, who continued her stance of stalwart refusal. "Renshai do leap joyfully into battle, but it's usually not to die. It's for the excitement of besting a challenging opponent, of honing our skills until the day we can die in ultimate glory, hopefully at an old age. Warriors remain aware of death and don't fear it, but the camaraderie that develops between those who face death together, especially repeatedly, is stronger than the ties that bind any other. Even in the heat of battle, we grieve for one another. And we're prepared to do everything we can to help one another."

"I hain't no warrior."

"Kevral?" Ra'khir pressed.

Kevral threw up her hands. "Rascal, you owe him."

"Hain't owin' nobody nothin'. An' hain't dyin' for a daid man. Cain't make me."

The urge to stuff Rascal through that hole became nearly irresistible. "You're right, Rascal. If your own sense of honor and fairness can't make you, no one can." With that, Kevral returned to the others. "Stubborn as a rock, with half the virtue. I caused this mess. I'm going in after him." She measured the opening with her gaze. The baby kicked wildly, a cruel reminder of why she could never fulfill her determined words.

El-brinith's voice glided through Kevral's discomfort. "If only we had the shard."

Kevral looked up. "We do." Concern for Tae had not allowed her to mention it sooner. Thrusting a hand into her pocket, she withdrew the blue fragment and offered it to the elf.

Taking it, El-brinith soothed. "Kevral, it's best if I go, and not just because of size or risk to an innocent infant. We might manage the transport magic separated, which would save whoever goes to rescue Tae from a return trip."

Kevral recalled the mission as an attempt to locate, not rescue, allowing Chan'rék'ril the details he needed to safely direct the unburying efforts. Hope formed an excited tingle in her chest. "You can still transport? From in there?" She gestured toward the pile.

"I don't know." El-brinith glanced at Chan'rék'ril for support. "Depends on how far Tae fell. How much weight pins him." She looked back at Kevral. "It seems worth trying."

The men clambered down from the rock pile, stepping as lightly as their own bulk allowed. Chan'rék'ril perched on a boulder, head in his hands, watching El-brinith float delicately to the top of the pile. She paused there, measuring the created cavity with a doubtful frown. She clasped her hands, holding her arms straight out in front of her. Without hesitation, she pitched herself through, pointed fingers leading. The darkness swallowed her arms, then she poised, shoulders trapped against the rubble.

Kevral mentally willed the elf forward, not noticing she had, herself, physically shifted until a stone rolled under her foot. El-brinith bobbed for several moments. A shoulder slipped through, dislodging a patter of rock. Kevral flinched, awaiting the deadly avalanche that might follow. Then the elf's second shoulder followed the first, and her body slipped behind it like a baby escaping the womb.

The moments that followed passed like hours while those left behind displayed nervousness in ways that had become characteristic. Darris paced. Andvari traced the haft of his ax with a finger that circled the same design a thousand times. Ra-khir smoothed wrinkles from his britches with palms that left sweaty marks. Rascal crouched, hands twitching at intervals. Chan'rék'ril sat perfectly still, head bowed into long-fingered hands. Kevral caught herself clinging to the hilts of her swords, tensed near to breaking.

Suddenly, Chan'rék'ril rose and calmly said, "We need to move as near the rocks as possible."

They all did as instructed, including Rascal. "Did she find him?" Kevral asked, nearly in concert with several others.

Chan'rék'ril sent brief *khohlar,* before starting into the familiar chant. *A glimpse. Can't get close enough to tell much. Spell is worth trying.*

Kevral braced for the blinding, disorienting moment of transport, squeezing her lids shut. The chant continued long past its usual time. The swirl of movement did not come, nor the bright flash that seemed to always accompany magical travel between worlds. *Not working.* Kevral opened her eyes. As if waiting for that moment, a brilliant blast of whiteness exploded across her vision.

Kevral's eyes snapped closed reflexively, etching a colorful web of afterimages over the darkness. She blinked desperately, needing to see the result of the elves' work. Gradually, she registered the moments of sightlessness alternating with the simple decor of the strategy room from which they had left for the task. She skipped her ruined vision over her companions, registering none of them until she found the limp figure on the floor. Tae lay with his arms and legs tucked against his abdomen, eyes closed. Dust covered every part of him. Gaze trained fanatically on him, Kevral watched for the subtle rise and fall that would indicate breathing; but the flecks of light that still spotted her vision foiled details. "Is he. . . ?"

Ra-khir caught Kevral's arm and steered her for a door she only now noticed was open. Heads poked through, waiting impatiently for the room to clear. "Let the healers work."

"Healers?" Kevral allowed herself to be led. "So quickly?"

"El-brinith used *khohlar* to alert them." Ra-khir politely worked the two of them around the rushing healers, human and elfin, apologizing for every movement. Andvari and Darris also blundered through the crowd. Kevral never saw Rascal leave, but soon only the elves and a horde of healers filled the room. She barely had time to notice Matrinka among them before the door swung closed, plunging the hallway into silence.

Ra-khir's grip left Kevral's arm, and she took his hand as it fell away. "Was he breathing, at least?"

"I didn't notice," Ra-khir replied, his voice thick with otherwise well-hidden discomfort. "I'm sure the healers will let us know as soon as possible. In the meantime, we need to clean ourselves."

Kevral nodded. She needed a bath, wishing it would scour away the guilt as easily as the dirt. At least, the knight's need to appear immaculate gained her a means to occupy her time until the answers arrived. Rascal's words returned to haunt her: "Gettin' daid hain't no big deal for types like ya . . . Why's ya gettin' so fussled now?" For all the times she had plunged into battle, she had seen death as a distant obsession. Tae's risk-taking had endeared him to her. She had always known it would likely kill him, yet that did not soften the blow when it happened. *Might have happened.* Kevral tried to put the sight of the tons of boulders from her mind, along with the still form on the strategy room floor. "Ra-khir, do you think Rascal's right? That we're insane to cry for one who came to grips with his mortality years ago?"

Ra-khir answered the only way his honor allowed. "No." He elaborated, "No one belittles the grief of those who lose elderly relatives to long-term illnesses, no matter how predictable their passing. No matter how honorable, the death of a loved one is tragic."

Kevral sighed as she walked, understanding the point, though it contradicted the Renshai teaching that a brave warrior who died in battle should be celebrated, never mourned. The method of Tae's accident allowed for sorrow.

Kevral did not notice Andvari until his soft voice filled the thoughtful hush. "Berserk. That's what we call soldiers who fight without emotion, without worry for the safety of self or companions. Most reach that state through drugs or deliberate mental isolation." He added carefully, "It's no coincidence that the word has come to mean 'crazy.' "

That point, though more subtle, did not escape Kevral either. Even among those who anticipated a sudden, violent end, the ones who did not lament fallen companions were the ones most would consider mad. "Thank you," Kevral said, meaning it. With Ra-khir, she headed to their room.

The *Sea Knighty* reached Nualfheim during the third week, hull scraping sand with a sharp and prolonged grating that set Captain's teeth on edge. He sprang over the gunwale to haul the ship to safety without destroying the planking. Homogeneous eyes followed his every motion, elfin spectators scattered across the beach. His crew joined him to assist, tugging at the mooring lines. The ship glided along the sand, leaving a triangular trail etched deeply into wet embankment. Captain secured the ship to a *doranga* tree, the rope snuggling between circles of roughened bark. Only then, he dared to face the many *svartalf* who had watched their approach and landing in silence.

Curving toward its zenith, the sun beamed down upon the beach, warming the sand where the waves did not touch it. Bits of quartz glimmered amid the tan chips of rock and shell. The tide kicked up shells, seaweed, and bracken, reclaiming half in its relentless return. Planted on the shore, a sea slug followed the receding waters, humping across the sand, dragging a shell the length of Captain's forearm. Sand fleas, uncovered by the surge, dug furiously back into the beach, disappearing beneath a shallow layer to emerge with every subsequent wave.

Only after the ship lay safely docked did Captain bother to address Nualfheim's masses with *khohlar.* Fewer than two hundred elves made their homes here, more than four times the number in Béarn; and it seemed as if every one now stood upon the sand or studied him from the branches of high trees. *Fellow elves. Greetings.*

No response followed Captain's call. He looked to his crew. Dhyano stood to his right, only two steps behind him. His blue eyes remained focused ahead, and his thin-lipped mouth remained pursed. Sal'arin clung to a line already taut and secure, and her amber eyes followed every slight movement. Reehanthan and Tel-aran stood together, their discomfort so subtle even he could barely read it. Irrith-talor kept a hand on the gunwale, looking as if he might attempt sudden retreat at any moment, driving the *Sea Knighty* back into the ocean. Ke'taros had gone below to assist their only passenger, a moronic elf who bore the name Khy'barreth.

Captain tried again. *My peers, we have come to make peace.*

Eight *svartalf* sorted themselves from the others, forming a semicircle in front of the grounded ship. Seven had served in the Nine, the elfin council, when Captain had sat among them. The last, he knew, had replaced him at the time of his exile. Apparently, they had not yet filled the slot Dh'arlo'mé had vacated. As usual, Vrin'thal'ros chose to speak for them. *You're not welcome here, Lav'rintir.* His attention barely shifted to the others. *And your lav'rintii. You were banished for eternity.* The wind fluttered a strand of silver hair over violet eyes that fixed back on Captain.

Circumstances have changed. Captain stuck with *khohlar,* though his speaking voice would carry to every ear. It seemed prudent to use uniquely elfin communication while convincing dubious elves that living among humans, or at least remaining at peace with them, posed no threat to elfin society. *Dh'arlo'mé has forsaken you as well as us.*

Lies! Clear disdain tainted Vrin'thal'ros' sending. *Dh'arlo'mé will return. And you must leave.* He started to turn his back.

Dh'arlo'mé exists no more.

Vrin'thal'ros whirled to face Captain again. *Are you confessing to . . .* He sent a convoluted concept of causing the death of one's own. Murder did not exist in elfin culture or language.

Captain explained without bothering to directly address the question, *He chose a new identify for himself. He joined with the Staff of Law to become Odin. If you continue to follow him, you no longer heed the words of an elf but of a god who is not your creator.*

Ke'taros appeared on the deck, herding Khy'barreth. Reehanthan and Tel'aran assisted the infantile elf to the beach.

Murmurs of *khohlar* suffused the crowd, and many more singular exchanges probably occurred.

Vrin'thal'ros would have none of it. *Dh'arlo'mé told us you would lie.*

"He's not lying, Vrin'thal'ros Obtrinéos Pruthrandius Tel'Amorak." Though soft, the voice carried. Captain knew it well. Hri'shar'taé, a female second in age only to himself, had spoken sooner in a dispute than he had ever heard her before. Known for slowness in emotion and decision, she rarely said a word until all of the others had finished. At times, she waited long enough that even the elves had forgotten the topic. "We all saw that creature summoned by Dh'arlo'mé'aftris'ter Te'meer Braylth'ryn Amareth Fel-krin. Human, it may have seemed; but he used demon-summoning magics to bring it. And it called him Odin."

Captain hoped Hri'shan'taé might prove more willing to listen. Like himself, she recalled, even still embodied, the unhurried joy of elves. He knew demon summoning brought the Prince of Chaos, and Colbey had claimed Dh'arlo'mé/Odin had evoked him more than once.

Dh'arlo'mé, Vrin'thal'ros sent. *Odin. It doesn't matter. We follow the ways of elves and you the ways of humans. Dh'arlo'mé led us through the worst times in our history, and he never turned against us.* Though elfin subtle, the look he turned Captain felt barbed.

Captain doubted he could convince Vrin'thal'ros of the truth, that Odin had performed the summoning in the hope of bringing a demon to destroy elves and humans alike. Instead, he indicated Khy'barreth. Raven hair hung barely below his ears, kept short because it otherwise grew too difficult to detangle. The blue eyes that stared out from his angular face looked flat and dead. Captain switched to voice, a subtle insult to Vrin'thal'ros and homage to Hri'shan'taé. "This is how Dh'arlo'mé cares for his own. He ruined Khy'barreth's mind, then left him to rot in Béarn's dungeon."

No! The *khohlar* wafted from the middle of the *svartalf*'s irregular ranks, in Tresh'iondra's mind-voice. *Now you are lying. Khy'barreth did that to himself—by grasping the Staff of Law and the one of Chaos at the same time.*

Captain bowed to one present at the time of the incident. *A misunderstanding, not a lie, though the facts do not wholly explain the result. Others have held both staves without damage.* He attempted to salvage his point. *Regardless of the cause, Dh'arlo'mé did abandon Khy'barreth when he most needed assistance.*

Pre-han, who had once impersonated Béarn's king spoke next. "We knew you would not allow the humans to harm him, and he seemed safest locked up until age can claim him and his soul can return to the pool."

"Best locked in a human dungeon for centuries?" Captain shook his head at the ludicrousness of the suggestion. "Do we not owe it to one of our own to assist when he needs us?"

"We could do nothing for him," Pre-han insisted. "He's mindless."

"No." Captain had worked closely with Khy-barreth in the months since taking residence at Béarn Castle. He had even taken the damaged elf on his trip through West and North lands to repair the damage the *svartalf* had inflicted. "Not mindless." He met Khy'barreth's sapphire eyes. "Khy'barreth, tell us about the dungeon."

The attention of every elf jerked to Khy'barreth. Seven *lysalf* watched from on and around the ship. The *svartalf* remained in various positions on the beach.

"The . . . cage?" Khy'barreth managed, his voice loud and dull.

"The cage," Captain confirmed, encouraging. "Tell us, Khy'barreth."

"Dark," said the feeble-minded elf. "Dirty. Stink. Not room. Need air. Trees." He pouted. "Not like."

Near the front, the lips of a few *svartalf* parted. They had seen Khy'barreth at his worst: staring with seeming blindness, incapable of *khohlar* or speech.

Captain explained. "He needed our time, our effort. With attention, he can relearn so much more. Perhaps even *khohlar*."

Vrin'thal'ros belittled the miracle. *Anyone could have made a mistake escaping amid human threats. Dh'arlo'mé and the others should have taken Khy'barreth. Instead they left him with someone with the time and inclination to help him. No harm done there.*

Captain swiveled his head to the speaker. *By luck alone, no harm. My point is that Dh'arlo'mé has abandoned you just like he did Khy'barreth. As Odin, he has no further use for you.*

That remains to be seen. Vrin'thal'ros continued to speak for the others. *What do you want from us?*

Captain smiled, the expression feeling right on features that had once harbored little else. *I want you to give up your bitter crusade against mankind. I want to unite* lysalf *and* svartalf *together again as elves.*

Lav'rintir, we have no interest in joining your betrayal.

A tiny voice barely rose above the lap of waves on the shore and the rustle of wind through serrated leaves. "I do."

All eyes zipped toward the sound. Even Captain did not recognize the speaker by voice alone. He followed the focus of every eye, zeroing in more easily as his gaze neared the proper position. A child no older than thirty-five years stood on the sand, red-black bangs dangling into golden eyes.

Oa'si, the elves' only child, quailed under the intensity of hundreds of gazes; but he did not back down. "I—I have memories of another time. When elves played all day and worried for nothing. I want to be a part of that again."

Captain knew those memories did not belong to Oa'si but to the elf whose soul he used. The elder suppressed a smile. Once the first stepped from the pack, others usually followed swiftly.

Yet, this time, no one did. Sad eyes followed Oa'si's course toward Captain, and several held out their arms as if to cradle the babe until he returned to his senses. Likely, they bombarded him with singular *khohlar* so thick he could read none of it. No one physically intervened; Dh'ar-lo'mé had sworn not to stop any elf who wished to join Captain's band, though he would name them traitor. They would all miss the child they had raised together.

Vrin'thal'ros' smile outdid Captain's own. *One taker. Too young to understand the folly.*

As Oa'si came to Captain, he placed long fingertips on the child's shoulders. *Youth clearly has nothing to do with this. The oldest and the youngest made the same decision.*

The oldest, Vrin'thal'ros said. *Is addled. Svartalf and lysalf are your terms. To us, your followers are the lav'rintii, the destroyers of our peace. We are the dwar'freytii, the chosen of Frey. Our creator.*

A poorly chosen name, Captain sent with a snideness that sent several recoiling. *You have abandoned Frey to follow Odin.*

When the Ragnarok threatened to destroy all of elfinkind, it was Dh'ar-lo'mé who intervened for us, not Frey. Your misplaced loyalty is understandable, Lav'rintir. You were not with us when the fires killed thousands and left the rest of us in agony. Others are young, born here after the tragedy. Vrin'thal'ros gestured Dhyano, Reehanthan, Tel'aran, and Ke'taros in turn. *Willing to violate our unity from ignorance.* He pinned Sal'arin and Irrith-talor with his piercing, violet gaze. *These two, I do not understand.* Vrin'thal'-ros' fingers traced a faded scar on his wrist, visible beyond his sleeve. He jabbed a hand toward the sea. *You're not welcome here. Now go!*

Captain glanced one last time over the nearly two hundred elves who had selected uniformity over ethics. Though he knew every name and face, they appeared different to him at that moment: squatter, harder, less fluid of movement. He had failed, utterly, to convince them. As he folded his arms over Oa'si, he consoled himself with the realization that saving one young life made the trip worthwhile for elfinkind, if not for Béarn. He sent a last wordless plea in *khohlar* for the *svartalf* to save themselves from the trap of their own bitterness. With all his soul, Captain wanted them to see Khy'barreth as a symbol for their society, crippled by a hatred that Dh'arlo'mé had fostered and exploited, then abandoned by the one they followed with steadfast and zealous blindness.

The *svartalf* gave Captain nothing but wordless stares.

The eldest of the elves gestured for his followers to assist Khy'barreth and Oa'si on board. Head low, smile vanquished, Captain turned toward the ship. The sails wilted, folding the Béarnian bear into unidentifiable, brown triangles. A flag at the front danced gaily in the breeze. Masts towered, arms opened like angry parents, demanding obeisance and promising the only salvation. Beaten, Captain shuffled toward the ship.

Odin was right! A voice boomed like thunder from the heavens. **You are unworthy.**

Captain froze. Elves rolled their eyes, seeking the speaker without jerking their heads about in wild, undignified confusion.

A moment later a tall figure appeared on the shore, not far from the Béarnian ship. His purple cloak flapped in the wind, snapping like a gale-tormented sail. His hood flopped free, spilling yellow war braids that swirled around handsome features. Blue eyes glared out from the perfect angles of his face, rolling from one pocket of elves to another.

Captain whirled to face Frey. He had not seen their creator in centuries, not since the god had lived among them on Alfheim.

Millennia ago, at the beginning of the mortal worlds, all of the gods submitted designs for the keepers of Midgard. Odin created a qualifying test on a world where time passes swiftly. Simply walking across the plain spans fifty years, at which time the aged being must confront its younger self and prove he bettered himself during the journey, for Odin wished to assure that only mortal creatures geared toward positive progress should populate the worlds we created. Frey's glare gained an intensity that made it impossible to meet. In waves, the elves turned their gazes to the ground. **Those creatures who passed returned to their youth. Humans accomplished most.** Faces rife with accusation spasmed upward to find Frey's eyes once more. Every elf who dared challenge the claim met Frey's angry features and looked away. **And won Midgard as their charge. Giants also passed, given to Jötunheim. All of the others failed. These remained fifty years older or died on the test plain.** Frey

paused, granting his charges time to understand the significance of his words.

Even Captain clenched his hands. All the knowledge of millennia, even in the company of Wizards, had not revealed this story.

Your salvation: I granted you near-immortal life spans at the expense of individual souls and character. Unlike the others, fifty years did not trouble your reproductive capacities. On Alfheim, elves thrived. Frey continued to stare at what remained of his followers. *Odin told me I would live to regret my deceit, but I never believed that. The happy, frivolous creatures I designed could never disappointment me. Or so I believed.*

A long silence followed, filled with the patience of gods and elves alike.

At length, Frey broke it. *Those of you who remained with Dh'arlo'mé'aftris'ter Te'meer Braylth'ryn Amareth Fel-krin because he convinced you he followed my expectations may still league with Arith'tinir Khy'-loh'shinaris Balishi Sjörmann'taé Or.* He inclined his head toward Captain, who took inordinately long to recognize his own given name. Millennia had passed since anyone had used it.

Elves drifted almost immediately, some with clear relief etched on their faces, other trembling with terror. And, when the shifting ended, Vrin'thal'ros remained staunchly in place, some forty elves still supportively ringed around him. Only one of the Nine had abandoned him; She of Slow Emotions joined Captain without her usual need for long consideration.

Frey watched the division with an air of wistfulness, yet he seemed pleased by the relative numbers. Captain worried more for his ship. It would require fifteen to twenty trips to ferry so many to Béarn.

Those who prefer the path of Odin shall become elves no longer, Frey explained. *I will find a dark quiet place where you can simmer in your hatred for eternity. One day, you will serve the gods with talents born of brooding, magical crafts, and secrets that must accompany such isolation and intensity. You may call yourselves svartalf or even dwar'freytii, for you are, in a way, my chosen. Chosen no longer to represent me. You shall remain a people, but no longer my people.*

Captain saw the solution to his own problem. If Frey removed the svartalf/dwar'freytii, the lysalf could remain on Nualfheim. Those who wished to live among humans could come aboard, and any who preferred to remain here, including his crew, could do so instead. Eventually, he would extend that option to those already living in Béarn and in Pudar. His discussion with Colbey gave him information that obviated Frey's visit and all of his plans. If Odin managed to destroy the world, nothing they did mattered, yet it made no sense to make plans based on this eventuality. Annihilation required no preparation. The re-creation of the elves did.

Captain turned to thank their benefactor. Unlike humans, elves did not worship gods, not even their creator. Alfheim's close proximity to Asgard had brought them in direct contact on many occasions, and their more similar lifespans made them less mysterious. But Frey had disappeared, taking the *svartalf* with him. Nothing remained but the lap of surf, a dying wind, and the mass of followers who awaited Captain's command.

CHAPTER 26

The Laws of Ascension

When circumstances change, I change my mind.
— Sir Ra-khir, Kedrin's son

KEVRAL had scarcely pulled on her clean clothes when a knock sounded on the door. Dashing past Ra-khir, she ignored the towel slipping from her head to jerk open the panel. "How is—" she started, not caring which of the healers had come to deliver the news. Then, recognizing Tae, himself, she bit back the question.

A bandage speckled with blood formed a band around his head. A cleaner one supported his right ankle, and cloth encased his right hand. "May I come in?"

Kevral stepped aside, finding speech impossible. The towel slid to the floor, and water dripping from her hair left dark spots on her tunic.

Tae limped inside, his every movement stiff. He walked only as far as the first chair, then plopped himself down on the seat. His dark eyes held a glaze Kevral usually associated with death. She let the door swing partway closed.

Ra-khir hurried to his friend's side. "Tae, what are you doing here?"

Tae smiled weakly. "Glad to see you, too."

"That's not what I meant." Ra-khir scolded rather than explained. "Did the healers say you could . . . I mean they haven't even reported—"

Another rap on the door silenced Ra-khir, and the panel swung open at the touch. A young Béarnide stood in the entryway, long dark hair tied back from broad shoulders. She wore the simple gray robe preferred by a group of Béarnian healers who believed it their god-sanctioned mission to end suffering. "The queen sent me to tell you the Prince of Stalmize is alive. You may come—oh!—" She broke off abruptly at the sight of Tae. "You're here, Sire." Her brows knitted in desperate consideration, and she looked back into the hallway.

Tae's smile turned sweet. "I thought they'd worry less if they heard it from me."

"Well, yes, Sire, but . . ." The healer licked her lips furiously. Pounding footsteps suddenly filled the corridor behind her. She stepped aside to admit Matrinka, two elves, and an unfamiliar Béarnide.

"Kevral. Ra-khir." Matrinka's gaze fell on Tae, and she stopped cold. Her expression went from alarmed to irritated, and she waved the others away. "Let them know we found him, and he's all right."

The healers scurried to obey, leaving Kevral, Ra-khir, Tae, and Matrinka. The Queen of Béarn closed the door. Turning back to her friends, she made a flourishing, though somewhat facetious, gesture of respect. "Thank you all for your service to Béarn. Another successful mission." She narrowed in on Tae. "You idiot! What do you think you're doing?"

"Think?" Tae said with a dismissive gesture. "I gave up thinking a long time ago."

"Clearly." Matrinka surrendered her attention to Kevral. Ra-khir managed to refrain from any grand displays, but he did stand at attention.

"Tae's alive and well?" Kevral guessed.

"Alive," Matrinka conceded. "Though obviously deranged and confused."

Ra-khir could not resist. "So he's normal."

"Hey!" Tae protested, without the strength to muster his usual sarcastic edge. Despite his bravado, Kevral noticed that he sat crookedly in the chair, allowing the back and sides to support him. For once, he did not look as if he could evade any threat in an instant.

Matrinka sketched out a scenario no one could confirm. "From what I can put together, his fall down the stairs caused all but one of his injuries but saved him from a crushing. Lots of scrapes and bruises, especially the ankle. Bashed his head on a step, I think. Opened a good-sized gash and knocked him out." She stared fiercely at Tae. "Not long enough. The only damage from the falling stone seems to be his hand."

The door quivered, as if in the wake of a guard patrol.

Tae raised the white bundle that represented his right hand. "Same one as on the ship." He had broken several fingers about a year previously falling off the mast of Captain's ship during a magical storm created by elves. Then, too, Matrinka had worried he might have crushed some bones in his hand. He replaced the damaged limb into his lap. "My left hand's jealous. Demanding equal punishment."

"And I'm sure you'll inflict it," Matrinka said tiredly. Her tone went deadly earnest, and she surely addressed all of them. "I'd like to tend some other patients for a change. I understand there're only two shards left. Please be careful."

"We'll do our best," Ra-khir promised.

The door fluttered again, and Kevral thought she heard a scratch.

"Tornadoes and hurricanes," Tae said cryptically, a reference that defeated Kevral.

"Yes," Matrinka returned. "But you were supposed to be the man of reason."

Tae opened his mouth, but Matrinka ran over his reply.

"Yes, I know you were reining in a tornado at the time, but you can't justify running away from healers in your weakened state."

"I thought—" Tae started, again interrupted by Béarn's queen.

"Yes, I heard. You thought our friends would worry less if they heard your condition from you."

Kevral shook her head, deliberately staying out of the conversation, as did Ra-khir. Matrinka and Tae had an unusual relationship that worked for them.

The door vacillated irregularly. Though soft and gentle, its persistence sent Kevral to the panel. She opened it a crack. No one stood in the hallway, but a yellow eye glared up at her through the opening.

Matrinka continued, "Not good enough, Tae. I don't believe it."

Kevral admitted Mior, who huffed out an indignant meow before stalking deliberately across the room.

Matrinka rolled her eyes to the cat, softening the demanding gaze once wholly on Tae.

Though partially freed from the queen's focus, Tae answered the ultimatum, though it forced him to show vulnerability. "I guess I thought if I could make it up here, I wouldn't die."

Matrinka knelt, holding out a hand to pet Mior. The calico ignored her mistress, pacing a deliberate arc around her, then leaping into Tae's lap.

"Ungrateful little furball," Matrinka muttered, only then seeming to notice she had spoken aloud.

"Me?" Tae asked facetiously, running his hand over the spotted fur while Mior purred loud enough for Kevral to hear.

"You, too." Matrinka could not wholly suppress a smile. Usually, she managed to keep her conversations with the cat wholly silent. Either she had become comfortable with her companions' knowledge, or she had grown tenser than any of them realized. "You could have died pushing yourself too hard too fast, and no one might have found you in the hallways."

The last assertion seemed ludicrous to Kevral. Obviously, Matrinka had surmised where Tae had gone and would have discovered him en route to, if not in, their room.

Tae shifted in his chair, wincing as he did so. "I kept drifting in and out of awareness. I worried I might not wake up, and I didn't want to die in a sickbed. So long as I'm moving, I'm alive."

Matrinka gave him a sidelong look, lacking its previous hostility. "Tae Kahn, I believe you're afraid of dying."

Kevral closed the door harder than necessary. The short distance allowed for only a sharp click, not a slam. Matrinka had essentially called Tae a coward, the worst insult in Renshai vernacular.

But Tae took no offense. "Not afraid exactly. Let's say I'm not quite ready to go. I've got a son to raise. A father to assist. A kingdom that might actually need me." He added hastily, "Not because of my vast wisdom, fine blood, and experience, but because of the hordes of criminals and ousted nobles who would fight over the throne if anything happened to my father. Because of the people—dangerous people—who would follow no one but my father and his chosen successor."

Ra-khir diffused the guilt that Kevral's training would not allow her to consider. "Tae, you don't have to justify wanting to live. It's perfectly normal and natural."

Tae's hand went still on the cat, his dark britches speckled with her short, multicolored hairs. "Then why does it feel so odd? And humiliating?"

Kevral hoped one of the others had the answer. She still did not understand.

Matrinka said, "The prime minister has often said that 'youngsters' like Griff and me believe themselves immortal. With age comes true understanding of mortality. From my experience, I'd say that serious injuries bring the same understanding."

"It's not the first time Tae's gotten hurt," Kevral supplied.

"No." Matrinka ran her hands over hair tied in the back. She wore it this way while she worked, to keep it from falling onto patients. "But there're other things to consider, like he said. His son. The Eastern kingdom. And we're all getting older."

"Twenty in three months," Tae said, shaking his head only slightly and stopping nearly as quickly as he started. "Twenty years old." He stared into space a moment, while Mior butted his good hand with her head.

"Landmark ages like that make a difference, too," Matrinka said softly, without referring to the detail they all now knew. Not only did it signal the end of a decade but also the age when Tae's father agreed that, if Tae survived, he would receive his inheritance. Though the details of that birthright had changed, and Weile had accepted his son back early, the date still had to hold significance for Tae.

Kevral cleared her throat. Her youth and upbringing stole import from the whole situation. "So does this mean you're not going to finish the mission with us?"

Tae's head jerked toward Kevral, then he loosed a noise of pain. "Of course I'm finishing the mission. I'm not becoming a different person, just changing the way I do certain things. Like, maybe next time Matrinka has a baby, I'll come visit through the door."

"Maybe," Matrinka repeated sadly. Unlike Kevral, she had chosen to sacrifice fertility to dedicate herself to the one child she had managed to carry. Though optimistic, the elves did not know for certain whether they could lift the sterility spell, even after the group regathered the Pica shards.

"And I don't want to get sent to Pudar." Tae spoke so softly the words would have gotten lost if not for the hush that followed Matrinka's lament.

Matrinka nodded her understanding. "Is that what's bothering you?"

Tae shrugged, without answer.

Matrinka mulled her next words so long that Tae finally filled the hush.

"My only crime was eavesdropping. I don't deserve execution for that."

"Execution's not an option. Even Pudar admits that." Matrinka meant to reassure, but the words raised questions.

"When did that get decided?" Tae sagged further into the chair, a gesture contrary to his obvious interest. Either his injuries, or the healers' elixirs, finally threatened to overtake him.

Matrinka glanced at Ra-khir and Kevral, as if begging them for an interruption. When none came, she elucidated. "We've exchanged messages with Pudar and your father. More than once. The council meets tomorrow to make a final decision."

"I want to be there," Tae said.

"You can't." Matrinka turned away. "Nor Leondis, either. But Darris and I will be."

Ra-khir read more from the exchange. "This isn't settled yet?"

"I'm afraid not." Matrinka sighed. "But at least we've gotten Pudar to agree to treat Tae like the prince he is."

"A prince." Tae laughed.

That did not satisfy Ra-khir. Features crinkled with irritation, he paced a few steps before heading for the door. Grabbing the latch, he opened it.

Kevral started after her husband. "Where are you going?"

Ra-khir walked into the hall. "I'm going to finish this." Without further detail, he shut the door behind him.

Matrinka looked worriedly at the silent panel. "Should we stop him?"

Kevral saw no need. "He's a Knight of Erythane. How much trouble can he get into? His honor won't let him do anything wild or stupid."

Tae needed only history to contradict. "As opposed to personally declaring war on Pudar?"

"He's not going to declare war on Béarn." Kevral shrugged off the concern. "Let him expend some anger however it pleases him. You know he won't endanger Béarn. Or its innocents."

"Not willingly." Matrinka continued to stare at the door. "But he doesn't know we're already on the verge of war with Pudar."

Kevral flinched. "Because of me?"

Matrinka chose not to answer, sparing her companions. Finally, she glanced at Tae, finding him asleep. Only then, she deigned to address Kevral's question. "Because of . . ." She inclined her head toward the Easterner. Either she worried that speaking his name might awaken him or that he had not fully passed beyond consciousness. ". . . actually." She lowered her head, sucking in a long, deep breath, then faced Kevral directly. "The baby is no longer an issue. It stinks, Kevral, but there's no legal way we can refuse Pudar." She paused, awaiting a savage reaction before continuing, "Griff has already promised to fully cooperate." Again she watched intently for Kevral's rage. "Of course, if you run, catching you becomes Pudar's problem."

Kevral had never considered such an action. She knew she would not have to go far. The Fields of Wrath would shield her, and she doubted even Pudar would attempt to breach the Renshai settlement. Then, she recalled the desperation that fairly defined King Cymion when he demanded Kevral's imprisonment and impregnation. The Renshai would battle to their deaths sheltering one of their own, especially once she convinced them the baby carried Colbey's blood. Eventually, they would succumb to Pudar's numbers, dying in glory but leaving no legacy behind, not even the baby. She dared not delve into the agony such action would cause Ra-khir, torn between love and honor. Once before, he had chosen her over his vows to the Knights of Erythane; but, then, the ethics of the situation had fallen far into her favor.

Matrinka did not await an answer, nor even reassurance. She had spoken the facts and left a way out; in the same situation, no friend could do more. "I'll send some people up to collect him." She waved toward Tae. "Shall I have them bring the twins?"

So much kept Kevral's concern for the babies buried: the excitement of the tasks, the lives of friends, the fate of the unborn; but only shallowly. "Please. Though I wonder how long till Tae's up here stealing Subikahn."

"At least a day or two, I hope." Matrinka gave Tae a motherly look. "He needs the rest."

Mior glanced toward Matrinka, yawned, stretched, then paced a circle across Tae's lap. Ignoring Matrinka, she lay back down, a self-appointed guardian.

Shaking her head at the cat's antics, Matrinka looked at Kevral. "And you need the rest, too."

Kevral knew Matrinka spoke the truth, yet a long time had passed since she had managed a full night of sleep. Physical and emotional pain had haunted every night since before her return from Pudar. She doubted this one would prove any different.

Standing between his seated king and queen, Darris scarcely noticed the familiar ministers and dignitaries clustered around the long, rectangular table in Béarn's Council Room. By convention, the walls remained bare, symbolizing the importance of the discussions that occurred here. An ancient prime minister had decreed it so, concerned for anything that might distract the council, even momentarily. For the first time, Darris wondered whether that strategy might not backfire intermittently. The plain gray walls stood in interesting contrast to the murals, tapestries, and finery of the remainder of the castle. Without something to exercise his eyes, he found his thought guiding his attention in a much more engrossing fashion.

Griff opened the meeting, as he must. He raised massive hands, his sleeves gliding backward to reveal sparse black hair growing nearly to his wrists. "I'd like to start by talking about the latest message from Stalmize."

Stall discussion of Tae as long as possible, Kevral had told Darris that morning, charging off before he could question. That practically assured Griff would start with it. Deliberately avoiding Kedrin's gaze, Darris made a broad, unmissable gesture that demanded the floor. The knight would not approve of interrupting the king, especially when he had barely commenced.

Despite the grossness of Darris' motion, proximity rendered it all but invisible to Griff. "King Weile wrote that he appreciated Pudar's reassurances, but . . ."

Darris repeated the gesture, this time punctuating it with a touch of his foot against Matrinka's ankle under the table. She looked up in time to catch the end of the signal.

". . . he prefers that extradition not occur."

Matrinka waited until Griff finished the sentence and took a breath before intervening. "The bard has requested our attention."

Griff lowered his arms, blinked twice, then crinkled his brow in confusion. He turned to Darris. "You may speak."

Darris cleared his throat silently, seeking the mellow, confident voice with which he taught morality in song. "Your Majesty, I'm sorry to interrupt, but I understood you wished to take matters today in order of importance."

Griff had expressed no such intent, but he accepted the comment without challenge. Either he believed he had mentioned it in private, casual discussion with his bodyguard or trusted Darris to have good reason for lying. He held out a hand to indicate the bard should continue.

"As most of you know, I've spent many months researching the ascension laws." Darris finally glanced at Kedrin, who returned his regard with a mild frown. "I'd like to discuss amending the law."

Suddenly, Darris had the full attention of every minister and the knight's captain. Only Thialnir seemed disinterested, studying the calluses on his massive hands. Regimentation concerned him little, except where it involved relations with his people. Kedrin demanded, and was granted, the floor.

"I respectfully submit that while modification of a Béarnian law does take precedence over nearly any matter of diplomacy, especially one we've been handling over so long a time; the amendment of a law should occur only when such has been rendered obsolete, unfair, or dangerous." Kedrin's lengthy and overly formal sentence sent Thialnir beside him into a disrespectful pantomime of sleep which, luckily, Kedrin did not seem to notice.

"Acknowledged." Darris knew he needed to focus on the most conservative members of the council: Minister Saxanar and the Knight of Erythane. If he could convince those two, the others would not argue. "I'm simply suggesting we add the word 'elf.' "

No one interrupted this time, awaiting details.

Darris pulled a folded sheet of vellum from his pocket. Opening it, he read words he knew by heart, ". . . Béarn's heirs may marry only a woman or man, in the case of the crowned ruler more than one, from the primary noble line of Béarn approved by a majority vote of the Council . . ." He lowered the parchment. "I'd like to add 'elf' to 'woman or man.' " He looked up, realization striking hard and almost too late. "In fact, I'd like to add 'elf' to several laws, granting them the same rights as other citizens of Béarn."

Minister of Foreign Affairs Richar seemed glad to have a positive matter to consider after longer than a month of balancing the East against Pudar. "The elves have helped us so much. We've invited them to live among us. The least we can do is give them equal rights and protections under our law."

Internal Affairs Minister Franstaine raised bushy brows. "Is there some reason why elves can't be people? Their males men? Their females women?"

The ministers considered in silence, some nodding immediately and others reserving the right to respond after further consideration. So far, Darris knew, the peaceful *lysalf* had done nothing to violate any criminal statutes. For day-to-day privileges and responsibilities, Béarn had simply granted them to the elves as they would to any guest of the castle. If anything, the guards had proved more lenient, accepting ignorance of law as excuse for minor infraction.

Pleased by the suggestion, old Saxanar bobbed his head. "It would place them on a level with every other citizen of Béarn, without necessitating a complete rewriting of every statute."

Darris stepped back, trying not to smile. The irony had become magnificent. He had focused so hard on fixing the one problem, he had missed the simple, more global solution.

The king took over the meeting. "I would entertain a vote on this matter, unless anyone wishes to speak. Or delay." He glanced around the group, but no one indicated an interest in saying more. "All right then. On the matter of including elves as 'people,' 'men,' and 'women' . . ."

Unanimous gestures of assent followed.

"Executed," Griff said. At the far end of the room, the sage's servant furiously scribbled the result.

Kedrin waited only until the king had finished. "Bard Darris, I applaud your raising a subject too long ignored, meaning how to reconcile elves to Béarnian law. But I believe we all know your real intent. Noble as it is, you have not accomplished it."

Darris winced, knowing it would not prove as easy. At least he had managed to stall. He only hoped Kevral realized he could not do so interminably.

"I'm certain I speak for all of us when I say that we treasure the happiness of our king and would like to see him married to the one he loves, especially since it would also benefit Béarn with another heir at a time when babies of any kind have become a cherished rarity." Kedrin paused to allow his lengthy objection to sink in before continuing. "Correct me if I've gotten this wrong, please. I believe among the tangle of definitions, 'primary noble lineage' requires a certain number of generations to pass after a person not born to nobility becomes honorarily titled before his or her offspring become acceptable for marriage to members of the king's direct line."

Darris pursed his lips. They both knew Kedrin had the circumstances exactly right. Certain marriages could render a line previously considered primary nobility to lose that status. And it took three generations of noble marriages to bring nobles who earned their titles honorarily to primary status. He had researched every loophole, every convoluted definition, discovering that some who could trace their line directly to Sterrane the Bear did not qualify while some who carried little of any king's blood did. "I'd like to disabuse that law on two bases." Sweat spangled Darris' brow. The service of a direct duty granted him the right to speak long discourses, even to teach, without song. His mother had explained it by demonstrating the ludicrousness of lapsing into accompanied poetry while fending off enemies from the king's person. Logistically, he knew he could present policy cases directly to the king and to his council, yet it felt inherently wrong and his lack of experience trebled an already difficult task.

Brows rose, and several ministers settled back in their chairs. No laws had changed during their service at all, and it seemed unlikely they would start with something as staid and respected as those that governed the ascension.

"First," Darris said, adopting a singsong tone to appease his perceived need for song. "If we hold elves to our generational requirements, it'll take millennia for any of them to become primary nobles." Recognizing the flaw in his reasoning, he amended, "Actually, it can't happen, since elves raise their children communally and don't acknowledge parentage."

Minister of Internal Affairs Aerean raised a new concern. "What about the neutrality?"

Several glanced at her with crinkled features. Darris suspected he appeared as puzzled as the others.

Aerean continued, "The Béarnian rulers maintain the balance of the world."

Darris waited expectantly for her to move beyond the obvious. When she did not, he stated simply, "Blood does not wholly determine the bent of a man. Perhaps not at all."

Aerean shook back her black locks impatiently, as if irritated with having to explain details that seemed perfectly plain to her. "The elves seem to have a more strict and . . . um . . . well, primitive system. *Lysalf* good; *svartalf* bad."

Franstaine broke in, "One could argue that we define *lysalf* as "good" solely because they're on our side, *svartalf* as "evil" because they're enemies."

No reaction. The philosophical argument was either lost on or immaterial to the others.

Darris tried to assist. "Captain maintained his neutrality even while directly serving the champion of all morality. Clearly, there are neutral elves. Besides, the inherent leanings of a ruler's spouse has never been addressed by the law. It's up to the staff-test to choose an unbiased heir."

"The staff-test," Thialnir reminded, revealing at least superficial attention to the matter, "no longer exists."

Aerean finished her point, "Perhaps, then, we could make excepting elves from the old laws' conditions dependent on restoration of the staff-test. Or give the human offspring of Béarn's rulers preference as heirs."

Saxanar waved briskly for acknowledgment, barely waiting for it before speaking. "One could argue that those not of strictly Béarnian bloodline should not become nobles at all."

That comment earned the elder statesman several angry glares. In Griff's cabinet, the honorarily titled outnumbered primary nobility. Only Saxanar and Franstaine qualified, the latter a second cousin of Griff's through his mother. Richar and Local Affairs Minister Chaveeshia had enough recent contamination to put their lines in doubt. Aerean, Zaysharn, and Davian carried only honorary titles, with little or no blooded gentry among their ancestors. Captain Seiryn claimed no nobility while Kedrin, Darris, and Thialnir bore no Béarnian blood at all.

Saxanar weathered the hostility. "I'm not claiming superiority, only that the laws clearly intended to keep the Béarnian ruler Béarnian in bloodline. Surely you can all see that that's the reason for defining primary nobility the way the ancient lawmakers did."

Wiping damp palms on his breeks, Darris looked at the king. He sat quietly, his demeanor uncharacteristically stiff and his swarthy features almost pale. He had much riding on the results of this meeting. The idea of disappointing the gentle king pained Darris, but at the moment he was clearly losing the battle. *I should have waited. Should have thought this out longer.* He cursed Kevral's need for time that had caused him to bring up the subject before he had fully prepared. Yet he also realized he had had more than enough time to ready words for this moment. If Kevral had not instructed him to stall, he might have dragged the matter out for years, long after the birth of Tem'aree'ay's baby.

Zaysharn claimed the silence, as he rarely did. "I believe, Darris, you said 'first.' That implies at least a 'second.' "

"Quite right." Darris tried to remember his intention, befuddled as much by Griff's discomfort as his need to make points without the support of a musical instrument. "Second, the current definition of who the king or queen can marry is so twisted it's almost incomprehensible."

"It's worked thus far," Kedrin pointed out. "For centuries."

Darris grinned. The knight had practically baited his trap. "Mistakes have been made."

Kedrin stiffened in clear surprise. The pale eyes, nearly white, widened in question.

Only the bardic quest to know everything had driven Darris to examine the minutiae of history, using the mass of knowledge his research had granted. "Zoenya, who ruled in AR 50-61, married Avishar as her third husband. He missed primary nobility qualification by one Béarnian ancestor. Yvalane, Kohleran's father, took a half-Erythanian fathered by a long-lineaged noble as his third wife of ten. Myrenex, AR 173-189, married ten times, including sisters who didn't meet the requisites because of a fine detail of law. He left no progeny, but that doesn't change my point. The convolutions of ascension have bewildered past councils. It recommends, I would even venture requires, rewriting."

"Well taken," Prime Minister Davian said, dark eyes shining. "I suggest we set up a group at once to consider the bard's proposal. At least, it could make the same laws easier to understand. And, if the group saw fit to change details, we could consider them in the future."

"Any other suggestions?" Griff said halfheartedly. Davian's idea, though difficult to fault, meant long delays.

"I would offer my support to that," Darris said, "but I still believe we need to address the issue of elves and the ascension, since we know the current laws contain nothing in this regard."

Saxanar gave Darris a look that suggested the bard had suddenly turned stupid. "We've already voted that they're included in 'people' for the purposes of Béarnian law? Why should we separate elves out for special treatment?"

Darris thought he had already explained that well enough. "Because of their lifespans. And their lack of lineages."

"Then we would have to apply that to all of our laws."

"Indeed." Davian conceded to Saxanar. "Life imprisonment, for example. Is it fair to span a punishment across ten kings' rules?"

Franstaine corrected the math, "Try a hundred kings."

The issue was not worth arguing as it depended too much on the length of the reign, the age of the elf at the time of confinement, and their lifespans, which he had heard ranged from a few centuries to multiple millennia. Ultimately it did not matter. Darris could not imagine *lysalf* committing a capital crime, even over the next several thousand years.

Saxanar did not let go. "We can deal with those issues on an individual basis, and I don't really believe we'll find many. If we can solve the problem by simply defining elves as people, without rewriting Béarnian law, why should we consider any other way? Why should elves receive special treatment over our other allies?"

A pause followed. Even the youngest ministers rocked their heads, without reason to contradict. Darris' heart sank, and he forced himself to look at his king. Griff's face seemed to shrink within the mane of hair. He wore an expression of ultimate sorrow, the type Darris had only seen from children who believed themselves betrayed by loving parents. He had tried too hard. And failed.

Darris' support came from an unlikely source. Unable to capture Griff's attention, Knight-Captain Kedrin accepted Matrinka's recognition. "Because, Minister Saxanar, the situation is different." He rose. "The bard, my son, and several others have risked their lives repeatedly to retrieve the tools necessary to reverse a spell that renders humans sterile." He repeated for emphasis, "Sterile." The pale gaze ran over the entire assemblage. "If they succeed, Captain never guaranteed he could lift the curse even then. We've found another way to escape it—humans interbreeding with elves. That's not a sure thing yet, either; but the elves say Tem'aree'ay's baby seems healthy. Friends, the time is already upon us. Our very survival as humans depends utterly on the *lysalf*. That other, darker, elves placed us in that position is immaterial. The *lysalf* are innocent, and they have risked themselves to rescue us."

Kedrin shook back a thick mane of copper-blond hair. "What message should we send our new allies: we'll use your women's wombs, but we do not find them worthy of marriage? Your offspring sired by our king are not good enough to sit upon our throne? If the sterility cannot be reversed, we shall be left with only one human heir. What if we regain the staff-test and she fails it? Even should she pass, the line of kings must end with her."

Only Saxanar did not fall victim to the spell of Kedrin's appeal. "Shouldn't we wait until we see whether or not the sterility spell can be lifted?"

"Ethically?" Though twenty years Saxanar's junior, Kedrin responded like a peer. "We can't. It would send the message that the *lysalf* only become worthy when we desperately need their reproductive capacity. Now that the issue has been raised, we're morally obligated to make the change in our law now. Or not at all."

Saxanar contemplated Kedrin's words more carefully than he would have any other at the meeting. They rarely disagreed on anything, especially matters of ancient design and protocol. "Doesn't that morally bind us to open the ascension to other allies?"

"No." Kedrin glanced apologetically at Griff as minister and knight took over the meeting. The king waved control into the captain's hands, appreciating his assistance as much as Darris. "There's nothing unethical about designing the royal line, per se. It's worked thus far. But as Darris pointed out, the elves present a special case with their magic, culture, and longevity. They should be treated as such."

Chaveeshia brought Saxanar's point down to a personal level. "So, if Saviar wanted to marry Marisole, it wouldn't bother you that he couldn't. But any elf could."

"My grandson's unhappiness would bother me, but I wouldn't consider it unfair. He wouldn't be the first non-noble to love an heir. I would hope his father would instill the morality to handle it as graciously as our fair bard has."

Darris turned scarlet from the roots of his hair to his neck. *If Kedrin only knew.* At the moment it pleased him that the knight did not. Matrinka looked away.

Griff smiled. "Do you all feel prepared to vote on the matter?"

Kevral, where are you? Darris found another means to stall. "Sire, might I suggest a short break for discussion and consideration prior to a vote?"

Griff's grin wilted. Surely, he wanted the voting finished, while the knight's words still hung strongest in every mind. Yet he would not use circumstance to bully through what he wanted. "All right. Let's take a break. Return when you feel comfortable with a stance." He rose to leave the room, the others skittering to their feet as well.

Darris waited until Griff left, ministers following in lines, their conversation a dull buzz of incomprehensible sound. Only then, Darris slumped into an empty chair, head sagging to arms folded on the table. *Kevral, where are you?*

CHAPTER 27

Parley

Kings who do not serve as their own generals risk losing their followers to heroes.
                                    —*Colbey Calistinsson*

SUNLIGHT warmed the purple glass in the fourth-floor study window where Prince Leondis reclined with a tome balanced across his knees. The histories of Béarn's kings could scarcely compete with green gardens just beginning to bud in patterns and rows. Children raced between flower beds and statuary with a carefree excitement that seemed wonderously misplaced. Leondis flicked an errant curl from his shoulder, the first smile in months easing onto his features. He envied the ignorance that underlaid their joy. He would give much to shed the burdens that weighted his broad shoulders, to regain his childhood—and his innocence—for a day.

A presence entered the zone of danger, stealing Leondis' attention. He tried to ignore it, maintaining his focus on the children, assuring himself that no one but Boshkin could come so close without challenge from his guards. Yet the instincts of a warrior would not allow the lapse. No matter how fanatically he trained his gaze on the children, the moment was lost. His interest trickled inexorably back to the one near enough to pass for threat. With a sigh, he looked at his steward.

The middle-aged, balding man in Pudar's colors gave a respectful nod to acknowledge the prince's regard. "Sire, Sir Ra-khir and Lady Kevral wish to meet with you as soon as possible. They say it's important."

Leondis' heart rate quickened, and possibilities marched through his thoughts. He hoped, but doubted, they had finally both agreed to present the baby without a fight. He knew he would get no apologies, nor would he give them. The best he could hope for was grudging conciliation. The negative possibilities spanned a larger spectrum, everything from a verbal battle to a physical one. He would have preferred to dodge the meeting and spend the day in the courtyard, enjoying the sun and the sweet aroma of new growth, watching nobles court and children play. The responsibilities of a kingdom already plagued him, and he wondered if he could ever learn to stop mulling situations, to live with his mistakes.

"They chose a suite on the fifth floor for the meeting, Sire. We've examined it minutely and have guards stationed at the door. It's safe. There's a second entrance from a separate hallway. Béarn has security handled there to our satisfaction."

"Thank you, Boshkin." Leondis vaulted gracefully to his feet. "Let's get this over with."

Together, they headed for the door. Boshkin knocked once, and it swept open to reveal two of Leondis' personal guard. The other four, he knew, stationed themselves at the meeting site. The prince and his steward headed down the corridor to the stairs, the guards taking positions at Leondis' either hand.

As Boshkin climbed a stairwell that contained a spiraling mural depicting the *Ragnarok*, he questioned. "Sire, would you like an escort for the meeting?"

Leondis would have liked to meet the Renshai with an army at his back, but circumstances demanded he confront the two alone. He trusted his wits and battle knowledge, as well as the knight's honor, to keep him alive. The thought brought his hand to his side, where the sword his father had given him hung at his hip. Lantern light reflected from the jeweled scabbard, winking highlights across the artwork that made the movement seem theirs instead of his. Kevral would respect him more for bringing the weapon. That slight edge might gain him much in these new talks. "No escort. Delicate negotiations. Just myself and them."

At the top of the stairs, Boshkin bustled down another corridor, glancing frequently at his prince.

Leondis kept his own gaze forward, resisting the urge to script the meeting in his head. He could only guess at Ra-khir's and Kevral's current mind-set, their reasons for calling a sudden conference now. His kingdom required that he learn to think quickly, especially in situations of greatest stress. "And don't let anyone hassle Kevral about her swords. I prefer to face a Renshai armed rather than angry." He headed toward the door where the other four members of his honor guard waited.

"Yes, Sire." Boshkin went still while the guards repositioned, then opened the door for his prince to reveal unoccupied guest quarters similar to his own.

A huge, square bed sat dead center, cedar columns supporting a royal blue canopy. Pulled taut and meticulously tucked, a blanket covered the bed, the same color as the canopy except for a central circle surrounding

Béarn's rearing bear symbol. Two well-oiled chests of drawers filled one wall, while a wardrobe and a personals box took up most of another. Above it, sunlight streamed through a glassless window that admitted an intermittent breeze and the occasional distant squeal of children. Two openings interrupted the last wall. The smaller one, set off by a door, obviously led to a privy. The other opened into a chamber nearly as large. Before taking a close look, Leondis ascertained that Kevral and Ra-khir had not yet arrived. Though never one for formality, it irritated him that they had defied this particular convention. The time of a crowned prince should take precedence over that of anyone but the reigning king and queen. He believed the disrespect, in this case, very deliberate.

Leondis gestured for Boshkin to close the door, which he did immediately. The panel clicked against its jamb, leaving him in a silence that amplified the muffled conversations and giggles from the courtyard. He preferred it to the sounds of his guards: the brisk swishes of their movements, the occasional clink of mail, the slap of leather sheath against greaves. Prince Leondis explored the second room. One door led into a hallway perpendicular to the one his guards protected. A desk near the window sported a delicately carved pattern that perfectly matched the chair in front of it. The opposite wall had a lengthy mirror. Beneath it, a table held a basin containing a pitcher, a comb, and a shaving knife. A bathing tub, flat on adjoining sides, fit perfectly into the corner, its semicircular lip jutting into the room. A second chair, much like the one at the desk, stood beside the tub. A rectangular rug covered most of the floor. Like the study, the wide ledge beneath the window held a cushion for those who wished to sit and study the courtyard below.

Leondis had just moved toward the window when the latch clicked. He smoothed his silks, feeling abruptly uncomfortable. Unaccustomed to being the first in any room not his own, he did not know how to greet them. Needing something in his hands, he reached for the desk chair, scooting it around to a more proper speaking distance from the window seat. The door glided open to admit Kevral, Ra-khir, and Tae.

Leondis froze.

Quietly, Kevral threw the bolt, locking the Béarnian guards out in the hallway. She wore her usual tan linens, designed to allow free movement, and a sword graced each hip. Ra-khir looked resplendent in his knight's garb, and he executed a bow appropriate for royalty. Leondis had never seen Tae wearing tailored silk before. A bandage enwrapped his head and another encased his hand. He limped forward, dark eyes questing the prince's.

Leondis glared at the Easterner for only a moment before moving on to Ra-khir. Of the three, the knight seemed most worthy of his attention. "What's *he* doing here?"

Kevral snapped a lock over the bolt, displayed the key, then placed it in her pocket. She answered for Ra-khir. "Tae's here to talk to you. Ra-khir and I are going over there . . ." She pointed through the entry. ". . . while the two of you work this out." She headed toward the bedroom.

Leondis' mouth fell open, though he had no intention of speaking. "What? How dare—?" He turned to watch Kevral leave. Then, realizing this placed his back to Tae, he whirled to round on Ra-khir. "You? A Knight of Erythane? Do you belittle your honor enough to keep a prince hostage?"

"Two princes, Sire," Ra-khir corrected. "To forestall a senseless war, I believe it well within my honor." He added with a smile, "Believe me, Sire, I won't be the one standing in front of the door to prevent your calling on your guards."

Leondis glanced toward the bedroom.

Kevral waved.

"This is preposterous!" Leondis lost track of Tae but refused to deliberately look for him. "If I shout loud enough—"

"They won't hear you." Kevral tapped the walls. "Why do you think we chose this room?"

Leondis glanced at the window, finding Tae at its ledge.

"Sire." Ra-khir bowed again. "I wouldn't advise screaming into the courtyard. It might make a dignified man look silly, and it seems extreme just to avoid a conversation."

Leondis felt a trail of sweat tickle down his spine. "I won't chat with my brother's murderer."

"I didn't kill Severin," Tae said.

"There," Kevral called from the opposite room. "You're talking already."

Finally, Leondis looked directly at Tae. The dark eyes held evident pain, accompanied by a gentle sincerity. They focused in on the prince's face and remained steadfast. Tae raised his right hand to brush away a clump of hair across his forehead, stopping before he bashed himself with the mass of bandages. "Your lie has brought three kingdoms to the edge of war. I confessed to a crime we both know I didn't commit, and I'm willing to die to spare the innocents who would otherwise die in that conflict. Doesn't that earn me a few moments of your time?"

"This is a trick." Leondis glanced around the room. Kevral and Ra-khir had left for the bedroom, and all else looked as it had when he first examined the room. "You're just trying to get me to admit you never attacked me."

"No trick." Tae eased the edge of his buttocks against the window seat. He clearly preferred to stand, but his injuries would not allow it. "Your own men searched the room. There's no one here but those who know the truth."

Guilt sent a flush of heat through Leondis. He looked away. "What you did or didn't do to me doesn't matter. You killed my brother." The weakness provided a crack through which a tidal wave of sorrow burst. Images of the elder brother he had admired filled his mind's eyes, accompanied by the tears he had once believed fully shed.

"You . . . murdered . . . Severin, you bastard." His voice emerged in gasps he desperately wished he could control. "You deserve to die for that, whatever it takes."

Tae made no move to comfort. Touching the armed prince of Pudar would amount to suicide. "I didn't kill Severin. How many times do I have to say that before you hear it?"

"I've heard it." Leondis spoke through gritted teeth. "I don't believe you."

"What makes you so certain I killed him?"

Leondis suppressed the urge to answer only with "because it's the truth." He breathed in a calming pattern taught by his arms instructor. A battle, verbal or physical, was never won by blind emotion. Eventually, he realized, he would need to learn how to bargain with enemies, finding compromise where none appeared to exist. The discussion would accomplish nothing if it consisted solely of Tae asserting his innocence and Leondis as adamant about his guilt. Instead, he presented the evidence. "Severin died of a knife wound across his throat. You were at the scene, swinging a bloody knife."

"Beneath a pile of Easterners trying to kill me," Tae reminded. "Any of whose blood could have been on that knife."

"The guards said Severin ran in to assist you."

Tae's eyes widened. "So I'm guilty of murder because I got attacked in Pudar's streets?"

Leondis fought for control of his temper. "You're guilty because your knife in your hand killed Severin."

"But it didn't."

Leondis stared through Tae, to the blue expanse of sky. "A dozen men swore that it did." He finally managed to pin an angry gaze on Tae, irritation fueled by the sincerity of the Easterner's expression.

"Exactly," Tae said softly.

The response confused Prince Leondis. "That's not in your favor, Tae Kahn." The name burned his tongue.

"But it is." Tae settled onto the ledge awkwardly. "Ask a dozen witnesses to a fist fight in the market what happened, and you'll get twelve different answers. They will disagree on everything, from the nationalities of the those involved to who made the first violent gesture."

"Your point." To Leondis, it only confirmed Tae's guilt.

"When twelve witnesses give you the exact same answer, it can only be because they rehearsed it."

Leondis blinked wordlessly for several moments. Finally, he managed speech. "My father says you didn't deny their accusations."

Tae had never been given the opportunity to explain. "Then, I didn't know whether or not I might have accidentally struck Prince Severin in the chaos. At least give me that if I had, it could only have been an accident."

"The witnesses said—"

"All of them? Consistently?"

"Yes."

Tae shrugged as if that explained everything. "Here's the truth: At the time, the elves sought the destruction of mankind and worked toward it by creating havoc in all the human kingdoms: the murders in Béarn; the stirring of war among the Northern tribes; assassinations in the East that left bickering, selfish nobility vying for the crown at the expense of the people. The elves set their sights on Pudar, and a criminal rival of my father's seized the opportunity to serve his own purposes as well." Tae kept his attention fixed on Leondis, as if to see that every sentence met its mark. "Working together, the elves and the criminals created a disturbance they knew would attract Severin who, as you well know, liked to police his own streets in the company of town guard. The elves used magic they call the "mind-fog" to confuse the situation beyond sorting. One of the Easterners killed Severin, then they all swore I did it."

Prince Leondis frowned, not liking the complication. In his experience, the simplest answer usually turned out correct. Many criminals had designed wild theories to explain how another could have committed their crime. "Interesting. Implausible, but interesting."

Tae rocked his head back against the framework.

Leondis wondered why it only occurred to him then how easily he could shove the irritant out the window to his death.

"I can prove it," Tae said softly.

Leondis' brows shot upward.

Tae rolled his head to the side to confront Leondis again. "First, the criminals eventually surrendered the one who murdered Severin. If you talk to some of those same so-called witnesses now, you would get a different story. Just as my father did."

"Because your father tortured them to a confession."

"My father? Torture?" Tae shook his head as if Leondis had said something remarkably stupid. "My father doesn't work that way. But even if he did, he couldn't control what they said under the protection of your father."

"So how did you get them to confess?"

Tae's lips came together in a line that contained a hint of smile. "I'm giving up a big secret here, which I guess proves Matrinka . . ." he corrected, ". . . Her Ladyship right." He swung his legs around so that they dangled into the room and bent forward as if to whisper. He kept his normal volume however. "To a street orphan, a gang becomes his family. They stick together, defending one another through anything, confirming anything another said. It's an honor-tie as strong as the knights', but there's a way through it."

Leondis nodded, surprised to find himself truly interested.

"Most of these boys and girls come from families without love. They never learn to trust." Tae balanced his elbows on his thighs to lean even further. "If you separate them, you need only convince one that one of the others will . . ." He paused, likely seeking trading words to replace the street slang that naturally came to mind first. ". . . inform on him before he informs on them. Then, suddenly, the whole thing collapses. They sing like bards."

"How do you know which one's telling the truth?"

The grin became real. "When eleven of them name the same one, but he names someone else, it becomes obvious."

"Unless they banded together and worked out a story together."

Tae spread his hands and rolled his eyes. "I simplified to make a point. Actually, it's more like seven refuse to talk, four blame the same one but tell the story as differently as any normal four witnesses, and the last blames someone else." He changed tacks suddenly. "More importantly, some of the elves have explained their role in the whole thing, which is how I got the details." He added emphatically, "And elves don't lie."

Leondis considered Tae's words, suddenly realizing his anger had fully dispersed. The foundation of a certainty built on his father's wavered. He turned away. "It still sounds far-fetched. I don't know who to believe."

"Believe the king of Béarn, whose judgments the gods rendered nearly infallible. Believe the queen, and the Knight of Erythane in the next room. If I'm a killer, how do you explain their loyalty?"

"You've tricked them?" Leondis suggested, not even certain he still believed that. "You're gaining their trust in order to make Béarn vulnerable to attack by the East."

Tae stared with a surprise that Leondis doubted even a con man could feign. He half-expected Tae to say that that explanation sounded much more implausible than the one he had given for Severin's murder. "Then believe this." Tae raised his bandaged hand. "And this." He pulled up one leg of his britches to show another bandage around his ankle. "This." He touched the bandage that enwrapped his head. "But mostly, these." He loosened the ties of his tunic, revealing the chest and abdomen riddled with knife scars. "I'm a survivor, Leondis. I'm not going to fling myself into the deadly affairs of Béarn just to gain their trust. There're easier ways than getting myself killed." He retied his shirt. "Believe me. I know them."

"The elves will vouch for your story?" Leondis pressed.

"They will."

"I'm going to check."

"I would think less of you if you didn't."

Leondis took no offense from the words, to his own surprise. Scant moments ago, he would have found their source enough to incite him. "You didn't kill Severin."

"No."

"And you didn't attack me."

Tae paused just long enough to get across the self-evident nature of that statement. "No."

Leondis studied the man in front of him, allowing the last vestiges of anger to diffuse. For the first time, he allowed himself to think of Tae as a crown prince, like himself, compiling life experiences to assist with a task the ignorant envied. The responsibilities of rulership had crushed many a man, ending their lives early, driving them to sacrifice morality for convenience, transforming loneliness and power into greed. A kinship between himself and Tae could strengthen both kingdoms, form alliances that would assist trade, and provide a bridge between their peoples. Letting go of vengeance and hatred had opened a vast chasm of opportunity. "Prince Tae Kahn." He smiled. "Your father is lucky to have you as a diplomat. Someday, you'll make a great king."

Tae seemed more distressed than gladdened by the words, his return smile forced. "I'm not at all sure I'm worthy of the honor, but thank you."

The moment disappeared beneath a flood of concerns. Leondis turned away. "I made a big mistake."

"Let's talk about how to fix it."

Leondis started to pace, then stopped, still with his back to Tae. "I'm not sure it's fixable."

"You could start by begging my forgiveness."

Affronted, Leondis whirled. The broad grin on Tae's Eastern-coarse features put him back at ease. "You're kidding?"

"Yes."

"I *am* sorry. Lying doesn't come easily to me, and I haven't slept well since I did it." Leondis explained with a statement that might seem unrelated, "I loved my brother." The next admission came harder. "And I was scared."

"Scared?" Tae prodded. His brow uncreased, and he addressed his own query before Leondis could do it. "That I'd use the information I overheard to reveal your father's mistake?"

"If you ever have need to talk to my father about it, don't call it a mistake." Leondis resumed his pacing. "If I ruined our chance to retrieve the heir to Pudar's throne, he would have killed me. Literally."

Tae could not hold bitterness wholly at bay. "So, better to have me killed."

"Yeah." Leondis would not compound his lie with another. "I'm not afraid of dying, especially for my own mistakes. But your presence in that room wasn't *my* mistake; it was yours. And I wholeheartedly believed you my brother's killer." He made a gesture over his shoulder. "Wouldn't you trade the life of the man who murdered your mother for your own?"

Tae sucked in a sudden breath, then choked on his own saliva. "That better have been a lucky guess."

Leondis reveled in gaining the upper hand, for once. "It's not. You're not the only one with connections." He did not explain further, inflicting the same troublesome discomfort Tae had on so many others, including himself. The Eastern tough might not understand that Severin had been more than a son to Cymion; he was the king's very hero. Since the killing, Cymion had scrutinized every fact and rumor about Tae to the point of obsession.

Tae regained composure more easily than the prince of Pudar expected, a sure sign of training. "As I promised the council, I won't tell anyone what I overheard. A wise woman pointed out that the problem belongs to the three of you."

Leondis could only believe that "wise woman" was Kevral, though Tae truly meant Matrinka. "I still don't see a way to fix this. A confession to the council might vindicate you, but it would create more problems at least as serious." King Weile Kahn might demand Leondis' extradition. King Cymion would never publicly accept the truth, not only blocking extradition but still demanding Tae. Leondis' chances of becoming a king the populace trusted would disappear forever. They would remember him only as a foolish, dishonest young man. His mother's words, so long ago, now emerged to haunt him: *One lie is enough to undo a man.*

"I don't need a confession." Tae remained calm, though a slight narrowing of his eyes suggested the words caught him as much by surprise as Leondis. "I need a way to keep my life *and* prevent a war."

Leondis pondered the matter, not liking the direction his thoughts took him. His own pardoning of Tae would prevent extradition but would enrage King Cymion, worsening the likelihood of war. Kevral's refusal to deliver the baby would absolutely assure it. "Just a moment." He continued the line of his pacing so that it took him to the bedroom. Ra-khir broke off from his conversation and snapped to attention at the sight of Leondis. Kevral placed herself between the prince and the exit. He ignored the actions of both to say, "Kevral, Tae and I have found a peace. We're working on extending that to Pudar's and Béarn's armies. I need to know now and for certain. Are you going to turn over . . . " He paused, searching for the right words that would not force him to face an armed *and* angered Renshai. ". . . our baby?"

Ra-khir glanced at his wife with a worried expression. He wanted to know the answer as badly.

Kevral's hands winched over her abdomen. She approached Leondis with the fierceness of a warrior headed toward certain death in an unfair battle.

The prince held his ground. If the Renshai wished to kill him, he would defend himself, though he would surely lose. He could not escape her in a locked room of this size.

Reaching down, Kevral took Leondis' hand and placed it on the bulge. Sharp, tiny movements flicked against his hand. "Be good to him or her," she said with a gentleness he would have believed outside her repertoire. "And teach him the warrior way. It's in his blood."

Leondis could have stood for hours feeling the flurry that defined his son or daughter, yet politeness demanded he remove his hand. He did so with obvious reluctance and a grateful smile. "On both sides." Historically, the greatest kings had led their own troops into battle. His father had kept up his training, and Leondis intended, even felt driven, to do the same. "I'll always love that baby. And he or she will never doubt it."

"I wouldn't let him go if I didn't believe that." Kevral walked back to Ra-khir. "And I will always love the baby, too." She fell into her husband's waiting arms.

Their grief saddened Leondis, but he consoled himself with knowing that their loss would become Pudar's greatest gain. Feeling like a voyeur, he left them to one another's tender mercy, returning to Tae with a renewed sense of purpose. Mind stimulated by this new victory, he found the answer that had eluded him before. "Tae, my father won't listen to you or even to me, but I believe there is someone who might convince him." He met Tae's eyes again, unable to differentiate irises from pupils. For the first time, no stirring of hatred accompanied the scrutiny. "I'll need your help."

Tae bowed. "I'll do my best, Prince Leondis."

Leondis returned the gesture of respect, with a flourish. "Call me Le."

CHAPTER 28

Measurements of Worth

*There are those who say that the worth of a man cannot be
measured. I say it depends on the scale.*
                                                    —*Colbey Calistinsson*

THE council's vote went, nearly unanimously, in Tem'aree'ay's favor.
Darris winched a hand around King Griff's chair, fingers blanching, to
keep himself from pacing even after the results became clear. He owed
much of his success to Kedrin and mentally noted the need to thank the
knight's captain after the meeting. He understood that much of Kedrin's
assistance stemmed from compassion for the king he served and loved,
yet he surely also considered the long-term effects on the kingdom of
changing ancient law. His honor would not allow otherwise.

While the council turned to the burgeoning situation among Béarn,
Pudar, and Stalmize, Darris' thoughts tracked off in a different direction.
Once they restored the staff-test, he realized suddenly, it could, once
again, determine the worth of the heirs, including any mothered by elves.
Time would tell whether the offspring of elf and human had the lifespans
of mother, father, or somewhere in-between, but it might mean the oft-
desired eternal reign of benevolent kings could become a near-reality. In
the excitement of discovering that the sterility plague did not affect elves,
and that they could interbreed with humans, Darris had not considered
beyond the excitement of rescuing themselves from imminent destruction. Now, he could not help wondering how those differences would
manifest and how well each group would handle them.

Griff's deep, young voice penetrated Darris' contemplations.
". . . trusts his son and, though Pudar has promised to try him as royalty,
the king worries that some overloyal fanatic might harm Prince Tae . . ."

Joy mingled inseparably with dread. Darris had accomplished a task
that had defied and obsessed him for months, yet concern for Kevral's
need tainted the excitement that should have followed such a feat. He

hoped she appreciated that he had stalled things as long as he could. She had pitted him against the stodgiest conservatives in all of Béarn, and he had played his every card.

Griff continued, "King Weile Kahn is on his way here to discuss the matter face-to-face."

The words caught Darris wholly off his guard. He had hoped the king would bring such matters to him for opinion, then realized the soft brown eyes did rest on him. *We're in council, stupid,* Darris berated himself. *What better place to solicit advice?* He nodded, forcing himself to concentrate on the matter at hand. If Griff could still think clearly after winning the battle for a desire he had believed unattainable, Darris should manage to concentrate also. "It would also give you a chance to discuss the possibility of war with Pudar. And establish an alliance."

The nods that traversed the room were somber. No one liked to consider the possibility of long-term colleagues going to war, yet the practicalities remained. If Pudar attacked, Béarn would need every new proponent it could muster.

"When do we expect him?" Richar asked the practical question. He would become responsible for the visiting king and his entourage at a time when he already had two princes to consider.

"I'm not exactly sure from his message." King Griff glanced around the bare walls. "But his answer came a week sooner than it should have."

"Which suggests he intercepted the message somewhere in the Westlands," Internal Affairs Minister Aerean said. The messenger lines consisted of stationed horses and riders, allowing galloping travel throughout the day and night. These royal messengers took priority over everything else. Interfering with their missions meant death, assuring no delays. In this fashion, they condensed months of travel to weeks. She mulled over her own words. "Could make it here in a month."

Less. Darris chewed his broad lower lip. Accustomed to light travel, Weile Kahn had once scattered his men through the Westlands in what had seemed like no time at all.

"We'd best let Prince Tae know," Aerean finished.

"He knows." Darris could hardly believe those words had come from him. Tae had made no mention of the impending visit. "I mean, he likely knows. He's been exchanging messages since his arrival. If the King of Stalmize wants his son to know, he surely already does."

A knock resounded through the room. Saxanar's brows knitted. Few would dare to interrupt a meeting of Béarn's Council. Captain Seiryn drifted nearer to the king, as did Darris. Only an emergency would prompt such rudeness, and it might pose a threat to Griff.

The panel swung open gently, and Prince Leondis poked his head through the crack, flanked by his guards and steward. "Please forgive the interruption." He bowed nobly. "May I speak, Your Majesty?"

"Certainly." Griff made a wide gesture.

The prince stepped into the room, leaving his entourage to crowd in the entryway. "Sire, I apologize for wasting the council's time, now and in the past. I would like to dismiss the charge I brought against Prince Tae Kahn."

Darris did not believe he had ever heard a hush as intense as the one that followed that pronouncement.

Protocol demanded that the king break the silence; but he only stared, eyes round as well-minted coins.

Darris gently nudged Griff, who finally found his tongue. "That is very generous of you, Prince Leondis." They all knew he did not just refer to Tae, but to the myriad who might die in the coming battle. "Thank you."

Leondis bowed again, his expression deadly earnest. "Do not thank me, Your Majesty. It is I who should thank you and apologize for placing you in this situation. Had I known, Your Majesty, how my father would react to the situation, I would not have reported it."

Griff looked contrite, like a sad-eyed puppy. "Prince Leondis, please don't apologize. I need to know what happens in my castle, especially things like . . . what happened."

Courtesy demanded an explanation for the change of heart, but Leondis did not give one. The knowing glances of most of the council suggested they believed he did so to avoid war. Darris suspected Kevral's need for stalling bore some relation to the prince's announcement, and he hoped she had not threatened Leondis' life. He looked toward Matrinka, who smiled at him. She had described Ra-khir's irritated storm from the room the previous night. The knight had assisted in some manner, and he would not allow intimidation.

Leondis went on, "Your Majesty, I believe I can explain the matter to my father best in person. I plan to take leave of your city in a few days and thank you for your hospitality."

"You're quite welcome, Prince Leondis," Griff said. "And I'm sorry about . . . what happened." He seemed stuck on the phrase. "Will all of your people take their leave at one time?"

"No, Your Majesty." Leondis' staunch expression left no room for compromise on this matter. "Lady Kevral has promised to surrender Pudar's heir at birth. Your Majesty, by your leave, the wet nurse and some others will remain to collect the baby."

Darris closed his eyes. Though he had suspected the outcome long ago, the news fell hard on his sensibilities. It now seemed likely that

Kevral and Ra-khir had surrendered the baby for Tae's freedom, yet the assessment seemed patently unfair. Pudar had demanded the baby *and* Tae, and King Cymion had made it clear he would not settle for only one. Leondis' willingness to do so demonstrated his love for the child, that he could sacrifice vengeance for peaceful fatherhood. Where Tae did not recognize the wisdom of his own father in choosing him as successor, King Cymion did not see the gem of a ruler he had for a second son. Darris shook his head at the irony.

Elves lined the walls of the conference room, surrounding the travelers in what had become an almost too-familiar pattern to Kevral. One hand draped casually over the hilt of the sword Colbey had given her, the other lightly touching Ra-khir's wrist, she shed the last vestiges of annoyance remaining after her argument with those who insisted she had become too pregnant to go. The same healers and worriers would claim her unfit after the birth as well, requiring months of rest. With only two tasks left to complete, Kevral refused to delay. Tae took less than a week to recover, and she insisted they leave the following day. Whether because he worried about delay or because he refused to argue with an irritable Renshai, Griff allowed the process to continue.

Led by Marrih, the elves' chant rose like a gentle chorus of wind-blown bells. Her harder-spoken words intertwined with the sound that was not quite a melody, as if shaped to fit it. Darris tipped his head sideways, clearly trying to capture the tones, though he did not forget to shut his eyes. Kevral squeezed her lids tight, feeling the brightness and warmth of the magical flash. Then the stuffiness of an overfull room disappeared, replaced by the delicate tug of wind.

Kevral snapped open her eyes. The ground stretched in every direction in a flat plane. No trees, hills, or rivers interrupted earth packed as flat as a trading route. She saw none of her companions nor any other signs of life. Worry went through her in a short, sudden flash. *The magic failed.* Captain had warned them of the impreciseness of the operation. It had worked so well until that moment, it had never seriously occurred to Kevral to worry for it. *Where am I?*

A voice rang over the plain. "You're on the proving grounds."

Startled, Kevral jerked so hard she strained muscles. She whirled to face a woman of immense proportions, half again as tall as Ra-khir. She bore features so seamed, Kevral could not have guessed her ancestry, although the creases held too little color for an Easterner or Béarnide. Recessed by wrinkles, the pale, watery eyes looked slitted. Thinning white hair curled around broad shoulders pinched by age. A simple dress of Northern cut dangled to her ankles.

The giantess raised her hand.

Kevral crouched, studying every movement. "Where are my friends?"

"They must pace their own courses." The voice boomed with a power that seemed impossible for one so ancient and apparently frail. The hand remained raised.

"Their own courses?" The words made no sense to Kevral. "What does that mean? And what is this proving ground?"

"A test, crafted by Odin, to measure the worth of the gods' living creations. Plot your course well, young Renshai." The giantess dropped her arm, then disappeared, leaving Kevral in a lonely silence so intense she wondered if she had imagined the other and her words; yet, the memory remained with her, strong and certain. The reality of the moment seemed less sure. The plain appeared impossibly flat and empty. A light film of fog lent it a ghostly quality that stole clarity and left a bland wonderment. Only the kicks of the baby seemed sharp, viable, and real.

Finding no landmarks, Kevral took a step in a random direction. Time flew in that instant, the future unscrolling with the speed and ease of a carpet at the feet of the king. Plunged into prospective tomorrows that seemed sharper than present reality, Kevral launched into discussions, into practices, and into battles with the fury that characterized nearly every action. An instant afterward, the memory faded from her mind, desperately dreamlike. Attempts to cling to the knowledge failed miserably, no more successful than capturing smoke.

Within three strides, another joined Kevral on the path, an infant who grew to childhood within a dozen paces. Golden hair flopped over comely features, sparkling with youth. The limbs grew from pudgy to slender overnight, and toddler clumsiness melded swiftly into remarkable grace. All else about him defied Kevral's memory, but she clung to the comfort of his presence. A second giantess appeared along the trail at intervals, her existence as fleeting as the betrayal of Kevral's memories. Kevral noticed only that she resembled the first closely, except that her face bore few lines and creases, her light eyes bright. From her, Kevral came to understand that she faced only one of a myriad possible futures and that the events, and even her reactions to them, mattered less than the end result. Understanding must flee like threatened wraiths from her attempts at recollection. True knowledge of one's own fate would drive any human to insanity.

The child abandoned Kevral after less than a thousand steps, leaving only a waning impression of a handsome youth with a hint of stony gray in his blue eyes, and a motherly wistful sense of loss. Then other things shifted in to fill Kevral's life and attention. These, too, faded into an unremembered blur, trailing impressions no more significant than a rambling tale told by a street drunkard. The impression of time slipping inexorably past remained, a life lived but unremembered. Age marked her physically, but memory shied from her mind like a frightened foal whipped by a previous master.

At length, Kevral reached an end, of sorts. The plain continued into a vast eternity. Or, perhaps, she had walked in a full circle around it without knowing. The scenery that had scrolled past as she walked belonged to her world, not this one; and nothing on this place seemed ever to change. A giantess stood in front of her, this one enough like the others to be a triplet, except for the youth that softened her features nearly to childlike innocence. Wind twined a full head of yellow hair, and the blue eyes studied Kevral with a mischievous playfulness. Though she wore a dress similar to that of the first giantess, it swirled about a firm and curvaceous figure. Around her neck she wore a tear-shaped blue stone strung on a thong.

Caught in the study of the immense and impressive figure, Kevral nearly missed another at the woman's side. Dressed in stained linens and leathers, the woman appeared tiny at the giantess' side, yet anything but frail. The creased features held a fierceness that defied their age, distinctly familiar. White hair hacked short barely stirred in the wind. She wore a pair of long swords, one at each hip, equally matched for grip, length, and, surely, balance. *Grandmama?* Kevral took a hesitant forward step, struck suddenly by reality. She did not face an ancestor. She faced herself: the end result of all that living she could not remember.

The giantess raised her arm, so like the gesture the other had used to begin Kevral's trials. Only then, the Renshai surmised her identity: Skuld. *Future.* And with that knowledge came more. The elder she had first encountered could only be Urdr, *Past;* and the one who had intermittently accompanied her on the path was Verdandi, *Present.* She had met the Fates, the very keepers of time and reality, those whom even the gods could not escape. Clear and solid, Skuld's voice resembled the crash of steel in wild sword play. "Only one of you can return to your world." A smile danced over the youthful features. "Begin." Her hand slashed downward, and she, too, disappeared.

The elderly Kevral stepped forward, and Kevral prepared to talk. It seemed only logical for her to return, still in her youthful prime. She would become the other soon enough.

Yet the older Kevral did not give her junior a moment for discussion. The swords sprang from their sheaths faster than Kevral's eyes could follow. She barely managed a back-step that rescued her from a head slash, her own swords freed an instant slower. She managed to catch the second attack on the blade of the sword Colbey had gifted, surprised by her elder self's strength. Any lesser sword would have suffered a damaging notch.

Kevral scarcely managed a riposte that the other dodged neatly. She charged in with a flurry of attack that, she hoped, would confound her older self. The elder Kevral met each attack with a block, parry, or dodge, returning a stroke for every one of Kevral's. Then came a complicated Renshai maneuver that Kevral had never managed to perfect. A desperate dance brought her through the flying blades unscathed, though not without a heart-pounding moment of desperate worry. A blade skimmed her cheek, stinging. Then, Kevral cut in with a bold frontal cut that all but impaled her on a stop-thrust. She retreated.

The elder pursued, grinning as she charged. Though perhaps a hair's breadth slower, her strikes contained a refinement Kevral could not match. Awe at the other's competence turned to pride. She had strived for the elder's abilities, had always hoped she would become this able. When she reached this age, she might actually manage her goal, to challenge Colbey himself.

The moment of thought became a fatal lapse. The elder cut through an instantaneous gap to slam Kevral's right sword from her hand. Faster than sight, she caught the hilt, now facing Kevral three swords to one. Yet, the battle still did not finish. Kevral dove in with renewed energy, challenged rather than defeated by the inequality. She launched in for a frenzied over/under combination, drawing on youthful vigor. The older Kevral evaded the complicated sequence with a minimum of movement, a dodge Kevral hoped she would live to analyze. Then, an invisible blitz stole her grip on the second sword. Both dove for the errant hilt. Kevral arrived first, foiled by a deadly weave of steel in front of her face. Forced into withdrawal, she watched helplessly as the elder claimed the last of her weapons.

No! Shocked, Kevral watched as her opponent raised her blades in triumph. She did not worry for her life or for the disgrace. The better warrior had triumphed, yet the cost would prove her youth. The baby would never exist. The future she had sped through on this world must become her past, whatever its unrememberable content. She would return to Midgard having accumulated fifty years, a sixty-six-year-old woman married to a knight not yet eighteen.

Skuld studied the combatants as if she had never left. The elder's shoulder seemed to disappear beneath the giantess' massive palm. "You have demonstrated betterment of self during your lifetime journey." A dizzying swirl of magic surrounded Kevral. She back-stepped several paces, but it gained her nothing. The spell intensified, stealing all sensation of position. Upended mentally and physically, Kevral howled and fought, clawing and kicking at currents that took no notice of her savage movements. The Northern rune for "success" swirled past her.

At Skuld's side, Ra-khir's red hair lay speckled with white, the foremost line receding. Eyes green as emeralds met those of his youth, and a smile split a face still handsome despite time's ravages. The years had proved kind to the skin of his face and hands, thinning with nary a wrinkle. The veins in his arms appeared more prominent, yet the skin did not sink between the tendons of his callused hands. Though still tall, his body had become more lean and sinewy than the muscular powerfulness that characterized his late teens. He wore knight-colored silks perfectly tailored to conform to this new figure.

Ra-khir tried not to stare, instinctively knowing, as Kevral had, that he faced himself fifty years in the future. Still, he felt the need to ask. "Are you me, sir?"

The figure spoke with the gently patient tone that characterized the best knight instructors. "Maybe."

Ra-khir's brows rose at an answer that seemed evasive when definitive seemed both possible and polite. "Either you are, or you aren't, sir." Though he challenged the response, he would remain always gracious to an elder, especially a Knight of Erythane.

The elder's tone gained an edge so slight it did not offend. Ra-khir found himself overattentive to the delivery, seeking to emulate. "Sir Ra-khir Kedrin's son, the future holds more than one possibility. Events and consequences have their own significance, but the wisdom we gain from them matters more."

"Thank you, sir." Ra-khir believed he understood.

"Come." The elder held out a hand. "Let me teach you."

Ra-khir obeyed, shocked to discover the discourses that followed, filled with guided demonstration, reminded him closely of his father's own patient wisdom. At times, the elder's comments seemed as cryptic as his father's own; yet the kindness of their speaking softened them to challenging puzzles rather than the frustrations that Kedrin often left him feeling. It seemed as if Ra-khir had, over time, refined his father's strengths and weaknesses, remembered from his youth.

The time ended too soon. Skuld made a gesture Ra-khir could not read, though his older self apparently could. The elder sat, tapping the ground to indicate Ra-khir should join him. With a bow of respect, Ra-khir performed as requested. The elder stared into the distance, as if seeing something interesting in the vast expanse of flat dirt. "Ra-khir, imagine that the love between Kevral and yourself becomes lost."

Ra-khir lost his breath. He jerked his head to the elder. *No!*

As if oblivious to the agony his pronouncement caused, the elder continued. "In fact, that it turns to desperate hatred."

"No," Ra-khir finally managed aloud. "That will never happen. It can't ever happen." He clung to that certainty, fighting the pain that hovered beyond self-delusion. If the elder Ra-khir spoke truth, he might just as well end his life now.

The elder continued, ignoring Ra-khir's response. "Kevral marries another, who claims Saviar as his own. And Kevral tells the boy nothing but evil about you."

Ra-khir froze, momentarily overwhelmed before his brows crunched downward in cynical disbelief. "You're baiting me. That's not what's going to happen to me. It's what happened to my father."

Skuld frowned judgmentally.

The elder raised his hands in a forestalling gesture, though whether to silence Ra-khir or Skuld, the younger man could not tell.

Ra-khir had never understood his father's absence from his childhood, had never agreed with Kedrin's methods then. "I would attempt to reason with Kevral."

"Kevral would prove unreasonable, her hatred gaining strength daily. She would refuse to speak with you except to hurt."

Ra-khir grew uneasy. His hands winched closed. "Then, sir, I would fight for my fair share of time with my son."

"Kevral would deny it."

"I would fight, not with violence, but with legality."

"And if Kevral used your fight as an excuse to speak bad things about you to Saviar?"

"I would deny them." Ra-khir's nails gouged his palm. "I would tell him the truth."

"That his mother is a liar?"

"If need be. If it were truth."

The elder shifted toward Ra-khir, the green eyes sober. "Kevral would never give you the opportunity. And if you did speak evil of her, truth or not, what effect do you believe it would have on Saviar?"

Ra-khir forced himself to think back to a time he would rather forget, when his mother and stepfather held sway over all he perceived as reality. He had always wished his father had fought harder for the right to raise him, had harbored bitterness over the choices his mother made him suffer, including the one, at sixteen, that had driven him forever from her and to his father. At one time, he had believed his father's decision not to fight a tragedy that had cost him too much time. He still did not wholly understand his father's strategy, to resist interference until Ra-khir grew old enough to separate truth from deception by himself, to never speak ill of his mother, no matter the extent of her evil. Yet, now, he finally believed he someday would.

"Success," Skuld chortled. And the magic began.

Withered fingers danced across lute strings, wringing out a deep and violent sorrow that defined raw grief. The words that trickled from the old man's throat bore a sweetness that blended perfect harmonies, matured but never gruffened by age. Darris' features had roughened. The hazel eyes settled deeply into their sockets, enhancing the large nose; and the broad lips had shriveled. Yet, for the first time since childish innocence and ignorance had allowed him to fall beneath the spell of his mother's voice, he found himself utterly spellbound by another musician. Tears sprang to his eyes, unbound by the primal beauty of his elder self's talent.

A few strands of gold tied elder Andvari's left war braid to his right, and the chime of steel barely reached ears that had lost their high range of hearing. Blue eyes still keen, he followed every movement of his younger self's ax, but he found his reactions frustratingly slowed. He fought a desperate battle for the sake of the very one who opposed him. Young Andvari could only believe he needed to fight to win at a time when losing would serve him better. If the old self failed to prove that he had bettered himself in some fashion, he would return to Midgard with fifty years behind him and only faded memories of the trip. Yet the Fate's laws gagged him. He could not warn young Andvari to lose. He could only find a way to use experience to outdo his young and vital self.

Wisdom had allowed the elder to anticipate the problem. Devoid of landscape, the plain gave him nothing. So, he had prepared the ground with a memorized series of holes dug by his own hand. The younger man's ax blazed repeatedly for critical areas, true to his training. The older man concentrated on the minimum of necessary evasion, conserving strength and energy. He kept his attacks to the necessary, bearing in only to keep Andvari off his guard and to steer him in the appropriate directions. A high strike pulled the younger man's gaze upward, and a feigned opening in defense sent him lunging forward. Young Andvari's foot slammed down on a hole. He stumbled, flailing a wild defense as he caught his balance. As he lost his footing, it proved easier for the elder to drive him to the second hole, then the third. Andvari tumbled to the ground, and the elder pinned him at the throat with the point of his blade. Andvari went still.

And Skuld, once again, worked the magic of success.

* * *

The testing ground unnerved Tae Kahn, and he found himself crouched nervously in front of the giantess and a coarse-featured elder with a snarl of salt-and-pepper hair. Like the others, he knew the identity of the other man, yet he found himself unable to study the end result of fifty years of living on himself. Inelastic skin proved more forgiving of the scars, which tended to fall into creases. Unlike his own, the eyes did not dart but remained as steadily focused as Tae's had when he confronted Prince Leondis. Until this moment, it had not occurred to him that he now tended to look directly upon those with whom he conversed. Though he still slept on the barest edge of awakening, a habit he doubted his gang training and need to escape enemies would ever allow to die, he had learned the importance of keeping his eyes still to garnering a trust that once did not matter to him.

Several moments passed in silence, during which Skuld turned increasingly measuring looks on the elder. The blue eyes seemed to burn, fiery pinpoints goading the older Tae to action.

"What do you want from us?" Tae finally demanded.

The head swiveled, owllike, to him. Unlike with the others, Skuld gave him a clue. "I want nothing from you. He is the one who must act."

Tae recalled the comment of the eldest giantess who mythology identified as Urdr. She had called this "Odin's testing ground." From only those two details, Tae surmised his fate. He lowered his head. "Fitting that my future has no betterment. My lifestyle would not allow me to reach his age anyway."

Finally, the aged Tae cleared his throat. "It is not that I haven't bettered myself." The words emerged in a confident tenor that startled Tae. It was the voice of a king. "Simply, I'm looking for the best way to prove it. Not only to you, but to myself." He gave the young Tae a smile that contained not the wisdom of the experienced elder but the conspiratorial unity of a friend. "Sometimes, there is betterment in sameness." The words seemed nonsense, but he continued, "The ability to appreciate, even embrace, youth long after it has faded. To love and respect, rather than only chide our children. To remember why we did the foolish things we did and why others deserve the chance to make the same mistakes."

Tae listened appreciatively, reading the mischief in dark eyes he was accustomed to seeing only in a mirror. Even time could not wholly dull the fire, though he would have believed otherwise in the days before they embarked on this leg of their journey. Fifty years later, he had still not forgotten the doubts, the excitements, the humor that had defined him at his current age.

The elder said, "I'll become a leader of men, without losing my humility. My judgments will remain always tempered by just enough self-doubt to keep me from becoming a King Cymion, from believing myself above the very laws I dedicate myself to uphold. Along the way, I'll search my soul for what's right: for myself, for my son, for those I love." He met Tae's gaze. "I'll come to fully understand my father and, from experience, avoid the same mistakes."

Tae felt a sudden, intense desire to return home and frolic with Subikahn. The compliments desperately embarrassed him.

"But, if none of that proves my betterment, here are two that might." The elder said something more, fluently, in a language Tae did not understand, though he recognized it as Renshai.

Tae grinned. The last holdout among the civilized human languages would not defy him forever.

"The other, Tae," the old man continued to gaze at his younger self, "is understanding. Do you remember when you asked Ra-khir if he would steal food if he would otherwise starve?"

Tae could not forget. "He said 'no.'"

"Someday, Tae, you will understand that answer."

Tae doubted that possibility. He had learned much of morality that he once would have found inconceivable. His association with Kevral, Ra-khir, Darris, and Matrinka had already changed him more than he would have believed possible. And, slowly, he was beginning to find ethics he could admire in the father who had organized criminals.

Apparently convinced, Skuld gave Tae, too, a pass.

Nameless, the fifty-year-old man stood alone in front of the youngest of the Fates. Golden hair, devoid of gray, lay hacked short in a battle cut across his brow. The delicate oval of his face gave no indication of his age, and keen blue eyes held a faint trace of gray. A long, slender sword hung at his waist, its make a subtle blur that matched his clothing. Other than his features, predetermined by blood, nothing about him felt concrete. His potential remained untapped and unlimited, his future a vast fog.

Skuld's voice boomed like thunder. "The law is clear on this. To return as your younger self, you must prove that you bettered yourself to him."

The man smiled. "How could I not have bettered myself? I have no younger self."

"Precisely." Skuld interpreted the situation differently. "Without a younger self to whom to prove yourself, you cannot earn your way back to his age."

The man felt his heart rate quicken and calmed it using the mental techniques his mother had taught. On the path, she alone could guide him, yet he understood his real future, if he had one, might not include the woman who bore him. "At the risk of displaying too much pride, I believe my life will have significance—whether as a fully trained Renshai or the heir to a major kingdom."

Skuld folded bulging arms across her chest. "I'm not debating the significance of your life, but Odin made his laws on this matter clear. Most humans do not believe the worth of an intelligent being can be measured, but this test does exactly that." Her pale eyes contained no mercy. "A month prior to your birth, I can only compare you to a baby. It's difficult to better an innocent who has no concept of chaos or the evils it represents."

The man returned the giantess' stare, feigning easy confidence beneath stark terror. He did not wish to return to Midgard with his life already mostly lived. Kevral's lessons would stay with him in instinctive ways, but the details of his life, the emotions, the love would remain an eternal blur. "Some would call infants ultimate chaos."

Skuld cracked a smile that she swiftly hid. "It matters not. You cannot prove you bettered yourself." She looked him up and down. "At least age does not seem to have touched you too hard."

"It has not because my life is eternal, and the soul I lost to the spirit spiders immaterial. Nonetheless, I deserve a childhood."

"I decide what you deserve."

The man pursed his lips, seeking the words to convince. He had little time. Already, the others likely waited and his mother would worry for the fetus absent from her womb. *Mother!* "Have you judged Kevral and Ra-khir already?"

"Yes."

"They bettered themselves?"

"Yes."

The man grasped for his only remaining hope. "Whether they have me a moment or a lifetime, our fates remain entwined."

Skuld frowned. "How so? I don't believe in blood as magic. Children are happily fostered daily, their fates eternally separated from those who gave birth to them."

"Indeed." The man persisted. At least he had her listening. "I may never know she whose blood I share or the knight who the law and I consider my father, whether or not we share blood. But Ra-khir and Kevral will never forget me. Consideration of my needs, and those of so many others, will have a profound effect on them." He delivered the coup de grace. "It will prove a strong factor in what they become fifty years from now and whether or not they better themselves."

Skuld's eyes narrowed, and a glow more fire than light flickered in them. "You're saying if I already passed them, I have to pass you, too? Even though you haven't met Odin's criteria?"

That being self-evident, the man gave no reply. He simply focused a sober-eyed gaze on the giantess.

Kevral arrived first amid lean, triangular stems poking from neat rows of dark earth. Birds trilled in a dozen different voices. The air lay saturated with the aroma of damp soil. The sun beamed down, gliding toward the horizon. The field stretched as far as her vision, then rose to mountains in the east, north and south. Westward, the world beyond the fields trailed into gray obscurity. Her body felt ungainly and awkward, strong with youth but hampered by the now-enormous bulge in her abdomen. She felt no movement from the baby. At first, this did not bother her; she had grown accustomed to not having it in the fifty years of life that had passed her on the testing plain.

Kevral examined her hands. They appeared callused and scarred, devoid of thinning or wrinkles. She touched her face. The wind blew the short feathers of her hair, tickling across her fingers. Everything felt normal. The memories of the trial had faded. She recalled nothing of her fifty-year trip across the plains, other than the baby. *A boy.* Kevral gritted her teeth, too grief-stricken to revel. Pudar had wanted her to bear them a girl. And still, the baby did not move inside her.

Ra-khir appeared a moment later, looking a bit disheveled but otherwise exactly as he had before their journey began. Darris came next, followed by Andvari, then Tae. They all began talking at once, describing their future selves and the method with which they proved their betterment. Only Tae remained silent on the matter, his discussion with the future-Tae sensitive and personal. And still, the baby did not move.

Chan'rék'ril arrived on the field next and El-brinith an instant later. Neither appeared different to Kevral, but appearance might not reveal the truth. Fifty years would not likely change either. The grin on El-brinith's face, so unelflike, gave a stronger clue. "The Fates told me that the elves originally failed this task, their frivolous joy not allowing them to better themselves. Near-immortality saved our people." The grin broadened, if possible. "But it didn't have to save me. My interest in feeling different types of magic will become a talent, with a lot of hard work. I'll become adept at separating and defining power."

"In this, apparently, humanity has had a positive effect on our people," Chan'rék'ril added. "I also returned to my younger self. I'll become more magically adept, especially at my favorite thing: artistic creations."

Their joy became infectious. Kevral smiled wistfully, wondering whether humans had truly benefited the elves or only made them more like themselves. The baby did not kick. In the past month, Kevral could not recall it lying still so long.

Darris asked the question Kevral had considered. "Is the change in the elves a good thing?"

El-brinith pinned the bard with her gaze. "I believe it is. We have no sentimental connection to our past. Whether we like it or not, Alfheim is gone forever, and we need to adjust to our new world. Finding betterment over a lifetime is one of the best traits of humans."

Tae returned, though Kevral had not seen him leave nor noticed him missing. Perplexedness scrunched his features. "This looks familiar. I'd guess we're in the Westlands. Around the fertile oval."

El-brinith confirmed the assessment with an elfin-subtle nod. "Skuld sent us back to Midgard. I can transport us easily from here, since I talked her into giving me this." She raised the thong the giantess had worn around her neck, with the tear-shaped Pica shard. "I appreciate her assistance. I might have had trouble transporting with a member missing."

Kevral's hands flew to her abdomen, even as she realized another had not yet joined them. As if in answer to the concern, the baby jolted into a wild flurry of movement. "Where *is* Rascal?"

At the question, Tae's gaze zipped around the group. "Yes. Where is she?"

El-brinith raised her brows, then shrugged. "She couldn't—"

"—better herself," Tae finished in a loud whisper. "She's . . . old?"

"She's gone," El-brinith corrected.

"Gone?" the Easterner repeated carefully.

"Her lifestyle did not allow for old age."

It took Kevral until those words to realize that Rascal was dead. "Gods."

Tae only stared in stark silence.

Kevral moved to his side, placing a sympathetic arm around him and surprised to find tears in her eyes. She refused to delve into their origin, worried that she cried only for Tae's loss and not Rascal's death. "You did your best."

"No." Tae buried his face into Kevral's shoulder, sobbing. "I could have done more."

Ra-khir moved to them, stroking Tae's hair with a gentle hand. "If you had, it would not have made a difference. You can guide one with blinders, but you can't force her to see. You can't better one who refuses to better herself." He glanced at Kevral over Tae, head rocking and eyes dropping to indicate the Easterner.

Kevral understood the wordless communication. If not for Tae's own strength of character, they could not have changed him either. The Tae they had known at the start of their mission to rescue King Griff would have died on the proving grounds as well.

So much remained to discuss and consider, especially those few events remembered. Kevral wondered whether time would bring back snatches of recollection from her journey, if those would merge with or confuse the reality of future, or if they would simply slip away. In the time before they searched for the last Pica shard, she would muse over what little she remembered of what she had lived and consider whether those events were truly predictive of the next fifty years. *A boy? Or just one possibility?*

Once again, Keveral felt herself enwrapped by magic, this time El-brinith's transport.

CHAPTER 29

The Stalking Horse

The larger the enemy, the larger the victory.
                                        —*Renshai proverb*

KING Cymion lunged at the padded and armored warrior in his practice room, sending his massive opponent into awkward retreat. The king pressed his advantage with a quick thrust. The soldier slapped it aside, a desperate defense. A tinny clang rose from the contact, sour compared to the crisp music of exchanged strikes and sweeps that had filled the room moments ago. Barely diverted, Cymion's blade wobbled through the opening, scoring a nonfatal touch on the thickly padded breastplate. The tip flipped to the man's throat. "Done."

When the threat disappeared, the soldier bowed, then strode to the "dead man's" corner to join six other casualties of the king's practice.

Cymion pulled a rag from his pocket, wiped beads of perspiration from the steel, then mopped his face. He turned to the door, with its water pot and dipper, only to find Javonzir waiting. Dressed in colors, the adviser clearly attended kingdom business, not seeking a spar. Cymion sighed and sheathed his blade. His cousin worked his arm less and less, and his skills slowly withered.

As the king's attention found him, Javonzir performed a flawless bow. "Your Majesty, I hate to interrupt." The seriousness of his tone warned Cymion not to delay.

"Dismissed." The king made a high gesture at the "corpses," then another at those still anticipating the chance to pit their swords against him. When only his personal guards and servants remained, Cymion peeled off his practice armor and padding, attendants scurrying to claim each piece and arrange for its cleaning. Others ran ahead while some hovered for a command. "What do you need, Javon?"

"Your son has returned, Your Majesty."

King Cymion froze in mid-movement, leaving a servant nervously reaching for a sodden undertunic. Ordinarily, Leondis' appearances did not warrant attention. Now, heat flashed through the king, not wholly attributable to exertion. He doffed and flung the tunic so suddenly, the attendant had to chase it. "What's wrong with that whelp? I didn't give him permission to return." His eyes narrowed at the only condition that would legitimize the homecoming. "Does he have my grandchild?"

Javonzir shook his head once, not in answer, but to indicate the king should not speak ill of the crown prince in front of servants who might gossip. A time would likely come when Leondis needed their respect. "The baby is not yet born; but the prince is not alone, Your Majesty. The King of Stalmize is with him."

King Cymion's pale eyes winched open in increments as the significance of the words trickled ever deeper. "King Weile Kahn is here?"

"Yes, Your Majesty."

"In Pudar?"

"In the Waiting Area."

"Gods." Cymion threw off the last of his clothes and lowered his voice. "What's his disposition?"

Javonzir hesitated. "He's a difficult man to read, Your Majesty." He addressed the servants. "Draw His Majesty's bath. Prepare the best clothes."

Those who had not already done so scurried to obey.

King Cymion managed to maintain a regal air despite his nakedness. The workout pumped his muscles into boulders. "Has he brought an entourage?"

"Two guards only, Your Majesty. And your son."

"My son." It made no sense. "Now how do you suppose Leondis. . . ?"

Javonzir's silken shoulders rose and fell. "Your Majesty, they surrendered weapons easily enough and haven't caused any trouble. I believe, as his other Majesty says, they've come for a friendly discussion. He claims the prince talked him into this visit."

The royalty became confusing. "His prince? Or my prince?"

"Prince Leondis, Sire."

Cymion headed toward his bath, servants and guards trotting to keep up with his long strides. "What in heaven's name do you think he's up to?"

Javonzir fell into step beside his king. "I don't know, Sire. I'm sure he has a good reason."

Cymion stopped dead. "What logic can there be to bringing a hostile king, the father of Severin's murderer, into my home without warning?"

Javonzir seized the king's arm and encouraged him to keep walking. It would not do to keep a king waiting nor to stand too long unclothed in open hallways. "Your Majesty, Prince Leondis has a good head. If he believes it best—"

"Threatened, no doubt," the king grumbled, though he had no proof. "Separate them. I trust you to do so tactfully. Find out what's going on." As he reached the bathing room, the door flew open. "Tell the king I'll be with him shortly. Apologize for not being prepared for him."

"Your Majesty, he's already expressed regret for coming unannounced."

Cymion stepped into the room, slamming the door as the servants positioned to close it dashed out of his way. *King Weile Kahn of Stalmize is here.* He clapped a hand to his face. And hoped the high king of the Eastlands had come in peace.

Nobles filled the benches of King Cymion's court, eager to watch a confrontation between kings, to observe the dealings that might finally bring closure to their beloved Severin's murder. On his throne, Cymion prepared for a verbal offensive as strong as his swordarm. He held the upper hand in his own court, surrounded by a dozen of his guards and with morality squarely on his side. He did not worry for Weile Kahn's arguments. Even another king would not dare attempt to bully him under those circumstances, and every run of possible scenarios through his mind went the same. Weile Kahn could only guess what had happened that night based on his son's description. Cymion had been there when his watch returned, wailing like banshees and cradling Severin's lifeless body. They had dragged Tae to the worst of the dungeons. Had he not already been unconscious from the beating he had received from rival Easterners on the street, the guards would have finished the job.

Cymion's thoughts slid to the image of Tae, striped with blood, lying still on the cold stone floor. Rimed with dirt, his hair a dark snarl, his clothes tattered rags, he had seemed the epitome of classless street scum. The urge to kick him beyond oblivion had seized the king then and every time since that he dared to recall the scene. Had he followed his instincts, succumbed to a father's honest rage, he would not face this difficulty now. And Tae would have died as the vagabond he was, gaining no benefit from his father's takeover, his crimes unforgiven, never protected and coddled as a prince.

Apparently sensing his king's distress, Javonzir clamped a placating hand onto Cymion's arm. He stood to the king's left, prepared to counsel and console as the moment required.

The great doors swung open. The court guards snapped to attention, spear butts clicking to tile. They carried the polearms only for show. Should violence ensue, the size of the room would require shorter weapons, and each also wore a sword crafted to Kevral's rigorous specifications. Two of Béarn's guards stepped through, followed by a page who announced loudly, "Prince Leondis."

Dressed in travel silks, Leondis stepped grandly into his father's court. The dark brown hair, so like his mother's, tumbled to his shoulders. He bowed with a grandeur befitting a Knight of Erythane, then took a position to the right of King Cymion's focus, leaving space for the visiting king and his entourage. No longer a foppish child, he had grown into a cultured man that Cymion might not have recognized except for the chiseled cheekbones, the proud nose, and the alert blue eyes that distinguished their line. For the first time, Cymion noticed well-defined sinews enhancing an otherwise slender body. Leondis could not have changed so much in a few months. Rather, the time apart had given the king new perspective.

Cymion did not have long to consider before the page stepped up again. "King Weile Kahn of Stalmize."

The audience of nobles rose with varying degrees of decorum. Cymion also stood, a formality the situation allowed him to violate. After discussion with the visiting king, Cymion's advisers and ministers had decreed it best to dispense with protocol of any type rather than attempt to define the boundaries of each king's obligations when it came to displays of respect. Low-born, Weile Kahn did not place proper significance on these gestures, which annoyed and pleased Cymion simultaneously. The missing "Sires" and "Your Majesties" would bother his ear; but he appreciated that he would not have to speak them himself either, nor bring a chair to properly place Weile Kahn at his level.

Another pair of Pudarian guards stepped through the courtroom door, followed by an imposing figure dressed in cleaned, tailored leathers lacking colors. Blue-black curls hugged his head, without a hint of gray. A stubby forehead curved to large eyes so dark they seemed to lack irises. A well-set nose perched above spare lips. His swarthy skin bore a healthy hue that made Cymion's guards seem sallow in comparison. A man walked at his either hand, both wearing expressions so densely solemn they appeared as if they never laughed. They made an oddly matched pair, the left one tall yet with a sturdy compactness. The other looked huge, even to a warrior king, taller than the first but more classically proportioned.

Despite his lack of finery, the man in the middle carried himself with an ironhanded confidence that identified him as the king. Cymion's first impression, that Weile Kahn was large, failed with comparison to his bodyguards and to his own warrior frame. The Eastern king stood a full head shorter than the smaller of his entourage, yet the impression defied logic. His largeness came wholly of demeanor, and his ability to carry himself in such a fashion fascinated as well as unnerved. Cymion found himself emulating the man's movements, attempting to memorize them for his own future use.

Cymion remained silent only until Weile Kahn came to a halt. The dark eyes whipped to Cymion's, depthless and unrevealing.

Unaccustomed to others directly meeting his gaze, Cymion fought the urge to shift nervously or to look aside. Instead, he attempted to distract Weile Kahn, the nobility, even himself, with speech. "Welcome to Pudar . . . " He caught himself about to tack on a "Your Majesty." "To what do we owe the pleasure of your visit?" Cymion felt it best to address his guest's agenda before his own, though likely they overlapped. Aside from Tae and the possibility of an alliance, no other business seemed conceivable.

The dark eyes never wavered. "We were en route to Béarn when your son suggested we stop here first and handle some unfinished business." Weile shook back his curls. "I was not opposed."

Nothing. Cymion still read no emotion in the Easterner's unwavering gaze nor in the pleasant tenor of his voice, even harshened by its accent. "Which business would you like to finish?"

Weile made a conciliatory gesture, yet still retained his authority. "You choose, King Cymion."

Cymion made a mental note of the movement, surprised that one untrained in the ways of rulership could manage so much nonverbal power. He sought a tactful way to raise the issue of Tae, without losing his vengeance or the chance for an alliance. He had worried for Béarn's kinship with the East; now, he grew concerned that he himself might drive it. "If I were King Weile Kahn of Stalmize, I would want my son to be brought to justice."

A slight smile crawled onto Weile Kahn's features. "If I were King Cymion of Pudar, so would I."

The words took Cymion aback, leaving him with none of his own for reply. He touched Javonzir's wrist, a plea for assistance.

The adviser's reassuring voice hissed into Cymion's ear. "I believe he's speaking of Leondis now, Sire. Meaning your own son is not wholly innocent."

The subtlety of the attack unmanned Cymion. He could not even raise anger. He tried to use equal tact, talking around the issue so as not to embarrass kings or princes. "Do you think things other than they appear?"

"The facts," Weile said carefully, "do not fit the outcome."

"He has a point, Your Majesty." Javonzir's whispering continued, "If

Tae could best Severin knife to sword, why would he have trouble killing Leondis with a surprise attack from behind?"

Cymion tossed off the question with a shake of auburn hair as curly as Weile's, though liberally flecked with white. He had a solid twenty years of age on the East's high king. The situations held little comparison. One had occurred on Pudar's streets, with myriad players. The other had taken place one-on-one in a castle room. "Prince Tae Kahn has not denied the charges."

Weile spread his hands. "An error in morality or in judgment? Not the first time my son has chosen to protect others over himself." His grin became sharklike. "He didn't learn that from me."

The assertion seemed outlandish. "Who is he . . . protecting?"

Weile gave nothing away, resisting the opportunity to implicate Leondis with a directed glance. "If I said, it would defeat my son's sacrifice, would it not?"

Cymion read relief on his own prince's face, and his certainty wavered for the first time. He revived it with the memory of his favorite son lying so still, so handsome, the hopes of a kingdom buried with his corpse. The chance to avenge Severin, even with cultured imprisonment, seemed worth any deception. The solution rose directly from Weile's words, and Cymion seized it triumphantly. "Refusing to allow justice would defeat that sacrifice also, would it not?"

Weile Kahn's grin disappeared, replaced by an expression that rewarded Cymion's success.

Now Cymion smiled. It seemed he had outwitted the master schemer, and the King of Stalmize's deference on this one matter pleased him more than he expected.

"Very well, then," Weile Kahn said. "If you insist, I will remove Tae from Béarn's law. And her protection." He glanced at his leftmost bodyguard, as if noticing the man for the first time. The dense guardian stood like a statue, his eyes as active as his body was still. "In Eastern tradition, the king is law. I can spare Tae for . . ." His hand flickered as he considered, then he lowered it. ". . . say five years. Let him work on your kitchen staff, serve as your personal steward. Or hold him in a cell; he might learn more as a prisoner."

Cymion had the distinct impression he had just received an agile insult, one too subtle to protest.

"Now, perhaps, we can move on to more important matters."

Another insult, Cymion believed, existed in the suggestion that discussion of trade routes should be considered more significant than regicide. Yet Weile's discretion rescued him from a hostile response. It would not, however, spare Tae from Cymion's pronouncement. He drew breath to suggest a more physical punishment accompany the imprisonment, prepared to bargain to acceptable compromise.

Before Cymion could speak, Leondis broke in. "Father, I apologize for disrupting the proceedings out of turn, but you must know one thing."

Cymion's eyes flitted to Leondis, his annoyance clear. He would not spare his son his wrath. "What is it, Leondis?"

"I pardoned Prince Tae Kahn."

"What?" The word was startled from the king.

"I pardoned him, Father," Leondis repeated. "I have conclusive proof that he didn't kill Severin, and he didn't attack me either. Under the circumstances, it was the least I could do."

"No," Cymion said, using a monotone to hide burgeoning rage. "The least you could do was nothing." He glanced at Weile Kahn, suddenly realizing that the whole of the Eastern king's casual generosity with Tae's future had been a sham. Surely he had known of the pardon before offering Cymion five years of his son's life. Pudar's king also understood now why Leondis and Weile Kahn had returned together. The Eastern king had become Leondis' "stalking horse," sent ahead to rescue Leondis from punishment. Irritation disappeared, replaced by grudging respect, for Leondis as well as Weile Kahn. Cymion suspected his expression closely resembled the one Weile Kahn had turned him moments before. Trapped, he gave the only answer he could, "Well, then. I suppose this matter is finished."

Javonzir leaned into the king. "Might I suggest we retire and reflect before we bargain away the greater part of the city to this aptly named king?"

Cymion caught the pun. Though the Easterner pronounced his name *Way*-lee, it came near enough to "wily" in Western dialect to make the point. Cymion prepared to speak as Javonzir advised. He would not bargain treaties with Weile Kahn until he amassed an army of wise men around him. One thing seemed certain. It might be worth the greater part of the city to have the King of Stalmize on his side.

A splash of warm water on Ra-khir's legs awakened him from sleep with his heart pounding. He jerked toward Kevral, finding her bolt upright in bed, face more pale than usual. A puddle soaked the sheets and blankets. "Kevral, are you well?" He reached for her.

Kevral nodded. "The baby's coming."

Ra-khir bit his lower lip. They had expected this for so long, yet he still felt unready. He had often lamented that he could not be there for the twins, offering his support to his wife and watching the miracle of birth. Now, the experience he had wished for in secret seemed more burden than joy. "How long?"

"I don't know." Kevral winced but showed no other sign of pain. "Matrinka said the second time happens much faster."

Matrinka. We need a healer. Ra-khir wondered why he seemed to have turned so muddle-headed. "Stay here. I'll get help."

Kevral bunched the blankets around her. "Thank you." Ra-khir dressed swiftly, hearing her mutter as he stepped out into the hall. "We'll see who arrives first, healers or Cymion's vultures."

Ra-khir closed the door. "Healers," he promised softly to the hallway. "I'll see to it." Swiftly, he headed toward the queen's quarters. His honor taught him never to bother royalty after dark, but he knew Matrinka would never forgive him if he allowed the baby to arrive without her assistance. He knew because she had made it abundantly clear with threats. And he knew that she alone could keep the Pudarians away. *At least we no longer have to worry about the prince.* The image of Leondis wringing his hands, hovering over Kevral and the baby like a properly concerned father stabbed his heart like a blade.

As Ra-khir hurried through Béarn's hallways, he thought of Leondis' last words as he left the castle for home: "Only fitting that you should attend mine as I did yours." At the time, it had made no sense to the Knight of Erythane; other concerns had superseded it. Now, he understood. The prince had stood by Kevral while she birthed the twins. And, now, Ra-khir would oversee the birth of Pudar's heir.

Pudar's heir. Ra-khir's hands drooped open, without the strength to bunch. He sought the inner strength the next several hours would demand. Weakened by childbirth, physically and emotionally vulnerable, Kevral would desperately need him at a time when he wrestled his own grief. The baby belonged to Pudar. He had no choice but to harden his heart to the tiny, helpless infant who had grown inside his wife, would be left with only the memories of its fluttering against him at night.

Béarnian guards in the hallway came rigidly to attention at the sight of Ra-khir, though he wore hurriedly donned, off-duty attire and his hair lay in sleep's disarray. One left the doors of the royal quarters to approach him with a greeting. "What can we do for you, Sir Ra-khir?"

"Please let Her Ladyship know Kevral's baby is on the way." Ra-khir ran a hand through the red tangles, suddenly self-conscious about his appearance. Knights properly remained dignified and in control at all times, not just during procedures and maneuvers.

"Thank you, sir." The guard headed back to his fellows. After a brief exchange beyond the range of Ra-khir's hearing, two entered the queen's chambers, the door clicking closed behind them. A moment later, they emerged, and another round of quiet discussion ensued.

Ra-khir shifted from foot to foot. Though the whole affair had taken moments, the delay felt interminable. He belonged at Kevral's side.

The guard approached Ra-khir again. "Sir, she says she'll meet you at your room."

Ra-khir resisted the urge to catapult himself back through the corridors to Kevral, relievedly leaving everything in the queen's hands. "What would she like me to do?"

The guard smiled. Apparently, Matrinka had anticipated the question. "She told us to tell you to just go. She'll handle everything, sir."

Ra-khir gave up a crooked grin in return. "Thank you." He would present Matrinka with a more enthusiastic show of gratitude when she arrived. His mind still refused to function normally, and though he knew much needed doing, he could think of nothing but holding Kevral's hand. Turning in a smooth motion befitting a march, he headed back down the corridor.

As during his trip there, Ra-khir noticed nothing of the magnificent murals, torch brackets, and tapestries that covered Béarn's walls. His concern for Kevral, the baby, and the situation unfocused his thoughts and interrupted all the streams of his consciousness. Nothing made sense but to dutifully follow the paths he had already determined as right. He plunged through the door to his quarters. The blankets balled in wadded disarray on the floor. Kevral lay on the center of the bed, her head balanced on both pillows, her legs drawn to her abdomen. The Béarnian-made nightshirt covered her, bulge and all. Tinged brown, a puddle stained the sheets, the bulk of it on her side of the bed.

Ra-khir pursed his lips, taking in the situation. He saw no reason for Kevral to remain in the damp spot left by the breaking of her water. "Can you get up?"

Kevral nodded. "I taught a class with stronger pains than this."

Ra-khir cringed at the memory of General Markanyin's description. More than one Pudarian soldier had witnessed Kevral's collapse after she had bullied through active labor with force of will and Renshai mind techniques. When the pain finally overcame her control, it had built to a crescendo that nearly killed her. "Let's do it the regular way this time, all right?"

"All right," Kevral agreed, rolling from the ticking. "Why did you want me up?"

"I'm changing the bed." Ra-khir headed toward the chest that housed the clean linens. "No reason for you to be wet or to have a baby on dirty sheets."

Kevral laughed, climbing back into place before Ra-khir could reach the chest. "The wetness and dirt have only just begun, my love. It gets pretty bloody from here."

"Bloody?" Ra-khir repeated.

"Bloody." Kevral confirmed. "Haven't you ever seen a baby born?" She cringed, clutching her abdomen.

Ra-khir swooped to Kevral's side, dragging one hand from her nightshirt to hold. He could feel the muscles beneath it knotting. "Are you all right?" He rolled his eyes at his own stupidity. "Sorry. You're having a baby."

"I'm fine," Kevral finally managed. "Contractions close and deep. It won't be long."

Ra-khir stared. He had no siblings, no young cousins. He had once seen a calf born but never a human. "I thought it took hours, sometimes days."

"Often." Kevral tightened her fingers around Ra-khir's. "But sometimes no time at all. I've heard of women who went to the privy to relieve a few stomach cramps and had their babies there."

Renshai, maybe. Ra-khir had always heard childbirth was a tremendously painful procedure. Kevral handled it as gracefully as all physical discomfort, and he wondered if she focused on the process of birthing to avoid thinking about the end result. One moment, they would sit as two people, three the next, then two again as the Pudarians bundled their child away for his new and better life.

"Easy, Ra-khir." Kevral wriggled her fingers. "I'm the one who's supposed to do the crushing.

Ra-khir loosened his hold on Kevral's hand, watching her fingers regain their rosy hue. "Sorry."

Then, as if to prove her comment, Kevral winched her grip so tight it smashed Ra-khir's hand. A flash of pain crossed her features. Drawing her knees toward her head, she spread her legs. "Ra-khir, my love," she said through clenched teeth. "You're going to have to deliver this baby."

"What! I can't . . . I've never even seen . . ." Then, realizing protestations would not change the timing of the baby's arrival, Ra-khir worked his fingers free and headed toward the foot of the bed. He hoped the right maneuvers would come to him, as they obviously did to Kevral. But as he arrived to a trickle of fluid and a film of blood, he found himself disoriented and light-headed. *People have been birthing babies forever.* Yet his mind naturally corrected itself. *Not people. Women.*

A knock sounded through the room.

Gods be praised. In his rush for assistance, Ra-khir nearly shouted for the other to enter without identification. "Who is it?"

"It's me, Ra-khir." Matrinka's voice wafted through the panel. "And others. May we come in?"

"Please." Ra-khir rose. Suddenly protective of Kevral's privacy, he blocked the very area the healers needed to see.

The door opened to admit Matrinka, a female elf, and a human healer whose name escaped Ra-khir for the moment. Mior skittered past Matrinka's attempts to bar her with a foot as the queen shoved the door closed. The cat leaped onto the bed, curling near Kevral's face.

"I'm glad you're here. The baby's coming now."

Matrinka glanced at Kevral for confirmation, frowning at the calico. Mior shifted position slightly, deliberately keeping her face from her mistress' view.

"I have to push," Kevral said, panting from the strain of another contraction.

Matrinka stepped toward the knight. "I think we can use you better at the other end." She flicked her chin toward Kevral's head.

"Huh?" Recognizing Matrinka's polite request to move him, Ra-khir felt like an idiot. He scrambled to Kevral's side as the healers moved in to attend the delivery. The other Béarnide, who Ra-khir now recalled went by the name Lysantha, snatched up the bunched blanket, spreading it over Kevral's knees to create a cave beneath which they worked.

"Don't push yet," Matrinka called, her voice muffled by the blanket. "You're not quite ready."

How does she know that? To Ra-khir it seemed like magic, and he appreciated Matrinka's arrival more than she would ever know. He would have just stood there and hoped he caught the baby. Using his sleeve, he wiped sweat from Kevral's brow and cringed with her at the next contraction. He wriggled a hand through her clamped fingers.

"Sorry about the cat hair." Matrinka looked over the blanket to address Kevral. "I couldn't keep her out."

"That's fine," Kevral returned, the cramp apparently finished. "I like having her here."

Matrinka rolled her eyes, surely in response to something smug from Mior. She disappeared back under the blanket.

Ra-khir stroked away blonde hairs clinging to Kevral's cheeks and forehead. He wished he could do more, his appreciation for Matrinka growing in bounds at that moment. Kevral groaned, admitting a pain she would surely rather have hid. Her nails gouged the side of his smallest finger. "I . . . really . . . have to . . . push."

The elf responded this time. "Go ahead, Lady. It's time."

Kevral shoved her chin against her chest and pushed with the power of a warrior, making no sound as she did so. Then she flopped back onto the pillows, releasing a gasp of breath. She opened blue eyes with a wet glaze of pain.

Ra-khir clasped both hands around hers, desperately wishing he could take the pain onto himself.

"Relax," Matrinka commanded. She rose again to look directly at Kevral. "A couple more like that, and it'll be over." She turned her soft brown gaze to Ra-khir, the look rife with sympathy. She swallowed, addressing a difficult subject. "Kevral, when the baby's born, do you want to know. . . ?"

"It's a boy," Kevral replied, her voice weak but without a trace of uncertainty. She grunted. "Another one."

Matrinka dipped below the blanket, without questioning Kevral's assertion. "Push."

The door creaked open. Six Pudarians, three male, stood in the doorway. Attention on pushing, Kevral did not notice them, but Ra-khir knew a sudden rush of irritation. First, they had not knocked, a simple courtesy. Second, they had no right to look upon his wife's undignified position. *What are they doing here?* he wanted to hiss, stopped by honor. Instead, he waited until Kevral's grip lessened and she settled back to the bed before easing his hand free. Before he could step between the newcomers and his wife, one of the women forced her way beside Matrinka and the elfin healer. "I'm the midwife supposed to birth this baby. Why wasn't I called sooner?"

Kevral's eyes snapped open at the Pudarian voice. "Get away from me," she said, her voice containing an edge that made warriors wary. Mior rose, back arched, expelling a high-pitched growl. "Only Her Ladyship and my husband may touch me down there."

"It's my job," the midwife insisted. "I've touched thousands of women 'down there.' You have nothing unusual or special."

"I have . . . " Kevral broke into a pant, fighting another contraction and the natural need to push. Sweat spangled her bangs. ". . . the heir . . . to Pudar's . . . throne . . . down there. And . . . he'll stay . . . there . . . until you . . . back away." Her voice gained strength as the wave of pain passed.

The midwife opened her mouth, but Matrinka interrupted. "You were called immediately. The baby came early. Now, do as Kevral said, or I'll have you bodily dragged from the room."

A look of strangled outrage filled the midwife's face. She jerked her attention to Matrinka. Ra-khir watched scarlet rage drain into blanched shock as she recognized the queen of Béarn crouched between Kevral's legs, hands sticky with blood, amniotic fluid, and vernix.

"Your Ladyship." The midwife backed away and curtsied simultaneously, an awkward gesture. "I—I didn't know."

Kevral gasped.

"I'm here," Matrinka said gently. "Push, Kevral."

Ra-khir planted himself between the healers and the Pudarians, preferring to face the visitors yet too fascinated by the proceedings to do so. Once he dismissed the blood and fluid, he concentrated on the head squeezing through an exit that seemed far too small. He watched in fascination as the top of a pale scalp appeared, sparse yellow hair matted with dark fluid. "Push, Kevral," he repeated, his voice too low for her to hear.

Then, suddenly, the head slithered from the birth canal, then stopped, wedged at the shoulders.

"Is he out?" Kevral asked dizzily.

"Just the head," Ra-khir called back before anyone else could answer. "Just the beautiful, beautiful head." Excitement battered down the sorrow, and he found tears of joy in his eyes. *Has to be a girl.* Yet he knew Kevral's claim had an irrefutable basis.

The baby gurgled, then blasted out a strong cry.

"Healthy, thank the gods," a Pudarian whispered.

"Don't push now," Matrinka instructed. She pulled the head upward until a shoulder popped free, then maneuvered the baby toward the floor. "Now, one more small push."

The baby glided fully free, accompanied by a rush of fluid. Lysantha and a large-breasted Pudarian held out blankets simultaneously. Matrinka drew the baby toward herself, oblivious to the blood this smeared across her sleeping silks. For several moments, she cradled the infant before placing it into Lysantha's arms. The Béarnide carefully folded edges of cloth over the infant while Matrinka tied and cut the cord. "It *is* a boy," she announced, then pointed Lysantha toward Ra-khir as she waited for the afterbirth.

Startled, Ra-khir accepted the package without comment. The baby smelled of blood and Kevral, a mix he found surprisingly pleasant. He stared at the tiny hands, the pursed lips, and blue eyes beneath partially opened lids. Long lashes curled in surprisingly dark semicircles for one so blond. He hugged the baby close, barely feeling its impression through the folds of the blanket.

A Pudarian male cleared his throat. "Forgive the questioning, Your Ladyship. But is there purpose to delivering the future prince of Pudar to an Erythanian who bears no relation to the boy?"

Ra-khir clutched the bundle closer, worried to crush it. He tried to ignore the comment, to fight the dull certainty telling him he held his second son. The Pudarian's words became more nonsensical than offensive.

Matrinka feigned engrossment with the afterbirth.

Ra-khir drifted to Kevral's side. "Do you want to hold him?"

The midwife made a horrified sound. "No! Please, I mean only the best for her when I say don't do that. If she holds him, it will only make his loss that much harder."

Kevral reached for the baby with genuine need. It was not just defiance that fueled her desire, and Ra-khir trusted Matrinka's judgment over the Pudarian's. He settled the blankets into her arms. A serene smile bowed Kevral's lips, and she stroked the baby with a finger, touching him all over as if to memorize the feel as well as the look.

"A cruelty," the midwife muttered, unable to directly condemn the queen whose decision had placed the infant into the arms of those who must relinquish it.

Lysantha brought the washing bucket, and Matrinka deposited the afterbirth into it. "We'll need another, with soap and water to clean her. And fresh sheets and blankets."

Matrinka's two helpers scurried to obey, while the Pudarians fidgeted with obvious discomfort. Finally, one man stepped from the group and bowed to the queen. "Your Ladyship, it's our job to take the baby. If you plan to deny us, we cannot fight you. But we must report back to King Cymion."

"I don't plan to deny anything." Matrinka freed the sheet from the edges of the ticking and used the slack to mop up blood. "You'll get the baby after his first parents say their good-byes."

"He'll need his first feeding soon," the large-breasted Pudarian, apparently the wet nurse, said.

Matrinka looked at Kevral, then smiled. "He's getting it."

Ra-khir watched Kevral's response to Matrinka's words. She shifted the blankets and worked a breast free of her nightshirt. Suddenly, it bothered him beyond bearing that these Pudarians were arguing over his wife's exposed body. No longer helpless or muddled, he planted himself in front of them. "Get out." He jabbed a finger toward the door.

All three women edged backward. One of the men took a threatening half-step toward him. "You can't order us—"

"I can," Ra-khir said. "And I did. Pudar will have a lifetime with their prince. We have our son only for today. You'll get him in the morning, no sooner. No later." He took a deliberate full step at the other man. "Now, get out."

The man stiffened, as if he might begin a battle Ra-khir had every intention of finishing.

"I got a good look at the baby," the midwife said. "They can't switch him for another without my knowledge." It was a warning disguised as information. "Let's go."

The Pudarians turned away, the one in front of Ra-khir last of all. "First thing in the morning," he said gruffly, "the prince travels to Pudar." Without awaiting a reply, they funneled from the room, closing the door behind them.

Ra-khir stared at the panel even after its closing, feeling a rage he never realized he harbored ebb into cold desperation. His pulse hammered in his throat. The whole world would watch this man grow to adulthood, projecting their hopes and dreams upon the future ruler of the West's largest city. Yet, to Ra-khir, he would remain always frozen in time, the innocent infant that filled his arms and heart for only the day his boldness had won him.

"Thank you," Kevral said.

When Matrinka and her assistants gave no response, Ra-khir turned his gaze to Kevral. She looked tired and radiant at once, and the last of his anger fled before a rush of love. For her and for the new infant. "You're welcome," he responded, refusing to cheapen her gratitude by belittling the actions he had taken. "I love you."

"I love you, too."

Matrinka allowed the words a few moments to sink in before breaking the mood. "Ra-khir, I'd like to leave the three of you alone . . ."

Guessing the reason for her reticence, Ra-khir reassured. "I can handle cleaning things up. Thank you for everything."

Matrinka did not worry for demeaning his appreciation. "It was truly nothing but my job."

Ra-khir smiled. "I thought your job was to rule Béarn."

Matrinka raised a finger in a marked gesture. "Not when I'm healing, remember. Then I'm just plain Matrinka."

Ra-khir did not mention how she had used her position and title to help keep the Pudarians at bay. He appreciated it too much to risk making her feel guilty. "Thank you, just plain Matrinka. Get some sleep."

"I will," Matrinka promised, herding the elf and other Béarnide from the room. The door closed behind them, leaving a silence that admitted the baby's quiet swallows.

Kevral rose, and Ra-khir stripped and replaced the bloody sheets and spotted blanket. Once finished, he patted the bed, indicating Kevral should rest. By that time, the baby had lost interest in the breast. It lay in Kevral's arms, tiny eyes unfocused, limbs flexed, fists tightly closed. Kevral remained standing, her stamina remarkable but not unexpected. She broke the hush. "I want another."

Ra-khir considered the words several moments, seeking logic in them. He looked at Kevral's face, but her gaze did not move from the baby. "Another . . . ?" he encouraged, but Kevral did not finish the thought. "Another . . . baby?"

Kevral nodded, still not raising her head.

Ra-khir placed an arm across his wife's shoulders and guided her to a sitting position on the bed. He reached for the baby. "I don't plan to go the rest of my life without coupling with my wife, so it's likely there'll be more."

Finally, Kevral gave him her attention, though she still clutched the baby. "I want to start as soon as possible. Two weeks. No longer."

Ra-khir cringed at the bare thought. He knew little of birthing, but he suspected the discomfort would last at least that long. "Kevral, I don't think that's a good idea." He sought words for his concern. "We can't replace this child. Like all children, he's unique, and he deserves an identity of his own. We need time to mourn, to deal with what happened. Saviar and Subikahn deserve our time and attention. And we need time for us, if we can find it."

Kevral relinquished the swaddled infant to her husband, removed her soiled nightshirt and used it to wipe clean her lower regions. The bulge in her abdomen had already shrunk, and he could not help noticing limbs and a torso honed by daily hours of sword practice. "I'm not trying to replace this baby." She made a gesture at her chest of drawers.

Ra-khir turned, cradling the baby in the crook of his left arm and opening the lowest drawer with his right.

"And I agree that it would be better to wait." Kevral sighed. "But if I cycle even once after this baby, I can't have another."

Rummaging through the drawer for another nightshirt, Ra-khir frowned at the idea of Kevral pregnant for longer than two years. The risk of death increased exponentially with each subsequent pregnancy less than a year after the previous one had ended. "We've only got one shard left, and we've succeeded so far. We'll restore fertility." Finding a nightshirt, he drew it out and closed the drawer. "We don't have to place your life in that kind of danger nor steal time from the twins . . ." Turning, he trailed off.

Kevral sat on the bed, back supported by the headboard, her eyes large with sorrow and her mouth fiercely pinched. "Captain only said it *might* lift the sterility spell. If I don't have another right away, I might never be able to."

Ra-khir passed Kevral the nightshirt. "You have two strong sons. That's more than any other woman your age. You didn't want this one." He did not add that most of her fight for the baby had come from anger and pride, not desire for another child.

Kevral donned the clothing, then reached for the baby. "Not at first. But now that he's here, I want him more than almost anything."

Ra-khir found himself not wanting to let go. The baby's warmth against him felt so comfortable, so right. If they had relinquished the baby because they could not care for it, he would still have suffered regret; but the joy of doing the best for the child would have diminished the pain. This loss left a void that he, too, wanted to fill—but not at the risk of Kevral's health and life. "I want him, too," he admitted, passing the bundle back to Kevral. He did not argue about creation of another child. High emotions, caused by childbirth and by the need to surrender the child, would not allow for rational discussion now. He had two weeks to convince her that the perils outweighed desire. It seemed ludicrous to insist on performing the last task while she still recovered from childbirth; yet it would likely prove less burdensome than another nine-month gestation. At least they would know whether or not the complete Pica, and the elves' magic, could counter the plague. If logic and circumstance failed to convince, and Kevral still wanted another baby, he could not deny her. "My love, should we name him?"

Kevral smiled. "Calistin," she said.

Ra-khir nodded, recognizing the name of Colbey's father, reserved all these years by the Renshai for one deserving. They would have been willing to bestow it upon Tae's son, so it only made sense that they would have granted it to a baby sired by Colbey's own son. "Calistin," he said. "Of course."

Kevral clutched the infant, savoring her only day with him. Ra-khir hovered close by, her strength, heroically hiding his own pain.

CHAPTER 30

The Fatal Mistake

Skill has no limits, and anything will come with practice. If it does not, look to your own dedication and will.
— Colbey Calistinsson

ASGARD seemed to scroll changelessly past Colbey, the sky a cloudless sapphire plain, the trees identical and evenly spaced, the grasses as steady and uniform a green as elfin eyes. Disoriented by a world that had served as his home for centuries, Colbey relied solely on pacing to bring him to the structure he sought, since landmarks failed him. *Has chaos affected me this much?* The thought raised buzzing alarm. If he had become so linked to his charge that the places of his past, those once familiar worlds of law, seemed utterly static, then chaos had gained a greater hold than he could bear. As he worried before taking on the responsibility of chaos, he might never manage to free himself from this burden he had grudgingly, but willingly, accepted. *I have to find Odin and end this. Soon.*

Odin's hall, *Valaskjalf,* appeared suddenly on the horizon, as if by magic. The break in the stable monotony eased Colbey's soul, and relief wafted from the chaos sword as well. He hurried toward it, prepared for an abrupt and angry meeting with the one who ruled the citadel. Freya had sent him many places in search of the one he needed to confront, without success. Colbey had anticipated that a simple transport to the world of Odin's rule would bring the gray father of gods to him in an instant. Yet, after longer than two months of intermittent searching, the confrontation still awaited. In the meantime, chaos gained strength, no longer requiring contact with his hand to communicate. Soon, he worried, it would break through his barriers and claim him, turning order into pain. His form would disappear, and he would flow into the primordial chaos like a vapor.

No one challenged Colbey as he entered Odin's hall and passed the many treasures of war that served as decoration in a place whose very name meant Shelf of the Slain. Now, as never before, the decor consisted only of pairs, trios, and quadruples set in perfect patterns. Colbey tried not to notice as he passed from room to kindred room, the scenery barely fluctuating. The sword focused in on tiny differences while he refused to study his surroundings, except to seek signs of life or movement among the displays. Odin's possessions had never required such definitive patterns during the time of his death. Since his return, he had rearranged everything he owned, Colbey felt certain, now realizing that the changes in *Valaskjalf* and Asgard came from Odin's bond with law, not from his own with chaos.

The thought intrigued Colbey. His ventures into Odin's mind made him certain the AllFather did not believe himself influenced by law at all. Odin had placed his essence into what he had believed was an essentially empty staff and he, not law, had joined with Dh'arlo'mé. Circumstances showed otherwise. Law had quietly integrated Odin while he lay quiescent in the staff through centuries. As Odin regained his power, so did law; and chaos had grown in necessary opposition. *He believes I have bonded with chaos, yet it is himself who has become hopelessly one with law.*

These thoughts brought Colbey to *Hlidskjalf,* the high seat from which Odin viewed the main worlds. When they lived, only Odin and his wife could sit upon that chair. After the High One's death, Colbey had done so a few times and other gods also, including his son, Ravn. No one but Odin had dared since his return.

Colbey approached the jeweled, stone seat in silence and discovered that someone occupied it now, blond braids flowing over the back. Colbey froze, hand creeping toward his hilt, heart pounding the calm cadence of war. From that position, Odin could see everything on nine worlds. Surely, Colbey's presence did not surprise him. "Finally, I've found you."

The figure on *Hlidskjalf* jumped, skittering to his feet. It was Frey. "I just—" He broke off at the sight of Colbey, then finished in a less defensive voice. "I just got here."

Colbey approached, uncertain which side Frey served. Two months could change much, especially those touched by Odin. "I'm sorry. I thought you were Odin."

Frey's brows rose in surprise.

"Because you're here," Colbey explained. "No other reason." He changed the subject, "Whom were you seeking?"

"You," Frey admitted freely. "And Odin."

"You haven't seen him?"

"Not since we spoke." Frey conversed freely. If Odin did not sit upon *Hlidskjalf,* he could not overhear them. "But this is the first time I've dared to come here. I believe he's out looking for you."

"I've hardly made myself scarce." Colbey walked around Frey to perch upon Odin's great chair. The view allowed him to study nine worlds, including the three destroyed by Surtr's fire at the *Ragnarok:* Alfheim, Jötunheim, and Vanaheim. He scanned painstakingly, pausing once to look at the infant in Kevral's arms with satisfaction. "A boy."

"What?" Frey ran his fingers over the rainbow of gemstones set into the arm of the chair.

"Over the past two months, I've divided my time between Asgard and chaos' world, with a few stops in Midgard in the hope I might find Odin there. I thought surely he'd come after me each time I transported onto his world." Colbey made a vast gesture, turning his attention to some of the lesser worlds that had never concerned him in the past. To his surprise, he found life on two tiny worlds that were previously unoccupied. He honed in, searching for Odin and finding only unfamiliar creatures not quite human. "What's happening on Nídavellír and Svartalfheim?"

"My doing," Frey admitted quietly. "Those elves who wished to return to the old ways have Svartalfheim, which I now call Nualfheim. Those once-elves who chose bitterness and Odin now dwell on Nídavellír, the dwarves for whom we prepared that place. The rest live among the humans on Midgard."

"Ah." Colbey did not need the details. The spreading and division of elves did not concern him.

Frey also seemed glad to let the matter of his creations rest. "I still believe he's seeking you, just in the wrong places at the wrong times. When you're on chaos' world, of course, he can't see you. That's not one of the places *Hlidskjalf* shows."

Having gazed over all of the worlds he could, including the lands of the dead, Colbey sat back. "Where would he go that I can't find him?"

Frey shook his head. "He might be searching some of the smaller worlds. The created ones. In case you might be hiding out on one of those."

He's on chaos' world, the sword supplied suddenly and with alarm.

Colbey sat bolt upright. *How do you know?*

I'm grounded there. There's a disturbance . . .

Take me back. To where Freya and Ravn are. Terror closed over Colbey's heart.

Why there?

Colbey's fingers clenched the hilt. *It's the only place there he can go.*

Gray clouds shrouded Béarn's sun, turning the late spring afternoon cold. Wind tangled the curtains of the window in the queen's chambers, smelling damp. Tae leaned against the cushioned arm of a couch across from Matrinka in a matching, upholstered chair. Subikahn toddled across the floor, falling whenever the paneling gave way to carpeting. In a flash, he pulled himself to a stand again, marching up to a half dozen steps before landing on his bottom again. Soft black hair fell crookedly to his ears, and eyes as dark as his father's showed a hint of mischief. Tae wondered how much of the soft roundness of his face came from Kevral and how much from age. He hoped his Eastern blood would never coarsen those gentle and handsome features.

Sitting at Matrinka's feet, Marisole laughed whenever Subikahn fell. Though three months behind him in age, she already outweighed him, rolls of fat hiding her joints and making her arms and legs look short. Bright brown eyes followed his every movement, and a smile stretched her tiny lips more often than not. Around her, no adult could help grinning and cooing like an idiot. Her dress flared around chubby thighs, and a bow held up her single tuft of dark hair. Flopped upside down on the couch, Mior batted Tae's hand.

Yes, I know you're there. Tae caught the paw, pinching it lightly between his second and third fingers before letting it slide free. He tickled under the calico's chin.

★Prove it.★ The words glided into Tae's mind, his best guess at Mior's reply.

"I expected to find you with Kevral and Ra-khir." Clearly oblivious, Matrinka informed. "The baby was born early this morning. Figured you'd climb the castle for a sight of him, too."

Tae had overheard guards in the hallway and already knew the news. Though angry with himself, not Matrinka, he could not keep an edge from his voice. "I don't want to see him. And I don't want to see my friends . . . " The word came hard, and he swallowed it until he could speak without crying. ". . . sad." Absently, he fingered the ruby he now wore on a chain around his neck.

"You're upset about Rascal's death," Matrinka guessed, her tone sympathetic, understanding.

"Yes." Tae needed no such reason to visit his friend, yet he would not lie. Recognizing the action that clued the queen, he released the gemstone he and Rascal had discovered in the demon's horde. He had promised it to the Pudarian after completion of the mission. "I can't help feeling responsible." He gathered Mior into his lap, running his hands in circles over her belly. "And that I could have done more. I could still do more."

★That's better.★ Mior purred, grabbing playfully for Tae's moving hands.

Tae's face jerked down to the animal, and he wondered if grief had driven him insane. "Are you talking to me?"

"I—I didn't say anything," Matrinka stammered. She turned Tae a curious look that contained guilt as well as sorrow. "I was still thinking."

Mior rolled, tumbling from lap to floor. Though she landed on her feet, she stumbled. Sitting, she licked at a foot with an air of disdain. *I did that on purpose.*

Tae shook his head, scarcely daring to believe. He tried thinking at the cat. *Can you understand me?*

Not usually, Mior returned, though a shocked joy trickled past the nonchalant answer. The lack of surprise at his ability to communicate with her was as feigned as her claim to have deliberately fallen. *You rarely make sense.*

Not quite ready to reveal his new talent, Tae returned the attention Matrinka more than deserved. "I'm sorry." He sought the dense and shameful grief that had brought him to Matrinka's room, shallowly buried beneath amazement. He caught one hand slipping toward the ruby again. "If I had worked a bit harder, tried better tactics, I might have prepared her . . ."

"No." Matrinka leaned forward. "Tae, you did as much as anyone could. Rascal lost herself long ago."

You can search forever in an empty well, but you will never find diamonds.

Mior's profundity complimented Matrinka's words. Tae lowered his head. "I was an empty well, too. And you never gave up on me."

Matrinka considered those words, obviously not privy to Mior's comment. The cat had clearly directed it to him. "You were never empty, Tae. We didn't do anything special to bring you to our side. Your own inherent morality did that for us."

"You didn't know me before."

"I didn't have to." Matrinka steadied Marisole, then approached Tae. Mior leaped into her lap. "Tae, think back. We didn't do anything for you, only for the mission and for ourselves. You changed yourself for yourself. Rascal had neither the will nor the strength to save herself. You couldn't do that for her." She clasped his hands. "Ultimately, Tae, no one ever can."

Listen to her. She knows what she's saying.

Tae wondered if the calico was giving an equal amount of commentary on his words to Matrinka and gained a new respect for the queen of Béarn. He envied how she managed to keep the thread of human conversations with a second one occurring in her head. "Weren't you the one who claimed every person has good in them? Didn't you tell me to keep trying, that I'd break through to her eventually?"

Matrinka's hands tightened around his, and Mior wound between the circle of her arms. "A mistake?" It was a question, not a statement. "I wanted you to strive for the impossible, and I wanted Rascal to have every possible chance." She released Tae. "I believe you gave her that."

"If only—"

"Stop." Matrinka arrested that line of thought. "You could have done things differently in hindsight, of course. I saw how you handled her. You did as well as anyone could."

If everyone knew how others would react to what they do, things might go smoother. But they'd be really, REALLY boring. Mior clambered from Matrinka's lap to Tae's, demanding attention with sharp butts of her head against his hands. *Pet me.*

Tae allowed the animal to distract him. *What if I say 'no?'*

I'll pee on your bed. Mior's happy rubbing seemed incongruous with her words. *I'll leap on your head in the dark.* She tapped his thigh with an extended claw. *I'll flip sharp objects into your boots.*

Tae pretended to consider. *I've suffered worse.* Nevertheless, he stroked the calico. "It just doesn't feel over. Like I could go back and make a plea to the giantess. Like I should try, at least." His thoughts slipped back to Loki's citadel and his mad rush to hurl himself between Kevral and danger. The others had reported Rascal's words: "I seed what happent when he try ta save ya. Now, he's daid an' ya's 'live. Hain't no one's life worth more'n mine." The idea of placing a price on humans bothered Tae. Once, every life had felt more significant than his own.

Matrinka shook her head. "Odin's not known for his mercy."

Tae knew Matrinka spoke truth. The cruel gray god had found pleasure in stirring war between societies and watching men die. "I know she's dead. There's just something about the way she went that makes me wonder . . ."

Subikahn waddled to his father, placing a tiny hand on Tae's knee. He reached for Mior with the other.

Immediately, Tae shifted to intervene.

I'm not going to hurt him. Mior seemed affronted.

I was more worried about him hurting you.

Mior stalked into harm's way. *Maybe I like my tail pulled. Maybe I like my whiskers tweaked.* Subikahn grabbed for Mior's face, and she back-pedaled instinctively before returning to her stalwart position. *I did that on purpose, too.*

Well, maybe I don't like when you purposely poke my son in the finger with your eye.

If you're going to grouse at me— Mior slunk onto Matrinka's lap, the baby following the movement.

"It's because you never saw Rascal's body."

Tae had never considered that.

"That's why you need to take a look at the baby before he goes." Matrinka consoled Mior with a hug and a series of rapid strokes. "Or it'll never seem quite real. Your feelings about it never quite certain or finished."

Tae racked his thoughts for an explanation from Matrinka's personal history. *She knows this too well.*

Grandpapa, Mior reminded.

Only then, Tae realized Matrinka had never seen the dead king's body, though many others confirmed his demise. "Thank you," he said. He might never come fully to terms with Rascal's death and with his failure at rescuing her from it. But, at least, he understood his own reaction to it.

"Take time to grieve, Tae."

"I will." Grasping the ruby in one palm, Tae rose and headed for the door. "Right now, I have a baby to visit." He stopped with his other hand on the latch. "Can you and Mior speak with elves?" The question sounded ludicrous. "Using your mind talking thing, I mean."

Matrinka smiled. "No, it's different. She can hear their general *khohlar*, like the rest of us, but she can't intercept their singular ones. Neither of us can communicate by mind, except to one another."

"And now, for Mior at least, with me."

Mior sent a concept of the past, how Matrinka and she had learned to share thoughts much the same way Tae and she had done: study and anticipation. She also gave him the realization that the bond would not extend between the humans, though she might agree to translate things silently for them—for a petting price.

Matrinka's grin broadened, no surprise at all registering on her features. "It was only a matter of time."

Colbey flashed into an empty room of his creation, the sparse furnishings toppled, food scattered and smashed. The heel of a boot lay immortalized in a smear of boiled roots, too large for Freya or Ravn. Terror exploded through Colbey and he stood, mind empty of action for the first time he could ever remember. *He's got them.* Hating himself for the situation he had allowed to happen, he clapped a hand to his hilt with an animal growl of frustration and rage.

There's a recent magic trail.

Colbey did not hesitate. *Follow it.*

Into Odin's trap? Are you insane?

Yes. Completely. Colbey regretted even that almost intangible delay. *Go! The less time we waste, the less time he has to make or complete said trap.*

Apparently convinced by the argument, the chaos sword triggered the transport. Light pulsed against Colbey's vision, swarming through the never-quite-familiar spectrum of color. Each time, he discovered new hues, fresh conformations that made the magic unpredictable. Then he stood upon the steady grasslands of Asgard.

The sword/staff loosed a sensation that approximated a human groan. The perfect sea of grasses, the regular glaze of the clouds, the steady golden circle of sun bothered Colbey's sensibilities as well. He swung his gaze over a plain he had left moments before, finding only one new thing. A short distance to his right, Ravn lay, his body arranged in perfect symmetry, arms at his sides and legs slightly parted. "Ravn!" Colbey leaped toward his son.

Trap! Magic! Though mental communication whizzed instantly into Colbey's mind, the Staff of Chaos shortened to the essentials. Colbey slammed against a barrier, pain flaring across his right cheek and shoulder. Ignoring it, he dashed rightward, skimming his fingers along the invisible magic to detect an end. When he did not find one after several running paces took the boy from his vision, Colbey turned and headed in the opposite direction. That, too, failed him. He gathered his mental presence.

Careful. The sword vibrated in his grip. *It's a trick.*

Colbey did not care. Need drove him to rescue Ravn before he no longer could. Once, he had grown close enough to chaos to allow it to drive him even against his son. He had vowed that would never happen again. Logic kept him cognizant; it did no one any good to save Ravn at the expense of the world *and* Ravn. Yet, the longer he waited, the more Odin could claim or destroy of his son. Colbey threw his mind into Ravn's.

A coating dense as cloth surrounded Ravn's familiar thoughts. The Renshai teachings, the love for mother and father, and the rebellious search for self that characterized most teens beckoned beneath the presence that enwrapped them like a greedy spider. Colbey jabbed for the intruder, drilling desperately through the darkness. As he entered, it enveloped him, stealing purpose and screaming of triumph. It echoed through him, forcing him to abandon his son to address it. Once it had his attention, it dropped him into a downward spiral as strong as any tornado.

Colbey felt himself falling at a fantastic speed, fueling fear into a bonfire that threatened to consume him even as the winds of his captor swirled wildly around him. Scenery whizzed past in a spectacular, unfathomable blur. The creature that embodied the shroud contained a mental strength that made his own seem puny, and it mocked him with a laugh distinctly Odin's. *You gave them to me, Colbey. And for that I thank you!* A laugh like thunder shook the world, and it would have quailed any man from reality.

But Colbey was not any man. Odin's taunts did not raise the hopelessness or desperate rage they sought, only forthright determination that jerked him from the AllFather's control. He became suddenly and intensely aware of the energy that drained from him every moment his mind remained separated from his body. He had to act, and swiftly. *There must be an exit.*

No way out! Odin sent.

The Staff of Chaos remained befuddled. *Nothing. It's impossible to find anything here.*

Colbey drove his focus to the passing scenery, closing his ears to Odin's badgering and even to the sword whose opinion he had solicited. Only as he concentrated fully upon it did he recognize the sword/staff's problem. The same scene zipped past them repeatedly, an endless wheel of corridors exactly alike, perfectly symmetrical and patterned. To the Staff of Chaos, it might just as well have been an impossible maze. *Find the one that's different,* he instructed. *The one with the exit.*

Odin's laughter hammered Colbey's ears, raw pain. Strength slipped inexorably away.

No exit! It's all dizzyingly the same. The staff's frustration became a howl of agony.

Colbey felt vigor disappearing at a horrifying pace. He forced thought, searching for the logic that might save him when all his sword training could not. *Dizzyingly the same.* He scrambled after the answer, dropping the reality his mind had previously built, from common sense. Once he stopped looking for the one difference that might signal the exit, he found it among the repetitive corridors. Caught in a circle, he had passed the very exit he sought more than a hundred times. This time, he dove through it.

Back in his own body, Colbey cursed the weakness his hesitation had cost. His arms felt weighted, and he had to concentrate on not staggering. Odin now stood between himself and Ravn, and hot pinpoints of magic streaked toward him.

Move! the sword/staff screeched.

Colbey struggled to do exactly that, slowed by the ordeal and its resulting frailty. He dodged aside, only to watch directed chaos slam against something unseen, shattered to sparks that bounced backward in lopsided steamers of color.

Odin shrieked. "You traitorous bastard! Has chaos caught you, too?"

Frey's reply came from Colbey's right, Odin's left. The god stood amid the patterns of trees and grasses, steady and fearless despite the threat of imminent destruction. "The sword calling the ax sharp, High One. We'll counter anything magic, nothing more. A start toward evening the fight." Only then, Colbey noticed Freya standing in a like position at the other side of the battle. Likely, Frey had released her from whatever trap she was to have served as bait. Sister and brother would need to work together to contain just one of the AllFather's powers. Colbey locked his knees to keep them from buckling and prepared to face all of the others.

Red flared across a face that now seemed more godlike than elfin. Though still Dh'arlo'mé's features, the expressions ill-suited him. "Die, then." Odin raised his hands.

Colbey charged. The barrier that had separated him from Ravn disappeared as Odin turned his concentration onto the god and goddess who dared stand against him.

As Colbey reached him, Odin dropped his hands, magic sizzling with a sound like a waterfall against the fires of *Ragnarok*. His sword jerked from its sheath, too slow for the Renshai's usual lightning speed. With Colbey hampered by fatigue, it proved fast enough. The blades slammed together with a force that pitched Colbey backward. He ducked the slash that followed, the breeze of Odin's passing sword peeling the back of his tunic free, no longer sweat-glued to his spine. The power behind the attack awed him. A single blow would shatter whatever it struck.

The chaos sword bucked against his control. *Can't hit law with chaos, remember? It'll destroy us.*

A second wind spurred Colbey, the reality of a true battle an excitement nothing could quell. He had not forgotten the sword's concern, only questioned its word choice. So long as he remained unbonded, the contact would harm Odin and the Staff of Chaos, not himself. He drove in, weaving a Renshai maneuver around Odin's steady defense. His blade scored a gash across the AllFather's wrist that the sword fought. God and sword screamed simultaneously.

Colbey spun in for a wicked stab, only to find Odin's sword in his path. Back-pedaling, he spiraled in for a different angle. A mental barb from Odin struck the barriers of Colbey's mind with an impact that flashed abrupt pain through his head. Lurching backward, he lost all control of his attack. He twisted, dodging a surmised riposte, nearly blinded by agony. He felt Odin's next blitz as a concentration of energy streaming toward his head. This time, Colbey forced his barriers down, accepting the barb through subsequent walls until it struck the back, nearly devoid of power. He barricaded it there, as he had in the past, holding it for release into the vastness of chaos' world, where it would cancel out an equal amount of disorder.

But this time Odin followed his first assault with another. A second probe, gently guided, slipped through behind the first, stopping after the first of Colbey's barriers. The physical battle disappeared as the two grappled mentally, Odin seizing hold of the intensity of emotion that Ravn's still form had evoked.

No! Colbey struggled to hold his thoughts intact. His mental control surged forward to war, yet he managed only to grip the presence that already held his. Odin's mental power dwarfed his in the wake of the trap he had barely escaped in Ravn's mind. The AllFather made slow, steady progress. The bank of emotion crept toward freedom. Colbey knew he had to jettison the piece of his thoughts that Odin gripped or risk losing everything. Once Odin had Colbey's full consciousness trapped, he could sit back and watch the Renshai's body die. His mind would follow instantly.

Colbey settled back to do as he must. Then, his eyes fell on Ravn, rising blearily, Asgard's grasses smashed to the shape of his body. The thoughts that Odin clung to, with which he adamantly extracted Colbey's mind from his body, were his love and respect for his son. Without those, Colbey could never feel the depth of emotion that had awakened the day Freya had birthed the baby into his arms, that had grown gradually from unconditional acceptance to an esteem earned by Ravn's own struggle and exertion. Throughout his mortal life he had yearned for a child, gained the responsibility for a boy swiftly lost to madness and later death. Soon the everything, the very world, that Ravn had become would disappear from him, leaving emptiness in its place. The boy would become as any other boy. And Colbey would never remember, never manage to rekindle, that missing adoration.

Never! Colbey clung to his love for Ravn, allowing himself to get sucked from his own head. Odin's excitement grew tangible. Thrust into another spinning void, Colbey caught a glimpse of the infinite and ordered cavern that represented Odin's knowledge before becoming plunged into a universe that consisted of Odin's victory, hearing nothing but the AllFather's words surrounded by ringing laughter: *"The only enemy will make/One small lapse; a fatal mistake/Leave the world at the mercy of Gray."*

In a moment, Colbey knew, all his energy would wring out, leaving not even a spark of life. He had made the exchange he had earlier refused: sacrificing his son to rescue world and son together. He cringed, waiting for the last of his strength to drain. In a moment, the sword would fall from his hand. His body would collapse, then his mind. Odin would destroy the Staff of Chaos, ruin and recreate the world in his image, then the law he did not even realize owned him would stagnate his creation to an oblivion worse than the one before. *Leave the world at the mercy of Gray.* Colbey knew Odin had no mercy. He never had. *At the mercy of Gray.* The word indicated the great gray father to most, once even to himself, yet Colbey's thoughts strayed to the sword he had carried for centuries. Harval, the Gray Blade. *Gray meaning neutrality.* Suddenly, the prophesy unraveled. *I am not the enemy, Odin is. The fatal mistake is his. The mercy my own.* Though Colbey never thought he believed in prophecies, this one raised a will that seemed impossible an instant earlier.

Colbey clung to the clinger, wrapping his consciousness around the other with all the violence with which he had fought it a moment earlier. *Home,* he told the sword/staff, struggling not to broadcast a hint of his intentions. If it knew the details of his battle, that this simple action would destroy Colbey and Odin, both essences in the staves, and much of chaos' world, the Staff of Chaos would never comply.

The chaos sword's understanding flickered to Colbey only as backwash, the concept of strategic retreat. Even as the magic flashed, the staff informed him: *Freya has returned home.*

Freya! Too late to stop the transport, Colbey redirected. *To her!*

The array of colors splashed wildly, then concentrated and, suddenly, Colbey was in the safe pocket of chaos' world he had crafted to house his family. Freya jerked aside as Colbey appeared, Odin materializing beside him. Jolted partially back to his body, Colbey realized nothing remained of his vitality. He collapsed, Odin's triumph still pulsing against him. *Transport!* He hoped the desperate message reached his wife in time. His world became a black oblivion, devoid of sight or sound. With the last of his strength, he reversed his creation. The walls fell, chaos roaring through the opening and meeting the very embodiment of law. The explosion crashed against Colbey, slamming him with the force of a thousand galloping horses.

Then every sensation disappeared.

CHAPTER 31

The Spring of Mimir

Those things most desired come at hefty prices.
—*Colbey Calistinsson*

THE warm comfort of spring seeped even into the windowless strategy room where Darris and his friends gathered prior to each search for a shard of the Pica Stone. Béarn's bard could smell the sweet, loamy odor of growing gardens as well as the mingled perfumes of the myriad flowers that graced the courtyard. Suffused with the excitement the warm seasons always inspired, as well as preparation for their last task, Darris found the wait interminable. He fought the urge to burst into happy song, fingers gliding over imaginary strings while his lute remained in place on his back. He glanced about the group, their moods a strange mixture of joy and sorrow, blithe anticipation and quiet concern. Kevral's head drooped, her color pale and her hair hanging in limp feathers. It seemed ludicrous to expect her to function as a warrior only a week after childbirth, yet she declared herself ready. When Ra-khir, her staunchest defender, made no protest, the others did not argue either.

The knight himself looked as haggard as Kevral, the rims of his green eyes swollen and pink. The pristine linens with their crisp gold, blue, orange, and black stood in stark contrast to slumping limbs and tired features. Tae, too, seemed subdued, though it did not blunt his wary scrutiny of a room filling with more elves than ever in the past. Captain had returned with many followers, expressing the need for a larger *jovinay arythanik* to trigger a spell linked to one fewer participant. His matter-of-fact manner poorly hid his concern for the ability of the magic to function properly.

El-brinith and Chan'rék'ril watched each new elf file in with clear interest, their eyes lighting for every one in turn. They wore matching broad smiles, their attitude closest to Darris' own. Andvari paced from Kevral to Captain, fingers moving nimbly over the lacing that held his ax in place. He clearly worried for the Renshai as well, their friendship strengthened by the resolution of long-held hostility. It was a phenomenon Darris had described more than once in song: hard-won friendships often discovered an intensity that regular relationships could never match.

Finally, when twice as many elves as usual pressed against the walls and the door could barely close, Captain gave a nod of wary satisfaction. Darris rescued a curl about to tumble into his eyes and focused on the chant that rose in heavily accented, alien voices yet seemed as gentle and fluid as a lullaby. Tae crouched. Andvari went still. The two elves stopped studying the newcomers to concentrate on the coming transport. Only Kevral and Ra-khir seemed wholly unaffected, standing in the same despondent hush, clutching one another's hand.

Captain's voice rose over those of the other elves. Darris listened intently, having nearly captured the syllables of the spell verbatim. As the familiar sounds rose over the *jovinay arythanik*, he covered his eyes with his hands. The dizzying sensation of movement brought a queasy feeling to his stomach. He released his eyes, suffering the concern Captain had not allowed himself to show. His companions stood all around him, most rubbing eyes assaulted by the magic's brightness. Otherwise, none seemed worse for the transport. If anything, Kevral and Ra-khir appeared more alive, forced to attention by new surroundings that could hold any sort of threat.

They stood beneath a massive ash tree, its branches stretching beyond sight, seemingly to infinity. Movement in the branches caught Darris' notice. At first, he believed massive birds skipped from limb to limb. Then, he recognized the movement as leaping, not flying. Flashes of white against brown fur identified the creatures conclusively as deer. They moved with a grace beyond anything of the mortal world, slender legs bounding, tails flickering, heads dipping to devour the bright green shoots on every branch. Even as Darris admired their grace, he recognized bulkier animals interspersed with the deer. Cloven hooves skipped over branches as solid as anything built by mankind, and the shaggy coats sported a variety of colors. Unlike the silent deer, the coarse song of the goats filled the air like birdsong. Bees as large as hummingbirds flitted around Darris' head, gathering droplets of dew stretching like honey from the lowest boughs.

Darris' lore gave him the answer even as Andvari spoke it in a breathless whisper, "Yggdrasill. The World Tree."

Darris stared at the axis of the world, memorizing every detail. A million songs described it, yet all of them remained vague for want of a witness to its grandeur. Now, he realized, none of them had come near to capturing the sparkling hue of its leaves, more precious than emeralds. Orange-pink fruit bowed the branches. He knew the tree touched every world, yet mere words had never captured its vastness. It rose in increments so subtle it appeared nearly flat, yet its umbrella of protection defied space and time, stretching and defining eternity. He could sit for hours observing and writing and still never capture its vastness.

El-brinith broke Darris' contemplation. "The shard is pretty much straight down, but moving."

"Moving?" Andvari's brow creased. "Why would that be?"

"Most likely in the possession of something living," Chan'rék'ril explained.

Darris perched on one of the three great roots that arched upward from the trunk before plunging into open caverns. The task seemed hopeless. The roots, he knew, led to the nine main worlds. They could never hope to explore all of that territory, and El-brinith's spell would only work one time. Resigned, he refused to let his concerns affect the others. "Where first?"

"The shortest." El-brinith tapped the central root, thicker than her entire body. "We can stop before we reach any of the worlds. If the shard lay in one of those, the *jovinay arythanik* would have sent us directly there."

Darris rose, wishing he had thought of that particular detail on his own, though it did not appease him. El-brinith believed the shard in the possession of a living creature, which meant it could move freely, even onto other worlds. Religious knowledge filled Darris' head, and he sorted out the references to Yggdrasill. The shortest root led to the worlds of gods and elves: Asgard, Vanaheim, and Alfheim. Past discussions with the elves suggested that, of the three, only Asgard had survived the *Ragnarok*. A body of water lay beneath each root, and these seemed the most likely places for creatures to visit.

A squirrel rushed up the longest root, zipping to the opposite side of the tree to clamber up its trunk.

Kevral led the way down the cavern, the excitement of visiting a place of deep and significant legend driving aside her sadness. They followed her through an echoing cavern filled with a light whose source Darris could not fathom. Prepared to memorize a maze as complex as the one that warded Béarn's dungeon, he found the task unnecessary. The cave surrounded the root, which did not branch. In fact, it barely arched as it delved toward the upper worlds. The idea of heading downward to reach Asgard repeatedly befuddled Darris, and he had to keep reminding himself that he no longer stood upon the ground of Midgard. Yggdrasill sheltered even the uppermost portions of the worlds the gods had created and in which they alone dwelt. Only now, Darris realized he had seen no sky through the interwoven branches of the great ash, only higher limbs in endlessly rising increments reaching toward the heavens.

The journey seemed to span moments and days at once. Then, suddenly, the root ended. A circular pool filled the area immediately below it. Beyond stretched a vast plain as far as Darris' vision. As the group arrived, three massive figures appeared from the shadows created by the meeting of cavern and meadow. Kevral and Andvari crouched. Darris instinctively placed himself between the elves and the giants, as he might do for the king. Ra-khir stood as ready as the other warriors, though he would not insult unidentified strangers by assuming them hostile. His hands stayed well away from his hilt.

As the others glided closer, their identities became clear. All three of the Norns stood together, guarding the well that bore the same name as one of them: Urdr, meaning Past or Fate. Skuld stepped forward, examining them as she might a flaw in her dress. "You again? Do you have more business here?"

Ra-khir glanced at El-brinith. Though clearly willing to return to his role as speaker, he knew she had had the last and longest conversation with the giantess whose name literally meant "Being" but who represented the future as well.

The elf rose to the challenge. "The same business that brought us to Odin's testing ground. We're seeking the last shard of the shattered Pica."

All three of the giantesses shook their heads together, Skuld still the one speaking. "I gave you the one I discovered on the testing grounds. I have seen no other."

Losing interest in the conversation, Verdandi seized a bucket, dipping it deep into the well. She dredged up clay as well as water, muddying the surface beyond visibility.

Skuld watched her sister from the corner of her eye. "If we're finished with you, we have work that needs doing."

Darris could not resist asking, "What exactly do you do here?"

Urdr fixed him with a sharp stare of her watery blue eyes. Wrinkles folded over her brows and into the sockets, taking all fierceness from the look. "We keep the Tree alive and, with it, all the worlds of gods, elves, and mankind."

Skuld shook the bucket, sloshing a small amount of silt-filled water to the ground. "The mud of the well preserves the branches that the stags and goats mangle and repairs the damage done by Nidhogg the dragon. The water nourishes Yggdrasill." She spoke the tree's name with the fondness of a mother.

Dragon. Darris' eyes widened. They had already battled one such creature, and the results had nearly proven fatal to more than one of them. He hoped this Nidhogg did not have the shard, and the expression taking shape on Andvari's features suggested he shared the bard's thought.

"We also guard the well." Verdandi gave the group a hard look. "You may not touch it."

Ra-khir made a conciliatory gesture. "So long as it does not contain the shard, we have no reason to disturb the waters or you."

"It does not." Verdandi fairly hissed. The others nodded their agreement.

Darris suspected they spoke truth. Although their need to oversee the well might drive them to lie, it seemed unlikely El-brinith's spell would have considered the depths of still water significant movement.

Ra-khir remained polite despite Verdandi's evident hostility. It seemed odd that one whose name meant "Necessity" did not seem to recognize the desperation that would drive this group even to battle the Norns for what they sought. "Then we shall look elsewhere, Ladies. Could you please enlighten us as to what lies beyond the well?"

"Asgard." Urdr gave Ra-khir a measuring look.

El-brinith gestured back the way they had come.

"Thank you," Ra-khir said, and the group returned toward the trunk of the World Tree.

The trip proved more difficult because of the steady upward course. Darris estimated that it took about twice as long, though time again passed in a strange, inexplicable blur that lacked meaning. He could not measure their progress by conversation as his companions kept mostly to themselves, Tae and the elves naturally taciturn, Ra-khir and Kevral quieted by circumstance, and Andvari choosing the company of his own thoughts over forcing Darris to arias. Darris kept himself engrossed by memorizing the events at the Well of Urdr, the look and feel of Yggdrasill's root and the cavern it occupied, and capturing the emotions of the group. No book yet contained the information the Norns had divulged. Now, all of it would become immortalized in song.

At length, the party reached the ground beneath Yggdrasill once more, startling the squirrel that clung, upside down, from the trunk. It leaped to a branch, scolding them with loud, repetitive chattering.

Only then, El-brinith spoke her opinion of the situation. "That root didn't delve far enough to account for the position I saw the shard, and I still maintain it's on this world. Let's try another."

Andvari flicked his war braids behind his shoulders. "Which one?"

"This one." El-brinith indicated a root by placing a small foot upon it. "It's the one that leads to Midgard, Jötunheim, Nídavellír, and Nualfheim."

A wistful look crossed Chan'rék'ril's face at the mention of the last two worlds, where Captain stated Frey had sent the remaining elves: those who wished to recreate Alfheim and those who embraced the darkness that Odin bore in the guise of Dh'arlo'mé.

"It may not be deep enough either," El-brinith confessed. "But I'd rather try it before facing the dragon or accidentally finding ourselves in Hel or Niflheim."

Even Kevral shivered at the mention of the worlds of the dead, the second more horrible than the first. Also called Misty Hel, it was the dark cold site reserved for the most horrible of those who died in disgrace.

No one challenged El-brinith's decision to attempt the route that seemed easiest first, which disappointed Darris.

Tae also noted Kevral's lack of enthusiasm. "Why isn't there a wild Renshai insisting we confront the dragon?"

Verdandi hauled herself from the cavern, supporting the bucket on the lip of the opening. Her sisters clambered out behind her.

Kevral sighed, tensing, mood rushing from sorrow to irritation in an instant. "I'm tired, all right? Aren't I allowed that after all that's happened? After losing my baby and my soul, maybe I'm willing to take the easy way, for once. I won't run from a confrontation with twenty dragons, if that's what you're implying."

Tae raised his hands in surrender, physically backing down. "Hey, I was joking . . . "

An answer came from an unexpected source. Urdr's voice boomed, caught beneath the ceiling of Yggdrasill. "Your soul was not lost, young Renshai. The spirit spiders got only that of your unborn baby, hence you lost him long before the day of his birth."

Kevral jerked around to face the Norns.

Verdandi softened her sister's pronouncement. "Indeed, the youngling gave up his soul, but he is not lost. He carries the blood of immortals. Like an elf, his years may span enough cycles to make an afterlife unnecessary."

Darris' attention went naturally to Skuld, the only one who could see the future and announce the true fate of the heir to Pudar's throne. But the youngest of the Norns only smiled as she clambered from the cavern. Even Odin, whose wisdom spanned all things, had his blind spots. Some who studied myth believed his great anger and merciless temper came of his powerlessness before the Norns, especially the close-mouthed Skuld. Even the all powerful AllFather learned the future the way every other did.

Kevral, too, awaited more that never came. She tensed. For a moment,

Darris believed she would charge the giantesses, demanding information rightfully hers; yet she did not. He doubted cowardice, or even her own depression held her back, but rather her respect for divine creatures her people had studied and worshiped for millennia.

"Let's go." Tae sprang through the second root's cavern.

Driven to take back the lead, Kevral hurried after Tae, and their companions followed. Much like the other, this root never divided, simply led through the cavern in a graceful arc that resisted an accounting of time. It, too, ended at a body of water. A spring that started at the tip of the root trickled over the wood and into a tiny lake at its base. A whiff of damp reached Darris' nose where he stood behind his friends, and his mouth went suddenly and painfully dry. Every fiber of his being yearned for a sip of that water.

Darris rammed into Ra-khir's shielding arm before he realized he had moved.

"The Spring of Mimir," Kevral explained.

"Where are you going?" Ra-khir asked.

"I'm thirsty." Darris suffered a rush of defensiveness. "I need a sip."

Tae casually slipped between Ra-khir and the lake, under the auspices of studying the water. It irritated Darris that now two of his friends prepared to stop him from performing the one act for which his entire life had prepared him. The Spring of Mimir contained all the knowledge of the universe. One mouthful would impart that to him as well.

Darris' throat became a fire that needed quenching. He had never known a need so great. His hand fell to his hilt. If necessary, he would battle through his companions. "I need a drink."

Andvari defined the problem. "Odin paid for his sip with an eye and nine days hanging upside down from Yggdrasill with a spear in his side. No doubt it will cost you as much."

"One sip . . . " Darris panted, his need as strong as the one for air. ". . . is worth that price and more." He retreated from Ra-khir, then galloped around the Knight of Erythane. He collided with Tae who had shifted directly into Darris' path. The Easterner collapsed beneath him, and they tumbled into a wheel of flailing limbs. Driven to madness, Darris hammered at the barrier that separated him from all that mattered. Tae swore, then yelped in pain. Suddenly, the blockade disappeared, and Darris staggered blindly forward. He slammed into another barrier, this one hard and cold. Pain lanced through his nose. He dropped to his knees, waiting for his vision to unswirl. The water beckoned him irresistibly, and he tried desperately to answer.

A voice speared into Darris' head. "Your price is different, descendant of Jahiran. A taste will cost your voice and your talent."

As Darris knelt, helplessly driven, in front of the barrier, strong hands seized him, pinning him to the ground. He fought wildly, kicking until a leg came free then connected with something firm and fleshy. A grunt followed, then more hands held him. He howled, foaming like a rabid dog, ripping at their hands and feet and snapping at anything that came within range.

"Darris." Ra-khir's voice hissed into his ear. "Get control. Darris!"

Darris went still, glaring at his captors. Andvari, Ra-khir, and Kevral pinned him to the ground. Tae crouched nearby, clutching his forehead. Blood striped his fingers where the wound from Loki's citadel had re-opened, with Darris' savage assistance.

Ra-khir's chiseled features looked down into Darris' face. "What in darkest Hel is going on with you?"

Darris stared fiercely, and his tone gave none of the ground his body must. "I just want a drink. Why are you treating me like a vicious animal?"

Kevral chimed in. "Because you're acting like one."

"Kevral," Ra-khir warned, unwilling to risk his hold on Darris' hands to glance at her. He softened his voice to address Darris again. "We're just concerned. We wonder whose will you're truly serving and whether you really understand what you're sacrificing."

A tidal wave of need struck Darris again. He struggled madly. His friends' hands gouged like shackles against his wrists and legs. Gradually, exhaustion worried at his battle lust, leaving him aching and tired. He stopped fighting.

"Darris, we're going to take you away from the spring."

The words pounded Darris like a hammer blow. "No!"

Ra-khir ignored the interruption. "When you're beyond its influence and can think clearly, you can decide if you really want this. If you still do, I won't interfere." He glanced around at the others, apparently seeking their support as well. "In fact, I'll help you any way I can. I just want you to make the decision using your own good sense, not driven to some fanatical frenzy."

Darris panted, trying to make sense of the words. Only the knowledge mattered, his goal since birth. Ignited by the gods' curse, his blood burned like fire in his veins. All his life, all the lives of his ancestors, had culminated in this moment. To deny him access to the Spring of Mimir was as cruel as teasing a starving dog with steak.

Lost in the hysteria of unbridled lust, Darris felt himself hefted and carried. With every step, more of his senses returned. He saw the well-lit cavern that contained Yggdrasill's root to the centermost plains, watched the grainy wood glide past him in a blur. He smelled the moist odor of soil and the crisp, sweet aroma of growing plant life. His companions' grips pinched him, though they supported him lovingly. They remained quiet, except to communicate an imbalance that needed correcting or an irregularity in the cavern that might affect others' footing. The reckless, headstrong urgency had died to a fascinated tickle of want. The chance to know all still clutched him, a desire he would never wholly lose. Yet, now, he felt he could consider the situation without surrendering self, family, companions, and anything else it might demand. "I'm all right now," he told Ra-khir, but no one responded.

Not until they hauled Darris to the trunk of Yggdrasill did his companions lower him to the ground. Their hands winched open, clammy from the enormous time spent clinging and carrying. Then they surrounded him, the largest taking positions between him and the cavern they had just exited.

Darris sat up but otherwise made no movements. "I'm sorry," he said, meaning it. "Odin's curse condemns the bard—"

"We know." Ra-khir did not let Darris finish. "We've suffered from your quests for knowledge in the past, though never as much as Tae does now."

Darris swiveled his gaze to the Easterner who closed the circle behind him, seated on the Asgard root with his head clutched between his hands. Blood matted the bangs that flopped over his fingers. Chan'rék'ril moved to assist.

Darris winced. "I'm truly sorry, Tae. I didn't mean to hurt you."

Tae released a hand to silently wave off the bard's concern. His voice emerged muffled through his palms. "I'm used to friends attacking me."

Kevral took offense. "Hey! I haven't done that for months."

"Months. Right." Tae raised his head, his bleary eyes revealing the intensity of his headache. "Sorry I complained."

"That's the answer," Andvari said suddenly, his attention beyond Tae, toward Yggdrasill.

Darris followed the Northman's gaze, watching the squirrel skitter up the World Tree again.

Andvari left his position, drifting toward the trunk. "Ratatosk, the squirrel. El-brinith located the shard deep below us but moving. Ratatosk carries insults from the dragon to the eagle perched at Yggdrasill's summit. Deep, but moving."

Darris considered, the thought clever but only one possibility.

Kevral voiced the same cynicism. "Isn't it as likely the dragon who has the shard? He moves, too."

"Well, yes." Andvari turned to Kevral. "But I saw something blue in the squirrel's mouth. That's what gave me the idea."

Now, every head swiveled toward the squirrel perched on one of Ygg-drasill's branches, tail twitching with the sharp, mechanical movements of a water clock. Darris stared at the mouth, seeing nothing. Then the paws flicked upward, and a flash of sapphire struck the light momentarily. Ratatosk shoved the sliver into his mouth, dropped to all fours, and skittered up the trunk in looping spirals.

An instant later, only Ra-khir remained with Darris, the others abandoning their charge for this new concern. Only the knight remained steadfastly between the bard and the Spring of Mimir.

"I won't run," Darris promised, watching his companions discuss the matter, though he could not hear their words.

"Under ordinary circumstances, I would believe you."

Darris tried to reassure. "I won't deny I want that knowledge more than anything in the universe, but you already promised I could have it if I thought the matter through on my own." The idea of repeating Odin's sacrifice no longer appealed to Darris, only because it seemed unlikely he could survive a nine day hanging with a spear in his side, which might explain why the spring had requested a different price from him. His music had often seemed a burden. Surrendering it for a chance at ultimate knowledge seemed more blessing than cost. "I have no reason to run away now."

Ra-khir shook his head. He did not understand. "The knowledge of the universe. It seems so daunting. Why would you want it?"

Darris found Ra-khir's position equally inscrutable. "Why wouldn't you?"

Ra-khir crouched near his friend. "You've sought bits and pieces of understanding your whole life. Wouldn't this take away any reason you have for living?"

"Not at all." Darris pinched grass spears between his fingers. "I still have Matrinka to love. Marisole to teach. The king to advise. And now, my advice would have the knowledge of the universe behind it." He grinned, the thought awesome. "The knowledge of the universe."

"But wouldn't it take away . . . I don't know . . . " Ra-khir struggled for his point. ". . . the newness of understanding. The joy of everyday learning." He considered, still seeking words. "Wouldn't everyone else seem . . . well . . . simple? In every way. Ordinary. Dim-witted. And wouldn't you feel obligated to solve everybody's problems and as if every mistake you made was a world-shattering failure." Ra-khir sighed, clearly frustrated by his inability to convince.

Darris resisted the urge to remind Ra-khir that having the knowledge of the universe would rescue him from moments like this one.

"Remember your ancestor?"

Darris pictured Jahiran, the madness that overtook the first bard except when engaged in song. "Age, not information, addled him. The Spring of Mimir grants past and present knowledge, not future or eternal life."

Ra-khir found another, more exact, comparison. "Look what drinking at the spring did to Odin." He clamped a hand over his mouth, surely worried he had spoken his sacrilege too loud and too close to Asgard.

"I believe," Darris said carefully, "that Odin was contemptuous and merciless long before he drank from Mimir's spring."

Ra-khir shrugged, without the knowledge to argue.

Kevral came to Ra-khir and Darris, crouching beside them. "Any thoughts?"

Darris managed a smile. "Many. Why?"

"I meant about Ratatosk." Kevral looked over Darris' head to Yggdrasill. "The elves have tried flying, but the squirrel won't let them near him. Tae's climbing up there now, but the squirrel's evading him, too. I think it's teasing him. And with those deer and goats whizzing about, I'm afraid he'll get hurt." Kevral released a deep breath through vibrating lips. "I'm ready to wait till it comes down and jump on it. None of us thought to bring a bow. Tae says he can throw stones with reasonable aim."

"My love, I don't think stoning a pet of the gods is the best option."

Kevral made a brisk gesture, accompanied by a harsh expression, to show that she had relinquished the matter to Ra-khir.

Darris rose. "Tell Tae to come down. I'll handle it."

Kevral also stood, pausing for an explanation. When none came, she headed toward Yggdrasill's trunk.

Darris unslung his lute and set to the strings. Notes chirped out, tuned well enough to appease most human ears; but Darris could hear the minuscule differences between nearly and right. He adjusted with movements so tiny they scarcely existed until every sound peeled forth as true as perfection allowed.

By the time Darris had finished his tuning, Tae stood among the others, a fresh bandage wound over his forehead. His eyes still held a glaze of pain; the need to focus on climbing had likely incited the headache Darris' wild blow had caused. Washed with fresh guilt, Darris started with a comforting melody and words that bore no meaning in sequence yet eased the worst physical agonies mankind suffered. An ancient bard had constructed it on a battlefield to soothe a dying prince, and his descendants had enhanced it through the centuries. Only when the creases smoothed from Tae's face and his eyes softened back to their dark normal did he launch into a song of the trees.

Darris' fingers moved as swiftly and jerkily as Ratatosk himself, weaving the corkscrew movements of a squirrel on a branch. His voice simulated the click of ripe acorns against their branches, swaying in a gentle breeze. He added ripe, juicy riffs, wordless description that conjured images of Yggdrasill's fruit dripping its sweet dew for the bees to gather. He launched into a wild mating dance, squirrels chasing one another at startling speeds through limbs that bowed and pranced beneath their weight. A contented chatter spoke off the fourth string at intervals, piercing the human words of Darris' song, which he hoped Ratatosk understood. It seemed likely that one capable of communicating a dragon's insults to an eagle should understand more than seemed otherwise logical for a squirrel.

Darris glanced through boughs thick with leaves. The stags and goats stood in place, listening. Ratatosk perched on a low branch, head cocked to allow one black eye full gaze at the bard below him. The Pica shard sparkled between his paws.

Darris changed his tactic, still stimulating squirrel play yet mixing in strains intended to tame and call it to him. The coaxing music rang softly beneath voice and melody, successful on the humans before the squirrel. Every one, he noted with amused satisfaction, took a half step toward him.

Finally, the squirrel, too, succumbed to the song. Moving directly over Darris, it released the branch. It plummeted, landing on the lute with a thump and jolt that nearly stole it from Darris' hands. He lost the thread of his playing; harmony disappeared. He managed to keep the song going with his voice, leaping octaves and rocking quavering notes to the gentle gibber of playful squirrels. Struggling to balance the lute, Darris abandoned his playing altogether, relying on voice alone to keep the animal in place. He reached for it with a slow, fluid motion devoid of threat. His fingers closed over the shard, feeling the sharp smoothness of claws against his fingers. He sang of its release.

Ratatosk clung, hind feet rattling against the wood, and the sound echoed deep within the instrument. Finally, he released the sapphire fragment to Darris' care, and the singing drew to a quiet close. "Thank you, my friend."

Ratatosk paused for a moment longer. Then, as if awakening from a spell, he skittered to the ground, bounded to the trunk, and launched himself up the tree.

Darris never knew who started the clapping. By the time he noticed, all of his companions were applauding his song with a raw joy that made him smile.

"My headache's gone," Tae announced.

"Mine, too," Kevral said, though she had never claimed to have one. "And I don't think I'll ever get another."

"I was going to heal him when he held still long enough." Chan'rék'-ril clamped a long-fingered hand to Darris' shoulder. "You have great talent, my friend. It is, in many ways, more powerful than my magic."

Though accustomed to others lauding his music, Darris flushed at the compliments. From these companions, all so capable themselves, the praise meant so much more. Their appreciation was genuine; he saw it in their eyes and expressions. For the first time, he recognized the joy his talent brought to so many; it had reached a new level of mastery this day. He only wished his mother could have heard it.

That thought brought memories shallowly buried. Darris could never forget the hours of practice his talent had cost him, his mother's loving hands guiding his at every step. She had taught him songs through the ages, the ones she had written and the ones of all the bards before her. He still measured the passage of seasons by the location of her teaching: summers in the gardens, striving to match her perfect harmonics floating with the warm and delicate breezes; autumns in woodlands seeking to capture the vibrant beauty of the multicolored wash of leaves, the stalwart finery of the trunks; winters indoors, chasing the power of roaring flames; and the tales of birth and wonder her voice brought with the spring. She had taught him not simply fingerings and notes. She had taught him to live and to teach, dragged him to depths of emotion that humans rarely plumb, and dredged forth a love and closeness that had set the foundation for his relationship with Matrinka, the very essence of his trust. He would always love his father; but nothing could ever match his time with his mother, the endless passing of bardic understanding, the desperate thirst for knowledge that others could not comprehend, the frantic frustration of teaching only with song. He would cherish her efforts and her memory forever.

Another idea struck Darris then, a ghostly wisp of a future that had faded from recollection. The man upon Béarn's throne bore the crown proudly upon thick black hair, his face enclosed in the standard mane. Darris could not remember his name. His face dulled to a detailless blur. Yet Darris did recall the bloodline, the second born child of Marisole by the son of Griff's third wife. Marisole stood proudly beside him, as robust and handsome as her mother, her hair white with age, her fingers callused by lute strings and swords. Marisole's firstborn, a daughter, watched proudly from amid the nobility, awaiting her chance to guard her brother when old age or accident claimed her mother.

Darris grinned at the many thoughts his mind filled in between, as the image disappeared from his memory forever. He imagined the rapport with his daughter, as strong and magnificent as the one he had shared with his own mother. And Marisole and her daughter would have that, too, and all of the bards through eternity. He glanced once more at his companions, the joy just beginning to fade from their faces. Through the ages, the bards had brought so much happiness to Béarn, had taught so many lessons they could not otherwise learn. Even Colbey Calistinsson spoke fondly of Darris' ancestor, Mar Lon, a man of peace who had brought knowledge through song to Colbey and the Cardinal Wizards in his time. *My gift with music is not mine to sacrifice. It belongs to my children and their children. It belongs to the many who needed it and will need it through past and future.*

Darris tossed the shard to El-brinith, who caught it gracefully from the air. "Let's go home."

Ra-khir nodded, this time understanding. He smiled broadly as he closed his eyes in preparation.

CHAPTER 32

Griff's Testing

The rulers of Béarn are neutrality incarnate, the very fulcrum of the world's balance.

—Colbey Calistinsson

EL-BRINITH'S magic brought the travelers back to the strategy room from which their many journeys began. A page stood beside a toppled chair, obviously aroused suddenly from a quiet vigil. On the table, a square of silk covered a lopsided object; and Kevral could make out several smaller lumps beneath that shroud as well. By its size and shape, she guessed it the malformed Pica Stone awaiting the uniting of its final pieces. Likely, Captain had covered it in case they could not locate the last shard, so it would not stand as a testament to their failure. El-brinith placed the newest piece beside the silk.

"Welcome home," the page tossed over her shoulder as she dashed from the room. No sound filtered through the open door, which suggested that some event must have disrupted the usual bustle of Béarn Castle. Kevral lowered her head in silence, unable to keep the worst possibilities from her mind. Though the season had not changed since their departure, the balmy warmth of late spring registered as it had not for the last week. The world seemed new and different, full of promises and a peace it could not have harbored even the previous day.

The page returned, a troupe of elves filing into the room behind her. Their descriptions defined a vast spectrum. They wore their hair in myriad styles, some even copying human bows and braids. Soft locks of blacks, golds, browns, and whites glimmered red in the torchlight. The canted, steady-colored eyes flickered from the newest shard to the returned heroes, and smiles decorated nearly every face. Captain entered among them, his features timeless, the smile wrinkles deeply etched by the largest grin she had ever seen. The chance to rid the world of the dark elves' magic, to restore joy to humanity, brought them more pleasure than she ever would have guessed.

"Thank you," Captain said. "For your sacrifice."

Kevral blinked. The words sounded odd from one who gained nothing but satisfaction from their success.

Captain explained, "King Griff asked me to say so. He apologizes for not being here to greet you. His wedding party yesterday tired him, and the new baby kept him awake through the night."

"Tem'aree'ay's baby?" Ra-khir guessed.

Darris rolled his eyes, though he could not hide a smile. "Only our king would spend the night with a wailing newborn when any of a thousand servants would happily take his place." The bard dashed for the exit. "Excuse me. The king needs me." He mumbled at Kevral as he ran, "Rantire's the last thing he should have to deal with right now."

Kevral watched Darris go, finally managing a grin of her own. She doubted her overzealous cousin would do anything but watch over Griff who, after suffering through two ceremonies led by Knights of Erythane, entertaining hundreds of guests, and settling in a new wife and baby was probably in a coma. She hoped Matrinka was happy with the arrangement, then wondered a moment later why she ever doubted.

Tae also headed for the door, stopped by Ra-khir's sudden proclamation. "If you don't fill in some details about the little one, you're going to force the Prince of Stalmize to climb a wall to find them."

Tae turned back sheepishly. Clearly, the search for information *was* the thing that drove him to leave before Captain worked his long-awaited magic.

"A girl," Captain informed. "A bit small even for an elf, but healthy. The consensus is that she looks like her father, but the elves can see some subtle things. No official name yet. He wants Ivana. She wants Shorith'na Cha-tella Tir Hya'sellirian Albar."

"At least they're close," Tae quipped.

Kevral looked at her feet, fighting bitterness. She wished them all well, yet she could not escape visions of the tiny blond boy she had placed into the arms of the Pudarians only a week earlier. Sensing her pain, sharing it, Ra-khir placed a comforting arm around her.

Captain paused a moment to assure the questioning had ended. Then he pulled the cloth from the misshapen lump of blue stone that represented most of the Pica. He gathered the retrieved shards, the nine parts of the sapphire together for the first time since its destruction nearly four centuries ago.

Ra-khir interrupted the proceedings, voice urgent. "You're not planning to restore it now, are you?"

Captain returned a tilt-headed stare. "Why wait?"

"The king and queen aren't here."

"They requested we begin without them."

Ra-khir pursed his lips, surely weighing the safety of Béarn's royalty against their right to a presence during such a spectacular moment. He glanced at Kevral. Apparently deeming her ready for battle, as well as himself, he fell silent and nodded.

Kevral worried more for Darris, who surely would have created a reason to stay had he guessed Captain might start the proceedings immediately. Nevertheless, she did not chase after the bard. His subsequent quest for the details would help focus his mind from the ultimate knowledge so recently sacrificed.

Captain sent *khohlar*: **Jovinay arythanik, begin the reconstruction.**

The whole room seemed to swell with elfin song, a pulsating wave of sound with its own special beauty, though it paled in the wake of Darris' squirrel serenade. Captain's words sounded gruff and harsh, his voice losing its usual rhythmical gentleness. Beneath his spread hands, the main portion of the Pica Stone glowed as if lit from the core, a cerulean lantern that seemed to darken, rather than lighten, the rest of the room in comparison. Gradually, each shard took on a similar light. One twitched. Another rocked on its rounded surface. Then, all but the largest portion floated from the table. They buzzed like insects, gliding across that last, main segment until they found their proper positions. As the final shard merged into place, the Pica shimmered. The inner glow blazed outward, the sapphire shining with the radiance of a tiny sun, dwarfing the torchlight.

Release.

The elfin chant died in an instant. Every human eye went to Captain.

"Did it work?" Kevral asked in a small voice.

Captain sat back, a bead of sweat forming on his brow. "It's repaired."

Kevral cocked her head, the answer incomplete. "The gem? Or fertility?"

"The gem." Captain rubbed his forehead with the back of his sleeve. "Whether we've lifted the sterility spell remains to be seen."

Ra-khir asked the obvious question. "When will you know for certain?"

Captain's amber eyes swiveled to the knight. "When the first human pregnancy is confirmed in a woman who has cycled since the placement of the curse."

Andvari bobbed his head at the obvious logic. Ra-khir pursed his lips. Words rushed from Kevral's lips before she could stop them, "But that could take months."

"Months," Captain confirmed with an elfin gesture Kevral could not read. The canted, unvarying eyes, fine hair, and high cheekbones had never seemed so alien. "Months will not affect even mankind's future, I don't believe?" It seemed more question than statement.

Not mankind's. But mine.

"Thank you." Ra-khir drew Kevral closer. "We appreciate everything you've done for us." He looked around the ring of elves. "All of you."

Nods and mumbles issued from the smiling outworlders.

The air vacillated near Captain, liquid-appearing waves, like those emanating from tar on a hot summer day. Then, quietly, Colbey Calistinsson appeared beside him. The ancient Renshai looked different than when Kevral had last seen him. His golden hair was shaven to stubble, revealing bruises and burns on his scalp. Healing lacerations scored his face and hands. He wore two swords at his hip, a matched set of S-guards different than the one had carried the last time she saw him. He seemed tired, but the blue-gray eyes remained hard as ice, reflecting a vigor and youth that age and experience belied.

Startled, Captain leaped aside. Concern sent his welcoming grin askew. "Don't tell me. You came to lay your claim on the Pica Stone."

"Just to see it." Colbey raised a hand over the sapphire and, for the first time, Kevral saw his fingers shake. Slowly he lowered his hand to his side. "My last touch shattered it."

"Bring it full circle," Captain insisted gently, like a mother encouraging a frightened child. "It won't happen this time."

Colbey studied the elf.

"Trust me."

Colbey's hand rose again, and this time he stroked the Pica Stone like a pet. The glow flickered and winked, then shone more steadily than before. Colbey sought out the page amidst a roomful of elves. "Record that the test of the Pica will now and forevermore choose the rightful ruler of Béarn. The Staves of Law and Chaos exist no longer."

Kevral looked up, too shocked to savor the news.

Captain asked guardedly, "Odin?"

"Destroyed utterly."

"You're certain?"

"Absolutely." The word carried the assurance of the gods.

"How?" Captain asked, but many needed to know. Kevral winced at the realization that Darris could suffer eternally for missing this moment and the chance to personally elicit the story.

Colbey's eyes rolled back, following his mind to a distant location none of them would ever see. "Wars and battles. Deceptions and deaths. We lost a few more gods along the way, and I could not have succeeded without the help of your creator."

The smiles on the elfin faces seemed eternal, yet natural and right.

"I never bonded with chaos." It was a promise. "But I did sacrifice myself. Freya rescued me at the final moment, more than I expected or thought possible. She transported us both from the destruction that claimed Odin and most of chaos' world."

"A special woman," Captain said, the description bordering sacrilege.

Colbey took no offense. "The best. I don't deserve her." He added with a twinkle, eyes returning to their proper position. "Thankfully, she doesn't agree." He removed his hand from the Pica Stone.

"What do you plan to do with the life Freya rescued?" Captain replaced the Pica's cover, and the room dimmed visibly.

"Guard the balance." Colbey reached to run a hand through his hair, then stopped mid-movement, apparently recalling that the feathers no longer existed. "Train and be tried by my adolescent son. Try to prove myself worthy of my wife's loyalty." Joy softened the coldness of his eyes. "And spend a lot of time in Valhalla." His gaze swung to Kevral. "Someday I'll see you there?"

The presence of Kevral's hero erased some of the pain. With the Fate's help, she now knew she still had a soul. "You can count on it."

"Perhaps you'll be the one to finally best me."

Under ordinary circumstances, Kevral would have vowed to that with the same certainty as her previous statement. This day, she felt beaten. "I can't even win my battles here." An image of the baby's tiny lips and fingers filled her mind, the brilliant blue of his eyes with just a hint of future gray. Until that moment, she did not realize how closely he physically resembled Colbey.

Though Colbey could not have guessed her meaning from words, the intensity of her sorrow surely reached him. "Kevral, that was never *your* battle."

Confusion filled many faces. Ra-khir squeezed Kevral's hand, his arm still wrapped around her. Like Colbey, he knew that she referred to losing her youngest son.

"Under the circumstances, you had to make that vow." Colbey's attention focussed on Kevral and Ra-khir simultaneously. "And once you made it, the battle was no longer yours."

"No longer mine?" Kevral repeated, now as bewildered as Andvari and the elves.

"No longer yours." Colbey swiped a finger between her and Ra-khir, indicating the plural use of the word "you."

"Then whose . . . ?" Kevral started, unable to finish.

"One appropriately concerned for the wellbeing of his grandson's mother."

His grandfather? Kevral followed the loop of Colbey's words. "You?"

Colbey shook his head. "I'm a grandfather only by blood. A real grandfather is the one who gives his time and love, who is there when the child needs his assistance and experience. I can't help taking an interest, but I will not actively interfere."

Kevral's mind turned to the next obvious candidate. *Kedrin?* She frowned. It would violate Ra-khir's honor for his father to get involved. *My father?* A smile eased onto Kevral's lips, crueler than those of the elves. She pictured Tainhar hacking his way through King Cymion and his guards, a Renshai battle cry ringing over Pudar.

As Kevral savored her conjured images, Colbey moved on to Ra-khir. "Are you going to make me beg, Sir Knight?"

Ra-khir's bow contained so many flourishes it spanned longer than any pause in conversation should. "Certainly not, *Sir* Colbey. Every Knight of Erythane should have his own charger, and Frost Reaver is the only one worthy of you."

Colbey laughed. "Perhaps he is simply the only one who will have me." He grew serious again. "I gave him to you in good faith. You would be within your rights to keep him." He added somberly, "Without angering immortals."

Ra-khir bowed again, demonstrating his own earnestness. "So long as you're alive, Frost Reaver would never be happy with me."

"Thank you." All of the fatigue seemed to fade from Colbey then. "Now that you know what I am, must I worry that your father will place me into the rotation?"

"I think I can talk him out of it." Ra-khir smiled now, too. "Somehow, I can't picture you taking part in five-hour rituals."

Colbey cringed. "Even immortality hasn't granted me the patience for that." He waved an arm, fading before Kevral could question further.

Colbey's final gesture, a signal of brotherhood, was clearly aimed at Andvari. Kevral could not ignore it.

Matrinka puzzled over her summons to the testing room, only moments after Griff had headed there himself. Dread gripped her heart as she hurried down the four staircases from her quarters to the first floor, leaving guards to scurry in her wake. From past experience, she knew the test seemed to take hours to the one undergoing it, only minutes to those waiting outside the room. It had never before occurred to her that Griff might fail, yet no other reason remained for him to call her. Success would simply result in a great celebration.

Darris, Prime Minister Davian, Rantire, Griff's mother and stepfather, and a page huddled outside the testing room door. Matrinka did not wait until she reached them before questioning, instead shouting down the corridor, "What's wrong?"

Darris rushed to her, though Davian chose to answer. "The king is asking for you. He wants you in the room for the testing."

Matrinka squinted. "The law doesn't allow spectators."

"Ravn's with him," Rantire explained, jerking a thumb toward the door. "He permitted it. Suggested it, in fact."

Ravn? Matrinka greeted Helana and Herwin with waves, then turned to the entry. She did not bother to knock. The thick door of the testing room would not permit the sound to penetrate. Tripping the latch, she pulled the panel open.

The glow of the Pica granted vision into every corner of the tiny room. Griff sat, cross-legged, in front of the sapphire, which lay on a gold stand on the floor. Ravn leaned against the back wall, leaving more space for Matrinka to enter. Once, before Griff took back his throne from elves, they had stuffed five people into this room. Now, Matrinka marveled at how they had managed such a feat. At Ravn's gesture, she closed the door.

Colbey's son radiated a golden presence nearly as illuminating as the Pica Stone. "I'm leaving," he promised. "Already used up my share of air. I just thought you earned the right of inclusion."

"I'm not sure I understand." Matrinka crouched at her husband's side. "I'm not getting tested again, too, am I?" She tried to hide fear. When all the available heirs had failed the staff test, the then-prime minister, Baltraine, had them all tested a second time. Only Matrinka, away on the mission to rescue Griff, had evaded that trial and the inescapable madness it inflicted on every victim. Her single failure had left her drowning in self-doubt, questioning her every decision and the value of her existence. She had gradually overcome the agony of that rejection and did not wish to revive the pain.

"You can experience his testing as a spectator. You can't influence the outcome." Ravn studied Griff's first queen. "Interested?"

Matrinka felt a tickle of excitement in her chest. "Yes," she admitted.

Ravn waved a hand to indicate they should proceed. A moment later, the room contained only Griff, Matrinka, and the Pica Stone.

"Ready?" Griff asked.

Matrinka smiled at his generosity. "Please. Proceed at your pace. I'm just a spectator, remember?"

Griff nodded, muscles knotting beneath silks. She had rarely seen him nervous, never more so than at this moment.

"You'll do fine," Matrinka assured, illogically certain.

Griff placed both hands upon the sapphire. Matrinka closed her eyes, bracing for the rush of pain that had accompanied seizing the Staves of Law and Chaos. She stood aside, unaffected while a whirlwind flung

Griff in wild spirals. His cheeks flapped with the motion, but no pain filled his eyes, to Matrinka's relief. She hoped Odin's presence in the Staff of Law at the time of her testing accounted for the discomfort and that her cousin would not have to suffer it.

At length, Griff fell on a familiar, little island, his hair whipped to tangles, his beard in disarray, his clothes a mass of wrinkles. Although he had started by clutching a gem, he held a staff in each hand, just as Matrinka had during her time of testing. Griff gazed out over a sea tousled by waves, its shore battered by bracken. Like her, he seemed not to question his location or arrival. Ruffled by wind and shielded by fog, the sea revealed a massive shadow in its midst. Matrinka knew its contents, waiting patiently for Griff to surmise the same. Way out in the sea, two humans stood balanced on a massive scale. They tossed their arms about wildly, desperately requesting help.

Unlike Matrinka, Griff did not secure the staves before leaping into the frothing sea. Waves slammed him, tossing him in ungainly circles, but he persisted. His strong strokes should have taken him triple the distance in the same time in calmer water, and the burden of the staves slowed him further. Matrinka smiled at the simplicity of his forgetting to release them, wondering if that act alone separated her attempt from his. Memory emerged: the man in the left pan lived a simple life with his wife and four children in a hungry but generous and loving household. The young woman in the opposite pan had lived a cruel and selfish life, shirking responsibility. Her credits already included theft and murder.

Matrinka recalled the dilemma in detail. Magic held both in their places, unable to descend without assistance. Left there, both would die of exposure and starvation; but saving one meant drowning the other as the balance dropped the weight in the opposite pan beneath the waves. Matrinka had measured her ability to pull one free, steady him or her, then rush to assist the other and found the necessary speed impossible.

When the victims spotted Griff, they called out to him as they had to Matrinka. "Please save me," the woman shouted first. "I can reward you. I can shower you with riches. My body and my soul as well." She peeled back the sleeve of her shift to reveal the greater portion of a large and finely proportioned breast. Matrinka recalled being offered the heart and soul of a fine, young man. "Whatever you desire, I can see that it becomes yours." Matrinka also remembered that, in testing state, she had never doubted the woman could deliver on her promises.

The man in the other pan spoke next, "I have nothing. Nothing but as many warm nights in my family's cottage as you desire. We would share what we have, but that would not be much, I'm afraid."

Matrinka held her breath, waiting for Griff's response. The test delved to the core of the tested's being, often placing him or her into a different persona or era, stealing knowledge of the testing, supplying details that the tested could not otherwise know. Oblivious, she had accepted all the test had presented: unquestioningly believing herself a previous king, an aged queen, and her placement into situations that would otherwise seem ludicrous. Her own version of this task had ended in condemnation when she had chosen the life of the honest man over the hardhearted woman. Even now, outside the scenario and with her faculties and memories intact, she still could not fathom her mistake.

"A moment," Griff said, giving the situation only a brief scrutiny as he treaded water that sloshed and roiled around him. He planted the staff from his left hand into the water, and its opposite end rose just high enough to brace the beam between the fulcrum and the man's pan. Griff then moved to the right, jabbing the second staff into the waves to brace the scale's other beam. Only then, he started climbing the contraption.

Matrinka gaped at a simple solution she had never considered. With the staves blocking movement of the scale's arms, he could shift weights freely. He could and would rescue both of its prisoners. Subsequently, he could try the woman for her crimes and return the man to his needy family. She never doubted that he would refuse the rewards both offered, having saved them only for humane and moral reasons.

From her own ordeal, Matrinka knew the test never rewarded the actions that pleased it, only condemned those that did not display the naive and neutral proclivities necessary for Béarn's ruler. Warmth suffused her, pride at her cousin's cleverness hidden beneath an innocent mantle of childlike simplicity. No matter how many times she saw him deliver brilliantly guileless judgments, she could not help finding them awesome and sweet. She sought the shame that had so often accompanied her thoughts of this task in the past, heightened by the realization of an obvious solution that she had missed. Instead, she found an inner warmth and peace. She had made the wrong decision for the ruler of Béarn, but not for Matrinka. And she could finally put the matter fully to rest.

Realizing she had lost track of Griff and his trials, Matrinka rejoined him in another familiar scenario. He perched upon his throne in the courtroom, as so often in the past. Darris stood at his one hand, Captain Seiryn at the other. In front of him knelt a cowed line of men and women in chains, their clothing ragged and their feet bare. Matrinka recalled a recent treaty with LaZar, a city of the East. Tae had told her that his father had outlawed slavery soon after taking the throne, but the staff-test made even anachronisms seem utterly real. This scenario required

LaZar and Béarn to exchange slaves, once a standard treaty-sealing practice of the East.

Like Matrinka, Griff had deftly substituted animals for humans, allowing the king's delegates to pick out the ones they felt constituted a proper, even trade. The LaZarian contingent had gone to do so, leaving Béarn's king with a dilemma that had appalled Matrinka in his place. He now owned slaves, a clear violation of Béarn's law. Matrinka recalled what she had done in his place, a solution that had brought more damnation from her divine testers. Embarrassed by her breach of law, she had commanded the slaves freed, then promised to deliver each and every one to a desired location or home.

One of the guards asked the same question of Griff that he had once delivered to Matrinka. "Your Majesty, what shall we do with these?" He indicated the slaves.

Griff glanced over, clearly taken aback by the question. "Unchain them, Zapara. Béarn has no slavery. When I accepted them, I could only have done so as citizens of the city."

The scenario ended, sweeping Griff into another warm spiral, carrying him gently into the next task, without imprecation. Brow furrowed, Matrinka contemplated the differences between Griff's handling and her own, this time more subtle. It seemed like an eternity before she discovered the two particulars that separated his success from her failure. First, he had never worried for breaking Béarn's law. Unlike her, he did not consider himself to have brought slaves that needed freeing into his kingdom but rather that the instant he accepted them as his charge, they were no longer slaves. Second, he had not suffered the empathy and resultant pity that forced her to promise those freed slaves special treatment. He had given them the exact opportunities of any Béarnian citizen. *The neutral solution, not necessarily the kindest one.* This understanding, too, placed her mind and soul at rest.

The time spent analyzing minutiae stole most of the third scenario. Matrinka rejoined Griff at the moment of judgment, memory dragging her back to her own desperate concerns. A Pudarian healer had come to Béarn at a time when the kingdom suffered from a plague of lumpy-consumption, promising a cure-all that Matrinka, and now Griff, allowed him to sell without tariff, even purchasing some for the castle staff. The Pudarian had skipped town with a large sum of money in exchange for a worthless tonic. Captured by the guards, he was hauled back for sentencing, his money confiscated and his panacea exposed as fraud.

Matrinka did not hear Griff's pronouncement of punishment, though she felt confident enough of her two year imprisonment followed by permanent exile to suspect his would be similar. Now, the final moment of judgment came, the place where she had made her mistake.

A guard approached and bowed, "Majesty, what would you have us do with moneys confiscated from the guilty?"

Griff answered without hesitation, the same as Matrinka, "Return it to those who paid for his product."

"Yes, Majesty. And what would you have us do with the extra?"

Matrinka pursed her lips. She had told the guard to divide the remaining hundred coppers between those who had suffered from the scam. Now Griff's hand stroked his beard. "Place it in a special fund to be used toward finding a real cure. And for victims of the disease."

The scenario ended with his words, yet again it did not label Griff the unworthy failure it had Matrinka. She discovered the differences more easily this time: Griff saw no reason to reward those duped by a scam artist when he could better use the money to rescue future victims of the plague. Though compassionate, her choice did not suit the ultimate neutrality that always characterized Béarn's ruler.

Matrinka's test had ended with that third failure and the one success that preceded it. Griff's continued through a hundred more scenarios, each more difficult than the one that came before it. After the first six, Matrinka breathed a sigh of relief that she had not needed to suffer these. The situations twisted her emotions in desperate knots. From that moment on, she became a quiet spectator, not bothering to guess how she would have handled each matter. She simply sat back and enjoyed Griff's triumphs.

Then, as the last objective drew to a close, Griff sat back. His hands fell from the Pica Stone, and he glanced at Matrinka. "Are you all right?"

"Me?" Matrinka stared. "You're kidding, right?"

Griff's face resembled that of a scolded puppy. "Did I say something offensive?"

"Not offensive," Matrinka hastened to console, rising to her feet and offering a hand to the king. "Just unbelievable. After all you just endured, you're asking me if *I'm* all right?"

Griff smiled tiredly. "I think I passed."

"Of course you passed." Matrinka took Griff's hand and pulled. "You performed magnificently."

Barely allowing any weight to fall on Matrinka, Griff stood, leaving the Pica in place. He flushed at the praise. "I didn't do anything special. Just what I had to do."

Matrinka shook her head, startled by a realization she could never have anticipated. With all its taxing quandries and harsh analyses, the test had not changed innocent Griff at all. But it had a profound effect on its spectator. At the time, she had believed every specific would remain with her for eternity, frozen in time by an intensity of emotion that spanned every gamut and beyond. Yet, already, the scenarios faded from her memory as if reclaimed by the stone for future use. Whether or not she remembered enough to coach her children made no difference. Once sucked inside the stone, they would respond with the raw depths of self and character. Circumstance could only shape so much. Like the myriad of kings and queens before him, Griff had, indeed, been born to rule.

Matrinka grinned. "The whole world is waiting for you to emerge from this room and give them an answer."

Griff nodded once, opening the door to a life that had not substantially changed. "I passed," he said in a small voice that barely suited the grandness of the claim. Yet, for him, it was enough.

Helana caught her son into an embrace, while the prime minister and the bard watched proudly.

Mior leaped into her mistress' arms. *You're fixed!*

Fixed. Matrinka cradled her best friend, the fur warm against her face and arms. *I'd say wiser. More at peace.*

I love you. Mior purred, rubbing her ears against Matrinka's chin. *And I have some happy news.*

Happy news? At the moment, Matrinka did not know if she could stand any more.

More babies in Béarn.

Matrinka's smile widened until it strained the edges of her face. Her heart seemed to flutter in her chest as she shared the joy of thousands of barren women, eventually celebrating her own gain as well. Someday, she hoped, she would carry another, too. *The elves lifted the sterility spell?*

I don't know about that. Mior turned in Matrinka's arms, settling her tail on the woman's hands and her nose in Matrinka's face. *These babies are mine.*

Epilogue

OVER the next two months, Kevral's sorrow settled into a dark corner of heart and mind, disturbed at intervals but no longer the center of her attention. Sunlight filtered through the window, striking gold highlights amid the red mop of Saviar's hair and adding a blue sheen to the sheer black of Subikahn's fine locks. The differences seemed more striking than ever. By size, Ra-khir's son seemed the older, yet he still clutched furniture to walk, toddling only a few steps unassisted before flopping on his bottom. Subikahn ran from Tae to Kevral, frequently returning to stroke Marisole's chubby leg, to pull at her dress, or simply to point.

Beside Darris, Matrinka clutched the nine-month-old in her lap, Marisole squealing with delight whenever Subikahn touched her. "Baby!" Saviar declared for the hundredth time, looking to his father for confirmation.

"Baby," Ra-khir repeated, also for the hundredth time. "Yes, Marisole is a baby."

"Say 'baby,' " Tae coaxed Subikahn. "Come on, say 'baby.' "

"Dada," Subikahn shouted, clutching his tiny wooden sword. "Da Da Da." Laughing happily, he dashed toward the corner of the room where Mior lay with her three kittens. The males, one black and one ginger, kneaded her belly as they nursed. The gray tabby female curled near her mother's tail.

Tae swooped in to rescue the cat. "No, no, Subikahn. You could hurt those babies." Playfully, he wrestled the toddler to the ground, growling like an angry bear. Subikahn giggled, joined a moment later by Saviar who scrambled over Tae's back.

Kevral smiled, counting her many blessings. Her promises in Pudar's dungeon had cost her a son but gained her two every bit as precious. Duty usually called at least one of their group away, making their quiet times together especially glorious. She pulled her legs onto the bed with an ease that still felt awkward. Even three months after the birth of Pudar's prince, she still expected the inconvenience of the familiar bulge in her abdomen. In truth, worry and the intensity of her practices had stolen a bit too much weight, leaving her unattractively thin. She had not cycled since the birth, but the elves had found no new baby growing inside her. Not for the first time, the rigorousness of her lifestyle had caused the irregularity. The weight loss had not helped either.

In contrast, Matrinka had managed to throw off only half of her extra girth. Only a few moments earlier, she had verbally surrendered to it, certain it had become a permanent part of her anatomy. Ra-khir and Tae had swiftly reassured her, but Darris' insistence, in song, that the extra weight only enhanced her beauty was the detail that finally put her at ease. The perfect flow of the melody left Kevral wistful for a few more pounds.

A bold knock on the door interrupted their quiet reunion. Kevral winced, dreading what would come next. She tried to guess whether political affairs, knight duties, or Renshai training would pull one or more of them away. Ra-khir rose from the floor, his manner resigned. "Who is it?"

In reply, the panel swung open to reveal Weile Kahn, resplendent in tailored silks and wearing a smile as fresh as the sunlight. He made a grand display of closing the door on the milling crowd in the hall, surely to the distress of Béarn's sentries and his own personal bodyguards. "Where's my grandson?"

Every adult but Matrinka skittered suddenly to their feet, Tae pausing to catch Saviar before he fell. Already standing, Ra-khir reacted first, the hurriedness of his bow stealing most of its grandeur. He fussed at his hopelessly wrinkled tunic.

"None of that formal crap," Weile bellowed. Then, his head whipped to the only Béarnide. "You must be Queen Matrinka," he said with a sheepishness Kevral would not have believed possible from him. "Sorry, Your Ladyship."

Matrinka hefted Marisole and finally stood also. "None of that formal crap," she repeated. "Bothers me as much as you."

"Great." Weile clapped his hands together. "Now, where's my grandson?" His eyes went directly to Tae and the twins clinging to either arm.

"Guess," Kevral said, certain he could pick the proper baby. Tae had claimed Subikahn closely resembled his paternal grandfather, but she had never believed it until that moment. Now, she could see the similarities in the stubby forehead, softly rounded cheekbones, and gentle chin.

The King of Stalmize crouched, holding out his hands. Tae turned Subikahn toward his grandfather. For a moment, the child clung. Growing braver, he took slow steps toward Weile Kahn, finally falling into his arms. As if uncertain what to do next, Weile consulted his son, who smiled. The arms closed cautiously around the toddler.

"No one told us you were coming." Matrinka broke the peace with necessary politics. "I hope you received a proper greeting."

"Absolutely." Weile Kahn did not look at the queen as he spoke, as if entranced. He rose, lifting Subikahn. "I met with King Griff. Told him not to bother any of you till I got here."

Subikahn turned a watchful eye to his parents and started to squirm.

Reluctantly, Weile released the boy, gaze following Subikahn's run back to his mother. Smiling, the king held out his arms again, this time for his son.

Tae came forward, greeting his father with a hug that contained genuine warmth. As soon as they separated, Weile approached Kevral. A strange light danced in his dark eyes. "Good to see you again, Kevral."

"And you." Kevral retook her seat on the bed, cradling Subikahn. Her relationship with Weile had, so far, been rocky.

"Well," Weile Kahn said. "Perhaps this will earn me a hug." Backpedaling, he opened the door and called into the hall, "Daxan."

The squatter of his bodyguards approached, clutching a bundle in his arms.

Kevral's heart quickened, and she fought against quashing hope. She rose for a better look.

Weile took the baby from his bodyguard, opening a corner of the blanket to reveal a closed-eyed blond breathing in the slow, quiet cadence of sleep. Though larger than Kevral remembered, she recognized him at once.

Kevral had the baby in her arms before she recalled moving. She stared at him, watching the blue eyes glide open, the tiny face screw into angry lines. Suddenly, he loosed a lusty wail that drew the toddlers' attention in an instant. Subikahn rushed back to his father and brother. Kevral clutched the infant to her shoulder, cooing and swaying to calm the screams.

"So I still don't get my hug," Weile lamented beneath the baby's cries.

Ra-khir seized the King of Stalmize into a massive embrace. "Maybe not from her." He released the king, unable to stop himself from a respectful bow. "But you have *my* appreciation."

"Not exactly what I was looking for." Weile Kahn reassured Ra-khir's uncharacteristic action with a friendly expression. It had taken a struggle for Ra-khir to shed his knight's formality to joke with a king.

Kevral could not take her eyes from the baby. Finding his fingers, he sucked avidly, eyes drooping closed again. Colbey had told her the battle belonged to one "appropriately concerned for the well-being of his grandson's mother." Over the ensuing months, she had tried to broach the subject with Kedrin and Tainhar. Weile Kahn had never occurred to her.

"Thank you." Ra-khir addressed Weile, but his attention kept slipping to wife and baby. "How did you manage such a thing?"

"Once the elves proclaimed Prince Leondis' wife pregnant, it wasn't that hard." Weile Kahn downplayed his role. "There was talk of keeping him until after the birth of a healthy baby, but I convinced Cymion that wasn't necessarily in Pudar's best interests." He smothered a smile along with details better left unspoken.

Finally, Kevral released the baby to Ra-khir and gave Weile Kahn the embrace he had earned. "Thank you," she said, choking around unexpected tears. "Thank you so much."

"You're welcome." Weile clutched Kevral with the pride of a father. "And now, my price."

Kevral jerked free. Tae groaned.

"I'd like to take my son and grandson back to Stalmize."

Kevral bit her lower lip. She had dreaded this moment.

"For a few months a year," the king added, softening the request.

Kevral shook her head. "His Renshai training—"

Weile Kahn interrupted with the answer. "—can be handled by you after a three-week training session. Or so Thialnir said."

Realization dawned. *I'm invited, too.* Kevral glanced at Ra-khir, who deliberately kept his face toward the infant. He would leave the decision in her hands, a difficult one that involved tearing up the family into pieces of varying sizes. To reunite them with the baby, then tear husband and wife apart seemed cruel. "Ra-khir—" she started.

Weile broke in again, "—can represent Béarn as the king's diplomat. Or so the council decided. His captain agreed to spare him, and King Griff requested him by name."

"Give up now," Tae told his friends. "He'll have an answer to every objection you can raise."

Kevral looked at Ra-khir, who shrugged. "If the king of Stalmize really wants to travel with three infants, who am I to tell him no?" The knight lifted his chin toward Tae. "I'll need diplomat lessons. I'm new to this."

Tae grinned mischievously, leaving the twins to explore the room without him. "You start by making a grand entrance. Say, climbing the castle . . . "

Ra-khir blanched, rocking the baby with the natural rhythm all parents seemed to know. "On second thought, maybe I'd better figure this out on my own."

Matrinka and Darris glanced at one another, smiling. They could spare their friends one season a year.

"And I'd iike to learn the Eastern language," Kevral announced, surprised to find herself excited by the prospect of a long trip with loved ones and a chance to visit Tae's home.

"Settled, then." Weile Kahn headed for the door. "I'll make the arrangements."

Tae went to Mior, stroking the calico from the backs of her ears to the tip of her tail. Kevral knew he would miss Matrinka's cat as much as the queen herself. After a moment, he hefted the tiny tabby with the delicate caution of a prized glass figurine. "Father, add one more to the group." He displayed the kitten. "She wants me to have her."

Weile Kahn paused, one hand on a slender hip. "She?"

"Mior," Tae responded.

The calico purred, seeming almost to grin.

Appendices

WESTERNERS
Béarnides

Abran (AH-bran)—previous minister of foreign affairs; killed in the elfin purge

Aerean (AIR-ee-an)—current minister of internal affairs; previously a renegade leader

Aranal (Ar-an-ALL)—a previous king

Aron (AHR-inn)—the Sage's apprentice

Avisha (A-VEESH-a)—Zoenya's third husband; an ancient king by marriage

Baltraine (BAL-trayn)—previous prime minister; deceased

Baran (BAYR-in)—an ancient guard captain who served King Sterrane

Baynard (BAY-nard)—an ex-soldier, turned renegade. Distant descendent of Baran

Charletha (Shar-LEETH-a)—previous minister of livestock, gardens, and food; killed in the elfin purge

Chaveeshia (Sha-VEE-sha)—current minister of local affairs

Dalen (DAY-linn)—a cooper; a renegade

Davian (DAY-vee-an)—current prime minister; previous leader of the renegades

Denevier (Dih-NEV-ee-er)—minister assigned to relay Knight-Captain Kedrin's orders from prison

Ethylyn (ETH-ell-in)—King Kohleran's daughter; killed during the second staff-test

Fachlaine (FATCH-layne)—King Kohleran's granddaughter; deceased

Fahrthran (FAR-thrin)—minister of internal affairs; descendant of Arduwyn; killed in the elfin purge

Fevrin (FEV-rinn)—a past sage; served Xanranis

Franstaine (FRAN-stayn)—current minister of household affairs; in-law uncle of Helana

Friago (Free-YAH-go)—a renegade

Griff (GRIFF)—the King

Helana (Hell-AHN-a)—Petrostan's wife and Griff's mother

Kohleran (KOLL-er-in)—previous king of Béarn; deceased

Limrinial (Lim-RIN-ee-al)—previous minister of local affairs; killed in the elfin purge

Marisole (MAA-rih-soll)—the princess; daughter of King Griff and Queen Matrinka; sired by Darris (see Pudarians)

Matrinka (Ma-TRINK-a)—Griff's wife and cousin; the queen

Mikalyn (MIK-a-linn)—previous head healer; killed in the elfin purge

Mildy (MIL-dee)—King Kohleran's late wife

Morhane (MOOR-hayn)—an ancient king who usurped the throne from his twin brother, Valar

Myrenex (My-RINN-ix)—a past king

Nylabrin (NILL-a-bran)—King Kohleran's granddaughter; deceased

Petrostan (Peh-TROSS-tin)—King Kohleran's youngest son; Griff's father. Died in a plowing accident

Richar (REE-shar)—current minister of foreign affairs

The Sage—the chronicler of Béarn's history

Saxanar (SAX-a-nar)—current minister of courtroom procedure and affairs

Sefraine (SEE-frayn)—a grandson of King Kohleran

Seiryn (SAIR-in)—the captain of the guards

Sterrane (Stir-RAIN)—the best known previous king of Béarn

Talamaine (TAL-a-mayn)—King Kohleran's son; Matrinka's late father

Ukrista (Yoo-KRIS-tah)—King Kohleran's granddaughter; deceased

Valar (VAY-lar)—Morhane's twin brother; Sterrane's father; a previous king murdered during his reign

Walfron (WALL-fron)—supervisor of the kitchen staff

Weslin (WESS-lin)—previous minister of courtroom procedure and affairs; killed during the elfin purge

Xanranis (Zan-RAN-iss)—Sterrane's son; an ancient king

Xyxthris (ZIX-thris)—King Kohleran's grandson; a traitor; committed suicide while imprisoned

Yvalane (IV-a-layn)—King Kohleran's father; a previous king

Zapara (Za-PAR-a)—a guard

Zaysharn (ZAY-sharn)—the current overseer of the caretakers of Béarn's livestock, gardens, and food

Zelshia (ZELL-sha)—a head maid

Zoenya (Zoh-ENN-ya)—a past queen

Erythanians

Arduwyn (AR-dwinn)—a legendary archer
Asha (AH-shah)—an adolescent girl
Braison (BRAY-son)—a young Knight of Erythane
Carlynn (KAR-linn)—an adolescent girl
Diega (Dee-AY-gah)—Carlynn's father
Edwin (ED-winn)—a Knight of Erythane; the armsman
Esatoric (EE-sah-tor-ik)—a Knight of Erythane
Garvin (GAR-vinn)—a Knight of Erythane
Harritin (HARR-ih-tin)—a young Knight of Erythane
Humfreet (HUM-freet)—the king
Jakrusan (Jah-KROO-sin)—a Knight of Erythane
Kedrin (KEH-drinn)—the captain of the Knights of Erythane; Ra-khir's father
Khirwith (KEER-with)—Ra-khir's stepfather
Lakamorn (LACK-a-morn)—a Knight of Erythane
Mariell (Mah-ree-ELL)—an adolescent girl; Sushara's sister
Oridan (OR-ih-den)—Shavasiay's father
Ra-khir (Rah-KEER)—a Knight of Erythane; Kedrin's son
Ramytan (RAM-ih-tin)—Kedrin's late father
Shavasiay (Shah-VASS-ee-ay)—a Knight of Erythane
Sushara (Soo-SHAR-a)—an adolescent girl; Mariell's sister

Pudarians

Boshkin (BAHSH-kinn)—a steward of Leondis
Brunar (BREW-nar)—a dungeon guard
Cenna (SEH-na)—an ancient queen
Charra (CHAR-ah)—a healer
Chethid (CHETH-id)—a lieutenant; one of three
Cymion (KIGH-mee-on)—the king
Daizar (DYE-zahr)—minister of visiting dignitaries
Danamelio (Dan-a-MEEL-ee-oh)—a criminal; deceased
Darian (DAYR-ee-an)—a lieutenant; one of three
Darris (DAYR-iss)—the bard; Linndar's son
DeShane (Dih-SHAYN)—a captain of the king's guard
The Flea—a criminal; deceased
Harlton (HAR-all-ton)—a captain of the king's guard
Harrod (HA-rod)—a surgeon
Horatiannon (Hor-ay-shee-AH-nun)—an ancient king
Jahiran (Jah-HEER-in)—the first bard

Javonzir (Ja-VON-zeer)—the king's cousin and adviser

Lador (LAH-door)—a locksmith

Larrin (LARR-inn)—a captain of the guard

Leondis (Lee-ON-diss)—the crown prince; Severin's younger brother

Leosina (Lee-oh-SEE-nah)—young daughter of the west wing maid

Linndar (LINN-dar)—the previous bard; Darris' mother; killed in the elfin purge

Mar Lon (MAR-LONN)—a legendary bard; Linndar's ancestor

Markanyin (Marr-KANN-yinn)—Pudarian general

Nellkoris (Nell-KORR-iss)—a lieutenant; one of three

Octaro (Ok-TAR-oh)—a guard

Perlia (PEARL-ya)—a merchant healer

Peter (PET-er)—a street urchin; deceased

Rascal—a street thief

Sabilar (SAB-ill-ar)—a blacksmith

Severin (SEV-rinn)—the late heir to Pudar's throne

Stick—a criminal; deceased

Tadda (TAH-dah)—a thief; deceased

Tanna (TAWN-a)—a healer

Renshai

Ashavir (AH-shah-veer)—a late student of Colbey

Bohlseti (Bowl-SET-ee)—a late student of Colbey

Brenna (BRENN-a)—false name used by Rantire while a prisoner of elves

Calistin the Bold (Ka-LEES-tin)—Colbey's late father

Colbey Calistinsson (KULL-bay)—legendary Renshai now living among the gods, a.k.a. The Deathseeker, a.k.a. The Golden Prince of Demons, a.k.a. Kyndig

Episte Rachesson (Ep-PISS-teh)—an orphan raised by Colbey; killed by Colbey after being driven mad by chaos

Gareth Lasirsson (GARR-ith)—tester of worthiness of Ra-khir and Tae to sire Renshai; Kristel's father

Kesave (Kee-SAH-veh)—a late student of Colbey

Kevralyn Balmirsdatter (KEV-ra-linn)—a late warrior; Kevralyn Tainharsdatter's namesake

Kevralyn Tainharsdatter (KEV-ra-linn)—a young Renshai

Kristel Garethsdatter (KRISS-tal)—first guardian of Matrinka, along with Nisse

Kyndig (KAWN-dee)—Colbey Calistinsson; lit: "Skilled One"

Mitrian Santagithisdatter (MIH-tree-an)—wife of Tannin

Modrey (MOH-dray)—forefather of the tribe of Modrey

Nisse Nelsdatter (NEE-sah)—first guardian of Matrinka, along with Kristel

Pseubicon (SOO-bih-kahn)—an ancient Renshai, half-barbarian by blood

Rache Garnsson (RACK-ee)—forefather of the tribe of Rache

Rache Kallmirsson (RACK-ee)—Rache Garnsson's namesake; Episte's father

Randil (Ran-DEEL)—a member of Béarn's second envoy

Ranilda Battlemad (Ran-HEEL-da)—Colbey's late mother

Rantire Ulfinsdatter (Ran-TEER-ee)—Griff's bodyguard in Darris' absence; a dedicated guardian

Raska "Ravn" Colbeysson (RASS-ka; RAY-vinn)—Colbey's and Freya's son

Saviar Ra-khirsson (SAV-ee-ahr)—Ra-khir's and Kevral's son

Subikahn Taesson (SOO-bih-kahn)—Tae's and Kevral's son

Sylva (SILL-va)—Rache Garnsson's wife; an Erythanian

Tainhar (TAYN-har)—Kevral's father

Tarah Randilsdatter (TAIR-a)—wife of Modrey and sister of Tannin

Tannin Randilsson (TAN-in)—forefather of the tribe of Tannin; Tarah's brother and Mitrian's husband

Thialnir Thrudazisson (Thee-AHL-neer)—a chieftain

Vashi (VASH-ee)—a late warrior

Santagithians

Herwin (HER-winn)—Griff's stepfather

Santagithi (San-TAG-ih-thigh)—long-dead general for whom the city was named

EASTERNERS

Alsrusett (Al-RUSS-it)—one of Weile Kahn's bodyguards (see also Daxan)

Chayl (SHAYL)—a follower of Weile Kahn; commander of Nighthawk sector

Curdeis (KER-tuss)—Weile Kahn's late brother

Daxan (DIK-sunn)—one of Weile Kahn's bodyguards (see also Alsrusett)

Jeffrin (JEFF-rinn)—an informant working for Weile Kahn

Kinya (KEN-yah)—a long-time member of Weile Kahn's organization

Leightar (LAY-tar)—a follower of Weile Kahn
Midonner (May-DONN-er)—previous king of Stalmize; high king of the
Eastlands
Monika (Moh-NEE-kah)—a fertile woman
Nacoma (Nah-KAH-mah)—a follower of Weile Kahn
Niko (NAY-koh)—a pregnant woman
Shavoor (Shah-VOOR)—an informant working for Weile Kahn
Shaxcharal (SHACKS-krawl)—the last king of LaZar
Tae Kahn (TIGH KAHN)—Weile Kahn's son
Tichhar (TICH-har)—a LaZarian emissary
Tisharo (Ta-SHAR-oh)—a con man working for Weile Kahn
Usyris (Yoo-SIGH-russ)—a follower of Weile Kahn; commander of Spar-
rowhawk sector
Weile Kahn (WAY-lee KAHN)—a crime lord
Zeldar (ZAYL-dah)—a pregnant woman

NORTHERNERS

Andvari (And-VAR-ee)—NORDMIRIAN; warrior and diplomat
Mundilnarvi (Munn-dill-NAR-vee)—NORDMIRIAN; *Einherjar* killed
in the war against the Renshai
Olvaerr (OHL-eh-vair)—NORDMIRIAN; Valr Kirin's son
Tyrion (TEER-ee-on)—ASCAI; an inner court guard of Pudar
Valr Kirin (Vawl-KEER-in)—NORDMIRIAN; an ancient enemy of Col-
bey's, long dead; Rache Kallmirsson's blood brother

OUTWORLDERS

Arak'bar Tulamii Dhor (AHR-ok-bar Too-LAHM-ee-igh ZHOOR)—the
éldest of the elves; a.k.a. The Captain; a.k.a. Lav'rintir
Arith'tinir Khy-loh'Shinaris Bal-ishi Sjörmann'taé Or (ARR-ith-tin-eer
KIGH-loh-shin-ahr-iss Bal-EE-shee Syoor-mahn-TIGH Orr)—Cap-
tain's given name
Ath-tiran Béonwith Bray'onet Ty'maranth Nh'aytemir (Ath-TEER-inn
Bee-ON-with BRAY-on-et Tee-MAR-anth Nigh-A-teh-mayr)—a *ly-
salf*
Baheth'rin Gh'leneth Wir-talos Dartarian Mithrillan (Ba-HETH-a-rinn
Gah-LENN-eth Weer-TAY-lohs Dar-TAR-ee-an Mith-RILL-in)—a
young elf
The Captain—the common name for Arak'bar Tulamii Dhor

Chan'rék'ril (Shawn-RAYK-rill)—an artistic *lysalf*

The Collector—a giant

Dess'man Damylith Char'kiroh Va-Naysin Jemarious (DESS-man Dah-MIGH-lith Shar-eh-KEER-oh Vah-NAY-sin Jem-AHR-ee-us)—a *svartalf*

Dh'arlo'mé'aftris'ter Te'meer Braylth'ryn Amareth Fel-Krin (ZHAR-loh-may-aff-triss-ter Teh-MEER Brawl-THRINN Ah-MAR-eth Fell-krinn)—the elves' leader

Dhyano Falkurian L'marithal Gasharyil Domm (ZHAN-oñ Fal-KYOOR-ee-an Lah-mah-EETH-all Gah-SHAR-ee-ill DOHM)—a *lysalf*

El-brinith (El-BRINN-ith)—a *lysalf* with a good feel for magic

Eth'morand Kayhiral No'vahntor El-brinith (Eth-MOOR-and Kah-HEER-all Noh'VAHN-tor El-BRINN-ith)—a *lysalf*

Haleeyan Sh'borith Nimriel T'mori Na-kira (Hah-LEE-yan Sha-BOHR-ith NIM-ree-ell Tah-MOOR-ee Nah-KEER-ah)—a *lysalf*

Hri'shan'taé Y'varos Fitanith Adh'taran (HREE-shan-tigh EE-vahr-ohs Figh-TAN-ith Ad-hah-TAYR-an)—a member of the council of Nine; a.k.a. She of Slow Emotions

In'diago (In-dee-AH-go)—a *lysalf*

Irrith-talor (EER-ith-tah-lorr)—an older *lysalf*

Ke'taros (Key-TAR-ohs)—a *lysalf*

Khy'barreth Y'vrintae Shabeerah El-borin Morbonos (Kigh-BAYR-eth Eev-RINN-tigh Shah-BEER-ah ELL-boor-in Moor-BOH-nohs)—a brain-damaged *svartalf*

Lissa (LISS-a)—a weaver

Marrih (MAH-ree)—a *lysalf* talented with magic

Mith'ranir Orian T'laris El'neerith Wherinta (Mith-RAN-eer OR-ee-an Tee-LAR-ihs Ell-ih-NEER-ith Whir-INN-tah)—a *svartalf*

Oa'si Brahirinth Yozwaran Tril'frawn Ren-whar (WAY-see Brah-HEER-inth Yoz-WAHR-an Trill-FRAWN Ren-WAHR)—the youngest elf

Petree'shan-ash Tilmir V'harin Korhinal Chareen (PEH-tree-SHAN-ash Till-MEER VAY-har-inn KOR-in-all Shah-REEN)—a member of the council of Nine

Phislah (PHEES-la)—a weaver

Pree-hantis Kel'abirik Trill Barithos Nath'taros (PREE-hahn-tiss KELL-ah-beer-ik TRILL BAR-ih-thohs Nath-TAR-ohs)—a *svartalf* impersonating King Kohleran

Reehanthan Tel'rik Oltanos Leehinith Mir-shanir (Ree-HAHN-than TELL-rik Ohl-TAN-ohs Lee-HIN-ith Meer-SHAN-eer)—a *lysalf*

Sal'arin (Sa-LARR-in)—older *lysalf*

Sassar (SASS-ahr)—a weaver

Tel-aran (Tell-AHR-in)—a young *lysalf*
Tem'aree'ay Donnev'ra Amal-yah Krish-anda Mal-satorian (Teh-MAR-ee-ay Donn-EV-er-a Ah-MAL-yah Kreesh-AND-ah Mahl-sah-TOR-ee-an)—a *lysalf* healer; King Griff's lover
The Torturer
Tresh'iondra She'aric Airanisha Ni-kii Diah (Tresh-ee-ON-dra Shay-AHR-ik Air-ANN-ee-shah Nee-KEE-igh DIGH-a)—a *svartalf*
Vincelina Sa'viannith Esah-tohrika Tar Kin'zoth (Vin-sell-LEE-na Sah-ha-vee-ANN-ith Ess-ah-toor-EE-kah TAR KEEN-zoth)—a *svartalf*
Vrin-thal-ros Obtrinéos Pruthrandius Tel'Amorak (Vrin-THAHL-rohs Ob-trin-AY-os Proo-THRAND-ee-us Tel-am-OOR-ak)—a member of the elfin council of Nine
Ysh'andra (Yah-SHAN-drah)—a member of the elfin Council of Nine

ANIMALS

Frost Reaver—Colbey's white stallion
Mior—Matrinka's calico cat
Silver Warrior—Ra-khir's white stallion
Snow Stormer—Kedrin's white stallion

GODS, WORLDS & LEGENDARY OBJECTS

Aegir (AHJ-eer)—Northern god of the sea; killed at the *Ragnarok*
Alfheim (ALF-highm)—The world of elves; destroyed during the *Ragnarok*
Asgard (AHSS-gard)—The world of the gods
Baldur (BALL-der)—Northern god of beauty and gentleness who rose from the dead after the *Ragnarok*
Beyla (BAY-lah)—Frey's human servant; wife of Byggvir
The Bifrost Bridge (BEE-frost)—The bridge between Asgard and man's world
Bragi (BRAH-gee)—Northern god of poetry; killed at the *Ragnarok*
Brysombolig (Briss-om-BOH-leeg)—Troublesome House; Loki's long-abandoned citadel
Byggvir (BEWGG-veer)—Frey's human servant; husband of Beyla
Colbey Calistinsson (KULL-bay)—legendary Renshai
The Fenris Wolf (FEN-ris)—the Great Wolf; the evil son of Loki; also called Fenrir (FEN-reer); killed at the *Ragnarok*

Frey (FRAY)—Northern god of rain, sunshine, and fortune

Freya (FRAY-a)—Frey's sister; Northern goddess of battle

Frigg (FRIGG)—Odin's wife; Northern goddess of fate

Gladsheim (GLAD-shighm)—"Place of Joy;" Sanctuary of the gods

Hel (HEHL)—Northern goddess of the cold underrealm for those who do not die in valorous combat; killed at the *Ragnarok*

Hel (HEHL)—The underrealm ruled by the goddess, Hel

Heimdall (HIGHM-dahl)—Northern god of vigilance and father of mankind; killed at the *Ragnarok*

Herfjötur (Herf-YOH-terr)—Host Fetter; a Valkyrie

Hlidskjalf (HLID-skyalf)—Odin's high seat from which he can survey the worlds

Hod (HODD)—Blind god, a son of Odin; returned with Baldur after the *Ragnarok*

Honir (HON-eer)—An indecisive god who survived the *Ragnarok*

Idunn (EE-dun)—Bragi's wife; keeper of the golden apples of youth

Ífing (IFF-ing)—river between Asgard and Jötunheim

Jötunheim (YOH-tun-highm)—the world of the giants; destroyed during the *Ragnarok*

Kvasir (KWAH-seer)—A wise god, murdered by dwarves, whose blood was brewed into the mead of poetry

Loki (LOH-kee)—Northern god of fire and guile; a traitor to the gods and a champion of chaos; killed at the *Ragnarok*

Magni (MAG-nee)—Thor's and Sif's son; Northern god of might

Mana-garmr (MAH-nah Garm)—Northern wolf destined to extinguish the sun with the blood of men at the *Ragnarok*

The Midgard Serpent—A massive, poisonous serpent destined to kill and be killed by Thor at the *Ragnarok;* Loki's son; killed at the *Ragnarok*

Mimir (MIM-eer)—Wise god who was killed by gods; Odin preserved his head and used it as an adviser

Modi (MOE-dee)—Thor's and Sif's son; Northern god of blood wrath

Nanna (NAH-nah)—Baldur's wife

Nidhogg (NID-hogg)—dragon who gnaws at the root of the World Tree in Niflheim

Niflheim (NIFF-ul-highm)—Misty Hel; the coldest part of Hel to which the worst of the dead are committed

Njord (NYORR)—Frey's and Freya's father; died at the *Ragnarok*

Norns—The keepers of past (Urdr), present (Verdandi), and future (Skuld)

Odin (OH-din)—Northern leader of the pantheon; father of the gods; a.k.a. The AllFather; killed at the *Ragnarok*; resurrected self by placing his soul in the empty Staff of Law prior to his slaying, then overtaking Dh'arlo'mé

Odrorir (OD-dror-eer)—The cauldron containing the mead of poetry brewed from Kvasir's blood

Ran (RAHN)—Wife of Aegir; killed at the *Ragnarok*

Raska Colbeysson (RASS-ka)—son of Freya and Colbey; a.k.a. Ravn (RAY-vinn)

Ratatosk (Rah-tah-TOSK)—a squirrel who relays insults between Nidhogg and the eagle at the top of Yggdrasill

Sif (SIFF)—Thor's wife; Northern goddess of fertility and fidelity

Sigyn (SEE-gihn)—Loki's wife

Skögul (SKOH-gull)—Raging; a Valkyrie

Skoll (SKOEWL)—Northern wolf who will swallow the sun at the *Ragnarok*

Skuld (SKULLD)—"Being," the Norn who represents future

Spring of Mimir—spring under the second root of Yggdrasill

Syn (SIN)—Northern goddess of justice and innocence

Surtr (SURT)—The king of fire giants; destined to kill Frey and destroy the worlds of elves and men with fire at the *Ragnarok*; killed at the *Ragnarok*

Thor—Northern god of storms, farmers, and law; killed at the *Ragnarok*

Thrudr (THRUDD)—Thor's daughter; goddess of power

Tyr (TEER)—Northern one-handed god of war and faith; killed at the *Ragnarok*

Ugagnevangar (Oo-gag-nih-VANG-ahr)—Dark Plain of Misfortune; Loki's world on which sits Brysombolig

Urdr (ERD)—Fate; the Norn who represents past

Valaskjalf (Vahl-AS-skyalf)—Shelf of the Slain; Odin's citadel

Valhalla (VAWL-holl-a)—The heaven for the souls of dead warriors killed in valiant combat; at the *Ragnarok*, these souls assisted the gods in battle

Vali (VAHL-ee)—Odin's son; destined to survive the *Ragnarok*

The Valkyries (VAWL-ker-ees)—The Choosers of the Slain; warrior women who choose which souls go to Valhalla on the battlefield

Verdandi (Ver-DAN-dee)—Necessity; the Norn who represents present

Vidar (VEE-dar)—Son of Odin; he is destined to avenge his father's death at the *Ragnarok* by slaying the Fenris Wolf; current leader of the gods

The Well of Urdr—body of water at the base of the first root of Yggdrasill

The Wolf Age—The sequence of events immediately preceding the *Ragnarok* during which Skoll swallows the sun, Hati mangles the moon, and the Fenris Wolf runs free

Yggdrasill (IGG-dra-zill)—the World Tree

Western

(gods of this pantheon are rarely worshiped anymore)

Aphrikelle (Ah-fri-KELL)—Western goddess of spring
Cathan (KAY-than)—Western goddess of war, specifically of hand-to-hand combat; twin to Kadrak
Dakoi (Dah-KOY)—Western god of death
The Faceless God—Western god of winter
Firfan (FEER-fan)—Western god of archers and hunters
Itu (EE-too)—Western goddess of knowledge and truth
Kadrak (KAD-drak)—Western god of war; twin to Cathan
Ruaidhri (Roo-AY-dree)—Western leader of the pantheon
Suman (SOO-mon)—Western god of farmers and peasants
Weese (WEESSS)—Western god of winds
Yvesen (IV-e-sen)—Western god of steel and women
Zera'im (ZAIR-a-eem)—Western god of honor

Eastern

Sheriva (Sha-REE-vah)—omnipotent, only god of the Eastlands

Outworld Gods

Ciacera (See-a-SAIR-a)—The goddess of life on the sea floor who takes the form of an octopus
Mahaj (Ma-HAJ)—The god of dolphins
Morista (Moor-EES-tah)—The god of swimming creatures who takes the form of a seahorse

FOREIGN WORDS

A (AH)—EASTERN. "from"
ailar (IGH-LAR)—EASTERN. "to bring"
al (AIL)—EASTERN. the first person singular pronoun
alfen (ALF-in)—BÉARNESE. "elves;" new term created by elves to refer to themselves
amythest-weed—TRADING. a specific type of wildflower
anem (ON-um)—BARBARIAN. "enemy;" usually used in reference to a specific race or tribe with whom the barbarian's tribe is at war
aristiri (ah-riss-TEER-ee)—TRADING. a breed of singing hawks

årvåkir (AWR-vaw-keer)—NORTHERN. "vigilant one"

baronshei (ba-RON-shigh)—TRADING. "bald"

bein (bayn)—NORTHERN. "legs"

berserks (bair-sair)—NORTHERN. soldiers who fight without emotion, ignoring the safety of self and companions because of drugs or mental isolation; "crazy"

bha'fraktii (bhah-FROK-tee-igh)—ELFIN. "those who court their doom;" a *lysalf* term for *svartalf*

binyal (BIN-yall)—TRADING. type of spindly tree

bleffy (BLEFF-ee)—WESTERN/TRADING. a child's euphemism for nauseating

bolboda (bawl-BOE-da)—NORTHERN. "evilbringer"

brishigsa weed (brih-SHIG-sah)—WESTERN. a specific leafy weed with a translucent, red stem; a universal antidote to several common poisons

brorin (BROAR-in)—RENSHAI. "brother"

brunstil (BRUNN-steel)—NORTHERN. a stealth maneuver learned from barbarians by the Renshai; literally: "brown and still"

chrishius (KRISS-ee-us)—WESTERN. a specific type of wildflower

chroams (krohms)—WESTERN. specific coinage of copper, silver, or gold

corpa (KOR-pa)—WESTERN. "brotherhood, town;" literally: "body"

cringers—EASTERN. gang slang for people who show fear

daimo (DIGH-moh)—EASTERN. slang term for Renshai

demon (DEE-mun)—ANCIENT TONGUE. a creature of magic

dero (DAYR-oh)—EASTERN. a type of winter fruit

djem (dee-YEM)—NORTHERN. "demon"

djevskulka (dee-yev-SKOHL-ka)—NORTHERN. an expletive that essentially means "devil's play"

doranga (door-ANG-a)—TRADING. a type of tropical tree with serrated leaves and jutting rings of bark

drilstin (DRILL-stinn)—TRADING. an herb used by healers

dwar'freytii (dwar-FRAY-tee-igh)—ELFIN. "the chosen ones of Frey;" *svartalf* name for themselves

Einherjar (IGHN-herr-yar)—NORTHERN. "the dead warriors in Valhalla"

ejenlyåndel (ay-YEN-lee-ON-dell)—ELFIN. "immortality echo;" a sense of infinality that is a part of every human and elf.

eksil (EHK-seel)—NORTHERN. "exile"

erenspice (EH-ren-spighs)—EASTERN. a type of hot spice used in cooking

fafra (FAH-fra)—TRADING. "to eat"

feflin (FEF-linn)—TRADING. "to hunt"

floyetsverd (floy-ETTS-weard)—RENSHAI. a disarming maneuver

formynder (for-MEWN-derr)—NORTHERN. "guardian," "teacher"

forrader (foh-RAY-der)—NORTHERN. "traitor"

forraderi (foh-reh-derr-EE)—NORTHERN. "treason"

Forsvarir (Fours-var-EER)—RENSHAI. a specific disarming maneuver

frey (FRAY)—NORTHERN. "lord"

freya (FRAY-a)—NORTHERN. "lady"

frichen-karboh (FRATCH-inn kayr-BOH)—EASTERN. widow; literally: "manless woman, past usefulness"

frilka (FRAIL-kah)—EASTERN. the most formal title for a woman, elevating her nearly to the level of a man

fussling (FUSS-ling)—TRADING. slang for bothering

galn (gahln)—NORTHERN. "ferociously crazy"

ganim (GAH-neem)—RENSHAI. "a non-Renshai"

garlet (GAR-let)—WESTERN. a type of wildflower believed to have healing properties

garn (garn)—NORTHERN. "yarn"

Gerlinr (Gerr-LEEN)—RENSHAI. a specific aesthetic and difficult sword maneuver

granshy (GRANN-shigh)—WESTERN. "plump"

gullin (GULL-in)—NORTHERN. "golden"

gynurith (ga-NAR-ayth)—EASTERN. "excrement"

hacantha (ha-CAN-thah)—TRADING. a type of cultivated flower that comes in various hues

hadongo (hah-DONG-oh)—WESTERN. a twisted, hardwood tree

Harval (Harr-VALL)—ANCIENT TONGUE. "the gray blade"

Hastivillr (has-tih-VEEL)—RENSHAI. a sword maneuver

jovinay arythanik (joh-VIN-ay ar-ih-THAN-ik)—ELFIN. "a joining of magic;" a gathering of elves for the purpose of amplifying and casting spells

jufinar (JOO-finn-ar)—TRADING. a type of bush-like tree that produces berries

kadlach (KOD-lok; the ch has a guttural sound)—TRADING. a vulgar term for a disobedient child; akin to brat

kathkral (KATH-krall)—ELFIN. a type of broad-leafed tree

kenya (KEN-ya)—WESTERN. "bird"

khohlar (KOH-lar)—ELFIN. a mental magical concept that involves transmitting several words in an instantaneous concept

kjaelnabnir (kyahl-NAHB-neer)—RENSHAI. temporary name for a child until a hero's name becomes available

kinesthe (Kin-ESS-teh)—NORTHERN. "strength"

kolbladnir (kol-BLAW-neer)—NORTHERN. "the cold-bladed"

kraell (kray-ELL)—ANCIENT TONGUE. a type of demon dwelling in the deepest region of chaos' realm

kyndig (KAWN-dee)—NORTHERN. "skilled one"

lav'rintir (lahv-rinn-TEER)—ELFIN. "destroyer of the peace"

lav'rintii (lahv-RINN-tee-igh)—ELFIN. "the followers of Lav'rintir"

lessakit (LAYS-eh-kight)—EASTERN. a message

leuk (LUKE)—WESTERN. "white"

loki (LOH-kee)—NORTHERN. "fire"

lonriset (LON-ri-set)—WESTERN. a ten-stringed musical instrument

lynstreik (LEEN-strayk)—RENSHAI. A sword maneuver

lysalf (LEES-alf)—ELFIN. "light elf"

magni (MAG-nee)—NORTHERN. "might"

meirtrin (MAYR-trinn)—TRADING. a specific breed of nocturnal rodent

minkelik (min-KEL-ik)—ELFIN. "human"

mirack (merr-AK)—WESTERN. a specific type of hardwood tree with white bark

missy beetle—TRADING. a type of harmless, black beetle

mjollnir (MYOLL-neer)—NORTHERN. mullicrusher

modi (MOE-dee)—NORTHERN. "wrath"

Morshoch (MORE-shock)—ANCIENT TONGUE. "sword of darkness"

motfrabelonning (mot-frah-bell-ONN-ee)—NORTHERN. "reward of courage"

mynten (MIN-tin)—NORTHERN. a specific type of coin

nådenal (naw-deh-NAHL)—RENSHAI. Literally: "needle of mercy;" a silver, guardless, needle-shaped dagger constructed during a meticulous religious ceremony and used to end the life of an honored, suffering ally or enemy, then melted in the victim's pyre

nålogtråd (naw-LOG-trawd)—RENSHAI. "needle and thread;" a Renshai sword maneuver

noca (NOE-ka)—BÉARNESE. "grandfather"

odelhurtig (OD-ehl-HEWT-ih)—RENSHAI. a sword maneuver

oopey (OO-pee)—WESTERN/TRADING. a child's euphemism for an injury

orlorner (oor-LEERN-ar)—EASTERN. "to deliver to"

perfrans (PURR-franz)—a scarlet wild flower

pike—NORTHERN. "mountain"

prins (PRINS)—NORTHERN. "prince"

ranweed—WESTERN. a specific type of wild plant

raynshee (RAYN-shee)—TRADING. "elder"

rexin (RAYKS-inn)—EASTERN. "king"

rhinsheh (ran-SHAY)—EASTERN. "morning"

richi (REE-chee)—WESTERN. a specific breed of song bird

rintsha (RINT-shah)—WESTERN. "cat"

Ristoril (RISS-tor-ril)—ANCIENT TONGUE. "sword of tranquility"

sangrit (SAN-grit)—BARBARIAN. "to form a blood bond"

shucara (shoo-KAHR-a)—TRADING. a specific medicinal root

skjald (SKYAWLD)—NORTHERN. musician chronicler

skulk i djevlir (SKOOLK EE dyev-LEER)—NORTHERN. "devil's brutal fun"

skulkë i djevgullinhåri (SKOOLK-eh EE dyev-gull-inn-HARR-ee)—NORTHERN. "golden-haired devil's brutal fun"

svartalf (SWART-alf)—ELFIN. "dark elf"

svergelse (sverr-GELL-seh)—RENSHAI. "sword figures practiced alone; katas"

take—a game children play

talvus (TAL-vus)—WESTERN. "midday"

thrudr (THRUDD)—NORTHERN. "power, might"

tisis (TISS-iss)—NORTHERN. "retaliation"

torke (TOR-keh)—RENSHAI. "teacher, sword instructor"

tre-ved-en (TREH-ved-enn)—RENSHAI. "Loki's cross;" a Renshai maneuver designed for battling three against one

trithray (TRITH-ray)—TRADING. a purple wildflower

Tvinfri (TWINN-free)—RENSHAI. a disarming maneuver

ulvstikk (EWLV-steek)—RENSHAI. a sword maneuver

uvakt (oo-VAKT)—RENSHAI. "the unguarded;" a term for children whose *kjaelnabnir* becomes a permanent name

Valhalla (VAWL-holl-a)—NORTHERN. "Hall of the Slain;" the walled "heaven" for brave warriors slain in battle

Valkyrie (VAWL-kerr-ee)—NORTHERN. "Chooser of the Slain"

valr (VAWL)—NORTHERN. "slayer"

Vestan (VAYST-in)—EASTERN. "The Westlands"

waterroot—TRADING. an edible sea plant

wertell—TRADING. a specific plant with an acid seed used for medicinal purposes

wisule (WISS-ool)—TRADING. a foul-smelling, disease-carrying breed of rodents which has many offspring because the adults will abandon them when threatened

yarshimyan (yar-SHIM-yan)—ELFIN. a type of tree with bubblelike fruit

PLACES

Northlands

The area north of the Weathered Mountains and west of the Great Frenum Range. The Northmen live in ten tribes, each with its own town
surrounded by forest and farmland. The boundaries change.

Asci (ASS-kee)—home of the Ascai; Patron god: Bragi

Aerin (Ah-REEN)—home of the Aeri; Patron god: Aegir

Blathe (BLAYTH-eh)—home of the Blathe; Patron god: Aegir

Devil's Island—an island in the Amirannak. A home to the Renshai after
their exile. Currently part of Blathe

Erd (URD)—home of the Erdai; Patron goddess: Freya

Gelshnir (GEELSH-neer)—home of the Gelshni; Patron: Tyr

Gjar (GYAR)—home of the Gjar; Patron: Heimdall

Nordmir (NORD-meer)—the Northlands high kingdom, home of the
Nordmirians; Patron: Odin

Shamir (Sha-MEER)—home of the Shamirins; Patron: Freya

Skrytil (SKRY-teel)—home of the Skrytila; Patron: Thor

Talmir (TAHL-meer)—home of the Talmirians; Patron: Frey

Westlands

The Westlands are bounded by the Great Frenum Mountains to the east,
the Weathered Mountains to the north, and the sea to the west and
south. In general, the cities become larger and more civilized as the
land sweeps westward. The central area is packed with tiny farm
towns dwarfed by lush farm fields that, over time, have nearly coa-
lesced. This area is known as the Fertile Oval. The easternmost portions of the Westlands are forested, with sparse towns and rare
barbarian tribes. To the south lies an uninhabited tidal plain.

Almische (Ahl-mish-AY)—a small city

Béarn (Bay-ARN)—the high kingdom; a mountain city

Bellenet Fields (Bell-e-NAY)—a tourney field in Erythane

Corpa Bickat (KORE-pa Bi-KAY)—a large city

Corpa Schaull (KORE-pa Shawl)—a medium-sized city; one of the
"Twin Cities" (see Frist)

Erythane (AIR-eh-thane)—a large city closely allied with Béarn. Famous
for its knights

The Fields of Wrath—Plains near Erythane. Home to the Renshai

Frist (FRIST)—a medium-sized city; one of the "Twin Cities" (see
Corpa Schaull)

Granite Hills—a small, low range of mountains
Great Frenum Mountains (FREN-um)—towering, impassable mountains that divide the Eastlands from the Westlands and Northlands
Greentree—a small town
Hopewell—a small town
The Knight's Rest—a pricy tavern in Erythane
New Lovén (Low-VENN)—a medium-sized city
Nualfheim (Noo-ALF-highm)—the elves' name for their island
The Off-duty Tavern—a Pudarian tavern frequented by guardsmen
Oshtan (OSH-tan)—a small town
Porvada (Poor-VAH-da)—a medium-sized city
Pudar (Poo-DAR)—the largest city of the West; the great trade center
The Red Horse Inn—an inn in Pudar
The Road of Kings—the legendary route by which the Eastern Wizard is believed to have rescued the high king's heir after a bloody coup
Santagithi—a medium-sized town, relatively young
The Western Plains—a barren salt flat
Wynix (Why-NIX)—a medium-sized town

Eastlands

The area east of the Great Frenum Mountains. It is a vast, overpopulated wasteland filled with crowded cities and eroded fields. Little forest remains.
Dunchart (DOON-shayrt)—a small city
Ixaphant (IGHCKS-font)—a large city
Gihabortch (GIGH-hah-bortch)—a city
LaZar (LAH-zar)—a small city
Lemnock (LAYM-nok)—a large city
Osporivat (As-poor-IGH-vet)—a large city
Prohothra (Pree-HATH-ra)—a large city
Rozmath (ROZZ-mith)—a medium-sized city
Stalmize (STAHL-meez)—the Eastern high kingdom

Bodies of Water

Amirannak Sea (A-MEER-an-nak)—the Northernmost ocean
Brunn River (BRUN)—a muddy river in the Northlands
Conus River (KONE-uss)—a shared river of the Eastlands and Westlands
Icy River—a cold, Northern river
Jewel River—one of the rivers that flows to Trader's Lake
Perionyx River (Peh-ree-ON-ix)—a Western river

Southern Sea—the southernmost ocean
Trader's Lake—a harbor for trading boats in Pudar
Trader's River—the main route for overwater trade

Objects/Systems/Events

The Bards—a familial curse passed to the oldest child, male or female, of a specific family. The curse specifically condemns the current bard to obsessive curiosity but allows him to impart his learning only in song. A condition added by the Eastern Wizards compels each to serve as the personal bodyguard to the current king of Béarn as well.

Cardinal Wizards—a system of balance created by Odin in the beginning of time consisting of four, near immortal opposing guardians of evil, neutrality, and goodness who were tightly constrained by Odin's laws. Obsolete.

The Great War—a massive war fought between the Eastland army and the combined forces of the Westlands.

Harval—"the Gray Blade." The sword of balance imbued with the forces of law, chaos, good, and evil.

The Knights of Erythane—an elite guardian unit for the king of Erythane that also serves the high king in Béarn in shifts. Steeped in rigid codes of dress, manner, conduct, and chivalry, they are famed throughout the world.

Kolbladnir—"the Cold-bladed." A magic sword commissioned by Frey to combat Surtr at the *Ragnarok*.

Mjollnir—"Mullicrusher." Thor's gold, short-handled hammer so heavy that only he can lift it.

The Necklace of the Brisings—a necklace worn by the goddess Freya and forged by dwarves from "living gold."

The Pica Stone—a clairsentient sapphire. One of the rare items with magical power.

Ragnarok (ROW-na-rok)—"the Destruction of the Powers." The prophesied time when men, elves, and nearly all of the gods will die.

The Sea Seraph—the ship once owned by an elf known only as the Captain.

The Seven Tasks of Wizardry—a series of tasks designed by the gods to test the power and worth of the Cardinal Wizards' chosen successors. Obsolete.

The Trobok—"the Book of the Faithful." A scripture that guides the lives of Northmen. It is believed that daily reading from the book assists Odin in holding chaos at bay from the world of law.